Shattered

Reflections

Shattered Reflections is Lyn's first published book.
This second edition has been published in response to
many requests for both eBook and print versions to be available.
In the meantime, her recently-released historical fiction for children,
While I Can Still Remember…Norfolk Island,
is being enjoyed by children and adults alike.
Readers can find more information about her other books
at www.lynduclos.com.au & on Facebook.

Shattered Reflections is a compelling and accomplished tale of longing, loss, friendship and betrayal that takes you through the full gamut of emotions. It will keep you reading till the last turn of the page then make you want to start all over again. Duclos' timing is impeccable and her eye for detail creates a world that is hauntingly familiar to us all.

Liam Davison (dec.)
(writer, critic and winner of the National Book Council Award for Fiction)

This powerfully written novel - *Shattered Reflections* - is absorbing reading. Lyn Duclos has created characters with an insightful determination and presents them to the reader in the most incisive way. WARNING! You should not take this compelling story to read in bed - you won't sleep until you've finished it.

Roger Stanley (author - *Spring Fever*)

This is a compulsive page-turner. A full-blown family saga that draws the reader in emotionally. Sensational!

Shane Bilsborough *(The Fat Stripping Diet,*
7 Days to Strip Fat Forever, Why Haven't I Lost Weight Yet?)

Shattered Reflections

a novel

by

Lyn Duclos

PilandPress

First published by Piland Press Melbourne, Australia 2006
This 2nd edition published by Piland Press
Melbourne, Australia 2016
2/11 Fowler Street, Chelsea, Victoria 3196, Australia
www.lynduclos.com.au

National Library of Australia
Cataloguing-in-Publication entry

Creator: Duclos, Lyn, author.
Title: Shattered reflections / Lyn Duclos;
Andrés Duclos Vargas, illustrator.

Edition: 2nd edition.

ISBN: 9780975780442 (paperback)

Subjects: Twins--Fiction.

Other Creators/Contributors:
Duclos Vargas, Andrés, illustrator.

Dewey Number: A823.4

Printed by Ingram (Worldwide)
July 2016

Cover design by Andrés Duclos Vargas
Line art graphics Danielle Jupp
Author photo by Pilar Duclos Vargas
Typeset in 10.5 pt Century Schoolbook

While I Can
Still Remember
... Norfolk Island
Lyn Duclos

Acknowledgements

- The late Bill McMurray, the most courageous man I've known, who generously gave of his thoughts and experiences via email whilst a locked-in victim
- Liz Bource, widow of Henri Bource
- Rasa Patupis & Steve Patupis, Eucla Motor Hotel, W.A.
- Moya Sharp, Librarian, Eastern Goldfields Historical Society Inc., Kalgoorlie, W.A.
- Michael Carter & Trevor Crouch, Dept. Road Transport, S.A.
- Graham Stokes, Historic Commercial Vehicle Club Aust.
- Pam & Barry Lambert, former Victorian primary school teachers
- Jack Andrews, former Principal, Mt Eliza North Primary School
- Angus McPhail, former Chelsea Primary School teacher
- Catherine Herrick, Education History Research Unit, Department of Education & Training, Victoria
- Leonie Taylor & Margaret Diggerson, Chelsea Historical Society
- Jody Harrison, Orchestral Coordinator, West Australian Symphony Orchestra
- Jack Harrison, former 2nd Clarinet, West Australian Symphony Orchestra
- Rudolf Osadnik, Principal 2nd Violin, Melbourne Symphony Orchestra
- Lyn Brodie, Manager, Community Development & Public Relations, Montefiore Homes for the Aged, Melbourne
- Duane Bell, Detective Senior Sergeant, Crime Investigation Support, Western Australia Police Service
- D'Arcy Evans, Justice Dept., W.A.
- Tim Hogan, State Library of Victoria
- Sue Gemmell, New Zealand Research Adviser, New Zealand Society of Genealogists Inc.
- Laura Cushman, Ph.D., Dept. Physical Medicine & Rehabilitation, University of Rochester Medical Center, NY, USA
- Jillian Simmons & Jackie Douglas, Stroke Association of Victoria
- Véronique Blandin, Association du Locked-in Syndrome, Boulogne, France
- Jean Hobson, Police Historian, Western Australia Police Service
- James Claiborn, Ph.D., American Board of Professional Psychology (via All Experts website)
- Wanda Steele, RNC (via All Experts website)
- Syed Hviqar, Psychologist (via All Experts website)
- Sister Patricia Williams, Catholic Archdiocese, Frankston
- Carmen Brooke, Longreach Library

- Angela Moffat, author of The Longreach Story, Longreach
- Elaine Britton, local historian, Longreach
- Joan Moloney, Mayor of Longreach
- Cynthia Cohen, Survivor Group Facilitator, Jewish Community Services, Jewish Care (Vic.) Inc., St. Kilda
- Evelyn Reid, Norseman Tourist Bureau Inc.
- Liam Davison (dec.), author & inspirational teacher at Chisholm Institute of TAFE, Frankston
- My thanks to Gavin Paterson who turned himself inside out to oversee the printing of the 1st edition of the book.
- Glenda Byrne (dec.), retiree extraordinaire, who guided me in getting the book out there.
- Shane & Fiona Bilsborough, your encouragement and faith in my writing pushed me to publish—my infinite thanks.
- Alex Bilsborough for his unfailing support.
- Danielle Jupp, talented graphic designer and wonderful friend – a million thanks for helping with the cover and all else.
- Aaron Wood, heartfelt thanks for helping to tweak the cover for this edition and provide tech support that was invaluable.
- To my loyal readers who always encouraged and believed in me: Annette Marron, Desiree Duclos, Gail Harber, Genevieve Koenig, Jennifer Robinson, Joy Duncan (dec.), Kath Dixon, Kaye Nolan, Leanne Paterson, Maree Hewish, Maria Capannari, Merrilyn Hayes, Mimi Sananikone, Nan Clydesdale (dec.) and Pat Luca. Thank you so much.
- Roger Stanley—mentor and dear friend—my love and heartfelt gratitude for your endless support and advice.
- To my step-dad, Hans Mulder, who printed off each chapter for my mother to read – my love and thanks for all you did.
- To my wonderful sister, Denise Hudd, to whom family means everything and who will go out on a limb to protect those she loves, including me—my love and appreciation.
- To my beautiful daughter, Pilar, who read the early manuscript in bits and pieces and who always believed in me—my thanks and love forever. May you achieve your dreams someday too.
- To my beloved son, Andrés, who created the cover and wanted my success so badly, I hope you can see this from wherever you are.
- And, finally, to my amazing mother, Rosalie Lillian Mulder (née Schultz), who always encouraged and inspired me. We shared so much of this story on the phone and it's mainly because of you that I finished it. If I could be an identical reflection of you, I would achieve perfection. My love always.

For my beloved son
Andrés Duclos Vargas
5 February 1981 – 11 April 2004

So beautiful, so vibrant, so incredibly talented
...but now my shattered reflection.

Part One

"Devotions Upon
Emergent Occasions"
Meditation 17, 1624.

*No man is an island, entire of itself;
every man is a piece of the
continent, a part of the main.
If a clod be washed away by the sea,
Europe is the less,
as well as if a promontory were,
as well as if a manor of thy friend's or
of thine own were:
any man's death diminishes me, because I am involved in mankind, and
therefore never send to know for whom
the bell tolls;
it tolls for thee.*

John Donne
1572-1631

Chapter 1   Perth

Sunday, 8th May 1955 - Mother's Day

The doctor hated this part of his job—when the mother didn't pull through. Especially when the father looked like this one did. The face was pale, crumpled. The eyes bewildered, haunted, bleak.

"We did all we could, Mr Schwartz. I'm sorry."

Gunter Schwartz looked down at the ivory face of the dead woman. The beautiful red hair curled around the forehead, perspiration drying. He remembered the marble face of his sister the last time he saw her. He hadn't said goodbye to her either.

Two nurses made as if to wheel the body out of the room.

"Please. Don't take her away yet. I want to be alone…with her."

The doctor signalled to the nurses and they left the room.

The morning sun rose up over the windowsill, painting his wife's face in a soft glow, but failing to warm it. It was already cold to his lips as he bent over her, the hands unresponsive to his touch.

"Hannah. You are so cold," he sighed.

The sun shifted along the length of the bed and disappeared above the roofs. Only the muffled sobs of the man disturbed the rasp of the brown blind as it rubbed against the top of the window frame in the faint breeze. The cord hung in the middle of the window, moving rhythmically, a silent witness to the sorrow contained within the room.

The door opened behind him, letting in the hospital sounds and the pungent smell of disinfectant. The white, stiff uniform leaned over him.

"Is there someone…?"

"Else? No."

"But surely you have family somewhere…?"

"Hannah and I…we have no family…in Australia. No family anywhere."

He closed his eyes against the memories, yet they intruded as they always did.

Gone. Family gone when my baby sister was thrown into the oven. Her marble face. Hannah looks the same. No—don't think of that. Push it out of your mind. We agreed. No more pain.

He had first seen Hannah in Auschwitz. Her red curls stood out amidst the sameness of the thin, anonymous faces and bleak, staring eyes. Her hair was the only glimmer of colour in that endless grey sea of hopeless humanity that poured into the camp—hungry, lost and frightened. She was ten years old and pretty enough not to have escaped her captors' attention. The lone survivor of her family, she wandered forlorn amongst her people in the stench of burning flesh; bewildered by the world she lived in.

At twenty-two, Gunter suffered the terrible loss of his parents and sister. His parents had already been killed when he was captured in the ghetto and taken to Auschwitz. He'd supposed his sister was dead too. His solid build, fair hair and pale green eyes saved Gunter's life when he was selected from the condemned and put to work labouring on excavations and underground building. Later, he was forced into the position of *Sonderkommando* where he was made to put the bodies of his fellow Jews into the ovens when they were removed from the gas chambers.

Gunter reasoned that he could justify his life by treating the bodies with as much respect as he could before giving them up to the flames. He was hated by his fellow prisoners for what he was doing, for the privileges he received, but the survival instinct drove him to continue the loathsome task amongst the greyness of human ash. What choice did he have, anyway? It was process bodies, or he would go to the gas chamber to die—an outcome that he expected daily as *Sonderkommandos* were routinely gassed. He tried not to think about the bodies. That they used to be people—mothers, fathers, brothers and sisters. He avoided the skeletal faces as he lifted them into the oven, but they haunted him in nightmares as accusing faceless people. In his waking hours, he learned to shut down his emotions from the reality of his situation and that of his fellow Jews as they were stripped of their hair and gold teeth before cremation. His jaw became set into hard lines, his mouth harsh and thin, and he remained detached, strong, unflinching. Until the day his sister's face appeared on the pile of bodies. The little, pale, thin face that used to giggle when he tickled her feet, the eyes half-closed in death's dream. The arms that would hug him bent back at an angle, already stiffening. The memory of her laughter tugged at his shrunken, empty guts and he retched foul bile, shaking, crying, sinking down to his knees, and covering the body that was his sister.

Hannah stood at the corner of a building, watching the young man grieve. She had seen him looking at her many times and wondered if he, too, would violate her body as the grey uniforms did. Somehow she didn't think so. He wasn't like the other men. His gaze had been soft and thoughtful. Another prisoner pulled the young man away from the girl's body and gently lifted her into the oven. Gunter turned and staggered towards Hannah. He retched again, the bile splashing on her feet, and he sagged onto his own vomit on the ground. She was afraid to move, to intrude upon his suffering, silently sharing their mutual losses. When his sobs subsided, he lifted his eyes to the small feet just inches from his face. As his eyes travelled upwards, he saw the red-haired girl with his own pain reflected in her desolate, tearful eyes.

When the Allies freed the skeletal living remains of Auschwitz, Gunter and Hannah walked hand in hand into a new beginning. They were all they had, and all they trusted. Gunter was the brother Hannah never had, and Hannah was the sister Gunter had lost. From the wreckage of their young lives, they united into a determined partnership that conquered adversity and allowed nothing to stop their flight to Australia. The land of sunshine and vastness beckoned them with its promise of freedom and peace. And out of that partnership grew a love that was fierce and eternal.

The nurse pulled the stiff white sheet over the red curls.

"Don't..." he reached for the sheet.

Insistent, firm hands took him away. Away from his wife. Away from his life.

Voices—soft, murmuring—enshrouded him. A hand appeared in front of him holding some white pills.

"Just a sedative to help you to..."

"No." He shook his head. The room came into focus. It was empty. The sun no longer caressed the window. His wife's body was gone.

"The twins are fine, healthy girls. Would you like to see them now?"

"Twins?"

"The babies."

"Babies?"

"Mr Schwartz. You have two beautiful daughters."

"Two?"

The realisation hit him in the stomach and he gagged, falling back into a chair.

"Hannah had twins? I didn't know."

Resentment twisted his gut in a painful lurch. *Two for the price of one.*

The doctor looked down at the distraught figure of Gunter whose black suit was crumpled from the long night and day. The black bow tie still sat under his chin over the starched white shirt. The blood had dried on the suit, making it stiff, and the metallic smell of the blood permeated the room.

Gunter slumped further down into the chair, memories of the past twelve hours seeping through his grief.

It had been so quiet on the other side of the door as he had fumbled with the key, a feeling of dread gripping him. A record spun neglected in the room, the needle tracing a circular path around the spindle. It rotated constantly in rhythmic clicks, the only sound in the room, other than his wife's moans as her full womb convulsed in painful waves. She was lying on the floor in a great pool of blood that seeped from between her legs.

No one answered his frantic knocking. The neighbours remained hidden in the dark behind closed curtains, the unintelligible guttural voice frightening them at that late hour. He had left her there, on the floor, while he ran along the deserted streets until a taxi appeared.

Reluctantly, the tired driver stopped when the crazy man ran out in front of his headlights. The driver had hoped to get home before midnight. It had been a long night and he had seen enough of drunks. He was wary of the frantic man until he saw the blood. They carried her unconscious body out to his taxi. The man cradled her in his arms in the back seat, mumbling in his own language as he stroked her face. The driver watched them in his rear-vision mirror afraid the woman would die before they reached Prince Alfred Hospital. He pushed the taxi faster and faster.

Helpless, Gunter stared down at the shiny brown lino as he waited. It filled his vision like a glossy chocolate pudding as tears seeped out from their hidden place. The place that had felt safe until now. The tea sat cold, untouched, in a white cup beside him. The milk was congealed in a layer on top. He waited, congealed in his own agony, waiting for the antiseptic mouths to end the nightmare, waiting for reassurance that failed to come.

His seed was torturing Hannah. The seed she so desperately wanted. The seed that was to create their own family. He had promised her that nothing else could ever hurt her. He had promised to protect her, but he had failed.

The twins bellowed lustily for the absent mother but were quieted with rubber nipples and warm milk. The nurse's arms calmed them in a firm embrace.

"Such a shame the mother died," said one nurse to another, "and on Mother's Day too. They're such beautiful girls—you can't tell them apart!"

"She was only twenty-one, you know. They've got her red hair."

"Have you seen the father? So handsome! I wonder what he'll do? How he'll cope with two little 'uns."

It was now dusk on that autumn day. The city of Perth was yawning and closing its eyes upon the leaden clouds that now scudded across the tops of its buildings. The clouds blustered over from the thudding, relentless power of the Indian Ocean as it completed its journey upon the cold, wet beaches of Western Australia. Driving rain surrounded the westward windows of the hospital. The white face of the man looking out saw nothing. He was alone. Alone in his grief.

The doctor was exhausted. It had been a lousy day and he was looking forward to going home to a less complicated and tragic world. First the wife, now the disappearance of the baby. How was he going to tell the man? The doctor turned the door handle reluctantly and entered the quiet room. He haltingly broke the news of the kidnapping to Gunter who listened in a silence more resigned than shocked. Grief and loss were a part of his life—always had been, except for eleven healing years with Hannah. Then he fell senseless to the floor.

Gunter went to visit his remaining daughter. The little bundle that was wrapped tightly in a pink rug made funny snuffling sounds, the tiny mouth working in random patterns. Wispy red curls protruded from the confines of the rug and the eyes of the baby opened to take in the first blurred image of her father.

The nurse objected as Gunter began to dismantle the tight wrapping from the baby. He looked up at her from a face that was desolate with grief, eyes shadowed black in an expression she could not read. The doctor held her back.

"Leave him be."

Gunter peeled back the layers and gently examined his daughter. The tiny legs kicked jerkily now that they were free of their confinement in a delighted burst of energy. He smiled down at her in wonderment, marvelling at the perfection of her body, except for a small brown patch under the jaw, shaped like a lightning fork. Her little fist grasped then clung tightly to his index finger, and their bonding began.

Chapter 2

TWIN GIRL KIDNAPPED FROM HOSPITAL! The headlines of the Perth papers announced the sensational story. Shocked pedestrians surrounded newspaper stands, hushed voices questioning. Mothers instinctively tightened their grasp on their own babies, wrapping them more securely against the chill autumn wind. The wireless carried the story into warm, protected Perth homes where housewives paused in their dinner preparations to hear the horrifying news.

George Chambers, the Detective Sergeant assigned to the case, had a distinctly bad taste in his mouth. This sort of crime did not happen in his district. A baby! Who would steal a baby? Chambers was disgusted because someone somehow had let the press in on it, and the kidnapping had made headlines in every paper in the city. The father was locked in a room somewhere with the dead mother, and everyone else in Perth seemed to know about it before he did.

George, whose solid build and forbidding height commanded respect, was a tough but compassionate cop with an amazingly shrewd mind. He had the perception to read people accurately and would wait like a panther, muscles tight, ready to pounce on any lie, mistake or clue that jumped in front of him. He was a man endowed with sweeping, thick eyebrows that made an emphatic statement above intelligent, brown eyes. They were brows that had a knack of rising independently of each other, especially at times when he was confounded. The left eyebrow would shoot up and collide with the lank, Brylcreamed, dark hair that had a habit of falling down over his forehead.

The list of hospital staff on duty at the time of the baby's disappearance seemed endless. It would be a long night. Little was known of who went in and out of the hospital, and the car parks and surrounds were being checked out with the help of the uniformed boys. There would be a lot of legwork on this case. George's pen drew a large question mark next to the name of the nurse in charge of the nursery at the time of the disappearance.

Winnie Edwards knocked on the door of the room the hospital had hastily assigned to the detective and waited, rocking back and forth on her heels.

"I said...come in!" came the voice, louder this time.

"You wanted to see me?" she asked in a whisper, but it came out in a muted croak.

"Yes. Yes. Sit down please. Over there." Chambers indicated the chair in front of the desk that the hospital had provided him with.

Winnie perched on the edge of the chair. Her right foot hooked over her left heel, her weight almost totally on her trembling left leg and foot. The Detective Sergeant was scribbling something on a note pad. A frown creased the bridge of his nose between the eyebrows. The mouth was harsh when it gripped the pencil from time to time as he gathered his thoughts. She studied the face, terrified, her hands twisting the hem of her white uniform into a crumpled mess.

"Ah, Nurse Edwards. Thank you for coming."

His eyes were kind and the mouth was no longer harsh. It turned up at the corners when he smiled at her, creating long lines that ran from his nose down to the chin. She shuddered a wan smile in return, and relaxed the grip of one hand.

Fifteen minutes later, Winnie Edwards quietly closed the door behind her and leaned against the wall. It hadn't been so bad after all. What a nice man the detective was. He didn't look at her accusingly as everyone else was doing.

She was tired out. Exhausted. What had started out as a very normal day had turned into a nightmare. Those beautiful little babies—so helpless, so tiny and so dependent upon her. It had been her responsibility to take care of them. And she'd lost one. It had never happened to her in all her working life. "Negligent," she'd heard them saying in the corridor. Negligent! Her? She'd been the most respected nurse in the hospital—anywhere she'd worked, in fact. How could one person be in three places at once? They were short-staffed and that new intern had called her aside to talk about the prem baby due from the labour ward. She hadn't noticed that one of the twins was missing until feeding time.

Winnie smoothed down her spotless white uniform, squared her shoulders, and patted her greying hair. *I'll just get my coat and hat and walk out of here. I'm innocent and that nice detective knows it. The others can go to blazes.* The corridor seemed unending and the normally friendly faces of her work mates shunned her as she passed them. *I will not cry. I will not cry.*

George was sick to his stomach. Later that night he wearily looked down at his own baby daughter and wondered how he'd feel if someone had taken her. Since Ivy had been born, four months ago, the bond he had formed with her had surprised him. He looked forward to going home and cuddling her if she was awake, and marvelled at the sweetness of her breath and softness of her skin. The eyelids were so translucent; he could see the tiny veins beneath. Because his training had made him a keen observer of the finest detail, he delighted in merely watching her. She was a constant wonder to him—a delicate miracle that he had partly created.

Dorothy led him gently out of the baby's room and put a large whisky in his hand.

"Poor, poor sod," he repeated over and over again.

Dorothy knew to wait. It would come out of its own accord—when he was ready. He'd had difficult cases before, but she knew this one had touched his heart.

"If you'd died too..." His mouth worked, his eyes bright with unshed tears.

"Shhh. It's all right, George."

"But you might have," he insisted.

"Well I didn't."

He stood up and walked quietly over to the baby's room again. The door squeaked slightly as he pushed it open and the light from the lounge room cast a soft glow on his sleeping daughter's face. The faint smell of baby powder met his nostrils and he sighed slowly, deeply. Dorothy was at his side, her arm around his waist as they stood leaning against the doorway. The only sound was the soft breathing and murmurs of the baby and the ice clinking in George's now-empty glass.

Chapter 3

The fact that Gunter was a musician was not lost on his neighbours. They were not accustomed to the muted sounds of a violin now escaping from behind the closed doors of the young German couple's home. Previous tenants in the street had been *ordinary* folk, working class people who were not artistically inclined. They eventually gave up trying to include Hannah and Gunter in their social gatherings as the young woman quietly declined in her halting English, careful not to give offence. They noticed that the man arrived home in the early hours of most mornings, violin case in hand, and was greeted by the red-haired woman at the door.

Gunter and Hannah spent their days together quietly, privately, in a warm tenderness that brooked no interruption. She would curl up on the couch with the mending and listen to him practice on his violin. Sometimes she would watch him when he didn't realise, his pale green eyes intent on the music score. She watched his straight golden hair fling about as he played, the long sensitive fingers as they guided the bow over the strings. Then sensing her attention, he would look up and they would smile as the pure notes filled the room.

They learned about the earth, digging into it in their back yard, watching it anxiously for the first green shoots. They delighted in the seasons that brought new perfumed growth and multi-coloured leaves that stunned the senses. They cooked together and ate together, and scrubbed their rented house until it shone with the love they lavished upon it.

The only thing that brought shadows into Hannah's eyes were memories of hard, brutal bodies that had violated her own—that tore her flesh as well as her soul. Her nightmares were quieted by the gentle kisses of her beloved Gunter as he held her trembling body, willing the demons to leave her as well as himself. His own nightmares left him shuddering with fear, the remembered voices of the SS shouting: *Raus! Raus! Alle raus!* indicating the prisoners should get out of the wagons and walk to their death. He choked on the smoke-laden air again as he was selected fit enough to work, and would awaken burdened with guilt for what he'd had to do to survive. And then Hannah's arms would cradle his head into the beating of her heart and he would find absolution in her love.

To have a child was Hannah's dream. A child that would be the harvest of their love, their desire to start afresh. They promised each other never to think of the past—what they had lost. They promised to look to the future, and a child was what they both craved to seal their happiness.

Hannah hid from Gunter the secret that she suspected. One Saturday afternoon, when he was with the orchestra, she left the house and walked two miles to a doctor's rooms. She had not been there before, and hesitated as she looked at the brass plate on the fence: **Dr Harold Barns**. The brass shone brightly in the afternoon sun and there were roses of every colour in the small, well-kept front garden. *This must be an omen—a good omen,* she decided. The doctor's wife smiled encouragingly at Hannah. She could see the young woman was extremely nervous and offered her the latest *Women's Weekly* to distract her. Hannah accepted the magazine but stared blindly at the pages that shook as she turned them. There was a roaring in her ears and her breathing became shallow. Suddenly her hand flew up to cover her mouth, eyes wide and panic-stricken.

"Are you going to be sick, dear?" asked the doctor's wife.

She had been watching Hannah and pushed a bowl into the young woman's hand. Hannah swallowed hard and tears rushed to her eyes.

"It's all right, dear. Just take a few deep breaths. That's right. Hold on—I'll get you a glass of water."

A blush stained Hannah's neck as it crept up to display her embarrassment. This had never happened to her before. She *always* kept a hold on her emotions—except when she was with Gunter. Those men at the prison camp. They never drew tears from her. Not even when she bled. Not even when there were a lot of them.

"Doctor Barns will see you soon, dear. You'll feel better then."

The doctor's wife was old. Maybe the doctor would be too. No man had touched Hannah after the camp—except Gunter. And, oh, when he touched her she was on fire, consumed by a passion she had never known existed. But he had never hurt her. She wondered if the doctor would hurt her.

The door opened and a woman came out holding the hand of a little girl who was crying softly and clutching a bandaged arm. Hannah looked from the girl to the doctor's wife in panic.

"You're next now, dear."

Hannah's legs struggled jelly-like to propel her into the room. Harold Barns, a man of sixty-five, looked up and smiled in greeting.

"Mrs Schwartz to see you, dear. She's feeling a bit peaky and nervous-like."

The doctor rose and walked around the desk. His well-fed paunch bulged over clean and well-pressed trousers. A stethoscope tangled in a fob watch chain that hung in a loop and disappeared into a pocket. His face creased into a myriad of craggy seams, laughter lines fanning out from the corners of his enquiring brown eyes.

"Now tell me all about it, young lady."

The laughter lines seemed less well pronounced when he began the examination. An expression of profound sadness washed into his eyes. He had never seen scars like these before.

Forty minutes later, Hannah stood outside on the footpath and breathed great gulps of wonderful, clear air. The doctor was the most marvellous man on earth—well, second most marvellous. He had confirmed what she had kept hugged close to herself for weeks, afraid to let it out in case she lost it. She and Gunter were going to have a baby!

She had never felt so well in all her life. This baby, this miracle, was inside her, communicating with her. It was hers—theirs—and they had created it. Her feet glided over the footpath, hardly touching the concrete. A joyous scream bubbled in her throat and the pedestrians she passed were treated to the most beautiful smile they had ever seen.

Doctor Harold Barns stood in the doorway shaking his head as he looked after the red curls dancing along the street. *With God's help and mine, I pray she'll get through this.*

When Gunter arrived home at four minutes past midnight, his hat was whisked off and his violin ceremoniously taken out of his hand and replaced with a glass of champagne. That night he fell asleep on her naked stomach, close to the woman he loved and the new life pulsing inside her.

Chapter 4

Winnie Edwards went to work each day with her head held high. She tried to ignore the whispered remarks that ended abruptly when she walked into a room. Gone was the familiar camaraderie and the laughter with her work mates. Her days dragged by with no one to confide in. Only the helpless demanding little bundles in the nursery gave her a sense of being needed or wanted. She satisfied their needs and received their trusting acceptance as she held them in her arms.

After each shift she returned to the empty flat that had been her home for fourteen years. The nights were cold and lonely as she sat staring sightlessly into the heater's elements. Bitter, disappointed lines surrounded her mouth. Lines that were not seen in the hospital. Lines disguised by cheerful smiles. It was only when alone that she let down the mask, gave in to the despondency she felt. Life had not been kind to her.

She was blessed with an hourglass figure, large bright blue eyes that looked out on life with merriment, and a personality that made people want to be her friend. Her lips were rather thin, and her hair a mousy brown—but they were nothing that bright lipstick and modern tints couldn't correct.

Winnie had had her fair share of boyfriends since she left school. She loved to dance and wore out many a pair of shoes on dance floors in her hometown of Kalgoorlie, and then in Perth where she'd moved to get her nursing qualifications. She was popular, being a naturally graceful and proficient dancer, and many of the young doctors held her in their arms as they guided her around the floor, hopefully anticipating a kiss—and more. They took her home, and were rewarded with kisses that set their hormones exploding but left her wondering what all the fuss was about. Groping hands at the picture theatre were put back firmly in their place, even though at times her own hormones stirred tantalizingly. Winnie carried romantic visions of the *perfect man* and the *right time* before she would succumb.

But Anthony Oxford was different. He came from a wealthy family, which gave him the advantage over the other young interns and doctors who struggled to achieve their qualifications. He had the money to impress the hospital's nursing staff and a date with Anthony was a date to die for. It was not long before Anthony noticed young nurse Edwards. He took her for romantic dinners, held her close as they danced, wooed her with flowers, and kissed away her fears of the unknown. After two months of courtship, she surrendered her virginity and his grip upon her soul tightened.

Then the whispers started. The handsome doctor had been seen with another nurse. He denied it, of course, kissing her tears away—and did so for the rest of that summer. But it seemed that he was busy more often, had less time for her. She sat waiting many times, hands folded over in her lap, the perfume that he had given her filling her tiny flat, eventually to fade as the clock ticked away her faith in him. His excuses were always plausible, and she tried to believe him, wanted to believe him. But the tight, twisted knot in her gut told her the truth. He was avoiding her; she knew that. She also knew she was pregnant.

Perth was a quiet, conservative, close-knit community in Winnie's youth. *Loose* girls disappeared for six months and came back decidedly thinner. Everyone turned their backs on the truth. They knew, of course, but it was tidier to believe that young so-and-so had gone bush to help her Auntie Nora for a few months. No accusations, no scandal, and everyone could hold their heads up in their neighbourhood—or at least try to.

Winnie found work at Geraldton Hospital, where she worked most of her pregnancy, and she returned to Prince Alfred Hospital thin, depressed and lonely after giving her baby up for adoption. Every time she passed the nursery she would hear the babies crying. She imagined her own little girl in the warm embrace of another woman, and her breasts ached with milk that would not be suckled.

It had not been easy to carry on at the same hospital with tongues wagging—and Anthony still there. It was as if she'd never existed. His charms were ladled out to the next pretty nurse, and the next and the next. Too late, Winnie saw the type of man she'd given up her girlhood to and she was bitter. Bitter with the taste of anger and rejection in her tears. Bitter with torment and longing for her baby. Life had given her a pretty rotten deal and she took that inside herself and nurtured it. It grew over the years until she regarded men as loathsome creatures who were never to be trusted. She would never allow another to pierce her armor. She would remain safe inside the wall that she had constructed around herself.

A week after the disappearance of the Schwartz baby, Winnie returned home late to her cheerless cold flat. There were three letters in the letterbox: one from her mother, a bill, and another that she turned over curiously. With the heater on and a cup of tea beside her, she opened the letter and read the five pages written by a remote cousin. They had lost touch over the years and Winnie had wondered at times what had happened to her adventurous cousin. She had married a cattle station manager and moved somewhere up in Queensland and the letters had petered out. Now her cousin was writing with news of the past ten years up to the present. Her daughter was ill and needed constant nursing. Would Winnie like a change of scenery and pace? Would she like to do something different? Would she be prepared to nurse her daughter?

Winnie had never been the adventurous kind. That's why she'd spent so many years in the same hospital, at the same flat, with the same circle of friends. Her first impulse was to write back and say no, she wouldn't do it. Then it occurred to her that maybe it wouldn't be such a bad idea. It would take her away from the scandal of the baby's disappearance. She would start afresh where she was unknown. She was wanted there. Needed.

She stared for a long moment into the brightness of the heater. It dazzled her eyes but they were glazed in deep thought. She took a deep breath and rose to put the kettle on. Another cup of strong, black tea would help her with her task. It was going to be a difficult one. In her bedroom was an old chest, which she dragged out in front of the heater. She hadn't opened it for years but she knew every item it contained as if they were listed on a sheet of paper in front of her. Empty perfume bottles, photos, letters, theatre programmes, stolen restaurant menus. They were mementos of her brief but ruinous affair with Anthony. Mementos that she had never had the heart to discard. Now was a time to turn her back on the past. Now was the time to face the future. She put everything into the rubbish bin and pushed the lid on firmly. Her treasure chest was empty.

That night she was unable to sleep. Thoughts ran riot around her head. Would the police let her go? She couldn't see why not. Longreach was thousands of miles away. Thousands of miles away from the humiliation, pain and loneliness. She would speak to that nice detective about it tomorrow.

Chapter 5

George Chambers consulted with hospital staff and security was tightened. Not that a kidnapping was likely to happen again. There was no gruesome discovery of a tiny body —the search showing no result. Of course there were the usual crank letters. They came from the same nuts who sent them every time there was a crime in the city.   People took to locking their doors and were more careful about leaving their babies unattended for any length of time.

George wondered when the ransom note would arrive. Why was the kidnapper taking so long? How much would he ask for? Surely he knew from all the publicity that Mr Schwartz had no money? There was a loud public outcry against the heinous crime and calls for donations towards the anticipated ransom. It was not long before money started to pour in to help the German man.

"There's a nurse out there to see you, sir."

The young constable waited for George to look up from his paper work.

"Oh?" He looked up.

"A Sister Edwards, sir."

"Show her in."

George stood up as Winnie was shown in to his office. He wondered what she had to say. Maybe she had a lead on the case. She looked tired and drawn. *The past few days have been hard on her,* he thought.

"Sister Edwards. What brings you to this neck of the woods?"

"Mr...er...Sergeant Chambers."

He made her nervous. They all did. It wasn't so much that she was frightened of authority, it was a feeling of being under a microscope. She knew he was watching her, searching for reactions. It made her aware of what she was saying, doing, and her tongue felt like it was going in the opposite direction to where it should be. She tried not to fidget. She'd read somewhere that it gave a guilty person away. But she wasn't guilty! There was the embarrassment, too, of enduring people's suspicions about her. And there was her anger—that she should be suspected of stealing a child. Honest, efficient, conscientious people like her shouldn't have to bear that.

"Yes?"

"Well, it's like this. I wondered if you'd finished with me. I mean all the questions and so on."

"Why would that be now?"

"It's just that…if you don't need me anymore…I thought I might go to Queensland." George looked at her in surprise and she rushed on, "I'm not trying to hide anything, mind you."

He waited for her to go on.

"I've been offered a job. In Queensland. My cousin."

His left eyebrow shot up. Winnie Edwards had not struck him as the type to go gallivanting off to Queensland at the drop of a hat. Maybe there was more to her than he'd thought.

"Would you mind telling me why you're going?" he asked gently. It had not escaped him that she was making a very determined effort not to cry.

"Since the Schwartz baby disappeared…things are *different* at work." She waited but George nodded for her to continue. "You see, they all think that I was negligent in my duties. Or that I was the one who stole the baby." Her bottom lip was trembling, and her hands worked furiously at the hem of her skirt. "It's not fair!"

"Yes…go on," he nodded.

"I've *never* been negligent."

"I know that."

She looked up, surprised.

"You do?"

"Yes, the hospital staff speak very highly of you, Sister Edwards. Your work record has been extraordinarily good—anywhere you've been."

"Oh yes. I suppose you'd know all that," she said weakly.

"I've no doubt that those babies were in good hands," he said kindly.

"Thank you. I wish everyone felt that way."

"I think most do. You get the odd one with an axe to grind—usually jealousy makes people cruel."

"But how could they even suggest that I'd steal that baby. What would I do with it anyway? I'm too old to look after a baby—at least at home."

"There is the money side of it," he pointed out.

"What money? You mean the ransom? Have you had a ransom note?"

"No. What I meant was, if you had stolen the baby, maybe you could make some money out of it." His eyes were watching her keenly as her face flushed bright red in indignation.

"Oh! Oh! I would never…" Her eyes filled with tears.

"I said, *if*, but I don't believe you could do that."

She searched vainly for a handkerchief in her handbag; he leaned over and handed her his own.

"Would you like a cup of tea, Sister Edwards?"

Winnie nodded as she blew her nose. She noticed her make-up had smudged his handkerchief and wondered what his wife would say.

The strong tea revived Winnie's spirits, as well as Chambers' permission for her to leave the State. He showed her out of his office fifteen minutes later after obtaining her forwarding address in Longreach and wishing her well. He sighed as he stared at the Schwartz file. They had absolutely no leads. The baby had disappeared without a trace.

Three weeks later, George decided to pay Gunter a visit. The new father opened the door to the detective with some surprise and invited him in. He'd been walking the baby around after a feed and she had brought up some milk on his shoulder. George recognised the not-unpleasant odour from his own little girl.

"Can I hold her while you clean that up?" he asked.

Gunter, reluctant to hand her over, was surprised at George's adeptness.

George laughed. "I've got a baby daughter too. Not much older."

"Ah," Gunter nodded in understanding.

"Pretty little thing. Such a lot of red hair."

"Yes. Her mother had the same hair."

George noticed a photo of a smiling Hannah on the wall. She had been beautiful.

"Oh, I see." The pain in Gunter's eyes was clearly evident. George hesitated. "What have you named the baby?"

"Ursula. It was my wife's second name."

"Are you still working with the orchestra?"

"Yes."

"Who's looking after the baby?"

"I am."

"No—I mean when you're at work."

"I take her with me."

Gunter was not about to let Ursula out of his sight. Somehow he knew that he would never see the missing twin—and he was not going to lose this one. She was a perpetual source of discovery for him as she responded to the stimulation of his love. He amused her, cuddled her, talked to her, played the violin to her, all of her waking moments. And when she was asleep he sat in a chair by her cot and just looked at her. He watched her even breathing, the rapid eye movements as she dreamed, listened to her murmurs, his index finger in her clutch as she slept. And he would weep for her dead mother and her missing sister.

The other members of the West Australian Symphony Orchestra were very sympathetic towards the violinist. They had liked Gunter's young wife, and understood his intense loss. So they did all in their power to enable him to keep Ursula close, recognising his determination not to leave her far from him with babysitters.

The typists' pool was next door to Studio 1 in the ABC building and it was there that Ursula was watched over by adoring eyes that flitted from their typed pages to her pram. The clickety-clack of the typewriter keys accompanied her dreams and her exploratory responses to her new world. She slept through rehearsals or lay quietly listening to the instruments as they began her classical education. Sometimes, when the typing pool was empty, the musicians turned a blind eye to the baby's presence in Studio 1.

The confines of her pram were her world where the sounds and sights of the orchestra embraced her senses. In her waking moments, eyes wide, she would watch the forest of pointed bows as they dipped and rose above the edge of her pram. The conductor's baton darted in all directions and light glittered on the ornate, golden harps as they moved with the caress of the fingers that plucked them. Varying shades of gleaming wood curved into the scrolls of cellos and double basses; pegs sitting out proudly; strings taut, thrumming, swift fingers dancing upon them, splayed, vibrating.

Soft melodies, waltzes, soaring strings, transported Ursula into a world of beauty that was as familiar to her as the soft warmth of the womb, where the sound of her mother's heartbeat had lulled and enfolded her and her briefly-known sister. Muffled music had arrived to their developing ears and was a part of their watery realm, as was their mother's voice as she sang and talked to them from the outside world.

Sometimes, when turned onto her stomach, Ursula called upon her strengthening arm and neck muscles to lift her head up to see over the edge of the pram. Flashes of light reflected off shining flutes, clarinets, oboes and horns; frenzied, dizzying drumsticks pounded tight skins; throaty double basses pulsed into the floor; radiant cymbals crashed and resounded. Ursula would shudder at the unexpected then squeal in delight, dribbling from her wet mouth onto the flat pillow, and a fist would ram her gums, working back and forth in excitement.

She associated her father with the pleasant, woody smell of resin and the creations of Mozart, Beethoven, Brahms, Tchaikovsky as the characteristic tone of Gunter's violin soothed her to sleep. Her eyelids would droop as she floated into the world of dreams where another being, identical to herself, drifted and tumbled in harmony with her.

When she was old enough to sit up, Ursula's eyes would dart from one instrument to another—absorbing, listening. Her arms would wave in excitement to the music, and she would gurgle her pleasure. Even when she could not see the instruments from the typists' pool, her delight in the music was evident to her custodians. She listened to the direct to air radio broadcasts from the room next door with the same attention given by listeners beside their wirelesses at home. There were always trusted volunteers backstage during performances at the Capitol Theatre who would watch over her, and they did so with the vigilance of the Queen's Guard. Even when the Orchestra toured, Gunter was never at a loss for a babysitter to accompany them.

Ursula's sunny nature shone from sea green eyes that took in all around her with a quick and curious intelligence. Her face was surrounded by a thick mass of ginger curls that bobbed up and down as she moved. She became the darling of the Orchestra, loved by even the most stone-hearted member. She wore the most splendid clothing fashioned by the hands of relatives and friends of the Orchestra. Books and toys overflowed in a huge basket at rehearsal—mostly given anonymously by those who loved and cared for her. They took Ursula and her father into their hearts and received infinite love in return.

Her father bought her a violin at the age of two and by the age of four she stood beside him in their lounge room, notes blending, soaring around both violins. Until death parted them, Gunter and Ursula shared the most profound of father-daughter relationships. He never spoke of the other baby.

Chapter 6

Sunday, 8th May 1955 - Mother's Day

Les Baker hadn't wanted his wife, Ruth, to visit her friend in the hospital. He said it was too soon. The crying had gone on every day since Ruth's baby had been stillborn. For ten days she'd been having nightmares, and last night had been no exception.

She had sat up in bed, screaming, drenched with perspiration.

"Shhh, darling. It's all right. It was only a dream."

Les Baker had held his wife tightly until her sobbing stopped and the nightmare receded. It was the same dream. It was the baby dropping into a bucket from between her legs. It was her baby. The one that died.

His Ruth, who laughed and giggled constantly, who was full of mischief, who loved him and made his life complete—she had gone. She had been replaced by a different woman. A woman with tear-filled eyes, who suffered exhausting, restless nights, and who spent nearly every waking hour in the empty nursery.

From the time Ruth had discovered her pregnancy, she had sat at her sewing machine creating the most beautiful baby clothes. The layette grew daily with beribboned, frothy, lacy dresses, jackets, booties, hats, gloves, singlets and pants all piling up in the chest of drawers and wardrobe made by Les. She made stuffed toys for the baby too. Their favourite was a fat little teddy bear made of soft brown leather with a bright red collar stitched around its neck. The continual hum of the Singer machine accompanied the hammering, sawing and sanding of the best wood Les could obtain. From rough, straight, inanimate pieces of wood emerged smooth, gracefully curved pieces of furniture. They glowed warmly under their varnish, waiting for the new addition to the family to breathe life into them by occupying them.

It had been a happy pregnancy. A pregnancy that gave their love purpose and promise. Now there would be a baby who would be their own. One they could lavish all their love upon as they watched the child grow. Then there would be another and another and another until they were one laughing, happy, close-knit family. Something that neither of them had ever had.

Ruth had been born to a young girl who should have known better. That young girl came from a 'good' family, which was overseen in a most dictatorial manner by a Methodist Minister and his pious wife. Their daughter had been brought up to follow the strictest codes of behaviour, along with her two brothers and three sisters and, until she met the new boy in town, her rebellious spirit had never surfaced.

The new boy was like a breath of fresh air. He was different: independent, free-spirited, nomadic, nonconformist—and he was extremely attractive. He impregnated the girl's mind and body with feelings and thoughts and questions that had never occurred to her before. She dared to challenge her father's beliefs and practices, and she criticised her mother for her blind obedience and lack of motivation. And she dared to experiment with her own mind, and with her own body. Not only did she find herself a more reflective and independent young woman, she also found herself carrying a baby she was not ready for.

The adoption process was thorough and swift. The baby's new mummy and daddy called her Ruth and any memory of her real mother passed into oblivion.

Ruth grew up in her adopted home with parents who knew and understood little of how to give and receive love. Her new father—a stern, closemouthed farmer who towered threateningly over the young girl—saw young Ruth as a servant for his wife. Sickly and morose, her new mother was a whining and demanding woman, bitter over her husband's absences working on the land. The attention she craved from him was transferred to Ruth who received the brunt of the woman's frustrations. From a young age, Ruth was made to clean and cook from the time she rose until she fell exhausted into her bed at night. She received only the barest rudiments of education as it was considered a waste of valuable working hours for a girl like her. As a result, young Ruth met very few people and made no friends. No time was wasted on childish games when there was always a meal to cook, clothes to mend, and floors to scrub. It seemed that each task was interrupted by the bell ringing, the bitter woman's thin lips snapping out more orders, complaining and finding fault.

"Don't forget we adopted you," she would say, "so you owe us your keep—and more." They never let her forget it.

Ruth's body was small and slender, like her real mother's, with fine, sparse dark brown hair framing a fairly ordinary face. Her nose had an unsightly bump in the middle, her brown eyes were a little too close together, and her skin was so pale it was almost translucent. Small though her frame was, she was strong—and she was a survivor. The solitary, endless hours of work gave her plenty of time to think, having no one with whom to converse. Inside her childish mind wafted the stirrings of furtive defiance, not yet understood, not yet tested.

She never had cause to smile in the presence of her adoptive parents whose cold regard rejected any attempts at affection that she may have instigated. Life was to be endured, not enjoyed, and her only escape to a better world was in dreams.

She was a secretive child, who had imaginary friends with whom she shared her lonely hours. She saw their faces in the soapsuds as she played silent games whilst washing dirty dishes. They entertained her when her arms ached holding the scrubbing brush, and they made her giggle as she smoothed out their images from starched white sheets on the beds. They spoke to her in the hiss of steam as she ironed the dampened linens, and they whispered to her in the leaves that brushed her windows on dark, cold, solitary nights. No shared warmth by the open fire for her. The stony faces of her adoptive parents would turn towards her, if she dared enter the lounge room, eyebrows raised in surprise at her temerity.

At the age of fourteen, Ruth decided she had had enough. Life on her own would have to be better than the constant drudgery in her loveless existence. Despite the fact that she did not inherit her natural mother's good looks, she did inherit her rebellious streak. And so she packed her meagre belongings, stole enough money to get herself started, and disappeared on a train to be absorbed into the anonymity of the city of Perth.

It took Ruth two days to find herself a job as a machinist in a blouse factory. When she was put to work on a power machine, it didn't take long for the owners of the small factory, Earl and Mabel Blackburn, to notice the young girl's accuracy. She had a habit, they observed, of cocking her head to one side when she was thinking, or about to make a decision. They knew she wasn't educated, but she had an eye for detail and enough faith in herself to make them pleased with their decision to employ her. Tired of waiting for Earl to cut fabric and noticing pieces incorrectly cut, Ruth had enough cheek to offer to cut the fabric herself. Her fine stitching and workmanship as a sample hand made her a valuable asset, co-operating well with the Blackburns' designer. By the time she was seventeen, Ruth had learned just about everything the Blackburns could teach her.

When Ruth's wages rose, she moved to a boarding house closer to the factory. She had liked the owner, Gladys Taylor, the moment the front door was opened and the welcoming aroma of a roast dinner assailed her nostrils. Gladys wasted no time in showing Ruth the only room left out of the five she had available for boarders. She liked the look of the young girl and instinctively felt she would fit in with the rest of her tenants. Ruth looked around the clean, airy room, her head to one side. The dresser had a lace runner along its length, and the large mirror reflected a vase of freshly-picked flowers that filled the room with their fragrance. There was a large wardrobe, an armchair, a small table and a pretty bedspread that matched the curtains. The window looked out over a large backyard where she saw a well-kept vegetable garden and fruit trees with benches under them where she pictured herself reading a book in peace.

"Can I please take it?" she asked Gladys anxiously.

"Of course, dear. When would you like to move in?"

"Tomorrow?"

Gladys was an indulgent, motherly woman in her late forties, who always had a sympathetic ear and a hug for a worried young mind. She was a surrogate mother to her boarders, and they all loved her dearly. Young Ruth was swept under Gladys' wing and into her confidence and life turned around and smiled upon Ruth for the first time.

It was at the boarding house that Ruth met the shy, sandy-haired young carpenter, Les Baker, who had a room on the floor below her. At first she only saw him at meal times when they sat at the table. She would look up to catch his grey eyes regarding her, and they would both duck their heads down to their laden plates, pushing the food around distractedly. Her heart would beat so hard and fast that she was afraid the girl sitting next to her would hear it. *Don't look up at him,* she would admonish herself, but the irresistible urge to do so would overcome her, and she would catch him doing the same. Their blushes were not lost on the other four seated with them who watched their antics with growing amusement.

One wintry night Ruth had finished her bath and emerged flushed and damp from the bathroom. At the same time Les was about to enter the bathroom but was bent over at the doorway picking up his dropped comb. Ruth didn't see him in front of her and tripped right over him, landing in a tangled heap of clothes and towels and talcum powder.

"Oh, I'm sorry…" they both began, and then he burst out laughing at the sight of her.

The tin of powder had burst open and landed in a white cloud over her hair and face. Ruth started to giggle, great ripples bursting out from pent-up emotions, uncontrollable and delightful. The more she giggled, the more powder shook loose from her hair. The powder landed on the polished brown linoleum, on the stair banisters, on the skirting boards and on Les' dark brown dressing gown. She sneezed and a cloud of powder flew off her hair and into Les' face. At his surprised look, Ruth's hand flew up to her mouth in feigned horror, stifling the giggles that gushed from her mouth.

"What a fright you look," she gasped.

"And what about you?"

"Oh my, look at the floor!"

They fell to their knees trying ineffectually to mop up the powder with their towels.

"Gladys'll have a fit," giggled Ruth. White streaks lined the floor where they had been wiping.

The pair spent the next hour cleaning up the mess, whispering so as not to disturb Gladys who had retired for the night. It was the most wonderful happy hour Ruth had ever spent. The restraints of their shyness fell away to reveal mannerisms and personalities that they liked in each other.

His grey eyes took in the slight, compact figure hugged by her dressing gown, the translucent skin contrasting with the dark, damp hair, and he longed to trace the blue veins that pulsed at her neck. Her breath was gentle, fragrant, as she leaned towards him to wipe the powder from his face, her voice melodious, caressing. Her soft, brown eyes laughed at him, teased him. Her giggles rippled soft and light over his mind, enthralling him, enticing him.

Ruth regarded his sandy hair, the light catching in gold flashes as his head moved. She longed to touch it. His skin was a deep tan, evidence of long hours working in the sun, his hands calloused and strong. She wondered what they would feel like on her body. If they would be rough. When they stood together, her eyes were level with his full chest and she felt small beside him, but protected.

It was the beginning of what was to be a life-long devotion to each other.

Ruth hadn't left the house since he brought her home from the hospital. Perhaps the fresh air would be good for her after all. One of Ruth's work mates, Jenny, had been in a car accident and had been admitted to the hospital in a critical condition. It was the only thing that had penetrated Ruth's consciousness. Maybe it would take her mind off the baby.

Les had been told not to talk about their baby's death with her. It would only upset her more.

"Don't let her dwell on it. She's better off if she goes back to work. She'll forget all about it then." The hospital staff had been adamant.

The pain in Ruth's mind and body was relentless. It had been the only thing that had kept her going. She clutched onto it. Tightly. It was all she had left of her baby.

She looked at Les through the mist of pain and wondered if he, too, felt it. If his throat was constantly tight, hurting. If his gut was ground into a pulp that dug acidly into his ribs. She knew he was trying to hold her up, to keep her alive, to give her a reason to go on. *Why not end it?* she asked herself. But she looked at him and knew she couldn't leave him. She was his world and there would be nothing left for him if she died. She couldn't leave him with the loneliness, the emptiness—which he, too, had suffered until they first met.

Les was the younger of two sons born to Adele and Tom Baker in the port of Fremantle in nineteen thirty. Les' father was a merchant sailor who was hardly known to his two sons, or, indeed, his wife, who barely scratched out a living as a cook. Tom appeared intermittently at their rented weatherboard house, sometimes with money and gifts, at other times drunk and demanding. By the time the boys were eight and ten, Adele had begun to move them from one house to another, each one declining in size and condition, until the money ran out. Their father had stopped trying to find them, and decided to stay in Singapore where he had another family. Adele met a farmer who persuaded her to marry him and start their own family. Somehow he never found out that she already had two sons and was still married. Adele, not about to give up the opportunity of a settled, respectable life, set about to solve the problem of her adolescent boys, Harry and Les.

Engines and motors had always fascinated Harry, and he spent most of his spare time tinkering with bits and pieces he'd retrieved from the local tip. They had lived next to a garage in one of their houses and Harry had kept in contact with the mechanic over the years. That relationship looked like the best opportunity for Adele's oldest boy, so she arranged an apprenticeship and board with the mechanic's family. That left Les.

Like his older brother, Les had shown a liking for a trade—not with engines, but with wood. He liked to build and carve, and a hammer, nails and saw were never very far from his capable hands.

"Always work with your hands, boys," their mother told them. "You'll never be out of work as long as you use your hands. Get a trade."

Les, too, began an apprenticeship with a carpenter, and he settled into a boarding house.

Adele began her bigamous marriage with the farmer, leaving no forwarding address with her sons. They had no idea what had happened to her and never bothered to try to find out.

Harry and Les saw each other every weekend, swimming at the beach in the summer, going to the pictures in the winter, until the older boy fell in love. Harry gradually slipped out of Les' life until Christmas was the only time left for them. The Bakers had drifted and scattered from each other with very little anguish suffered by any of them.

Les grew up a likeable young man, who was eager to please. He was a hard worker who became a very talented and expert carpenter. He considered every piece of wood as if it were a living thing that needed to be coaxed into life. He saw its innate beauty and instinctively knew how to produce a masterpiece. Woodturning was a delight that filled his free time. His work was his only interest. He appeared an untroubled, uncomplicated young man, with not a care in the world. No one pierced the shell he had skilfully constructed around him, the shell that hid the longing for someone to love him, the longing to be needed, the longing to love.

Les shifted from one boarding house to another. They were occupied by shifting, unfriendly people—nobody who could satisfy his hunger for love. His luck finally turned for the better when he found Gladys Taylor's boarding house. She was the mother he yearned for and the two other young men and girl were a nice change. They were good mates and the girl, even though she had a boyfriend, was like a sister. Meal times were fun, the food was great, and they laughed a lot.

When Ruth moved in, Les was twenty-two and had been living at Gladys's for eighteen months. He was a tall, heavyset young man, with thick sandy hair cut short above a handsome straight-nosed face. His wide mouth revealed large, white teeth when he smiled— and that was often—and his firm chin was cleft with the deepest of dimples from which there was always an errant bristle sticking out. For those eighteen months, Gladys and the boarders had tried to match Les with numerous girls, but to no avail. He was awkward around girls, never knowing what to talk about. They were mysterious creatures to him that smelled good and talked incessantly about things of which he had no knowledge. They weren't in the least interested in his job, and the few times he had spent with a girl had been an agony of fixed smiles and weighty silences. It was easier to go to a brothel for relief. He didn't have to talk to those women. They wanted to get it over and done with as quickly as possible anyway. He would return home physically satisfied but mentally despondent.

But Ruth was different. She looked at people when they were talking and appeared interested in whatever they had to say. She actually listened to them, usually with her head held to one side, like she was thinking very seriously. She made him feel as if he mattered and, once their initial shyness had melted away, he was more comfortable with her than anyone in his life. They talked about anything and everything, tripping over their words trying to get them out fast enough. They laughed together, finding so many of the same things funny. Silences were contented sharings of time spent in each other's company, saying nothing, doing nothing, just being together.

Ruth was the best thing that ever happened to Les. He wanted to wrap her up in a protective sheath that would keep her from harm, that would give her warmth, that would answer her needs. She accepted his love and gave back to him her soul, her life. They were two unloved, lonely people who had never belonged, and now they dared to look at the future with hope—together.

Ruth watched Les through the kitchen window as he got into his old truck. He looked up at her and raised his hand to hers that rested tightly on the window glass. Neither of them smiled. The corners of their mouths felt heavy, tired. Her red-rimmed eyes moved scratchily in their sandpaper sockets as she gritted her teeth in the tight, aching jaw in an effort to stop the tears yet again.

"You go," she'd told him.

"I don't like leaving you—especially today." What he meant was—Mother's Day. He wasn't sure if she realised.

"It makes no difference. And you promised."

"Yes, I know. But he'll understand."

"You can't put it off forever. And you don't have any other time to do it."

It was one last favour he had promised Harry, his brother. Harry and his wife were selling their house to move interstate, and there were a few repairs that needed doing to it before it was shown to prospective buyers. Ever since Ruth had lost her baby, Les had kept delaying and time was running short for his brother.

"If you're sure..."

"Go," she had insisted. "He needs you."

As the sound of the truck faded into the traffic, Ruth began to get ready. *I owe it to him. I must make an effort,* she told herself. She looked at the haunted face in the mirror as she dug into her mouth with the toothbrush. She noticed idly that more hair had fallen into the basin. It seemed to be coming out in clumps. Her lipstick looked gaudy on her pale face, and she wiped it off leaving a smudge that wouldn't rub off. Her breasts were agonizingly engorged with ten days neglected milk stretching her dress tightly across them. She dismissed the thought that she would have to do something about it.

She sat in the train carriage, looking out at houses that blurred past the window reflections. She tried not to look at the mothers and their children sitting near her but her eyes were drawn towards them. Everywhere she looked she saw babies. In the train, in the station, in the streets. They jumped into her vision unbidden—a cruel reminder of her loss.

Ruth hesitated at the foot of the hospital stairs, looking up at the windows that stared blankly out over the city. One window revealed a ghostly face looking out. The wind had risen cold and insistent, and she thought it might rain later that afternoon. She entered the foyer and climbed the stairs to her friend's ward without asking anyone for directions.

Jenny was very tired. Her right leg was encased in plaster and raised on a pulley and her head was heavily bandaged.

"Jenny. It's me. Ruth."

"Thanks for coming," she whispered. Her eyes fluttered open momentarily then closed back into healing sleep.

Ruth sat beside her for a few minutes holding her hand, then stood up to kiss her cheek before turning away.

The sound of babies crying lured her away from the exit. She was like a moth irresistibly drawn to a light. *They look so helpless,* she thought looking at them through the glass. They were all crying, their little fists waving in futile jerks, their hunger creating havoc in the nursery. *Why doesn't somebody feed them?*

Ruth watched an harassed nurse talking with a doctor in the next room. Her breasts were aching with untapped milk. The front of her dress was soaked. The little red face in front of her screwed up in anger, the body convulsing inside the tightly-wrapped cloths. Beside the baby's head was a stuffed toy. It was a fat little teddy bear made of soft brown leather with a bright red collar stitched around its neck. Ruth was so close that she could see inside the baby's wide-open mouth. The glass stopped her outstretched hands.

When the nurse returned, the urgent hunger of the crowded nursery claimed her attention. It wasn't until she got to the twins, that she noticed one was gone.

Chapter 7

Les returned from his brother's house a worried man. After the baby died he didn't like leaving Ruth on her own. She wasn't the same anymore. She stared into space, not talking for hours on end, silent tears trickling slowly down her face, then down onto her milk-soaked dress. And the nightmares. They woke her up every night. He felt desperate, unable to cope with the closed shell she had erected around her pain. He couldn't reach her, and he felt alone for the first time since he had met her. His pain was different from hers, he knew, but it was there all the same.

The loss of their baby had devastated him. Their hopes, their dreams, were shattered and torn. The nursery stood empty, a grim reminder of the tiny being who had failed to come home with them. Who had failed to breathe life into that room. Who had failed to fill their lives. Who had failed to even establish an identity. The doctors told him to be patient, but Ruth didn't seem to be getting any better. Perhaps they should leave Perth and their grief behind. A change of scenery would be good for both of them—make a new beginning.

Before Les opened the door he could hear her singing. It was a lullaby. She was seated on a lounge chair holding a soft pink-wrapped bundle to her breast and her smile when she looked up at him was...ecstatic. Her eyes held the old sparkle; joy and love greeted his stunned stare.

"What on earth...?"

She continued to sing softly, rocking back and forth, winding red curls gently around her fingers, pulling them out and letting them snap back to the tiny scalp.

"Where did you get it?"

"She didn't die, Les. They made a mistake. Isn't she beautiful?"

He dropped to his knees beside her and gazed in wonder at the baby feeding sleepily at his wife's breast.

"Ruth. Darling. Where did you get this baby?" he asked gently.

"She's ours, Les. You know that."

Her arms tightened around the bundle as she resumed her lullaby. He sensed that she would not argue about it. She was convinced it was hers.

This was the scene that he had imagined when Ruth was still carrying their own baby. But not now. Not with this baby. Where did she get it? How? His mind raced in confusion, questions bombarding him. There had to be an explanation, but he knew he wouldn't get it from Ruth.

He noticed the fat little brown leather teddy bear with the bright red collar around its neck. He hadn't seen it since Ruth was admitted to hospital for the birth. Neither of them had bothered to look for it when they left their dead baby behind. And now here it was.

All right. Let's think about this logically. I went to Harry's. Ruth was here. I saw her at the window when I left. I come home and now she's got a baby. Where did she go in the meantime—the hospital!

"Ruth."

"Umm...?"

"Did you go to the hospital today?"

"Umm..."

"Did you see Jenny?"

"Yes. I promised you I'd go."

"Did you go anywhere else?"

The only sound in the room was the baby's sucking and his own harsh breathing.

"Did you visit anyone else?"

He saw a fugitive shadow dart across her eyes as she looked up at him. A frown creased her forehead for an instant and then smoothed out, gone as quickly as it had come, an intruder no longer. A smile began in her eyes and melted into her face, the corners of her lips turning up slowly until her face radiated with it.

"No. I just went to pick up the baby. I couldn't leave her there, could I?"

Les sat back on his heels in resignation.

"No. I don't suppose you could," he said slowly.

He grudgingly recognized that Ruth's mind now teetered on the edge of insanity and it frightened him. He didn't know how to handle it. The past ten days had shown him a side of Ruth that he never knew existed. So withdrawn, so depressed, so—apart. He hadn't wanted to admit, even to himself, that she might be somewhat...*affected*...by the death of their baby. The word *crazy* had flitted through his head, but he had rejected it with repugnance. Not his Ruth. She was far too sensible to lose her mind.

Her head was now bent over the baby as she rocked in time with her lullaby, touching, stroking the soft pink skin. Les studied her in an agony of indecision. He was convinced that she had taken the baby from the hospital. There would be an uproar. She would be found out. It was a terrible crime, he knew. She would be taken away from him. Perhaps for years. No, he couldn't let that happen. Take his Ruth away from him? Never! Especially not now. Now that she had a baby—all right, not her own—but she would make it so. She looked so fulfilled, so calm, so free of pain. No one would take that away from her, not if he could help it. A fierce protectiveness for Ruth clenched his jaw. *No one will hurt you,* he promised her silently. *No one will take you away from me.*

It wasn't very long before his suspicions were confirmed. That night the news on the wireless announced the disappearance of one of a pair of twins. Les sat with a mouthful of steak, unchewed, as he listened to the story of the stolen red-haired baby from Prince Alfred Hospital. Pity for the German father of the twins made it impossible to swallow. Les knew what it was like to lose a baby—but a wife as well? He couldn't bear to be in that man's position. Les's mouth was dry; the meat stuck like a heavy sponge in his throat. He felt like he was choking.

"Is the steak tough, Les?" Ruth asked him, concern in her eyes.

He shook his head mutely, listening to the newsreader's voice going on and on...*Mr Schwartz collapsed when told...*twisting the news into his gut...*having suffered at the hands of the Nazis...*turning the knife edge...*distraught hospital staff...*words, more words...*police having instigated investigations...*torturing him. Ruth eating unconcerned. Smiling.

Les' chair fell back with a clatter on the floor, the baby shuddering at the unexpected noise, as he stumbled to the bathroom. Deep, convulsive retching left him exhausted, eyes streaming, legs weak, trembling. He leaned against the wall gasping.

"Are you all right, Les?" she called out.

"Yes...yes...I'm all right."

"What happened?"

"The meat...got stuck in my throat," he called back weakly.

He returned to the table, sitting heavily on his chair, and pushed the fork around in the congealing gravy on his plate. He noticed the wireless had been turned to another station. Soft music created a deceptive cheerful background, a lie to the upheaval touching so many lives.

She's not even aware of what she's done, he thought. He looked at her, marvelling at her returned healthy appetite, and total oblivion to the trauma she had caused. And he was afraid, terribly afraid.

Ruth refused to be drawn into any discussion about where the baby had come from. She laughed at him as though he was being ridiculous. It was her baby and no one was going to persuade her otherwise. The bassinet was beside her at the table, her eyes hardly leaving the baby's face. She chattered animatedly, laughter bubbling at her lips, the dark circles already receding from beneath her eyes. He could see that her pain was gone.

He felt like they were actors on a stage as he carefully watched her. His mind seemed to be floating above him—detached, analytical—while his body responded like a puppet whose strings were tangled. She played the part of the mother with ease and competence, her movements flowing, assured. And he the new father—tentative, awkward—in awe of the power of maternal love.

The nursery was now inviting, warm with the personality of the tiny being who occupied it. The soft smell of baby powder rose to his nostrils as Ruth replaced a wet nappy with a dry one and then slipped on a frothy lace nightdress and matching booties. She bent over the baby, gently holding the clutching fingers, and kissed the pink forehead, her eyes half-closed in ecstasy.

"Can I…"

"Hold her?"

"Yes."

"Of course, darling. She's your daughter too."

"How do I…?"

Ruth showed Les how to pick up the baby, supporting her head. He cradled the soft wriggling bundle in his arms, amazed at the emotions that exploded in his mind and heart. The tiny mouth worked in a muffled language that included him and yet confounded him. The eyes looked up at him, seeming to search his face as much as he did hers.

"Can she see me yet?"

"No. Not yet. Perhaps your shape."

"Oh."

"She knows it's you, though. She knows it's her daddy."

"How can you know that?"

"I just do."

"Ruth…"

"Yes?"

"Are you sure…?"

"Isn't she perfect? Isn't she beautiful?"

"Yes, but…"

"She's everything I dreamed she'd be."

"But…"

"And I'm so happy, Les. I'm just so happy!"

Her eyes shone with tears that came from pure joy—not the painful tears of the past ten days. She kissed him lingeringly and he could taste the salt of her tears. Her arms were around him, encouraging him. She gazed at the baby for a long moment, then up at him.

"You know, Les. We really are a family now. We have each other, and we have her. You—and she—are my whole life. My joy. If I died now, I'd die happy."

"I know," he said softly. There were tears in his eyes too.

"Les?"

"Umm...?"

"Can we call her Joy?"

"Joy?"

"Yes. Joy. She's our Joy."

Les lay awake listening to his wife breathing beside him. Her sleep was untroubled, deep and peaceful. The faint glow of a lamp from the nursery next door to their room was a welcome hint of the addition to their married life. He smiled to himself in the dark, overwhelmed by love for the woman he had married. She was everything to him. He would do anything for her.

He thought of the German couple with guilt, but reminded himself that the mother was dead. She'd had two of them, hadn't she? Surely the natural father couldn't cope with two, didn't need both. Ruth and he could give the second baby as much love—no, more—than the natural father could. They would both work hard, give the baby all she needed in life. The natural father was only one person. He had no wife to support him, to bring up two babies. Of course...two would be almost unmanageable for a man on his own. He and Ruth were probably doing the man a favour.

Yes. They would keep the baby. Joy—it was a perfect name for her. Ruth was always right about things. She just knew what was for the best. She was so capable. Always capable. Except when their own baby died. It was like she'd died with the baby. And he'd been acutely terrified that he was going to lose her too. If not physically, certainly mentally. He couldn't have borne that. Not after all their dreams. Their plans for a family. A future together. But his Ruth had come back to him. She'd come back with the German man's baby. It was meant to be. These things didn't happen just by chance.

Les had never been a God-fearing man, preferring to answer to his own demons about the difference between right and wrong. His mother had never taken him or Harry to church. It was a place he went to for weddings and funerals, and there hadn't been many of those in his lifetime. People spoke of God and urged him to take up a religion, but Les had resisted, uncomfortable with their talk of heaven and hell. He supposed he would be punished on Judgement Day for being an unbeliever. They told him so. But Les was never a hypocrite and he wasn't about to start being one now. If he was going to burn in hell there wasn't much he could do about it.

When Ruth lost their baby, when their hopes were dashed, Les looked up to where heaven was supposed to be and shook his fist at a vengeful God. Ruth was a good woman—had never done a rotten thing in her life—and she was being punished. After all she'd suffered during her life, she was being punished cruelly. Les couldn't understand—if there was a God—why their baby had been taken from them. Ruth had never clung to an ethereal figure for comfort during her desolate childhood and quietly shared Les's scepticism. Was she now being tortured for that?

During the ten days before Joy came into their lives, Les conducted many muttered conversations with God. He accused, berated and scorned the God that others loved as he worked, each hammer blow driven by his fury. Every nail disappeared into its wooden tomb, followed by another and another and another. Curses punctuated each blow, a sob lurking behind them but denied release. The handsaw bit into timber that seemed like melted butter, enraged strength empowering his arm muscles. His hands that had been so gentle, almost caressing the wood as he shaped it, now took on a brutality that sanded rough edges without love, without care.

In his agony and desperation, Les accepted the existence of the God he had denied. Ironically, it helped Les to work through his grief. If there was someone—or something—he could blame, he could focus his fury and impotence upon it. If God was *all-seeing and all-knowing*, how could He rob Ruth, who was good, of a baby and give one to any woman who was not worthy? There were plenty of unwanted children on earth—wasn't his Ruth living evidence of that? Why deny her, especially her, the chance to replace the love that had never been hers? Les would look up contemptuously, past gathering clouds towards infinity, and spit in his mind at the God he didn't believe in.

Merciful, they call You! They don't know the meaning of the word. You don't exist. I don't believe You exist. I'll never believe You exist.

The baby began to cry out her hunger. Ruth stirred and sat up instantly awake.

"The baby!"

"She must be hungry," Les murmured, switching on the bedside lamp. "Do you need some help?"

"No. I'm fine. I'll just get her."

The cries were more insistent as Ruth got out of bed.

"I'm coming, little one," she soothed the baby as she picked her up, then returned to bed with her.

Les sat up against the pillows, and watched in wonder as Joy fastened onto the already leaking nipple that Ruth offered her.

"How does she know what to do?"

Ruth laughed.

"Instinct, I guess."

This must be the closest thing to heaven, thought Les as he watched mother and child bond in the most simple of actions—giving and receiving. A warmth spread slowly from the pit of his stomach right up to his throat and he choked on tears that engulfed him. He sobbed his relief and his love into the shoulder of his wife and he knew she understood. *I do believe in you. You have given me back my Ruth.*

Les arose early without disturbing Ruth or the baby, and went out to buy the morning newspapers. He sat in the truck reading them, hands trembling as he read the sensational headlines.

TWIN GIRL KIDNAPPED FROM HOSPITAL

BABY TAKEN BY FIEND!

FATHER COLLAPSES WHEN DAUGHTER STOLEN!

...German immigrant, Gunter Schwartz, was unavailable for comment after the death of his wife in childbirth...Detective Sergeant George Chambers, assigned to the case, holds grave fears for the safety of the newborn baby girl...the stolen twin has disappeared without a trace...staff, in and around the hospital, are being interrogated...the question being raised as to how Mr Schwartz will bring up the surviving baby on his own...whether

the death penalty should be imposed when the
kidnapper is caught if the baby is...

Les stared for a long while at the photo of Hannah and Gunter
Schwartz. It was a close-up in which the couple was in profile, looking at each other. Gunter's hand was touching her hair and she was
laughing up at him as he smiled into her eyes. His straight fair hair
had been carefully parted and combed, in stark contrast to the pro-
fusion of curls that surrounded her face. His was a strong face with
a firm chin that, although young, bore lines of hardship and sorrow.
Her face was softly contoured around high cheek-bones and her long
neck disappeared into a roll collar. The photo had been taken outside; there was a clear sky behind them and a blurred image of two
birds as they flew behind the couple. It was a loving picture taken
at a time when the couple was free, enjoying each other immensely,
and when their life was full of promise.

Les tried to put himself in Gunter's place but Ruth's image
blurred out any feelings of guilt. It was not hard to persuade himself that he was about to do the right thing.

He knew that he would have to move fast. Before anyone suspected. Melbourne was far enough away to make a new start. There
were always jobs for good carpenters and Ruth could take in sewing.
It wouldn't take him long to settle into a new job once they arrived
there, and they could save up a deposit on their own home—
somewhere near the beach. It would be good for the baby and Ruth.

Chapter 8   W.A. to Victoria

"Ruth! Ruth! I've got a great idea."

Les burst in through the back door, false enthusiasm lighting up his face. The grin felt stiff, phony, but he had to convince her it was the right thing.

"Les, where've you been so early?"

"I bought the papers to have a look at the jobs columns."

"Whatever for? You've got plenty of work here."

"Yes, I know. But it's time to move on. Start a new life."

Ruth was holding the baby up against her shoulder as she walked around the kitchen. Motherhood suited her. She took to it naturally like she'd had lessons. But as always, since they'd first met, she stopped what she was doing and gave him her full attention. He guided her to the table and they sat down opposite each other. The baby's head wobbled on Ruth's shoulder, and she cupped it in her hand as she lowered her into the crook of her arm. Smelling milk, the baby turned instinctively towards Ruth's breast, the mouth working excitedly. Ruth opened her dressing gown and pushed her leaking nipple towards the mouth. She experienced the tingling sensation of the let-down reflex as the baby suckled and the milk surged spontaneously.

"Now tell me what you've been up to," she prompted him.

He was distracted, marvelling at the picture before him. He'd never been so close to a woman breast feeding until now. It was beautiful. Mother and baby looked so close, you'd think nothing would ever part them. He wondered idly if his mother had breast fed him. Perhaps his mother had used a bottle for him and Harry. Why else would she leave them like she had? God knows where she was now, what she was doing, if she was happy, if she'd had any more children. It didn't matter to Les anymore—now that he had Ruth and little Joy.

"Well, I woke up with the idea that it would be good to see a bit of the world, you know...a bigger city."

"Go on."

"Haven't you ever wondered what the east coast is like? We haven't been out of Western Australia."

"No, we haven't."

"And I thought, now that we're parents...we should look to Joy's future."

"Yes."

"It's pretty small here in Perth. We could offer her more in Melbourne or Sydney. Education, jobs and so on. The east coast has more going on."

"That's true."

"So, what do you think?"

"I think it's a very good idea."

"You do?"

"Yes. I do."

It was that easy. Ruth sat there holding the baby, looking at Les with trusting eyes, her head cocked to one side.

She's listening. Really listening, he thought.

It took Les two weeks to finish up his most important jobs, sell the old truck and buy an American 'Lend Lease' Chevrolet truck at the Army disposals auction in East Perth. It had been painted a dull red-brick colour on the exterior, but reminders of the war were evident in the khaki-painted interior. The chrome work had been painted over but he left it as it was thinking he would restore it to its former condition, as well as painting his name, address and business description on the doors once he was established in Melbourne. He was pleased with its neat and tidy appearance and its apparent good condition, and wondered where it had seen service. He'd been lucky, he thought, to pick it up at such a reasonable price. He built up the tray with a height of four boards to surround it so that their belongings would survive the trip—which he knew would be rough—without bouncing off the sides. When he looked out of the kitchen window at the truck, it seemed to sit there proudly beckoning to him to be loaded and on its way with its new owners to the other side of the continent, some two thousand-odd miles to the east.

Les sold their furniture, taking it piece by piece to auction rooms and private homes after answering advertisements in the newspapers. Included were the chest of drawers and wardrobe he had worked on so lovingly for the baby's room, but he comforted himself that he could make new ones when they arrived in Melbourne.

He bought supplies for the trip with the money he raised from the sale of the furniture: a Coleman lamp, Primus stove, drums for water and petrol, jerry cans, a spare battery for the truck, a shotgun, temperature gauge, maps, chains, extra ropes, plenty of canned fish, corned beef, fruit and vegetables. He checked his tarpaulin for tears and made sure that the spare truck tyres were in perfect condition.

Their rent paid up, Les told the landlord that he and Ruth were moving down to Albany. The landlord was sorry to see the young couple go. They had been good for the house, making improvements to it with Les building a verandah around it and fixing the fencing, and Ruth putting up pretty curtains in all of the windows. During the two weeks it took Les to finalise everything for the trip, he chafed at any delay, desperately anxious to get away before the authorities caught up with them.

"Don't go out unless you have to, Ruth. It's getting chilly now and Joy might catch a cold."

Ruth was only too willing to oblige. He wondered if she realised the danger they were in.

"Try not to have any visitors. They might give the baby a cold."

He hoped their neighbours were too busy with their own lives to notice that Ruth hadn't returned with her baby at the expected time. She hadn't gone out during those ten days, so he hoped people would assume Joy's cries were those of the baby that Ruth had carried. He prayed there was nothing to connect them with the missing baby. They must get out of Perth—and fast.

On Sunday, 22 May 1955, at 4.00 a.m., the packed truck drove out of Perth with Les and Ruth sitting in the front with their baby. They never looked back.

Joy slept in Ruth's arms as her new parents spoke over the unfamiliar noises of the Chev truck. It seemed to bite into the road effortlessly, strong and determined to sweep its passengers into a new beginning. They watched the sunrise ahead of them, heralding in the new day in a blaze of light that flamed the red-barked gums, as if golden powder had been sprinkled on everything before them.

They made good time during the 160 miles to Merredin, reaching there in three hours on the bitumen road surface.

"Are you going to pull over to have a rest, Les?" Ruth touched his arm as they were about to enter Merredin.

"Not unless you want to, love. I'd rather go as far as Southern Cross where the bitumen stops. We could have a cuppa then, eh?"

After they had driven along the main street of Southern Cross, a ghost of its former bustle in the gold rush days, the road changed to a single lane of bitumen. Les pulled over carefully in the loose red sand on the side of the road.

"How about a cuppa now?"

It was good to get out and stretch their legs in the fresh morning air. Ruth busied herself with the thermos she had packed, and they stood by the roadside easing their cramped muscles and enjoying the steaming tea and homemade biscuits.

"She's been so good, Les. Not a murmur out of her."

"That might change when we hit the gravel. It's not going to be easy."

"She'll be fine. I'm sure of it."

I wish I could be as sure, he thought, knowing that what lay ahead of them was going to be a very difficult journey. *Just so long as no one catches up with us.*

They were lucky that morning, not passing a single vehicle on the way to Coolgardie. Les was pleased with their progress and the ease with which Ruth and the baby took to the adventure. He decided to give them frequent stops, however, and they ate their pre-packed sandwiches with a healthy appetite. By late afternoon they were approaching Coolgardie through mostly undulating plains of red sand covered by mulga scrub and eucalypts with the occasional hill here and there. Rabbits darted between the scrub as eagles, cockatoos and crows soared above them, waiting for their opportunity to feed on any unwary creature that failed to look skywards. Kangaroos thrust themselves in huge bounds across the road in their journey towards food and water.

Les slowed the truck as they drove along the quiet wide main street with its stately stone buildings from a bygone era. He searched the street looking anxiously for a fuel supplier. It was better to top up the drums of petrol when he had the chance, as he knew that petrol stops were scarce.

"I'll just drop the two of you off out of town a bit, then I'll come back for some petrol," he said. "Keep low."

"Why, Les? Is there something wrong?"

"No, love. I'd just rather people don't remember us along the way."

Ruth looked at Les in puzzlement, but said nothing.

He wanted to make sure that no one would remember a couple travelling in a Chevrolet truck with a baby. So Les drove out of town and left Ruth and Joy sheltered behind some scrub on a groundsheet. This was to be the pattern for each town that they passed through.

"Will you be all right?" he asked anxiously.

"Of course. Go," she reassured him.

"I'll be as quick as I can."

He turned the truck around and sped back to Coolgardie, feeling very guilty leaving his wife and baby alone. *What if a wild animal attacks them?* He tortured himself with thoughts of disaster befalling them without his protection.

"Where're you off to, mate?" asked the man as he filled the petrol drum and the truck's tank. "We don't get many strangers around these days."

The man was slow, happy to while away the time in conversation, leaning on the side of the truck. He peered over the side of the tray, curious.

"Going a fair way by the look of it."

"Esperance," Les lied.

"Got a good deal of stuff back there," said the man indicating the supplies packed into the back of the truck.

"Yeah. Stuff for my brother's property."

"Oh? What's his name? I might know of him," the man persisted.

"Rogers. Bill Rogers."

"No. Can't say I've heard of him. What's he do there?"

Will this bloke never give up!

"Fishing mostly."

"Got family?"

"Yeah. Three or four kids."

"What about you, mate? You hitched?"

"No. Too ugly."

Les settled up and took off before the man could ask more probing questions. He was aware of the man's curious stare following the truck along the street. Thank goodness Ruth and the baby weren't with him.

To his relief, Ruth and Joy were where he'd left them—unharmed and quite rested.

"Are we going to Kalgoorlie, Les?" she asked, happy to be next to her husband again in the truck.

"No. No point going that far out of our way—unless you want to see it, do you?"

"Not particularly." Ruth snuggled into Les's left side. "Where are we going next then?"

"Norseman. It's about a hundred miles from here. But we'll sleep beside the road tonight before we get there. No sense pushing ourselves too much."

The road was in very poor condition, being gravel and sand, and he had to concentrate carefully on the miles ahead. He felt they should face the difficult conditions fresh the next day and looked for a suitable place to pull over. Half an hour later, Les spotted a clump of eucalypts off the road.

"This should do us," he said as he headed the truck over loose red sand behind some scrub.

It didn't screen them entirely, but it was far enough off the road for the truck not to be readily visible, and he thought it unlikely that there would be any traffic that late in the afternoon. The sun was setting behind them and they saw on the gauge that the temperature had dropped to a cool forty-eight degrees. Ruth began to shiver as she stepped down from the truck, and they donned jumpers quickly.

By the fading light Les unpacked their supplies and positioned a rolled-up rubber mattress on the base of the tray. In the meantime Ruth had a frying pan on the Primus stove with large slabs of beef, tomatoes and onions sizzling in butter, and a billy boiling on a tripod over a fire.

"That smells great," Les enthused, hugging Ruth. "I never realised how hungry I was."

"Come and get stuck into it. It's our first and last steak, so we'd better enjoy it. It kept all right considering it was such a nice day."

Washed down by hot tea, they made a good meal of their beef steaks, followed by canned peaches.

"I wouldn't be dead for quids," Les grinned. "Not with such a bonzer wife, a beaut little daughter, and all this."

He swept his arm around to indicate the West Australian bush surrounding them in the fading light where the horizon turned a misty amethyst. As one, they both stood and embraced tightly. Joy watched their shapes blend into one and waved her arms and legs as she lay on her back on the ground sheet. She, too, had a full belly and was content.

"Look at those stars," breathed Ruth, looking at the canopy above them. "There are so many of them. It's beautiful."

They lay on the mattress, Joy tucked safely in beside them, listening to the sounds of crickets and birds settling down to sleep in the velvety deep blackness of the bush.

"Are you afraid?" Les murmured.

"No."

"The eggs are ready," called Ruth.

Les was packing the truck the next morning as the sun began to rise over the horizon casting light on their surroundings. It was cold but the morning sky was cloudless above the mist, promising a warm and sunny day.

He sat down beside her, devouring the eggs and bacon with a voracious appetite.

"I'll be getting fat at this rate," he said, soaking up the egg yolk with his fourth piece of bread.

His mouth full, and holding out his mug for a refill, his gaze settled on one of the back wheels of the truck.

"Oh, no!"

"What?"

"Hell's bells."

"What, Les?"

"Look at that," he pointed. "We've got a flat tyre."

"We've got two spares, though, haven't we?"

"Yes, but we need to get this one fixed before going too far. We can't risk having just one spare."

"How long to Norseman?"

After consulting the maps, Les realised they still had around one hundred miles of very poor conditions before them. It was too dangerous to risk another flat tyre on the gravel road.

"We'll have to go back."

"To Coolgardie?"

"No. Too risky. The fellow who sold me the fuel was too nosy. We'll have to go to Kalgoorlie."

Although out of their way, Les knew he had to turn back. With only one spare tyre left, they could be sitting on the side of the road for days if they had another flat. Ruth smoothed the anxious lines along Les's forehead.

"Don't worry. It'll be all right."

"I expect so. Come on then, we'd better get started," he said as he made for the tools to change the tyre.

It was still early when they passed through Coolgardie, the sleepy town not yet astir, and Les heaved a sigh of relief as they passed the fuel depot. There was no one about.

"You can get up now," he told Ruth.

She had been lying down out of view. Joy gurgled contentedly in her arms, unaware of her parents' concern.

Like the day before, kangaroos and emus darted across the red sand plains where isolated hills and low scrubby vegetation were the only features on the endless countryside. One car passed them, going in the opposite direction, honking its horn loudly, the driver waving at them with a grin on his face. His car was soon lost to sight in the dust cloud raised by the two vehicles.

Ruth and Les were amazed at the size of Kalgoorlie and the number of historic hotels in Hannan Street.

"There'll be no problem getting our supplies here," said Les, noticing Fernie's grocery shop in Hannan Street and Matzig & Jarvis butchers shop. "We can have steaks again tonight."

Finding the sign for Kambalda, Les headed out of Kalgoorlie, past rickety buildings and tin sheds rusted brown on the red soil, until he found a suitable place to leave Ruth and the baby.

"Why don't you stop at that Exchange Hotel? Have a beer, Les. You'd enjoy it. You might find out more about the road conditions there too."

"I couldn't do that thinking of you two here waiting. I'll be back as soon as I can. Don't leave without me."

"Silly," she laughed, kissing him resoundingly on the mouth.

He was back after two hours worried sick that he had been so long. He had to wait for the tyre to be fixed, so topped up their water drums in the meantime at the pipeline along the roadside. The shops weren't open at that early hour, so he had to wait, not wanting to leave without the promised steaks. He bought canned fruit, cheese, bread and eggs in Fernie's and looked for a newspaper, but they were a few days old so useless for the information he was seeking.

"You know why Hannan Street is so wide?" he asked Ruth when he returned to her. "It's because camels can't walk backwards!"

"What are you talking about, Les?"

"They used to have camel trains there, and they had to have the extra-wide streets so that they could turn around. How about that?"

"That sounds reasonable," she said, her head to one side, listening to him.

Passing through Kambalda, the road rejoined the highway to Norseman almost fifty miles out of Kalgoorlie.

"Are you hungry?"

"I could eat a horse," Les answered laughing. "It must be the country air."

"Where do you think we'll stop for lunch, then?"

"How about just before Norseman? Can you wait that long?"

"You're the one who's hungry, not me." Ruth poked him in the stomach.

The noon sky was cloudless and they drove in a pleasant silence in the warmth of the autumn day.

Being the last major town in Western Australia before heading east across the Nullarbor Plain, Norseman was an important stop for the Bakers. Les was mindful of the need for water and petrol for the long journey ahead of them and topped up his tanks yet again, as well as checking all the truck tyres. He worried whether he should have three spare tyres and tubes instead of just the two, but space was at a premium on the tray.

At midafternoon, Les turned the Chev towards Balladonia, some one hundred and thirty miles east of Norseman.

"Are you ready for this?" he asked Ruth anxiously. "It's going to be rough."

"I'm ready for anything, as long as I'm with you and Joy," was her reply.

They were lucky it wasn't the rainy season. The Eyre Highway was just a dirt road with tracks made by cars and trucks as they passed along it, in some places as many as three tracks to choose from. Les had been warned that if it rained they would get stuck and have to wait until the road dried out, and that they could not afford to do. He looked up at the sky and was reassured by the endless expanse of blue.

It was hard going. The rattling of the truck, constant gear changing over the uneven tracks, the drumming of the motor, all made it difficult for conversation. Ruth fell into a light sleep, jarring awake from time to time as the truck bounced over ruts, and the baby slept with her, more cushioned by Ruth's body than Ruth was by the truck seat. Les stared ahead, eyes constantly on the alert for any sign of danger that might put the truck out of action. He winced each time a stone thudded against the underside of the truck, but it happened so often that the winces became a continual frown that remained stamped upon his forehead. Fine red dust coated everything inside the cabin. It was hot in the afternoon sun and he wiped at trickles of sweat that ran down his dirty face. The low green and brown scrub lined the road as it pointed ahead towards the uninterrupted horizon in the distance.

Les wondered what had been going through Ruth's mind since he had announced they would leave for Melbourne. Not once had she questioned his motives or objected to any suggestion. She'd calmly packed up what they could take and helped him sell or give away what they couldn't. He'd kept newspapers away from the house and turned the wireless off when the news was broadcast at the usual hours. It was as though the outside world no longer existed for her.

He had scanned the newspapers in great detail, looking for any clue that might betray them to the police, but it was apparent that there was no sign of a culprit. It baffled the police and the media.

At times, Les wanted to talk to Ruth about it, but he sensed that it was a closed subject—one that would create a rift between them if brought to the surface, and that he was not prepared to risk. Their relationship was almost exactly the same as before their own baby was stillborn. They laughed together, they loved together, and they shared the wonder of the baby they had in their keeping. There was just a faint chink in her armour, like a door slightly ajar, and he was tempted to wedge his foot in it to find out what lay behind it. Would he release insane demons that would send her back to the despair she suffered before? Probably. He decided he could live with the chink. If she kept it closed up, then the madness would stay away and they would live a normal life—with Joy. The small part of Ruth that he could not access would have to remain hers alone in the world of her forgotten nightmares. If her brain could make her believe that Joy was theirs, then he would pretend along with her.

As the sun began its slow descent over the land they had left behind them, Ruth sat up and looked at Les enquiringly.

"Where are we?"

"Oh, about a third of the way to Balladonia Homestead, I reckon. You want a break?"

She nodded, "I think you could do with one too."

Les swung the Chev off the track and ground to a halt, letting the dust settle before opening the doors. In no time Ruth had tea poured from the thermos and cut pieces of chocolate cake. It was a good opportunity to change the baby's nappy and play with her for a while and walk a few yards to exercise their cramped legs.

"Do you think you can go on a bit longer?" he asked her. "I'd like to get a few more miles behind us before stopping for the night."

Les drove another hour and, guiding the truck over broken branches and small rocks, he pulled it over behind a clump of scrub where they could gather some kindling. He sat back with a sigh.

"Tired?" she asked with concern.

"A bit. I'm all right though."

"How about a steak to revive you?"

"Now you're talking," he smiled. "And a wash would do wonders."

That night Les slept soundly, not even stirring when animals scuttled around their camp-site.

They awoke in the morning to find their store of bread and powdered milk vandalised, and Ruth berated herself for being careless.

"Never mind. We'll just have to drink black tea until we can get some more," Les comforted her.

"We must be careful to stow the food away from wildlife at night. Inside the front of the Chev with the windows up," Ruth decided.

After a satisfying breakfast they were on their way again, bouncing over the seemingly endless tracks. Les made frequent stops to rest Joy. She was becoming fretful and Ruth was concerned that she might be suffering from the constant jarring of the Chev. During one stop, an old truck approached from the east, visible well before it was close to them by the dust cloud it raised.

"Quick! Take Joy for a walk and try to keep her quiet."

Ruth's eyes betrayed the fear Les felt and she turned wordlessly into the scrub, walking quickly away from the road.

"Look out for snakes," he called out.

By the time the truck pulled up beside them, Ruth was a distant indistinct figure squatting behind some bushes.

"How you going, mate?" the two men greeted Les, getting down from their truck. "You in trouble?"

"No. We're fine, thanks." Les traced patterns in the red soil with his boots, watching swarming ants in their thousands make their way around and over everything in their path.

"Going far?" the younger of the men asked.

"Adelaide. How about you two?"

"Oh, we're headed for Perth. You come from there?"

"No. We're going back to Adelaide. Been visiting family in Kalgoorlie."

"The missus all right?" asked the other man, indicating Ruth's distant figure.

"It's my mum. Got a bit of a bellyache. A bit embarrassed. She'll walk all the way to Darwin to get away from us," laughed Les.

"Oh, she doesn't have to worry about us," the young man chuckled.

"You know women. Can't tell 'em. Stubborn as mules."

"Know what you mean, mate. My mum's the bloody same."

After more inane conversation, the two men decided to get on their way and leave the poor woman to her bellyache.

"Good luck, mate," they called back as they took off in a cloud of dust.

"Yeah. We'll need it," mumbled Les to himself.

Around noon they passed Balladonia Homestead and the old crumbling stone fences built by pioneer farmers. There was no point in stopping as he had been told there was no fuel there. Next was the longest straight stretch of road in the world: Balladonia to Caiguna—nearly one hundred miles.

During the afternoon, they refreshed their mouths with apples, avoiding the water can in the hope of saving their precious supply. Progress was very slow, the road being in such poor condition. Les decided to make an early night of it to give Ruth and the baby a rest. It had been pretty hard going.

The next morning, refreshed and well fed, they headed for Caiguna and passed through it without incident. Between Cocklebiddy and Madura, another hundred miles towards the east, the road climbed to the escarpment allowing magnificent views. They opted to stay up there where they had a good view of the road ahead, which gave Les a sense of security in being able to see if any vehicles were coming their way.

And so they continued: slowly, agonizingly, on the road of a thousand nightmares. A tyre blew out and Les had to use one of the spares that left him a very worried man with only one back-up tyre left. The fan belt frayed, then broke, but he had two others. The truck began using water and he had to keep topping up the radiator with their precious supply, and they were very low on petrol. Les was glad of the hessian water bag he had hung in front of the radiator—that at least was helping to keep it cool. The constant bumping of the truck broke their eggs, which ran into flour packed beside it, but they decided they could manage without bread for however long it took for them to replenish their supplies. Bad luck only served to reinforce their determination to succeed and they laughed at themselves and thumbed their noses at the gods who tormented them.

Time ceased to matter so much for Les. The further they drove away from Perth, the more secure he felt. Although he worried about their survival in that hostile landscape, he felt they were far enough away from any connection with Gunter Schwartz and the missing baby to be chased by the law.

Ruth had sensed Les's fear and accepted it unquestioningly. When he told her to lie down on the seat so that no one would see her or the baby, she did it because he wanted her to, and for no other reason. Whatever Les wanted was all right with her.

On Friday, May 27, they drove through the Madura Pass and continued until Les found a suitable spot for Ruth and Joy to pass some time while he retraced his steps to get supplies. When he was reunited with his family, he was sporting a smile from ear to ear.

"They had some?" asked Ruth.

"Yes. Water, petrol—and I even got some bread!"

"Wonderful! We'll have toast with sardines tonight for supper. And we've got some canned fruit left."

"And I've got another surprise for you."

"Ooh…what is it?"

"Powdered milk. We can have a decent cuppa again."

They finally reached Eucla on Saturday, seven miles from the border of Western Australia and South Australia. Miles of clean, white sandy beaches stretched west and east along the Great Australian Bight where extraordinary limestone cliffs rose to a height of over three hundred feet from the ocean. Refreshing, strong sea breezes made it an ideal spot to stop and take welcome relief from the endless road. Les was bent on having a complete day there and took the truck as close as he could to an old jetty on the beach.

It was another sunny day—perfect weather to enjoy some hours in the sun and water. They swam in the invigorating sea near the jetty with Joy on a towel in the shade. Oh, how good it was to feel clean again. Les knew they were taking a risk, but they had been through enough not to take a few chances. The place was dead anyway—practically a ghost town. They could see that it had once been a thriving settlement, but now shifting sand dunes mostly covered the old telegraph station and some buildings. Les looked from time to time in the direction of what looked like an inhabited house, but no one appeared to be about. He hoped it would stay that way.

As the afternoon wore on, they reluctantly turned back to the Chev and prepared to be on their way. Suddenly they were aware of footsteps scrunching in the sand coming towards them. Les went over to greet a young man as Ruth piled up tins and folded ground sheets to hide the sleeping baby. She walked over to join them.

"That was close!" Les breathed as the young man turned back to lead them to a ground water tank.

They thanked him, went about topping up their water drums, and made a quick escape before any other people emerged from the house. Fortunately, the baby had slept right through the incident.

Rested and cheerful, Ruth and Les smiled at each other as they passed over the border into South Australia. The old life had been left behind and they faced the future together with their child as they drove across the continent. They had survived this far, and they had every intention of continuing to do so.

54

The enormous ocean swells rolled towards the towering limestone cliffs, hurling their awesome might at the horizontal lines of colour that stretched as far as the eye could see—carving, biting, shaping the edge of the great continent. Clear, variegated shades of blue/green water extended to the darker hues where the vast depth of the sea hid the busy survival of marine life from the gaze of the human watchers. They stood, hand in hand, on the cliff edge so flat it appeared to have been cut straight across with a gigantic scythe in the hand of a pre-historic god. They stayed there, in silent homage to the force of nature, until the horizon melted into the night sky and hunger beckoned with an ever-increasing urgency.

Les had driven through Border Village and continued slowly along the appalling road for some time until they reached the lookout and had discovered the remarkable view.

"We must stay here. See the sunrise tomorrow," Les shouted into Ruth's ear so that she could hear him over the booming of the waves and the wind.

They were strangely subdued, humbled by the beauty that spread out in front of them. The constant pounding of the ocean on the cliffs was like a symphony, repeated again and again. It lulled them, soothed them, and they listened as they lay looking at the stars parading across the sky's dome.

"I love you, Les," she murmured as sleep claimed her.

"Struth, how I love you," he replied, tightening his arms around her. She still smelled salty from the sea they had bathed in at Eucla. He knew he did too, despite their thorough stand-up washes, but her own special smell was perfume to his nostrils and, as he nuzzled her neck, it tickled his senses as he, too, fell asleep.

With great reluctance they packed up the Chev after breakfasting the next morning.

"I wish we could stay right here, Les. It's so beautiful."

"I know. But there's nothing else here. We'd starve."

"We could live on rabbits. Goodness knows there are enough of them."

"They'd bugger our guts, like they have the land," he joked. "We've seen the proof of that." He was referring to the damage the millions of rabbits had made to the landscape by eating the ground cover, causing sand dunes to take over and partly bury vast areas of land as well as towns like Eucla.

"And there's the problem of the water. The nappies."

Nappies had been a constant worry to them, mainly because of the water shortage. Ruth put the soiled nappies into a bucket of water, which Les tied securely onto the tray at the back of the truck. The rough ride agitated the water and the nappies enough to wash them in Velvet soap and at the end of each day Ruth rinsed them out and hung them to dry. The cool nights weren't long enough to dry the nappies, but Ruth pegged them on a line Les rigged up over the tray and, if they saw another vehicle approaching, they would stop and get them down in time so that the nappies weren't seen. But there were so many of them—as well as their own washing.

At Eucla Les hit upon the idea of using salt water to wash the clothes in, and just rinsing in fresh water. The water drums were low and he had filled one up with salt water. But they weren't able to refill the drum from the high cliffs.

"You're right, Les. Let's move on."

It was another ninety miles until the road veered away from the coastline, and it took them three days to get that far. Their rest stops took longer as they drank in the view, unwilling to lose sight of it and continue on their bone-jarring way. The stiff breeze coming off the ocean blew the dust away from them and sent it across the flat landscape.

Joy amazed Ruth and Les at how well she travelled. She settled into their routine easily, sleeping through the nights beside them in the back of the Chev. She woke early, gurgling as she watched birds swoop overhead in the clear blue skies. Then hunger brought whimpers that were easily quelled by Ruth's full, dripping breasts. Joy would doze in Ruth's embrace and wake bright-eyed and full of energy. Before Ruth prepared the breakfast for herself and Les, she lay Joy on a ground sheet and washed her clean. Ruth let the baby kick her strong little legs without the restraint of a nappy and she kicked with the abandon of a can-can dancer. They laughed at Joy's own language as she squealed and babbled, eyes alert to anything that moved, ears attuned to sharp sounds.

Motherhood had given Ruth a certain fullness to her usual slender body. She appeared less fragile and her voice was deeper— except when she giggled, and that happened more often now. Her face softened into a slow, wide smile that seemed to smooth out the bump on her nose when she looked at Joy.

"What are you looking at?" Ruth caught Les inspecting her closely.

"I don't know. It hasn't got tickets on it," teased Les.

She flicked a clean nappy at him, catching him on the shins, laughing up into his face.

"Oh, really? Perhaps I should put a label on my forehead: Wife. Mother."

"Lover," he continued, wrapping his arms around her, pulling her close. "My beautiful lover."

Her translucent skin had a healthy honey-coloured glow to it from constant exposure to the sun during their journey. Her short, dark hair grew in fine, wispy waves around her face and he teased it out with his fingers as he looked seriously into her dark eyes.

"You are everything to me. You know that."

A black face split by white teeth peered over the side of the tray where Les, Ruth and Joy were asleep. It watched them for some moments, then disappeared as silently as it had appeared. The sleepers remained in the world of their dreams, unaware of their soundless visitors—until the next morning.

"Les? What did you do with the fruit cake? And the tins of...?"

"I haven't touched them, love."

"But, they're gone."

"What do you mean gone?"

"And the sugar...the flour...and the Spam!"

They stared in horror at each other as the realisation dawned upon them. They had been warned about the aborigines; not to leave anything unguarded, especially on Yalata land where they'd camped.

"Is there anything left?"

"Oh, Les. They took the tinned fruit too."

"As long as we've got the water, we're okay. It's about another eighty miles to Penong. We should be right for supplies there."

He was relieved to see the water hadn't been touched. Ruth held up some tins of fish and peas that were in the back of the truck.

"I said I was sick of these but we'll just have to put up with them," she said pulling a face.

"I'll see if I can get a rabbit," said Les picking up the shotgun, "or a 'roo."

Ruth watched him as he made his way around clumps of salt-bush on the flat land.

"Don't get lost," she called after him, smiling. He waved at her, jiggling the shotgun in the air.

"Well, joy of my life," said Ruth waving back to Les, "we'd better get you cleaned up, hadn't we?"

She busied herself with the baby, confident that Les would find them something to eat. Ruth trusted him implicitly, knowing him to be a capable and resourceful man. She sat on a ground sheet holding her fingers up and moving them slowly from side to side for Joy to follow with eyes, eager and observant. They both jumped at the sound of a gunshot, and Ruth looked up to see Les in the distance dodging around trees in the direction of a cloud of red dust. His obscure figure stopped then bent over and was almost lost behind some shrubs, and then he stood up holding something.

"Daddy's got us tea, little one. I knew he would."

The dirt road presented a variety of tracks to choose from, each one offering no better condition than the other did. The Chev bounced and ground its way towards Penong as they gritted their teeth with each pothole that Les guided the truck down and out of. The truck was tough but Les wasn't sure if it would survive the trip. Each night he spent quite some time under the truck making sure there were no oil leaks, tightening bolts, checking the tyres and water. So far so good. His luck had held.

The day was long and gruelling, not only due to the dreadful condition of the road, but because Joy was becoming fretful. She jarred awake after a particularly big pothole, followed by several more that were unavoidable. Les's eyes swept back and forth over the tracks looking for any easier route. His body was tense, his jaw tight. Cushioned against Ruth's breast, Joy had slept well, but she suddenly screwed up her face, pulled up her legs and screamed piercingly.

"What...?" Les pulled the truck to a stop.

"She's in pain, Les. Look at her!"

He jumped down from the truck and opened the door for Ruth.

"Maybe she's hungry?"

"She shouldn't be. I only fed her a couple of hours ago."

Ruth felt the sharp stab of the let-down reflex and opened her blouse to Joy's eager mouth.

"Funny...she must have been."

But after a few moments, Joy stopped sucking and screamed again, her legs working in stiff, jerky movements pulled up to her chest and then stiffening out straight. The worried parents looked at each other in dismay. Joy had never acted like this before.

"A nappy pin? Could one be sticking into her?"

Ruth undressed the baby carefully, finding the pins still done up. Then they noticed Joy's abdomen, tight as a drum, bloated with wind.

"I think it's colic. Some babies get it. I'll walk her around a bit—see if I can work the wind out of her."

Perched over Ruth's shoulder, the baby seemed to gain some relief as Ruth patted and rubbed her back. Les made them a cup of tea from the thermos and they took it in turns walking the baby around. Little burps escaped, along with gushes of milk that wet her parents' shoulders.

"She seems better now. Will we get going again?" asked Ruth.

No sooner had they settled down in the truck and resumed their journey than Joy began screaming again. Ruth assured Les that he should continue while she did her best to placate the baby.

"Gripe Water. That's what she needs."

"What's that?"

"For colic—helps relieve it."

"How does it do that?"

"I don't know, Les. It just does."

"But what's it made of?"

"Dill, I think. You know, the herb."

"I don't think they'll have it in Penong," said Les anxiously.

"We might have to wait until we get to Adelaide. But, if it is colic it won't harm her. Lots of babies get it."

And so they continued on their tortuous way, the sounds of the truck's engine and gears and the screaming baby disturbing the stillness of the undulating landscape. They met no other traffic and saw no living thing other than countless rabbits running helter-skelter between the scrub and kangaroos bounding gracefully away from them.

That night they all fell asleep exhausted—Joy had given them an anxious four hours when they stopped for their evening meal. Unless held up on their shoulders and walked around, the baby cried fitfully, obviously in pain, until finally she passed wind and they were all able to lie down in the back of the truck and get some rest.

Ruth looked at Les over their breakfast, noting the redness of his eyes as he rubbed them, and the tired lines that suddenly made him look much older. He had taken to running his fingers through his sandy hair and that usually meant Les was worried.

"Are you feeling all right, Les?"

He looked up at her in surprise.

"Yeah. Why?"

"Oh, you look tired—worried."

"I'm all right. Just a bit knackered."

"We could stop here today. Give you a rest."

"No. We need to get to Penong. Get more supplies. Maybe even the gripe stuff for Joy."

"Well…if you're sure."

"Yeah. I mean, look at this place. There's nothing here."

They both looked around them. It was a relief to pack up and get going. It would have to get better. They'd been pretty lucky so far. If Joy became no worse then they would manage. Les hoped Ruth was right and that it was only colic bothering the baby. If it were some-thing else—something serious—what would they do?

In the short time since Joy had been in their lives, he had be-come very fond of her. She tugged at his paternal instincts as he watched her develop her own routine, her reactions to the world around her, and the close bond that was already created between her and Ruth. And when he held her, felt her softness, her innate trust in him, he felt himself melt into the clear, beautiful eyes that searched his face. He wondered if she could see him yet. Was he still a blur? Did she recognise his voice? His smell? He thought that he knew every inch of her, every expression, every movement, her baby fragrance. And he knew that he would be able to pick her out of a hundred babies—even if they were all redheaded. This was what it felt like to be a father. And he loved it.

The stab of fear that exploded into his stomach and chest each time Joy screamed left him shaking and nervous—anxious. He wondered how Ruth seemed to cope with it so well. She was so mat-ter-of-fact. So sure of herself once she was satisfied that she had the correct label on the problem: colic. How did she do it? Were women given something at birth that made them so…capable? And men so helpless?

But what if Joy died? Or the police discovered them and she was taken from them. What would happen to Ruth? He knew without doubt that she would lose her mind forever. Joy had healed her, bridged the gap between normality and insanity. Joy was essential to Ruth. If they lost Joy, he would lose Ruth. No—they must move on. Ruth would be happy and he would be happy. That's all he wanted.

The next day followed the same pattern of bumping along the impossible road, the baby crying and Les tiring from the long hours of concentration. Penong looked close on the map, but their progress was so slow that they felt they would never reach it. As the sun disappeared behind them, wheat fields loomed large on either side of the road and they knew they were close to Penong. Les drove through the tiny town and left Ruth and Joy a mile past it, hating leaving them in the darkness.

He returned to their hiding place with relief lighting up his face, and a truck full of supplies to replace what they had lost. He had searched the general store in Penong for Gripe Water, but to no avail, and was afraid to ask not wanting to draw attention to himself.

"We've got water!"

Ruth smiled at him. "Enough to rinse out the clothes?"

"Plenty. And we can fill up again at Ceduna."

It would be a vast improvement to have soft clothes again. To conserve water, Ruth had washed their clothes only in salt water but their skin itched from the roughness of the salty residue on the material. She had tried a nappy on Joy without having rinsed it in fresh water, but the baby's soft skin had looked irritated.

Les held up some tins. "Corned beef, carrots, Sao biscuits...and tinned peaches for tea."

Ceduna 70 miles The signpost swept past Les' vision and was gone. The headlights stabbed relentlessly into the night, a wall of darkness on either side of the nightmare highway. Eyes shone at him from the edges of the road and he wondered sleepily what sort of animal they belonged to. He suddenly pulled on the wheel to avoid a kangaroo that bounded into the light, narrowly missing it. Then bumping over another seemingly bottomless pothole, he slowed the truck and pulled over to the side of the road.

"What is it?" Ruth stirred.

"We're not far out of Ceduna. We can rest up there."

"Oh good."

"I have to sleep, though. Too tired."

"Do you want to get in the back?" she asked, sitting up.

"No, just an hour or two. I'll be all right then."

"Joy's asleep. I won't disturb her now," Ruth murmured, settling back into her former position.

Les was already asleep, leaning against his door.

The sun glared on the windscreen and into Les' face, waking him with its welcome warmth. His mouth felt furry and tasted revolting. He rubbed his face and eyes; the inevitable dust mixed with dried sweat and grease caking his fingers. *What I'd give for a shower,* he thought for the hundredth time since leaving Perth. He stretched and looked over at his sleeping wife and baby. *How do they do it?* he wondered. They seemed almost oblivious to the hardships of the journey.

He started up the engine, thankful for its reliability, and swung the truck onto the road. Ruth awoke and looked up at him smiling, then found a comfortable spot with her head on his lap, the baby cuddled into her breast.

"Not long until we can have a good wash," he said quietly, touching her face with his left hand. He ran his fingers along her nose, rising at the bump and then down to the tip.

She squeezed his hand and kissed it.

The dust rose behind them as the truck made its laborious way around the potholes. It promised to be another glorious day on this uncompromising land where the long, straight road stretched as far as the eye could see. Thoughts of Melbourne occupied him as they headed closer to their destination. The uncertainty of what lay ahead worried him but excited him at the same time. Would he find work quickly? Where would they live? Had he covered their tracks sufficiently? Would Ruth stay 'normal' or would she slide back into that deep depression?

The baby woke, gurgling her pleasure at the new day. The smell of breast milk turned her head back towards Ruth and she was soon feeding contentedly.

"Well, someone's having breakfast early," Les laughed.

"I'll have to put a certain young lady on a diet if she continues with this huge appetite," joked Ruth.

"Not long now and we can have ours."

"How far?"

"About sixty-odd miles. According to the map, it looks like there are some safe beaches at Ceduna. It might be warm enough to have a dip. Fishing's supposed to be good there too."

Although they needed to drive a few miles away from Ceduna off the main road, Denial Bay seemed an ideal spot for a quiet day. Sheltered by white sand dunes with mangroves and cocklebeds, the inviting calm cool water refreshed their tired, dirty bodies. Joy took to the water with delight, kicking and splashing her fat little arms and legs, her parents captivated by her antics. They had the beach to themselves and made the most of the opportunity to relax without the fear of being seen. The baby slept in the shade as Les made love to Ruth, the sun, seagulls and black swans the only witnesses to their passion. The water beckoned again and they frolicked like children in its invigorating buoyancy, dazzled by coruscating reflections that bounced off its surface.

Ruth sat with Les as he fished, and Joy lay naked on a towel in the sun at their feet gurgling as she watched the swooping flight of seagulls passing in and out of her vision. Whiting filled Les's bucket, elating them with the anticipation of a change of diet. As the sun began its descent towards the land behind them, it cast an orange light over the sand dunes and their barbecue. The aroma of freshly-caught fish cooking over the flames stirred their hunger and they ate with pleasure. Regretfully, they packed up and got back into the truck. It had been a glorious day.

On the way through Ceduna, Les bought more fuel, checked the tyres, refilled the water drum, and stocked up on more canned food. Ruth smiled her pleasure when he put a loaf of just-baked bread on her lap—she wouldn't have to make damper for a few days.

After having driven for some hours, Les pulled over to the side of the road. He felt pleasantly tired as he arranged the back of the truck with Ruth's help. The night sky spread out endlessly above them, the stars and moon casting a soft glow on their faces as they talked.

"I wonder what Port Augusta's like?"

"Pretty big, I reckon. The bloke in the store at Ceduna said it's all wheat country around there. It'll take us a good three or four days, at least, to get there, though."

"How many days after that, do you think?"

"To Melbourne?"

"Yes."

"I don't know...a week...or two, maybe. Are you sick of it...the trip, I mean?"

"No, Les. I'm loving it. I've never had a holiday."

"Come to think of it, neither have I."

They slept well on their mattress in the back of the truck. Joy's colic seemed to have settled somewhat and her parents were no longer so anxious when it did trouble her.

Port Augusta was a big enough town for the three of them to be seen together without drawing attention to themselves. They bought more bread, powdered milk, eggs, and even picked up some bacon. They were very pleased with themselves.

"Do you want to stay here, or go on to Adelaide?" Les asked Ruth.

"How far is it?"

"About a hundred and seventy miles."

"Let's go to Adelaide. I'm curious to see it."

"Would you like to stay in a hotel there? We could have a shower."

Ruth needed no persuading and, after counting up their dwindling money supplies, they decided they could afford one night away from the truck. With eager anticipation, Les headed the truck towards the capital city along the highway's poor bitumen—at least it was some improvement from the ghastly conditions they had now left behind them.

The bathroom in the small, modest hotel in Glen Osmond Road was heaven to their salty bodies. They stood in the shower, faces upturned into the fresh water, revelling in the luxury of foaming soap. Then it was Joy's turn to splash and touch and enjoy the water in her bath. The pleasant smell of baby powder filled their small room and Joy slept as her parents made love in the soft clean bed.

The next morning Les awoke early, luxuriating in the novelty of the comfortable bed. He looked up at the ceiling, studying the opaque light fitting, the shadows playing on the flowered wallpaper, the hook set into the picture rail that held a framed photograph of the hotel when it was first built. There was another picture hanging there: a faded painting of a house on the banks of a river. The grass around the house was green—not dry like the country they had driven through—and there were flowers growing at the front door. The water was high in the riverbed and looked to be flowing rapidly. He wondered idly where the house had been—in Adelaide, or maybe somewhere in England. It didn't look like anywhere he'd ever been. Maybe it was in Melbourne.

They breakfasted on copious quantities of fried eggs and bacon on hot, buttered toast, with a huge pot of strong tea. The other guests smiled at their appetites, and made a fuss of the pretty red-haired baby. The publican engaged Les in conversation about the possibilities of extending his crowded dining room, once he realised Les was a carpenter.

"And he's the best carpenter this side of the Black Stump," boasted Ruth. "You should see the beautiful furniture he makes. He's so clever."

"Not as clever as she is. She makes everything we wear...and made to last too." Les tugged at his shirt-front.

"I was admiring your dress. Did you make that?" asked Mrs Sloan, the publican's wife.

In no time at all, Ruth and Margaret Sloan were firm friends, chatting on as if they'd known each other for years. With Joy balanced comfortably on Ruth's hip, Margaret Sloan led her out of the dining room to show Ruth where she could wash out nappies and the rest of their dirty clothes. The two men watched them with grins on their faces.

"No doubt about bloody women. They'll talk the leg off an iron chair, given half the chance," laughed Bert Sloan. "You won't see the little woman for hours now."

His big frame supported a large stomach that wobbled when he laughed—and that was often. His grey hair was cut short over a round, creased face, with blue eyes that regarded the world around him with much amusement. And the young man beside him wore such a concerned expression on his face that Bert bellowed with laughter.

"Don't worry, young fella. She'll be back...eventually." He slapped Les a resounding blow on the back. "Come on, mate. Let's go and have a beer."

"It's a bit early for me..." protested Les, but Bert wouldn't hear of it, leading Les into the public bar, which was deserted at that early hour.

Les felt let down, almost betrayed by Ruth's disappearance. They had been together constantly for the past three weeks and he felt her absence keenly. Would she give them away? Would she know how to answer the inevitable questions that Mrs Sloan would ask her? Could she manage without him to protect her? And did she feel torn from him, like he did her? She hadn't even looked over her shoulder as she'd walked out of the door with Mrs Sloan. He felt hurt—stupid—but hurt. He shook his head in disbelief at himself. *The first show of Ruth making a go of it and I feel left out.* He felt ashamed, and gave himself a mental kick in the pants, having recognised his own need to be needed. *I should be happy that she's come out of it.*

Les lifted his glass—foaming beer spilled down the sides and over his fingers. Bert Sloan looked at him quizzically as he waited for the verdict on his own brew. The young man had been lost in thought.

"Penny for them?" he asked before downing his glass in one long gulp.

"Oh, nothing." Les gulped the cold, refreshing amber liquid. "Hey, that's bloody beautiful."

"Best in Adelaide. Make it myself. Another one?"

Les laughed and the tension flew out of him. "You trying to get me drunk?"

After lunch, Les and Ruth explored Adelaide on foot, pushing Joy in an old pram that Margaret Sloan had borrowed for them. The first breath of winter swept gently along the streets and Ruth was glad of the woollen twin set and heavy skirt she had changed into. It was good to walk openly in the streets together with their baby, and they took full advantage of the new experience.

They found a chemist shop in King William Street where Gripe Water was readily available, along with plenty of good advice from the kindly chemist. They marvelled at the wide, straight streets and parks, and spent most of the afternoon walking in the gardens that flanked the Torrens River as it wound its way across the northern part of the city. Ruth and Les entered St. Peter's Cathedral and stayed there for some time, thinking about the journey that had seen them safely halfway across the continent. The beautiful stone building was quiet and cold in the afternoon light that shone in colourful splashes through the stained glass windows, and picked up specks of dust and danced them towards the spired ceilings. Les couldn't help wondering if there was a god listening to them. If he really existed.

"I like it here," Ruth sighed as she ran her fingers absently through his thick sandy hair. She was sitting against a tree trunk on the grass with Les's head in her lap.

"Would you like to stay longer? At the hotel?"

"I'd love to, but we can't afford it."

"Well, the old man...Mr Sloan...he offered us free board and lodging if I'd help him with the dining room. He was asking my advice about extending it. I told him he should just knock the wall down between the dining room and the storeroom they don't use. Easy job."

"Would you like to do it?

"Yeah. Why not? And we'd have showers every day and that bed to sleep in."

"Heaven."

The following four days passed by pleasantly for Ruth and Les. She caught up on all the washing and drying of clothes while Les worked at what he did best. Bert Sloan watched Les work with a mixture of admiration and respect and felt a growing fondness for the young man who he imagined he would have liked as a son. Daughters were all right, and he loved his two, but a son...now that would have been something. Especially one as handy as this young fellow.

Margaret and Ruth spent many a happy hour in the kitchen together, Ruth insisting on helping with the cooking to pay for their keep. The older woman was lonely for female company since her two daughters had married and moved away, and the arrangement suited her. Thick, steel-grey hair fell over her forehead constantly, despite the many bobby pins stuck in it at all angles in an attempt to tame it, and her floured hands left white blobs all over her face and hair when she pushed it back. Her face was covered in wrinkles that moved in soft folds as she talked, and Ruth longed to touch them—trace them with her fingers. But she didn't dare. Margaret was a shrewd observer of the female temperament, after having brought up two vivacious girls, but Ruth puzzled her. She saw a young woman who was obviously adored by her husband, who loved being in the role of mother, who giggled a lot, who was enjoyable company and was very handy around the house. But there was something missing. Something...not quite right. Maybe she'd get to the bottom of it one day. She hoped they'd stay long enough for her to do that.

Margaret liked the way Ruth stopped what she was doing to listen when she was relating one of her many stories about her daughters, one of whom lived in Hahndorf, up in the Adelaide hills. Everyone else she knew had heard the stories before and was bored with them.

"Heysen. Hans Heysen. He paints those landscapes of the bush. Well, she knows him, you know. Cleans his house."

Ruth's hands hovered over the chopping board, waiting for Margaret to finish her story.

"You should go up there some time. See the paintings. They're beautiful."

"I'd like that."

"Take that young husband of yours. My Bert's had him working too hard."

Ruth laughed. "He loves it, Margaret. Put a hammer or a saw into his hands and he's happy."

"Nevertheless...and little Joy, she's feeling better now with the Gripe Water, isn't she? Didn't she set up a ruckus when you first got here."

"Yes, I'm sorry about the noise. Did the other guests complain?"

"No, love. You've got to expect that with babies. It's natural, like."

On the fifth morning, Les picked up *The Advertiser* and read it leisurely over a large pot of tea. The dining room extension was finished and he was about to help Bert put on a new coat of paint to complete the job. At the bottom left-hand corner, on page 12, a small article caught his eye:

NO NEW LEADS ON

KIDNAPPING

D/Sgt. George Chambers indicated last night that even though the investigation has been wound down he will never give up the hunt for the missing twin girl. "I will leave no stone unturned...no clue left uninvestigated, even if I have to hunt down the kidnapper—or murderer—in my own time." The father, Mr Schwartz, is caring for the other twin alone. He remains unavailable for comment. D/Sgt. Chambers went on to say that he, "...will never rest until this case is solved. Someone, somewhere, must have the answer to the disappearance of the child. And I mean to catch that person before I die."

A cold feeling of dread gripped Les's stomach. He placed the cup carefully in its saucer and picked up the pot of tea, then poured it slowly over the article, scrunching the page tightly until there was left only a sodden ball of newspaper, the newsprint staining his calloused hand.

The rest of the newspaper sat in a wet puddle, tea oozing over the table and dripping over the edge and onto the floor.

"My goodness! What happened, Les?" Margaret pushed the swinging door as she went into the kitchen and came back out again with a cloth to mop up the mess.

Les was standing, tea dripping onto his work boot, and looking out of the window.

"What...?"

"The paper. You've got tea all over it. Never mind. It's all old news now. There's always tomorrow's paper..." She prattled on heedless of the chaos that raced through Les's mind.

"Yes...tomorrow," he said in a flat monotone.

Suddenly, he turned and hurried out of the room. "Sorry, Margaret. Sorry about the mess."

"That's all right, love." She looked after him. "Something put the wind up that young man, if I know anything about anything."

"Ruth! Ruth! Come on; let's get packed. We're leaving." Les burst into their room, banging the door open.

Joy woke up with a fright. Ruth was frightened by his voice, his urgency. "What is it?"

"I...I've finished the job. We'll get going now. To Melbourne."

"All right, Les. If that's what you want to do." She looked at him curiously.

He was pacing the room, pulling down their cases and bags, throwing things furiously into them. Joy began to cry and Ruth picked her up. He looked at them both and saw his panic mirrored in Ruth's eyes.

"I'm sorry, love." He sagged onto the bed. "I'd just like to get going now."

"Have you told Bert?"

"No. Not yet."

Within an hour they were packed and ready to go. Margaret wrung her hands around her apron, tears leaping to her eyes.

"You'll write? Let us know where you are?"

"Yes, of course. And thank you...for everything."

"Oh, son. We'd have loved to have you longer—as long as you wanted."

Bert and Margaret stood watching the truck as it disappeared amongst the morning traffic.

"Hell of a nice fella that...her too." Bert felt as stricken by the young couple's departure as his wife did. "I don't understand it. One minute he was getting ready to paint, and the next he was packing up the truck.”

“I know. He seemed quite upset. Spilt his tea all over the floor.”

“Something put the wind up him, all right.”

“It must have been something he read in *The Advertiser*. He was all right until then.”

“I hope they keep in touch, those Bacons.”

“Who?”

“The Bacons—you know, Les and Ruth.”

“I thought they were Bakers.”

“No. You got it wrong, love.”

“I was sure she said Baker...”

The road climbed steeply into the hills, but the going was easier than before with a sealed road that provided a smoother passage in their flight eastwards.

“Margaret told me about an artist up here, Les,” commented Ruth quietly as they drove through Hahndorf. “She said her daughter works for him. That he paints beautiful landscapes.”

Les seemed preoccupied. He’d hardly spoken since they left Adelaide. He sat hunched over the steering wheel, his jaw tight.

“Les?”

“Umm?”

“I left Joy back with the Sloans.”

“That’s nice.”

“I knew you weren’t listening,” she laughed at him.

“What? I’m sorry, love. Just thinking.”

“I know you were. I was saying about the artist. Margaret’s daughter works for him. Could we see his paintings while we’re here?”

Les looked at Ruth for a moment, then turned back to the road. He sighed heavily.

“I wish we could, love. No time, though.”

Ruth was silent for a while.

“Sorry.” Les felt guilty. He would have done anything to make her happy—he’d give her the world if he could. But he couldn’t risk the Sloans’ daughter seeing them. He’d told them he and Ruth were going to Perth and Hahndorf was in the opposite direction. He would take Ruth to every art gallery in Melbourne if she wanted.

By late afternoon they had driven past Murray Bridge and then Tailem Bend where the road branched off to the Mallee country and Mildura. Instead Les headed the Chev along the highway in the direction of Bordertown, another hundred miles or so towards the border of South Australia and Victoria. They camped that night just after the branch in the highway, behind a clump of trees that provided enough privacy for Les to feel reasonably safe from prying eyes. The traffic was much busier on the Dukes Highway and it would become more so as they entered Victoria and neared Melbourne.

Joy slept fitfully that night in the back of the truck, crying loudly each time wind woke her in painful bouts of colic. Les hoped the people in the farmhouses he'd noticed nearby wouldn't be able to hear her. She settled down finally when Ruth gave her some Gripe Water, and they slept for a few hours until the sun rose.

"It's like old times, eh?" said Les with a mouthful of egg and toast. "I'd kind of missed it, you know."

"Me too. It's lovely to wake up with the birds overhead and the sun on your face. The smells of the country. It's so peaceful here, Les."

They packed up and were on the highway again before eight o'clock. It was a relief to drive without having to dodge huge potholes and corrugations in the road and the red dust coating everything. Les felt that after what they'd been through, he could face just about anything, but he thought things would be easier for them from now on. The five days in Adelaide had cleared the grime from their bodies and rested them. They were well fed and very healthy. But he was still determined to get to Melbourne as quickly as possible. He had made the mistake of being lulled into a false sense of security in Adelaide—his guard had been let down—but the article in *The Advertiser* had jolted him out of his complacency. That detective was like a terrier at his heels, and the more distance he could put between themselves and the detective, the better. Melbourne was a big city and the more people the better to hide amongst. No...he mustn't waste any more time. He would get them to Melbourne within the week.

Twenty-four hours later, Ruth opened one eye to see a very few nondescript buildings slide past the window ledge of the passenger side of the truck. Bordertown was a drowsy blur, and she went back to sleep.

Les shuddered a sigh of relief as the truck surged over the border into Victoria an hour later. Ruth heard Les mutter: "Goodbye South Australia. Good riddance," and she smiled to herself.

The road that led to Melbourne sliced through rolling plains of wheat fields, and on either side sheep grazed on extensive pasture-land. They saw that the land was the colour of straw, but it was not like the red Nullarbor—this land supported growth and livestock. It supported mankind—and in an ordered and immense way. Evidence of man's industry and his ability to conquer the land was everywhere they looked with great fields fenced in symmetrical precision.

As they drove through Nhill, Ruth noticed gigantic round cylinders that towered over the landscape on the left of the town.

"What do you think they are?" she asked Les.

"I'm not sure," he shook his head, "unless they're those silos I've heard about...for wheat."

They stopped after Nhill for a break. Ruth poured out steaming cups of tea from the thermos she had filled that morning.

"The flies are terrible here!" Ruth swiped at persistent bush flies.

"Must be the sheep," said Les. "There's always more flies in the bush where you've got sheep and cattle."

"I hope it's not like this in Melbourne."

"As long as there aren't any sheep walking down the streets, we should be all right," he laughed.

By the time they reached Dimboola, the winter sun had emerged from behind a wispy cloud cover and warmed them through the windscreen of the truck. They were both hungry. Les found a suitable spot to stop beside the road and Ruth made chunky sandwiches with thick slices of tinned meat and fresh tomato that they had bought in the township.

"I'll get a paper in Horsham. See what the jobs are like in Melbourne. Real estate...that sort of thing."

"You might get a big map of Melbourne, and the suburbs, there too, Les. Maybe someone will be able to give us an idea of a good place to stay."

"Good idea. No point us just driving around like a pair of silly galoots with nowhere to go."

With their bellies full, they fell into a comfortable silence. The ever-present buzzing of tireless insects had a hypnotic effect as they idly regarded the muted tones of the bush around them. Strips of mottled bark hung from the trunks of gum trees, their shady olive-tinted branches arching over the road.

"It's nearly over, Les."

He looked up at her, suddenly afraid. "What is?"

"The trip, silly. We'll be settling down again soon."

"Oh, yeah." He breathed a sigh of relief. *Funny,* he thought, *I'm just as jumpy as ever.* He wasn't quite sure what he was afraid of—being caught? Ruth coming to her senses and realising what they had done? What would he say to her? Oh, never mind, no one knows it was us? There's nothing wrong with stealing a baby?

Ruth was singing softly to Joy as she fed her. The baby's eyes were fixed on her face, drinking in her every movement and sound. Her mouth drew strongly upon Ruth's nipples with wet, practiced movements, until she was content and she drifted into an easy nap, secure in Ruth's surrounding warmth. A warm rush of emotion took hold of him, and he sat beside them and added his arms to the enclosure that protected his new daughter.

When they reached Horsham, Les spent some time with an elderly estate agent who had a shop in Firebrace Street. The kindly man knew Melbourne well and gave Les some good advice on suitable suburbs for a young family to make their home in. They poured over the classified advertisements in the Melbourne paper, drawing a ring around the most promising situations vacant as well as houses for rent.

"Thanks very much," Les shook the man's hand as they parted company.

"She's right, mate. Know what it's like setting up again. But you'll be right, being a carpenter and all."

"I hope so."

"There's plenty of work for young blokes like you. Just stay on the other side of the bay, though. This side's bloody awful. Flat and ugly."

"Much obliged. I wouldn't have known where to start looking."

"Yeah. The southern suburbs—and down towards the Mornington Peninsula's nice. You've got the beach, like I said, and there's plenty of building going on. They're fixing up the road between Oakleigh and Dandenong...here," he pointed on the map, "so watch out for that. It's a bloody mess. It'll be good, though, when it's finished."

Nice young fellow, the older man thought to himself as he watched Les cross the road and get into a packed truck that looked like it had travelled half-way around Australia. He stood thinking about their conversation with his hands dug deep into his trouser pockets, absentmindedly jiggling the coins there. As Les swung the truck onto the road, the estate agent's forehead creased under the rim of his felt hat, and he wished he were as young as Les with such opportunity before him.

Now that Les had some idea of where they were heading for in Melbourne, and what they might expect to find there, he steered the Chev back onto the highway with enthusiasm rather than a need to escape. They passed through undulating pastoral and wheat lands, noticing the peaks of the Grampians dominating the skyline to their right. He drove through Stawell without stopping; Les was determined to reach Ararat before nightfall. The nights were cooler now, and he wanted to get a big fire going to ward off any chills.

Conscious that this was probably to be their last night under the stars, Les resolved to make it a special evening for both of them. He stopped in Ararat and bought beer, a custard tart and something he kept hidden from Ruth until later that night.

The night was still, except for the sounds of the Hopkins River as it gathered momentum for its long journey to the coast. Its waters kissed the banks softly and were gone to be replaced immediately by more icy water originating from nearby mountains. It slid over exposed roots that jutted out from the banks, nudged leaves and broken branches from their temporary prisons to join it and the fish it caressed.

Les filled the billy from the river and hung it on the tripod over the fire he had lit. The flames glowed brightly, keeping the cold at bay as night mist settled over the land. The aroma of lamb chops and onions sizzling in a frying pan tormented their rumbling bellies.

"Struth, that beer tastes good." Les wiped his mouth with the back of his hand. He had wedged the bottles in the river where they had cooled very quickly.

The fire cast cavorting shadows over Ruth's face as she drained her glass. They smiled at each other and she held out her glass for a refill.

"You'll get drunk, and I may have to take advantage of you," he warned in mock seriousness.

"You might get drunk too—and I don't know who'll be taking advantage of who."

Wrapped snugly, Joy lay sound asleep lulled by the peace of the surroundings and a contented, full stomach. Her parents lay beside her, their pleasure in each other replacing the need to eat. Ruth pushed Les's thick hair out of his eyes as he leant over her. The fire light painted his muscled shoulders and arms with a soft copper glow and her lips traced along them, feeling the tautness of his skin and the full, pumping veins that ran underneath it. She lingered there; delighting in the sensation of the life force that was so strong in him, his maleness, and his physical perfection. Then his mouth found hers, gently, tasting of the beer they had both enjoyed. Her lips tingled as he teased them with his own in feather-like strokes, then their mutual urgency captivated them and carried them beyond their camp site into a world of their own making.

"The chops!" Ruth sat up suddenly, the smell of burning meat disturbing the shallow slumber they had fallen into. "Oh, Les, they're ruined."

"Never mind," he chuckled. "It was worth it."

"Silly." She pulled a face at him. "You still hungry? I can cook some more."

"I'm starving, woman. Where's my dinner? Can't a man get a feed around here?"

Six more chops began to brown in the frying pan and they sat back to wait for them to cook. Les fished another bottle of beer out of the river and they enjoyed it, slaking their thirst after their lovemaking. Soon after, their teeth ripped into the tender lamb, and they gnawed at the tasty bones until there was nothing left on them. The custard tart finished off their meal with plenty of hot tea to soak it up.

Ruth busied herself in cleaning up after their meal, while Les rummaged inside the cabin of the truck until he came out carrying a small parcel.

"A special gift for a special lady," he handed it to her with a flourish.

"What's this?"

"Open it."

She untied the string around the flat parcel and carefully opened the brown paper. Inside was a shiny black single-play gramophone record.

"Oh, Les." Her brown eyes were suddenly moist as she looked at the record. "*When I Fall In Love*. Our song."

"I know. I saw it in Ararat when I was buying the things and it just begged me to buy it for you."

Ruth hugged him tightly.

"It still means just what I feel about you."

"I wish I could play it."

"Until you can, I'll sing it."

Ruth laughed as he jumped up on top of a nearby log and started singing but the performance came to an abrupt halt as Les overbalanced and fell behind the log.

They awoke simultaneously to raucous laughter. Joy's eyes followed the boisterous sound above her that continued in a long surging peal and was taken up by another until the treetops were full of it. When it stopped the silence was almost as deafening. Two kookaburras were perched on an overhanging limb, looking down at them curiously. Ruth and Les could see the birds' white heads quite clearly with streaks of brown across the eyes. Then the kookaburras opened their long, heavy bills and gave an encore, proclaiming ownership of their territory, their thunderous laughter startling Joy anew. But the laughter was so exhilarating, so infectious, that Ruth joined in, her giggles hatching into full-blown bursts of laughter that were added to by Les's own. Tears sprang to their eyes as they shook with abandoned mirth, clutching helplessly onto their stomachs that ached with the spasms. Joy's head moved from side to side, following the chaotic sounds of her parents and the birds, eyes stretched wide. But she sensed no threat, only vitality and cheerfulness, and she gurgled her own response with her arms waving excitedly.

"I think it's time to get up," gasped Les.

"Oh. Oh. It hurts," Ruth giggled, exhausted.

Les looked at his watch. "It's only six o'clock but I don't think I could go back to sleep after that."

"Me either."

"And I'm ravenous."

"What again?"

The road continued on, lined with gum trees, through farmland where sheep grazed. Shade fell in ribbons across the road as the sun rose higher towards a noon sky. Flashes of sunlight glanced across the windscreen of the truck in almost hypnotic rhythm. The tree leaves that reflected the sunlight in shining silver dazzled Ruth's eyes. Bark peeled back, hanging in strips, from eucalyptus trunks like layers of skin to exposed bone that was smooth in varied colours of ivory through to grey, brown and olive. Sap oozed its way through thick, crusty ochre bark clinging to tall, straight trees where magpies squabbled. Some were blackened by bush fires with stubborn renewed life pushing its way through with bright green shoots.

"Look at all the trees." Ruth pointed along a line of winter-bare trees as they approached Ballarat. The line extended for miles and miles along each side of the road with small plaques at the base of each tree. Curious, Les pulled over and they got out to have a look. Each bronze plaque was bolted to a steel stake driven into the ground.

"What can they mean?" Ruth puzzled as she bent over one.

It read: E.A. Dingle   2818   3rd T.C.

Les called back to her as he walked from tree to tree. "They're all names...of soldiers I guess. These look like regiments, or something."

They stared out of the Chev's window in awed silence as Les drove slowly along the road between the trees. They felt a reverence towards those names, without understanding why, as their eyes searched each plaque for the inscribed letters that told an incomplete story. The noise of the truck's motor seemed an intrusion upon the hushed scene of ghostly sentinels guarding each plaque. Those sentinels stood proudly, their exposed limbs pointing skywards like long witches' fingers...perhaps pointing to the ultimate destination of those names.

As they approached Ballarat, some thirteen miles later, the trees ended at a large archway constructed over the road. The words *The Avenue of Honour* stood out proudly over the arch.

"Let's see what it's about," Ruth said at the same time Les slowed the truck and brought it to a halt at the side of the road. They walked back to the arch and read from a plaque set into the side of the archway.

"It says here that every tree has the name of a Ballarat citizen who served in the Great War," Les observed. "They planted 3,900 trees. Imagine that!"

"Nice idea. It would be lovely to have your relatives honoured like that—if you had any." She pulled a rueful face.

"I wonder if there's a Baker on one of them," Les laughed.

"Probably. It's a pretty common name."

"It wouldn't be my father, though. He was no hero."

"I doubt mine was either—whoever he was."

"Let's have something different for lunch," Les said as they strolled along the main road in the city of Ballarat.

"You know what I fancy? A pie. A meat pie."

"What a great idea. With lots of tomato sauce."

They bought their steaming hot pies and, finding a bench seat on the footpath, ate them there watching the busy traffic and pedestrians. It was a delicate juggling act trying to eat the pies without the meat and sauce spilling out of the opposite side from which they were biting. Les took a big bite and hot minced meat oozed over the side and onto his hand, burning him.

"Jesus!"

Ruth giggled as he licked it off his hand and around the sides of the pie. Some of it had dripped onto the footpath and hungry sparrows dashed around it, vying with each other for the tasty prize.

"I've lost half of it."

"Go and get another one, Les. Just one'll never fill you."

They were surprised at how big Ballarat was with its stately old buildings, and were tempted to spend time looking around the shops—Les feeling safe amongst so many people—but decided to press on to Melbourne. They were impatient now to get to the city before nightfall and find accommodation. As Les filled up at a BP service station, Ruth bought some maps of the outer suburbs and the city. She knew Les would need some help in navigating their way around the sprawling capital.

Les drove down through low hills that parted to give glimpses of the flat plain that extended to where the city of Melbourne spread out; the blue/grey Dandenong Mountains climbed beyond it over the horizon in the distance.

As they passed through Bacchus Marsh, another avenue of trees extended beyond the town carrying plaques on their trunks. Once again they stopped to read some of the plaques which were attached to wooden blocks nailed onto the tree trunks.

"I wonder who Pte. H.N. Blake was and if he survived the war?"

"Must be like in Ballarat—an Avenue of Honour or something like that," Les commented.

"They're very patriotic here."

Names strange to them—Melton, St. Albans, Albion, Footscray—were suburbs of their new city. From farmland to industrial estates they travelled; sheep and crops in wide fields to built-up, busy streets, huge factories, trams joined to overhead wires as they rattled along tracks in the middle of the roads, buses, and so many cars. The wheels of the Chev caught in tram tracks and Les, unfamiliar with the experience took some time to work out how to negotiate them. He stopped at an intersection, watching the traffic signals, when they heard a bell dinging insistently behind them. They turned back to see a tram right on their tail, the driver gesticulating angrily.

"Keep off the tracks next time, mate," a driver in the lane next to Les called out. "Bloody tram drivers have a fit if you block 'em."

"Thanks, mate," Les called back laughing. He turned to Ruth who looked back at the tram anxiously. "Can't upset the locals, can we?"

The traffic thickened as they drove along Ballarat Road, passing Flemington Racecourse on their left. Les was tense, eyes darting everywhere, wary of the vehicles coming at him from all angles.

Some blocks further along, they approached a busy intersection. Ruth looked intently for street signs. "Damn...we should have turned right here, into Flemington Road."

"Nice park," Les observed.

"I know where we are. We're in Royal Park. Just keep going until you hit Royal Parade, turn right, and then straight along until you strike a roundabout. That should be Elizabeth Street."

"Where are we going, by the way?"

"I don't know, Les. I'm just heading us for the middle of the city. We should be able to find our way from there out to the other side."

"What about a night in the city before we go further? We could start fresh in the morning looking for a house. The estate agent in Horsham told me about a hotel in the city that's supposed to be all right. Young and Jackson's I think he said. Said to ask for a girl named Chloe. Said he knows her well."

"Oh, good. She might give us a few hints about Melbourne too. Like where to buy food, clothes—that sort of thing. Prices and so on."

Les pulled the Chev over to the side of the road and got out. A policeman was directing traffic at the intersection of Elizabeth and Collins Streets where a car had broken down. Les waited patiently until the blockage was cleared, and then walked up to the policeman. Ruth saw them in animated conversation as she waited in the truck. She smiled as she watched Les ply the officer with questions—saw the officer waving his arms and pointing all around the intersection—and wondered what was causing such pantomime.

"Very helpful fellow," Les commented as he slammed his door shut. "We're not far from the hotel. Just a few blocks away."

"What was he waving his arms around for?"

"Oh, he was explaining about the weird right-hand turn they do here in the city at some of the intersections. You turn right from the left-hand side of the road. Just as well he told me."

They continued on down Elizabeth Street until they could go no further, and turned left into Flinders Street.

"It's down here on the left. The copper said we should get parking further along Flinders Street, beside the railway tracks."

They crossed Swanston Street and continued along over Russell Street. Les noticed plenty of empty spots on their right and steered the truck over the tram tracks and parked.

They looked over at the myriad train tracks intertwined in seeming confusion that separated and wound their way off into the distance, going to many different parts of Melbourne. They led through suburbs and streets and past houses that protected families. Families that lived an ordinary existence without fear. Families that nurtured and prepared their young for the future. Families just like them.

"Do you think the truck will be safe here? I mean, all our things are in it." Ruth had stopped, reluctant to leave it alone.

Les turned back and saw a very dirty, very battered-looking truck. It seemed to be settling there, creaking in all its joints as it relaxed on worn tyres.

"I'll come back for any valuables. I don't see anybody bothering with it, though. Probably not worth pinching."

Les picked up their suitcase and, holding Ruth's hand, they walked back up Flinders Street towards the hotel. Flinders Street Station rose large on their left, its many clocks adorning the gaping entrance.

"It's huge, Les," Ruth breathed in awe as she looked up at the station.

They stood at the corner of the intersection at Princes Bridge—a couple in dusty clothes with a baby and a shabby suitcase. They looked out of place there as office workers jostled past them in their rush to get home after their busy workday. Streams of people crossed the road as cars queued up at the left of each street waiting to turn right. Suit-clad people were disgorged from trams and they flowed into the station oblivious of the young couple staring at them.

"Well," said Les. "We'd better get on with it."

And they crossed the road and stood in front of the stairs leading up into Young & Jackson's Hotel.

"After you, my lady," he smiled at her, and she began to climb the stairs. They led up to a comfortable room, plentiful water for a good hot bath, and a satisfying meal. They led up to their first night in their new adopted city. And they led up to the beginning of a new life of promise and final refuge.

The unfamiliar sounds of a busy city morning seeped in through the closed window. Ruth stretched lazily, wondering what the clanging noises were outside. *I'll get up in a minute and have a look,* she thought as she snuggled back down into the warmth of Les's body. It was a cold morning. Soft murmurings came from the cot in which Joy was awakening and Ruth knew she didn't have much longer to lie there before getting up to start their new day. Les's arm, heavy but reassuring, circled her body as he nuzzled into her neck breathing deeply in an easy sleep.

A cacophony of sound—car horns beeping loudly, whistles shrilling, intermittent clanging, footsteps pounding, voices shouting, car engines revving—were too much for Ruth. She had to get out of bed and see for herself. Parting the curtains, she looked down onto the street below where green trams rattled along their steel tracks. Crowds of train travellers appeared from inside Flinders Street Station, streamed down the steps and crossed the intersection at Flinders and Swanston Streets. A sea of felt hats wended their way amongst the crowd that was in constant motion, dodging cars, buses, trams and each other.

"Come on, lazy bones. Time to get up," Ruth said as she got back into bed with Joy, and put her cold feet onto Les's warm legs.

"All right, all right. I'm awake," he groaned. "What time is it?"

"Ten past eight."

"Struth, I haven't slept this late for donkeys' years."

"You must have needed it. What with all that driving."

"I'm starving."

"You're always starving," she laughed. "And I know someone else who's starving too."

Les kissed them both before getting out of bed and crossing to the window.

"Busy down there, isn't it?" he observed.

"I'll say."

"You hungry?"

"I am a bit peckish."

"Well, I'll go downstairs and see what the story is about breakfast, get a newspaper, and see if I can find that Chloe sheila."

"Can we afford breakfast here? I mean, we've just about run out of money, haven't we?"

"For you, love, we can afford anything."

"No, really, Les. We've only got a few quid left." She was frowning now, her head to one side as she watched him.

"I reckon we'll be all right. I'm going to get a job today—remember?"

Les buttoned up his shirt and pulled a jumper over it then ran a comb through his hair.

"See you soon."

Twenty minutes later, Les opened the bedroom door with a huge grin on his face.

"What?" she asked, puzzled at his obvious delight.

"I met that Chloe sheila. Bloody good sort."

"Oh?"

"Must have been freezing though."

"Why?"

"She didn't have any clothes on."

"What?"

"Not a stitch."

"What are you talking about? No clothes, indeed."

"No, really. She was just standing there naked, leaning on a table, and looking out the window. Wouldn't talk at all."

"What sort of place is this?" Ruth was indignant.

"Oh, quite decent. The Manager introduced me to her, all proper-like."

"Why would anyone be walking around naked, much less in this sort of weather? It's disgraceful. Is she a prostitute or something?"

"No. A very nice young lady. She's got gold all around her too."

"Gold?"

"Yeah—a gold frame." Les started to laugh, enjoying the joke. "She's a painting, love. A beautiful painting."

"You bugger!" Ruth threw a pillow at him and he fell to the floor. He lay there, not moving.

"Come on, get up, you dill."

He remained there, breathing heavily, eyes rolled up in the back of his head.

"Les? Come on...Les?"

She kneeled down, concern smudging her eyes. He hadn't moved. She ran her fingers across his face, felt the pulse in his neck, rising panic causing her to pant. Then she noticed the corners of his mouth beginning to tremble and his chest started to jump up and down with mirth.

"You rotten bugger," and she punched him hard in the belly.

By now Les could contain himself no longer and rolled around the floor in helpless laughter.

"Got you," he laughed, while she pretended to be angry with him. But she couldn't remain angry for long and burst out laughing along with him.

By ten o'clock they were back inside the cabin of their faithful truck, the engine running smoothly as it idled while Les had another quick look at the map. He swung out into the traffic and turned left at Swanston Street, drove over the Princes Bridge and then along St. Kilda Road passing the Shrine of Remembrance on their left.

They had noticed a house for rent in *The Weekly Times* in the suburb of Bentleigh and they headed in that direction.

The advertisement had read:

HOUSES TO LET
BENTLEIGH. Fully furnished house.
Long lease. Must be garden lovers.
8 GNS. PER WEEK. RING MO5774.

Ruth pointed out the red brick house with a low fence in Centre Road to Les. Rose bushes lined the driveway and three small conifers stood proudly in the front lawn. Minutes later they were in the back yard looking in astonishment at fruit trees.

The owner, Mrs Davenport, laughed. "There are an awful lot of lemon trees, aren't there? This area was a market garden years ago."

"How many lemon trees are there?" Ruth asked.

"Thirteen. And four apple trees, an apricot, two plums, and an almond."

Ruth was busy thinking of all the lemon meringue pies and lemon puddings she could make, and stewed apples and apple pies. Les was interested in the large brick garage, pleased to see that it was big enough for his truck and a workshop as well.

The woman smiled. "Well, if you want it, it's yours. I'd be very happy to see a young couple like you, with that adorable little baby of yours, in our home to look after it."

"You mean we can have it?" Ruth's eyes were shining.

"Yes, dear. You can move in tomorrow."

The older woman walked them to the gate and directed them to a nearby guest house where they could stay overnight.

"Pat'll look after you there. She's an old neighbour of mine. She'll let you use the telephone to ring up about a job. I'll ring her and tell her you're coming now."

"I can't believe our luck, Les. Such a nice woman, and the house is just the sort of place we wanted."

"Yeah. With three bedrooms, you've got the space for a sewing room, and I've got the workshop out the back. I'll be making you a sewing table in no time at all, and a new cot for Joy."

They found the guest-house ten minutes later in a street that ran alongside the railway line. Pat Lewis was in the front garden filling a large wide basket with a colourful array of flowers. She smiled as they got down from the truck.

"Mr and Mrs Bacon? Helen Davenport told me about you both...and this little bundle of joy here."

"Joy she is. That's her name," laughed Ruth.

"Oh, what a coincidence. Come in. Come in, before it starts pouring," she said looking up at the threatening clouds that scudded across the southern skies.

Their room for the night was simple, clean and comfortable, and faced onto a backyard that bordered on the railway line. Mrs Lewis settled Les down at the kitchen table with his newspaper near the telephone, and she went outside to join Ruth who was looking at the garden.

"I hope the trains won't disturb you or the little one too much. We're used to it, you see, living here so many years."

Her face showed concern but Ruth quickly allayed her fears. She liked Pat Lewis and they slid into easy conversation as they walked around the backyard. Short, dark, thick hair perched in wavy chaos over friendly brown eyes in a tiny oval face. She was a petite woman of fifty-five years who enjoyed the company of her guests, with a vigorous curiosity about their lives and welfare. Although a busy woman, she had time for anyone who needed help or who asked her for a favour. A *soft touch*, people often labelled her affectionately. *Soft in the head* was what her husband called her, worried that people took advantage of her good nature.

A stranger looking over the fence at Ruth and Pat could have mistaken them for mother and daughter, their build and hair colour being almost identical. They were both good listeners and shared the same sense of humour, giggling in similar tones at the incongruities of life.

They drew their thick cardigans across their chests as the wind gathered strength bringing a few drops of rain across the backyard, then turned as one and made their way to the back door.

"I wonder how Les got on?" Ruth mused. "I do hope he can get something today."

"He should do. There're plenty of jobs around, and if he's as good as you say..."

"Oh, he is that. He can fix or build anything."

"Well once word gets around, he'll get plenty of work to set himself up on his own. That's what he wants, isn't it?"

"Eventually. We have to get back on our feet first though. We've got very little money left...oh don't worry, we can pay you for tonight..."

"I'm not worried, love. You can leave it until you've got a bit more if you like."

"No, we'll be right. Once Les gets a job and I start sewing again..."

"You sew?"

"Yes."

"What sort of sewing? Frocks? Blouses?"

"Yes, anything really."

"Are you any good?"

"She's the best there is," Les interrupted them as they joined him in the kitchen. "You looking for a dressmaker? She's right in front of you."

"Well, yes, I am," Pat smiled at Les's open adoration of his wife. "I'm useless with a needle and thread. Jim...he's my husband...he reckons the only thing I'm good for is cooking and cleaning as his clothes are hanging off him 'cause I can't and won't repair them. You can't be good at everything, can you?" she laughed at herself. "And, seriously, if you're looking for customers, you've got one all ready...and I can recommend you to lots of my friends."

Ruth and Les looked at each other in delight. Things were going to be all right. They all sat down around the kitchen table in the welcome warmth of the heater. Pat put out her arms to hold Joy and Ruth passed the baby to her. She saw that Joy settled easily with Pat and she smiled as the older woman caught Joy's attention playing with her fingers. Les showed them one of the notices in the newspaper:

CARPENTER, good tradesman;
£20 per wk. Centre Road,
South Oakleigh. UW1940.

"The bloke who advertised—a Mr Healey—said to drive straight up Centre Road and it'll only take about twenty minutes to get there. I'll be passing our new place on the way."

"That's good money, Les. Are you going now?"

"Yeah. Said I was lucky to catch him. He'd called in to his house to pick up some extra tools and a tarp."

Ruth watched Les from the front door as he swung the Chev out onto the narrow street and turned right into Centre Road. Rain fell lightly, quietly staining the road and footpaths, and causing the flowers in the garden to quiver with each drop as they landed. She shivered as she turned back into the house, silently hoping that Les would be successful. After having paid a week's rent in advance, and their night's accommodation to be paid tomorrow, she knew they had less than £5 left to their names. It was cutting things pretty finely. They still had a week to go before Les could pick up his first wage packet—if he got the job, that is, and started tomorrow—and there were groceries to buy to keep them going. They had a hard week or two in front of them, she knew.

Ruth rubbed her forehead absentmindedly with cold fingers. She was only faintly aware of the beginnings of a headache as she stood deep in thought. Her mind conjured up an image of Les in the Chev finding his way to the builder's home, talking with the man, being questioned about his credentials. Les wouldn't have papers to show Mr Healey, she knew—he didn't have any in their new name. She couldn't understand why Les had wanted to change their name from Baker to Bacon. She had liked being Mrs Les Baker. She was a part of him and his surname. It was difficult to identify with the Bacon name and to remember to call herself Ruth Bacon. It had something to do with making a complete change, he'd said. Cutting the ties from their past. Not that either of them had a past worth clinging onto. But it's what Les had wanted and she'd gone along with it.

She smiled to herself as she remembered how they'd chosen the name. They'd been talking one day in the cabin of the truck as they bumped and shook over the countless potholes in the nightmare road across the Nullarbor.

"What about Bakewell? Or Bottomly? Or Bumsbrigade? Or Buckingham Palace?" Les had joked.

"I like Brandon," she replied.

"Branding Iron?"

"No, silly."

"I'm starving."

"You're always starving."

"What I'd give for a plate of chips, with a big lump of steak, fried onions, eggs and a heap of bacon," he sighed.

"Bacon!"

"Yeah, bacon. I can almost smell it."

"That's it. Bacon...we could call ourselves Bacon."

"Beauty. I like it. Mr and Mrs Les Bacon. Has a nice crackle to it."

She was brought back to the present by the soft touch of a hand on her shoulder.

"You all right, love?"

"Oh, yes. I'm fine. Just wondering how Les is going."

"You come back in the warm kitchen and have a nice cup of tea. That husband of yours'll be back in no time at all. And I think this little miss is after something too."

Joy was squirming in Pat's arms, becoming fretful with hunger. They returned to the kitchen and sat at the table with a large pot of tea. Ruth fed Joy while Pat described the variety of local shops in Bentleigh—which butcher to go to and which one to avoid; the best greengrocer; the *nice man* at the chemist shop on the corner; the helpful people in the wool shop; where to buy fabrics—and explained the routine of the buses along Centre Road and the train timetable.

Pat had a basinette to put the baby in and within a short space of time Joy was contentedly sleeping off a large feed. The rain had settled in to a steady drumming on the roof, and Ruth added a heavy jumper to what she already had on. *The Weekly Times* had predicted a maximum temperature of 48° Fahrenheit with cold-snap conditions and she wondered if it would become much colder in Melbourne with winter only just beginning. The change of conditions seemed strange to her as she looked out at the leaden sky after having slept under the clear, starry Nullarbor heavens. They had been fortunate with such mild weather during their journey from the west.

A door banged outside and a minute later Les entered the kitchen. Both Ruth and Pat looked at him expectantly. There was a big grin on his face.

"Well?" both women said at the same time.

"I got it!"

That night the small dining room was crowded with Pat and her husband, Jim, Les and Ruth, and three more guests. It was a celebratory dinner for Les and Ruth now that their worries were over as far as a place to live and a job were concerned. The vegetable and barley soup warmed them, as did the lively conversation at the table. They felt lucky to have fallen on their feet so quickly and to have found such friendly people to guide them. The steak and kidney pie followed by a rice pudding had them groaning in defeat when pressed for a second helping, and they went to bed satisfied both physically and mentally.

The rain eased through the night as Ruth slid in and out of dreams. Her face was relaxed, with a faint smile on her lips, and she breathed deeply. Jumbled images of endless roads merged with orchards of lemon trees, nappies became rolls of fabric, a robust red-haired baby struggled from between her legs gasping for its first breath and was laid on her breast—and an empty bucket kicked over and rolled away into the darkness where it disappeared forever.

Part Two

© Danielle Jupp 2006

Chapter 12   Bentleigh & Chelsea

Saturday, 18th January 1960

The needle in the Singer sewing machine bit into the fabric at a dizzying speed. It was a blur as Ruth's shoe pressed the foot pedal while she guided the long seam over the needle plate. Her movements were practiced, controlled, competent. She was at home working at the machine and she loved it.

"There," she exclaimed as she inspected her work with satisfaction. "Almost finished."

Piles of neatly folded garments surrounded her. A pleasant smell of clean, new fabric filled the room despite the open window and the warm, summer breeze that lifted the lace curtain.

The curly red head bent over a small desk beside Ruth. The curls hung in ringlets over a face that concentrated on an array of buttons before it.

"Is this a green one, Mummy?" Joy asked, holding up a small button.

"Yes, sweetheart. It's a light green one. It's almost the same shade as your eyes."

Joy put it with a group of green buttons, then continued to take one button at a time out of a large jar. Her hand stuck in the opening and, as she tugged it back out, the jar tipped over and all the buttons spilled out onto the desktop. *Just like lollies in the milk bar,* the child thought as she scooped them up in her hands. She regarded the shapes and colours that not only looked pretty, but also were a pleasure sensation to touch. Some had two holes in the centre, others had four, and some had a shank at the back with a hole. Some were smooth and some lumpy. Some reflected the light in shiny sparkles and others had dull flat surfaces.

Joy picked up a pink glass button and held it to the light. "I like this one," she said.

"Can you find any others just like it?" Ruth asked her.

Joy's hand scooped up a handful and let the buttons fall through her fingers one by one. She spread them out on the desk, her fingers hesitating over every pink button, discarding, picking up and holding each one next to the original one.

"Here, Mummy. This one's the same," she cried in triumph.

She separated them by colour and then arranged them in rows from smallest to largest. Ruth paused for a moment to regard her daughter holding a mauve button indecisively over a group of pink buttons and a group of red. The tip of her tongue peeped out from the corner of her mouth as she wavered back and forth until she found a shade that was a close match. It was an occupation that Joy never tired of. Sometimes she would sort them by colour, other times by shape, and others just because she liked the button and wanted to find others that were exactly the same. And sometimes her mother would thread a tapestry needle with thick cotton, tie a large knot in the end, and Joy would poke the needle through her chosen buttons to make a great string of them.

As Ruth worked at the machine, Joy sat at her own little desk made by her father. It had four drawers on one side and a cupboard on the other. There was a shelf built over it where Joy's favourite books resided, and a lamp that cast a good light over the desk area. It was Joy's special place to play while her mother worked beside her on the many garments that she was paid to make. Sometimes they hardly spoke, each absorbed in her own tasks and thoughts. At other times they had long conversations about anything and everything during which Joy would ply Ruth with an inexhaustible list of questions.

But today they were lost in their own reflections about the morrow. Ruth's mind was busy sorting and prioritizing the chores that had yet to be done. And Joy sensed the change that was about to take place in their lives.

A month earlier Les had arrived home one afternoon from work in an excited state.

"Ruth! Ruth! Guess what?"

Les banged the door of the truck as he made his way out of the garage and scooped up his daughter to plant a large kiss on her forehead. His arm went around Ruth and he kissed her upturned face.

"You know those bathing boxes we started building today in Chelsea?"

Ruth watched him, her head inclined to one side, waiting to hear his news.

"They're on a real nice stretch of beach and there are all these short little streets that lead to it...some only have eight or ten houses in 'em...and I saw a nice little house with a *For Private Sale* sign up and I reckon it would be just the ticket for us. I asked the lady if I could have a look inside, like, and she didn't mind. It's got three bedrooms, an inside dunny...some of 'em don't, you know...a good gas stove in the kitchen, a stainless steel trough in the laundry, a gas heater in the lounge room, nice Axminster carpet, and, and..."

"Slow down, slow down! You're going at a hundred miles an hour," Ruth laughed.

"Daddy, you're funny," Joy giggled.

"So I am, daughter of mine. So I am."

"You obviously liked it, Les," Ruth smiled at him. "When can I see it?"

"Now. Right now."

They drove down to the Nepean Highway and followed it to the bayside towns that ran beside the railway line. When the highway crossed Mordialloc Creek, they caught a glimpse of the bay beyond colourful boats moored on either side of the creek. As they headed towards Chelsea, Joy excitedly pointed each time they passed one of the many streets on their right. She was rewarded with a momentary view of sparkling blue water at their end.

The traffic slowed as they approached Aspendale Railway Station where Les pointed with amusement to the traffic signal.

"Struth...look at that, will you? I didn't notice it before."

They watched the traffic signal—which resembled a clock face—as a white arrow moved slowly around its face on a red section towards the green. A horn bipped from behind the truck as the three of them watched, fascinated. Les rolled forward slowly in first gear while Ruth and Joy turned to look out the back window of the cabin. They saw, on the other side of the clock, the arrow reach a smaller amber section and the traffic slowed once more to a stop as the arrow entered the red.

Joy remained on her knees looking out the back window intrigued by the strange-looking clock until it was out of sight.

"What time was it, Mummy?"

Ruth and Les were still laughing as they drove through Edithvale and arrived at Chelsea. Les turned right into a short street that led behind the shops, and pulled up in front of a small weatherboard house. From where they sat, in the cabin of the truck, they could see Port Phillip Bay at the end of the tiny street.

"Mummy, look at the water," Joy squealed with delight. "Can we go and see it?"

"Soon, sweetheart. We have to have a look at a house first. Then we'll go for a stroll on the beach. How does that sound?"

They walked up the driveway of the property looking around them at the neat garden. Multi-coloured petunias alternated with impatiens and daisies in a border lining the pathway and more petunias spilled out of large pots on either side of the front door. Les knocked and the door opened to an elderly woman who smiled in greeting. The late afternoon sun played on the stained-glass window of the door, casting multi-coloured patterns across the floor. Joy played with the colours, passing her hands through them.

"Mrs Hyland, I've brought my wife and daughter, like I promised." Les introduced Ruth and Joy.

"What a beautiful child," the elderly woman commented. "Come in and have a good look around."

She led them down a narrow passage that separated two bedrooms at the front of the house. The walls were covered with striped maroon wallpaper and family photographs hung from picture rails along the length of the passageway.

The doors to the bedrooms were open and they paused to look into them. The master bedroom was dominated by a double bed with solid wooden ends that matched an imposing wardrobe and dressing table. A white crocheted bedspread touched the flowered carpet. The other bedroom had a single bed under the window and a dressing table with a large mirror that reflected a wardrobe on the opposite wall. The sun streamed in through open Venetian blinds, lighting the room with soft orange stripes.

The passageway opened into a lounge room crammed with worn stuffed chairs and couch. Doilies covered the top of each piece as well as the armrests. A knitting bag sat open on one of the chairs, with long steel needles sticking out of balls of blue wool. A pipe sat in a clean ashtray on a glass-topped table, next to a framed photograph of a handsome man with the same pipe in his mouth. A faint reminder of that pipe hung in the air, so faint they had hardly noticed it until seeing the pipe brought awareness to their nostrils. The lid of a Stromberg-Carlson radiogram was piled high with records. Ruth picked one of them up.

"Doris Day," commented Ruth. "I like her."

"So do I, dear. I go to the Mentone picture theatre and see all of her films there. I've seen *Calamity Jane* four times."

Facing the lounge room were a third bedroom, which had the same Venetian blinds as the rest of the house, and a bathroom and toilet. Ruth's mind was busy thinking of curtains to replace the blinds that she hated. *Dust catchers,* she thought to herself. *A nice pale pink paint would brighten this up in no time,* she reckoned as she mentally ripped off the faded patterned wallpaper. *Good light in here…big enough for the machine.* Yes, this room would make an excellent sewing room.

Behind the lounge and third bedroom was the kitchen. The plentiful cupboards were painted cream. Green lino, peeling at the edges, covered the floor as well as the surface of a wooden kitchen table. The benches were topped with a green Laminex not unlike the colour of the lino. Over the gas stove was a mantelpiece with tin canisters announcing flour, sugar and tea on their embossed labels. An old mantel clock sat beside them ticking loudly.

Joy clasped her mother's hand as they walked through the house. The rooms smelled faintly musty with an overlying aroma of tobacco, cooking smells and flowers. Joy liked the welcoming feel of the house and the old lady who kept on smiling down at her and patting her head. The kitchen, especially, smelled good. Underneath the kitchen window there was a wire rack placed on the sink with biscuits cooling on it. Joy looked up at them, her mouth watering.

"Would you like one, dear?" the old lady asked.

"Thank you very much," Joy said in a clear voice as she accepted a biscuit.

"What a dear," exclaimed Mrs Hyland.

Suddenly the mantel clock began to chime: slow, even, loud chimes that filled the house with their vibration.

"What's that, Mummy?" Joy stood listening intently with surprise.

" A clock, sweetheart."

"It's a loud clock," she said earnestly as the chimes faded.

"You should hear it when it strikes the hour, dear. And it strikes for a lot longer…especially if it's twelve o'clock."

Mrs Hyland opened the wire door that led to the back yard and an outside laundry. Les inspected the house carefully with a trained eye. It was a small house, but had possibilities for extending as the block was long. In the backyard was a lemon tree…*thank goodness for that,* thought Ruth, after being used to having lemons on tap…and a huge apricot tree which was laden with fruit. Blue, white and pink hydrangeas grew outside the back door, and a large vegetable garden extended halfway down the length of the block. Lettuces, tomatoes, cucumbers and parsley grew in healthy abundance. The sunlight sloped across the backyard casting an orange shadow across the garage at the end of the driveway.

"Do you mind if we walk along the beach and have a talk first?" Ruth asked.

"Of course not, dear. Take as much time as you like."

They walked hand in hand, with Joy in the middle, to the end of Sandalwood Avenue where clean white sand led down to the water's edge.

"Here they are. The bathing boxes we've been working on," Les pointed out.

The beach stretched flat into the distance on either side of them, covered with shells of all shapes and sizes. A jetty reached out towards the horizon where blue water shone like silver with the sun's rays melting into its surface. A molten sun, low in the sky, stained the stark blue with streaks of golden pink. They walked along the water's edge, shoes off, kicking in the waves as they rolled softly over their feet. Joy collected shells into the skirt of her dress, which she gathered up until water dripped through it down her legs.

"I like this place," she said, standing on a jellyfish and watching it squish through her toes.

"So do I," said Ruth squeezing Les's hand.

"How much did you say you were asking?" Les stood with his hands in his pockets, trying not to show his enthusiasm.

"£3,750," replied Mrs Hyland.

"£3,750, eh? And what sort of settlement? Thirty—sixty—ninety days?"

"Whatever would suit you best, dear."

"Well, thirty days would be good for us, wouldn't it, Ruth?"

Les looked at Ruth and she nodded imperceptibly. They could just manage it, they both knew, with what they'd saved. Joy sensed the tenseness of the situation and looked from one adult face to the other. They seemed very serious.

Les took a deep breath. "All right. We'll take it."

The month had flown by in a haze with Ruth finishing off sewing jobs while Les put the finishing touches on pieces of furniture which had been commissioned by neighbours and friends.

During the five years they had lived in Bentleigh, Pat and Jim Lewis had been the means of opening up a whole new world for the young couple and their daughter. They had introduced them to prospective clients who would help to set them on their feet financially.

"Ruth, love, there are two ladies in the football club who would each like a frock made for the social club dance. Can I send them over?"

"The kinder has got a concert going next month. The littlies have to have costumes made. Have you got time, love?"

"Jim's split his trousers, love. He bent over to tie his shoelace in the hardware shop and...rip. He had to walk home down Centre Road holding the newspaper over his bum. I split my sides laughing when he got home. Can you run them up for him?"

"Mabel, next door, asked me to ask you if you can sew curtains. I told her of course you can sew curtains. There's nothing you can't sew."

Ruth's expertise as a dressmaker soon became common knowledge and before long the telephone rang constantly for fittings. The women stood stiffly in the third bedroom, which had been made into a sewing room, while Ruth, with pins poking out of her mouth, pinned them into a perfect fit. Sometimes Joy handed pins to her mother, and the ladies fussed over her for being 'such a good little helper'.

It hadn't taken those women long to notice the extra pieces of custom-made furniture around the house.

"Where did you get that dressing table?" they would ask, or: "Who made that wardrobe?"

Ruth would smile proudly and say: "Why, my Les made them. He's a beaut carpenter. Best anywhere. And he does wood turning, too. He can make anything in any style you like."

They would look at her in amazement, and then the orders came in thick and fast.

Next morning, Joy woke early and tiptoed into her parents' bedroom, holding her teddy bear closely to her.

"Shush, Teddy, we'll get in and have a cuddle with them before they wake up," she whispered.

"Before who wakes up?" Les muttered with his eyes closed, a grin on his face.

"Oh, Daddy, I was going to surprise you."

"Oh were you now? You'll just have to surprise your mother instead."

Ruth lay with her eyes closed, trying not to laugh. Joy climbed up on the bed warily, dragging Teddy with her. She wriggled in between her parents and pushed Teddy's nose up against Ruth's face.

"Wake up, Mummy. It's time to get up and go to our new house."

Still pretending sleep, Ruth found it harder not to giggle with the bear's fur tickling her nose.

"Mummy won't wake up, Daddy. Is she tired?"

"I'll see what I can do about it," he said seriously.

And with that he reached over and tickled her ears, then down her neck. Still no response, except for her diaphragm bouncing up and down.

He reached under the covers and whispered: "Here, tickle her on the knees."

Joy scrambled down the bed and tickled a knee. Suddenly Ruth sat up exploding in laughter.

"All right. All right. I surrender."

They frolicked around the bed until the bedclothes fell onto the floor with Ruth ending up on top of them. Les and Joy bounced up and down on the bed in triumph, laughing at Ruth giggling helplessly on the floor.

"Can we go to our new house now, Daddy?"

Chapter 13   Chelsea

She was up and dressed before the familiar sounds of her mother preparing breakfast in the kitchen began. It was too early for the delicious aroma of Sunday's bacon and eggs to waft into her bedroom. She chose bright red ribbons for her long dark chestnut pigtails. They matched her red cotton dress. She pulled on white anklet socks and turned the frilled edges over, making sure that they were equal lengths, then pushed her feet into black patent leather sandals. They were her new ones. The buckles were hard to do up and she had to content herself with leaving them with just the strap pushed through. The holes punched into the leather were still too tight to find with the metal pin. Perhaps her mother could do them up for her if there was time.

The heat had not yet penetrated the bathroom but she could see the sun begin its solid glare on the window as it rose up the side of the house warming the bricks. She remembered to brush her teeth an extra twenty strokes to make them especially white. She stood on tiptoe until she could just see the top of her head in the mirror above the basin, and she parted her hair from her forehead right down to the neckline at the back. The parting ran a little to the right as it reached the crown of her head, went back towards the middle, and then ran riot in jagged abandon for the rest of its journey. She gathered two thick hair bunches into rubber bands and tied the ribbons around them. One pigtail was tied behind her left ear, and the other was in front of her right. Grasping the edge of the basin, she jumped up and down to catch a glimpse of her handiwork in the mirror. It passed.

The tap dripped in time with her thoughts: *Today's the day. Today's the day.*

The door handle squeaked as she tiptoed out of the bathroom and into the passageway. She stopped, one foot suspended over the floorboards, trying to remember which one creaked. She let her foot down slowly, letting out her breath in jagged relief. She had not disturbed her father's snoring. She could hear his slow whistling exhalations followed by thunderous intakes of air and she covered her mouth tightly to stifle her giggles.

The wooden drawer in the kitchen cupboard stuck halfway out as it always did. From her vantage point, standing on a kitchen chair, she could see the scissors amongst a muddle of string and gadgets.

Carefully she eased the drawer back in and tried again, edging it out on an angle, an inch to the right, an inch to the left, until it was open just enough to get the scissors out.

She put the scissors in the basket her mother used for cut flowers and dragged the chair over to the back door. It grated on the linoleum floor and she stood frozen for a moment, listening. The snoring continued uninterrupted and she climbed up on the chair to reach the handle.

"Louise?" her mother called softly from the bedroom. "Is that you?"

"Yes, Mummy."

"What's the matter? Are you all right?"

Her mother appeared in the kitchen, sleepily pushing her hair back from her eyes.

"What are you doing up at this time of the morning? And dressed too."

"It's today, Mummy. She's coming today."

"Oh, I know, Sweetie. But not for a long time yet. It's only seven o'clock."

"Is that near lunchtime?"

"No, Louie," her mother laughed. "We haven't even had breakfast yet. And your father's still asleep."

"I know. I can hear him," giggled Louise.

"What are you doing up on the chair?"

"I was going to pick some flowers for her. Some sweet peas."

"What a nice thought. But they'll wilt by the time she gets here, especially in the heat. Why don't you wait for a few hours? Have some breakfast first."

"I want to wait for her. Outside. In case I miss her."

"You won't miss her, Louie. I think they're arriving after lunch. Tell you what: I'll give you plenty of notice before she comes, so you'll have all the time in the world to pick the flowers. How about that?"

"Well, if you're sure..."

Louise got down from the chair reluctantly, and her mother put it back beside the table. She sat down and pulled Louise onto her lap, hugging her closely.

"You've been looking forward to today, haven't you?"

"For years and years," Louise responded seriously.

"That long, eh?" Her mother tried not to laugh. "I hope you won't be disappointed."

"Disappointed?"

"Yes. When something doesn't turn out to be as good as what you'd expected. You may not even like her, you know."

"Oh, I will, Mummy." Louise shook her head emphatically. "Mrs Hyland said she's very nice. She's got red hair, too."

The humidity sat heavily, like a thick wet cloak, on those not fortunate enough to spend the afternoon in the refreshing waters of Port Phillip Bay. The sun's rays glittered like diamonds skittering across the surface of the bay, dazzling the eyes of the beach goers. The sounds of children squealing excitedly and the splashing of water from the beach reached Louise's ears. The allure of the cool water tempted her, but she remained resolute.

She sat on the top step outside the front door of the house in the shade of the verandah. In her hand she gripped a large bunch of sweet peas—red, pink, white, blue and purple fragrant blossoms—tied with a pink ribbon. For an hour she had sat there, after finishing her lunch, waiting to see a truck pull into the street. A slight breeze ruffled the sweet peas that grew over the low picket fence between her house and number twenty. Louise looked at her wilting bunch and back at the fresh ones. Should she pick a new bunch? She stood up and swapped the bunch over to the other hand, wiping her sweating palm on her dress.

Just then a movement caught her eye and she saw a dilapidated truck and a removal van cross Camp Street and enter Sandalwood Avenue. The truck was piled high with boxes and tools sticking out at all angles making the truck look like it might tip over at any moment. Inside the cabin were a man, a woman and...a red-haired girl. The man stopped the truck outside number twenty, climbed down and walked around the truck to open the door for the woman. He helped her out and the girl jumped down after her.

Louise held her breath and her grip on the bunch of flowers tightened. She leaned against the picket fence, almost lost amongst the sweet peas, afraid to speak, afraid to utter the words she had rehearsed in her head. The girl appeared excited, looking down to the end of Sandalwood Avenue at the water. Then she spied Louise at the fence and walked up to the gate.

"Hello," Joy said.

"Hello," Louise whispered, shrinking further back into the sweet peas. She was stunned by the red hair as it flashed golden-rust lights with the movements of the girl's head. She had never seen hair like it before.

"What's your name?" Joy asked, leaning over the gate.

"Louise."

"You look like a flower," Joy said, matter-of-factly.

"You look like a princess," came the whispered reply.

Louise felt the flower stalks oozing in her palm and she was reminded of her intention. Slowly she approached Joy and held out the flowers to her, mute with shyness.

Joy's hand tentatively reached for the flowers, hesitating, unsure if they were meant for her. She looked at Louise questioningly.

Louise found her tongue: "Welcome to our street," then burst into tears.

Horrified, she looked at Joy's startled face, pushed the flowers into Joy's hand and dashed inside her house, banging the front door behind her.

When the removal truck had finally left, and the last of the Chev's contents had been unloaded, Ruth, Les and Joy sat down wearily on the steps outside the kitchen and looked out over their back yard. A breeze had sprung up, bringing some relief to their tired, sweat-soaked bodies.

"What do you reckon about a swim?" Les asked.

"Yes, Daddy. Let's go."

"But I don't know where all our bathers are," Ruth sighed. "We haven't unpacked the clothes yet."

"We'll find them," Joy said confidently, standing up. "Come on, Mummy...Daddy...let's go to the beach."

Half an hour later, with the contents of nearly all the clothing boxes upturned, they found their bathers and changed into them quickly. The thought of the water washing their sticky bodies and cooling their blood was irresistible. Les carried the towels as they made their way out of their new house and walked past the gate of Louise's house.

"I wish she'd come out," Joy said wistfully looking at the front door.

"Oh, I'm sure she will when she feels a bit better, sweetheart," Ruth reassured her.

"But what if she never comes out again? I liked her."

"I think she liked you too," Les said.

They stayed at the beach for the rest of the afternoon feeling wonderfully refreshed. Joy played at the water's edge building sandcastles, studding the sides with pretty shells and digging moats around them that filled with water. The bay was calm sending tiny ripples to wash the sand around Joy's legs as she sat absorbed in her games. Ruth and Les swam out into deeper water with strong strokes, always turning back to watch their daughter. The beach was less crowded now and they noticed the little dark-haired girl sitting on the sand in front of a bathing box. She stayed there for a long time just watching, not moving. The next time they looked, she had moved a little closer to where Joy played. Then they saw her get up and walk a few steps, hesitate, and sit down on the sand again. She repeated these steps a number of times until she was sitting just behind Joy. Then Joy turned around to look for more shells and she noticed the girl there.

Ruth and Les trod water waiting to see what would happen. The girls were in deep conversation and then they sat on the sand together and started building a new sandcastle.

"Looks like she got over her shyness," Les laughed.

"Poor little thing. I felt so sorry for her."

"I hope Joy's got a good little friend there. She's been on her own too long."

"On her own? She's got us."

"That's different, love. She needs friends her own age. You know...talk each other's lingo."

"Oh? Do you think so?" Ruth frowned as she watched the two girls playing together.

Les disappeared into the water and surfaced some yards away, squirting the salty seawater out of his mouth. He was surprised to see Ruth still looking towards shore. She looked tense...worried.

"What's the matter?" he called back to her.

"Nothing."

Chapter 14

Bright sunlight bounced off the surface of the placid waters of the bay, shattering the rays into a lavish display of dazzling reflections. Children's shouts of excitement mingled with the cries of sea gulls and the soft murmur of the tide as it rippled towards shore.

The white, clean sand reached as far as one could see to the left and right, with a barrier of marram grass and bathing boxes separating the beach from the houses. The pier was often crowded with children dangling lines over the edge, waiting hopefully for the nibbles that sometimes tugged at an eager hand.

The weather continued hot and humid over the following days but Joy hardly seemed to notice it. Every spare moment she was up and out of the house playing with Louise and, when she could persuade Ruth to accompany them, she would frolic in the water with her new friend. Les left for work early in the mornings with Joy making him promise to come home as soon as he possibly could so that he could have a swim with her and Ruth.

During the daytime, the beach was crowded with young children enjoying their school holiday break. Colourful beach towels were spread at intervals on the sand from which recumbent parents cast a watchful eye over their children. Small buckets and spades were busily employed by eager sand castle builders, as were shining black rubber tyre tubes supporting the slippery bodies of young swimmers in the water as they fought for their turn. Smaller blown-up rubber rings supported learning swimmers, and flippers propelled them through the water seemingly faster than the darting fish that tickled their ankles. Snorkels, attached to submerged heads trundling in the shallows, puffed and sucked at air.

Joy envied the bubble bathers that Louise wore to the beach. They were made of cotton with square bubbles of the fabric popping up between machined rows of shirring elastic. When Louise bent over, a smooth layer of cotton covered her bottom. When she stood straight, the bubbles would appear again without the fullness of her bottom to push the bubbles out. It fascinated Joy to see this phenomenon, and she had Louise bending over and standing up, over and over again, to the accompaniment of shrieks of laughter and much giggling from both girls.

Joy and Louise introduced their mothers to each other over the fence one morning. Olive Fletcher was pleased that her daughter finally had a playmate and that they obviously took to each other so quickly. She liked Ruth's friendly manner, her sense of humour and devotion to Joy. But she was puzzled at Ruth's reluctance to allow Joy the freedom to play with Louise more often, even if Olive herself was supervising the girls. She noticed an exaggerated protectiveness that she found cloying, and she felt a slight sense of unease that she shrugged off as merely not knowing Ruth enough.

A few days later, Ruth enquired about the bubble bathers, asking if she might borrow Louise's pair to copy and make a pair for Joy. Olive was only too pleased to oblige, delighted to learn that Ruth was a dressmaker.

"You know, there's not a decent dressmaker anywhere in Chelsea. You'll do pretty well out of it, I reckon, especially with school starting in a couple of weeks. The kids'll all need new clothes for that. Good strong ones. They charge too much in the shops for them."

"School?" Ruth said weakly.

"Yes. It starts on the second of next month. Young Joy, here...she'll be going to Chelsea Primary, I assume? That's where Louise is enrolled. It's the closest to here."

"I suppose so. I hadn't really thought about it..."

"She's not enrolled?"

"Les...my husband...he said something about it."

Olive looked at Ruth in surprise. She wondered at Ruth's apparent lack of interest—or knowledge—about Joy's entry into the world of education. She had been feeling quite excited at the prospect of her daughter starting school, and Louise was excited too, especially now that it appeared she would have a friend to go with.

"When's Joy's birthday?" Olive asked.

"Eighth of May."

'You're kidding! Louise's is the ninth. What a co-incidence." Olive called to Louise who was making a daisy chain with Joy on the front lawn of the Fletcher's house. "Girls...did you know that your birthdays are a day apart? You're almost exactly the same age."

"I'm going to be five," Joy said seriously, pushing a daisy stalk through the stem of another in which Louise had made a hole with her nail. "I'm four now."

"Me too," said Louise, selecting another daisy from a heap in her skirt. She pushed a hole through its stalk and handed it to Joy, who then threaded it with another daisy stalk. She pulled the stalk through until the head of the flower stopped at the hole. The chain was long enough to join and, when she had done so, she placed it on top of Louise's head.

"Fairy queens wear crowns just like that." Joy sat back on her heels, inspecting her handiwork. "There's one who looks just like you in one of my books. She's pretty, like you, too."

Louise blushed as she raised her hands tentatively to touch the daisy crown. Her mother smiled as Louise stood up slowly, her head and shoulders held stiffly, for fear that she might disturb the flowers.

"We could have a party for the two of them. What do you think?" Olive asked Ruth enthusiastically.

"If that's what Joy wants," Ruth replied a little stiffly.

"Oh, of course..." Olive trailed off uncertainly. "If you had other plans..."

"No. It's just that we haven't talked about it yet. It's four months away. Things change."

Ruth hated herself at that moment when she saw the hurt expression on Olive's face. *Why'd I say that?* There was a feeling of...panic...as if Olive was taking Joy from her. But how could she? She seemed a nice enough young woman and why would she want to take Joy from her anyway? Ruth wondered at her sudden feeling of insecurity. There seemed to be a threat in the background but she couldn't understand what it was. She had been talking about school, the girls' birthdays, a party...where was the threat? She shook herself mentally and turned to the girls.

"Well, how about it, you two? Would you like a joint party?" Ruth called over to them.

Olive stared at Ruth.

"What's a joint party, Mummy?" Louise asked.

"It means that the two of you would have one party instead of two separate ones."

"Why?"

"Because your birthdays are so close together, it would be a bigger party if we joined the two. So it would be a double celebration at the same time." Olive looked sideways at Ruth to see if she agreed.

"That's right," Ruth nodded.

"And we could have it exactly between their birth times—as long as it's not at midnight," Olive laughed.

"Can we? Can we, Mummy?" Joy asked jumping up and down in excitement.

"If that's what you both want."

"Oh, yes." Joy turned to Louise. "Do you want to have a big party with me?"

"The biggest!" Louise squealed. "With balloons? And streamers?"

"And party hats? And games?" Joy looked from Ruth to Olive.

"Yes, and a big cake for the two of you," Olive laughed, then she looked at Ruth. "What time was Joy born?"

"What time?" Ruth looked puzzled.

"Yes. The time she was born."

"I...don't remember." She hadn't been asked this before and the question stumped her. She realized she ought to know. Why didn't she? She must have forgotten, but it would come back to her. Of course it would. Every mother *must* know when her child was born. It was less than five years ago, after all. "I'll ask Les. He'll know..." Quick tears sprang to her eyes and she blinked them away fiercely, suddenly infuriated with herself.

"What time was I born, Mummy?" Louise asked.

"Ten minutes after one o'clock in the morning. I'll never forget it." Olive bit her lip, regretting her thoughtlessness. She didn't miss the slight wince that passed over Ruth's face. She puzzled again over the other woman's behaviour; it wasn't quite right. There was something mysterious about her—something hidden behind those brown eyes in the expression that lurked suddenly—a childlike bewildered facade that disguised what really was going on behind the words.

When Les returned from work later that day, Joy told him excitedly about the big birthday party she and Louise would have. He was pleased that the two girls seemed to get on so well together and was amused at the coincidence of their birthdays being so close. After Joy had gone to bed that night, Ruth and Les sat out on the back door step enjoying the early evening breeze. He had noticed that Ruth seemed preoccupied since he arrived home from work. His arm rested loosely around her shoulder and he leaned over and kissed her cheek lightly.

"Ruth?"

"Umm?"

"Are you happy here?"

"Of course I am. Why?"

"You seem worried about something."

"No, not really."

She sighed and stood up, brushing her skirt absentmindedly again and again, then walked over to the lemon tree and picked up a ripe lemon that had fallen on the grass. She gripped it so tightly that the knuckles stood out white on her thin fingers, the tendons and veins raised tautly on the inside of her wrist. He waited, knowing that she would talk when the time was right. Two gulls swooped over the back yard, squabbling over a prize held in the beak of one. Their appearance startled Ruth and Les saw the tension ease from her as she dropped the lemon unnoticed. She looked up at him and smiled tremulously as she returned to sit beside him. Her eyes were bright with unshed tears, he noticed.

"Les?"

"Yes, love?"

"Am I a bad mother?"

"What...?" Les felt a cold tremor ripple through his body and his heart began to thud wildly in his chest.

"I mean, do you think I'm a proper mother to Joy? Like other mothers?"

"Of course you are," Les hugged her reassuringly. "You're a wonderful mother. What on earth makes you ask a question like that?"

"It's something that Olive, next door, asked me today."

"And what could she possibly ask you that would make you think you're not the best mother this side of the Black Stump?"

"She asked me what time Joy was born."

Les sucked in his breath.

"Les...I couldn't answer her. I...don't know. How can that be?"

"Oh, love, you've just forgotten..."

"But every mother should know when her child was born. It's one of the most important times in a woman's life. And it wasn't that long ago. I don't understand..." Tears began to slide slowly down her cheeks, dripping into the corners of her mouth.

"You were in a lot of pain when you gave birth. They gave you stuff...it's a wonder you can remember any of it." He searched desperately for the right words. "I'll bet lots of women can't..."

"What time was it, Les?" she asked quietly.

"It was...it was..." He suddenly noticed his watch sitting amongst the golden hairs on his tanned arm, the hour hand pointing to eight. "Eight...yes, that's it...eight. Ten past eight...at night." His smile disarmed her.

"Are you sure?"

"Of course I'm sure. Wouldn't I know the time my own daughter was born?"

"I don't," she replied in a small voice.

"Oh, love, I wasn't suffering the pain you were. You were too busy to be worrying about anything other than pushing her out."

"Les?"

"Yes?"

"I don't remember that either."

Next door, at the Fletcher household, Olive opened the oven door and took out a plate piled high with lamb chops and vegetables.

"Careful, it's hot. It's been there that long," she warned as she placed it on the table in front of her husband, Jack.

He grunted his thanks and watched as she poured strong tea into his cup from a china teapot covered with a brightly coloured tea cosy. He dealt two full teaspoons of sugar into the cup, added some milk, and stirred the tea three times clockwise, then three times anti clockwise. He shook a thick covering of salt over everything on his plate, and then gave two short shakes of the white pepper. He then pulled his chair close to the table, and began to eat. It was a ritual that he repeated every night. Every movement was precise, deliberate and boringly predictable, and they annoyed Olive immensely. She blew some strands of hair out of her eyes, pulled her dark hair back tightly and jammed two hair combs impatiently back into the thick wavy mass. Her hazel eyes darkened as she restrained herself from snatching his plate up and throwing it in the sink.

"Busy at work again?" she asked calmly, sitting down to her third cup of tea.

"Yeah."

"You seem to be working back a lot lately."

"Yeah."

"Are they paying you overtime?"

"Bank managers don't get overtime. It's part of the job."

"It's ridiculous. You're never home."

Jack put down his knife and fork carefully on the sides of his plate and glared at her.

"Can't a man eat his dinner in peace without you nagging?"

"It's just that..."

"Well?" he demanded.

Olive finished her tea and took the cup and saucer over to the sink without answering. She stared out of the window, looking over the backyard, and noticed two seagulls squabbling over something held in the beak of one of them. They disappeared over the fence next door where the Bacons lived. *I'll bet they had an early dinner together*, she thought to herself bitterly. *I'll bet everyone else in the street ate early.* She wondered idly what Les and Ruth were doing now. They seemed devoted to each other—more so than most couples who'd been married for as long as they had—seven years, Ruth had told her. *They're probably making love right now*, she thought ruefully, with a mental image of a naked Les springing into her head and making her blush. She hadn't missed the sight of his tall, tanned figure, clad only in bathers, as he passed her front window on his way to the beach with Ruth and Joy. *What a dish*, she'd thought, wondering how a plain woman like Ruth could catch him. She turned to watch her husband cutting each vegetable into equal portions and positioning them on his plate in the order he would eat them. The tines of his fork impaled five peas lined up in a row and he directed them to his mouth. The overhead light shone on a bald patch on top of his head; she saw it was widening noticeably through the hairs he combed over it. She knew it worried him but he never mentioned it.

"Funny thing happened today," she sat back down at the table opposite Jack. He looked up at her without speaking. "Turns out that Louie and Joy next door have their birthdays a day apart. Imagine that."

"And that's funny?"

Olive ignored the hint of sarcasm in his voice. "No. But when I asked her—Ruth, that is—what time Joy was born, she didn't know. Fancy that."

"So?"

"Well, what I mean is, how could she forget something like that? She really didn't know."

"Jesus. You bloody women. You're not happy unless you're bitching about one another. They moved in five minutes ago and you're already having a go at her."

"No, I'm not. I'm just saying how strange it is...she's hard to figure out. That's not running her down."

"What's for pudding?"

She looked at him in disappointment—not for the first time. What had happened to them? Where had the magic gone—if there had been any at all? It seemed that they just lived in the house together, keeping a distance between them so they didn't touch, didn't love. She envied couples like Ruth and Les. What they had, though, was more than she'd ever had with Jack. She wondered for the umpteenth time why she had married him in the first place. He'd been a charming prospect, going places in the bank, with a promising future for them as a family. Five years her senior, he'd tamed her flighty character with his serious courtship, taking her up to the city for a meal as well as the pictures, making her the envy of her friends. The local boys took their dates to the pictures and the dance, and a cuddle on the beach when the opportunity arose, but Jack had been more impressive with a car to take her around in. If only she'd listened to her mother who'd wanted her to have more fun before settling down.

She opened the fridge and took out a bowl of pink junket. It wobbled as she put it down in front of him, the smooth surface cracking down the middle and splitting the moulded dessert so that the daub of whipped cream fell into the crack.

"What, bloody junket again?" he said in disgust.

At midnight the clock noisily struck the hour in the kitchen. Mrs Hyland had asked Joy if she would like it, not having a place for it in her smaller quarters at her daughter's house. It stood two foot tall on the kitchen mantle, where Mrs Hyland had left it; a dark-stained wooden cabinet with two large clock faces sporting black letters on white backgrounds. The top face had twelve roman numerals that indicated the hour and minute as the hands swept around it. The bottom face had two little windows: the one on the left showed the day of the week and the one on the right showed the month. There were thirty-one numbers and a long single hand that alighted on each day of the month. Joy had loved it immediately, calling it her own special clock. Every morning she raced into the kitchen to see if the date hand had moved on to the next day and if the day window had turned over. As yet she could not recognise all of the words, but she knew they looked different every day. She spent many moments waiting for the clock to strike—which it did every quarter hour, half hour and hour—and she learned to tell the time, probably earlier than she might have done without it.

The chimes did not disturb Joy's slumber as she dreamt of a party where hundreds of balloons were spread out along the beach and she skipped amongst them holding hands with Louise.

Ruth was dreaming of huge clock faces lined up against a wall. She ran from one to the other searching for the hands but each face was blank. The kitchen clock's chimes broke her dream and she snuggled closer into Les's body.

Next door, Olive dreamt of a smiling, tanned man who stroked her body with gentle hands and held her with arms that had golden hairs growing on them. They were in the water as she gave herself up to him, and he pulled her down beneath the surface, their mouths joined. She couldn't breathe, and tried to break away from him, but he held her down. She fought to the surface, gulping air, and woke with her husband's arm across her face, a dead weight. She pushed his arm back and turned away from him, getting as close to the edge of the bed as she could with her feet over the side.

The street slumbered, the windows of each house curtained as if they were eyes closed to the worries of an outside world. A dog barked twice but settled down again when its master called out to it sharply. And the waters of Port Phillip Bay sighed softly into the sand before a fresh wind gathered strength to pull the waves up into choppy little hard-edged tufts with white tips. They raced toward shore, biting into the sand cruelly, changing the shape of the beach ever so slowly, toppling decorated sandcastles left by childish hands, and obliterating footprints left by those who hoped for a perfect day tomorrow.

Chapter 15

The day was pleasantly warm with a light breeze blowing off the bay, so Ruth and Pat Lewis decided to take Joy to the beach after lunch. The two women spread towels on the sand and watched from under the shade of a beach umbrella as Joy and Louise (who had joined them as soon as she'd seen them making for the beach) frolicked in the shallows.

"It must be a relief to you Joy having such a nice little friend to play with," Pat commented, "and being a neighbour too."

"Yes, I suppose so," Ruth agreed.

"And it'll be much easier on her, starting school and all. I mean, it's going to be a big change for her not having been to kinder."

"Sometimes I wonder," Ruth said wistfully, "if she's too young to go to school. She's not even five yet."

"She will be in a couple of months though. And little Louise, being the same age, they'll help each other. I don't think it'll be too dreadful for our precious Joy."

Ruth gazed across the sand to where the girls played. Their shrieks of laughter carried across to her and, despite herself, she smiled. Pat watched her young friend, concerned that all was not quite as it should be. She had wondered why Ruth had been so adamant about not sending Joy to kindergarten when they lived in Bentleigh, and had put it down to the impending move to Chelsea. It wasn't any of her business anyway, she thought. But there was a sadness in Ruth's eyes that worried Pat. It was a sadness that belied the words of assurance that she was happy living in Chelsea, having their own home, Les doing so well with his trade and already getting new customers since the move. There was a great deal of orders coming in for dressmaking, too, from the new neighbourhood as well as the established customers at Bentleigh. Everything looked like it was working out extremely well for the young family and for that Pat was very happy.

The relationship that had developed between the two women since Ruth, Les and Joy had stayed the one night at Pat and Jim's house had become very close. The Lewises had been a never-ending source of information about Bentleigh and Melbourne, which had eased the way for the young couple's establishment into their new life.

"The sewing machine shop is down past the station, love," Pat's reassuring voice had sounded clearly on the phone. "They've got plenty of spare parts for your machine, bobbins, needles and so on. We could go for a walk after lunch today. Joy'd enjoy the sights."

"Fancy a trip to the city today? Myers has got a sale on. You might pick up some cheap fabric."

Many times the Lewises were invited for a barbecue, which would give Ruth and Les the chance to repay some of the kindness they had received. Jim and Les attended to the cooking of the lamb chops and thick rump steaks, downing a few bottles of icy cold beer in the process.

"Wanna come to the game on Sunday?" Jim asked Les. "My grandson's playing half forward. He's a chip off the old block...his dad was kicking the longest drop kicks in the team when he was his age."

"Beauty, Jim. Ruth'll enjoy it too, I reckon, won't you, love?" he said turning to her as she came out of the back door, arms laden with salads. "Are we doing anything Sunday?"

"What?"

"Footy. We could go and see young Greg kick a few."

"That'd be nice. Joy had a good time when we went last time," Ruth smiled.

"Course she did," laughed Jim. "What with all the young-uns fighting over who was going to take her next around the field in the pusher."

"And not least of all your three granddaughters, Jim Lewis." Pat teased her husband.

"You love the kids, don't you, little one?" Pat picked Joy up and swung her around.

Joy squealed her excitement. "More, Nana, more."

She adored her adopted grandmother—calling her 'Nana' as she had heard Pat's own granddaughters address her. There was always a small gift for Joy in Pat's hand, be it a flower or a bag of lollies. "You spoil her," Ruth would admonish Pat, but the older woman would smile and say, "It's a *joy* to spoil her." And Ruth felt it churlish to refuse the gifts in the face of such kindness.

"How about having a go at umpiring, Les?" Jim asked him. "We need another one for the juniors on Sundays."

"I haven't done it before, though." Les looked doubtful as he handed Jim another beer bottle.

"You'd pick it up in no time. "

"You reckon?" Les was hopeful.

"Course you would, love. Any drongo can umpire," Pat laughed.

"And thank you, Mrs Lewis," Jim bowed to her.

"Don't mention it, Mr Lewis," she curtsied back.

Joy copied them, but fell awkwardly on the grass—much to the amusement of the adults. Ruth quickly picked up the Brownie box camera and took a photo of the group. *Such a happy day*, she thought, *and we're so lucky*.

Pat had been captivated by the red-haired baby from the first time she had held her, taking a keen interest in the child's progress as she grew into a little girl with whom she could converse.

"You're so good to her...to us," Ruth said. "You've got grandchildren of your own to worry about without us as well."

"Nonsense. There's plenty of room in here," she touched her chest, "for everyone."

"You're going to miss that little tyke when she starts school," Pat observed.

Ruth nodded, unable to answer. Pat didn't miss the rapid blinking of the eyes and the clenching of the jaw. *Oh, so that's it*, she thought.

"That's not to say your life comes to a halt, love. I remember when my boys went off to school. I howled my eyes out the first time I left them there. But you get over it. And there's always so much to do at home. You've got your dressmaking, and that lovely husband of yours to look after."

Ruth smiled brightly, but the expression in her eyes did not match the smile, the older woman thought. There was a look of...panic. If Pat knew her onions, and she reckoned she did, something was wrong.

"What about another baby, love? Have you thought about having another one? It would be a good time now that you're settled."

"I'd like to, but Les said the doctors told him I couldn't have any more. I was lucky to have Joy at all."

Les looked up as Joy twirled in front of him. He put down his knife and fork and applauded her.

"You'll be the best dressed and prettiest girl in school," he declared.

"Thank you, Daddy," she curtsied him solemnly. "Louise will be too."

"Oh, of course, we mustn't forget Louise." He gestured to his plate. "Want some bacon and eggs?"

"I'm not hungry."

"What? My big girl isn't hungry?"

"Don't you feel well, sweetheart?" Ruth knelt down beside Joy, feeling her forehead. "She's a bit hot, Les. Perhaps she shouldn't go today."

"I'm hot too, love. It's boiling outside already."

"Yes, but..."

"She'll be fine...won't you princess?"

"Yes, Daddy."

"But if she's sick, Les..."

"She's just a bit nervous. Every kid's nervous their first day at school." He turned to Joy, searching her face. "Is that what it is, little one?"

"Yes, Daddy."

"You see?" He stood up from the table, hugged Ruth, and scooped Joy up in his arms. "Nothing to worry about. She'll have Louise to look out for her, too. They'll look out for each other."

Ruth bit her lip and Les kissed it. "I don't know who's more nervous...you or Joy. I think it's you!"

Ruth felt the rising hysteria subside while Les's arm was about her. His grey eyes met hers and he smiled reassurance while Joy poked her finger into his dimple.

"Why did your mummy give you a dimple?" she asked him for the hundredth time.

"So that Father Christmas would know it was me and not give someone else my presents by mistake."

"And did he?"

"No."

"How do you know?"

"Because he brought me you."

Ruth and Olive walked the short distance to the Nepean Highway with Joy and Louise skipping along the footpaths, hand in hand, in and around the two women. Their excitement had them twirling around, giggling, running backwards and forwards, trying to hurry their mothers. They knew the route by heart as they had walked it before with Ruth and Olive, who had timed it so the girls wouldn't be late for the first day of school. Many other first-day children were taking the same path. Some held their mothers' hands tightly and were subdued. Others walked more confidently, seeming not to suffer the nervous dread of the unknown that many others did. Ruth took Joy's hand firmly, Olive doing the same with Louise, as they negotiated the morning traffic to cross the Highway safely. Once over the railway line, they entered Argyle Street and walked up the block to reach the double-storied, red brick Chelsea Primary School.

A steady stream of children and parents filed through the gate and found the teachers for the appropriate year levels. The grades were allocated by alphabetical order and both Joy and Louise spent some anxious moments waiting to see if they would be in the same prep grade.

"Lucky our surnames are pretty close," Olive commented. "Fingers crossed, girls."

And luck was with them as Joy Bacon and Louise Fletcher were herded into a group of thirty-five children.

"Say goodbye to your parents now, children," Mrs Grant encouraged them. "Don't cry, Wendy, love. Mother'll be here at three o'clock, won't you, Mother?" She looked at the mother concerned, who gave her daughter a final hug and backed away.

Ruth held Joy closely, her fingers digging into her daughter's arms.

"Mummy...you're hurting me!" Joy tried to wriggle out of Ruth's clutches.

"Oh, sweetheart, I'm so sorry. I didn't mean to hurt you." Ruth bit her lip in embarrassment as the other parents looked aghast at the red marks left on Joy's fair skin.

Olive turned away, uncomfortable with what she had seen. Louise touched her own arms where the marks showed on Joy's.

"You have a wonderful first day at school, Louie," Olive hugged her. "I want to hear everything about it this afternoon, so pay attention to Mrs Grant, won't you?"

Louise swung her school case back and forth waiting for Ruth to let Joy go. By now, most of the parents had said their goodbyes and were leaving the school grounds. Their children were lined up in class groups and were standing at attention. The Headmaster cast an eye over the grounds to see if all were in readiness for the national anthem. Mrs Grant touched Ruth on the shoulder gently. "Come on, Mother. Your little girl will be fine. Everyone's waiting for her."

Ruth clutched Joy even more tightly as she sank to her knees to look into her daughter's eyes. Tears streamed down her face unheeded and she planted kisses on Joy's cheeks while stroking the red curly hair.

"I won't leave you, sweetheart. I'll wait right here. Don't be frightened," she whispered.

Joy's face flushed a bright red and she looked over her shoulder to where Louise waited in line with the other children. "I'm not afraid, Mummy. I have to go now," she whispered back, tugging her mother's clutching hands away from her. "They're waiting for me."

A silence had fallen over the playground and it seemed to Joy that all eyes were on her and Ruth. After having looked forward to this day for so long, talking with Louise about what it would be like, imagining the new world they were about to enter, her mother was ruining it. She could hear tittering and sniggering coming from the lines of children behind her and wished that she could disappear in a puff of smoke—like they did in her fairy story books. Why was her mother doing this to her? Why wouldn't she go out of the gate with Louise's mummy? Mrs Fletcher hadn't made a fuss, had she?

"Do you want to come home with me?" Ruth hissed at Joy. "You don't have to stay, you know. We can go for a swim. I'll buy you an ice cream. Some lollies..."

The Headmaster leaned towards a microphone on a stand in front of him. "Mrs Grant, are we ready?" he asked.

"Mummy, get up." Joy looked around her. "Stand up, Mummy. They're looking at us. Everyone's staring at us." She pulled at her mother, trying to get her on her feet.

"You really must let her go now, Mother," Mrs Grant insisted quietly. "You're making it very hard for her, you know." She extricated Joy from Ruth's grasp and pointed to where Louise was lined up. "Go and wait over there...what's your name again, dear?"

"Joy." The voice was very small—mortified.

"Joy. Go and join the others, there's a good girl." She pulled Ruth to her feet. "Go and wait outside the gate, Mother," she whispered. "I'll send the Infant Mistress out to have a chat with you after assembly."

Ruth looked desperately at Joy whose eyes were downcast, her face still bright red. She was standing next to Louise. "But she needs me..."

"Not now. She needs to be independent. Stand on her own two feet. All the children do. You're making this hard for little Joy. Do you realise that?" She pushed Ruth discreetly towards the gate. "Go on. For her."

Mrs Grant turned her back on Ruth and joined her children. "Ready, Mr Roberts," she called over to the Headmaster.

He nodded, then turned to the microphone. "Good morning teachers, boys and girls. Welcome back. We hope you had a good holiday. We will now sing the national anthem."

Music crackled over the PA system and hundreds of voices joined to sing *God Save the Queen*. As the anthem finished, the children stood with the right hand over the left breast for the oath of allegiance as they saluted the flag:

I love God and my country;
I honour the flag;
I will serve the Queen,
And cheerfully obey my parents, teachers, and the laws.

"Come on, Ruth. She'll be all right," Olive put her arm around Ruth's shoulder as the girls disappeared inside the building. "She's got Louie with her. They'll look out for each other."

"You go. I'll just stay here for a while." Ruth gripped the iron fence, staring at the school buildings. Her eyes searched every window, wondering which room Joy was in. She felt as if part of her had been ripped out, leaving her raw, bleeding.

Olive looked at her watch, conscious that she had little time left before she was due at the hairdresser's. "Are you sure? There's nothing you can do here."

"Yes. I'm sure. Go on…you'll be late."

"Why don't you come with me? Have a trim and set? I'm sure they'd fit you in. It'd make you feel better."

"No. I'm staying."

Ruth had not turned away from the school buildings. Olive knew she couldn't budge her. She began walking back towards Nepean Highway.

"See you later, then," she called back to Ruth.

There was no answer.

Chapter 16

"She's still there," Louise whispered as she leant back over the milk bottle and took a sip through the straw.

"Are they still talking to her?" Joy whispered back. Her head was bent over her untouched bottle of a third of a pint of milk.

"No, they've gone. She's holding onto the fence and looking over here."

Their intimacy was broken by Mrs Grant calling out to the class.

"Come, children. Finish up your milk and then I'll show you around the playground."

Joy grimaced at the straw that pierced the silver foil top. She hated plain milk. Especially milk that had become warm sitting out in the sun. Louise held up her bottle, which was now empty.

"Good, girl, Louise," Mrs Grant patted her shoulder. "You can go out and play now." She looked at Joy's bottle in surprise. "Why, Joy, you haven't drunk any. Have you got a broken straw?"

"No, Mrs Grant," Joy answered in a small voice, her eyes downcast on the bottle which became a blur as her eyes focused on the white fluid inside it.

"Well, drink up so we can go outside and you can play with the others." Her voice was firm, insistent, demanding obedience. "They're waiting for us."

Joy pushed the straw back into her mouth as she looked sideways at the classroom doorway. Louise stood there, making frantic signals for her to hurry up. She sipped at the tepid, white liquid. It filled her mouth in a slightly rancid pool and her throat closed in protest. Her eyes filled with tears as she looked up in mute appeal to Mrs Grant, her cheeks puffed out with unswallowed milk.

"Come on, dear. You must drink it up. It's good for you."

Louise had disappeared from the doorway. Joy held her breath, then forced the milk down past her curling tongue by sucking strongly on the straw and not stopping until the bottle was empty. Her stomach gave a lurch but she gulped and pushed it back down where it belonged. She tried not to swallow again, afraid to taste or smell the milk that sat uncomfortably inside her, and her mouth filled quickly with saliva.

"There now, that wasn't so bad, was it?" Mrs Grant beamed at her. "Pop the bottle back in the crate over there, and you can go out and join the rest of the class in the playground."

Joy dropped the bottle into the wire crate. It made a loud clang in the now quiet classroom, making her start, and she swallowed the saliva involuntarily. She walked slowly out of the classroom and made her way to the playground behind the school. The hot morning sun hit her as she crossed the yard to join Louise in the shade of a tree. Nausea rose threateningly with each step she took. Her hair clung to her clammy forehead and neck and perspiration dripped down between her shoulder blades.

"What's wrong?" Louise noticed Joy's distress.

"I'm..." and, with a cry of distress, Joy deposited the milk at Louise's feet, splashing her shoes and socks.

Horrified, Joy clamped her hand over her mouth as her stomach threw up the rest of its unwanted contents in aftershocks. It spurted out from between her fingers and dripped down the front of her dress. A group of children encircled her, shrieking in laughter, pointing at her and beckoning others to join in the excitement.

Louise looked in dismay at her friend and down at her shoes. She stamped them, trying to shake the vomit off, but it seeped hotly through her socks around the ankles.

Joy looked around at the jeering faces that seemed to dance in hot waves around her, making her dizzy. Her ears buzzed and she sank down to the ground suddenly, her stomach still heaving. The sound of someone retching repeatedly reached her, as if through a tunnel, and she realised it was herself. Tears spilled down her face and her nostrils ran with mucus.

Mrs Grant hurried over to the group and made short work of shooing the children away from Joy. She pulled out a handkerchief that was tucked into her bra. It was one that her husband had given her for her birthday. It was an expensive one with flowers embroidered around its edges and it was folded in starched stiffness that was difficult to shake out. She thought, stupidly, that her husband would be disappointed at what she was going to do with it.

"Oh, dear. You really didn't want that milk, did you?"

She dabbed at Joy's wet face and the handkerchief collapsed into a slimy ball.

She felt sorry for the child. She'd had a pretty rough start with the mother causing such a nuisance and embarrassing the poor little mite. The children had taken it all in, too. They missed nothing. And now this. She shouldn't have insisted that the child drink the milk, but rules are rules. Well, she'd see about that. She'd have a talk with the Infant Mistress. Get a note from Joy's parents to say she could be excused from having to drink it.

"Come on, dear. We'll get you cleaned up before class. You too, Louise."

She led the two girls into a nearby toilet block and washed the vomit off their clothes and shoes. She showed Joy how to splash her face with cold water and rinse her mouth out to refresh it. Neither girl spoke as Mrs Grant's voice echoed hollowly in the toilet block. "There, that's better. Good as new." She knew she sounded pompous and hated herself for it. It was times like this that she wondered if she'd have made a better stenographer than a teacher.

Joy looked at Louise in mute appeal. She was appalled at what she'd done to her friend, afraid that their closeness would be lost, that she would have no one to play with or talk to at school or at home. Louise looked back at her and the corners of her mouth turned up into a smile. It grew until it reached her eyes and they, too, smiled at Joy, reassuring her. Joy's green eyes widened in surprise then they flickered back to the door from where the sound of children playing reached them. Louise's eyes followed hers and she frowned as she realised what might greet them out there. She knew enough of the cruelty of children, even at her tender age. Fear gripped both of them and they turned to their teacher.

Mrs Grant saw their expressions. "Are you going to be sick again?"

Joy shook her head, tears welling up anew.

"Don't worry. It's all right now." She looked down at the distressed child. "Do you like drawing?"

The child nodded.

"Well, we're going to do some drawing when we get back into the classroom. Would you like that?"

The child nodded again.

"And what about you, Louise?" Mrs Grant smiled, steering the two girls towards the classroom. "Do you like drawing with crayons?"

"Oh, yes, Mrs Grant."

The rest of the day passed by without further incident, any sniggering in Joy's direction sternly taken care of by Mrs Grant. Joy made sure not to look out of the window in case her mother was still visible. She kept her head pointedly turned away ignoring Louise when she tried to convey a whispered message to her about Ruth. Louise respected her feelings and said no more about the matter, but she looked back over to the window from time to time. She could see Ruth standing there in the hot sun, holding onto the fence, looking from window to window, searching for a glimpse of her daughter. She saw the Infant Mistress speak with Ruth, gesticulating towards the school and then back towards Nepean Highway. She saw the Infant Mistress try to prise Ruth's hands away from the fence. She saw the Headmaster join the Infant Mistress and then lead Ruth into the school grounds and they disappeared from view. Later, she saw Ruth walking slowly down the street towards the Highway and then turn back to stand at the fence again.

Joy was aware of Louise's head turning back to the window time and again. She knew that her mother was still there. And she knew that this was the worst day of her life. What she had looked forward to for so long had turned into a nightmare. She was shocked that her mother would embarrass her in front of the whole school and, more importantly, in front of Louise and Mrs Fletcher. Her friendship with Louise had become, suddenly, vital to her and the thought of living in Chelsea without Louise was unbearable. In the few short weeks that they had known each other, they had bonded remarkably quickly. Louise was the first real friend Joy had had and she was afraid that spraying her friend with vomit would not be forgiven. She remembered Louise's smile of reassurance in the toilet block, and was aware of Louise's concern over Ruth standing outside. She pushed some stray red curls away from her eyes, tucking them behind her ear, and took a sideways peep at Louise. Her friend was bent over a drawing she had been creating, her long thick plaits brushing the paper. Joy had to lean over to see the picture. There were two stick figures in the middle of the page and a long squiggly blue line through them.

"What's that?" Joy whispered.

"That's you and me playing on the beach. See the water?" She turned the page around so that Joy could see it. The faces on the stick figures both had mouths that were turned up at the corners.

At three o'clock that afternoon, Joy and Louise made their way out of the crowded school building and walked towards the gate. Olive and Ruth stood together waiting, one with a relaxed, smiling face and the other with a tense, relieved grimace.

"Louie! How was it?" Olive hugged her daughter. "Can you read yet?"

Louise laughed and hugged her mother back. "Yes, Mummy. And I can add up, too."

Ruth gripped Joy in a fierce embrace. "Oh, my baby. My baby. Are you all right?"

"Mummy...let go." Joy squirmed away from her mother, a bright red flush staining her throat.

Olive began walking towards the Nepean Highway, chatting animatedly with Louise, who turned back to make sure Joy was following. She saw her friend standing awkwardly beside Ruth who was inspecting the front of Joy's dress and then putting her nose to it.

"...so did you?" Olive asked.

"What?"

"You haven't been listening to a word I've said," her mother laughed. She followed Louise's line of vision turning back to see Ruth who was questioning Joy and pointing agitatedly back at the school buildings. "Oh, come on, Louie. Leave them alone for a bit."

Louise tugged on Olive's hand. "Yes but..."

"She'll be all right," Olive insisted. "Hey, how about a swim before tea?"

Louise's normally ecstatic response to the suggestion of a swim didn't arrive as it usually did.

"And Joy, too, if she's allowed."

At that, Louise walked a little more quickly, occasionally turning back to check on her friend.

"Go and see if Joy's allowed to go for a swim," Olive called out to Louise as she began to change out of her street clothes and into a swimming suit. "I'll meet you out there as soon as I'm ready."

"Come on, slow coach," Louise called back over her shoulder as she raced out of the front door.

"I'll slow coach you, you little devil."

Olive tossed beach towels over her shoulder, slid her feet into sandals, and stopped in front of the hallway mirror. She took out her hair combs and ran her fingers through her thick hair as she shook it out. The trim had done it good, she observed. It was thicker than ever. She thought of Ruth's fine sparse hair and wondered what it would feel like to have Les run his fingers through her own thick hair. *He'd notice the difference,* she mused, and then slapped herself as she caught her thoughts drifting to a half-naked Les frolicking in the waters of the bay. *Stop it!* She pulled a face in the mirror and laughed at herself as she stepped outside the front door.

Louise was sitting on the top step next to the sweet pea with her chin in her hands. She looked up at her mother who sat down beside her.

"What is it, Louie?"

"Mummy, why isn't Joy allowed to come and play with me like you let me go and play with her?"

"Well…"

"She wants to come with us but she's not allowed. Why's that?"

"Sometimes it's not the right time…" Olive floundered. "Sometimes she might have to do some things, some chores. Maybe her mum just wants to be alone with her to talk about today. It was the first day of school, after all."

"Yes, but…"

"Don't worry, Louie. She'll be out later. You can make up for it then."

"Mummy?"

"Yes?"

"Do you love me very much?"

"Why, of course. Why do you ask?"

"Why didn't you cry when we had to go inside school…like Mrs Bacon?"

Olive looked at her daughter's upturned face, searching her own with worried eyes. She was aware that none of what happened today made any sense to either of the girls, and was careful not to add to the confusion.

"I love you more than anything else on this earth," Olive replied earnestly. "But I love you enough to let you go when you need to. I can't keep you with me all the time. That wouldn't be right. You have to do some things on your own. Just like I had to do when your grandma took me to school for the first time."

"But why didn't you cry?"

"Because I was happy for you. You were about to start something special…your education. I wasn't sad."

"Then why was Mrs Bacon sad?"

"Because…sometimes it's hard to say goodbye—to let go."

"But Joy wasn't going anywhere. She was just going into school with me."

"I know, Louie. I know. I think Mrs Bacon was just having a bad day. She'll probably be all right tomorrow."

Before Louise could answer, Olive jumped up and pulled Louise up after her.

"Come on, last one in's a three-legged drongo."

Les arrived home hot and tired but eager to hear all about Joy's first day at school. He was surprised that Joy didn't run out to the truck to throw her arms around him, like she normally did. He surmised that she and Ruth were at the beach. He stopped to take his work boots off and put his head under the hose for a few moments. It felt good. It would feel even better to peel his heavy overalls off, put his bathers on, and join his family on the beach.

The house was quiet as he let himself in the back door. He blinked in the dim kitchen, his eyes adjusting from the glare outside, and was astonished to see Ruth sitting at the kitchen table. She was staring, glassy-eyed at the table in front of her where her hands rested clenched tightly. She looked up at him.

"Ruth? What is it?"

Fear gripped him instantly. He looked around for Joy.

"Where's Joy? What's happened?"

Ruth took a deep breath. "Oh, she's in her room." Her voice was slow, emotionless.

"Why?" He sat down beside her, gripping her hands. "What's wrong, Ruth?"

"Nothing. Everything's all right."

Her hands worked convulsively under his grip and her bottom lip was caught between her teeth. He could see that it was bleeding. He bent towards her and kissed her lips gently, then moved back slightly to force eye contact between them. She drew her eyes towards his and he smiled at her. He kissed her again and felt her lips relax slightly under his, and then a shuddering breath surged from her mouth as her eyes brightened with tears to reveal an expression of anguish.

"Hey," he whispered as he put his arms around her. "You can tell me."

He waited, cringing inwardly with dread. He was aware of faint sounds of sniffling coming from Joy's room and was impatient to go to her, but he knew that Ruth was more fragile, that she needed him more.

"It's..."

"Yes?" He moved back onto his chair, smiling encouragement.

"Joy."

"Has she been hurt, love?" he asked carefully.

"No."

"Then...?"

"She hates me."

Tears spilled over her bottom lid in a torrent, and streamed down her cheeks. Les never failed to marvel how she could cry without apparently moving a muscle in her face. She did it as if the crying mechanism was totally separate from her. Other women, so he'd observed, screwed up their faces in ugly grimaces, their mouths opening wide with their cheeks rising to meet half-closed eyes. And they wailed. But not Ruth. Her crying was totally controlled by her other self...and silent.

"Hates you? How can you say that? She loves you."

"Not anymore."

"But why?"

"She said she never wants me to go with her to school again." She looked at Les. "She said she wants you to go with her."

"Love..."

"She said she's ashamed of me. She said she wants another mummy."

"She'd never say that...she adores you."

He held her face tenderly and kissed her tears. Whatever it was that had upset Ruth really had her confused. She must be mistaken. It wasn't like Joy to talk like that to her mother. There'd never been a cross word between them. Maybe Joy had had a bad first day. Yes, that was it. Something had happened at school. Well, he'd get to the bottom of it. Sort it all out. Probably something silly. Bullies, maybe? He'd get Joy to tell him what happened. No use upsetting Ruth any more than she was already.

He stood up and wet a clean tea towel.

"Here, love. You're hot," he said wiping her face. "I'll get you a nice glass of cold water."

He reached inside the refrigerator and took out a jug of water.

"How about a swim to cool off? You'll feel better then."

He watched her drink the water slowly. Her tears were drying and the glazed look had returned to her eyes.

"Yes," she said woodenly.

"Come on, then." He led her to their room and sat her on the bed. "Where are your bathers?" He searched inside the drawers of the dressing table until he found them. "Here. Do you need a hand?" He put them on her lap.

"No."

"I'll just go to the lav. Back in a minute."

He closed the door quietly behind him and stood for some moments listening outside Joy's bedroom door. The sniffing had stopped. There was no other sound, other than the shrieks of children from the beach and gulls squawking overhead. He tapped softly on the door.

"Princess?"

He opened the door to see Joy lying on her bed, holding her teddy bear tightly against her face. She looked at him, eyes filled with sadness. He crouched on the floor beside the bed and kissed her cheek. She was hot, flushed and smelled of...vomit?

"Have you been sick, princess?"

"Oh, Daddy." she began to cry as she put her arms around Les's neck. The bear was squeezed between them, it's head wet with tears and perspiration.

"Why's my girl so sad?"

"Do I have to go to school again?"

"Why...yes."

"Why can't I stay home? I don't want to go." She was crying harder now.

"Everyone has to go to school. Don't you like your teacher?"

"Yes," she sobbed.

"Did someone hurt you?"

"No."

"Well, what happened to make you cry, little one?"

"The milk..."

"Milk?" He was puzzled, then realised what she meant. "Oh, the milk. They gave you milk to drink?" She nodded. "And that made you sick?" Another nod. "Oh, my princess, they didn't know you hate it so much. We forgot to tell them."

She was listening now. "You mean I don't have to drink it?"

"No. Mummy can tell them not to give you milk. It'll be all right."

"Can you tell them?"

"Well, I'll be at work, love. Mummy'll be taking you to school anyway. She can tell your teacher."

"I want you to take me."

"I can't, princess. But why not Mummy?"

Joy hesitated. "They laughed at me...at her..."

"Why?"

"She was naughty."

"Mummy was naughty?"

Joy nodded. "Everybody saw her...and she was on the fence...and...why's it bad to be a *mummy's girl*, Daddy?"

Her face turned towards him, searching his for understanding. After nearly five years her life had been turned upside down. Gone was the feeling of security of the family unit, the unquestioned certainty of her place in the world. Her mother's behaviour had made her feel ashamed and embarrassed for the first time in her life, and it was a feeling that confused and terrified her. Ruth had always filled her days with love, laughter and belonging, but now she stood back and saw her mother differently...as perhaps others saw her. It was a picture she couldn't interpret.

Chapter 17

The clock above the mantelpiece struck the half-hour. Its metallic clatter caused Ruth to look up at Les over the table. She had been stirring her tea for the past few minutes, looking intently at the whirlpool within the wide cup, her thoughts matching the liquid's pattern. He had been watching her silent contemplation of the cup, wishing he could get inside her head and share the secrets that tortured her mind. Her sleep had been disturbed by nightmares— nightmares that had made her cry out in anguish. He knew she'd not had nightmares like that since she'd taken Joy from the hospital back in Perth. When the alarm rang at six o'clock, she'd looked exhausted and dragged herself out of bed without her usual vigour.

"You don't need to get up, love. I can get my own breakfast," he'd pushed her back onto the bed.

"No..."

"You look tired. Get a bit more rest before Joy gets up."

She shook her head. "I have to make your lunch...her lunch."

"I can throw a sandwich together for myself," he laughed. "And one for Joy, come to that."

"No. I'd rather get up. I don't know what's the matter with me. I feel so washed out."

"No wonder. You had a rotten night's sleep."

"Did I?" she looked at him vaguely.

"Don't you remember?"

"I...not really."

He looked at her closely. "Was it about...Joy?"

"Joy?" She took a deep breath and sighed.

"I mean, after yesterday...school, and so on?"

She looked up at him. "It was a disaster."

He sat back down beside her on the bed and put his arms around her. She turned towards him and buried her face in his shoulder.

"I feel so...ashamed," she whispered.

"You don't need to..."

"Yes, I do." She sat up and looked at him earnestly. "I do, Les. I made a rotten mess of it."

"It'll be all right. She'll come round."

"She was so quiet last night. So distant. And she kept on looking at me...as if she didn't know me."

His calloused fingers ran through his hair, worry etched into his expression. He was out of his depth, wondering what to do about this change in the relationship between Ruth and Joy. He sensed a regression in Ruth's behaviour towards the despair she had suffered when losing her own stillborn baby. To his untrained mind, he supposed it had something to do with Joy going to school, but why? Why would she get all het up over a normal thing like that? All kids went to school, didn't they? Well, he hadn't—and neither had Ruth, but that was beside the point—it was the law now. You had to go to school. So why would it affect Ruth like that? She'd known all along that Joy would be going this year. And you'd think she'd be less worried seeing as how Louise was there with Joy. At least she wasn't going alone. Besides, Joy had been looking forward to it. No, it had to be something else, something to do with back then, back when she lost the other baby. But why now? Well, he'd have to think about it a bit more, when he was at work and had time to mull it over in his mind. In the meantime, he'd have to try and fix up the rift between Ruth and Joy. He wasn't sure how he was going to do it and was afraid of putting his foot in it and making it worse. But kids always bounced back, didn't they? And his little princess was a plucky little thing. She'd be all right. So would Ruth. She'd survived the *other thing*. Sure, it'd been touch and go for a while—he'd even thought he was going to lose her at some stage—but she'd pulled through. She'd been bonzer for years now, hadn't she? Maybe this was one of those *women* things. Maybe Pat would know. Perhaps he should give her a ring—see if she could shed any light on it. Yes, he might just do that.

"Come on, love. She'll get over it. Things'll be back to normal in no time. You'll see."

She sighed, unconvinced. "I hope you're right."

Ruth stopped stirring her tea and put the spoon back onto the saucer slowly. "I'd better get the little one up."

"You want me to do it?" Les offered.

"No. I'll go. Otherwise it will look different, and I don't want to make things any less normal."

Les watched her as she walked out of the kitchen, heard her walk resolutely up the passage past the sewing room and bathroom, then hesitate outside Joy's room. He fancied he could hear her sharp intake of breath before opening the door.

"Sweetheart? You awake?"

He absentmindedly pushed the remains of his breakfast around his plate, ears straining for any clue as to what was happening. The murmur of voices slipped along the passageway like leaves snatched by the wind and tossed carelessly in random directions. Then there was silence.

The fingers of one hand traced repeated furrows through his thick hair as he waited; the other hand held his fork, rubbing a bread crust through dried egg yolk on the plate. The rustling of footsteps stilled his hands and he pushed back his chair as he stood. The chair legs scraped noisily on the green lino floor. Ruth and Joy appeared in the doorway, hands linked as they stood together. Les's eyebrows shot up in question, and Ruth nodded imperceptibly. He let out his breath gradually, unaware that he'd been holding it for some moments.

"Good morning, my princess. Did you sleep well?" He held his arms out to her and she ran into them. His eyes met those of Ruth over the child's head.

"Do you have to go to work today, Daddy?"

"Yes, I do."

"Can I come with you to work?"

"No, little one. You've got school to go to."

"Do I really have to go?"

"Oh, yes. You'd get daddy and mummy into trouble if you didn't go. You wouldn't like that, would you?"

"No." Her voice was small, timorous.

"Well, then. Besides, there are lots of beaut things to do at school. And you can make new friends with the girls and boys there."

"I don't like them. I only like Louise."

"You don't want to disappoint Louise, do you? I mean, imagine if you didn't go to school and Louise had to go all on her own. I think she'd be very sad without you, don't you?"

Joy pulled away from Les's arms and looked up at him. "Does Louise have to go to school too?"

"Yes, sweetie. She does," Les laughed.

"Oh."

"Come on, then. How about it? Mummy's got some nice fresh orange juice all squeezed and waiting for you. That'll make you feel better. And you can have your breakfast and then put on one of those pretty new dresses Mummy made for you. You don't want to keep Louise waiting, do you?"

"No, Daddy."

Ruth poured orange juice into a glass in front of Joy. "Would you like some scrambled eggs, sweetheart?"

Joy shook her head. "I'm not hungry."

"Toast, then? With Vegemite?"

Silence. Joy's hands clenched onto the glass of juice.

"Tell you what," Ruth said sitting down next to her. "I'm not very hungry either. How about you have one bite, and I have another. Then you have another bite, and I have another. Maybe between us, we can eat one whole piece of toast together."

It was a game they had played many times when they had been feeling the opposite with ravenous appetites, endeavouring to eat a piece of toast faster than the toaster could produce another one. Joy looked up at her mother and the beginnings of a smile turned up her trembling mouth. Her fingers relaxed on the glass.

"All right, Mummy. Who goes first?"

Louise waited with Olive outside their house for Joy and Ruth to appear. She had spent some anxious moments wondering if her friend would come out, and to fill in the time she picked a bunch of sweet pea. She grasped them tightly as her mother tied them around the stems with some lengths of grass.

"There, that should hold them," Olive declared.

Louise turned the bunch around, eyeing them critically. "Do you think she'll like them?"

"Of course she will—just like she did the day they first arrived here."

Louise remembered how she'd burst into tears when she gave the flowers to Joy that day. Well, she wouldn't do that this time.

Olive looked at her watch. *If they don't hurry, we'll be late,* she thought. Just then Ruth and Joy emerged from their front door. *Ruth looks just as tense as yesterday.* Louise ran to meet them, holding out the bunch of flowers for Joy, who held them up to her nose and smiled. The colours reflected prettily on her pale skin. The girls walked on ahead of the women, heads together in conversation. Olive put her hand on Ruth's arm.

"Are you all right, Ruth?"

"Yes. I'm fine, thank you," Ruth replied rather stiffly.

"Can I do anything?"

"No." There was a long pause as they walked towards the end of the street. "Look...I'm sorry about yesterday."

"There's no need..."

"No. I'm really sorry. I made a frightful drongo of myself…and in front of everybody, too."

"It's normal to feel that way when they first go to school," Olive floundered.

"Did you?" Ruth looked at her quickly.

"Oh, yes." The reply was too quick, not convincing.

"But you didn't embarrass your daughter, did you?" came the quiet reply.

Olive stopped in her tracks, helpless to know what to say. Ruth stopped too. She looked so miserable that Olive impulsively put her arms around her. Startled, Ruth stepped back and Olive dropped her arms, flustered, wondering if she'd over-stepped the mark. Ruth was so hard to fathom.

"I won't do it again, though. I've messed things up enough."

She felt Joy's hand stiffen in hers when they said goodbye at the school gate. The hand was saying: *don't hold me, don't touch me,* and she let go before the urge to gather her child to her breast and take her home again became irresistible. She watched Joy's back— ramrod straight, defiant—as it drew away from her in the crowded schoolyard. It said: *don't embarrass me, don't smother me,* and she recognised her own rebellion when she was Joy's age. She mustn't let Joy draw away from her and retreat into her own secret world— as she had done, when she had no choice. She couldn't bear for Joy to shut her out. No, she must grit her teeth and try to hide the hysteria that bubbled up inside her.

Olive sensed Ruth's turmoil but allowed her the space to sort out her thoughts and feelings without interruption. She felt instinctively that Ruth would turn to her if she needed her, but that she mustn't rush any intimacy between them. Ruth was like a frightened bird that flittered away at the first movement it sensed in a threatening environment. The song was full of bravado, but the head still darted in every direction on the lookout for danger.

She tentatively suggested that they both attend the Chelsea Primary School Mothers Club. She showed Ruth a notice in the local paper, *City of Chelsea News.*

"Here, Ruth. It says they meet at the school at two o'clock on Tuesday the sixteenth. What do you reckon?"

"Well…"

"It'd be handy to know what's going on. Have a say in the school. It'd be good for the girls. They're asking for mothers of new pupils to go along, too."

"Yes, it sounds like a good idea. All right, Olive, I'll go with you."

Each morning Ruth steeled herself for the same ordeal. The pain of parting with Joy seared her mind and body, but she called upon the resolve that had served to see her through her childhood years with her adoptive parents. She would overcome it. She *must* overcome it. She didn't understand the crushing panic that shook her each time Joy disappeared inside the school building. There was a fleeting memory that she was unable to snatch. It rushed past her consciousness, leaving a stain on her mind that rubbed off before she could read it. If it was the clue to why she was behaving like this, she was unsure. All she knew was that her relationship with her daughter had suffered because of what she had done on that first day, and she must heal that wound before it festered and became a permanent disfigurement between them.

When Les arrived home from work each day, he would look warily at Ruth and Joy searching their faces for any sign of tension between them, if there had been any repeat of the first day's disaster. The seemingly *normal* atmosphere reassured him. Ruth had pulled herself together admirably but he knew the line she walked was a very fine one and that he must stay alert for any sign of trouble. Typically of a child of five, Joy had quickly bounced back to her usual cheerful self, but sometimes Les would catch her looking at her mother in a puzzled way, as if trying to sort something out in her mind. He preferred not to approach her about it, careful not to open wounds that might be healing over naturally. Instead, he tried to distract her so that she would not torture herself with events that she didn't understand.

"Pooh! Doesn't it smell?" Joy pulled her head back from the bowl.

"Yes, it's horrible!" Louise agreed.

"Are you sure it'll work?"

"Umm...Mummy showed me a long time ago. They grabbed on to it like mad."

"But it's so yucky!"

"I know." Louise nodded agreement as she tied a knot in the string that held a small lump of meat.

"Now you hang it over the edge here..."

They both bent over the end of the jetty to watch the meat descend towards the water as Louise played out the length of string.

"...and wait for them to stick it with their claws."

"How do you know they've got it?"

"You feel it."

"Feel what?"

"A tug on the string. Do you want to hold it while I do another one?"

"All right." Joy took the string from Louise and held on to it tightly. She looked eagerly at where her string entered the water. "Does it take long?"

"No."

Louise's fingers were sticky with blood as she tried to tie another piece of meat onto a string. Flies buzzed around her.

"Get away!" she waved at them impatiently. "Leave me alone!"

She bent over as she let her string down beside Joy's, raising her shoulder up to her face to prevent the flies from settling on it and blowing at them at the same time. The meat disappeared into the water with a little plop.

"Here." She passed her string to Joy to hold while she put a plate over the bowl and washed her hands in a bucket that held seawater. She took back her string and sat beside Joy to wait.

It wasn't long before both strings began to tug at their fingers.

"Louise! Louise! Mine's tugging!"

"Mine too! Pull it up."

They pulled their strings up, hand over hand, until the ends emerged with a crab hanging on to each of them. The girls stood up, pulled their crabs up and over the jetty, and lowered them into the bucket of seawater.

"Shake it and it'll fall off," Louise instructed. "Like this."

And her crab did just that. Joy's crab held on to the meat tightly but some determined jiggling on the string had it fall off to join the other in the bucket. The girls were so excited; they danced around the bucket shrieking in delight.

Olive sat up on her beach towel and shaded her eyes as she looked in the direction of the jetty.

"Looks like they caught some."

"Yes, they're dancing around the bucket like a couple of Indians doing a rain dance," Ruth laughed.

"It should keep them occupied for a while."

They could see the girls frantically tying meat onto their strings and then throwing them over the jetty into the water to catch more crabs.

"They'll be stinking hot sitting up there by the time they fill that bucket," Olive observed. "At least they can cool off after in the water."

"Joy's not going in."

Olive glanced at Ruth, surprised. "Oh?"

"I'd imagine you won't let Louise in either, after those sharks were sighted last week."

"But that was last week. They've always been around, Ruth," she said looking at Ruth closely. "These beaches are pretty safe...besides, the girls don't go out into deep water. They only play around the shallows."

"No. I'm not taking any chances. She's not going in the water. Not unless both Les and I are between her and the deeper water, and she's in our arms."

"What about if the two of them are just playing around here in front of us?"

"No. A shark is too quick. It could take her just like that." She snapped her fingers.

"Gee, she'll miss splashing around with Louise."

"She'll do as she's told." Ruth's mouth was firm, brooking no argument.

"How many do you think we've got?"

"Five hundred," Joy replied seriously.

"Yes."

"I wonder if the bottom ones are squashed."

"Oops...they might be."

"They might be dead."

They both looked aghast at the bucket of crabs.

"We'd better put them back in before they all die," Louise said attempting to lift the bucket by the handle. "That's what Mummy did, anyway." She struggled with the weight of it, so Joy took one side of the handle and they dragged it across the wooden boards and tipped it over the side of the jetty. The crabs fell in the water with a great splash, and the girls laughed in relief when they saw the creatures scurrying sideways on the sandy bottom, which they could easily see through the clear, clean water.

"What do we do now?" Joy was slightly crestfallen, the fun now over.

"Catch them again!" Louise giggled.

"Again?"

"Yes!"

And with that, they tied more meat on their pieces of string, and hurled them over the end of the jetty.

"Why won't your mummy let you go in the water?"

The girls sat on Louise's front door step threading daisies into a long chain. The sun sat low on the bay, casting an orange glow over them.

"I don't know."

"Is it because of the sharks?"

"Yes."

"Oh."

"I can go in with Daddy and Mummy though."

"But not me?"

"No. Mummy said so."

"Oh." They worked on the chain in silence for some moments. "I think your mummy doesn't like me."

"I don't know."

"Do you like me?"

"Yes."

"Good."

Louise joined the last daisy to the end of the chain and they picked it up and put it around both their necks.

"You're my best ever friend," Louise said gravely.

"You're mine, too."

"Would you like some sweet peas? I can put them in your hair."

Joy nodded and sat with her head very still while Louise pushed flowers of many colours into her red curls.

"I've got a secret name for you," Joy whispered.

Louise stopped what she was doing and sat down again beside Joy.

"What is it?" she whispered back.

"Sweet pea…'cause you gave them to me our first day here."

"I like that."

"We mustn't tell anybody. It's our very own secret."

"Not even Mummy?" Louise looked behind her quickly.

"Nobody. It's our secret until we die."

"All right."

"Have you got a name for me?"

Louise sat back and put her chin in her hands while she thought, a frown growing deeper with each moment. Joy looked at her expectantly.

"Have you?"

"Not yet. It's in here, though." She rubbed her forehead with the flat of her hand. "It's magic, you see."

Joy held her breath, waiting for the revelation, her tongue pushing a loose tooth backwards and forwards. Even Louise could hear the faint sucking sound the tooth made as it moved in the gum. She looked up at Joy, a smile radiant on her face.

"That's it!"

"What? What?"

"Tooth Fairy."

Joy looked puzzled. "Tooth Fairy?"

"Yes. Hang on a minnie…" and she disappeared inside the house. Moments later she darted back out of the front door with something in her hand.

"Louie? It's bedtime. Come and get into your nightie," Olive called from inside.

"I'll be right there," Louise called back.

"Look—my Tooth Fairy glass."

She passed it to Joy who turned it over in her hand. It was a tiny, gold-rimmed glass with a hand-painted figure on one side. It was of a beautiful fairy wearing a long, bright yellow dress and matching yellow shoes that peeped out from under the hem of the full skirt. The fairy's shoulders and arms were bare, the bodice of the dress being strapless, and she held a silver wand that radiated light from its tip. She wore a silver tiara with a star on the top and her lips were painted a bright red. And her hair that fell in long waves around her shoulders…was red.

Joy looked in wonder from the glass to Louise.

"Don't you see? Every time I see my glass, I'll think of you. The Tooth Fairy is you."

"Louise Fletcher, I'm waiting," Olive's voice was louder now.

Louise popped her head inside the door. "Coming." She turned back to Joy to whisper quickly, "I'll lend her to you whenever one of your teeth comes out, and she'll give you lots of money for it."

Joy carefully handed the glass back to Louise.

"I love my secret name," she whispered to her friend.

"But you must promise never to tell," Louise hissed. "Cross your heart."

"Cross my heart and hope to die," Joy declared.

"Spit on it."

They both spat on the ground.

"What are you girls doing?" Olive was at the open door.

"Just showing Joy my Tooth Fairy glass."

"Oh…come on then, Louie. I'm sure Joy has to go to bed too."

Half an hour later, both girls were in their beds listening to the receding footsteps of their mothers as they made their way back to their respective kitchens. In a trice, Joy jumped out of bed and put her head out of her open window. She was rewarded with the sight of Louise straining through her window to see over the sweet pea draping the fence that separated their houses. Louise mouthed: cross your heart, and Joy responded by making a cross over her heart. Then they both spat out of their windows. Giggling, they waved, then returned to their beds. They were happy to have such an important secret to share. And nobody would ever know.

Chapter 18

"Jack? Jack? Are you listening to *anything* I say?"

Olive glared at her husband as he sprawled out in an overstuffed chair in front of the television set. He'd not moved from that position since he'd arrived home late, as usual, and finished the dinner she'd kept warm for him.

"What?" He half-turned towards her, his eyes still on the screen.

"Jack Fletcher. I may as well be talking to a brick wall."

"What *is* it, woman?" She had his attention now.

"I *said*, did you know that a hick town like Mornington has had the sewerage on since 1936? It's bloody ridiculous that, with a population of seventeen thousand, Chelsea still can't get it."

"And where did you get that fascinating morsel of information?" His voice dripped with sarcasm.

"Aren't you interested in *anything* that happens in your home town? Or are you too busy with that job of yours to care?"

"Oh, don't start your bloody nagging again." He turned back to the screen.

"You're never home. It's a wonder you even recognise your own daughter. This one anyway." She jerked her head towards Louise's bedroom.

"And what's that supposed to mean?" His eyes glittered dangerously as they turned towards her.

"You know what I mean. Do you think I'm stupid? I know what's going on."

"And would you like to enlighten me?" He leaned over and gripped her arm, twisting it painfully.

"I'm sick of pretending all the time. I know you're sleeping with that...that...*secretary* of yours. Or is it more than one?" She wriggled her arm out of his grasp.

"That's enough." he stood up surprisingly quickly for a man of his expanding girth. His hand swept down towards her, where she sat on the couch, and she ducked.

"Do you hit her too?" she taunted, reckless now that she'd finally spoken out. She darted away from him, around the other side of the couch.

"Why you..."

He lunged for her, grabbing at her arm. He missed, his hand hooking into the armhole of her dress. A ripping sound accompanied the tearing of the side seam as he pulled her towards him with a fistful of fabric. She stumbled and fell over the back of the couch, landing on the floor at his feet. He bent down and hit her across an ear. Pain exploded in her head.

"Mummy?"

Louise stood at the door, rubbing her eyes sleepily.

Jack stepped back and made as if to help Olive up from the floor. She brushed his hand aside and sat up on the couch.

"Mummy? What's happening?"

"It's all right, Louie. I fell over." She looked up at Jack, eyes glaring hatred. "Daddy was just helping me up."

Jack stood panting and wiped sweat off his forehead.

"Go to bed," he roared, pointing at the door.

"I was just..."

"I *said*, go to bed."

Louise turned around and made for the door. Olive sidled past Jack and took her daughter's hand.

"Come on, Louie. I'll give you a cuddle."

"Are you all right, Mummy?" She looked up at her mother, eyes concerned, puzzled, taking in the torn dress.

"Yes, I'm fine. Just a bit of a sore ear. I must have hit it on something."

Joy opened her door slowly, crossed the hallway, and put her ear to her parents' bedroom door. Satisfied that they were still asleep, she tiptoed past the lounge and sewing room and into the kitchen. The clock ticked loudly from the mantel and she looked up at it, putting her forefinger to her lips and whispered: "Shush." The big hand was on the lowest part of the upper clock face, right next to the little hand. She frowned in concentration as she read "S-u-n-d-a-y" on the left of the bottom face and "M-a-y" on the right. The large single hand was level with the "8". Yes, she was satisfied. It was her fifth birthday...and Mother's Day.

She carefully put her gift on the kitchen table and then took out a tray from a cupboard under the sink. She placed the tray on the table, opened up a drawer from where she took a small embroidered cloth, and put it on the tray. The gift sat in the middle of the tray and she surrounded it with a glass of milk; a slice of bread spread thickly with butter that tore holes in it and covered with a fair layer of Vegemite; a bowl of raspberry jelly; a sweet biscuit; and a scattering of flowers that she broke off from a blue hydrangea in a vase. She stood back and looked at it, broke off some more flowers and rearranged them on the tray, and then picked it up and made her way back to her parents' bedroom.

Balancing the tray gingerly on her left arm, she opened the door and entered the room. The soft murmur of Ruth's breathing contrasted with the noisier exhalations that puffed from Les's mouth. Joy giggled as she placed the tray on the bed beside Ruth. Les's arm was wrapped around Ruth's shoulder. Joy reached over and tickled his arm. He jerked awake with one eye popping open to discover her just inches from his face. His smile was as radiant as hers.

"Shush," she cautioned him. "Don't wake Mummy yet."

"What are you up to, princess?"

"Mother's Day."

"And I believe someone has a birthday today. Do you know who that could be?"

Joy covered her mouth to stifle her giggles. "You?"

"No. I think it might be...you," he whispered digging her in the ribs.

She shrieked with laughter, squirming away from him, and Ruth sat up sleepily.

"What's going on?"

"Happy Mother's Day, Mummy." Joy pushed the tray closer to her mother.

"Ooh...what a surprise. Breakfast in bed...and what a lovely tray."

"Aren't you lucky?" Les said, pulling a face. "Where's mine?"

"You're not having Mother's Day, Daddy," Joy giggled.

"What's this?" Ruth held up the parcel. "Is this for me?"

"Yes."

"Can I unwrap it now?"

"Yes."

"Well, go on, woman. I want to see what it is." Les took hold of the tray while Ruth unwrapped her present.

"Such pretty paper," Ruth exclaimed, examining the decorated paper that Joy had made. "And what's this?"

She carefully pulled the paper away from a little cardboard box entirely covered with shells of all shapes and sizes. Joy looked at Ruth's face expectantly.

"What a beautiful box. I shall put all my favourite things in it. Thank you, sweetheart."

Ruth hugged Joy while Les examined the box.

"Where's my box?" he whined, pretending to cry.

"I'll make you one, Daddy. Don't cry." She took his hand, concern clouding her eyes.

"Daddy's joking," Ruth said giving Les a punch in the shoulder. "Don't take any notice of him."

Joy laughed in relief, and then gasped as Les pulled out a gift for her from under the bed.

"Happy birthday, princess," he said handing it to her.

"Happy birthday, sweetheart," Ruth kissed her.

Joy tore at the paper excitedly and found a large box inside it. She opened it to find tissue paper scrunched up around a smaller box, which she opened in turn to find more tissue paper and another box. By now Ruth and Les were laughing so hard the bed was shaking and Ruth's breakfast tray was threatening to lose its contents. Joy squealed with frustration each time she opened a box and found more tissue paper and yet another box. Finally she found a tiny box with lots of sticky tape around it and it took her some moments to get the lid off. Inside was a gold key. She held it up to her parents, puzzlement pulling her face into a frown.

"What's it for?"

"Something." Les looked up at the ceiling and scratched his chin, pretending indifference.

"Mummy?" Joy pulled at Ruth's arm. "What's it for?"

"Would you like to know?" Ruth was trying to keep a straight face.

"Yes." Joy bounced on the bed, Ruth catching the glass of milk just in time.

"Should we put her out of her agony?" Les asked nonchalantly. "Or should we wait for her next birthday?"

"No. Daddy...tell me. Tell me."

"All right. Let's go and have a look in the lounge room and see if you can see anything there that it might fit."

They jumped out of bed all at once and raced for the door, where they were caught in a muddle with Les trying to stop Joy getting out. She ducked under his legs and ran down the hallway and into the lounge room. She let out a piercing shriek.

Les looked at Ruth. "I think she found it."

They came upon Joy in the lounge room fitting the gold key into the lid of a magnificent roll-top desk. The polished oak gleamed in the morning light, a deep red with flecks of a darker colour that reflected on Joy's face as she bent close to it. The key turned in the lock with an audible click; she slid the lid back smoothly along its curved grooves to reveal the working space and pigeonholes of varying sizes set into the back wall. She pulled a chair over to the desk and knelt on it so that she could reach inside the workspace of the desk. Her hands darted to four tiny drawers built into the topmost shelf. She opened and closed each one, her fingers exploring the interiors, then ran her hands over the shelf and then down to two slightly larger drawers on each side of the middle shelf that had vertical and horizontal pigeonholes. Down again to the last shelf that had a larger drawer on each side. The central kneehole recess was flanked on either side with four deep drawers and a long shallow one above it. Two recessed rectangular panels adorned either side of the lower half of the desk, and the recessed panels were repeated in the smaller upper portion shaped to follow the contour of the roll top. At the very top of the desk was a small solid gallery made of the same burnished oak. And seated inside the gallery was a pretty blonde-haired doll who looked down at Joy with her mouth half-open, tiny white teeth peeping out from under red lips, looking as if she was about to speak.

Joy lifted the doll down and examined its clothes. It was dressed in a frothy multi-layered white short-sleeved dress with pink and green ribbons worked into the layers. It had a matching bag hung over its right arm and wore socks and little white sandals. Over the other arm it carried a long coat made out of the same material with a heavy white lining. Joy held it in her arms and noticed that the eyes closed and, when she sat it up, the eyes opened. She turned it over and was surprised to hear it say *Mummy*, which was unusual for the day when most dolls uttered *Mama*.

Les and Ruth stood watching Joy, waiting for some sort of reaction that would tell them if they'd made the right decision in making her a gift of the desk. Was she too young for it, they had wondered? Would she appreciate it? It had taken Les the best part of a year to construct it in secrecy behind a partition in his workshop when she was asleep. Every piece was lovingly created as it grew from carefully selected raw timber that was sanded, measured, sawn, fitted and finally polished to enhance the grain and colour. Les had wanted to make the desk for Joy to begin her education with. It was something he'd never had—a desk or an education— and he wanted it to be her constant companion for all of her learning years and beyond. Perhaps it would be something she would value.

Joy turned to them, her green eyes radiant.

"This is the bestest birthday ever. You made it, didn't you, Daddy?"

Les nodded, suddenly embarrassed.

"I know you did. You're the best maker."

She ran her free hand over the desk, tracing its contours with her fingers.

"And the dolly, Mummy…you made her clothes. I can tell."

"She's the best dressmaker this side of the Black Stump. Everyone knows that." Les hugged his wife.

"That's nothing beside the desk, Les," Ruth pushed him in front of her. "What your father has done is…utterly miraculous. You're a very lucky girl."

Joy hugged her parents in turn and then quickly returned to the desk with her doll.

"Look," she said to it. "This is our desk. We'll do some writing together. And some drawing. And sums. And everything."

Ruth and Les smiled at each other in satisfaction.

"I've got another surprise for you, princess."

"What?" Joy whirled around to see what he had.

"It's to do with the desk. Look." He leaned over and pulled the long middle drawer open. "Can you feel something at the back?"

Joy climbed on the chair and put her hand right in the drawer. At first she could find nothing, but upon searching around, she stopped when she discovered a small lever.

"You found it?" he asked, seeing the look of surprise on her face. "All right. Now push it to the right. That's over towards the kitchen. Yes, that's it."

Suddenly, a panel to the right of the small drawers and the pigeonholes slid open to reveal a long flat compartment that ran right back to the rear wall of the desk.

"Now push it back the other way, and you'll see it close."

She pushed it back and the panel slid quietly back into position. Once closed, there was no indication that the empty space existed behind it.

"It's magic!"

Les grinned as she tried to open the panel with her fingers but she could find no way to open it. She opened the drawer again, found the lever, and pushed it to the right and the panel slid open again.

"And there're two more," he said leaning over and indicating the pigeonholes. "See if you can find them."

Joy ran her fingers all over the open compartments, opened the drawers, felt for levers, but could find nothing.

"Give in?" he laughed.

"Where? Where?"

"Here."

He showed her on the middle shelf. He gripped the dividing wall between two of the pigeonholes and pushed it inwards. There was a faint click and a panel opened behind the rear wall of the desk between the two larger drawers on the bottom shelf. Joy clapped with delight.

"Look, Mummy...another magic door!"

"It *is* magic," Ruth replied.

"Where's the other one?" Joy turned to her father. "Is it another magic door?"

"Let's see."

He pointed to the gallery on the top of the desk.

"See if you can find it here."

Joy stood on the chair and pushed at the gallery, pulled it, ran her fingers right along it, but could find nothing.

"I can't find it," she pouted.

"All right. Watch this."

Les grasped the piece of gallery where it began on the left side of the desk. He lifted it up and then swung it around away from the desk. Nothing happened...or so it seemed. Joy searched the desk with her eyes but could find no secret opening.

"It didn't work." She looked up at Les, disappointed.

"Look around a bit," he said. "Hop down and have a good look."

She got down off the chair and looked inside the large side drawers and under the kneehole recess. Having no success, she crawled out from under the desk and walked around the side. There she saw the recessed side panel had disappeared to reveal a compartment with shallow shelves built into it.

"See?" Les swung the gallery piece back into place, and the panel shut.

She ran her hands over it and found no way to open it.

"Daddy, you're so clever."

She hugged him tightly.

"No one will ever know that you've got secret hiding places for your most treasured things," Ruth said. "You must tell no one about them. They are your secret and no one else's."

"I can tell Louise, can't I?"

"That's your decision, princess," Les knelt down beside her. "But remember, they're secret places for only you and..."

"You and Mummy know about them."

"Yes, but we're going to forget about them as soon as we can," Ruth assured her.

"...and if you tell other people about them, they won't be a secret anymore, will they?"

"No. But Louise won't tell anyone."

"Well, you have a good think about it. Don't tell her yet. Wait until you're really sure."

"All right, Daddy."

She looked at her parents, searching their faces, realising that it was an important decision she had to make...and it was hers alone. Taking her doll in her arms, she turned back to the desk.

"Do you want me to show you how to open the secret magic places?" she asked it. Then concern coloured her face as she realised something. "Can I tell my new dolly?"

"I think so," Ruth smiled. "She won't tell anyone."

"Have you got a name for her?" Les asked.

"Oh. Let's see." She studied the doll for some moments then turned it over and back again. It said, *Mummy* and Joy giggled hugging the doll to her. "She has the prettiest blue eyes I've ever seen in a hundred years. I think I'll call her *Blue Eyes*."

Hundreds and thousands, their colours bleeding into left-over pieces of butter-spread fairy bread, and flakes of pastry from sausage rolls on plates sporting pools of uneaten tomato sauce, sat dejectedly on the stained table cloth. Streamers uncoiled in ringlet ropes over the edge of the table and joined the rest of the remnants of the party on the lawn. Deflating balloons danced across the back yard as playful breezes urged them on, and sea gulls swooped daringly upon sausage and baby frankfurt ends, half-eaten sandwiches, and anything else that had been left.

The party had been a happy one. Both Joy and Louise had greeted their ten guests excitedly, squealing each time the doorbell rang and running to receive another gift that would be ripped open with eager hands. Their shared birthday celebrations were held in the backyard of Louise's house, where the children drank copious amounts of soft drink and cordial and ate a mountain of party food on a long table set up by Olive and Ruth. They played Pin the Tail on the Donkey, hide-and-seek, chasey, pass the parcel and treasure hunts. And both Louise and Joy blew out the two rows of five candles on a pretty pink-iced birthday cake made by Olive. The two girls blushed as everyone sang *Happy Birthday* and posed for one of many photos Ruth took with her Brownie camera. Their arms were around each other as they laughed into the camera, a gap in Joy's lower front teeth showing clearly.

Chapter 19

"…If the person who has my son is a father and has a child of his own, all I say is, for God's sake, send him back to me in one piece." [1]

The man broke down and covered his face with his hands.

Ruth stared at the screen, eyes focused on the parting in Bazil Thorne's dark wavy hair. Slowly she turned to Les, her face pale and her body shaking.

"My God."

"Poor bugger. I'd hate to be in his shoes."

"Les, what if that'd been Joy?"

"Well, it wasn't."

"Yes, but what if it had? What would we do? How would we cope?"

"No use getting yourself all het up over something that hasn't happened. We're just lucky it wasn't Joy."

"But, Les…"

"No buts. That's Sydney. This is Melbourne."

"The kidnapper might come here. Might take Joy!"

Les was shocked at the sudden hysteria in Ruth's voice and the panic in her eyes. She jumped up and made for Joy's room. He caught her at the door, put his arms around her shoulders and drew her away. "Calm down, love. You'll wake her up."

"I just want to see that she's all right."

"Of course she is. She's only been asleep for an hour or so."

"I want to see her." Ruth was shouting, struggling in his arms. "You can't stop me."

"Ruth…look at me." He pushed his face close to hers making her look at him. "Stop it."

"No! No! I want my daughter," she screamed, lunging wildly out of his grasp and making for Joy's room.

Joy appeared in the doorway yawning, her doll in her arms.

"Daddy?"

"It's all right, princess. Go back to sleep."

"What's wrong with Mummy?"

"Oh, my darling. You're all right," Ruth sobbed, dropping to her knees and clutching at Joy.

"Ruth," Les said quietly. "She's all right. Let her go."

---

[1] *Sydney Morning Herald, 9 July 1960*

"Why's Mummy crying?"

"She...saw something sad on the telly and it made her cry. She's all right now, though. Come on, off to bed."

He pulled Ruth up, supporting her with one arm, and gently pushed Joy back towards her bed. Ruth sagged heavily, her eyes rolling back in her head.

"Whoops. Mummy's gone to sleep," he said lightly, hoping Joy wouldn't notice the growing panic he was now feeling.

He picked Ruth up in his arms and carried her to their bedroom and put her carefully on the bed.

"She's going to bed now, too." He turned around to Joy. "You hop in and I'll come in in a sec and tuck you in."

"Is Mummy sick, Daddy?"

"Just a little. She'll be all right in the morning though. Don't you worry."

After Joy settled down again for the night, Les sat beside Ruth waiting for her to wake. She had fallen into a deep sleep, not waking from her swoon, and he watched her progress through one nightmare after another, each one appearing to grow worse than the previous one. He was unsure whether to wake her or not, afraid that he might disturb a natural mental process that was working through her fears. He decided to undress and lay beside her. The warmth of his body and arms seemed to calm her and she gradually drifted into a less troubled slumber.

Lying there, holding her, thoughts raced through his head. He was horrified at the violence of her reaction to the kidnapping of the Thorne boy. Of course, he had felt compassion for the parents. What father or mother wouldn't? What those people must be going through was beyond Les's comprehension, and he could only imagine what it would be like for him and Ruth. Well...maybe not Ruth. How could he possibly know what was in her mind? It was closed even to her, he suspected. But to react so frantically. It was like she was losing her mind.

He'd noticed the difference in her since...since...Joy started school? Yes, that was it. When Joy started school. Since that first day, when she'd dragged Joy back home, she'd been acting strangely. He'd thought perhaps she had it under control, but obviously she hadn't. His mind returned to that dark period in Perth when he'd almost lost her, when the Ruth he'd known had nearly disappeared. It mustn't happen again. She was everything to him...more than the house, his job, their new life on the other side of Australia…even more than Joy who he loved dearly. The thought of Ruth withdrawing from him to that other world that had all but claimed her before was too much to bear.

Ruth stirred in her sleep, mumbling unintelligible words that he strained to decipher. The darkness of the room was lit faintly by the luminous night sky as it filtered through the lace curtains. Soft rustlings of prostrate waves nuzzling the sand reached his ears as he gazed at the curtains moving lazily in a slight breeze. It seemed to him as though the waves echoed Ruth's mental state. Each murmur, each rhythmic movement, brought her back to him and then took her away, retreating into the depths of her hidden world.

He knew he would have to do something about it, but what? Take her to a doctor? Risk discovery of what had caused her unbalanced state…her illness? Yes, he admitted it to himself. She was ill. Mentally ill. But if she were questioned, would she reveal her crime…their crime? And if she did, would the authorities take Joy from them? Put Ruth in gaol? Separate them? That was something he would avoid at all costs. From the first moment he had seen her at Gladys Taylor's boarding house, and when she had sprayed him with talcum powder, he had known she was for him. Both their lives had been such pitiful existences until they met, but they had answered a need—a hunger—in each other that he was not prepared to surrender. Not for anything. So, what could he do? Where could he go for help? He'd thought some time back that he might have a chat with Pat Lewis. Perhaps now was the time to do so.

Next morning Ruth sat at the kitchen table in silence staring at her hand that held a slice of uneaten toast. Les had hidden *The Sun* with its glaring headline: **KIDNAPPED! Son of £100,000 winner**, before she could see it. There was no mention made of what had transpired the night before. Joy ate her breakfast quietly, looking up from time to time to see what her mother was doing, and then glancing at Les with a question in her eyes. It was a question he didn't know how to answer.

"We'd better get your sandwich cut for school," he said to her softly. "What would you like, Vegemite or corned beef?"

"Isn't it Saturday, Daddy?" she whispered.

"Oh. I forgot."

"You're a silly duffer," she smiled.

"I know," he grinned. "Do you want to run out and play with Louise?"

"No." Ruth straightened against the back of her chair. "No!"

"What?"

"She must stay here. Where it's safe."

"Ruth, darling. She's safe in our street."

"No!"

"Come on, love." He pulled his chair closer to hers and put his arm around her shoulders. "She's fine with Louise. It's all right."

Tears perished in her tear ducts before they could surface, pushed back by an unconscious frozen resolve to concentrate on one thing—and that was to protect her child.

"I don't want her out there, where that monster can get her." She spoke slowly, deliberately, as if thinking before uttering each word.

"What monster? Mummy? Daddy?" Joy looked from one to the other, fear intruding into her world.

"No. No. There's no monster." Les tried to laugh it off. "Mummy's only...joking." *Struth, can't you manage something better than that,* he thought, disgusted with himself.

"The monster who took that poor boy," Ruth declared. "He mustn't get to you. I won't let him." She gripped Joy's arm tightly.

"Daddy, I'm scared." Joy started to cry and clutched at Les's legs.

"It's all right, princess. Mummy's mistaken. There's no monster..."

The sudden clamour of the doorbell broke them apart. They looked at each other, startled.

"Struth!" Les struggled to the front door dragging Joy with him, who still held onto his legs, and with Ruth holding onto Joy.

He pulled the door open abruptly to see Louise standing there with Olive who held the newspaper out in front of her.

"Isn't it ghastly," Olive said. "Did you see that poor man on the news last night? I could have cried."

"Yes. Yes." Les pulled a face at her over Louise's head. "As a matter of fact, Joy was about to see if Louise was allowed to play."

"Of course...yes." She looked from Les to Ruth uncertainly, instinct making her put the paper behind her back. "Joy, how about helping Louise make some biscuits?"

"No!"

It was a cry of agony that turned each of them to Ruth. They froze, uncertain what to do next.

"She mustn't...mustn't..." Ruth was shaking her head, eyes wild, as she looked up and down the street. "There." She pointed to a young man walking towards Bath Street. "That could be him."

"Love...that's young Bernie from over the road." He prised her hand from Joy's arm, holding it firmly in his grasp.

Joy rubbed her arm where a large red mark was left from Ruth's grip.

"Go on, princess," he pushed Joy towards Olive and Louise. "Make some nice bikkies."

He made frantic signals to Olive to take Joy with her. She took the child by the hand and led her down the front step and out of the driveway, talking as fast and as loudly as she could to cover the commotion behind them. Les turned Ruth firmly around, taking her inside again, and propelled her towards the kitchen. She was sobbing now, her body trembling violently, as he sat her down on a chair at the table. He reached up to a cupboard over the bench, took out a bottle of brandy, and poured a good measure into a glass.

"Here," he put it to her mouth. "This'll do you good."

He could smell the fumes of the brandy as he stood over her. Some of it trickled through her lips and she swallowed involuntarily. She coughed and spluttered between sobs but he managed to tip some more down despite her hands waving the glass away.

"No, love. I want you to drink it. All of it."

She looked up at him as tears rushed from her eyes.

"At least do it for me...huh?"

She nodded and took hold of the glass. It rattled against her teeth as her breath shuddered between sobs. He could hear each mouthful stop in her throat threatening ejection, but he held her eyes with his own, willing her to drink it all.

"Come on. It's nearly gone," he urged, sitting down beside her.

He could tell the warm glow had hit her stomach as the sobs gradually subsided. His arms went around her and her head rested on his chest. His familiar smell comforted her, as did his calloused hands scratching through her hair. She stayed there, their two bodies rocking together slightly, until he could feel the tension seep out of her. The only sound now was the loud ticking of the clock. He watched the minute hand move slowly around the face until it had almost reached the top. He braced himself for the nine loud chimes he knew would arrive as the hammer hit the gong to strike the hour. He hoped it wouldn't startle her now that she was seemingly calm.

The whirring sound heralded the first clang. Her body jerked slightly, and he could tell that she was counting each boisterous clang as it split the silence in the kitchen. As the last chime's vibration faded, she sat up and looked at him.

"What's wrong with me, Les?"

Les swung the truck down the familiar street that ran alongside the railway line. Pat Lewis was waiting at the front gate, anxiety written on her face.

"Come on in, love. A nice cuppa will do you the world of good."

"Thanks."

"Jim's inside. Is that all right, or would you rather a chin wag—just the two of us?"

"No, no. That's fine. The more the merrier." His words belied the worry he carried with him.

He sat down at the kitchen table facing Pat and Jim. They waited for him to speak.

"As I said on the phone, it's Ruth."

"Go on, love," Pat said, pouring him a cup of tea.

"She's not quite…you know…the full two bob."

"What do you mean, mate?" Jim scratched his head, looking somewhat uncomfortable.

Les looked down at his cup, embarrassed too. "I mean, she's got problems. Mental problems, I think."

"I know, love," Pat nodded. "You can sort of tell."

Les looked up in surprise. "You can?"

"Oh, not on the surface. But once you get to know her, you know there's something…" she trailed off.

"Yeah, well. She's getting worse." No one spoke. "She's doing peculiar things."

"Like what?"

"Well, for instance, that poor sod, Thorne. You know…the kidnapping case up in Sydney?"

"Oh, terrible thing, that," Jim agreed. "You heard they had a call from the bastard who took the kid?"

"No."

"Yeah. Said if they don't pay up, he'll feed the kid to the sharks. Mongrel."

"Bastard."

"Yeah."

"Well, Ruth's gone funny over it…"

"Funny ha ha, or funny peculiar?" Jim asked.

"Peculiar."

"Oh."

"And she's got it in her mind that the bastard's gunna come down here and pinch Joy. Doesn't want to let her out of our sight."

"But that happened up in Sydney," Pat said, topping up their cups.

"That's what I said to her. Didn't make any difference though. She's sort of panicking. She even fainted last night. Out to it—just like that," he snapped his fingers.

"Jesus," Jim whistled quietly.

"Won't let her swim in the bay, either."

"Why ever not?"

"Says a shark'll get her. Remember those sightings off the beach?"

Jim snorted, "That's all they were though."

"What about our little Joy, love?" Pat put her hand on his arm. "Does she know what's going on?"

"Can't fail to. Ruth's clinging on to her like a leech...ever since Joy first started school. I've told you about that before, haven't I?" Pat nodded and he continued, "I'm running out of excuses for her mother."

"Poor little mite."

"I don't know what to do about it."

"A doctor?"

"No," he said shaking his head. "Can't do that."

"Why not, love?" Pat looked at him sideways.

"I...don't think she's strong enough."

"But a doctor—a psychiatrist, even—would make her stronger, don't you think?"

"Those bloody psychos—they'd make anybody nuttier still, I reckon," Jim put in.

"Don't be silly, Jim. They're there to help people."

"Help their pockets, more like it."

"Les," she ignored her husband. "What about your local doctor? Is he any good? Like...can she talk to him?"

Les shook his head. "She wouldn't open up. Not to a doctor. Doesn't trust 'em."

"Well, Les, love, if she won't talk to a doctor, who else could help her? A minister, or something?"

"Not religious," Les shrugged.

They sat in silence for some moments, thinking hard.

Jim blew his nose. "Bloody cold. A man's nose runs all the bloody time." He turned up the kerosene heater. "You haven't got any relatives, have you?"

"No."

"None at all?"

"No."

"Either of you?"

"No."

"What a bugger."

"Pat?"

"Yes, love?"

"Could it be...you know...women's problems?"

"Twenty five, isn't she?" Les nodded agreement. "No...too young, love."

"That's what I thought," Les said glumly.

"Unless it's something else. God knows what, though."

"Well, we're not getting very far with this problem, are we?" Jim asked looking from one to the other. "We're no bloody help at all."

"I appreciate your..."

"Les, love. We're here to help if we can at all," she tapped his arm. "I just can't think what else to suggest. Other than take her to the doctors. I think that's about your best bet, you know. Maybe you can go and see him first, like. You could sound him out first—without her knowing."

"I don't like doing anything behind her back..."

"I know, love. But it's for her own good. Talk to the doctor, then send her along and see if he can find out what the matter is. It might be something simple after all."

Pat and Jim stood at their front gate watching the truck until it disappeared around the corner of the street.

"Poor bugger. He's got a big problem there."

"And I don't think it's going to get any better."

Chapter 20

Les's eyes widened in alarm at what he read on page two of *The Sun*. It sent a chill through him.

> ...and despite the failure of finding any trace of the missing twin, Detective Inspector George Chambers says he has not forgotten the case. "The Schwartz case has been one of the most puzzling crimes of the century," Chambers commented after hearing about the Thorne kidnapping. "I doubt the cases are linked," he said, "There was no demand for ransom here in Perth, and there was no body ever found. The kidnapper will make a fatal error one day...and when he does I'll be there to put him away."

He sipped distractedly on his mug of tea, the hot liquid scalding his mouth.

"Bloody hell." It spilled down his chin and onto his overalls.

"You all right, mate?" the electrician working on the same job asked.

"Yeah, yeah. Missed my mouth," Les laughed at himself. He put the cap back on his thermos flask, and stood up. "Well, better get back to work, eh? We'll finish this job today, I reckon."

"Finished with the paper, mate?" The electrician threw the butt of his cigarette away as he stood up, wiping his mouth with his sleeve. As Les handed him the paper, the other said, "Want to have a read up about the Thorne case. Rotten luck kids finding the body, eh?"

"Yeah."

"Glad it wasn't my boys. Jesus, they'd never get over a thing like that. It'd make a kid nervous, like. Don't you reckon?"

"Yeah."

"They reckon it's a New Australian did it. Our lot don't do things like that."

"What?"

"Kidnap kids. Mongrel act that. Imagine how the kid's parents are suffering. They should hang the bastard when they find him."

Les held a nail ready, the hammer poised in mid air. He belted the nail in one hard strike. "Yeah," he said under his breath.

"Are you listening to me, Louie?" Olive gently pushed Louise's chin up so that their eyes were level.

"Yes, Mummy," she said, putting down her crayon.

"I want you to promise me. Never, never, never get into a car with a stranger. Do you hear me?"

"Yes."

"Not that you're on your own much, mind, but just in case. I want you to know that you can't trust every adult you meet. You have to just stick with those you know."

"Why?"

"Oh, just...just...because."

"Because why?"

"Because...there are some bad people in this world."

"Who?"

"No one you know, thank goodness."

"Oh." Her head was bent over her drawing again and she picked up a red crayon and drew a large stick figure next to a small one. "Is this the bad person?"

"Could be," Olive nodded.

"Is it a lady or a man?"

"Probably a man."

"Why?"

"Just is."

George Chambers was no stranger to the Schwartz household; in fact, he visited Gunter and Ursula at least once a month. It was his way of making up for what he considered to be his failure to return the missing twin to her father and sister but, rather than being a penance, the visits resulted in the formation of a solid friendship. It was a friendship that was confined to the three of them, without spilling over to the detective's own family or workmates. It was an indulgence that George preferred to keep to himself because his professional and private lives had never connected—ever—until this one case. He had the utmost admiration for Gunter's ability in raising his daughter alone and wondered if he'd be as successful, given the same circumstances; he seriously doubted it. But, then, he'd never been through anything like Gunter had in surviving Auschwitz and getting to Australia with Hannah. The indescribable horror of the prison camps was out of his league and he sensed that Gunter would not speak of it.

A few weeks after Ursula's fifth birthday, George arrived with a clumsily-wrapped gift.

"Sorry it's late," he said, thrusting the package at the excited girl.

"Thank you, Uncle George," she beamed, before reaching up for a kiss.

"You are too kind, George," Gunter said, shaking the detective's hand. "You spoil her—us."

George shook off the compliment as Ursula unwrapped the package to reveal a stuffed toy. She squealed with delight, "A puppy! A puppy!" and threw herself at George for more kisses.

Not long after, she proudly showed him her father's gift: a quarter-size violin that threw a flamed maple reflection on her pale skin as she positioned it under her chin.

"Yes," Gunter nodded, "it set me back a little in my savings for her university education, but she had outgrown her first. We will save very carefully, however, for the day we move to Sydney or Melbourne." He sighed. "That will be a long time from now, though, I fear."

"Do you want to know a secret?" Joy whispered in Louise's ear.

They were sitting on the floor of Louise's bedroom, putting a building together with coloured blocks of wood. The blocks were different shapes: rectangles, squares, triangles, circles, columns, and arches. It was one of the girls' favourite occupations. It gave them a chance to do something together and talk at the same time.

"Yes." Louise looked up expectantly, her hand hovering over a wall with a block in her hand. "What is it?"

"Promise not to tell. Not anyone."

"I promise."

"As Sweet Pea?"

"As Sweet Pea," Louise held her hand over her heart, eyes serious.

"I've got a secret hiding place."

Louise's eyes opened wide. "Where?"

"In my desk."

"Can I see it?"

"Come on, I'll show you."

They raced into the kitchen where Olive was standing at the bench, cutting up vegetables.

"Can I go to Joy's house?" Louise asked her mother.

"Of course, Louie." She smiled to herself as the girls ran outside, banging the back door after them. *They're in a tearing great hurry,* she thought. *Girl things. How long ago it seems since I did things like that, since life was simple.*

Her thoughts returned to the question of her marriage. It was in a shambles and she didn't know what to do about it. Louise knew that her father wasn't like other fathers—like Les, for instance. Jack was hardly ever at home and, when he was, the atmosphere was strained. He found fault with everything Olive said or did, and he took practically no notice of Louise when she spoke to him or attempted to show him something she'd done at school. He just didn't seem interested, much less involve himself in the school community. Olive was glad to see the back of him when he left early for work of a morning—that is, if he'd been home the night before. Sometimes he came home late smelling of alcohol and perfume. And far from appearing sheepish or guilty at those times, he was belligerent and sometimes resorted to violence. He was clever, though, in mostly only hitting her where the bruises wouldn't show. They played a silent battle in their bedroom where their respective parts were those of aggressor and victim. She played the passive role in which she tried to avoid antagonizing him, but there were times when it seemed just her presence was enough to set him off. Last night had been no exception.

His pale hazel eyes had narrowed as he took out his underwear for the next day and put it precisely on the chair next to his side of the bed, as he did every night. He had noticed a hole in the heel of one of his socks.

"What's this?" he demanded, straightening up and pushing it in her face. "What's the idea of leaving a hole in it?"

"I didn't notice it, Jack," she answered quietly, taking the sock.

"Didn't notice it?"

"Shush, Jack. You'll wake up Louise."

"Don't tell me shush. Who do you think you are?" He grabbed her by the arm, squeezing it painfully.

"For God's sake, it's only a sock. You've got plenty more."

"Oh, is that right?" He twisted her arm behind her back, making her gasp.

She looked at the door, worried in case they'd woken Louise. His voice was becoming louder.

"I'll fix it, Jack."

"You make damned sure you do," he roared. "What are you doing here all day? A man works like a dog to keep a lazy bitch like you and that's the thanks he gets."

His eyes were bleary as he tried to focus through the wine that had clouded his brain. His grip on her arm loosened slightly and she wriggled away from him.

"I'm going to fix it now," she said, and was out of the door and had it closed before he could answer.

He sat down suddenly on the bed mumbling to himself, then lay face down, dribbling into the starched crispness of his pillow. He was snoring before Olive had reached her sewing basket.

Louise had heard the argument. It had woken her up, as she had been woken on other nights. It was happening more often now. She buried her head under the blankets, hoping the shouting would go away. Tears wet her sheets at the sound of the muffled cries of her mother. With a feeling of relief, she heard light footsteps leave her parents' bedroom, walk over to the spare room, and the light switch turn on. Her mother would probably sleep in the spare bed again. Louise felt guilty for the hundredth time because she shouldn't feel this way, but she hated her father. He was a very nasty man.

Olive wiped her eyes with her apron. They had been watering, but she wasn't sure if it was from the onions that she'd been cutting up, or from what she'd been thinking about. Or both. She sighed. If only he'd take off with his floozie and leave Louise and herself alone. But he wasn't about to do that. He had his bread buttered on both sides. Not only that, if he did leave, how would she and Louise survive financially? Here she was, twenty-five years of age and all washed up. Not for the first time, she caught herself thinking what it would be like to be married to Les. He was a real family man. One who couldn't wait to get home to his wife and daughter, one who was passionate about his work and was handy around the house. That man could do anything. And on top of all that, the way he looked at Ruth was almost indecent. Olive could tell that he still desired his wife, even after the way she'd been acting lately. Some women had all the luck.

Les fiddled with his ear lobe while sitting in the waiting room. He felt uneasy being there as if he was sneaking around behind Ruth's back. He wondered how she'd feel if she knew.

A month before, Les had summoned up the courage to speak with the doctor. It had taken him some time to work out what he was going to say. There was the problem of what he'd told Ruth those five years ago—why she couldn't remember having the baby—

and the real truth of the matter. How was he going to get around that with the doctor? And if the doctor examined her internally— which Les supposed he might—could the doctor tell that she'd had a stillbirth instead of a normal one?

"...and she was so down in the dumps after Joy was born—real miserable, like new mothers get sometimes—that I didn't like to tell her. She didn't even remember giving birth to her."

"Hasn't she asked you since?" Doctor Armstrong had prompted.

"Oh, yeah. I told her that she'd had a hysto...hysto..."

"Hysterectomy?"

"Yeah, that's it."

"And she remembers nothing?"

"No. See, they had her doped up...the pain."

"So they gave her a general anaesthetic?"

"I...think so."

"And why did she need the hysterectomy?"

Les looked at the doctor's head bent over the desk as he was writing something on the card. The almost-bald pate shone through a few tufts of grey hair that grew right at the top. There were what looked like freckles on his skull—age spots, Les reckoned. It reminded him of the time, five years ago, when a similar doctor had sat down with Les and told him of their dead child.

They'd been listening to the wireless when she gasped and clutched her stomach. He saw her translucent skin go deathly white, like a bleached sheet. "I think this is it," she'd said, and she got out of the armchair. As she turned, her foot caught in the chair leg and she fell heavily over Les's toolbox, the solid wooden handle digging into her abdomen. He'd felt a chill dread when they both looked stupidly at the pool of blood that gushed from between her legs as he helped her to her feet. With each contraction, more blood came, so much so that he wondered where it was all coming from. Did a person have *that much* blood? He had a gut feeling that the baby was in trouble. It wasn't normal to bleed, was it? Ruth's eyes had mirrored what he was feeling and her screams came from her lips soundlessly; she was screaming inside, he knew.

"Mr Bacon?"

Les's head snapped up, his mind shaking the memories aside. "Yeah?"

"The hysterectomy." Les looked puzzled. "Why did she need it?"

"Oh. I don't really know. I don't understand these women things. You know..." he finished off lamely.

"Surely they explained it to you?"

"I suppose they did. I can't remember now. It was probably too technical for me."

The doctor looked at him closely. Les wondered if the man could tell he was lying. He must sound like a real drongo otherwise.

"Anyway, as I said, I don't know how to handle her right now." He hesitated. "Is there a tablet, or something, you can give her that would make her more...normal?"

"Well, Mr Bacon, I'd have to see her first. Examine her. Maybe order some tests."

"You won't tell her I've spoken with you?"

"No. If you'd rather I didn't. How are you going to get her here though?"

"If I ask her, she'll come."

So here he was, a month later, waiting to know the outcome of Ruth's visits. She hadn't said much. Just that she'd spoken with the doctor, had some blood tests, and that she was waiting on the results.

The doctor frowned at the card. "Mrs Bacon's tests didn't show anything abnormal. It could be just a phase she's going through that'll pass soon enough. Maybe you're worrying a bit too much?" He peered at Les over his glasses. "She seems to be quite a confident young woman. Not at all like you paint her." Les waited. "But, if you're sure she is having these *episodes*, or going mental as you call it, then I think Largactil may be of some assistance."

"Largactil? What's that?"

"It's a tranquilizer. It could help her get over a difficult time. Iron out the wrinkles, so to speak."

"What about the nightmares?"

"Well...I could prescribe Phenobarbitone. It's a sedative. It may give her a better night's sleep."

"All right," Les said slowly. "So you think if she takes these tablets, they'll make her better?"

"They should. I'll write out a script when I see her, for the Largactil—three tablets a day—and the Phenobarbitone—two at night—and let's see how she gets on. I'll see her again in a month's time. I'm sure she'll be much better by then." He stood up and walked across to the door to signal that the consultation was over. "And you won't be such a worried fellow either, eh?"

"I hope not. I just want her back to normal. For her sake as well as young Joy's."

"And what about your sake, Mr Bacon?"

"Les."

"Les. You matter in this young family of yours too, you know. Pity Ruth can't have another baby. That'd iron her out. It'd make her as happy as when she gave birth to Joy." He slapped Les on the shoulder.

Les grunted, then shoved his hands in his pockets, and walked out of the surgery.

The late afternoon sun warmed the two women's faces as they walked slowly through the shallows ahead of the girls. They each carried their sandals in their hands, swinging them in time with their footsteps. The water was refreshing around their hot feet. It had been another beautiful spring day; a day that had brought Ruth and Olive to the beach after they'd picked up the girls from school.

"You'd think they'd get sick of building sand castles," Olive laughed as she saw the girls stoop to pick up shells.

"They must've built thousands of them in the last four years," Ruth smiled. "No wonder they almost always win the sand castle competitions."

"It's embarrassing. Did you see young Beverley last Saturday?"

"Beverley Miller?"

"Yes. She cried when the girls beat her at it again." Olive looked back to see if the girls could hear them. "Sore loser."

"She might have been feeling a bit emotional still."

"Because her brother might get called up?"

Ruth nodded. "The whole family's pretty upset about it."

"They're counting their chickens before they hatch, don't you think? They may not even draw his birth date."

"If it was Les who had to go, I just don't know what I'd do. I couldn't bear to be without him—for even a week, much less two years. I'd go bonkers."

"Well, Les is way past twenty..."

"And Jack too."

"Yes..." *Pity. Some Vietnamese bullet might do me a favour and finish him off.*

Ruth looked sideways at Olive, not missing the wistful tone in her half-answer. Both she and Les had noticed Jack's behaviour— probably everyone else in the street had too—and wondered what was going on in Olive's mind. How did she hold her head up when Jack treated her so badly? It was common knowledge that he played around on Olive, plus the fact that he was never at home to help out with the general maintenance around the house. Les had falteringly offered to pitch in from time to time, careful not to embarrass her. At first Olive had been reluctant to accept his help, but there were times when she couldn't refuse, especially when her fence had been falling down, when the spouting leaked, when the back door wouldn't shut. They were problems that were easy for Les to fix, and he was only too happy to do them. Ruth was proud of her husband. Nothing was ever too much trouble for him and, even though the other neighbours were probably taking advantage of him when they too asked for help, he never looked at it that way. He regarded his neighbours as family—the family he never had—and it was nice to be needed.

Now, with Bob Menzies getting the National Service Act passed in Parliament, Ruth supposed Les's help would be needed more around the neighbourhood with the young men of Australia going to Vietnam. She had been terribly afraid that Les would be called up until she realised that, at thirty-four, he was well out of it. She'd tried to imagine what life would be like without him—without his easy-going presence around the house, his warmth, his loyalty, his love. The last twelve years with Les had been her only life. What had been her existence before she'd pushed out of her mind as though it had not happened. As if she'd been born on that day in 1952 when she had sat down at the table at Gladys Taylor's boarding house and seen the shy young carpenter regarding her with his grey eyes.

She often wondered why Les loved her so much—she knew that he did unreservedly—especially when there were so many other women much better looking than she was. Take Olive, for instance. She had a full figure that Ruth knew men found attractive, along with a thick wavy mane—not like her own fine sparse hair—and a pretty face with a straight nose. But Les had never shown even the slightest inclination towards Olive—or any other woman for that matter. He genuinely liked Olive, but that was it as far as Les was concerned. It was obvious he just couldn't see past Ruth and she was confident in her trust of him.

It was beyond Ruth why Jack would cheat on his wife. Since they'd become neighbours, Ruth had grown to like Olive and they had formed a fairly close relationship. It had been tentative at first, with Ruth's near-collapse during that uneasy period when Joy had first started school. With a shudder Ruth tried to push out the memory of how she'd behaved then—like a mad woman. Thank goodness for those tablets the doctor had given her. He'd said they would iron out the wrinkles. They certainly had. She remembered how at first she'd seemed to drift in a fog where nothing could reach her, not even in her dreams. Then gradually she'd cut down on the number of tablets and things had just seemed to be easier, less worrying. The panic that had shattered her had receded, pushed away by the tablets, and the nightmares had left her in peace once more. She'd been able to cope better with Joy's attendance at school, feeling less abandoned and afraid. Les had been supportive, as always, and Olive had been a surprising tower of strength as well. Yes, she had a lot to be grateful for and, not for the first time, she wished the same happiness for Olive.

Though the relationship between the two women was reasonably close, neither confided in the other about what was troubling them most. Not that Ruth had anything troubling her now that the tablets masked what before had come bubbling up from her netherworld.

Ruth had seen the bruises. They appeared regularly in places where Olive assumed they wouldn't be noticed. Ruth imagined how many others existed in places less obvious. And, of course, there were the mental bruises. The ones that would never show unless Olive decided to bring them out for others to see.

"Olive?"

"Yes?"

"Are you...all right?"

"What do you mean?"

"Oh...just...is everything all right?"

"Why shouldn't it be?"

"I...nothing."

She wondered if Olive would ever trust her enough to talk about Jack.

The front-page headline in *The Sun* newspaper screamed the fear that all swimmers felt when reminded of their vulnerability in the waters around Australia:

SHARK ATTACK ON DIVER; GIRL TO AID [2]

"Gee, look at this, Ruth. That poor man. Fancy losing a leg." Olive held out the paper she'd just bought on the way back from taking the girls to school. "Did you see it on the telly last night?"

"No, we missed the news. What happened?"

"He was an experienced diver yet a white pointer got him. A fourteen footer!"

"How horrible."

---

[2] *The Sun*, Monday, 30th November 1964

"Yes, and his girlfriend saved him. Jumped in and pulled him out."

"Where did it happen?"

"Near Port Fairy. It zoned in on him through some seals he was playing with."

Ruth stopped walking. "Port Fairy! That's not far from here."

Olive stared at her. "That's a fair way away, Ruth. Near Warrnambool."

"Yes, but that's still in Victoria. We've become careless, you know."

Olive noticed the old wild look in Ruth's eyes...a look of panic filled them with her head moving from side to side as if looking for a shark in the street. *Oh no*, she thought. *Not again.* She remembered how Joy had been kept out of the water when those sharks had been sighted off their beach four years back. Les had had a hard time convincing Ruth to let the child swim in the bay until Ruth had been taking the tranquilizers for a few months. Even then she had found it difficult to relax when Joy was in the water with Louise.

A gust of wind blew Olive's hair loose from the ever-present combs.

"Damn." She stooped over to pick one of them up from the pavement. "It's hot already. It's going to be ninety before the cool change—if it comes at all."

Ruth didn't comment as she stood staring at the photograph of Henri Bource in the paper. Her pale skin had become even whiter than normal. Olive noticed that she didn't even look hot, whereas Olive could feel the perspiration dripping down the back of her neck from the heavy weight of her hair, and her dress was staining around the armholes.

"How about a swim after lunch?" No answer. "Ruth?"

"Huh?"

"A swim?"

"In those shark infested waters? You must be kidding."

Joy and Louise sat in the shallows at the water's edge, looking longingly at the sparkling bay. They felt a little cooler now that they'd arrived home from school and they could sit in the water, but it would be much better, of course, if they were able to dive in and swim as they had done every other day. Today was different, though. Today Ruth had forbidden her daughter to swim.

"Do you want to lose your leg too? Or your life?" she had screamed at Joy.

"But, Mummy, they've got the shark planes. And we always look out just in case."

"That's not enough."

"But it's so hot," Joy grizzled. "I've been dying to go for a swim."

"I'm sorry, Joy, but the answer's no. It's too dangerous."

Joy glared at her mother resentfully. Why did that man have to lose his leg? Why did her mummy have to see it in the newspaper? Why couldn't her mummy be like other mummies? Why did she have to be so scared something would happen to her? Mrs Fletcher wasn't scared. Mrs Fletcher said Louise could go in the water. Joy's bottom lip trembled as she turned away from her mother. She knew Ruth wouldn't be budged. All she could hope for was that her father would talk her around.

Louise lay in the water beside Joy and rolled there with the small waves lapping over her chest and neck.

"Oh, that feels good."

"Lucky."

"Can't you even lay down in it?"

"No. I wouldn't be able to see the sharks. Anyway, she'd see my hair's wet."

"I'll hold your hair out of the way."

"She'll see me."

"No she won't. She's got her back turned talking to Mummy."

'You reckon?"

"Let's do it quick before she turns around."

Louise held Joy's plaits up over her head while she lay in the water. She kept looking towards Ruth and Olive while Joy sighed gratefully in the water.

"Oh, this is scrummy."

"Didn't I tell you?"

"Is she looking?"

"No. Better get up, though. Just in case."

Joy sat up. "You can go in. Your Mummy didn't say you can't."

"No."

"Why not?"

"I'm not going in without you."

When Les's truck pulled up in the driveway that afternoon, Joy ran outside to greet him.

"Gee, what'd I do to deserve such a big hug?" he grinned as he picked her up and swung her around in a circle.

"Daddy, can I go for a swim?"

"Why, sure, princess. Of course you can. Why shouldn't you?" Les looked somewhat puzzled.

"Thanks, Daddy."

Joy raced around the side of the house and was banging on Louise's front door before Les had taken off his boots and stuck his head under the tap outside the back door.

Ruth stepped quickly out of the door. "Where's Joy?"

"Hey, where's my kiss first?"

"Did you see her?"

"Yeah, sure." Les bent towards Ruth to kiss her, water dripping off his head. "She's gone next door."

"What's she gone there for?"

"For a swim."

"What!" Ruth exploded in fury. "I told her she couldn't."

"Oh, sorry, love. I told her she could."

"What business do you have going against my word?" Her eyes blazed.

"Love...I didn't know you'd said she couldn't. Has she got homework or some chores to do?"

"Didn't you hear about the shark?"

"Oh, yeah. That poor bugger lost his leg."

"There you are then." She turned to follow Joy next door.

"What's that got to do with the price of fish?"

"I can't have her going in the water."

"Why not?"

"A shark'll get her."

Les reached out to stop her. "Ruth, love, you're not going to start that again, are you?"

"Start what?"

"That smothering business. I thought we had that sorted out long ago."

"Don't you care about your daughter?"

"Of course I do."

"Then show it. Anyone'd think you didn't give a hoot about her."

"Love...that's not fair."

"It's not fair that you'd tell her to do the opposite of what I did."

"But I didn't know you'd told her not to."

"Well, why don't you ask in future? Instead of just jumping in and saying what you bloody well like."

Les gritted his teeth. This was a side of Ruth that he'd not seen before, and he didn't like it. She strained against him as he gripped her arm; he could feel her body trembling.

"Have you stopped taking your tablets?" he asked in desperation.

"What do you mean?"

"You seem...upset. Not like your usual self."

"Oh, so you think I'm bonkers, do you? You want to get me committed, do you? Get me out of the way, huh?"

"Ruth, what the bloody hell are you talking about? What's got into you?"

"That's right. Turn it all around. It's my fault now, is it?"

"Jesus, Christ!"

Her face was drained of colour, and the bump on her nose seemed to stick out more than he'd ever noticed before. She looked thinner, too, but her fury gave her the strength of a horse.

Les let go of her arm and stood back to look at her. He jabbed his fingers through his hair. It was then that he noticed Joy and Louise standing at the corner of the house with horrified expressions on their faces. They looked from him to Ruth and back again. Ruth stood with her hands clenched at her sides, chest heaving, lips pressed together in a thin line. Les looked ashamed, saddened, bewildered, all at the same time.

"Daddy?" Joy's voice was small, confused.

"It's all right, princess. Just a misunderstanding."

That night over dinner the table was quiet. Joy could hear the clock ticking loudly. It counted off the hour: one, two, three, four, five, six. Each clang seemed like a hammer pushing her stomach further away from her throat. She shoved her peas around the plate, then squashed them with her fork.

"Eat up," her mother ordered.

She dug her fork under her mashed potato and held it half-way up to her mouth for some moments until she saw the disapproving look Ruth gave her. The potato slid off the fork into her mouth and she left it there, dissolving slowly with her saliva, until it began to fill up her throat. She swallowed. The potato felt dry as it was forced down. Her eyes filled with tears as she regarded her parents. The silence was terrible.

"Please may I be excused?"

"What about your dinner?" Ruth frowned.

"I'm not hungry."

"Neither am I." Les pushed his plate away and stood up. "Let's all go for a walk along the beach. Blow the cobwebs away."

"I don't feel like walking," Ruth said to her plate.

"Come on, love. It'll do you good." He held out his hand to her.

He forced a smile down at Joy, holding his other hand out to her. She took it and they looked at Ruth, each waiting for her to take his offered hand. Some moments passed—long, agonizing moments—before he reached down and took her hand brusquely. She looked up, startled, and saw the frustration in his eyes.

"You've got to try," he snapped.

Joy felt guilty. Very guilty. She knew she'd caused an argument between her parents and, as she lay in bed, she wished that she hadn't kept on about the beach.

It was the first time she'd ever heard her parents argue. It gave her a scary feeling in her stomach, like butterflies flapping their wings in there and trying to get out. Maybe the butterflies had something to do with the tears that came up and wet her pillow. She knew that other parents had arguments—Louise had told her about her mother and father—and she'd always felt rather special that her own parents never did. They really loved each other. You could tell. They were always kissing and hugging, which was something that Louise's parents never did.

But this time the old sickness had come back to her mummy, like it had when she first took Joy to school. When her mummy made her feel awful, simply awful, in front of the whole school. That nasty Robert still reminded her of it at times in the playground. The other kids laughed, too, and called her names. Louise had stuck up for her and kicked Robert in the shins only last week when he teased Joy and said that her mummy was a loony. Well, her mummy wasn't crazy. She just got a bit funny at times. Joy wished she wasn't like that though. It made her feel horrible. Ashamed of her mummy.

She thought of her daddy's face when she and Louise had walked up the driveway and seen her parents arguing. He looked so hurt and mixed-up. Why did her mummy hurt her daddy? She yelled at him. It wasn't fair. He wouldn't hurt a flea. And why did her mummy get so silly about the water? Her daddy would protect her. Nothing could get her then.

Maybe Mummy wouldn't be so naughty tomorrow after she'd had a good sleep. Then everything would be all right again. Daddy would fix it. He could fix anything.

Chapter 22

"Why did you stop?"

"I didn't think I needed them anymore."

"But you know what the doctor said. To keep on..."

"Yes, but he said if I felt better I could wean myself off them."

"I don't remember him saying that."

"Well, he did. You've just forgotten."

Les paced up and down the bedroom, his fingers constantly combing through his hair.

"Aren't you coming to bed?" Ruth was feeling sleepy. The tablets were doing their work.

"Yeah."

He sat down on the edge of the bed, his body sagging with the mattress. That's just how he felt: like a sagging lump of crushed matter—the spring all gone out of it.

He looked at her lying back on the pillows. She had a bit more colour in her face now and he could see that she was struggling to keep her eyes open. He wondered if he could take one of her tablets...if he'd get a better sleep. How lucky she was to be able to push it all away. Pretend it didn't happen.

"Ruth?"

"Umm?"

"I want you to promise me something."

"Umm."

"You'll always take your tablets."

"Umm."

"All right?" Her breathing was even as she settled into sleep. "Because if you don't, I think you really will go bonkers," he mumbled.

Louise and Joy sat on the front steps of Louise's house. Their voices were subdued as they threaded a daisy chain. Their movements were mechanical, therapeutic.

"Did she say you could swim again?"

"Not really, but Daddy said I could."

"Will she go crook?"

"I don't know. Daddy'll fix it, though."

"Are you allowed to go in today?" Louise swiped at a fly. "It's so hot."

"I think so."

"What'll you do? Ask him?"

"All right. You want to come with me?"

Louise looked over the fence at Joy's house. All was quiet.

"Oh, I don't know."

"She's still asleep."

"All right."

They draped their daisy chain over the front door knob and walked over to Joy's house, making sure not to make any noise as they passed Ruth and Les's bedroom. Les was reading the paper as he sat on the back doorstep sipping on a cup of tea.

"What are you two up to?"

"Nothing much. We just wanted to know if we can go for a swim," Joy said insinuating herself under his arm.

"Isn't it a bit early?" He looked at his watch. "You've only just had your lunch. You'll get a cramp."

"Later then?"

Les opened his mouth to reply when Joy gave a sudden cry of pain and clutched her left elbow.

"What?"

"My arm!"

"What did you do to it?"

"Nothing." Tears sprang to her eyes as she rocked her arm back and forth. "Oh, it hurts."

Les prised her right hand away from the elbow and tried to straighten the arm. "Does this hurt?"

Joy screamed in pain.

"What's wrong with her, Mr Bacon?" Louise looked up at him.

"I don't know, little one." He picked Joy up in his arms and hugged her. "Can't see any blood. You didn't get a bite, did you?"

Joy shook her head violently, her tears splashing onto Les's arms.

"How long's it been like this?" he asked Louise.

"Just now. She was all right before."

"Doesn't make sense," he muttered. "Come on, we'll go inside and put some ice on it. See if that helps."

They went inside and Les gently put Joy down on one of the kitchen chairs.

"Can I help, Mr Bacon?" Louise tugged at his arm.

"Tell you what. You look after Joy—that's a very important job— while I get the ice out."

Louise pulled up a chair beside Joy, putting her arms around her and patting her back. Les smiled down at the imitation of an adult's concern. He took an ice cube tray from the freezer and pulled the tray's metal handle back to break the cubes free. He shook them into a clean tea towel and wrapped them up into a cold bundle that he placed around Joy's elbow.

"Does that feel better?"

"A bit," Joy sniffed between teary short breaths.

"What're you doing?" Ruth stood in the doorway yawning.

"Joy's hurt her arm," Louise said, patting Joy on the back again.

"How?" Ruth was wide-awake now. She took in the ice pack and the distressed look on Joy's face, and went to her side.

"She didn't fall over or anything. I can't see anything wrong with it, either." Les pushed his fingers through his hair.

"Let me see." Ruth gingerly took the ice pack away from Joy's arm and examined the elbow. She looked into Joy's eyes as she prodded. "Does this hurt?"

"Ouch!"

"Sorry, sweetheart. Can you put your arm out straight like this?"

"No!" Joy clutched her elbow close to her body.

"All right. I think we'd better take you to see Doctor Armstrong."

"No...he'll give me a needle."

"Princess," Les dropped to his knees beside her. "He probably won't. But if he does, I'll be right there with you."

"Promise?"

"Promise."

"I can't see anything wrong with the arm, Ruth, but I'll order an X-ray to make sure. There's no sign of injury, or a bite, and she's not got a temperature," Doctor Armstrong said as he took a thermometer from Joy's mouth and held it up.

"Are you going to give me a needle?" Joy looked at the doctor, fear showing plainly in her eyes.

"Not unless you want me to, young lady."

"Oh," she sagged in relief.

"See? I told you," Les laughed.

The doctor turned to Ruth. "She's not had rheumatic fever, so I think we're pretty safe there. I'm more inclined to think it's just growing pains, but it's unusual to suffer them during daylight hours. They mostly occur at night. I suspect she's about to have a growing spurt."

"So, is there anything we can do for the pain?"

"A bit of gentle massage and exercise of the arm could help relieve it."

"My arm's not broken, Doctor Armstrong?" Joy asked.

"No, my girl. Not broken. We're going to take an X-ray of it, though, just to see what's going on."

"Will it hurt?"

"Not a bit. It's just like taking a photograph."

Over the next few days, Joy suffered recurring pain in the elbow at odd times and then, just as suddenly as it had come, the pain disappeared. The X-rays showed very healthy bones, much to the relief of Ruth and Les, and the doctor confirmed his diagnosis of growing pains.

Ruth settled back into a calmer state once she had resumed the tablets, taking the dosage prescribed, and the argument was forgiven, if not forgotten, by all three of them.

The weather continued hot and humid and both families—except for Jack—spent most of their free time in the waters of the bay. The girls were now strong swimmers and joined their parents in the deeper water as well as jumping off the end of the jetty. Despite the fact that they made new friends at school, Joy and Louise stuck almost exclusively together, preferring each other's company to that of any other child. Their heads were always bent close, sharing secrets and planning activities. They kept nothing from each other, confiding the troubles of their families, offering childish advice and comfort.

One afternoon, when they had arrived home hot from school, and headed for the beach with their mothers, Joy came up from holding her breath under water.

"I just had the strangest feeling."

"What?"

"Like there was someone else beside me."

"Well, I am," Louise responded.

"No, I mean someone else. Under the water."

"What...a shark?"

"No. A person."

"Did you see them?"

"No. I just...felt them."

"What do you mean?"

"I don't know. When I opened my eyes underwater, there was no one there."

The pain in Joy's stomach had taken her by surprise. It pulled her from a deep sleep where she had visited someone who was her and yet not her. Sometimes she woke up in the mornings with a strange feeling about herself. Almost like she was two people. She would talk to Louise about it, ask her if she ever had dreams like that, but Louise didn't really understand what she was trying to say. It didn't matter anyway. They were only dreams.

The pain was right under her belly button. Her eyes fluttered open and she turned over to return to sleep, but the pain gradually increased and shifted over to her right side. She pulled her knees up to relieve the pain but it wouldn't go away. The clock ticked on the bedside table and she held her breath for thirty ticks to see if the pain would go when she started to breathe again. The curtains cast shadows over her desk in the dim early morning light. *Blue Eyes* sat on the top of it, looking down at her. A groan escaped her lips as she sat up and swung her legs over the side of the bed.

It seemed a long way to the door of her room. She turned the knob, bent over double, and made her way over to Ruth and Les's room. She could hear the sound of snoring through the closed door. It was then that she threw up.

Three hours later, Joy was back in her bed, drifting off to sleep. An anxious Louise sat beside her, holding *Blue Eyes* in her lap.

"Are you going to be all right now?" Louise whispered.

Joy opened her eyes again. "Yes."

"Does it still hurt?"

"No."

"Come on, Louie," Olive murmured. "Let her sleep."

They left the room as Joy's eyes closed again and her breathing became even in sleep. Les led them down to the kitchen where Ruth was making a cup of tea.

"What'd Doctor Armstrong say?" Olive asked.

"He was a bit puzzled," Les replied. "He reckoned at first it was probably appendicitis—which is what we'd thought—but she's got no fever, and never had the pain before."

"And the fact that it went away again," Ruth chipped in, "made him think it was a false alarm, or something. Said to keep an eye on it."

"Yeah. We're to race her back in to him if it happens again. Just in case it is her appendix."

"She's as good as gold now, though. Just a bit tired, eh?" Olive accepted the cup of tea that Ruth handed her.

"It's not growing pains again, is it?" Louise asked.

"No, love. Just a belly ache, I reckon," Les laughed.

"She's fine now, Mr Schwartz," the doctor assured him. "The operation was just a simple appendectomy. She'll be back at school in no time."

Gunter sank back onto the waiting room chair. The disinfectant smell reminded him of the last time he'd been there...when Hannah had given up her struggle for life. No, it wasn't going to happen again...he still had his Ursula. But it would be better to leave such painful reminders behind; give his daughter more opportunities. He calculated again how long it would be before they could move to Melbourne or Sydney. *Two more years at the most.*

Les turned off the television set and stood for a moment looking at the floor. Then he went outside to join Ruth who had been taking washing off the clothesline.

"Love?"

"Yes?" she half-turned towards him as she was bent over taking weeds out of the garden where she had placed the clothes-basket.

"There was something on the news." He hesitated, searching for the right words.

"What?"

"About some kids. In Adelaide."

"And?"

"They've disappeared."

Ruth's hand stopped in mid air, a bunch of weeds in her grasp. He saw them crush and her knuckles whiten until green fluid ran out from between her fingers. Her back was to him. It stiffened.

"Ruth?"

Her body began to tremble as he approached and lifted her up at the elbow to a standing position. Her fingers were still clenched tight. He prised them open and the weeds fell at her feet.

"It's all right, love. They'll find them."

"Adelaide?" Her voice was harsh.

"Yeah. A long way from here."

"How?"

"They were at the beach..." He could have bitten his tongue off as he said it. *Jesus!* "But..."

Ruth turned abruptly. "Where's Joy?"

"Drawing pictures at her desk."

"I must..." she gasped, trying to break free from his arms that had gone around her shoulders.

"Now listen, Ruth. Don't start that again."

Her head snapped back towards him, her eyes wild.

"You've got to control yourself. This is not happening to us."

She said nothing, searching his eyes with hers, trying to find something there that would reassure her.

"Don't do this to Joy again. I don't care how you do it, but you have to face this like the rest of us."

"Who?" she gasped.

"The rest of us poor bloody sods who're scared shitless and glad it's not our kids," he grated out. "Now you get a grip on yourself, take a couple of tablets, but don't for Christ's sake go all stupid over Joy again."

The hurt in her eyes drove a hammer into his gut.

"She's my daughter too, you know. I love her just as much as you do. But I'm sure as hell not going to drive her away from me by smothering her."

"Is that what I'm doing?" Tears welled in her eyes.

The hesitation was momentary.

"Yeah."

The news that weekend had most of Australia in its grip. The disappearance of Jane, Arnna and Grant Beaumont in Adelaide renewed the fear in the hearts of every parent, reminding them of the tragedy of the Graeme Thorne kidnapping six years before. It was also an event that had Les scrutinizing every newspaper he could lay his hands on, afraid that the terrier in the name of George Chambers would surface again to snap at Les's heels.

He was relieved to see only a small reference to the Schwartz twin's disappearance. After all, he reasoned, it was more than ten years since they'd made their escape from Perth and he hoped the case was shut and forgotten as far as the police were concerned. Maybe Chambers was dead, he thought guiltily, knowing that it was a wish he shouldn't entertain.

What worried Les equally was whether Ruth would act up again, as she had when the Thorne boy disappeared. He wondered how best to get her over the insecurity he knew she already felt. He considered getting her to take double the dosage of her tablets in the hope that they would dope her up enough so that she wouldn't be quite so aware. But would she co-operate?

Les knew the relationship between Ruth and Joy had been deteriorating slowly ever since they moved to Chelsea and Joy had started school. Anything that had Joy out of the house and away from Ruth's side started her inner demons screaming for the child. That was when she would behave so frantically—like a mad woman—and it would drive that wedge between her and Joy just a little bit further. It saddened him to see that happen, and it seemed there was little he could do about it, other than make up excuses for Ruth. But he was running out of them...and he knew Joy didn't believe him.

All too often, Joy would opt to spend time in Les's workshop in the garage, passing him nails, helping him sand furniture, brushing the sawdust off the floor, hanging up his tools...anything rather than spend the time she used to with Ruth. He was aware that Ruth was bewildered by the rejection—and hurt. Very rarely did Joy embroider while Ruth sewed, chat for hours as they both bent over fabric, their hands busily occupied with needles and thread. Sometimes Joy would say she had homework to do, when invited to spend time in the sewing room, and would disappear into her room and sit at her desk for hours.

On the last day of January, Jim Beaumont made an appeal on national television for the return of his three children. The scene was almost a replay of Bazil Thorne's appeal. The same desperation, the same anguish, the same terror, of a wretched parent already grieving the loss of a child.

The first weeks of February drifted past Ruth as if she were living in a fog. Protected by an increased dosage of Largactil during the day, as well as Phenobarbitone for the night, Ruth slept away most of the Beaumont tragedy. Les didn't care that his wife was out of their family life for those weeks, as long as she coped in her own way without making things worse between her and Joy.

He postponed a job on a building site he was about to start, but when Olive heard of it she insisted that he go back to work and allow her to sit with Ruth while he was out. She took Joy to school with Louise, and Ruth was only vaguely aware that anyone had left the house. A few anxious phone calls from Pat saw her and Jim arrive on the doorstep to help. No one questioned Les's decision to increase the dosage of Ruth's tablets—they all knew of her obsessive behaviour and were frightened by it. Not even Ruth questioned it. Les's insistence had her cave in very easily. After all, it was a way of blocking out the panic she'd been feeling.

When Ruth was awake, Les would put her in front of the television set while he and Joy busied themselves with the housework. Ruth's protests were slow, half-hearted, drugged, and they relinquished their hold upon her lips as her eyes drooped gradually and her head fell back on the cushions. She would see the first few minutes of one film and wake up at the end of another. Time had no meaning for her. The days ticked past until she woke to the new decimal currency and the Beaumonts' suffering was old news.

Olive stood in the back yard with the hose, giving the tomatoes and lettuce a good soaking. She looked up at the fence when she heard the back door slam shut at Ruth's house. *That'll be Les coming out to water his vegies,* she thought. She opened her mouth to call out, then thought better of it. *Poor bugger. He's running around in circles with Ruth out of action.* She knew it really wasn't Ruth's fault. She couldn't help being the way she was. *By God, if I had a husband like Les, I'd make damned sure I kept him happy.* No hysterics for her. She'd be too busy making love with him, having a string of kids, and making him laugh. Olive supposed he hadn't laughed much over the past few weeks...months.

Not that Olive had done much of that herself lately, what with Jack and his shenanigans. His behaviour had worsened, if anything, and Olive had taken to sleeping in the spare room the nights he came home. When he did come home, it was usually late and he was on the way to being drunk, if not totally. Thank goodness he hardly seemed to notice her absence from the bedroom. In the mornings he was too busy nursing a hangover to worry her overmuch, and then he would be off to work. She assumed his nights with the floozie were keeping him happy, if it was possible to make him happy.

Thank goodness for her diaphragm. When things had started to go wrong between them—and that was pretty soon after the honeymoon when she discovered she was pregnant—she had made a conscious decision not to have any more children by him. He never found out that she was using the diaphragm. She would just shrug her shoulders and say that she couldn't have any more children. And he believed her. Not that he cared about children anyway.

She moved over to turn the tap off when Les stuck his head over the fence.

"How yer going?"

"All right."

"Pretty dry."

"Yes."

"You want me to run the mower over?"

"Oh, Les, you've got enough on your plate without worrying about my lawn."

"Only take a couple of minutes."

"No. Really. I can do it."

"Shouldn't have to."

"You know how it is," she said, avoiding his eyes.

"Yeah. Bloody crime."

"There's a lot worse off than me."

"You going to do anything about it?"

"How can I? Where would I go?"

"Yeah. It's a bugger, that."

Olive made for the back door and then turned back to Les who still hung on the fence.

"How's Ruth now?"

"About the same."

She hesitated. "It's none of my business, but…"

"What?"

"Are you going to knock the pills off? I mean, she can't stay drugged up like that forever. She'll have to come out of it some-time."

"Yeah, I know."

Chapter 24

One cold winter's day Les had been on a job out at Flinders and was returning home via Main Ridge and Red Hill. The roads were wooded with eucalypts and pines; the fields were a brilliant green in the weak, late afternoon light. Everything looked washed and fresh after heavy rain and wind the night before. Some of the older trees had lost their weaker limbs in the storm. They either jutted out at strange angles, still hanging from the thick trunks, or lay discarded on top of pine needles and rotting leaves on the soft damp ground. The perfume of the trees and undergrowth was strong as he drove slowly along Shands Road with his right elbow stuck out of the open window. He was thinking about how peaceful the area was, how beautiful, how good for the soul it was, and how he'd like to bring Ruth and Joy there for a picnic one summer day. Yes, he must do that…bring them there. They would lie on a rug on the forest floor and look up at the treetops above them. They'd be so full of good food that they'd feel lazy and doze off for a while, breathing in that pure, perfumed air. Then they'd wake up and have a nice cup of hot tea from the thermos they'd packed. Maybe read a bit, cuddle a bit, eat a bit more, and go for a walk. They'd put everything back into the truck and finally drive back home. It'd be a good day. A happy day.

As the road wound around the side of the ridge, Les changed gears constantly, the truck climbing and descending as it passed clumps of trees and fields. An imposing, two storey white building, set well back on the slope of a hill, came into view on Les's left. It stood in extensive gardens, partly surrounded by a hedge. A low brick wall followed the property's perimeter. He noticed that the grounds and building had a decayed look about them, that the wall needed repairing, and that the building could do with a coat of paint. Driving past the main gate, a movement caught his eye. A man lay on the ground with something over him. It looked like the branch of a tree. He'd raised his arm as the noise of the truck's motor had reached his ears.

Les pulled over, turned off the motor, and was out of the truck and running up the driveway, reaching the man's side within a few moments.

"You all right, mate?" he asked the poor fellow who groaned under the weight of a large branch.

"Can't…get out…from under…," the man grunted.

"It's a big bugger," Les frowned, walking around it. "Are you hurt?"

"Don't know…my back…"

"You lie there, mate." Les looked up at the building. "I'll get some help."

"Only women…not much…"

"What d'you mean…only women?"

"Nuns…only nuns."

"Shit!"

"Yeah," the man agreed.

Les scratched at his head. "Is there a doctor around here anywhere?"

Les could see sweat on the man's forehead as he shook his head.

"Well, the nuns'll have to do. Stay here," he said, then grinned at the ridiculous statement. "Can't go far, can you?"

He took off at a run along the driveway and banged on the solid front door. There was a bell hanging to the side of it and he yanked on it as hard as he could. His ears strained for the sound of footsteps, but he could hear nothing, so he alternately yanked on the bell and pounded on the door.

"Can I help you?"

The soft, clear voice came from behind him and he whirled around.

"Jesus," he exclaimed, as he took in the figure in front of him.

The face of an elderly woman, possibly in her seventies, looked back at him from beneath a black veil, the white folds of her wimple draping around her neck, cheeks and chin. Her long black habit swept around her body, and her rosary made a soft clinking sound as she moved.

"Can I help you?" she repeated.

"Oh, yeah," Les recovered himself. "There's a bloke over there in the garden. He's in a bit of trouble."

"You mean Mr Middleton?"

"Who?"

"Mr Middleton. Anthony Middleton," the nun said. "Our handyman?"

"I don't know his name, Miss…?"

"Sister Margaret Mary," she smiled at him. "And you are?"

"Les. Les Bacon." He looked over his shoulder, back where the injured man lay. "Look, this bloke over there…"

"Mr Middleton."

"Yeah, Middleton. He's had an accident. A branch's fallen on him."

"Oh, Father in heaven," Sister Margaret Mary exclaimed. "Where is he?"

"Over here, Miss. I'll show you."

They both hurried through the garden to where Anthony Middleton lay, with Les leading the way and the elderly nun seeming to float along the grass behind him.

Before long, two more nuns joined them, tut-tutting over the unfortunate Middleton. Les realised that shifting the weight of the branch was beyond the capabilities of himself and the three women combined. He decided to back the truck into the driveway and tied a length of rope around the branch and towed it off the body of the man, with the nuns guiding it. Afraid to move Middleton, the nuns insisted he stay where he was while one of them rang for the local doctor.

They waited until the doctor arrived who, after a careful examination, proclaimed Anthony Middleton as an extremely fortunate man in that he would escape with mere bruising from the tree branch.

"Thanks to Mr Bacon," smiled Sister Margaret Mary. "What a godsend he was. And such a quick thinker too!"

"Well, if there's nothing else I can do..." Les shuffled his feet, embarrassed.

Sister Margaret Mary turned to Les. "Can we offer you a cup of tea, Mr Bacon?"

"No, thanks. I'll be on my way. The wife'll wonder where I am."

"Would you like to ring her so that she won't worry?"

"Yeah, thanks. That'd be good."

Les followed Sister Margaret Mary into the old building, and looked curiously around him.

"Old building this," he commented.

"Yes, it was built in the late 1800s. A wealthy farmer owned it but he sold it when his wife died. Terrible thing. Suicide, I think, or so the story goes."

"What are you ladies doing here?" Les asked as Sister Margaret Mary led the way along a dark corridor through to a spacious kitchen.

She indicated a telephone on a long bench near an open fire. "We spend our lives in prayer and contemplation, mostly in solitude and silence."

"What for?"

She smiled at his naiveté. "Because we have chosen this type of life, in service to God."

"Oh," he said, not understanding.

"You're not a religious man, Mr Bacon?"

"Les."

"Les."

"No. Never got around to it," he mumbled awkwardly.

"Well, religious or not, you're a Christian man, Les Bacon."

Sister Margaret Mary's face creased into one of the most beautiful smiles Les had ever seen. It started at the corners of her mouth as they turned upwards and travelled up to pale blue eyes that lit up with the kindliest of expressions as she regarded him. He suddenly thought that she would be a nice person to be held by—like the mother he never had—that she'd be soft and warm and comforting. He had to resist the impulse to touch her face; the folds of her wimple seemed to dissolve into the folds and creases of her old face. He wondered which would be the softest—the wimple or the skin.

"Yeah, well..." He scratched his head.

"Go on, Les Bacon. Ring your wife and I won't embarrass you anymore."

Sister Margaret Mary turned to the wood stove where a large kettle was spouting steam up into the chimney. She opened a door in the stove and pushed some small pieces of wood into the fire, nudging them into place with a blackened poker. Then she took a canister down from the mantelpiece and spooned tea leaves into a waiting teapot. Taking a thick potholder, she gripped the hot metal handle of the kettle and poured the boiling water into the teapot. Les watched her practised movements as he waited for Ruth to pick up the telephone at the other end.

"Hello, love...Just got held up...Yeah, be home in about an hour...no, no problem." Sister Margaret Mary held up a milk jug and Les nodded. "Tell you about it when I get home."

Les spent the next half an hour chatting with the elderly nun as they sipped their strong, hot tea. He learned that Anthony Middleton was a parishioner who helped out around the buildings and grounds whenever he could, although his expertise was more in a gardening capacity. Les could see, just in the kitchen alone, that a lot of maintenance work needed doing, not least of all on the table at which they sat. It wobbled alarmingly and, taking a quick look underneath, he saw that one of the legs had broken and been bound up with thick tape. As his eyes travelled around the room, he noticed an alignment problem with one of the windows, and a number of chairs were stacked up in a corner in varying states of disrepair.

"I could take those chairs home with me," he nodded in the direction of the stack. "Fix 'em up a bit. You'd have more than these three left to sit on then."

"Oh, Mr Bacon, we couldn't trouble you with…"

"No trouble. I'll be passing here every day for the next week or so, depending on how long the job I'm on takes."

"We can't afford…"

"No. No charge."

"You really are a Christian man," she smiled.

Over the following couple of weeks, Les fell into the habit of dropping in to see Sister Margaret Mary and the other nuns at St Agatha's Convent. He repaired the chairs and the kitchen table, and systematically went through the rest of the building doing what he could to make life a little easier for the women. Although their religious purpose made him slightly uneasy, he was grateful that they didn't push their beliefs upon him. Each nun had her own special fascination for him: Sister Dominique made delicious fruit scones that she always produced fresh from a warm tray no matter what time of the day he called in; Sister Francis Mary was a green-fingered wonder who grew every vegetable imaginable in the garden she tended, and gave Les some very sage advice on the growing of his own vegie patch; the Reverend Mother never said much, but she would take his hand and pat it with her own frail hand—the skin paper-thin, transparent and velvet soft—and her eyes would express the gratitude she—they—all felt. Les suspected that she was slightly demented and, for that reason, it seemed to fall upon Sister Margaret Mary to make most of the decisions around the convent.

But Les's very favourite was Sister Margaret Mary—or, 'Maggie' as he affectionately called her in his head—during the subsequent months that expanded into two years. Her pale blue eyes looked into his with a penetrating understanding, and he found himself confiding in her, the words tripping out of his mouth of their own accord. She drew out his concerns about Ruth, the growing rift between Joy and her mother, his growing helplessness with Ruth's state of mind. Sister Margaret Mary never had the solution to his problems, but she absorbed them and handed them back to him seemingly washed and scrubbed and smaller than he'd originally thought they were. Les would return home to Ruth and Joy, calm

and at peace with the world. He figured that Ruth had her tablets...and he had Sister Margaret Mary.

Chapter 25

The elderly couple looked at him with disgust. The wife moved a little closer to her husband as they turned their heads away to avoid the alcohol fumes.

"Waddayer looking at?" Jack mumbled before his head drooped again onto his chest.

The woman stood up, and she and her husband moved to another seat further down the carriage.

"I don't know what the world's coming to these days," she complained.

The other passengers tut-tutted in sympathy, looking with raised eyebrows at the very drunk man who lolled on the seat.

Each time the train rattled to a stop, Jack raised his head up long enough for him to read the station name and then it dropped back down again. His mumblings were almost unintelligible:...*stupid bitch...doesn't know what's good for her...never satisfied...work work work...I'll fix 'er...*

The train came to a stop again and, just as it moved on, his head raised slowly. The station name raced past his bleary eyes as a smudge.

"Was it Chelsea?" he called over to a young man a few seats away.

The young man shook his head. "Edithvale," he said abruptly.

Jack peered at his watch, trying to focus with the rocking movements of the train. He tapped at the watch and put his ear to it. He looked up.

"What's the time?" he asked the young man.

Jack was ignored as the man buried his head in a newspaper.

"I said...what's the time? You there! Are you deaf? I said, what's the time?"

"A quarter to eleven," the young man grated out, ruffling the pages of his paper. He stood up and moved closer to the elderly couple.

"Humph. Unfriendly bunch," Jack muttered.

The train lurched to a halt at Chelsea. The passengers saw that Jack's head was now firmly down on his chest and he was blowing bubbles as he breathed. They looked at each other, anxious that he would become more belligerent if he missed his station.

"Chelsea," the young man called out.

No response.

"I say, we've stopped at Chelsea."

The young man stood up and went over to Jack. He shook him by the shoulder. Jack's head wobbled to an upright position.

"Huh?"

"Chelsea. Didn't you want to get off here?"

"Oh, quite right. Quite right." He spoke in a mock English accent and, thinking himself funny, chuckled heartily.

He pulled himself up off the seat and staggered to the door that the young man had pulled open. The station attendant whistled and the train started to move. The young man supported Jack's arm as he shoved him out of the door and Jack landed in an untidy heap in a puddle on the platform. He looked up at the face of the man staring back at him through the window of the train carriage. Rain made the face look distorted as water trickled down the glass. A few moments later, the train was just a smudge in his vision as it disappeared along the tracks in the darkness.

"Sorry, mate. Didn't see you getting off." The station attendant helped Jack up. "You all right?"

"What?"

"Are you hurt?"

Jack swayed on his feet, looking in bewilderment at the station attendant.

"Oh, it's you, Mr Fletcher. I didn't recognise you."

"Yep, that's me all right."

He stumbled along the platform and made his way down the ramp to where he would cross over the tracks. The station attendant disappeared back inside the station to warm his hands against the heater. Jack bumped into the fence and swung around, fists up, ready to fight. Seeing no one there, he turned and started to cross the tracks. He fumbled in a pocket for his comb and, not finding it, stopped and looked around.

"Where'd I put the bloody thing?"

He peered down at the tracks. Something red was sticking out from one of the rails.

"Ah!" he bent down to pick it up.

Discarding a wrapper from a Cherry Ripe bar, he bent down to look at another item between the tracks. The rain was heavier now, and the longer hair that he usually combed over his balding patch fell forward over his eyes. He swiped at it before feeling around in his pockets again for the comb. Finding it at last, he sagged down on his knees, his body heavy under his soaked overcoat. He belched, smelling and tasting again the red wine and overlarge T-bone steak he had had for dinner. He swallowed as the remnants of it rose to his throat, burning his oesophagus.

Jack thought of his secretary, Carmel, as she had twirled her glass seductively in front of him over the dinner table. She had licked her brightly painted lips and looked at him over the rim as she sipped the wine. The promise in her eyes had excited him, as it always did. Later, they had returned to the office for a bit of *slap and tickle*, as she called it, before he left her to catch his train. In his confused state, he thought Carmel would be at home waiting for him and half-rose to go and meet her there.

The comb was still in his hand and he reached up to tidy his hair. Then he saw the full moon. It was huge, he thought, blinking at it through the rain—just like a big shiny light. It glared at him as it drifted towards him and he sat back on the track to watch the phenomenon, marvelling at how close it was.

He heard a roaring noise and the track started to vibrate under him. It was a pleasant sensation. Almost sensual. His whole body started to vibrate and the roaring filled his ears before the moon struck him.

The train driver rubbed his hands over his eyes. It had been a long day and he was looking forward to getting home. Then he saw the man sitting on the track in the rain. Too late, he applied the brakes. The sound of metal screeching on metal filled the air. The few passengers heard it as they were thrown from their seats, and wondered at the abrupt stop only yards from the station.

The mess splattered on the tracks was all that was left of Jack Fletcher. The face was crushed, but where the top of his head had come off, the bald patch could be plainly seen as the rain washed it free of hair. His right hand still held the red comb.

Les paced up and down Olive's lounge room, a glass of brandy in his hand. It had been a tough night—having offered to identify the body at the morgue—and now he was back to help out if he could. He looked at the ruby dress ring that had always been on Jack's right hand and that now rested on the coffee table. The stone glowed in the light of a lamp that someone had switched on. He'd never liked the ring. It had always seemed ostentatious...threatening. Now it looked harmless, almost beautiful.

The police had finally gone, and Olive had persuaded Louise to go back to bed after reassuring her that what had woken her up could be left until the morning. He could hear Olive talking faintly to Jack's parents on the phone in the kitchen. He stopped in front of Olive and Jack's wedding photo. They'd been a handsome couple—Jack with his hair parted neatly on one side and wearing a dark tuxedo with satin lapels, and a beautiful Olive with her thick wavy hair pinned up at the sides and wearing a long satin gown. As Les looked at the couple, his eyes lingered on her full breasts that pushed at the tight-fitting material of her gown. He wondered why Jack had strayed from such a pretty bride.

"Funny how things change," Olive breathed huskily beside him, making him start.

"Yeah." He tossed down the rest of his brandy.

He turned to her, expecting anything but the seemingly controlled woman in front of him.

"You all right?"

She nodded, sipping at her own drink.

"Is there anyone else you should call to come over? Your sister?"

"No. Sydney's too far away, and she couldn't do anything anyway."

"I could wake Ruth up?"

"No, Les," she laughed softly, her tone velvety. "You'll do."

He stepped back involuntarily. Her eyes were dark, shaded by the thick curtain of hair that rippled around her face, so that he couldn't quite read the expression in them. Her mouth trembled and he wasn't sure if she was about to laugh or cry. His heart began to thud in his chest and the palms of his hands suddenly felt wet.

"A minister...?"

"Les, I'm all right."

"Are you going to be able to sleep?" He tried to turn away from her, but it was as if a magnet were pulling him back. "Should I get a doctor?"

"No, but I could do with a shoulder to cry on."

As she looked up at him, he noticed how her bottom lip seemed more full than usual. Her whole mouth looked different. He saw her eyes move to his mouth and linger there.

"I..." His tongue felt like sandpaper.

"Yes?" she whispered. Her eyes touched him, building a bridge between what separated them.

"I'd better go...if there's nothing else...?"

Suddenly her eyes filled with tears. They spilled onto her cheeks and ran tracks down to her mouth. She looked at him in mute appeal and his arms went around her. She melted into him—soft, warm, trembling—and his eyes shut as the perfume of her hair filled his nostrils. They stayed there, hardly moving, each acutely conscious of the other. The only sound was their breathing and the steady downpour of the rain and the overflow of the spouting outside the window. Her dark red velvet dressing gown provoked his fingers as he stroked her back to comfort her. The fabric seemed to accentuate the curves of her body, and there was a heat that radiated through it that set his pulse racing. He was confused as his mind screamed at him: *What are you doing?*

Her arms went around him. She had stopped crying and her upturned face looked flushed and radiant. Her lips fascinated him; he wondered how they'd feel if he touched them...with his own. His head bent to her. He could feel her breath on his face. Their lips brushed each other, so softly that the sensation was no more than a mere feather's touch, and yet it radiated throughout his body. *No!* His head jerked back, his sharp intake of breath breaking the spell. He looked down at her closed eyes, her lips parted, as her weight was taken up by his arms.

"Olive...I can't..."

Her eyes snapped open and she looked at him, hurt showing plainly in her eyes.

"Ruth..." he whispered, sweat forming in his armpits. It felt cold as he released her.

She turned away. He could see that her breathing was as laboured as his own. *How did we get into this? What sort of monster am I?*

"I..."

"Don't say anything."

"I'm sorry. What with Jack..." he said to her back.

"Jack?" She turned to face him.

"Yeah. You must be feeling pretty bloody awful."

"Relieved," she whispered. "Relieved."

Les stood with his hand caught in his hair.

"Do you hear me?" Her voice was louder now. "Relieved."

He lowered his hand slowly, deliberately, and rammed it into his pocket.

"Are you shocked?" she taunted.

"No."

"Yes, you are. I can see it in your face: the grieving widow isn't so sad after all." Her eyes became hard. "There's nothing to grieve. He was a bastard. I'm glad he's gone. He's done me a favour."

She started to laugh, quietly at first, then rising hysterically. Les stood watching her helplessly, uncertain what to do. He looked in the direction of Louise's room, fearful that Olive would wake her.

"Come on..."

He put his hand out to her in appeal, but she continued to laugh until the laughing changed to a mute shuddering of her body, with tears pouring down her face. *What do they do in the pictures? Slap their face to stop it?* He couldn't bring himself to strike her. He'd never hit a female in his life and he wasn't about to do it now. She had sunk onto the couch and he sat down beside her, taking her hand and patting it ineffectually.

"I can get you some of Ruth's tablets, to calm you down?"

"Ruth's tablets? Oh, that's rich, that is."

She was laughing even harder now, but still barely a sound escaped her lips as she held her stomach, the muscles protesting against the constant lurching.

"Ruth's tablets," she mouthed, falling back in mirthful abandon against Les.

His arms went instinctively around her to catch her and she suddenly stopped laughing. An abrupt shock shafted through his body and their mouths fused violently, hungrily, until their reason was lost.

The sky opened and heaved its contents upon the bay, the land, and the houses. It washed the dirt from the roads, the dust from the plants, the blood from the tracks. And it drummed its primitive beat upon the tin roof of Olive's house. The rain created a barrier of sound that separated them from their responsibilities, their fears and their sin. It engulfed them in the taste, the smell, the touch of each other, and they floated there.

He let himself out of the front door and stood in the rain. It pierced his skin with stinging needles that punished, chastised, and bit into his swollen lips. The wind slashed at his clothes, his body, and propelled him towards the beach. He staggered to the water's edge and sank to his knees.

Chapter 26   Perth to Melbourne 1968

Gunter closed the door behind his last pupil for the day...and for good.

"Liebling, that's it finally." He handed her the money for the lesson. "Here, add this to our savings."

"Have we got enough?" Ursula asked, taking a tin down from a shelf.

"More than enough," he laughed. "Stop worrying. We must now begin packing."

"What about the car?"

"The nice man assured me that we can keep it until the day before we leave."

"And he still paid you?"

"Yes. What a trusting man, no?"

"Who wouldn't trust you, Dad. You're the nicest man alive."

"Oh, my liebling. What a flatterer you are." *Nicest man alive.* His cheerful words belied the images that hurtled across his mind: images of huge piles of shoes tied in pairs by their laces, bloodied gold teeth, hair cut from corpses, bodies twisted and charred in ovens, mounds of human ash thrown onto fields and into a river. Shame, guilt, everlasting horror...*no, I will not allow these thoughts...not now, not ever.*

The following two weeks were a frenzy of activity as Gunter and Ursula packed their possessions and arranged for a removal truck to take everything from Perth to Melbourne. Each morning, Ursula took the train tickets from their envelope, which leant against a potted geranium on the kitchen windowsill, and checked the date of their departure.

"You'll wear those tickets out looking at them," Gunter would tease, and she would smile at him before tucking the tickets back into the envelope.

"Just making sure," she would say.

They attended a round of farewell parties that included members of the West Australian Symphony Orchestra, as well as Ursula's school friends and their neighbours. The father and daughter had been popular in their street, not least of all for the music that floated out of the windows of their house and drifted past the nearest neighbours. A mother would stop in her baking, flour-coated hands paused in mid air, as she listened to the strains of Tchaikovsky; a husband would lift his eyes from the woes of the world reported in the newspaper to reflect upon the beauty of Beethoven's notes; children would look up from their games, from a crayoned drawing appearing upon a page, and their ears would cling to the music created by the two violins.

Ursula's curly, red hair swept around her face in chaotic disarray as she leant out of the train carriage window.

"Bye," she called out to the receding faces of her friends. "I'll write as soon as we get there."

The train pulled out of the station and, after a mere half-hour, Perth was lost to sight. She settled back onto her seat.

"Finally, Dad," she linked her arm through his. "We're on our way!"

Ursula's excitement showed no signs of abating as the train took her and Gunter away from the city of her birth and towards a new life in Melbourne. Little did she suspect that she was also travelling towards her unknown sister. She could not know that her sister had passed through Southern Cross thirteen years before. Or that their paths diverged at Kalgoorlie, when the train headed straight across the Nullarbor Plain. That at Port Augusta their paths crossed once again, as they did in Adelaide.

Gunter had no way of knowing that his lost child had travelled this path—or indeed that she was still alive. Nor did he sense that she had passed through Bordertown, or Nhill, or Dimboola or Horsham. As he gazed out of the carriage window, those names meant nothing to him. And as he looked out over Ballarat, his eyes could not see into the past when a young couple with a baby paused in their journey to puzzle over an avenue honouring fallen heroes. He looked, instead, at the green of the landscape, the spread of the country towns, and the promise of a future for Ursula. He turned to the face of his daughter as she stared out across the land, and he felt the familiar stirring of love that filled his days with happiness. His life was for her and only her. She was, after all, the only living link he had left with his beloved Hannah. What would have been the point, otherwise, of his having survived the war years when his parents, sister, family, had perished? Hannah had been the only positive aspect of the stinking hell he'd struggled to survive. He'd roused himself from his cocoon of self-imposed emotional anaesthesia that had made his physical survival possible so that he could protect her. And he had done that...until his seed had taken her away from him. *No, you promised,* he rebuked himself. *You will not think of the past. Only the future.* He turned his attention once again to his daughter and the memories receded back where he could place a lid on them.

The train finally pulled in to Spencer Street Station, where Gunter and Ursula ended their journey.

"I've booked us into a hotel," he said as they slid onto the back seat of a taxi. "We should be comfortable there until we find somewhere permanent to live."

The following morning, Gunter and Ursula searched through the newspapers for flats to rent. Luck was with them as they found one on a short lease that Gunter felt was suitable for the time being, until they had settled in and had a feel for the city and its suburbs. Perhaps after six months they would find a nice house in a good area to buy. In the meantime, he wanted to spend as much time as possible in practice for his audition with the Melbourne Symphony. They returned to the hotel, after having signed the lease papers at an estate agency, packed their belongings, and paid the bill.

Gunter gave their new address in Kew to the taxi driver, and sat back against the seat rubbing his forehead.

"You all right?" Ursula looked at him.

"Yes, I'm fine."

"Not another headache?"

"No. No pain. Just those flashing lights again."

"You really must go and see about it."

Gunter waved at her in protest, and went back to rubbing his forehead and blinking his eyes.

"You keep saying you will, but you don't, you know."

"Don't make a fuss, liebling. It's nothing."

"But you should find out what it is," Ursula insisted. "You're getting more and more headaches."

"I'm just tired."

"You're not coming down with something?"

"Maybe, my Ursula. Maybe. But I don't have time for that." He smiled at her, taking her hand in his. "I have to pass this audition now, don't I?"

Chapter 27   Chelsea 1968

The whirring of Ruth's sewing machine had been constant ever since the breakfast dishes had been washed and put away. The lengths of fabric and their matching buttons, zips, cottons and ribbons, were in the process of being transformed into two party dresses: one each for Joy and Louise. The day after tomorrow was to be a special day, the day of the girls' thirteenth birthday party, and preparations were at a fever pitch.

Joy poked her head into the sewing room.

"How're they going, Mum?"

"Getting there."

"Can I go and have another look up the shops to find Louise's present?"

"Yes, love. Just be careful. No talking to strangers."

Joy rolled her eyes without replying then bounced out of the house clutching her purse.

Traditionally, the girls gave each other their presents on the morning of their joint party and time was running out for her. So far, she'd been unable to get a present. Everything she saw in the shops in Chelsea was either not quite what she wanted for her friend, or else it was too expensive. She'd saved her pocket money for most of the year, and was ready to spend it. Joy knew that Louise, too, had been window shopping all along the same stretch of shops. There was little available that either girl had seen that could surprise as a gift. Perhaps today would be different.

Please, please let Dad get the job, Ursula said over and over to herself as the train rattled along the tracks after leaving Flinders Street Station. *Richmond...six more to go.* The commercial area of the city gave way to backyard fences of residential homes. She wondered at the lives of those who lived in the houses as she caught glimpses of clothes drying on rotary hoists, bedraggled gardens and children's toys. Had they lived there for long? Did they like Melbourne? Had they, too, come from Perth? *From Auschwitz?* Did the mother go to work? *Was* there a mother? How many children did they have? *Hawksburn...that was quick. Next should be Glenferrie.* Her thoughts strayed back to her father's interview and audition. What would happen if he didn't pass? If they didn't like him? *Of course they'll like him...they'll love him!* The train slowed for the next station. *If I don't look, the train'll get there quicker.* She checked her purse again to make sure she had enough money to buy meat for their dinner. *A nice stew,* she yawned, *he'll like that.* The steady swaying of the carriage lulled her into a light doze, her head resting on the windowsill. Each time the train pulled into a station, her heavy eyelids didn't quite open enough to read the signs, until a more profound sleep overcame her.

The train lurched suddenly as it approached a station, tugging Ursula out of her slumber. She stood with two other passengers at the door, expecting to have arrived at Camberwell, but was puzzled to see Mordialloc signposted. *Mordialloc? I don't remember that one.* She shrugged and sat down again, surprised to notice a creek leading out to the sea. Uneasiness crept over her as each station slipped past her window. *I'm sure the stationmaster said to get on this train.* The train slowed again and she decided to get off.

"Excuse me," she said to the guard collecting tickets, "I think I'm on the wrong train. I want to go to Camberwell."

The man's eyebrows shot up. "Camberwell, love? Struth, you're way off beam. This is Chelsea. You been on a joy ride?"

"Oh, no!" Ursula was dismayed. "How do I get to Camberwell?"

She crossed the tracks to get the next train back to Richmond. Her eyes meandered back along the platform, taking in the other waiting passengers, then across the tracks where litter scurried in the light breeze, and then back over the road where shops sprawled along Nepean Highway. There was a girl standing outside a shop directly opposite her. Staring at her.

She was conscious of a pounding in her ears, and her heart raced in concert with it. Her tongue suddenly stuck in her throat as her eyes widened to their fullest. She blinked rapidly, attempting to re-focus. Her bag slipped unheeded from her fingers and dropped to the platform with a soft thud.

The girl on the footpath was...herself!

Joy stared openly at the girl on the platform. The girl was doing exactly the same, her face mirroring the utter shock that Joy was feeling. They stood absolutely still, their eyes disbelieving as they took in each minor detail of the other: long, red, curly hair; the shape of the eyes, mouth, nose, face; the height; the build. They both wore flared jeans, platform shoes and thick roll-necked jumpers—different, but similar in taste. Joy's jumper was a deep old gold that reflected the golden lights in her red hair, whereas the girl who stared back wore a lime green wool. Long strings of beads complemented their outfits.

"Stay there," the other girl called out. "Don't move!"

She turned and ran along the platform and out of the gate. Joy stood, quite stunned, as she watched the girl cross the road before suddenly coming to a halt. Twenty feet separated them. They both took hesitant steps towards each other—closer and closer, until they could see the colour of the other's eyes: the colour of the sea at its greenest. They were identical.

"You..." Joy stopped.

"...look like me," the other girl finished.

"How...?" they both said at the same time.

They laughed.

"Do you...?" Again they spoke as one.

Joy waited and the other girl spoke.

"You go first," she giggled.

"Who are you?"

"My name's Ursula," she said with the slightest of accents. "What's yours?"

"Joy."

They regarded each other for a moment, confused thoughts whirling around in their heads.

"You realise we're absolutely the same?" Ursula said, suddenly serious.

"I know," Joy nodded. "How can that be?"

"I've heard of look-alikes, but this is spooky."

Joy reached up and touched Ursula's hair. "It even feels the same."

They both turned as Ursula's train rumbled into the station.

"Where're you going?" Joy asked hurriedly.

"Camberwell."

"Do you have to go now?"

Ursula looked at her watch. "I've got an hour or so. My dad won't be home until dinner time."

"Where do you live?" Joy asked.

"Kew. We've just moved there...from Perth."

As one, the girls swung away from the Highway and Joy led the way to the beach, some streets away from her own. The hour they spent there was enough to cover their thirteen years in excited revelations, words tripping over each other in their eagerness to get out as much as possible. They examined each other minutely, comparing their hands, their arms, their legs—they rolled up their jeans to reveal the same slim ankles and now-faded honey-tanned legs—hair, teeth. Suddenly, Joy grabbed hold of Ursula's chin and pushed it upwards.

"Hey! What's that?"

She pointed to a tiny brown patch under the jaw, shaped like a lightening fork.

"My birth mark. Have you got one?"

Joy shook her head. "No." She touched her own neck. "Never noticed one. You were born with it?"

"Yes."

"When were you born?"

"1955."

"Me too!"

"What date?"

"Eighth of May."

Ursula's mouth dropped open. "So was I," she whispered.

They both paled.

"Do you think we're sisters?" Joy's question was hesitant.

"Did you ever live in Perth?"

"No."

They thought about it for some moments in silence.

Ursula took Joy's hand in hers. "Did you ever feel like you were missing something…or someone?"

Tears sprang to Joy's eyes. "Yes…especially when I was under water, or dreaming."

"Me too. And no one knew what I was talking about."

"Same here. And—I know this sounds silly—when I got sick, I always felt there was someone close to me. I'd look under my bed, behind the curtains, but there was no one there."

"Yes! Like when I broke my arm. It was the same feeling. I had these peculiar dreams of floating in water with myself."

"Which arm?"

"This one," Ursula pointed to her left elbow.

"When…?"

"…did it happen? Oh, about four years ago."

Joy touched her own left elbow, casting her mind back to the time she had suffered a sore arm for no apparent reason, other than growing pains.

"Have you had your appendix out?" Joy asked quietly.

"How did you know?"

"This is really weird. Was it in the summer? About two years back?"

"How did you know?" Ursula repeated.

"I felt it. It hurt me too."

"How?"

"I don't know. It just did."

"Did you have appendicitis too?"

"No."

They watched seagulls squabbling over a prize that one had fished from the water. It soared into the sky, triumphant.

"Where were you going when you got off the train?"

Ursula pulled a face. "I was lost."

"How come?"

"We've only been in Victoria for a few days. Dad's having an interview today with the Melbourne Symphony before his audition tomorrow. I went in to the city with him and he bought me a birthday present." She held out her arm. "See? A new watch."

"It's gorgeous."

"Yes. And I promised to cook him something special for dinner…"

"For his audition?"

"Yes. You see, if he's accepted—and I know he will be—he's going to play me my favourite violin concerto…"

"What?"

"Violin. He's a violinist. The best on this side of the earth."

"I don't think I've ever heard one."

"Really? Gee…I grew up with one in my hand, I reckon."

"What? Do you play one too?" Joy was awed.

"Yes. Dad taught me. We play together—at home—a lot."

"So what's he going to play you?"

"The Tchaikovsky."

"Oh, I've heard of him."

"Well, that's a relief. Anyway, he plays me something and I cook him a nice meal—because I like to cook."

"So, how come you got lost?"

"I was going back to our new place to buy the stuff we need, but I must've got on the wrong platform. I went to sleep on the train and ended up here instead."

"Camberwell! That's the other end of the earth to Chelsea."

"I know," Ursula agreed. "The station master here…he showed me on the map. I reckon I've been all over Victoria."

"We live just up there," Joy said, pointing in the direction of her street.

"You're lucky. I love the water."

"Me too," Joy smiled at her.

They regarded each other for a long moment.

"I still can't believe this," Ursula said. "It's the biggest mystery ever."

"Curioser and curiouser..."

"Said Alice who forgot her English," laughed Ursula.

"You like reading too?"

"Of course."

"Hey!" Joy jumped up from the sand, suddenly excited. "What about you and your dad come to my birthday party on Sunday?"

"But we don't tell anyone?"

"That's right...a surprise."

"Won't that be a blast?"

The girls hugged each other, dancing around in a circle.

"Imagine the look on Mum and Dad's faces and Louise's," Joy giggled. "They'll have a fit."

"My dad too." Ursula looked at her watch. "Oh, the time's going too fast."

"Have you got to go?"

"I'd better. I wish we could see each other again tomorrow." Ursula looked at Joy hopefully.

"Hang on," Joy said slowly, "I've half-arranged with my Nana to meet her in Bentleigh tomorrow to buy a present for Louise if I couldn't get anything here today. Mum can't go as she's too busy sewing. Dad said he'd pick me up at Bentleigh after work but I could tell Nana a white lie...which I know she'll forgive me for when she knows why...that I'll have a return ticket on the train. That way, we could spend some time together in Bentleigh after I say goodbye to her." She bit her lip. "Can you get to Bentleigh tomorrow, though?"

"Yes, sure," Ursula nodded, thinking. "I'll tell Dad the truth—that I've met a new friend—and he'll be so pleased for me. I just won't tell him what our big surprise is. He'll be at his audition anyway and he won't mind me going to visit you."

"He doesn't mind you going out on your own?" Joy was incredulous.

"Not that much. He worries about me, of course, but he says he trusts me to be a 'grown woman' and that I should be independent sometimes."

"Gee, my mum's psycho about me going anywhere without them. You should have heard her when I said I wanted to go to Bentleigh in the train. She just about fainted but Dad said I'd have to go on my own sometime and if Nana meets me at the station what could possibly go wrong?"

Chapter 28

The next day, after many warnings of dire consequences if Joy disobeyed *the rules*, she boarded a train for Bentleigh. She waved to her mother through the window and then settled down on a seat. It felt strange to be in the carriage without her mother or Louise and Olive. She was acutely conscious of every passenger near her, especially the men. Ruth had lectured her about not speaking with anyone, least of all men. Joy sat with her back straight against the seat, her legs clamped firmly together. Her feet just reached the floor, ankles touching. Her bag rested on her lap, tightly clasped between both hands.

After stopping at Edithvale, Aspendale and Mordialloc, Joy began to relax a bit. There was a lady seated opposite her who smiled when their eyes met. She didn't look so bad, and Joy smiled back. The lady reminded her of Nana with a riot of wavy hair around a tiny face that radiated kindliness.

"Going far, dear?"

"Bentleigh."

"On your own?"

"Yes, but I'm not allowed to talk to strangers."

"Oh, of course, dear. I'll just make sure you're all right. I go past Bentleigh. You don't have to talk to me."

"I'm sorry..." Joy blushed.

"Shhh," the lady put her finger to her lips. "Nothing to be sorry for."

And they both looked out of the window, turning back from time to time to smile at each other. *I've got a secret. I've got a secret.* It was hard not to jump up and down with excitement thinking of her clandestine meeting with Ursula. They'd plan the surprise for the party down to the nth degree for maximum effect. *Oh boy, won't Mum and Dad go spaz. Their eyes'll pop out!* At last the train pulled into Bentleigh station. Joy stood up, holding onto the back of her seat.

"Thank you for looking after me," she said to the lady.

"Have you got someone to meet you, dear?"

"Yes," Joy pointed to the platform. "She's right there."

Joy pulled open the doors and stepped down onto the platform. Pat hugged her and they walked out of the station and began their search of the shops. It was an enjoyable time for both of them, delighting in each other's company and chatting all the while. After about an hour's fruitless searching, Pat took Joy into a milk bar where she treated the girl to a blue heaven spider—a concoction of blue heaven flavouring and lemonade topped with a scoop of ice cream—while Pat had the proverbial cup of tea.

"What about the jeweller's shop, love?"

"Jewellery? That'd be a bit dear for me, wouldn't it?"

"Sometimes they have little things that you wouldn't expect to be cheap, and yet they are. I know Mr Henderson, anyway. If I twist his arm, he might give you a cut off the price of something you like."

"I suppose so," Joy looked doubtful.

"Don't worry, love. We'll find something for Louise, or my name's not Pat Lewis."

Ten minutes later they were peering over the counter at precious stones that sparkled up at them from intricate settings. Pat explained their mission to Mr Henderson and he disappeared out to the back of the shop, reappearing in a moment with a felt-lined tray of brooches. Joy began her inspection of each one: a gold butterfly with wings extended, inside each of which were painted in a bright enamel red, blue and white around miniature diamantés; a tiny silver horse with its rider sitting low on the saddle hugging the animal's head; a swirl of gold-tone curves intersecting each other and painted in a dark blue enamel with the gold edges just showing; a yellow rose, half-opened, with a pale pink centre and two green leaves poking between the petals; and then an oval bar with a gold-tone scroll around its edges. It had a spray of multi-coloured flowers curved around the left edge seemingly pointing at a blank space in the centre.

Joy's gasp was audible as she picked up the oval brooch.

"What is it, love?" Pat peered closer over Joy's shoulder.

"These flowers," Joy touched them gently with her index finger. "What sort are they?"

Mr Henderson took the brooch from her and placed it on a felt pad by itself.

"They're sweet pea. Do you know them?"

Joy nodded. "We have them on our fence."

"Pretty things," the jeweller said. "My wife likes them."

"What's this for?" Joy pointed to the blank space on the bar.

"A name."

"Any name?"

"Yes, of course. I would engrave it, if you wanted."

Joy sighed as she stared at the brooch. "Oh, it'll be too dear for me. It's so pretty, though."

"How much have you got, young lady?" the jeweller asked, smiling at Pat over Joy's head.

"Five dollars and forty-five cents."

"I think you've got just about enough," he said.

"Really?"

"Really. What name would you like me to engrave on it?"

Joy and Pat walked back to the station with ten minutes to spare before Joy's supposed train was due at three thirty. Her eyes darted from face to face in the street searching for Ursula. If she were already there, Joy was afraid Pat would see her. They walked on to the platform and Joy assured Pat that she would be all right to leave, knowing that Pat had to get back home before her grandchildren arrived.

"I've had the best time ever, Nana. Thank you so much."

"Me too, love. We must do it more often."

"If Mum'll let me," Joy pulled a face.

"I'm sure she will. She did this time, and we've proven we didn't get lost or anything disastrous like that. Now, don't forget what I told you, love. You get straight on the train and no talking to any strangers."

They hugged goodbye and, as soon as Pat was out of sight, Joy darted back out onto Centre Road. There! Her mirror image jumped out of a phone box near the post office. They hugged.

"Glad you wore the same jumper," Joy giggled. "I wouldn't have known you otherwise."

"Does anyone suspect?" Ursula asked.

"No," Joy said, taking Ursula's arm, "but Dad kept looking at me funny. I was scared he could read my mind. Did you tell your dad?"

Ursula nodded. "He was so pleased for me..."

"But you didn't..."

"Tell him about us? No. He's got no idea—just that you're a new friend."

The girls made their way to a nearby park, enthusiastically recounting their lives, trying to find a possible link, a reason for their identical likeness.

"You know," Joy said thoughtfully, "we're dead ringers for each other in almost every respect, but your voice is slightly different to mine."

"Is it?"

"Yes. You've got an accent."

"Oh that," Ursula laughed. "I picked up a bit of my dad's."

"Isn't he Australian?"

"He was born in Germany. Still sounds it too."

"Was he a…a…"

"Nazi?"

Joy nodded, embarrassed.

"No. He was in Auschwitz."

"What's that?"

"A concentration camp. Where they killed a lot of Jews."

"Are you a Jew?"

"Not really. I mean, I am, but I'm not. Dad is…was…a Jew, but he doesn't want to be one anymore."

"Why?"

"Because he doesn't believe in it anymore. Not after what happened to him and my mother in the war. And then her dying when I was born. I never knew her."

"Gee, that must have been awful for him."

"He doesn't talk about it much."

"Have you got any brothers or sisters?"

"No," Ursula shook her head. "Have you?"

"No."

Joy took the box out of her bag to show Ursula the brooch that now had the word Louise engraved on it in flowing script.

"She's lucky," Ursula smiled, "to have you for a friend."

"Oh, I'm sure you'll like each other," Joy said with excitement. "You can be her friend too and make sandcastles with us on the beach. You do know how to make sandcastles, don't you?"

Ursula was interrupted by a loud blast of a horn. They looked up to see Les's truck as it pulled over to the side of the road.

"Oh, bugger…he's early!" Joy stood to hide Ursula's face. "Now the surprise is ruined."

Les got down quickly and walked around the truck to join the girls. Joy hugged him and then stepped aside. "Look what I've got, Dad."

His mouth dropped open as he stared at Ursula.

"I know," Joy laughed at his expression. "It's a real blast, isn't it?"

Les cleared his throat, unable to speak.

"Dad, this is Ursula. If I didn't know any better, I'd reckon we were twins."

Les offered to drive Ursula home. She had hesitated at first, but was reluctant to lose sight of Joy so quickly. She figured she was safe enough—after all, Mr Bacon was a family man, wasn't he? And she and her father were going to the party the next day, weren't they? The atmosphere in the truck was tense, though, as Les drove along Centre Road towards Nepean Highway. It didn't take the girls long to notice that he wasn't exactly thrilled about the co-incidence of Joy finding a girl who looked exactly like her. Les's teeth ground savagely together as his jaw clenched, the muscles rock-hard. His heart raced, hammering fitfully in his chest cavity, and the roaring in his ears was deafening as his fingers gripped the steering wheel like a vice to steady their trembling.

"Don't you reckon it's weird, though, Dad?"

"What?"

"Well, what do you think could explain it? I mean, we're so...close."

"Don't know."

"Even our birthdays are the same."

"Yeah."

"We never lived in Perth, did we?"

"No."

"Never?"

"No."

He turned to look at Ursula as he waited for a car that was turning right at an intersection. It was uncanny.

"Where're your parents?" he ground out.

"Dad's at home..."

"He's a violinist, Dad," Joy interrupted. "Imagine that."

"Is there anyone else?" Les noticed her mannerisms which were so like those of Joy's.

"No. Just us."

"Who are you staying with?" Les put the truck into first gear and it moved forward. A bottle of Ruth's tablets that he had picked up from the chemist rolled across the dashboard.

"Just Dad. It's always just the two of us."

"No. I mean, are you in a house? Hotel? Boarding house?"

"We've just moved into a flat until we find somewhere more per-manent."

"How long've you been here?"

"In Victoria?"

He nodded, eyes on the road ahead.

"Only since Wednesday."

"Three days," Les muttered. "Not long."

"Pardon?"

"You haven't been here long, I said."

"No."

"Won't your father be missing you?"

"No. Dad's rehearsing—and he knows I was meeting Joy."

The truck turned right into Nepean Highway, and then right again into Hawthorn Road. The tablets rolled back and forth across the dashboard, hitting each side with a rattling thump. Annoyed, Les picked the bottle up and shoved it in his pocket. They bumped along for some time in silence as Les avoided the tram tracks.

"Is it far to Kew, Dad?"

"Yeah."

"It's very nice of you to take me home," Ursula said hesitantly. She had a strong feeling that Joy's father didn't like her. It made her uneasy.

Joy looked up at Les. "If Ursula was my sister, you'd have a hard time telling us apart. We could play all sorts of tricks on you and Mum."

Les stared at the road ahead, his mouth a grim, thin line. He looked unfamiliar to Joy—older somehow—and she felt disappointed that his usual easy-going nature wasn't with them in the truck. She was normally so proud of him, with his good looks and ready smile. As she studied his face, he almost seemed a stranger to her. It was a puzzle that her father wasn't more interested in Ursula and the co-incidence of their resemblance. It was almost as if he was angry with them. It embarrassed her because she felt sure that Ursula could feel his tension too.

"I hope your dad's at home so we can meet him," Joy said in an attempt to change the atmosphere.

"He'd be very interested to see you," Ursula declared. "Imagine the surprise he'd get."

"Maybe you and he could find some family link between us, Dad? What do you reckon?"

"I don't think so."

"Yes, but, don't you think it's weird, Ursula and me being so alike?"

"They say everyone has a double."

"But this much of a double?"

"I don't know, Joy," Les snapped. "Some things have no explanation. They just happen."

Joy turned away from him, hurt and close to tears. *What's wrong with him?* He was ruining this special moment—this mystery. Ursula touched her arm lightly and they faced each other. Joy instinctively knew that Ursula understood what she was feeling and they smiled. Their eyes studied the face of the girl looking back at them and the wonder of seeing the mirror image captured them again. Their thoughts, their feelings, their emotions, were as one— shared by two bodies. And they felt whole.

Les was panic stricken as they crossed North Road and passed Brighton Cemetery on their right. Each intersection brought them closer to the moment of revelation. The moment when his and Ruth's crime would be discovered. And he would be face to face with the man whose child they had stolen. What could he do to avoid disaster? There was nothing that he could think of that would put off the moment. He looked at the speedometer and realised he had slowed down quite considerably. No wonder motorists behind him were bipping their horns and passing him impatiently once the road was clear of trams. The traffic lights changed to red as they approached Glenhuntly Road and he moved the gear stick into neutral.

He didn't look at the girls sitting quietly beside him. He could feel the truck's motor vibrating evenly as they waited, his eyes fixed on the traffic signal. A faint rattle reached his ears as the bottle of tablets moved with his body each time his foot pressed the clutch and brake pedals. His eyes strayed from the scene ahead and slowly travelled along the shops lined along the busy road. A milk bar filled his vision with its garish signs plastered across its windows: Fresh Bread Daily; Eggs sold here; Things Go Better With Coke; Get Your Sun Today!; Buy Your Creamy Malted Milks Here.

"You want a malted milk?" he asked the girls as he suddenly swung the truck to the side of the road and parked outside the milk bar.

"Yes please," they said in unison, and then broke into relieved giggles.

Les seemed a little friendlier.

"What flavour?" he asked as he held his door open.

"Blue heaven, please Dad," Joy answered. "What about you, Ursula?"

"I like blue heaven too," she said digging around inside her bag for some money.

"No. It's my shout," Les managed a smile. "You two stay here. I'll be back in a mo."

He jumped out of the truck as a tram shambled past.

"Three malted milks, thanks," he said to a woman behind the counter.

Her head disappeared as she bent over to dip a scoop into a deep ice-cream container.

"Cold out there?" came her muffled voice before she stood up again.

"Yeah. A bit nippy."

"Been out for the day?"

"Yeah, to the footy." Les frowned at her curiosity. "I'll just get a *Herald* too."

"All right, love."

Les helped himself to the top copy of the *Herald* from amongst a pile of newspapers in front of the counter and walked over to a table and chairs. He spread the paper out and sat down while he waited for the malted milks. The loud whirring of the machine as it whipped up the milk mixture made any conversation impossible. His right hand fingered the bottle of tablets in his pocket.

"Here you are. Two blue heavens and a strawberry."

"Thanks."

Les paid the woman and walked back to the table juggling the three malted milks.

"Mind if I drink one here? A bit hard holding it while I'm driving."

"Sure. Take your time, love."

Les pretended an interest in the news, holding the paper up in front of him as he sipped his malted milk shake. The woman didn't see him take the bottle of Phenobarbitone out of his pocket. Nor did she see him shake some of its contents on to the table. The rattle of a tram passing by masked the noise as the tablets spilled out onto the Laminex table surface. *How many?* He looked nervously at the tablets. If two were enough to knock Ruth flying at night, how many would it take to knock a thirteen year-old girl out for, say, four or five hours? And knock her out totally...without causing any damage? Two? Three? Five? Ten? Would it kill her?

He turned to look out of the window. The girls were deep in conversation in the truck. He sighed in relief.

"Who won?" The woman's voice intruded upon his frenzied thoughts.

"What?"

"Who won? The footy?"

"Oh. I don't know."

"Didn't you say you went?"

"Oh. Yeah." She looked at him in surprise. "I left before they finished."

Les rustled his paper, drawing it up around his face. The woman shrugged and returned to her cleaning behind the counter. The phone rang shrilly. Les jumped.

"Glenhuntly Milk Bar."

Come on. Make up your mind. His fingers hovered over the tablets and then he separated six from the pile before putting the rest back into the bottle. He looked up. The woman was still nattering on the phone. The tablets were rock-hard. He tried to crush them with his fingers and then his nails, but they resisted. He looked wildly around him, then grabbed a glass sugar container with a metal pourer. Watching the woman carefully, he pressed hard onto a tablet with the bottom of the sugar container. The tablet collapsed suddenly into a rough powder. Two more followed and Les scooped up the powder into his hand and emptied it into one of the malted milk shakes. The remaining three tablets followed quickly, once crushed, into the other milk shake. His hand brushed the tabletop clear and he stood up. He saw his fingers were covered with the powder and he wiped it on his pants, leaving one finger still covered. His tongue darted out to taste the powder. It was bitter.

"Excuse me," Les interrupted the woman.

"Hang on, love," she said into the phone and then put it down.

"Can I have some extra flavouring? And malt?"

"What's wrong with it?"

"No. Nothing. Just...you know what kids are like. Never satisfied."

The woman nodded in sympathy. "Know what you mean, love. It's more, more, more." She took one of the milk shakes from Les. "Both?"

"Yeah. Thanks."

"You want them beaten up again?"

"If you don't mind."

She picked up the phone. "Won't be a minnie, love. Don't go away."

Les took the milk shakes back from her and put new straws in them. He looked at his watch. It seemed like he'd been in the milk bar for hours, but he was relieved to see that it was less than ten minutes.

"This malted milk tastes funny, Dad," Joy said, pulling a face.

"Oh?"

"What about yours, Ursula?"

Ursula silently agreed with her, but was too polite to say so. "Mine's fine."

"See? You must be imagining it," Les said. "Drink up. Can't waste it."

They crossed Glen Eira Road, Balaclava Road, Inkerman Road, and then turned right into the Princes Highway. The late afternoon light began to wane as Les turned the truck left into Glenferrie Road. A tram dinged furiously at them as Les became caught in the traffic over the tramlines.

"Your trams are noisy," Ursula commented.

"Don't you have any in Perth?"

"No."

Joy yawned. "God, I'm sleepy. Can hardly keep my eyes open."

"Must be the excitement," Les muttered.

"What excitement?"

"Your birthday tomorrow."

Ursula tried to stifle a yawn. "Must be catchy," she said, her eyes watering.

"You too?" Joy smiled at her sleepily.

Ursula nodded.

"We've got a way to go yet, girls. Why don't you have forty winks?"

"No. I'll be fine," Joy yawned again.

Les snatched a look at her. Her eyelids looked heavy and she continued yawning. Ursula looked exactly the same, giving in to a huge yawn. A car honked behind Les and they all jumped. Joy's eyes became glazed as she attempted to keep them open, then her lids fluttered down. She opened them a few times, with each effort managing to get them open to a lesser degree until they were mere slits. Finally, she gave in to sleep and her head slumped to one side. Les continued driving towards Kew, more slowly now, so that infuriated drivers glared at him as they passed. He swung the wheel carefully to the left and pulled over, bringing the truck to a halt. With a deep breath, he turned to the girls. They were fast asleep, leaning upon each other, their arms linked.

He looked at the two identical girls as they slumbered. Their faces rested in identical poses, their lower lips slack as they breathed heavily. Their red curly hair tumbled around their faces, and he watched as their eyelashes moved in sleep. Inspecting every detail, he marvelled at the duplicate noses, eyebrows, mouths, chins, and pale skin. It tore at his heart to see them there together, finally, after thirteen years. And he knew the guilt that he'd tried to suppress for all those years would never leave him. *What am I going to do now?*

Chapter 29

The milk shake containers still rested on the girls' laps. Les picked up the containers and inspected the contents. Ursula had finished hers. Joy's had an inch of milk left. He was satisfied to see that there was very little of the crushed tablets left on the bottom of either container.

He sat watching the girls for some moments, wishing he knew something about human vital signs. How would he know if they were in trouble? If the drug was hurting them in some way? His heart raced suddenly at the thought of anything happening to Joy. He rammed his shaking hands between his knees in an effort to control them. The containers crushed in his grasp and some of the leftover milk seeped out, running heedlessly down the leg of his pants. The girls looked normal, he thought, reassuring himself. God knows he'd watched Joy fall asleep often enough and she looked pretty much the same. He wondered how deep their sleep was. He looked at his watch; it showed 5.15. They had started drinking their milk shakes about half an hour ago.

"Joy?" he whispered tentatively. "Joy? Can you hear me?" Louder this time. "Ursula?"

Neither girl stirred. He shook Joy gently, then more vigorously, but she merely mumbled a few unintelligible words before her mouth slackened again in repose. Ursula's response was exactly the same.

He sat back on his seat, the bottle of Ruth's tablets digging painfully into his hip. *Ruth*! He'd have to find a phone box. Ring Ruth. Tell her something…what? Tell her that her daughter isn't her daughter? Never had been? That her daughter-who-isn't-her-daughter has a sister? That they are both here, right next to him, drugged by his own hand? That if the other girl tells her father about Joy, then the game's up? That they'll both go to gaol and lose each other—and Joy?

The truck's engine ticked over, as if waiting for him to make a decision. The rhythmic vibration rocked the girls' bodies slightly, like the movement of the pram when he and Ruth had taken Joy for strolls when she was a baby. It had soothed her when she was teething and they'd watched her settle into a peaceful sleep under the frilly covers. A stuffed toy would be clutched in her hand, as indeed Ursula's arm was clutched in her hand now, but whereas the toy would have been let loose as her fingers relaxed in sleep, her twin was still firmly grasped. Even in her drugged slumber, Joy's hold on her lost twin seemed purposeful, desperate. He saw that Ursula's right hand gripped a fistful of Joy's jumper.

Neither girl stirred as Les pushed the right blinker and did a U-turn over the tram tracks. He drove carefully back down Glenferrie Road, avoiding bumps as much as possible, until he saw a phone box. He pulled up next to it and got down out of the truck with the milk shake containers, which he pushed into an overflowing litter-bin.

"Hello?"

"Ruth, it's me."

"Where are you? You should be home by now!"

"I can't find her."

"What?"

"I went to the post office, where she said she'd be."

"Les?" Her voice cracked.

"Look. Don't panic. I'm hunting around for her."

"What do you mean, don't panic? She's missing!"

"She can't be far. I must have been mistaken. She might have said somewhere else."

"She said the post office, didn't she?"

"Yeah. I thought so."

"Les, it's dark outside."

"Almost."

"Do you think she's all right?" Her voice was shaded with tears.

"Yeah, of course. She's around somewhere. I'll find her."

"What about the police? Have you told them?"

"Not yet, love." His palms were sweaty and he could hear his heart thudding in his ears. "Too early for that."

"Where've you looked?"

"Around the shops, the station..."

"What about Pat?"

"She...she...hasn't seen her."

"I'll ring her."

"No. She's gone...out."

"Out?"

"Yeah."

"Where?"

"Jesus, I don't know."

He could hear Ruth breathing into the phone—sharp, intakes of air—trying to control dry sobs.

"I'm coming there," she declared suddenly.

"Love, you need to stay at home next to the phone. In case she rings."

Silence.

"Ruth?"

"I suppose so."

Les put his head out of the box to check on the girls. They hadn't moved.

"...do now?"

"What'd you say?" he asked as he put his ear back to the receiver.

"I said, what are you going to do now?"

"Go up and down Centre Road again...the station...see if anyone's seen her."

"What if she's not there?"

"Maybe she caught a train instead, forgetting I was picking her up. There was one had just left before I arrived."

"So she might have come back to Chelsea?"

"Yeah, maybe. If there's no sign of her around here, I'll drive back to Chelsea and look around there. She's probably got distracted or something."

"I'll distract her when I get my hands on her."

"Yeah, well, I'll get going. See you at home."

"Les?"

"Yeah?"

"Find her? Please."

As Les drove towards Nepean Highway, his movements were automatic, without thought of what he was doing. His hands and feet obeyed the instructions given by his brain to guide the truck forward towards Chelsea. He knew he couldn't return to Ruth with the girls as all hell would break loose. *Oh, hi Ruth—Joy's a twin and she's not yours.* His thoughts whirled in a furious storm as each possible answer to the problem would flick through the squall and then be thrown out again just as quickly.

Sudden rain splattered the windscreen as a cold wind rushed in from the south-east. Les reached out to touch Joy's face and hands. They were still warm, but he turned the heater on anyway. He shivered as he looked ahead, his headlights picking out the shafts of rain as they hit the bitumen.

He wondered how long he had before the girls awoke. What would he do then? And what had he achieved by drugging them?

He'd only bought himself some time to think, and he didn't seem to be achieving much from that. Saturday night diners joined Les on the road in their cars as they made their way to pubs and restaurants and parties. He could just make them out through their rain-streaked windows laughing and talking in their safe worlds as they passed him—happy, carefree people seemingly without a trouble to mar their lives—and he envied them.

It seemed like a hundred years ago that he'd laughed and listened to Ruth's excited chatter on their way out to a meal. When she'd been a free and easygoing young woman who'd giggled all the time, who'd kissed him, made love to him. How long was it since they'd made love? *Really* made love. Not just the satisfying of their animal urges, but spending time indulging each other, delighting in each other's bodies. He sighed, and then an image burst into his mind of Olive's long, thick hair as it brushed his chest. It was an image that had haunted him these past two years. An image he had tried to eradicate from his memory. But it kept slinking back near the surface where he had to acknowledge his sin. The memories of the taste of brandy on her full lips, the hunger to explore her hot mouth with his tongue, the heat that radiated from her body as his hands slid over her incredibly soft skin, the memory of her ample breasts that his hands had eagerly cupped, the erect nipples gliding over him...as always sent blood surging to his genitals and he was afraid, so desperately afraid, that he would never be free of his lust for Olive.

It was a night that was never referred to again by either him or Olive. His eyes had avoided her questioning ones until, with a sinking feeling, she knew how it was. She could tell that he regretted it—their lovemaking—and that he tortured himself because of it. She was relieved that he obviously hadn't unburdened himself to Ruth, as the relationship between the two women had remained unscathed. And the girls...it would have been disastrous if they'd found out. Les dodged her when he could without the others noticing, but he still kept up his neighbourly attitude when it came to maintenance around her house. She was aware of the fact that he always tried to keep someone with them when he went into the house, though, and she felt ashamed of what she had done to him. For she blamed herself. She knew that he had tried to resist her that night, but his courage was too fragile at that moment when she needed him most. He'd had his own demons to contend with as Ruth see-sawed back and forth from normality to depression. And yet,

despite the fact that Olive had a conscience about what she'd instigated, she had her memories, and oh how she clung to them! When
she was alone at night. When her body ached with longing for what
Ruth had. She remembered the male smell of him; his hard, yet
gentle hands that had awoken powerful responses in undiscovered
places Jack had never visited; the multiple climaxes that terrified
her with their intensity yet left her gasping for more. She had no
memory of Jack's inept fumblings—only the instinctive passion that
Les had driven into her with his body. Their one night of lovemaking had left her craving for what she couldn't have and she turned
each moment over and again in her mind, leaving her shuddering
with lust.

Les dragged his mind back to the problem of the sleeping girls. He
knew what he had to do but, like his memories of Olive, he tried to
shun the thought that kept coming back to shake him. He wished
his mind could become numb, like his fingers that gripped the steering wheel. He wished he were back on the Nullarbor, driving forever on that nightmare road, with nothing else to worry about except where they would next find fresh water. Or before that, when it
was just him and Ruth. When they were young, lighthearted, and
flirting over the table at Gladys Taylor's boarding house. He wished
he were anywhere but in the truck with the girls and with his problem.

He slowed the truck as they passed through Chelsea, his foot
hovering indecisively over the accelerator and the brake, then he
pressed back down on the accelerator and continued along the Nepean Highway. As they crossed the bridge over Patterson River at
Carrum, he could just see the flash of wind-whipped waves lurching
drunkenly towards the beach. The rain blustered across the road
and he could feel the tug of the wind as he fought to keep the truck
in the left lane. Frankston looked almost deserted as he drove past
empty cafés with neon signs flaunting their garish messages to
passers by. The only sign of life was around the pubs on the corner
of Davey Street and the Highway, where drinkers and diners
dodged the traffic and the rain as they retreated to the warmth inside.

What the hell am I doing here? He drove past the pier where it
jutted out into the bay. *You know what.* The Highway passed the
round house, just past Sweetwater Creek, and climbed up steeply to
Olivers Hill. He ignored the view of the bay as he gripped the wheel.
Whenever he took that route, on his way home, he always made

sure to take the time to stop at the lookout and gaze over the water where he could make out the tall buildings of Melbourne in the distance. He would think how lucky he was to live in such a beautiful part of the world.

For Christ's sake, turn around! He pulled over to the left when he'd reached the summit of Olivers Hill and the road levelled out once more. The girls' faces were dimly lit by the dashboard lights. He saw they were still heavily asleep. His fingers raked through his hair as he sat deep in thought. Nausea rose in his throat and he swallowed quickly. He looked at his hands. They were trembling, as was his whole body. The muscles in his face worked; his jaw clamped shut; his mouth formed a hard line. *Get a grip on yourself.*

One, two, three, four cars passed and then there was a gap. The windshield wipers slashed at the rain. He peered through fog formed on the windows and rubbed at it with a handkerchief he pulled out of the pocket with the tablets. The bottle fell out and rolled on the floor around his feet as he turned the truck around. The opening to the lookout loomed in his headlights. He turned off the road and stopped just short of the safety rail, and switched off the engine and the lights. The darkness of the night seemed to envelop them in a blanket of anonymity, as if there was nothing else in the world except them. Even the lights of Frankston had disappeared behind the membrane of rain and wind.

He looked over at Joy and Ursula, marvelling once more at their identical faces and bodies. Then he thought of the rotten luck that had brought Ursula to Melbourne. How he and Ruth and Joy had lived a fairly carefree existence—except for Ruth's occasional mental collapses. How they'd made a new life for themselves in Victoria. How he'd tried to forget the face of Gunter Schwartz. How he'd tried not to think of the German man's loss of his wife and then his second daughter. How he'd justified their actions by the threat of Ruth's insanity. And now here was this girl beside Joy, threatening to shatter his family life just because of what she looked like. No, he'd gone too far for that. Ruth might not be the full two bob sometimes, but he still loved her. He loved her with the same intensity he always had. Maybe even more so because of what he'd risked to keep her.

His thoughts jumped back to the time he and his brother, Harry, had lost their mother. When she'd left them to marry again and made damned sure they couldn't find her. The rejection he'd felt was something he thought he had forgotten, but it suddenly came back to him, digging into his guts. It was something that neither he or Harry had actually ever verbalised, but their closeness had been important to him. For a short time, he had clung emotionally to his older brother until the fear of being without his mother had washed away. Life wasn't all that bad in the boarding house where he was staying at the time and his frustrations were played out on nails that he hammered into wood. The feeling of rejection was revisited when Harry took up with the girl he later married and meetings between the two brothers became fewer and fewer. When Harry sold up and left Perth, there was nothing left of Les's childhood to cling to. Any communication that might have continued between them was severed by the flight to Victoria. With no father, no mother, and also no brother, Les was grateful that Ruth was in his life. Now that she and Joy were his only family, he was not about to end up alone again.

His eyes left the face of the girl and lingered over the face of her sister. His daughter. His beloved Joy. The thought of losing her was more than he could bear. He'd cuddled her when she'd cried as a baby, hadn't he? He'd kissed her tears when she fell over. He'd watched her excited surprise each birthday and Christmas. He'd seen her grow from the naked baby that kicked the air enthusiastically on the beach at Ceduna to this thirteen-year-old who would soon sprout into the shape of a woman.

The door creaked as he opened it and stepped out into the rain. The roar of the wind and the slap of the waves against the rocks below filled his ears, as did the steady drumming of rain on the gravel. His footsteps crunched as he walked around the truck and opened the passenger side door. Ursula instinctively moved away from the cold as it entered her side of the cabin. His hands slipped under her legs and shoulders and he lifted her out of the truck, bending over to shield her face from the rain. She murmured in protest and her eyes struggled to open but failed to achieve a window to consciousness.

Les stood, swaying slightly, as he held the girl in his arms. A car passed the lookout, driving towards Frankston. Its headlights stabbed into the needles of rain as they hit the road ahead. The yellow arc swept momentarily into the lookout, highlighting the back of the truck, and then continued on down the hill. Les and Ursula remained shrouded in the blackness outside of the lights.

As he looked over the safety rail, he could make out tussocks of grass and low-growing shrubs clinging to parts of the cliff face. They were ripped in a crazy dance from side to side in the wind. Further down he could see white foam flare on the rocks as the bay's waters groped higher up the cliff.

Ursula stirred in his embrace, mumbling in her drugged state. He knew he was running out of time. Keeping his balance, he lifted his left leg over the safety rail, steadied, then lifted the other over. He shook his head to clear the rain from his eyes when another car passed. He froze, holding his breath, until it disappeared over the rise and continued on towards Mount Eliza. He was sure he hadn't been seen. Stumbling over the bumpy terrain, he found the steepest point on which to stand and, looking down at Ursula, he tensed his biceps.

Forgive me.

And he hurled her out over the cliff.

Chapter 30

He watched as her body fell in loose abandon, tumbling from each outcrop, momentarily halted by clutching bushes, then gathering momentum carrying it further down the cliff. It reminded him of a rag doll—arms and legs somersaulting crazily—that Joy had once lost over a bridge. They had watched it bounce off rocks and fall into the water far below where it had been carried downstream and out of sight. Ursula's outline diminished as his eyes strained to follow her erratic plunge through the blinding rain. He fancied he could hear a scream that the wind tore at and hurled back into the bay. In those split seconds he lost sight of her. He cupped his hands over his eyes to shield them from the rain. Waves died on the rocks in a tumultuous roar, in accompaniment with the gusting wind and hurtling rain, masking most other sounds from human ears.

Uncertain what to do, Les climbed over the safety rail again and looked through the windscreen at Joy. She appeared to be asleep, but he could see her moving her head from side to side as though in disagreement with something. He glanced at the safety rail. What if Ursula was coming back up? He had to make sure.

He stopped suddenly, remembering Ursula's handbag. Where was it? It must be in the cabin of the truck. Opening the door carefully, so as not to disturb Joy, he saw it on the floor, under the dashboard. Joy's handbag was beside it. And then he noticed the bottle of Ruth's tablets on the floor near the accelerator. He reached over and grabbed it, his hand brushing against a parcel of books hidden under the seat. He absentmindedly pushed it out of sight and retrieved the two bags before closing the door quietly behind him. He put the tablets in Joy's handbag and closed it, then stashed Ursula's bag in the back of the truck, pushing it under some old rags behind a ladder that was roped into place.

He hoisted himself over the rail again, grabbed on to some bushes and lowered himself down the cliff face. Slipping on loose soil, he went catapulting downwards, just managing to stop himself going over a last outcrop by hanging onto a broken stump. Joy's handbag had fallen out of his grasp, and he had no idea where it was. Soaked through to the skin, his body shivered violently as he regained his breath. He peered down at the rocks and made out Ursula's body lying across them. Her head appeared to be at a strange angle. Peering through the curtain of rain, he saw that she was face-up and he imagined he could see her eyes looking at him, though he couldn't be sure from that distance. A wave broke over her body and she was jerked back over the rocks as the water receded into the bay. He stayed suspended on the cliff-face, his arms trembling as he held himself there, while he watched the water gradually take possession of Ursula's body. It went, without protest, just like the rag doll, bobbing up and down with the movements of the waves. He watched it, squinting against the rain, until it was out of sight.

Les screamed. He screamed in agony for the act of murder he had just committed. He screamed for what he had become.

He stood outside the truck, the rain scouring at him like the waves scouring the rocks—except that his hard edges would become harder, rougher, dirtier. Urgent nausea rose inside him. His stomach heaved brutally, ejecting its contents so forcefully that it came out of his nostrils and mouth at the same time. The blood from his grazed hands dripped on the gravel, forming red rivulets, and the rain carried it and the vomit over the cliff edge. He sobbed—deep racking sobs—that tore at him, burned him, overwhelmed him. And he felt alone, so terribly alone, in his wrongdoing.

"Hello?" Ruth's voice was a whisper as she listened to the crackle in the receiver. No one spoke. "Hello?" She could hear someone crying. "Is that you Les? Joy?"

"Ruth."

"Les? Is that you?"

"Yeah."

"What? What?"

"Ruth…"

"Les, I'm out of my mind here. Tell me what's happening, for God's sake."

"I can't…find her."

"Oh, my God."

"I've looked everywhere."

"Where are you?" Her voice was shrill, threatening hysteria.

"Back in Bentleigh."

"What are you doing there? I thought you were coming to Chelsea."

"I did. I did. But I couldn't find her, so I turned back."

"Les?"

"What?"

"What're we going to do?"

She started to cry. He knew it would only get worse for her.

"I'm coming home. We'll go and see the cops together."

"You'll be home by seven, then?"

"No, it'll be later than that. I've got a flat tyre," he lied. He had to buy some time. "I'll probably be at least another hour."

"What am I going to do until then?"

"Look. She might ring. Just stay there."

"Les, I'm frightened," she cried. "And you are too. I can hear it."

"Yeah, love. I'm frightened too."

Les put down the receiver and leaned back against the wall of the telephone box. His mouth tasted disgusting and he felt more exhausted than he'd ever felt in his life. He craved the oblivion of sleep, escape from his scrambled brain, but he knew that he had to keep going, and face the ordeal ahead of him. He needed to think quickly and carefully. He was hardly conscious of the cold anymore even though his body shook under its covering of sodden clothes.

The truck started up again without protest. *Thank Christ there's plenty of juice in it.*

Joy stirred and mumbled, "Where are we?"

"Go back to sleep, princess," Les patted her arm.

"Umm?"

"It's all right. Go to sleep."

Her eyelids sank back down and she returned to her dreams.

They were passing Mount Eliza and headed along Nepean Highway towards Mornington. There was only one place Les knew he could take Joy. A place where he could leave her in safety and anonymity. Aggie's place.

The rain continued to pelt the windscreen of the truck. The wipers swished back and forth rhythmically as Les peered through them, driving more slowly along the narrow, winding roads that climbed the higher ground of the Mornington Peninsula. The headlights lunged into the night, clearing a path for the truck to follow. His thoughts clung to the past two years, to the comfort of the sanctuary that Sister Margaret Mary had given his mind when he had doubted his reason for living. When he had breached the trust in his marriage. When he had betrayed Ruth with his body. Aggie's place was where he had been able to find some measure of peace with himself, if not forgiveness, and it was the only place that he could turn to now.

It was strange, he'd thought on many an occasion, that he'd never gotten around to taking his small family to Red Hill for that picnic he'd promised himself that first time he drove past St. Agatha's. He'd told Ruth and Joy about it—about his dream of a picnic there, Anthony Middleton's accident, and the nuns—but those two different worlds of his never converged. He knew Ruth approved of his relationship with the nuns at 'Aggie's place', as he referred to it, because she always asked him about them, as if she knew them herself. As if she understood the need in him. As if she understood that Sister Margaret Mary was the mother he still unconsciously craved. Les always said, "One day I'll take you both to meet them," but that day was always tucked just around the corner.

The last time Les had called in to Aggie's place, the Reverend Mother had taken to her bed. There was a serene acceptance of the sad expectancy of her death. The nuns were quiet, introspective; their smiles didn't quite reach their eyes.

"Can I do anything?" Les had asked helplessly. "Get the doctor?"

Sister Margaret Mary shook her head. "No, Les, dear. She'll be in God's hands soon."

"Is there anyone...?"

"No, just us. We're her family. We'll be with her."

"Well, can I get you some groceries? Meat? The papers?"

"We've got enough," she smiled at him. "And we don't read the papers. Only the Reverend Mother does that."

"Why?"

"Because we are unworldly. We are gifted with a natural solitude. The outside world distracts us from our prayers and contemplation."

"Oh."

"It's all right, Les." She touched his arm. "We're grateful for your concern. But we really don't need anything." Her eyes searched his and saw the sadness there. "And the Reverend Mother...she's going to where she wants to be. With God."

Les covered her hand with his own large, calloused one. "Say goodbye to her for me, will you Maggie?" He turned away so that she wouldn't see the sudden tears that filled his eyes. He didn't realise that he'd called her Maggie.

She'd never been called that before, and she kind of liked it. "Yes, Les. I will," she said quietly.

He saw the low brick wall loom faintly ahead. The truck bumped to a halt at the entrance, and he sat for a moment before driving in. The branches of the old trees overhead danced in a frenzy with the wind threatening to snap them. Leaves scuttled across the gravel driveway, busy in their confused escape from the branches that had held them prisoner for so long. A dim light flickered behind the movement of the trees on the second storey of the convent. It was the Reverend Mother's room, he knew, and he wondered if she was still alive. It had only been three days ago that he'd been there last, and yet it seemed like a lifetime between then and now. If only he could go back to then, but what difference could that possibly make to what had happened?

His foot pressed on the accelerator again and the truck slowly edged forward along the driveway, coming to a halt at the front door of Aggie's place. The bell hanging next to the door swung wildly on its chain in the wind, but its ringing was mute in the roar of the wind and rain. He remembered the first time he had rung it. There had been another storm then, but it had been a lucky one for him. It had brought him Sister Margaret Mary.

The door stood out sharply in the headlights, beckoning him with a promise of the solace he knew would be given him. But did he have the right to knock there? Did he have the right to intrude upon their grief over the Reverend Mother, whether she was alive or dead? Did he have the right to involve them?

He looked down at the sleeping girl lying on the seat beside him. The dashboard lights illuminated the curves of her face, a ringlet of hair, the tight fist as if still holding her twin. He felt such an overwhelming love for her that he had to resist the impulse to take her in his arms and hold her. His throat ached as he choked back a sob, and he swallowed the foul vomit-tasting saliva that rose from his gullet. How could she look so peaceful when her life had been turned upside down? What was he going to say to her when she awoke? What was he going to say to Sister Margaret Mary and the other nuns? What was he going to say to Ruth?

He closed his eyes for a moment and took a deep breath. Nausea simmered in his gut and throat, but he pushed it back down, gritting his teeth. *Think, man! Think!* Bending over, he brushed his mouth lightly over Joy's cheek. Its warmth surprised him as it seeped into his lips.

"I love you," he whispered,

Then he opened his door and stepped out into the rain.

Chapter 31

Sister Margaret Mary hung Les's jumper over a chair in front of the fire in the kitchen. As the heat reached it, steam rose with a woolly smell. He stood with his back to the flames and sipped on a hot strong cup of tea that she'd made him. His body and hands shook as he warmed, and the tea spilled onto the floor from his cup. He made as if to clean it, but the old nun produced a rag from somewhere and mopped it up despite his protests.

"Shush, Les Bacon. You drink that up first and then tell me what's the matter."

Les's hair dripped and he wiped at it impatiently with his shirtsleeve.

"Here," she said, handing him a towel.

"Thanks."

Les finished his tea in silence and the shivering slowly subsided. Sister Margaret Mary took his empty cup and she sat down in front of him, hands hidden inside her habit, and waited. He took in her tired eyes and saw that she looked older than the last time he'd seen her. A sharp pang of guilt spread through him and he wondered what else he could do if he left now.

"The Reverend Mother?" he asked quietly.

"It won't be long now."

"Oh." He hesitated. "I shouldn't worry you..."

"Les. Tell me what's troubling you."

Her eyes had that way of seeming to penetrate his soul. He would be lost in them and tell her the truth. He couldn't do that. He had to lie to her, but would she believe him? He sat down next to her at the table.

"It's Ruth."

"Yes?"

"She's gone off her rocker." The nun waited. "She...she...found those old newspapers I'd hidden...about the Beaumont kids. You know...I told you about them? They were supposed to turn up in Dandenong...in February." Sister Margaret Mary nodded. "I'd meant to burn them, or throw them out. I must've forgotten about them. She was looking for something out in the workshop...before the party tomorrow..."

He trailed off, uncertain as to what Sister Margaret Mary's reaction was. She remained silent, waiting, as was her manner.

"She hadn't taken her tablets lately," he continued on. "She...wouldn't stop going on about it. She was raving."

"What about Joy, Les?"

"She'd already gone out. To buy a present for Louise."

"Alone?"

"She'd caught a train to Bentleigh. A good friend of ours met her there."

"I see."

"Well, Ruth found the papers. She'd been sewing the frocks for the two girls for tomorrow. Their birthday party," he explained. "And she took to the frocks with the scissors. Yes...the scissors. She stabbed them, and ripped them and made a bloody mess...sorry...a mess of them. Ruined them."

The nun sat looking at him steadily. He avoided her eyes as he searched his mind frantically for a convincing story.

"I was afraid for Joy when she came back. What if Ruth did the same to her...with the scissors?" He got up from the chair and started pacing the kitchen. "I couldn't let that happen." He saw that Sister Margaret Mary's eyes followed his every movement. "I took Ruth to the doctor's...to see what he could do about her. You know...quieten her down. He...he...decided she should go into hospital. For treatment. Of some sort. He thought she was a bit...dangerous. He stopped and looked at the nun to see if she was accepting his story.

"Yes, I can see that," she agreed softly.

Les dug his fingers into his hair and resumed his pacing.

"The doctor said she'd be in for a couple of days. Until she's right."

"And where is Joy now?"

"She's...out in the truck."

Sister Margaret Mary raised her eyebrows. "Out in the truck?"

"Yeah."

"What is she doing there? Why didn't you bring her in?"

"She's asleep. I didn't want to wake her."

"She'll be freezing, the poor child." She got up from her chair and made for the doorway.

"Ah...she...I haven't told her yet. About Ruth."

The nun turned around and walked back to where Les was standing in front of the fire. She waited for him to speak.

"I wondered. I mean, I hoped you ladies might be able to help me out...for a couple of days." His eyes met hers. "Could you put her up? I know this is a bu...stinker of a time for you. She wouldn't be any trouble, though," he hurried on. "She just needs somewhere quiet. She's gonna be pretty upset about her frock, the party, her birthday, and her mother. And I can't work, run back and forth to the hospital, and look after her at the same time."

"What about school?"

"She can miss a day or two. That's all it'd be. She could help you out. Do some cleaning or something. She's a good kid."

"I'm sure she is, Les. But how will she feel about staying here?"

"Oh, she'll..."

"We are very quiet, you know. We don't have television...you remember how poor the reception is here...and we don't listen to the wireless. We spend most of our time in prayer and solitude when we've finished our work."

"Have you got any books?"

"The Bible."

"Oh." He thought of the books hidden in the truck. "Well," he turned towards the fire. "I suppose..."

"Les, it's not that we wouldn't want her. God knows how much you've done for us. It's just that she would be frightfully bored. And we're strangers to her. Would Louise's mother be able to have her, or someone more familiar to her?"

"Olive's got her own problems at the moment," he lied. "And I couldn't ask our friends in Bentleigh. They've got a sick grandchild staying with them. Joy knows all about you. I've done nothing but talk about you these past couple of years."

She turned him around to face her. "Les...if you feel the poor dear child won't suffer too much in our hands, I'm sure I can speak for the other sisters when I say it would be our pleasure to have her. It would normally be Reverend Mother's decision, but I think I can speak on behalf of her, and the others."

Les sagged against the wall next to the fire. His eyes closed momentarily in relief. Sister Margaret Mary didn't miss the gesture.

"Come on, Les Bacon. You looked exhausted. Let's get your child in out of the cold."

The room on the second floor was small and bare, except for a narrow iron bed and a hard-backed chair. Sister Margaret Mary brought in clean linen and a pile of blankets, which she and Sister Dominique soon made up into an inviting place to rest. Les carried Joy up the stairs and placed her gently onto the bed. Sister Dominique knelt down and removed Joy's shoes, placing them neatly on the floor beside the parcel of books Les had decided to take from their hiding place, and then covered the girl with the blankets, drawing them up under her chin. Joy's hair was a splash of golden-red on the pure white pillowslip. The two women looked down at her in wonder.

"What a beautiful child," Sister Dominique whispered.

Sister Margaret Mary nodded. "Just as you'd described her, Les Bacon. She's an angel." She turned to the other nun as Joy stirred in her sleep. "Come, we'll leave Mr Bacon with his daughter."

They glided soundlessly out of the room. Les watched them go with the same amazement he always felt when he saw them walking. It was as if they were walking on air. He wondered again how they did it.

Joy's head was moving slightly and her eyelids were fluttering as if trying to clear them from the weight of sleep. Les pulled the chair over to the side of the bed and sat down, taking her hand in his. He looked at his watch. It was 7.15. Ruth would be frantic by now. He had to make this as quick as possible.

"Princess?" he stroked her cheek. "Princess, can you hear me?"

"Umm?"

"You all right?"

"Umm?"

"Open your eyes, love. I want to talk to you."

One eye opened slowly, and saw him sitting close to her. Suddenly both eyes popped open in alarm when she saw her surroundings.

"Where? Where are we?"

"It's all right, princess. Just listen."

"Daddy?"

"We're at Aggie's place."

"Aggie's place?" She yawned widely, her body quivering in a cat-like stretch.

"Yeah, love."

"What're we doing here?"

She tried to sit up but Les pushed her back down.

"I've got some important things to say to you."

Memory came flooding back suddenly. "Where's Ursula? Why're we here? What's happened?"

An image of Ursula's body on the rocks, in the water, cold and lifeless, flashed across his mind. *Mongrel,* he screamed within. *Child killer!* The numbness was wearing off as the horror of his actions seeped into him now that he'd passed the hurdle of where to leave Joy.

His hesitation was momentary. "Ursula's at her place."

"But, we were supposed to…"

"Yeah, I know, love. You were too sleepy and she was in a bit of a hurry. Said she'll be in touch." He marvelled at how easily the lies rolled off his tongue, how his brain seemed to be functioning on multi levels. It seemed that he was somewhere above himself, looking down at his performance. On one hand there was utter chaos which scared the hell out of him; on another, he was making decisions, taking charge, being someone he didn't know, yet it was someone who reminded him of a younger Les who had lied his way across the Nullarbor. Now here he was lying his head off to the nuns and his daughter—well, someone's daughter—while his stomach threatened to dredge up more bile and hurl it out. Had he really done *that?* Thrown that beautiful child over a cliff?

He swallowed, pushing the bile back where it came from. "You can see her some other time."

"But…"

"It suited me better too. I had a few problems to sort out."

"What sort of problems?"

"Your mother, for a start."

"Mum? Why, what's wrong?"

And Les told her the same story he had told Sister Margaret Mary. Joy's eyes widened in bewilderment when he told her about Ruth attacking the frocks.

"Why would she do that? They were so pretty."

"I don't know. But the doctor said because it was your dress, he couldn't guarantee your safety—or Louise's. He said to get you out of the house."

"Has she really gone crackers this time, Dad?"

"I don't know, princess, but they've got to do something about her. She's a danger to herself—and you."

"Will she get better?" Her eyes were full of concern.

"I'm sure she will. But you know how she is sometimes. She can't go on like that forever. Maybe a stint in hospital and the right treatment will sort her out. She might even need a new lot of drugs."

"Was she taking her tablets?"

"I don't think so."

"Oh."

"So that's why I brought you here."

"But why, Dad? Why can't I stay at home?"

"I can't leave you there on your own, love. I've got jobs on still, and I'll be at the hospital a lot."

"What about Louise's? Why can't I stay there?"

"Louise is going to stay with an auntie somewhere. Your mother might only be in hospital for a day and neither Mrs Fletcher nor I want you or Louise around when your mother gets home. Just in case, like."

"You don't really think Mum would hurt us, do you?"

He shook his head. "I just don't know."

"What about Nana? She'd have me."

"Yes I know, love. But she can't have you right now." He was conscious of Joy's eyes searching his face. "She's got a sick grandchild to look after."

"Funny...she didn't mention it to me," Joy mused.

"She must've forgotten," Les said lamely.

"Dad, I don't understand..."

"What?"

"How come I slept like that?"

"You were tired?"

"Yes, but I wasn't tired before. Why would I be tired at that time of the day?" Les shrugged. "What time is it?"

"Twenty past seven."

"What!" She sat up suddenly.

"Yeah, and I have to get going. Back to the hospital."

"Are you really leaving me here?"

"Have to, princess."

"Dad, I promise to be good. Take me with you. Mum won't touch me."

"I haven't got time to argue." He stood up. "You'll be here a day or two. That's all. I'll be back in the morning to see you. In the meantime, I want you to promise me you won't speak about anything to do with your mother or Ursula—to anyone. And you're not to use the phone. You promise me?"

"Yes."

"Now I mean that. No phone. No gossip. Say you promise."

"I promise."

"I'm holding you to that."

"Dad?"

"Yeah."

"I'm frightened. I don't understand..."

I'm frightened too. "Well. I'm sorry about that."

"Is it to do with Ursula?"

"No." *I wish it wasn't. If only she'd never come to Victoria, if only they'd never met...*

"You didn't like her, did you?

"It's not that," he floundered, "...just bad timing."

"Are you angry with me?"

"No, love."

"What about my birthday tomorrow? The party!"

"We'll just have to postpone it, love."

"But I bought a present for Louise. A nice brooch. I have to give it to her."

"Where is it?"

"In my bag." She looked around the room. "Where's my bag?"

"Must be in the truck still."

"Can we go and get it?"

"Not now. Look, the nuns are going through a hard time with the Reverend Mother dying, so don't make things more difficult for them. I want you to help them if you can, and keep quiet. They don't make much noise, so just amuse yourself as best you can. They're nice old sticks. You'll get along all right." He took her hand again. "I'm depending on you."

"What about Ursula? I wanted to show her to Mum and Louise."

"I don't have time for this!" he exploded suddenly. "Stop arguing with me and do as you're told."

Joy looked as if he'd slapped her. It tore at him as she searched his eyes with her own for some explanation of his behaviour. He knew it didn't make sense. He wondered if she even believed him. Could she see the guilt in his eyes? Did they reflect how he'd changed, the monster he'd become? Did they echo the thirteen years of fear that had now surfaced? He was flying again by the seat of his pants but he didn't know if he was up to the task before him. What was he going to do once he walked out of the convent? Would the police be waiting for him when he got home with that poor sod, Schwartz? He wished he could stay there with Joy and the nuns, hide from his world and responsibilities, from the enormous crime he'd committed. *If only I knew what to do.* He bent over to hug her and she struggled away from him, rejection in her eyes. Her bottom lip quivered.

"I think I don't like you."

"I don't either."

Chapter 32

Les slammed the door of the truck behind him. *Now she hates me. Can't blame her.* He turned the key in the ignition. The motor kicked into life. The warmth of his jumper, from the fire in the kitchen, was already gone and he started to shiver again. He bent over, holding his watch to the dashboard lights. *7.30—shit!*

"Ruth?"

"Oh, Les. Tell me you've found her."

"I wish I could, love."

He leaned against the wall of the telephone box, surrounded by light. Exposed. The concertina door squealed in protest as he pushed it open and held his foot against it. The light went out.

"Where are you?"

"In a phone box in the middle of bloody Iceland, or that's what it feels like."

"Come home, Les."

The storm's fury matched the workings of Les's mind. The wind whipped at the truck, trying to force it off the road and the rain sliced through the wind like the blade of a cutthroat razor. He fought the storm, the road, the time, the place. He was caught in emotions that churned him around, pulling at him, tearing at him, smothering him.

The lights along Nepean Highway flashed past like unfocused, forgotten dreams. In the cabin of the truck, it was as if time stood still. There was the comforting churning of its engine, the slip-slap of the wipers, the faint squeak of the clutch as his foot pushed the pedal, the subtle glow of the dashboard lights. If he stayed there forever, nothing could touch him. If he just kept driving, he'd never have to get out; never have to face Ruth, or Joy, or...anyone.

Another telephone box hurtled past the passenger window. A solitary world surrounded by four walls—a link with the outside. He saw it disappear in his rear view mirror. Washed. Washed away from view. He slowed at Seaford. There was another box somewhere along the Highway.

"Trunks. Can I help you?"

"I'd like a number in Longreach."

"Queensland?"

"Yeah. Queensland."

Metallic sounds dug into Les's eardrum. Muted sounds of voices, connections, pauses, clicks. His heart thudded. His hands shook. His mouth was dry.

"I'm putting you through, sir."

"Hello, Harry?"

"Who's that?"

"It's me. Les. Your brother."

The truck swung into the driveway of their Chelsea house at 8.15. Les saw the movement of the curtain in his and Ruth's bedroom, and a moment later she dashed out of the front door and into the rain. He wound down his window.

"Go inside love. Don't get wet. I'll just park the truck."

Her face was turned up to his. The rain flattened her hair against her scalp.

"Nothing?" she called to him shrilly above the sound of the rain.

He shook his head and she turned slowly, shoulders sagging, and walked back to the front door and disappeared inside. He stared dully at the closed front door. Water dripped onto his right side from the open window and he slowly wound it back up again. The steering wheel felt cold and hard as he sank over it, leaning his head against his arms as they surrounded the wheel. Suddenly the engine spluttered and died and he looked incredulously at the fuel gauge. It was on empty. It struck him as decidedly funny that the truck had just managed to get him home and no further. All those miles and now he was stuck with his problem. His body shook with mirth and he laughed great soundless heaving guffaws that hurt his stomach muscles, until they evolved into tearing sobs. He leant back over the steering wheel and sobbed into his jumper. Tears and mucus ran unheeded into the wool and his shoulders shook with each howl of mental anguish.

The door clicked and Ruth's arms were around him, pulling his head to her chest. And they stayed there, rocking in their pain and fear, together.

They hesitated under the blue and white sign and then entered the police station. An officer was seated beside an electric heater, with a newspaper spread out on a desk in front of him. He looked up.

"You folks after someone?"

"Yeah. We'd like to report a missing person," Les said.

The officer stood up and walked over to the reception desk.

"A missing person, you say?"

"Our daughter," Ruth said through chattering teeth. Her body shook with cold and fear.

"Your daughter? I'm sorry to hear that."

He raised up part of the counter. "Why don't you come in, sit down in the warm and tell me all about it."

They sat down on the chairs in front of the desk.

"How long's she been missing?"

Ruth and Les looked at each other.

"Five…six hours," Les calculated.

The clock struck twelve times in the kitchen. They heard it, counting each stroke as they lay in bed, their eyes wide as they took in the dim forms of the furniture in the dark bedroom. They hadn't spoken since the last time the clock struck the hour. Lost in their own thoughts, they'd lain in each other's arms as the trembling of their bodies gradually subsided in their shared warmth.

"Do you think she's cold?" Ruth whispered.

"No," he said truthfully.

"Do you think she's in pain?"

"No."

"How can you be so sure?"

"I just feel it."

"I wish I could."

They sat staring at the table. Dark circles smudged beneath their red-rimmed eyes. Neither spoke. The ticking of the clock filled the kitchen with a metallic clamour. It entered their minds and their hearts seemed to beat in time with it. A whirring began and the clock struck six times. The sixth stroke faded slowly. Their ears clung to the sound, straining, until the last echo soaked into the walls, the ceiling, the floor. The ticking seemed louder now, along with a steady drip, drip, from the spouting outside the window.

The cold front had passed over Bass Strait and was heading for the open sea. The wind and rain left silence in Chelsea as a weak autumn sun rose reluctantly in the east, painting the landscape with soft brush strokes of daylight.

Ruth stood up and, with mechanical movements, she filled the kettle and turned it on at the switch. She leaned against the sink, massaging her right temple with cold fingers. The headache was getting worse. She heard the front door slam next door and the familiar squeak of the gate as someone opened it. She realised it would be Louise or Olive coming in and walked slowly to the front door. She opened it before they reached the front step.

Olive and Ruth looked at each other. Ruth shook her head. Louise understood what it meant. No one could think of anything to say. Ruth stood back for them to come in and they passed wordlessly through the house and into the kitchen. Les looked up.

"Nothing."

"I know," Olive said quietly.

Silent tears ran down Louise's cheeks. "Where is she?" she whispered.

"I wish I knew," Ruth started crying too.

"Hush, Louie. We mustn't upset them." Olive put her arms around Louise.

"I'm upset too. She's my very best friend," Louise sobbed.

She remembered the first time she had seen Joy who looked like a princess; how she'd been so overawed by the red-haired vision that she'd burst into tears. She remembered swapping secret names for each other; fishing for crabs off the end of the jetty; their first day at school when Joy vomited all over her; their conversations as they sat on the beach and plucked at shells that peeped out of the sand. She remembered the many sand castles they'd built; the beach contests they'd won when they'd hugged each other and run into the water and screamed under it so that only they knew how thrilled they were. And she thought of almost every evening when they hung out of their windows and waved at each other across the fence where the sweet pea grew. If no one found her friend, if she never came back, Louise didn't know how she'd ever enjoy a single day again.

The phone shrilled making them jump. Les got to it first.

"Hello? Yeah...yeah...oh. No. Nothing here either...All right...I suppose so...You will...? Yeah...Bye."

He put down the phone slowly and turned to the three pairs of waiting eyes.

"Nothing."

Ruth's body shook violently and her skin had turned a sickly grey colour.

"Would you prefer to be alone?" Olive asked.

"No. No, it's all right. Stay," Les said. "She needs all the support she can get."

He looked at Olive over Ruth's head and she nodded. There was a faint wailing coming from Ruth. She rocked back and forth on her chair, her arms clutched around herself tightly. They saw that she was dry retching, her tongue curling up inside her mouth each time it opened and her throat contracted.

"Where's a bucket?" Olive asked quickly.

"The laundry," Les replied.

She was back with a bucket a few moments later. Ruth continued to dry retch, and the wailing rose until it abruptly changed to a whimpering, interspersed with hiccups.

"Why can't the police find her?" Louise cried.

"It's still early, Louie," Olive reassured her, putting her arms around the girl's shoulders. "It's only just light."

Pat and Jim arrived to sit and wait with Ruth and Les.

"It's my fault," Pat sniffed. "I shouldn't have left the platform."

"Of course it's not," Les soothed her. "You couldn't have known I was supposed to pick her up after work—though why she said she was catching a train's beyond me. Still, it was safe enough."

"Apparently not," Ruth said quietly.

Tears filled Pat's eyes and she swiped at them impatiently with a handkerchief. Jim patted her hand with no effect.

Ruth appeared to be controlling herself reasonably well, but Les knew differently. Her eyes were too bright and shifted continually from side to side. Her hands shook, when she allowed them to be seen, and she was grinding her teeth unconsciously. Everyone pretended they didn't notice.

"Here, throw this down," he said, handing her a small glass of brandy. He'd poured a brandy each for all of them and they took their glasses gratefully.

Louise lay curled up on the couch with her head on Olive's lap. Louise felt guilty that Joy had disappeared after she'd bought a birthday present for her. She learned of Joy's mission to Bentleigh on her behalf and wished she didn't have a stupid birthday. She wished it was just an ordinary day when she and Joy would wake up and go to their windows and lean out with a whistle and wave to each other. She wished Joy was her sister and that they could live together for always. Well, they'd do that when they grew up. Once the police found Joy.

Les cringed at the thought of the previous night and at the prospect of what Ruth must now go through. What they all must go through. He wished it could be any other way, but he was in too deep and there was no turning back. He sat with his elbows resting on his knees, looking at the pattern in the carpet. He wondered what each one of them was thinking, if they suspected that he'd had anything to do with Joy's disappearance. But why should they? None of them knew about Ursula—not even Ruth—and there was nothing to link her with them.

He looked up at Pat's anxious face, feeling sorry for her, for the guilt he knew she was feeling for not having waited to see Joy board the train. If only he could tell her that it wasn't her fault, that Joy was safe and alive. There were so many times they had spent with Pat and Jim, treated as if they belonged in the Lewis family—the warmth and generosity of the welcome they always received. What Les had done would always affect Pat, like it would if Joy had been her own granddaughter.

His eyes met Olive's who raised an eyebrow in question. He instinctively understood the question and shook his head. The question slowly dissolved from her eyes and face. He could see her relief. *No, Joy never found out. That's not why she's gone.*

Ruth tipped her glass up to her lips. It was empty. Les reached over and refilled it and she drank the liquid, grateful for the slow burning that seemed to chase the panic away. At least for the moment. How she regretted allowing Joy to go on the train alone. If only she'd put down those frocks for a couple of hours and gone with her. She could have sat up all night and finished the frocks, if need be, and the two girls would have woken up early today in excited anticipation of the party. They'd be here safe and getting under everyone's feet, laughing and opening presents.

When the call came, Les picked up the phone and faced the wall. It was a quarter past two in the afternoon. They waited, listening, instinctively knowing it was the police.

"...all right, I'll be there right away."

He put the phone down and turned slowly back to face them.

"Olive." He looked at her and then at Louise.

She understood.

"Louie," she said, standing up and bringing Louise to her feet. "Come and help me get something to eat."

"I'm not hungry."

"Yes, but everyone else is. We must do what we can to help."

"All right," Louise said reluctantly. "But we're coming back, aren't we?"

"Yes, sweetheart. Right back."

Les sat down beside Ruth and took her hands. She looked at him, eyes searching his, her mouth working in meaningless spasms. He waited until Olive and Louise let themselves out of the front door. They all heard it click shut.

"Love."

Ruth moaned, "No. No. No."

"Love. You have to be strong."

"No. Please don't tell me. I don't want to hear."

She clamped her hands over her ears, shaking her head from side to side, and began to hum, louder and louder. Les took her hands away from her ears.

"Ruth. They've found a body," he said quietly, his eyes riveted to hers. He heard a gasp from behind him.

"No. No," she shouted at him. "It's not Joy."

The scream climbed up from somewhere inside her, gathering volume as it reached her throat and erupted from her mouth. It pierced their ears painfully. It was a scream of fear, of pain, of separation.

"Ruth…"

The scream stopped as suddenly as it began.

"It's someone else," she said in a normal voice, as if the thought had just occurred to her.

"I hope so. I have to go and see."

Pat appeared on the other side of Ruth, putting her arms around Ruth's shoulders. Tears filled her eyes as she looked at Les. Ruth was teetering on the edge, and they all knew it.

"You'll stay with her?" he asked.

"Of course, love."

"I'll come with you," Jim said from behind him.

He heard a sob beside him in that cold silent room and he turned around to see Jim with tears pouring down his face. They splashed over his large fingers as he covered his mouth with his hand. Les felt as if everything was moving in slow motion. He saw a shower of fine needles follow the movement of his arm, as he raised it to touch Jim's arm. It took him hours to reach the arm. And his voice came out like a muffled horn. It didn't sound like it belonged to him.

"Are you all right?" his voice said, slow and deep. It echoed in his head.

He touched Jim's arm, and he was acutely conscious of the rough feel of the wool, the fibres sticking up from each stitch, the tingling of the texture on the pads of his fingers. Jim turned his head towards him. It was slow, like in a dream. His head seemed to float around on his neck. His mouth opened to say something, but Les couldn't hear it. He could only hear the roaring in his ears. There was a whirling tunnel that pulled at him and he could feel himself falling into it, turning around and around. The roar turned into a long wailing cry and it came from between his ears. Suddenly, he was jerked back into the room. The white glare of the overhead light stabbed at his eyes. Hands were holding him, supporting him. He looked in bewilderment at the faces regarding him.

It shocked him to see her lying there. He looked at the red hair surrounding the chalk-white face, its curls reflecting the overhead light with life that no longer belonged to the body. Bruises marred the perfect skin and he brushed at them tenderly as if to wipe them away. He didn't notice the small brown patch under the jaw, shaped like a lightning fork.

She looked as though she was asleep, as he'd seen her hundreds of times, and he felt if he touched her, kissed her cheek, she would open her eyes and say, "Daddy." It tore at him to see her so cold, so lifeless, so detached, and it took him a moment to remember that it wasn't really her. It was a reflection of his daughter.

He saw Jim's mouth say, "He loved that child".

Another face nodded in sympathy.

Les wondered whom they were talking about.

Chapter 33

The Chief Conductor, Concert Master, Associate Concert Master and other string principals took in the figure of the forty-six year-old man with the intense pale green eyes who stood before them. They noticed the jaw that was set into hard lines, the thin mouth, the serious expression, the neatly-combed fair hair copiously sprinkled with silver highlights. He slowly raised the violin, his long fingers gripping the scroll. His jaw settled into the chin rest as he raised the bow in his right hand.

Gunter's reputation had preceded him. He was a talented musician, a conscientious and valued member of the West Australian Symphony Orchestra, a dependable and good man. Nothing had prepared the panel, however, for the harsh face that stared back at them. It appeared as stone, with erosion cutting deep lines into its landscape. It was a face that had suffered, that had been sorely tormented, but it was not a face that looked for pity. Resignation lay in those lines, but not submission. Strength, but not defiance.

And yet, when he closed his eyes to the panel's scrutiny, when his violin began to sing, the lines smoothed a little, blended back into his features. The jaw softened, the lips rounded minutely, and the artist, the craftsman, spoke to them of beauty and joy through his music.

Gunter sat in the train impatiently, counting off each station. The train pulled out of Hawthorn. Next would come Glenferrie, Auburn, then finally Camberwell, where he'd board a tram that travelled along Burke Road to Cotham Road, and then a walk of a few short blocks to home. Ursula would be waiting for him. For his good news. His hands gripped the violin case on his lap as the train lurched suddenly. A dizziness and nausea swept over him and his vision blurred momentarily. He shook his head to clear it and noticed how heavy his body felt. As if it were being dragged down into the seat. *I must be coming down with something. Ursula was right,* he thought.

He closed his eyes and his body sagged in surrender to the feeling of malaise. It took all his willpower to stop himself from falling asleep. *Must not miss the station,* he kept reminding himself, over and over again. He rocked with the hypnotic motion of the train as it clattered along the railway tracks. Twice he felt the train come to a standstill, heard people getting off it and others boarding, the guard's whistle and the doors closing, then the train pulling out of the station. Still his eyes remained closed. Rock, rock, body tense, body heavy. Rock, rock, clatter, clatter. *Tired, so tired.* Flashing lights behind his closed lids. Rock, rock, clatter, clatter. Slow, slow, rock, rock, clatter, clatter. His stomach muscles pulled against the sideways lurch of the train as it ground to a halt at Camberwell. *Get up. Get up,* he told himself. *Open your eyes.* Heavy, so heavy. He swayed to his feet, dropping the violin case as he did so. A pair of hands in front of him picked up the case and handed it to him.

"You all right mate?"

"Yes, yes. Thank you. Thank you."

His fingers wrapped themselves around the handle of the case. It felt so heavy. Other hands guided him out of the train. His feet bumped onto the platform like jellied rubber and he had difficulty in directing them to carry him forward.

I am a robot—an automaton. I can walk. I can breathe. I can...

Gunter staggered in staccato footsteps out of the station. At the tram stop a pole held him up. He clung to it, barely feeling its cold, metallic rigidity on his cheek. Outside of his body were other hands and bodies. He saw them through the flashing lights and sudden rain as his legs propelled him up and into the tram. Rock, rock, clatter, clatter, screech, screech. A violin case swayed with the tram's passage along Burke Road. It was attached to his fingers, he saw. *Ursula will be so happy.*

"Cotham Road!" reverberated in his ear.

Oh, Cotham Road. Get off. Get off.

Footsteps rattled behind him, beside him, around him. They stamped in time with his legs. He knew because he could see his feet come out in front of him on the footpath. Right, left, right, left. His shoes. His feet. Funny...he couldn't feel them.

His right hand went to dig in his pocket for the key, but there was a violin case attached to his fingers. He saw his left hand reach out in front of him and was surprised to see the violin case now attached to it. He lifted up his right hand in front of his eyes again and saw that it was empty. There was no sensation in it. He wondered if it belonged to someone else, but it looked like his. It disappeared again and came back in front of his face, between the flashing lights. It had a key between its fingers. He looked down and saw his feet climbing some stairs. Right, left. Right, left. Something must be carrying him up, because he couldn't remember doing it. A brass figure '8' was on the door. Right in the middle. He saw a hand pushing a key into the keyhole. It turned with a nice clean click. He liked that. The door opened easily and the hand pushed it inwards. *Ursula,* he called out, but the sound was in slow motion, deep and unlike his voice. *I have good news.* His mouth twisted in the wrong direction and the words came out corrupted—incomplete.

He fell against the wall, sliding along it. *Why are there no lights on?* His shoulder brushed against a light switch and the apartment flared into blazing white. *Ursula! Liebling!* His legs refused to hold him upright and he slithered down to the floor. His whole body felt numb, heavy, useless.

As he clung to a shrivelling consciousness, his last thought was of Ursula. He knew she was not in the flat.

He lay on the floor. He'd been there all night and most of the morning. The light was still on. He could see it as he wafted in and out of consciousness. When he tried to get up, his body wouldn't obey him. It refused to stand up, turn off the light, close the door. A draft blew in from the landing. He knew because it danced across his face and made his right eye dry. At least he could close it, rest it, then he drifted off somewhere else, until a noise woke him and his eye would open again. He didn't know if his left eye was open or not.

The ringing in his ears was interrupted by the sound of footsteps on the landing.

"The door's still open," jangled a disembodied voice from somewhere. "Do you think something's wrong?"

"Goodness knows," another voice clattered. "He only moved in a day or so ago. Don't know anything about him, though. Do you?"

"Someone said he's from Perth."

"Just him?"

"I don't know. Kept to himself."

"What if he's been broken into?"

"In this neighbourhood?"

"We'd better check."

The draft whooshed in over his eye. He could see a pair of brown high heels where the door had been. He thought the ankles were very nicely shaped. The landing was behind them, and another pair of shoes—black court, with thick ankles attached—were coming closer.

"Hello?" came the jangle from above him.

"Goodness gracious!"

"Oh, my. He must have had a..."

And the jangle faded, along with the fear.

The concert hall was filled to capacity and every face was turned towards him. His jaw fitted comfortably in the chin rest as he looked along the strings to where his left hand gripped the scroll. The fingers jumped nimbly from one string to the other and his right hand flashed past his vision, driving the bow across and back, across and back. The orchestra members seated around him played better than he'd ever heard them. The music soared, filled his ears, and lifted him off the stage where he floated above the audience. Each note that he created was more pure than the one before.

The lights were bright...too bright, as he floated towards them.

"No, he can't hear anything. No response," said the voice behind the light.

He screwed up his eye against the blinding white.

Ursula. Where is Ursula? He looked down at the audience from his floating place, where upturned pink faces emerged from long V-necked bodices, shirt collars, rows of pearls, and jacket lapels. Some of the faces continued back onto bald pates, or ended abruptly at fringed, thick arrangements of hair. He searched among the audience, first along the front row, then back to the next row. Right to left. Across the aisle. Right to left. Back another row. Right to left. Across the aisle. Right to left. He stopped playing and dropped his violin. It fell like a leaf, drifting slowly from side to side, until it reached the floor where it sank through the carpet, swallowed up gradually until there was nothing left of it. The pattern in the dark red carpet was perfect.

"He won't last the night," said a jangle behind the white light.

Who won't? he wondered.

He tightened his eyelid against the light and looked through the slit.

Ursula, he screamed at the light. *You've got to find her.*

But his mouth didn't move.

He looked at the white, starched uniforms as they hovered near with needles, tubes, and other things that reminded him of Auschwitz, of Hannah's scars, of Hannah's death. They stuck them in, cut him. Cold. Cold terror.

Why doesn't my body move?

He tried to open his mouth to speak, lift his arm to attract their attention, scream, yell, curse.

"...a nursing home. Only place for someone like this."

Who?

"...a mere vegetable..."

A hand shook his shoulder, waking him out of a dreamless sleep.

"Mr Schwartz. We're moving you today."

His eye opened.

"Look, he's awake. Perhaps he heard me."

"No. He's most likely deaf. He can't talk, can he? It's a reflex from your shaking him."

"You think so?"

The thin white uniform nodded. "He's probably mental now. I mean, he's been here...what...two days? And he hasn't responded."

"Poor thing," said the other white uniform with long dark hair. She stroked his forehead and it tingled pleasantly as her fingers brushed it.

Help me!

The nurses moved over to the window and looked out over St. Kilda Road.

"Did you see the photo of that poor little girl in the papers?"

"Who? The one they found near Frankston?"

"Yes. A pretty kid, too. A redhead. What do you think if I tint my hair that colour? Be a nice change..."

Gunter woke up as his body was jostled onto a trolley. The sheet under him was cold. Rails were lifted up beside him and locked into place with a clatter. His chin was itchy and he tried to lift his hand to scratch at it but it was locked under a heavy weight and wouldn't move. The smell of disinfectant reached his nostrils as the trolley was pushed along a corridor. It bumped against a wall as it was turned into a waiting lift, and his head hit the rails. A man, two women and a young girl were in the lift. They parted to give the trolley room and stopped talking to look at him. The man was holding up a newspaper, reading the sports page, and he lowered it slightly as he, too, looked at Gunter. Just as he did so, Gunter saw the headline on the front page that faced him. It read: **BODY OF GIRL FOUND IN BAY** and there was a photograph of a young girl below it. The photograph was of Ursula. It took him some moments to realise the significance of the photograph. And then he screamed inside his head. The photograph of Ursula was without the birthmark.

The pile of bodies was never ending. The more he put into the oven, the more the pile grew. Flames belched out of the opening, and flickered over his face. The bodies in the oven sat up; their arms extended outwards for him to take their hands. The flames licked around them. His sister's pale, thin face grimaced at him. He reached over to tickle her feet so that she would giggle like she always did, but she drew her feet back out of reach. He followed her into the oven and sat there beside her as the flames warmed him. A hand touched him and he turned to see Hannah. Her hair was the colour of the flames and it drifted around her head like fairy floss. It tangled with the hair of a person sitting behind her. The colour of the hair was identical. The person turned around and he smiled to see it was Ursula. *Oh, there you are, liebling,* he said. He reached out for her but her eyes were closed and her body was stiff and cold.

"...yes, a coma..."

"Are you sure?"

"It's been ten days now."

"Poor man...doesn't have anyone..."

Mud encased his whole body. It was heavy, had dried hard, and he couldn't break free of it. *Why am I in mud?* His eye opened. He could see a tube coming out of his nose. He tried to swallow, but couldn't, and it hurt. It felt like something was stuck there. A white uniform bent over him. The faint smell of perfume reached his nostrils. *What's happening to me?* he asked her, but his lips refused to form the sounds. She looked down at him for a moment, and saw his eye watching her. She turned around.

"His eye's open again. Do you think he's conscious?"

"No. Look," and the other white uniform came into his line of vision; "he's got absolutely no expression, no emotion, on his face."

"I suppose so..."

"He won't last." She turned to adjust his IV. "I'll bet he won't even last a month."

Are they talking about me? I'm going to die? No. No, you're wrong! We've got to find her...Ursula!

Chapter 34

The door closed behind Les with a soft click. It was the only noise that Joy could hear, other than the rain spattering on the window. No television set or radio blared in that whisper-quiet building. Sitting there, on the narrow bed, she felt abandoned and afraid, and burst into tears. Why had he left her? Why couldn't she go with him? Maybe if she caught up with him, he'd change his mind. She dashed out of the room and looked along the gloomy passageway that led both left and right. Which way had he gone? The threadbare carpet silenced her footsteps as she hurried barefooted past forbidding closed doors, and she instinctively quieted her tears in the hushed surroundings. She came to the top of a staircase and looked down to the ground floor. A cold flurry of air brushed over her thinly-clad figure and she shivered. The familiar sound of her father's truck, as the motor kicked into life, reached her ears. She quickly ran down the stairs and flung open the heavy front door to see the truck's tail-lights disappear down the driveway and into the rain.

"Bugger!"

The forbidden word helped to vent her frustration, but she looked over her shoulder in case she'd been overheard. A light shone under a doorway at the end of a passage, and she decided to investigate.

"Hello?"

Her voice sounded small in the high-ceilinged passage.

"Hello?" she said again, knocking on the door this time.

Receiving no answer, she pushed the door open and poked her head around the doorway to discover the empty kitchen. The fire drew her to it and she stood close to calm her shivering. Looking around the room, it seemed familiar to her and it took some moments to realise it was because of some of the furniture. She had seen it at home—the chairs, a firewood box, some shelving—when Les had been repairing or making it in his workshop. The kitchen was just how he'd described it to her and Ruth. Even the table was familiar because Les had told them about the broken leg and how he'd sanded the table down and re-stained it. And the kettle—Les had mentioned how every time he called in, the kettle was always spouting steam up the chimney as it stood on the old wood stove in a permanent boiling state. Despite her fear, her confusion, Joy felt somewhat comforted to see the kettle steaming on the stove.

"There you are, dear."

Joy whirled around to see Sister Dominique and Sister Margaret Mary gliding towards her. The soft susurrations of the nuns' habits and the faint clicking of their rosary beads blended with the crackle of the fire in the stillness of the convent kitchen.

"Oh...I..."

"Are you all right, dear?" the older nun asked.

"Yes. I was just..."

"I know. You're frightened."

"And no wonder," the other nun exclaimed. "You're in a strange place, don't know any of us, and it's cold and wet outside."

Joy looked from one to the other.

"You must be Sister Margaret Mary," she said to the older nun. "You're just like Dad described you."

"Oh, my goodness! And how was that?"

"Your face, your eyes. Just everything."

"And I'm Sister Dominique," the other nun said, with a smile making the corners of her eyes crinkle.

"You conjure up fruit scones all the time," Joy laughed, more relaxed now.

"Well, yes, I suppose I do," Sister Dominique agreed, bafflement written all over her face.

"Dad told me. He said no matter what time of the day or night he calls in here, there're always hot scones. He doesn't know how you do it. He thinks you've got a magic wand."

Sister Margaret Mary smiled serenely. "I think Sister Dominique has some divine secret, dear. None of the sisters—nor I, in fact— have quite discovered it yet."

Sister Dominique glided over to the wood stove and took down a thick pot-holder from a hook in the wall. "Would you like a nice hot scone, dear?" she said over her shoulder. She grasped the handle of a door in the stove and opened it, taking out a tray of scones. The aroma that wafted over to Joy was delicious.

"If it's no trouble..." Joy suddenly realised how hungry she was.

"And a cup of hot milk? Or tea?" Sister Margaret Mary asked. "And we'll get you something warm to put on."

Twenty minutes later, Joy sat back a little ashamedly, having eaten half of the scones on the tray, washed down by two cups of hot tea.

"I didn't mean to eat so many," Joy exclaimed in dismay. "I'm terribly sorry."

"You must have been hungry, dear. And there are plenty more where they came from." Sister Dominique's eyes crinkled up again. "It's such a pleasure to see a healthy appetite."

"Just like your father," Sister Margaret Mary nodded.

Joy sat back, warm now, both inside and out. She understood why Les enjoyed visiting the nuns at Aggie's Place. They made you feel calm, and she wasn't nearly so frightened as before. They were such adorable old ladies who fussed over her like Nana did, but in a quieter way. She wondered where the other nuns were. If they were with the Reverend Mother. If she had died yet. Joy felt guilty suddenly as it occurred to her that Sister Margaret Mary and Sister Dominique might want to be with the Reverend Mother.

"Is the Reverend Mother...?"

"No, child," Sister Margaret Mary said softly. "But very soon." Her pale blue eyes were touched with sudden sadness.

"Do you want to go up to her?" Joy stood up and began to gather up the dishes on the table. "I can clean up here."

"What a charming child," exclaimed Sister Dominique.

"Thank you, my dear. I would like to sit with her."

She rose smoothly from her chair, the folds of her habit falling softly around her figure.

Sister Dominique also stood. "Would you like me to stay with you?"

"No. No, I'm fine," Joy assured her.

"Please make yourself at home," Sister Margaret Mary said, touching Joy on the arm. Her eyes seemed to look into Joy's mind. "We don't have much, but what we have is yours to share."

"Thank you, Magg...I mean, sister," Joy said, catching herself before calling Sister Margaret Mary *Maggie,* as her father did when he talked about her at home.

"Will you be afraid, child?"

"No. Not anymore," Joy replied honestly.

The two nuns glided across the floor to the doorway and paused to look back at Joy.

"One of us will come down to see to you later," Sister Margaret Mary said. "In the meantime, you'll find something to read in the library, if you like to read."

Joy nodded.

"The library is down the passageway, last door on the left. We mainly have religious books, but you might find something to your liking."

"Thanks," Joy smiled, wishing the two nuns wouldn't leave her. The kitchen suddenly seemed empty, colder.

She stood in front of the fire for a while, thinking over what had happened that day. She'd woken up to the excitement of the party preparations, and had been thrilled at the sight of the two frocks as they took shape under the capable hands of her mother. It seemed so long ago since she'd sat on the train alone, gone shopping with Nana and finally found the perfect present for Louise. And then meeting up again with Ursula.

What a strange and wonderful happening to discover a person who looked exactly like her. It was weird. Yes, that's what it was. Weird. They'd both thought so. It couldn't just be a coincidence. Of course, she'd heard people say that everyone has a double. But identical? *That* identical? It wasn't possible, and yet they had met and seen each other. They were living proof that nature could make an exact replica of their bodies, their faces, their hair—except for the only thing different they could find: the birthmark.

There was something spooky about her father's reaction to Ursula, too. Almost as if he was angry, or wished Ursula hadn't turned up. He'd acted so differently from his normal self. Wouldn't you think he'd be just as fascinated as Joy was about the likeness? After all, it didn't happen every day that you met somebody who was your mirror image. Joy was disappointed and hurt that her father hadn't been swept up in the excitement that both she and Ursula had felt. He'd let her down for the first time in her life. She was always so proud of him, so happy to show him off to her friends, confident that they'd like his easy manner, envy her for the wonderful dad he was. Ursula was proud of her dad, also. You could tell by the way she talked about him, how clever he was playing the violin, how she knew he'd pass that audition. From what Ursula had said, they seemed very close. Just the two of them.

Joy puzzled over the fact that she'd become so sleepy. How could she have fallen asleep in front of Ursula? What must she think of her? The last thing she'd felt like was falling asleep. She had absolutely no recollection of Ursula getting out of the truck, or how she arrived at the convent. It was eerie how she'd just woken up in that room upstairs.

As Joy thought of Ursula, a peculiar sadness swept over her. It rushed into her mind and spread down to her stomach. Her heart beat faster. She felt as if she were choking. Tears welled in her eyes, and the melancholy spilled out with the notion that she would never see Ursula again. Why she should feel such grief over Ursula, who was almost a complete stranger to her, was beyond her understanding. It felt like she had missed the only opportunity to solve the riddle of their sameness. That something important had been about to reveal itself to her, and it had slipped through her fingers. But her father had said Ursula would ring her. That she'd be in touch again soon. Surely then they could spend more time together, compare the events in each other's lives, become friends. Would Louise be jealous, she wondered. No…she'd like Ursula, too. And she was certain that her mother would love Ursula. After all, she loved Joy so much, and now there'd be two of her to love. Maybe then her sickness would go away.

The thought of Ruth jolted Joy back to the picture of her mother stabbing the frocks with scissors, as Les had described. She couldn't understand her mother doing that. She always took such pride in everything she made. To destroy the frocks was inconceivable. And what would her mother be like when she returned from hospital? Would she be drugged and lethargic like those other times? And for how long? Where had Louise gone? What was Mrs Fletcher doing about her mother? Was she mad at her for ruining the frocks? Was Louise mad at her for ruining their party? Was Louise mad at Joy? Would she talk to her again?

Some thirteenth birthday, Joy thought dejectedly, as she wiped her face with her sleeve. *Here I am, stuck in a convent with no one to talk to, and no party.* She sighed as she moved over to the sink to wash up the few dishes. It was then that she noticed the telephone. *No phone. No gossip*, her father's voice reminded her as she lifted the receiver. She began to dial. *Say you promise.* The phone was ringing. *I'm holding you to that.* She put the phone down just as Louise picked it up at the other end.

The library was a cold, silent room, with little to entice a thirteen year-old girl to stay and linger over the few books on the mostly empty shelves. Joy took out a bible and it opened at a colour plate that caught her attention. A large, bearded man was holding up a baby, and there was a distressed woman on either side of it, each clutching an arm. A soldier was holding up a sword. His eyes were questioning the man, as if waiting for a decision. Joy understood that the two women wanted the same baby, and with distaste she realised that the soldier was prepared to cut the baby in two, if so ordered, to settle the argument. Shivering with cold she moved over to a lamp to read the text about the picture. It was King Solomon—yes, she'd heard about him; he was supposed to be a wise man—and he proved the identity of the real mother when she put her baby's safety before herself. She had been willing to allow the other woman to take her baby rather than have her child cut in two. *How clever*, Joy mused. She wondered if Solomon would be able to work out the puzzle of her identity and Ursula's. If he'd come up with something so simple, something so certain. *Pity he's not around these days. I'd go and see him.*

Joy didn't hear Sister Dominique when she entered the room. She jumped in fright when the nun touched her hand.

"You're like ice, child."

"Oh!"

"Did I frighten you? I'm sorry."

"No. I was just reading..."

"You found something to interest you?" Sister Dominique bent over the book that lay open on the table in the lamplight. "Oh, you're reading about Solomon? What a wise man he was."

"Yes. I could do with someone like him."

"You need someone wise?"

"Yes."

"What about that wonderful father of yours?"

"I suppose so."

Sister Dominique looked concerned as Joy's teeth began chattering.

"We can't have you catching a cold. Come, child. We'll go back to the fire...or would you rather go upstairs to bed?"

"I'm not tired. I feel like I've slept for a week," Joy said, pulling a face. She suddenly remembered the dying nun. "What about the Reverend Mother? Is she all right? I mean..." she trailed off uncertainly. How was she supposed to ask?

"She's slipping away quietly."

"Oh, I'm sorry. Look, don't worry about me. I can sit by the fire. Read a bit more." She held up the bible. "Can I borrow it?"

"Of course, dear."

They turned off the lights and went back to the warm kitchen.

"Make yourself another hot drink. And there are more scones there if you'd like some."

"Thanks. I'll be right."

Joy watched Sister Dominique as she swept out of the kitchen. It was a soundless, smooth, hovering over the floor. Like her father, Joy wondered how they did it, how their feet never seemed to touch the floor. She made herself a cup of steaming hot tea and hesitated over the remaining scones before she gave in to the temptation and buttered two. Taking them over to the fire, she pulled up a chair and sat back to read some more, sipping on the tea and feeling much better in the warmth. After a while, she put another chair in front of her, and settled back comfortably with her legs up.

Despite herself, Joy started to nod after another hour of reading. The hushed atmosphere of the house, punctuated by the hiss and crackle of the fire, and the steady downpour from outside, lulled her into a light doze. She started if a log fell or exploded with a pop, showering sparks against the fire screen, and then settled back, her chin dropping onto her chest again.

Gentle hands coaxed her awake and guided her out of the chair. She looked at her watch and was surprised to see that it was after midnight. Sister Margaret Mary's eyes held a calm sadness and instinctively Joy knew that the Reverend Mother had finally slipped away. She impulsively hugged the nun.

"I'm sorry," she cried, sudden tears coming to her own eyes.

"It's God's will," the nun said softly. "She's at peace now."

"Can I...do anything? Get you a cuppa?"

"No, child. I think we'll all go to bed now. It's late."

They ascended the stairs together in a comfortable silence. Joy felt reassured and protected in Sister Margaret Mary's company. She remembered how her father had spoken of the nun, how he'd enjoyed visiting her and talking to her. He'd said it was a real tonic visiting Aggie's Place for a chinwag with Maggie. Joy turned at her bedroom door.

"Thanks for everything. I'm sorry to be a nuisance."

"Hush, dear. You're not a nuisance. It's our pleasure to offer you shelter." She took both of Joy's hands in her own. "We don't often have young company, you know."

"Don't you get bored here?"

Sister Margaret Mary smiled at Joy's naiveté. "Not at all. We're fortunate to live in such a beautiful part of the world. We have each other's company, and that of Our Lord."

"Oh."

"I hope you won't be bored while you're with us."

"I'll be right. It's only a day or so anyway."

"And what will happen then, child?"

"What do you mean?"

"Will you be going home?"

"Oh, yes. Sure."

The old woman's watchful eyes regarded Joy solemnly. They seemed to bore into her, read her fears, her uncertainty. She looked down at the floor.

"Mum'll be all right. The doctors'll fix her."

"Of course they will."

Joy hesitated. "Do you really think so?"

When she closed the door behind her, Joy noticed the parcel next to her shoes. Curious, she opened it to discover three books. *He's left them for me,* she thought, not sure whether to be pleased or angry with her father. Despite her yawns, she read the synopsis of each book, staying the longest on *The Diary of Anne Frank.* Then, forgetting her troubles, she became immersed in the drama of the horror of World War II and the ghastly circumstances in which the Frank family found itself in Amsterdam.

Thirty minutes later Joy slipped gingerly between the sheets of the bed. She was surprised to find three hot water bottles arranged along its length and was delighted to sink into the warmth they left rather than the icy welcome she'd been expecting. Things would be better in the morning, she decided. Her dad would be coming to see her, maybe take her home straight away, and her mum would be better taking some new tablets. This time tomorrow night she'd be in her own bed, looking at her desk with *Blue Eyes* sitting on the top, and her parents would come in and kiss her goodnight. Then she'd dart out of bed again, as soon as they'd closed her door, pull back her curtains, stick her head out of the window, and whistle softly to Louise. They'd wave at each other, grin, spit, wave again, and go back to bed. She turned on her side, putting her hand under the pillow. Her last thought, before she drifted off to sleep, was of someone who looked just like her.

Chapter 35

She was looking at herself in a mirror. At first, everything she did her reflection copied, but then their movements began to falter, become jerky, out of sync. The mirror's surface became distorted, and the face drooped and stretched into an ugly shape. She reached out a hand to stop it warping, but her fingers became caught in the mirror and, as she pulled them back, they bled onto the distorted reflection. The green eyes turned red and stared back at her, leaking tears of blood. The mouth screamed at her for help, but she couldn't move. Her father was sitting on her.

Joy's eyes snapped open. She looked around the unfamiliar room, heard the rain slapping on the window, felt the now-cold hot water bottles glugging wetly inside their jelly-like rubber envelopes. She reached down and pulled them out of the bedclothes, dropping them one by one onto the floor where they wobbled into stillness. Her arm darted back inside the covers and she snuggled into the warmth of the bed.

Her eyes were open under the water so that she could see her double floating beside her. Their red hair floated around their heads, moving in sinuous undulations. Music penetrated the water, playing around their ears, and they moved in unison with its melody. They smiled at each other as the sun filtered through the water lighting up their faces. Suddenly, Ursula was jerked backwards, away from her. Joy tried to follow but the distance between them became greater until finally Ursula was lost to sight. Joy was caught under the water. She tried to surface but was pushed back down. Her mouth filled with water. She was choking.

She sat up in bed, swallowing convulsively. It was Ursula who had been in her dreams all those years, she realised. It was Ursula who was the shadowy companion of her unconscious. But she'd never had such vivid, tearing nightmares about her before. Why was it that after their meeting yesterday, everything had gone wrong? Why did she feel that her world had come to an end?

Weak sunlight slanted through a gap in the plain curtains that hung on the window, painting a gold streak across the bed. Dust motes cavorted through the streak and she automatically held her breath to stop them travelling up her nostrils. She and Louise always did that when they saw dust motes. They used to pretend that the motes were evil fairies trying to take hold of their bodies, and they would have to turn away from the bands of motes before they could breathe again. Suddenly she wished Louise were with her. They could talk about all that had happened. Work it out. Then she remembered that her father had told her Louise had gone away. If they'd waited, Joy could have gone with her, instead of being in this deathly-quiet place.

The hands on her watch indicated that there was only an hour and a half of the morning left. With a start, she jumped out of bed and dug her arms into the woollen coat that Sister Margaret Mary had loaned her the night before. Her father should have arrived by now. He said he'd be here to see her in the morning. Perhaps he was waiting in the kitchen downstairs. Waiting for her to wake up. She shivered as she splashed her face with water in the cold bathroom, and rinsed her mouth out, brushing around her teeth with her index finger.

The kitchen's warmth was a welcome enticement to enter, along with the aroma rising from bubbling pots on the wood stove. Sister Francis Mary and Sister Dominique, who were busy chopping vegetables and adding them to the pots, looked up from their work.

"There she is." Sister Dominique smiled as she put down her knife and moved around the table to greet Joy. She turned to Sister Francis Mary. "This is the dear child you've been waiting to meet."

Joy tried to hide her disappointment at not finding Les in the kitchen.

"Hello. Sorry I slept so late."

"There's not much else for a young girl to do here," Sister Dominique crinkled her eyes at Joy. "This is Sister Francis Mary."

"Good morning, dear. I imagine you're hungry," she said gliding across the floor towards her. She took Joy's hands in her own, squeezing them in genuine welcome. They felt rough, Joy noted, looking down at the cracked nails and calloused fingers.

"Oh, hi. You're the gardener. Dad told me how terrific you are with plants."

"Bless his heart," Sister Francis Mary beamed. "What a lovely man your father is." When she smiled, creases darted across her face from the corners of her mouth to just under her ears. Her forehead was likewise creased as her eyebrows shot up above very round eyes, giving her a startled air.

"Yes."

"Now, what about a couple of fried eggs?" Sister Dominique asked. "We have our own chickens, you know."

"That'd be nice, thanks. Can I help?"

Joy forgot her disappointment for a while as she chatted with the two nuns, their lively conversation distracting her thoughts from Les. After she'd eaten a hearty breakfast, she joined them in preparing soup and washed up the dishes. The hour before lunch was served for the convent nuns, Joy's companions disappeared for spiritual reading, so she went upstairs for a while to continue reading her new books. It was difficult concentrating, waiting for her father, and she wondered what Louise was doing. Well, she'd show her *Sweet Pea* next time they saw each other that she'd been thinking of her. She opened *The Diary of Anne Frank* and wrote a message on the inside cover—one that only Louise would understand.

She looked out of her window and decided to take the opportunity to explore the grounds now that the rain had stopped. Walking along the driveway, she wondered where it was that the tree branch had struck the man when Les had rescued him. The extensive property dripped and gurgled under its coating of rain, and birds flittered busily from tree to ground, pecking out worms from the damp soil. Her breath hung on the air and she hugged the coat around her, digging her hands into the deep pockets.

She looked up at the old building, trying to pick out the room where the Reverend Mother had died. She hadn't liked to broach the subject when she was with Sister Dominique and Sister Francis Mary and, seeing as how they didn't either, she assumed they'd rather not talk about it. It wasn't even clear to her if the old nun's body was still in the convent. She thought about death. *What's it feel like?* she asked herself. *Does it hurt?* She remembered Louise's father, Jack. How he'd been killed by a train. *Gee, that must've hurt.* And there was one of her school friends whose mother had died. *That must've hurt.* Then she realised that the one who was hurt was her friend. How her friend had hurt missing her mother. And Louise had hurt thinking of the train smashing her father to bits. She'd cried a lot even though he wasn't a very nice person. Joy didn't know about Mrs Fletcher. She never saw her crying. It was a puzzle about the nuns though. They probably hurt too, missing the Reverend Mother. She was their boss, after all. *Was she a nice boss?* And what would they do with her body? Bury her here? There was a small area in the grounds, she'd noticed, with some gravestones standing up out of the ground. There had been no weeds around them, and she saw that flowers had been laid on the graves quite recently because, even though the rain had weighed them down and the wind had torn at them, their colours were still vivid, not yet faded into a rotting brown. The most recent gravestone was dated

1962—obviously another nun by the name inscribed upon it. Joy lingered there, studying each inscription, fascinated by the stories of the women who had come from goodness knows where and ended up dying in Red Hill.

Finally reaching the road, she stood for some time looking up and down it, expecting at any minute to see the familiar truck appear from around the bend. *Why's he taking so long?* For the umpteenth time she looked at her watch. *He said he'd be here in the morning.* She reasoned that he may have been held up at the hospital, that he was talking with doctors about her mother's treatment, that maybe he was settling Ruth in at home again, that his truck had broken down, that he had a flat tyre, that...

It was time for lunch, she realised, so she turned back and walked along the driveway and around the side of the building to enter the back door. The table was surrounded by five nuns sitting in the straight-backed chairs, two of whom she didn't know. There was an empty place waiting for Joy and Sister Margaret Mary beckoned her towards it.

"Good day, Joy. I trust you slept well?"

"Yes, thank you."

"Come, child. Sit. We're about to say grace."

They each bent their heads over folded hands and Joy copied them. She looked sideways up at Sister Margaret Mary, who was saying grace, to see what the others were doing. As their eyes were closed, Joy bent her head back down and closed her own.

"You can open your eyes now, dear," Sister Dominique said softly beside her.

"Oh, ta."

Lunch was a simple, but wholesome affair, of which Joy consumed her fair share, despite the fact that she'd had a large breakfast a little more than an hour before. During the meal, she was introduced to the two other nuns, and found them as easy to talk with as she did the others.

Joy turned to Sister Margaret Mary. "Have you heard from my dad? He told me he'd be here this morning."

"No, my dear." The nun studied Joy carefully. "Are you feeling concerned about it?"

"No...well...I thought he'd be here by now..."

"The poor man has a lot to contend with at the moment. I'm sure he'll arrive as soon as he possibly can."

"I'm not complaining..."

"I know, dear. You miss your father, though."

Sister Margaret Mary didn't miss the suggestion of tears in Joy's rapidly blinking eyes. She guessed that there was more to it than that, but unless the girl approached her, she was reluctant to pry. She thought it best to keep Joy busy while she waited for her father.

"Sister," she said, turning to Sister Francis Mary. "Am I not mistaken in thinking that you need a hand in picking some flowers for the chapel?"

"Why, yes, Sister. And who would you suggest could help me?"

The next hour passed by pleasantly for Joy in the company of Sister Francis Mary who allowed her the choice of which flowers to pick, and then showed her where to arrange them in the chapel. Joy stood back and admired her work, pleased that she was able to do something.

"What else can I do?" she asked, reporting back to the nun.

Sister Francis Mary looked up at her doubtfully from where she knelt beside a garden bed. "Do you like weeding?"

"Oh, I don't mind that at all," Joy grinned, crouching down beside her. "Mum and Dad both taught me which ones are the weeds and which ones are the good plants."

"Well, if you don't mind..."

"No. Really. I reckon it gives you time to have a think about things that you mightn't have time to think about at other times. You know, you're listening to the hit parade on the radio or watching TV, or doing your homework." She looked at Sister Francis Mary. "I don't suppose you would know about that."

"Yes, I do, dear. It is a wonderful time for contemplation without the interruption of the outside world."

"Yes, that's it exactly."

"I often pray when I'm out here with nature."

"Do you? What about?"

"Oh, many things...for continued good health for my fellow sisters; thanks for the beauty I see around me; the strength to help those less fortunate than myself; for the soul of our Reverend Mother..."

"Oh, yeah. Sorry about that." Joy looked sideways at the nun. "You all right?"

"Yes, dear."

"Do you feel...very sad?"

"Yes and no. Sad because I'll miss her terribly. We all loved her very much. But happy for her now that she's with God."

"Oh."

"You see, dear, she was a very old lady. She'd lived a full life, giving so much of herself to others, and now it's her turn. When the body is so frail, it's an encumbrance. I think it must be a relief to her that she's finally shed it. Where she's gone, she doesn't need it."

"You mean in heaven?"

"Yes, dear."

"Is it up there?" Joy turned her head up to where clouds scudded across the autumn sky.

"It's everywhere. It's here," she put her hand over her heart. "It's where you put it."

A bell sounded softly across the garden. Sister Francis Mary looked up.

"I'll have to leave you now. It's time for our solitude and contemplation."

"How long?"

"Quite a while, dear. We also have readings, then prayers until three o'clock."

"Can I carry on here?"

"Of course, dear. If that's what you would like to do."

The nun slowly rose to her feet, an involuntary grimace of pain marring her tranquil features. Joy was quick to help the old woman.

"Are you sick?"

"No. Just a bit of rheumatism and old age."

Joy watched her make her way along the path to the back door. Despite the stiffness of her advanced years, the nun still managed to give the impression of gliding across the ground with the utmost grace. *Nice old stick.*

Time lost its flurry as Joy worked in the garden, turning over the soil with a small rake and painstakingly picking out weeds from between azalea bushes, pansies, violas, and rose bushes. The pleasant earthy smell, the birdsong, the rustling of the leaves overhead, the monotonous movements of her hands as they worked, all lulled her troubled thoughts into a stupor. Here she could push her anxieties aside for a brief respite, breathe in the fresh cold air, and dwell solely on her senses.

Something white and moist landed on her arm. She looked up at an overhanging branch where a group of birds sat squawking and tittering at her.

"Thanks a lot," she called up at them, shaking the worst of it off her sleeve.

Her watch peeped out from under the cuff of her jumper and she looked at it in surprise. Ten past two! She hadn't realised she'd been in the garden for so long, but then she looked back along the garden bed and saw how far she'd come. It suddenly hit her that her father still hadn't arrived. A frown guttered across her forehead. *Where is he?* A sudden fear clutched at her that she'd never see him again, never see her mother, or Louise, or her home. *That's it. I'm ringing.* She put down the gardening tools and made for the kitchen. There was no one about as she washed her hands in the sink. The kettle still spurted steam up the chimney, she noticed, and wondered if it needed refilling. She took down the pot-holder and lifted the kettle up. Yes, it did. The fire had died down and she decided to carry some logs in from outside and stoke it up again.

By then, some of her fear had subsided, and she looked at the telephone uncertainly, her hand hovering over it. *Dad did say not to use the phone.* Would he be angry with her if she rang him? Surely he'd be here if he could. He'd never let her down before—at least not until yesterday. But he wouldn't make a habit of it, would he? A thought struck her: of course—it was her birthday. She'd forgotten all about it. *How could I forget that?* He was planning something for her. Yes, a surprise. That's what it would be. A birthday surprise. Maybe all this was a way to get her out of the house—an elaborate plan to fool her. Probably Louise was in the dark too. It would be for both of them. And what about Ursula? Maybe she was a part of it. A sudden gloom hit her in the gut at the thought of her double. She felt afraid for Ursula, but couldn't understand why. It was like the dream, she abruptly recalled, where Ursula was jerked away from her. The feeling was still with her, having seeped from her dream into her consciousness. *Don't be stupid,* she told herself. *It was only a dream.*

Her hand moved away from the telephone and she stood looking in the fire, its flames dancing hypnotically now that the logs had caught. *Thirteen...a teenager at last!* There would still be a party, she reckoned. Probably a different sort from what she and Louise had thought—had planned. Maybe something more adult. Not just a kid's party. Her mum was probably frantically finishing off the frocks, and Mrs Fletcher would be in with her decorating the house, baking, answering phone calls. Yes, she was convinced that was what it was all about. *All right, then. I'll go along with it.* Even if her father were terribly, terribly late, she'd be waiting as a grown-up thirteen year-old would. No tantrums or going crook. It hadn't been so bad here at the convent anyway. The nuns were really friendly and she hadn't suffered at all being with them. It was a blast, really. Something different. What a story she'd have to tell everyone at the party. She'd have to admit that she'd been hood-winked, and everyone would have a good laugh. Louise would probably be in the same boat. *I wonder where she is now.*

Returning to her spot in the garden, Joy knelt down and continued on with the weeding. The flowers looked really nice in the freshly-turned soil, she thought. She'd have to get her mum to buy some pansies. They came in so many different colours, and she could just picture them decorating the garden beds around the front steps of their house. She felt sure that her parents would allow her to take over the garden there. After having spent so much time on this garden, she felt more interest than she had before when she'd weeded just because it was a chore. This was different. This was a beautiful garden and she would like to make one just like it at their place. Maybe Sister Francis Mary would give her hints about planting. She'd like to come back and visit the nuns anyway...bring her mum...and Louise. They'd like the old ladies too. And wouldn't it be fun coming with Ursula? Just imagine how surprised the nuns would be. They'd think they were seeing double.

Sister Francis Mary appeared beside her.

"You're still at it, dear. Aren't you tired?"

"No, Sister. I'm enjoying myself."

"Really? I didn't think young girls stayed still long enough to weed. I was always running about playing, doing things, at your age. How old are you?"

"Thirteen. Today."

"Today? Holy Mother of God! It's your birthday today?"

"Yes."

"Well, many happy returns," she said, hugging Joy. "This is wonderful. We must celebrate. I don't think anyone has had a thirteenth birthday here before."

"I suppose not," Joy laughed.

"Come on, dear. You've done enough gardening for one day. We must tell the others. It will cheer us all."

They headed for the kitchen, Sister Francis Mary gliding over the paths and Joy attempting to glide and getting nowhere.

"How do you do that?"

"What's that?"

"Glide like that."

"Glide?"

"Yes. Your feet don't look as if they touch the ground."

"Don't they?"

Joy laughed at her puzzled expression.

"Never mind. I think it's terrific anyway. Makes you special."

In the kitchen, Joy was surrounded by the subdued excitement of the nuns as they regarded the teenager in front of them. Sister Margaret Mary held both of her hands in her own and sighed softly.

"On a day of mourning we are lifted from our sorrow with the celebration of a life. You have been sent to us, child."

"Pardon?"

"We wish you much joy." She smiled at the pun. "Yes…and a long and fulfilling life. And I must apologise for forgetting that today is your birthday."

"No need…"

They all turned to the door as a loud knocking rattled it furiously.

"What in heaven's name…?" Sister Dominique said as she moved across the kitchen to open the door.

"Dad?"

Les stood in the doorframe swaying drunken-like on his feet, his ashen face streaked with tears. He lurched over to Joy, and his arms wrapped around her so tightly, so desperately, that she squirmed uneasily. He stroked her hair, kissed her, checked her face over and over again, murmuring, "My princess. My princess. You're all right."

"Dad. Of course I'm all right."

She felt a blush creep up from her neck and into her face as she saw the embarrassment of the nuns who had turned away pretending to be busy with preparations for the evening meal.

"Dad? Are we going home now? Is Mum all right?"

"No, love," he said slowly. "I can't take you home."

He looked at the face of Ursula. *You're dead.*

Chapter 36

Les and Jim signed forms on lines that had no meaning. Kind faces mumbled words of sympathy. Words that had no meaning. The two men left her silent body on its cold slab with the mysteries of death.

Outside, they sucked in gasping breaths of fresh air, the autumn sunlight warming their upturned faces. Jim opened the passenger side door of his car for Les and helped the younger man in. They arrived back in Chelsea without having uttered a word, each lost in his own thoughts.

As Jim pulled up outside the house, Les said, "Would you do me a big favour?"

"Anything, mate."

"Would you and Pat look after Ruth for me for a while?"

"Sure, but..."

"I just need to be on my own for a bit." He looked down at his shoes. "I don't want to go in there just now. I don't know how to face her, what to say to her."

"Yeah, but she needs you."

"I know. I know. I'm going to see if I can drum up the doctor. He'll tell me what's best."

"What'll I say to her, then?"

"Don't tell her anything. Say I'm still there. I told you to go home, or something like that."

"Well, if you're sure..."

"I'm sorry to leave you with this, mate."

Jim waved his hand in negation. He stood back on the footpath looking after the truck as it disappeared from sight. He shook his head in bewilderment. Surely he'd want to be with his wife at a time like this? He could have rung for the doctor instead of going for him. Still, Jim had never been in this sort of situation—never wanted to be either, he thought—and he couldn't really say what he'd do himself. Maybe Les had caught some of Ruth's mental problems. Who knows? He steeled himself for the questions he knew he'd have to face and walked slowly back along Sandalwood Avenue and entered the house.

As the truck turned into the Nepean Highway, Les put his foot down. He was starting to panic, remembering that he'd told Joy he would see her in the morning. What if she disobeyed him and used the phone? He couldn't imagine what the repercussions would be. Ever since the night before, he'd been torn between wanting to go to her and having to be with Ruth, having to carry on the charade, wishing he could tell Ruth the true story.

He felt as though he were on a roller coaster: the more he did to hide the truth from Ruth and to cover his tracks, the more problems turned up. If only he'd taken Joy back to the hospital when she was a baby. But how could he have taken her away from Ruth? She had been so desolate after the stillbirth, he remembered. He'd thought she was losing her mind. *I wasn't far wrong.* But when he'd come home that day and found her with the baby, she'd changed so drastically. She'd become her old self. She'd healed with the love she could give that child. He was damned if he did take the baby away from her, and damned if he didn't. Well, he had to live with it now and do the best he could to avoid detection by the authorities. He had to think clearly and go ahead with his plans.

What a difference in the journey to Red Hill now with the sun warming him through the windscreen, he thought, compared with the previous night's struggle on the roads. A light breeze teasingly ruffled the water when he crossed Patterson River at Carrum. Being a Sunday, there was very little traffic on the road and he had a clear run through to Frankston. The truck slowed as it climbed Olivers Hill and his eyes were inexorably drawn to the cliff. Suddenly, he was back there, hanging onto the cliff face, as Joy was taken by the sea. No, it wasn't Joy—it was Ursula.

As his body relaxed and the driving became automatic once more, his thoughts returned relentlessly to the ordeal he had just endured. It was difficult to push aside the image of his daughter's lifeless form lying in the morgue. How he wished he could have breathed life back into her, mended her bruises, warmed her, put a smile back on her cold white lips. How could he kill his own daughter? See her dead...and yet, not dead. *It was the twin, the twin, the twin,* he repeated over and over again. How could he kill anyone? *Murderer! Murderer!* He longed to hold Joy, to know that she was alive, warm, safe. The sun's warmth made it difficult to keep his eyes open. They were heavy with exhaustion. The road blurred momentarily, his head lolling towards his chest—*the doll dropped slowly, turning time and again, bouncing off the rocks, until it hit the water. It looked up at him, screaming*—his head snapped back up again as the tyres hit gravel on the side of the road. He swerved back onto the bitumen just in time, a clump of bushes scraping the side of the truck.

It took another thirty minutes of concentrated driving with the window down, pushing all thoughts of Ursula out of his mind, before he reached Red Hill. Rounding a bend on the narrow winding road, he turned to watch two spirited horses gallop around a paddock, their manes and tails flying out behind them, when he felt a thud as the truck struck something. *Jesus Christ!* Getting out, he walked around to the front of the truck to see a cat lying under it. It looked up at him, its eyes frightened. Its weak mewing tore at him as its body quivered with pain. *Oh, shit. Oh, no.* He couldn't reach it and had to get back in the truck to reverse back a bit.

"You poor little bugger," he whispered as he lifted it up. "I'm sorry. So sorry."

Its beautiful gold-flecked eyes looked back at him without reproach. *Help me,* they seemed to say. He tucked it into the crook of his arm. It hissed and spat suddenly in pain with the movement, but Les soothed it with soft strokes around its head and it settled there in his warmth. Its eyes followed the movements of his hand and fingers moving back and forth over its body. Blood oozed from somewhere—it was on Les's sleeve and hand. The cat lay very still, accepting what little reassurance Les could give it. He marvelled at the softness of the fur, which was the colour of marmalade, and he thought how like Joy's hair it was. And Ursula's. He wondered where the cat had come from and looked up and down the road in the vain hope that someone would materialize to take it from him and make it better.

"Hang on, puss," he said. "I'll take you to Aggie's Place. They'll fix you up there."

But when he looked down at it, the cat's eyes were glazed and the shallow breathing had ceased. Its body lay limp against him and, in the stillness of the country road, he could hear the steady drip-drip of blood as it splashed on the bitumen.

"Nooooo." His cry reverberated through the treetops, disturbing the birds, and bounced off the nearby hills. Standing in the middle of the road, cradling the dead cat, Les wept. Guilt added upon guilt weighed heavily upon him. He felt as though everything he did was a disaster—the harder he tried to make things better, the worse things became. It seemed that he was on a path of destruction where the innocent were killed or hurt beyond imagination. And he was the cause of it all. Everything that had happened was his fault. Maybe Ruth would have become better eventually if he'd taken the baby back. Maybe they could have adopted a baby. If she had fooled herself into believing Joy was hers, couldn't she have done that with an adopted baby? Why hadn't he thought of that then? How could he have been so stupid? Then none of this would have happened. They could have stayed in Perth in safety without looking over their shoulders all these years. And he wouldn't have become a murderer. He looked down at the cat and wept for its owners—for their grief and loss. He wept for the pain and fear the cat had endured. And he wept for himself—for the person who he used to be, for the person he had become, and for the person he knew he would have to be. As he looked at that person in his mind's eye, it was a person for whom he had no respect or liking.

Joy stood back and looked at her father in dismay. "Why can't I go home?" Then she saw the blood. "Dad! What's happened? Did you hurt yourself?"

"What?"

"You're covered in blood."

"Oh. Yeah."

"What have you done?"

"I...hit a cat...on the road."

"Oh, no."

A pair of hands, with skin like thin soft parchment, guided Les to a chair beside the fire. He looked up at Sister Margaret Mary who regarded him with the hint of a smile mixed with pity, concern, love.

"What has become of you, Les Bacon? You look as though you had lost your soul."

He couldn't trust himself to speak.

"Are you hurt?"

He shook his head.

"The cat?"

He sighed. "Yeah."

"Where is it?"

"In the truck." He stood as if to go to it.

"No," she pushed him down gently. "We'll look after it. You have a daughter here who needs her father."

Joy put her arms around Les. "Feeling pretty crummy about it?"

His head dipped as he blinked away tears that were becoming more insistent, and Joy guided his head to lean on her chest as she stroked his hair.

"Poor Dad. Poor cat."

A plate of scones later—for which he had had little appetite for once—and two cups of strong tea saw Les and Joy, arms linked, strolling around the garden together.

"How's Mum? Is she in hospital still?"

"Yeah. She's in hospital. They've got her drugged up."

"Is she all right?"

"I think so."

"How long'll she be there?"

Les shrugged. "Don't know, love. Your guess is as good as mine."

"What about me, though? When can I go home?"

"I'm picking you up tomorrow arvo."

"To go home?"

"Not really…"

"Well, what then?"

"A surprise," he said dryly.

"I knew it! I knew you wouldn't let my birthday go without doing something."

"What?"

"My birthday surprise."

"Oh, Jesus."

"You didn't…?"

"Oh, Princess, I'm so sorry," he said hugging her.

"You didn't forget…did you?"

"How could I forget? I mean…it's just that with so much going on…"

"You did!"

"It just…slipped my mind a bit."

"Oh." She took her arm away from his. "What about the surprise then?"

"It's something you've never done before." He looked at her doubtfully.

"Is Louise in the surprise?"

"No." He looked up at the trees.

"Ursula?"

If only…if only she could be. If only you could've been the sisters—twins—that you are…grown up together. "No."

"Dad?"

He took his eyes away from the trees that had provided a refuge from her probing eyes.

"What?"

"Why do I feel that nothing will ever be the same again?"

Chapter 37

The truck scrunched along the driveway and came to a halt in front of the garage. Les looked in front of him at nothing for a moment, summoning up the strength that he knew he needed, took a deep breath, and got down from the truck. By the time he reached the back door, Jim was there to greet him.

"She all right?"

"So, so," Jim shook his head.

"She doesn't know yet?"

"No...you find the doctor?"

"Who?" Les had forgotten that he was supposed to look for the doctor.

"The doctor."

"Oh, yeah. I mean, no. He was out. I've been trying to find him."

Jim looked at Les strangely. He opened his mouth to say something and then thought better of it.

They walked into the lounge room where Ruth and Pat sat together on the sofa. The older woman rose slowly to her feet and then she and Jim left the room. It was so quiet that Les could hear the clock ticking in the kitchen and Ruth's sharp intake of breath as she looked up at him.

"Ruth..."

Her eyes were riveted to his face, searching for anything but the truth. What she saw was more than she could tolerate. Suddenly her head began to shake from one side to the other, so violently that Les thought it would snap off her neck.

"Stop it, Ruth."

He tried to still her head with his hands, fighting against the shaking. Her eyes became wider, the irises surrounded by huge amounts of white, so that it seemed they would burst out of their sockets. The shaking had extended to her whole body making it difficult for him to keep holding her head.

"Ruth, don't make this any harder than it has to be."

The shaking stopped as suddenly as it had begun. Her shoulders slumped back as they rested against the sofa, her hands rested in her lap, and her eyes stared ahead away from his own.

"Love...I saw her. She's...she's...gone."

Her eyes were glazed as she stared unblinking at a point beyond his shoulder. He hadn't expected this. Maybe she hadn't heard him.

"Ruth? Ruth?"

She remained unresponsive.

"We'll get through this. Somehow." He took her hands in his own. "Together. Like we've always been."

He looked behind him in the direction of Ruth's gaze but there was nothing apparent to hold her attention. The wall, that had striped maroon wallpaper when they first moved in, they'd stripped and painted a soft lemon. Photographs of he and Ruth and Joy hung from the picture rails along the passageway—a history of their life together from their marriage, through Joy's baby days and toddlerhood, sitting on Santa's knee, her first days at school, proudly crouching beside sandcastles with Louise, sandwiched between Ruth and Les waving at the camera, blowing out candles on a cake with Louise, dressed in a frilly frock that Ruth had made. But Ruth's eyes were not focused on those captured memories, or through the open doorway to her sewing room where Joy and Louise's birthday frocks hung ready. Ruth's eyes reached somewhere else beyond the lounge room, away from the house, perhaps even Chelsea. And where they reached was far from Les's grasp or knowledge.

A chair scraped in the kitchen and he remembered Pat and Jim. Ruth sat still, breathing evenly, her mouth relaxed.

"Ruth?" he whispered.

There was no acknowledgement of his presence beside her. He stroked her face lightly and brought his own close to hers so that he would be in her line of vision. Her stare was blank, without recognition of him or her whereabouts. This frightened him more than the shaking. He had no idea how to deal with it. Ruth's expression didn't register the fact of his standing up and leaving the room.

"You told her?" Jim asked.

"Sort of."

"And?" Pat guided Les to a chair and put a cup of tea in front of him. "What did she say?"

"Nothing. Absolutely nothing."

"Is she all right? I mean, she hasn't fainted, has she?"

"No. It's as if she's stunned."

"She's in shock, you mean?"

"I guess so."

"You don't look all that good yourself, mate," Jim commented, sitting down beside Les.

Les looked up at him. Tears welled in his eyes.

"I just don't know what to do," he said.

Pat walked quietly into the lounge room and stood for some moments looking down at Ruth.

"Are you all right, love?" she asked.

Ruth stared, unblinking in front of her, without acknowledging Pat who waved her hand in front of her.

"You poor little mite," she said shaking her head, fighting tears. She felt overwhelmed by the loss of Joy and Ruth's reaction, but she knew she had to be strong for Les's sake. She stayed there for a moment clenching her teeth.

"We'll get that doctor of yours," she touched Les's arm as she returned to the kitchen. "He must be home by now."

Chapter 38

Les walked slowly out of the hospital with his hands shoved into his pockets. He paused to look up at the clear night sky that flaunted a billion twinkling worlds that he could never reach. He wondered if there were people up there—like him and Ruth—who had the same sorts of problems that they had. Did they know how to go on when things were so tough that your head spun? Did they have somewhere or someone to go to who could find a solution to insurmountable problems? Did they hurt, shed tears, dream, laugh, love, die?

"Ah, shit." He shook his head in frustration.

"Pardon?" came a voice from within shadow cast by the glaring lights of the hospital entrance. A woman in nurse's uniform stepped out into the light.

Les looked at her in embarrassment. "Sorry." He ducked his head and hurried away.

"Can I..." she said to his back "...help?"

He didn't hear her as his quick footsteps carried him out of earshot. His figure was swallowed up in the darkness and the nurse shrugged as she entered the hospital.

As he drove along the Nepean Highway, he kept thinking with horror of what the doctors had recommended they do to Ruth. *Shock treatment*! To think it had come to this.

"...is highly effective in the treatment of major depression...especially in patients who've previously failed to respond to medication...," the pompous doctor had said as if delivering a lecture. Les noticed his clean, soft-looking hands and perfectly creased grey trousers over highly-polished leather shoes.

Les had looked to Doctor Armstrong for confirmation, who nodded his head in agreement with his colleague.

"Are you sure?" he'd asked. "Isn't there any other way?"

"I'm afraid not, Mr Bacon," said the mouth of authority. "If you want your wife to recover from this episode then we must proceed. Given Mrs Bacon's history..."

"Doctor Armstrong?"

"Ruth's shut down, Les. We have to find a way to bring her back and have the ability to cope with what's happened."

"How? How can giving her an electric shock make things better for her?"

"She possibly won't remember for a little while. About Joy's death. She'll have more time to get used to the idea."

"Will it hurt her?"

"Come, come, Mr Bacon." The other doctor was showing signs of impatience. The woman's admission to hospital had delayed his dinner and his stomach was rumbling. "It's just a little shock. For only a second."

"But..."

"Look, she can't be left in the state she's in. Or would you rather she was?"

Les felt his face flush with anger. "Of course I bloody well don't."

"Well, then," the doctor said, pushing the consent form in front of Les. "Sign here and we can begin making your wife well again."

Les looked sideways at Doctor Armstrong who was examining his fingernails. *The bastards always stick together.* He picked up the pen, his hand hesitating over the page. *Jesus, Ruth, what would you want me to do?* Then he remembered her blank stare, the expressionless face. With a sigh, he wrote his name.

He pulled out the ashtray from the dashboard where he always tossed his spare coins, and saw with relief that he had enough. He got out of the truck and placed the ashtray on top of weathered phone books with torn front covers and pages that curled up at the edges. The dial tone was loud in his ear as he balanced the heavy black receiver between his upraised shoulder and head.

"Trunks."

He waited until the tinny voice told him how much to put into the slot. Each coin dropped with a clink, telling the operator that he'd followed her instructions, he supposed.

"Go ahead please."

"Harry?"

The house was quiet as he walked aimlessly through its rooms. It struck him as strange that this was probably the first time he'd ever been in it without either Ruth or Joy. The emptiness bounced off the walls, the furniture, the floor. It flung at him, entering his body with each breath, like a plague. He was afraid of it.

The phone shattered the silence.

"Hello?"

"It's Pat here, love. How'd you get on?"

"Oh, Pat," he started to cry.

"What is it, love?"

"It's lousy…"

Her voice caught. "Do you want us to come back?"

"No, you've done so much as it is."

"What happened, then?"

"They're going to give her shock treatment," he sobbed. "And it's all my fault."

"You can't blame yourself, Les." She waited for him to answer, but all she could hear was his crying. "Les?"

"You don't know what I've done."

"All I know is that you've done everything you could. You're a damned good husband and you were a damned good father."

"No. You don't understand."

"Yes, I do, love. You're all done in. What you've been through is just awful. Anyone would be upset. Ruth's just packed it in, love, and there's nothing else for it. Why, I'll bet Jim would act the same in your shoes."

"No, he wouldn't."

"Of course he would, love."

"Not what I've done."

"Agree to the shock treatment?" Les didn't reply. "Now listen here, Les Bacon. I know you, and I know you wouldn't hurt a fly. And just let anyone try to tell me otherwise."

After Les hung up the phone, he sat on the sofa, where Ruth had sat earlier that day, looking in the same direction that she had. He realised that he couldn't see what she'd seen or enter her world, that private world to where she retreated when life was too difficult for her to handle. Only this time he knew that she had shut the door behind her. He couldn't blame her really. He almost wished he could do the same. But then he remembered Joy, and reminded himself that they hadn't really lost her, that when things settled down a bit they'd be reunited. They'd begin all over again.

He started as he heard the Fletcher's gate squeak. It would be Olive on her way in, he thought wearily, to find out the news. He ducked into the bathroom to splash his face with cold water. His eyes, he saw, were blood-shot, and dark circles smudged the skin under red rims. Stubble from more than a day's growth made his face look dirty, and he grimaced ruefully at the thought of Ruth's disapproval if she could see him now…or even cared enough to look. The front door bell echoed down the passage.

They stood there, behind the fly wire, waiting for him to say something—anything—that would deny what they saw written on his face. He opened the door and they preceded him into the lounge room.

"We stayed away...thought you'd have enough to cope with..." Olive said, trying to control her bottom lip.

"Mr Bacon?"

"Yes, love."

"Is she...is Joy coming home?"

He glanced at Olive and then steered Louise over to the sofa. He crouched down on the floor beside her and put his hands on her shoulders. Olive sat down next to her and covered her daughter's hands with hers.

"Louise, love. I don't know how to tell you this." He met Olive's eyes briefly and saw her nod. "But, no. Joy's...not coming home."

"Why?" Louise cried. "Why not, Mr Bacon?"

"She's...she's...been killed."

"No." She looked at him in disbelief, turned to her mother to see silent tears running down her face, and then back at him. "Joy's dead? She can't be!"

"I'm sorry, love."

"It's true, Louie," Olive hugged her.

"No! You're lying!" she shouted squirming away from Olive.

"Louie..."

"It's her birthday. She can't be dead!"

"I saw her," Les said.

"No. No. No," Louise sobbed. "She's my best friend."

Chapter 39

Les closed the door behind them and sagged against the wall in relief. The police officers had been very sympathetic, almost gentle with their questioning. He saw the pity in their eyes as they took in his haggard looks, the nightmare-tossed bedclothes as they passed his bedroom doorway, the quick tears that threatened with each probing question. Why was she in Frankston? How could she have reached Olivers Hill on her own? Did she have a boyfriend? Was she...forgive us for saying this...promiscuous? *Who? His daughter? Struth, no.* His confusion grew as they talked of an autopsy—he couldn't bear the thought of cold instruments cutting into his daughter's body—and delaying the funeral. *What funeral? Oh, yes. Joy's funeral...no, Ursula's funeral...no, Joy's.*

The front gate next door rasped on its hinges. He went into Joy's bedroom and looked through the lace curtains to see the police officers going in to Olive's house. Would she crack under their questioning and admit that they'd betrayed Ruth? Would Louise find out...Ruth...Pat and Jim? Would that one night of lust destroy his family—in addition to what he'd done in murdering Ursula? *No,* he shook his head, *she'd never tell.*

The springs on Joy's bed gave a muffled screech under his weight as he sat on the bedspread. *Must buy her a new mattress.* But then he realised he wouldn't have to. He looked up at her doll perched on top of the desk. Its eyes seemed to be following his every movement, as if in surprise at what he'd done. Its mouth was open slightly, as it always was, but it looked like it was about to say something, lose its half-smile, accuse him, mock him. It had watched the policeman as he'd riffled through Joy's things on the desk. Les had felt violated. He imagined Joy would feel the same way too. He noticed one of the drawers in her bedside table hadn't been closed properly, and he stood up to push it in. A small vase of flowers toppled and fell over, saturating the crocheted doily and the base of her lamp.

"Shit."

He looked around him for something to mop up the water with but finding nothing suitable rushed out to the bathroom and grabbed a hand towel off a hook. The hook came off the wall with the towel, as he'd pulled at it so hard, and he stood there looking at it stupidly. Then he crumpled up on the floor and cried into the towel until there were no tears left.

The kitchen clock proclaimed the hour with nine clamorous strikes as he slowly prodded himself off the floor and went back into Joy's bedroom with another towel. Ruth would be needing him, he remembered. He must get to the hospital to see her. The thought of food made him feel nauseous, and there was a burning sensation in his chest; his mouth was dry, his tongue coated. He decided he would have just enough time to have a cup of tea. As he waited for the kettle to boil, he thought about what he had to do: pack some things for Joy, do some shopping, fill up the truck.

Joy's bag lay on the kitchen table, where the police officer had put it, along with the clothes she had been found in...that Ursula had been found in. Les had to choose something for her to be buried in. How could he do that without Ruth to help him make that decision? He had no idea, until he stared at the two frocks hanging in the sewing room. Of course, that was the only choice. The birthday frock. He took it off the hook, turning it around to examine the beautiful work Ruth had put into it. It was only right that Joy's sister be buried in it.

The chest of drawers and wardrobe were brimful with the garments that had adorned the body of his daughter. It seemed intrusive of him to take them out, to discover the underwear she wore, to touch and sense their powdery perfume. What would she need? How many? Which were her favourites? The most comfortable? Bewildered, he chose jeans, skirts, jumpers, a coat, shoes, socks, blouses, panties, and put them on the bed in a pile. He wondered if they all went together. There was a box of Ruth's cast-off make-up on the dressing table. He knew Joy used it sometimes, when she and Louise were shut up in the bedroom giggling, but would she need it now? He decided against it. *Toothbrush.* It stood up in the mug beside his and Ruth's in the bathroom. There was a holder somewhere, he knew, as he sorted through the crammed drawer of the vanity basin.

Back in the bedroom, he looked around for something to put it all in. Her small suitcase was on top of the wardrobe and he got it down, brushing the dust off it. The pile of clothes just fitted into the suitcase. He snapped the catches shut and picked it up, but stopped suddenly. *Stupid bastard.* The realization hit him that he could hardly take Joy's belongings out of the house. It would be noticed. A corpse doesn't need a toothbrush. He sighed as he unpacked and returned everything to its original place. *Waste of bloody time.*

A metallic smell reached his nostrils and he raced out to the kitchen to see the kettle had boiled dry. *Jesus Christ, what else can go wrong?* There was milk in the fridge and he poured himself a glass to settle his stomach that betrayed him with nauseous growlings of hunger. He noticed briefly that the burning in his esophagus eased when he drank the milk.

The strong odour of disinfectant greeted Les as he entered the hospital. Ruth's eyes were closed, so she failed to see him stop at the doorway, awkwardly clutching a rose from their garden, and nod at the three women in the other beds. He stood over her slight, still figure which was dwarfed by the bed it rested on. She lay back amongst white pillows—a white that matched the colour of her face—and her forehead was crumpled with a headache, he knew. At her temples the hair looked damp, then he saw what looked like a clear jelly there. It puzzled him. His lips brushed over hers lightly. Her eyes snapped open with confusion clouding them, mere inches from his own.

"Gidday, love. How do you feel?" He stepped back.

She frowned.

"You all right?" he asked again.

"Les?"

"Yeah, love. It's me all right."

"Where am I?" she asked, looking around her at the other women.

Les noticed that they hung onto his and Ruth's conversation. It made him feel uncomfortable, and he pulled the curtain around the bed to give them some measure of privacy.

"In the hospital."

"Hospital?"

"Yeah. Don't you remember?"

"What?"

"You came here last night."

"Where?"

"The hospital."

"Where's the truck?"

He looked at her in surprise. "Outside."

"Have we got enough water?"

"What for?"

"To wash the nappies in."

"Nappies?" He scratched his head. *What the hell is she talking about?*

"And to have a wash. Fresh water, I mean."

"Wash?" said Les stupidly.

"Yes. We haven't had one for a few days, have we, since we left Eucla?"

A salesman hovered around Les as he stood undecided at a rack of jeans hanging near the cash register.

"Can I help you, sir?"

"Yeah. I need a pair of jeans. For a boy of thirteen."

"Your son, sir?" asked the salesman, appraising Les's stature.

"Yeah, but he's a little runt. Takes after his mother."

Once having decided upon a pair of jeans, Les moved over to a display of woollen jumpers.

"A pullover for your son, too, sir?"

"Yeah."

"And what colour would he like?"

"Pink..." Les said without thinking.

"Pardon?"

"Only joking."

"I see," said the man, who didn't see at all.

"Oh, I don't know. Blue, red, or this green one here."

The man found the correct size.

"Will that be all, sir?"

"No. I want a pair of casual shoes, too. Runners. And socks. A few of those. And a couple of T-shirts. Also a duffle-coat. A warm one. And one of those beanies over there."

"Your son's a lucky boy. Is it his birthday?"

"Something like that."

The lingerie shop didn't get many customers like Les walking through its doors. He hesitated in the doorway as the two sales-women looked up from the counter. One of them was holding up a frothy piece of black lace with suspenders attached to it.

"Excuse me," he croaked, clutching his purchases.

"Anything we can help you with?" one of the women smirked.

"No. Thought the missus was in here."

He turned to escape and collided with a customer about to enter the shop.

"Sorry."

He felt his face grow hot as he hurried along the street towards a Coles store. *They should have them there.*

With some embarrassment, he picked out half a dozen pairs of underpants, and quickly piled on top of them singlets, a towel, face washer, bar of soap, soap holder, tooth brush and holder, toothpaste, hair brush and comb, bobby pins, and a shower cap. He passed a stack of bras on a table, faltered, a frown on his face wondering whether Joy used them or not, and decided it was too big a problem for him to handle.

He queued at a cash register behind three other people. *Come on, hurry up!* When it was his turn, he began to put everything down on the counter when he remembered something. *Shit.*

"Sorry," he said, picking it all up again. "Forgot something."

It took a few minutes to find what he was looking for, but when he did, he added a pair of scissors to his pile of things. He walked back down the aisle where the hair products were and put back the bobby pins.

Last stop was a news agency, where he bought the morning's newspaper. On the front page was a photograph of Joy under the caption: **BODY OF GIRL FOUND IN BAY.** He went outside and threw up in the gutter.

Chapter 40

Everyone sitting at the table looked towards the door at the sound of the knock, their spoons at varying heights between the soup bowls and their mouths.

"It's Dad!" Joy jumped up in excitement as Les poked his head around the door.

"Can I come in?"

"Les Bacon, of course you may come in," Sister Margaret Mary smiled. "And how's your dear wife?"

"Not too good. But they're trying to sort her out."

"Please send her our very best love for a speedy recovery."

"Yeah, thanks, Sister."

"Would you like to join us for lunch?" She turned to Sister Dominique. "We've plenty left for a hungry man, haven't we?"

"Yes, of course." Sister Dominique was already up and about to ladle some of the steaming soup into a bowl.

"No, thanks, Sister."

"Did you have lunch already, Dad?" Joy put her arm through his.

"No. Just not hungry, that's all."

"That's not like you, Les," Sister Margaret Mary said quietly, her eyes searching his face.

He looked down at the floor, afraid that she might be able to read his thoughts, then he ruffled Joy's hair.

"Have you finished eating, princess?"

"Just about."

"We've got to get moving."

"What about your bread, child?" Sister Francis Mary was all concern as she peered over the table to where Joy had been sitting. "And you haven't finished your soup."

"Sorry, Sister," Les said. "Go on," he prodded Joy. "Finish up your lunch and then we'll go."

"A cup of tea then, Les?" Sister Dominique held up the teapot.

"All right, ta."

"And what have you been up to since we last saw you?" the older nun said as he sat down beside her.

"You wouldn't believe me if I told you."

She looked him squarely in the eyes. "I trust you, Les Bacon. Whatever you tell me I will believe."

Quick tears sprang to his eyes and he blinked them away, embarrassed.

"Would you like to talk about it?" she asked softly.

He glanced at the others who were busy chatting around the table.

"I wish I could," he whispered with a heavy sigh. "But I can't."

"I'm always here if you need me, Les Bacon."

"I know," he said.

She took his hands in her own. Their warmth surprised him. "God will help you, even if I can't."

"If only I could believe that."

Les put his foot down, checking the rear vision mirror constantly in case a vigilant police officer might catch him speeding.

"Aren't you going a bit fast, Dad?" Joy asked looking at her father strangely.

"Yeah, a bit. Can't be helped, though."

"Where are we going?"

"You'll see."

They sat in silence for a few moments.

"They're such lovely old ladies," Joy said, turning to him. "Everything you always said they were." Les nodded. "And even though I wasn't all that happy about being there at first..." she watched him for a reaction, and then getting none, continued, "...I really enjoyed staying there. I got stuck into these books you gave me," she said, clutching them to her, "and I spent quite a bit of time out in the garden with Sister Francis Mary. She taught me heaps."

"Yeah," he nodded. "She's got a green thumb all right."

"My teeth feel green," Joy said, running her tongue over her teeth and looking at her reflection in a mirror on the back of the sun visor. "I'm dying to go home and brush them. I think I'll do it for half an hour at least."

"We're not going home, love. But I've got a toothbrush and toothpaste for you in the back there." He indicated the pile of shopping in the back of the truck that she hadn't noticed.

"Oh, what's all that stuff?"

"Stuff for you."

"Birthday presents?" She was all smiles.

"Yes and no."

"Can I have a look?"

"Yeah, we'll be stopping in a minute when I find a good place."

Joy kept on turning back to look at the bags, trying to guess their contents from their shapes.

"Good place for what?"

"For you to change."

"Change?"

"Yeah. Your clothes."

"Why?"

"I'll tell you soon."

She knew it was useless trying to get more out of her father until he was ready to tell her.

"Are they really giving Mum electric shocks?"

"Yeah, love."

"Wouldn't that hurt?"

"I suppose so."

"How does she feel about it?"

"Not thrilled."

"What's it supposed to do, though?"

"Make her cope better with things. Iron her out a bit I think."

"Will it work?"

"I bloody well hope so."

He suddenly took his foot off the accelerator and swung the truck over to the side of the road, where it bumped along a narrow track which then opened out into a large paddock. There was no one in sight.

"This'll do," Les said, getting out of the truck. "Come on, princess."

Joy jumped down and walked around to where Les was getting the things out that he'd bought.

"Here…there's some jeans, T-shirts, a jumper, duffle-coat. Oh, and some shoes and so on. Put them on love, and make it quick, will you?"

"But, Dad," Joy exclaimed, frowning at the clothing, "these are boys' clothes—not girls'."

"Yeah, I know. Will they fit all right?"

"I suppose so, but I'm not wearing boys clothes." Her eyes flashed warning signals at him. "No way."

"Yes you are. No arguments."

"But why? What's going on?"

"You get changed and I'll explain once we get in the truck again." Les was rummaging around in the Coles bag.

"No."

"What?" His head snapped up to look at the defiant girl.

"No. I'm not putting that stuff on." She dropped the bag of clothes on the grass and walked around the side of the truck and sat back on the seat, staring in front of her through the windscreen. She slammed the door shut.

He yanked the door open. "Now listen here. I don't have time for this," he shouted, looking at his watch in fright. "You bloody well get changed or...or...I'll do it for you."

"You wouldn't dare!"

"Oh yeah?" He pulled her roughly back out of the truck. "Just try me."

He grabbed at her jumper, as if to pull it over her head, but she locked her arms over her chest.

"Let go," he yelled. "Joy, do as I say."

"Leave me alone."

He smothered an impulse to hit her. It shocked him. He'd never hit her in thirteen years. And she knew that he'd been about to hit her. He could see it on her face.

"Oh, my princess," he groaned, as he put his arms around her. She held her body stiffly against him. "I'm sorry, so sorry."

Joy burst into tears and tried to squirm out of his grasp.

"What's wrong with you?" she shouted. "Are you mad, like Mum is?"

"Maybe I am."

He slumped down onto the grass, his breath shuddering as he fought to regain self-control. A sudden pain hit him in the chest. A burning pain. It knifed through him in a searing wave and reached through to his back, between the shoulder blades. He gasped as he clutched his chest.

Joy turned at the sound of his gasp. She saw him double over. "Dad?"

His breath stopped as the pain spread through him, and then he let the air out slowly, afraid to inflate his chest in case he made it worse.

"Dad!" she screamed. "Are you having a heart attack?"

He puffed air in minute mouthfuls, unable to answer her, until the waves of pain slowly receded and he could tentatively relax his chest muscles.

"I...don't...know," he groaned.

She crouched down beside him, supporting him. "You need a doctor," she cried, looking around the paddock in desperation. "How am I going to get a doctor? Tell me what to do, Dad. I don't know what to do." Her tears fell on his hair, wetting it.

He looked up at the sky. "Is it raining?"

"No," she said through her tears. "No, it's me."

She started to hiccup and cried more as Les started to shake. She didn't realise that he was laughing, because his laughter was silent, until he fell over sideways clutching his stomach with his chuckles becoming belly laughs.

"You're laughing," she stopped crying. "You're laughing!"

Les looked at her helplessly.

And then she started too. They rolled on the grass together in mutual joyless mirth, laughing until their sides ached, until exhaustion gradually brought them back to normality.

They hugged each other.

"Are you all right?" she asked, touching his chest.

He nodded.

"What was it?"

"I don't know," he said slowly. "Never had it before."

"Is it a heart attack?"

He shook his head. "I don't think so. It was like a red-hot poker in my chest. Burnt like hell."

They stood up, helping each other. "All right, Dad. I'll put the rotten things on."

"Thanks, love."

Once Joy had put her new clothes on, Les showed her the other things he'd bought at Coles.

"Are we going on a holiday?"

"That's right, love. A holiday."

"Oh, I knew it! You did remember my birthday. That's what it's all about, isn't it?"

The pain was hovering around his chest again, but he gritted his teeth and ignored it. "Not exactly."

Her face fell in disappointment. "Oh. Well, where're we going then?"

"It's you going on a holiday."

"Only me?"

"Well, your mother's in hospital. I can't leave her."

"Can't we wait until she's better and we can all go?"

"No, love. You've got to go today."

"But..."

"No buts. Now," he said holding up the scissors, "I'm afraid I'm going to have to cut your hair."

Chapter 41

The traffic was heavy as they travelled along Mount Alexander Road. Les turned the truck left into Keilor Road and then right into Matthews Avenue. They could see the runway and windsock to their right. The control tower stood above the conglomeration of airport clutter—stationary aeroplanes, trucks, trailers, luggage trolleys, and people scurrying like soldier ants intent upon their business.

Les cleared his throat. It was slimy from the milk shake he'd drunk to quell the burning pains. It had been a long time since Joy had said anything—since he'd cut her hair. He resisted the urge to sneak another look at it. It was a rotten job. No wonder she'd screamed at him. No wonder she'd looked at herself in horror and dissolved into tears again. No wonder she wouldn't talk to him. She'd even thrown the milk shake he'd bought for her out of the window, container and all. "It's probably poisoned," she'd said, her bottom lip jutting out in a furious sulk.

During the long drive to Essendon Airport, Les had explained his plans for her—where she was going, with whom, for how long, and his version of why she was dressed as a boy. She'd turned her head away from him without comment and looked out of the window, with the beanie pulled right over her ears.

A tram dinged impatiently at him from behind.

"All right, all right, don't get your nickers in a knot," Les muttered.

The tram driver continued to ding at him.

"Where the hell do you think I can go? Straight over the bloody traffic?"

Finally, Les was able to turn right and into the airport. The tram waddled along the tracks in a triumphant huff.

Les parked the truck and turned off the engine.

"I wish I could make you understand..."

She turned to him, glaring.

"Nothing you can say will ever make me understand why you did this," she spat out, tugging at what was left of her hair.

"Princess, I only want the best for you. I love you..."

"I hate you. I hate you." She started to cry again. "I wish I was dead."

"Don't say that. Everything'll be all right in the end. I promise you."

"All right for who? Not for me."

"Look," he said glancing at the sky, "we have to go now. I think that's his plane." He looked at his watch. "Two o'clock. Right on time."

She looked upwards, despite herself, to see an aeroplane seemingly hanging in the air. It descended gradually until it was lost to sight behind the airport buildings.

"Couldn't care less," she pouted.

"Well, I'm sorry, love, but you'll have to come now, like it or not."

The lean, tanned man hesitated for a moment at the bottom of the steps, then walked in an easy stride across the tarmac over to the terminal. As he came through the doorway, he caught sight of Les immediately.

"Les, you old sod." He clapped Les across the back. "You haven't changed a bit."

"Jesus, you have. Where'd all your hair go?"

Harry's eyebrows shot up into deep creases as he looked upwards. "Lost it in the sun, I reckon," he laughed. "Burnt it off."

Joy stood away from Les, trying not to appear interested, as if she didn't belong to him.

He turned to her. "This is my brother, love." He pushed her gently towards Harry. "This is your Uncle Harry."

"Crikey, Les, I thought you said you had a daughter."

"Yeah, well. I have to talk to you about that," he said, leading Harry away from the crowd.

"You look like shit, mate," Harry said out of Joy's hearing.

She lagged behind them, and wandered over to a magazine stand where she picked up a copy of *True Confessions*. It was suddenly ripped out of her hands.

"Sorry, love. You're a boy now…remember?" Les hissed at her.

He guided her away from the magazine stand and a stack of newspapers with Joy's photograph on the front page. She hadn't seen it.

An hour and a half later, TAA flight 461 to Brisbane was called for boarding. Joy looked at Les with panic on her face.

"Dad, please," she whispered. "Don't send me away. I won't know anyone."

"I'm so sorry, love," he gripped her shoulder. "It won't be for that long. And you'll have your cousins for new friends."

"I don't want any new friends," she said stubbornly. "I've got Louise...and what about Ursula?"

"We've been over this."

"I know, but..." She looked up at Harry and then whispered in Les's ear, "...I'm scared, Dad."

"Uncle Harry'll look after you. He's a nice bloke."

"I want to stay with you." Tears filled her eyes as she clung to her father.

"I wish it didn't have to be this way, love."

Harry coughed as he neared them. He couldn't leave it any longer.

"Sorry...er...Jim," he said to Joy. "We've gotta get on now. They're calling us."

Les hunkered down and put his arms around Joy. "I love you more than anything, princess," he whispered. "You've got to believe that." He could feel her shaking in his arms as she cried. "I would do anything for you, anything. That's what I'm doing now. I know it doesn't look that way, but I am. This is for you, your mother...us. I promise you, it'll all turn out in the end."

"Oh, Dad," she cried into his chest. "I love you too."

"I know that, love." He wiped her eyes with his handkerchief. "Now, you've got to be brave. For me. All right?" She nodded uncertainly. "Go on, then." He stood up. "I'll ring you. Every day, if I can."

"Promise?"

"Promise."

"Look after Mum."

"You can be sure of that."

Harry put his hand on Joy's shoulder.

"You haven't been on a plane before, have you?" Joy shook her head. "Well, you're in for something bonzer."

The brothers shook hands, then Harry turned quickly and guided Joy through the doorway. As they walked across the tarmac, Joy turned back to look at Les. Her face was pale and small under the beanie still jammed down over her ears. Les wished he could run after them and get on the plane too, fly away from all the problems, start a new life. But he wouldn't do that without Ruth. He would do nothing without her. *She might be 'round the twist,* he thought, *but I'll never leave her in the lurch.*

He watched Joy and Harry climb the steps and reach the top. They both turned and waved—Harry's wave was an expansive, cheerful wave, Joy's a small, sad one. Les raised his hand to them. He was glad they couldn't see the tears running down his face. Or the pain that he felt. The burning had started again and he rubbed at his chest ineffectually, feeling as if he might belch or vomit.

Harry ducked his head as he entered the plane. Joy followed him backwards, looking all the time at the figure of her father, until she disappeared inside the aircraft. *Hang on, little one. Be brave.*

Les waited until the plane took off. He watched it until it flew through the clouds and disappeared. He suddenly felt very lonely— as if a part of him had been ripped out—and he realised that, apart from Joy staying at Aggie's place, they'd never been separated. He hated the feeling. It made him anxious, fearful, and he determined to carry through his plans so that his family could be reunited again, and the sooner the better.

Chapter 42

By the time Les had battled through the peak hour traffic in the city, and had reached the bayside suburbs, his stomach was growling at him murderously. Along with the realisation that he hadn't eaten all day, was the insistent pain in his chest. It ground at him, sapping from him what little strength he had left. He was tired. Buggered.

During the long drive, his thoughts whirled in kaleidoscopic confusion as images of Joy, Ursula, Ruth and then Gunter drifted through his consciousness. Shades of those thoughts were guilt, remorse, sorrow, bitterness, but the glimmer of hope was what sustained him. The hope that it would all have been worth it.

His eyes were drawn time and again to where the newspaper lay hidden under the seat beneath him, where he'd put it before fetching Joy from Aggie's place. He'd not had time to look at it, but he knew he had to. Not only to see what the media was saying about the death of his daughter—no, Ursula—but to see if Gunter Schwartz's daughter had been reported missing. *Jesus Christ...his daughter!* It suddenly dawned on Les that Gunter had lost two daughters, and Les was to blame. *Poor, poor sod.*

Les shook his head in self-loathing. He'd been so busy thinking about saving their skins that he hadn't had much time to consider what Gunter would be going through. Les felt linked to Gunter because they had shared identical daughters but, of course, both those girls were Gunter's and not his own. He had always faintly consoled himself with the justification that Gunter wouldn't have been able to look after the two by himself. So Les and Ruth had sort of done him a favour—no, he couldn't stretch it that far—but they'd cared for Joy, given her everything possible, brought her up in a decent home—hadn't they? But Les certainly had no business taking the other twin from the poor blighter who'd lost his wife as well. What must the man be going through now? And, more importantly, had he seen the photograph on the front page of the newspapers?

Les's palms suddenly became sweaty. If Gunter saw Joy's photograph, then it'd be curtains for Les. All Gunter Schwartz had to do was go to the police and report his daughter missing and tell them that the girl who was killed was his and not this Les Bacon chap's. That'd raise all sorts of questions and then they'd realise that Joy was the missing twin. Les could almost hear the slam of prison gates behind him. He'd even bet that bloody detective—George Chambers, wasn't it? —would be over from Perth frothing triumphantly at the mouth. Ruth would end up in a psychiatric prison, perhaps not even knowing or understanding what all the fuss was about. And Joy...what would happen to their girl? She'd go back to her real father, he supposed, and she'd hate him and Ruth for the rest of her life. He wouldn't blame her.

Suddenly, he was afraid to go home. The police would probably be waiting for him. Waiting to arrest him. Olive and Louise would watch, along with the rest of the neighbours, as he was marched off—perhaps in handcuffs. He wouldn't be able to look at them. And he wouldn't be able to visit Ruth. The thought of her lying in the hospital bed—alone, frightened, confused, perhaps for weeks—was more than he could bear.

Another wave of pain brought him back to the immediate world around him—the noise of the truck's motor, the traffic bustling around him, his hands on the wheel. With a start he realised he was already in Mordialloc. A chemist shop was still open where he bought some Mylanta for dyspepsia.

He drove into Sandalwood Avenue slowly, holding his breath as he looked at his home and the rest of the houses in the vicinity. He exhaled with relief when he saw no police cars waiting outside. His heart slowed gradually as he pulled into the driveway and turned off the motor. The backyard and house were quiet but he felt reluctant to go inside as the late sun broke through the clouds that hung over the bay. He walked back down the driveway and out into the street. Minutes later he was sitting on the end of the jetty, looking down at the water. The soft slap-slap of little waves against the pylons lulled him into a stupor and he rested his head on folded arms over his knees. He watched the ever-changing patterns in the water through a gap in his arms. They distorted and blurred into one as his eyes fought to stay open, and finally closed.

He shivered and sat up, momentarily confused as to his whereabouts. It was almost dark and the breeze across the water was cold. He pulled his hands up into his jumper sleeves and stood to jump up and down to get the circulation going again in his stiff joints. He wondered how long he'd been there. His watch showed ten past seven. *Ruth!* She'd be looking for him, waiting in that white cold hospital bed. He'd have a quick shower to warm him up—he'd smell better too—and get over to the hospital as soon as he could.

As he walked past the truck, he remembered the newspaper under the seat. He was surprised to see Joy's books left forgotten on the floor. *Shit!* He picked them up with the newspaper. The photograph of Joy on the front page looked back at him as he took it inside. Ruth had taken the photo on Joy's first day of high school. She was standing in the driveway beside Louise; she looked vigorous, happy and very pretty with her hair curling around her face and falling into soft waves around her shoulders.

Les thought ruefully of the ghastly job he had made of cutting her hair. He reckoned a blind man with a pair of hedge clippers could have done a better job. There were tufts sticking up next to gaps where the scalp showed through. Jim always said that it was only a fortnight between a good and a bad haircut, but Les thought it would need more than a month to recover from that butchery.

He glanced at his watch and then looked down again at the headline. He'd have to hurry if he hoped to be allowed into the hospital, but he really needed to go through the paper.

BODY OF GIRL FOUND IN BAY

The body of teenager, Joy Bacon, 13, was found today in Port Phillip Bay in the area of Olivers Hill, Frankston, by local fishermen. The cause of death is unknown. A postmortem is to be held...

The pain threatened again. He poured out a glass of milk and sipped it slowly as his eyes ran back and forth across each line. His hands shook and his stomach rumbled loudly. He didn't know what he could eat, afraid that he might make the pain worse. There was some leftover casserole in the fridge. *Might be all right.* He ate hurriedly as he searched the paper for any news of the missing Ursula. A small article in a column, halfway down page ten, caught his eye.

MUSICIAN COLLAPSES

Residents of a block of flats in Grange Road, Kew, discovered Mr Gunter Schwartz lying unconscious on the floor of his flat yesterday morning. He was taken by ambulance to Prince Henry's Hospital in St. Kilda Road, where he is undergoing tests. He has not yet regained consciousness. Newly arrived

> to Melbourne, Mr Schwartz was a prominent vio-
> linist with the West Australian Symphony Orches-
> tra. It is believed that he was about to take up a
> position with the Melbourne Symphony.

The fork Les held in midair finally entered his mouth, the piece of meat now turned cold. He let his breath out in relief. He was safe for the moment. It was anyone's guess whether Ursula had been seen since she and her father had arrived in Melbourne and, if so, whether that person had seen the photograph in the newspaper. *Sometimes I wish I believed in God,* he thought, looking up at the ceiling. *People pray when they're in trouble, don't they?* He wondered if prayer would help him, but he didn't know how to go about it. And that would be being a hypocrite, wouldn't it? It was the whole deal—you believed in God and you got the help. Well, he'd have to keep struggling on his own, he reckoned. His thoughts moved to the sisters at Aggie's Place—he hoped that they hadn't seen a paper. With the Reverend Mother dead, he mulled over whether Sister Margaret Mary would be the new boss and if she'd have access to newspapers. Instinctively, he knew she would say nothing, but he hated the thought of her disapproval—her horror—if she knew the truth.

Thankfully, there seemed to be no mention of that Chambers detective in the article. Les turned over more pages until he reached the comics and he read *Bluey and Curley* without anything registering. It normally made him laugh so much, he would show it to Ruth and then explain it to Joy. He thought that he'd looked far enough. There'd be nothing about Chambers after the comics.

Suddenly he remembered Ruth. *What the hell am I doing?* He dropped the fork back onto the plate, which toppled over and fell to the floor with a crash. The plate broke and the uneaten food splattered over the lino and onto his shoes and trouser legs. *Shit!* The dishcloth cleaned up most of it and he threw it into the rubbish bin along with everything else. Ruth always told him off for using a dishcloth on the floor. Now he really did need a shower and a change of clothes.

Sixteen minutes later, Les bounded out of the house, slamming the back door behind him. He jumped into the truck, backed it out of the driveway and tore up the street as if the very devil was after him. A neighbour across the road looked after him in astonishment. Les Bacon never drove like that.

When he arrived at the entrance to the hospital, it seemed like an avalanche of people coming out of the doors. Visiting hours were just about over. He'd have to sneak in without the nurses noticing him—look as if he'd been there for a while.

Ruth's ward was still lively with three visitors grouped around one of the beds, talking loudly and laughing raucously. Ruth lay without moving in her bed; her eyes fixed at a point which appeared to be at her feet.

"Gidday, love," Les said cheerfully as he approached the bed.

Ruth looked up at him and sat up suddenly.

"Les. Les." She clutched at his arm in a vice-like grip. "Don't let them take me. Don't let them." Her eyes were wild, frightened, her voice loud with distress.

"Who? Take you where?"

"In that room. They'll hurt me again. They'll put that thing in my mouth," she shouted. "They'll hold me down. Three of them."

A nurse came into the ward quickly.

"Mrs Bacon," she said sternly, "you'll disturb the other patients."

"They're already disturbed," Les observed dryly.

Ruth was struggling to get out of the bed. "Take me home, Les."

"Now be a good girl, Mrs Bacon. Shush." The nurse pushed Ruth back onto the bed and touched a button that rang out at the nurses' station. Another nurse rushed in and went around to the other side of the bed. They put side rails up and leather straps appeared from nowhere, which they fastened around Ruth's wrists and ankles and then onto the rails.

"Is that really necessary?" Les frowned.

Ruth fought against the straps as she shouted at the nurses.

"I said, do you have to do that?"

"Are you a doctor?"

"No, I'm her husband."

"Well, then, please leave Mrs Bacon's medical care to us. We know what we're doing."

"I bloody well hope so."

The nurse sniffed, turning her back on him.

The other patients and the visitors were watching the commotion. Les thought he heard a snigger and he glared at them until they turned away.

"I'm afraid you'll have to leave," one of the nurses said to Les. "Mrs Bacon needs her rest." She was preparing an injection.

"No," Ruth screamed. "Les, stop them."

He stood helplessly, not knowing what to do, wanting to take her home, afraid for her, wishing he could help her. Her screams were louder as the nurse neared to give her the injection. She struggled, her body flexing like a stiff board and then collapsing back onto the mattress, her head shaking violently from side to side as she screamed. Moments later, her body relaxed and she sank back into the pillows. Her eyes flickered, watching him, and then closed.

"Visiting hours are over," a nurse said loudly to Les and the other visitors. "Please leave the patients to their rest."

Les bent over Ruth and kissed her. Her eyes quivered as a half-smile touched her lips.

"Sleep well, love."

He walked out of the ward slowly, wondering how long this nightmare would continue. Then the pain hit him. It stabbed cruelly into his chest, crushing the breath from him. He gasped as the wall jumped out and the floor tilted up to meet him.

Chapter 43

This time Les had no hesitation in entering his house. Lonely as it was, all he could think of was the irresistible lure of his bed. His exhaustion dragged him slowly into the kitchen where he helped himself to a glass of milk. He sipped it cautiously, waiting for some relief from the pain, and then measured out a dose of Mylanta. He didn't care if it was too soon to take it. He was beyond caring about anything other than sleep.

He sank into the bedclothes feeling as though his body must surely melt into the mattress. When he stretched out flat on his back, he could feel where the pain had been—it was like the indentation left in paper after pencil marks had been rubbed out—so he curled up into the foetal position, cuddling the remainder of his agony. His worn out body sagged into a dreamless sleep.

Something woke him. At first he wasn't sure what it was, then he felt the pain gnaw inside him—a relentless warning to get up and do something before it became unbearable. It was ten past four, he noticed, as he pulled himself out of bed and padded down to the kitchen. His stomach felt bloated, even though he'd eaten next to nothing over the past few days. He finished the rest of the milk and poured out another dose of Mylanta.

The house was cold, silent, as he made his way back to his bedroom. He stopped in the passageway and looked in at Joy's room. He missed the sound of Joy's soft mumblings as she slept, and wondered if her sleep was tranquil in her temporary home. Was she desperately unhappy?

The sheets were still warm as he slid back into them, but he shivered without the presence of Ruth beside him. Her haunted eyes last night as she'd begged him to take her home, her resistance to the nurses, his inadequacy, swirled through his mind denying him sleep. The thought of the shock treatment distressed him. He felt he'd let her down, failed to protect her.

His eyes closed as he drifted into sleep, but a nagging thought nudged at his consciousness. At last it kicked him awake. What would he tell Ruth and Joy finally? How could he justify telling Ruth that Joy was dead when she really wasn't? How could he fend off Joy's questions? He could hardly tell them the truth. *Oh, it'll all come out in the wash...I hope*, he told himself wearily. Tossing and turning, he drifted in and out of a nightmare-laced sleep that woke each time to a dull ache in his stomach. When the kitchen clock sounded six times, he swung his legs over the side of the bed and sat leaning his elbows on his knees with his head in his hands. His fingers raked through his hair time and again until the finger pads were coated with oil from his scalp.

Doctor Armstrong finished reading the note from Ruth's hospital then peered over his glasses at Les who was seated opposite him.

"Are you in pain now?"

Les shook his head. "I've been drinking that Mylanta stuff and milk. Seems to help."

"We need to investigate it, Les. Find out exactly what's causing it."

Les nodded, then looked down at his hands under the doctor's close scrutiny of his face. He wondered what could be read in his eyes—guilt?

The doctor began writing on a printed pad. "I'm ordering a barium X-ray for you."

"What's that?"

"You swallow a thick liquid—it's a bit like cold porridge, but doesn't taste as good," he grimaced, "so they tell me. As it travels down your gastrointestinal tract, they'll take X-rays. If there are any abnormalities, they'll be able to see them then."

"Like what?"

"Tumours, ulcers, hernias, strictures..."

"What do you think it is?"

"From what you've told me, I think it could be an ulcer...or at the very least, the lead-up to one."

Just what I need right now. Les's stomach rumbled loudly. He grinned and rubbed it. "Sorry."

"Les, when did you last eat?"

"Eat?"

"Yes, a good meal."

"Oh, I dunno really." He scratched his head. "But I've been drinking milk."

"You need to eat. You won't be any good to Ruth if you don't."

"I suppose..."

"And no Aspirin."

"Oh, I don't take much of that stuff. Don't get sick."

"No, you don't."

"Just have the occasional Bex powder if I get a headache..."

"None of those. They've a disastrous effect on stomachs."

"But if I eat, it'll bring the pain on, won't it?"

"No. You need something in there for the acids to work on. If you don't eat, the acids attack the lining of the walls." He looked over his glasses at Les. "Just don't eat the wrong things...no spicy food..."

Doctor Armstrong's voice receded behind the pounding of Les's heart, and the jumble of panicky thoughts. Does a crime show up on an X-ray? What if I get sick? Real sick. What'll happen to Ruth? Have to ring Joy. Have to...

"...to fast tonight, though, so you've got an empty stomach for the technician to look at."

"What?"

The doctor tore off a sheet from the pad and handed it to Les. "Go and see them at the laboratory now, make an appointment for tomorrow morning, and they'll tell you what you need to do."

"All right," Les said as he rose to his feet. "Doc, why would I suddenly get this pain? Never had it before in my life."

"It's no wonder, Les. After your bereavement..."

"What?"

"Joy."

"Oh."

"And Ruth's problems. You've got a lot on your plate. Stress can bring on an ulcer just like that," he snapped his fingers, "and you've got to deal with it so that you can go on."

On the way home, Les called in at the local milk bar and bought two bottles of milk and a newspaper. Joy's death was shifted back to page three and there was a small article about Gunter Schwartz. Les's heart sank at the mention of George Chambers' likely arrival in Melbourne. He'd expected it, given the times Chambers seemed to pop up whenever there was a kidnapping, and now that Gunter had collapsed, Les thought the detective would be interested. Maybe the Schwartz case would be reopened. Still, Les convinced himself, there was nothing to connect him and Gunter—yet.

The afternoon sun warmed Les's head and shoulders through the glass of the telephone box as he waited to be put through. During those few seconds, he almost dozed off.

"Hello?"

"Harry. How was the trip back?"

"Les, old son...not the most cheerful trip I ever experienced."

"Oh?"

"Yeah, she's not a happy little chappie."

"Sorry to dump this on you."

"Well, I'm all you've got by the sound of things."

Les grunted.

"Look, you need to explain things to her, so she's not so confused."

"Can I talk to her? Is she there?"

"I'll get her. Hang on."

He heard Harry calling out for Joy, using the name they'd agreed upon—Carol. Once the trip was completed up to Longreach, they'd realised she would have to return to the persona of a female, but would have to be known by something other than her real name.

Les heard the receiver changing hands and he thought she had put it to her ear. She didn't speak. He waited.

After some moments he said, "Jo...Carol? Is that you love?" No answer. "Carol? Can you hear me?"

"My name is Joy," she hissed into the speaker, "or have you forgotten me already?" Her voice dripped with sarcasm.

"Princess, you know we can't call you that anymore..."

"Why bother to call me anything?"

The line went dead.

He looked at the receiver in surprise. *She bloody-well hung up on me!*

Chapter 44

Les found himself back on the jetty as the sun disappeared behind a curtain of clouds and horizon. As soon as it did, the last traces of warmth left with it and he shivered. He knew he should return to the house, have a shower, and go to visit Ruth, but he stayed, pacing up and down, the boards creaking under his footsteps. Joy's voice still echoed in his head, spitting hatred at him. He had suspected that she would be upset by all that had happened to her—especially with the lack of explanations—but he hoped that their closeness would heal the gap eventually. A seagull squawked at him as he walked towards it. He watched its wings flap as it swept into the air and hovered effortlessly on air currents. He envied its freedom.

He walked back slowly along the beach and then turned up into his street. As he passed his letterbox, he noticed something on the front steps, and stopped in his tracks. The something stood up and walked over to him.

"Mr Bacon?"

"Oh, Louise. What are you doing sitting here in the dark on your own?"

"I just...wanted to see you."

"Well, come in," he said and they walked around to the back door together. "Does your mum know you're here?"

"Yes. I told her I'd wait for you."

"I was on the beach..."

"Yes, I know."

"Why didn't you come over and join me?"

"I didn't like to interrupt. I thought you might like to be alone."

Les looked at her keenly. "That's nice of you, love." He saw tears in her eyes. "You all right?"

Louise looked up at him. Her mouth quivered. "Why? Why did it have to happen to her?"

He sighed. "I don't know. She..."

"It's not fair," she sobbed. "It's not fair."

He put his arms around her and held her for some moments until she calmed a little. They sat down at the kitchen table. "Some things happen for a reason. I don't know what the reason for this is. Some people believe in fate. Maybe it's that. Things happen. And they damned-well hurt. Like hell."

"What about Mrs Bacon? Is she going to be all right?"

"I hope so," he sighed. "I'm going to visit her now."

"I'll go then," she said, standing up. Her eyes lit upon a handbag slung over the back of a chair. "That's Joy's, isn't it?"

"Yes, love. The police brought it over."

"It's damp," she said, running her hand over it.

"It was in the water, not far from the...her...body."

Fresh tears welled in Louise's eyes. "It's ruined."

"Yeah."

"Mr Bacon?"

"Yeah?"

"Did she...I mean...was she...you saw her, didn't you?"

"Yeah, love."

"You're sure it was her?" Les looked at her in surprise. "I mean, it couldn't have been anyone else, could it? There couldn't be a mistake, could there?"

His forehead broke out into a cold sweat. "No, 'course not."

"It's just that..." Tears ran down her face. "...wouldn't it be lovely if the whole thing was a big mistake—that the body was someone else—and Joy walked in here right now and asked us what we were carrying on for?"

"It's just not gonna happen," he frowned.

The pain was starting again and he stood up to get some milk from the refrigerator. He held up the bottle in mute question but she shook her head and he poured himself a glass. The cold milk slid down his gullet, taking some of the pain with it.

The clock struck the half-hour. They both looked up at it and Les took the truck's keys out of his pocket.

"Sorry, Louise. I've gotta get going."

"Oh."

As she got up from her chair, her arm caught on the handbag's strap dragging it to the floor. The clasp burst open and some of the contents spilled out—a brush, a sodden handkerchief, bobby pins, a lipstick, and a small box. They both bent to pick the items up, putting them back into the bag. Les turned the box over curiously and opened it.

"Oh, I know what this is," he said with a forced smile. "It's your birthday present."

"What?"

"She bought this for you."

Les handed the box to Louise. Although the cardboard box and the lining inside were wet, the brooch sat where it had been pinned, undamaged. She looked up at him, uncertain if he would want her to touch it, but at his nod she reached inside the box with trembling fingers. "Louise," she whispered to herself as her finger traced over the engraved letters. The gold scroll gleamed dully under the kitchen light as she turned the brooch from side to side to see it better. It was then she saw the flowers.

"Oh," she cried, tears blurring her vision, and she wiped at them impatiently. "Sweet pea. They're sweet pea."

"Take it out, love."

She unclipped the brooch from the lining, put it up to her lips and kissed it. *Oh, Tooth Fairy. Why did you have to die? I wish you were here.*

"It's the best present I've ever had," she sobbed. "I'll always keep it."

"I'll tell her you said that." Les handed her a handkerchief.

"What?" she looked up at him, confused.

"I mean…she'd love to hear you say that…she'd…if she was here, she'd have loved to hear you say that."

Louise sat on the front steps of her home shivering in the cold, but preferring to be alone for the time being. She rocked back and forth as her tears dwindled, holding the brooch to her face. She imagined Joy's excitement at finding such a perfect gift for her and wished her friend had been the one to give it to her. If only Joy was sitting beside her, sharing secrets as they always did, planning things, laughing with her, crying with her.

She tried to imagine Joy lying in a coffin. It would be so dark. Did she have clothes on? What must it feel like to be dead? Did it hurt? Louise looked up at the sky between the clouds, and wondered if one of the twinkling stars was Joy. Or, was she an angel instead? Did she fly around the sky with other angels? Have lemonade with them? And Vegemite sandwiches? Did they eat at all? Could Joy see her? Hear her? *Tooth Fairy, are you there?*

Chapter 45

The funeral director shook hands with Les and watched him as he walked down the rose-lined driveway, past the manicured lawns and a small cascade that splashed over huddled stones into a pond. The man thought Les looked a lot older than his thirty-eight years. He walked slowly—almost shuffled—and you could see he was in pain by the way his red-rimmed eyes half-closed as waves of pain hit him. He was slightly bent over and his shoulders sagged. *Well, no wonder. If I lost my little Emily, I'd probably be the same.* The beauty of the grounds was obviously lost on Les as his head hung down, defeated. A parcel was clutched in his right hand. It contained the clothes that had been found on Ursula's body.

"Crikey, Les," Harry said quietly. "She doesn't want to talk to you."

Les leaned his shoulder against the door of the telephone box, bent over his agony.

"What do you want me to do?"

"Just leave it." Les slumped down on his haunches.

"Yeah. No use forcing the kid."

"No."

"She'll get over it. Kids do."

"She getting on with yours?"

Harry laughed mirthlessly. "Not exactly. It'll take her a while to settle in. Doesn't want to have much to do with any of us."

"Shit."

"Yeah, well. What can a body do? Just wait, I reckon. After all, she doesn't know us from a bar of soap. Strange faces...strange place." He waited, then went on. "Great hair cut."

Les coughed. "Thanks."

"Don't mention it."

There was a pause when neither of them spoke. Les put more coins into the box. They clattered loudly as they travelled down the slot.

"Why don't you ring from home?"

"Too risky," Les grunted. "They can trace calls, can't they?"

His feet stuck out over the end of the couch, hovering in mid air, moving occasionally with the rise and fall of his lungs. His mouth had fallen open and snoring punctuated his mutterings. His arms were folded protectively over his stomach.

The phone rang beside him, startling him into wakefulness.

"Hello? Hello?"

He could hear breathing, and—was he imagining it?—crying.

"Who's this?"

He sat up.

"Hello? I said, hello."

His hair prickled and his skin stood up in goose bumps. *Joy?*

"Is that you, love?" he whispered.

There was a click and the phone went dead.

Next door, the phone rang and rang in the empty house. Olive hurriedly pushed her key in the lock of the front door as the phone stopped ringing.

"Wonder who that was?"

"Well, Les, it is an ulcer, like I suspected."

Les waited, watching Doctor Armstrong.

"At least we know how to treat you now."

The doctor explained Les's treatment and then sat back and looked at him carefully.

"You know they did an autopsy?"

Les nodded.

"They'll be asking me questions...as her family doctor."

Les looked up, suddenly afraid.

"I can only tell them the truth, you know. I'm sorry, Les, but she was like her mother. She was showing signs of mental instability."

"What?"

"Those imagined pains...so many of them." Les looked at him stupidly. "Puberty can bring it on. Mental problems."

"Joy?"

"I'm sorry. I can't lie to the authorities."

"No."

"The stigma...no one has to know."

"No."

"Have you thought about...a change of scenery? A new start?"

"Moving?" Les's mouth dropped open.

"I know it's early yet, but think about it, Les. It could be the best thing for Ruth."

Les looked down at his hands, not trusting himself to look at the older man. Here he was wondering how he would get Ruth away without it looking suspicious, and Doctor Armstrong was suggesting it. The doctor took it as a further emotional hurdle. He walked around his desk, sat on the corner, and placed his hand on Les's shoulder.

"You've been to see Ruth?"

Les bobbed his head up and down.

"Of course you would." The doctor hesitated. "How did you find her?"

"Mixed up."

"That's to be expected."

Les shoved his fist into his mouth, not daring to look up. He smothered an absurd impulse to giggle. It threatened to explode from his mouth and, at the same time, he was afraid that he would burst into tears.

"Look," the doctor said, "I know this is a rough time for you. But it will get better. After a couple of weeks, Ruth'll be like new."

Les was standing in Joy's bedroom when he saw a movement next door that shook him out of his thoughts. Louise and her mother came out of the front door of their house, carrying something with a tea towel over it. He looked down at Joy's exercise book that he'd been holding. There was a half-written essay on the open pages entitled: THE PERFECT HOME. She had started it with the words: 'My home is a perfect home because of my parents and...'

I'd better open the door to the Perfect Home, he thought grimly as he heard his neighbours' footsteps outside. *My poor princess...if only she knew the truth about her rotten dad. Not only does he cut her hair and send her off to the outback and commits murder, he also roots her best friend's mother. That'd really put the icing on the cake.* He steeled himself as he opened the door wondering if he'd ever be able to put Olive's body back where it belonged. Certainly not with him, although the very thought of the way she'd quivered under him as he'd thrust into her...

"Mr Bacon," Louise held up her bundle carefully, "we made some dinner for you, so you'd have something decent to eat."

"Oh, Louise, anyone'd think he ate rotten food," Olive smiled.

Les smirked, despite himself. "Thanks. I could do with something decent." He took the offered casserole dish. "What is it?"

"Devilled Beef," Louise said proudly. "And with lots of curry powder in it, just how you like it."

"Louie made it herself. Wouldn't let me touch it. I hope she wasn't too heavy-handed with the spices."

"Is this what you made when we had that card night a few months back?"

Olive nodded.

"Well, thanks. I did like it."

"You were the only one who did," Olive shrugged. "Everyone else was in agony."

They followed Les into the kitchen where he put the kettle on. Louise kept looking at the handbag still hanging over the back of one of the chairs while Les and Olive talked about the funeral arrangements for the following day.

"Mr Bacon?"

"Yes, love."

"Can I see Joy?" Her bottom lip trembled and she bit it looking from Les to Olive. "Can I see her before…?"

"No," he almost shouted. Then he looked at her in contrition. "I mean…no." He regained control as his heart thudded furiously in his chest. "She…the autopsy…I haven't…"

"But…"

"Louie." Olive put her arm around the girl. "Let it be."

"I just wanted to touch her…" Her voice was a mere whisper as she stared at the handbag. "…kiss her goodbye."

"The coffin's not open," Les said quietly. "I'm sorry Louise."

On their way out, Les suddenly stopped at the sewing room door where Louise's party dress still hung. On an impulse, he grabbed it and handed it to her. Her eyes filled with tears as she took it.

"She's got hers," he said awkwardly.

"She's wearing it?"

"Yeah."

There was an uneasy silence between Les and Olive as their eyes met over the weeping girl. He felt helpless in the face of such cruel grief that Louise was suffering. His eyes looked away from Olive's penetrating stare to fall upon the tight parcel of clothes that lay discarded on an easy chair in the lounge room. The parcel had opened and a sleeve dropped out and over the side of the chair to almost touch the floor. It embarrassed him because it looked so careless, so dejected, so unloved.

"Her clothes," he mumbled as he hastened to tuck the sleeve back in. He was too quick, too rough. The paper split and the jumper burst out with a life of its own, followed by a leg of the jeans. He tried to stuff them back but the paper ripped further, leaving the contents exposed.

Louise stared at them, then back to Les, and again at the clothes. *What's she looking at?* She started to say something but apparently thought better of it. *They're only clothes,* he thought, puzzled, as he gathered them in an untidy heap in his arms. He threw them on Joy's bed as he walked Louise and her mother to the front door.

"Thanks again for the meal."

"Hope it's okay," Olive said.

He shut the door behind them and walked back to the kitchen, and looked longingly at the casserole.

Bloody pity. He dropped the contents into the rubbish bin, and poured himself out a generous dose of Mylanta.

Olive and Louise walked slowly arm in arm back to their house, lost in their own thoughts. As they climbed the front steps, Louise stopped and leaned against the verandah post.

"Mum?"

"Yes, Louie?"

"Mr Bacon said they were Joy's clothes, didn't he?"

"Yes."

"Could he be mixed up?"

"I don't think so."

"Where did he get them from?"

"Probably the funeral people." Olive looked at her curiously. "Why?"

"They weren't her clothes."

Chapter 46

Ruth's breathing was uneven as she slept. Her fears and nightmares twitched at her subconscious, tearing at the oblivion of deep, restful sleep. Images of white-coated monsters holding her, hurting her, flitted across her mind. She moaned softly and her limbs jerked.

Les watched her for half an hour until she awoke, startled. She looked at her surroundings—puzzled, frightened. Then she saw the tired sandy-haired man sitting beside her—a handsome man, she thought—with a deep cleft in his chin. His grey eyes smiled at her as he bent over to kiss her.

"Gidday, love. How are you?"

She wasn't sure whether to pull away from him or not. He seemed to know her and she immediately liked him. There was something protective about him.

"I'm all right." She looked at the patients in the other beds. "I think I am."

Instinctively, he knew she didn't recognise him. They'd warned him this might happen—just temporarily—but it threw him nonetheless.

"That's good."

She smiled at him and his heart lurched. It was a smile that reminded him of when they first met—shy, yet flirtatious.

"You know who I am?"

She smiled a little uncertainly and then shook her head.

"That's all right. It'll come." He took her hand gently. "I'm Les. The lucky bloke who's your husband."

Her head inclined to one side as she looked at him, waiting for him to go on. He resisted the urge to trace the bump on her nose. He desperately wanted to take her in his arms and hold her. He needed her body, her smell, her strength—the strength she used to have.

He talked quietly about himself, her dressmaking, their friends, where they lived, the beach, and she lay there without interrupting him, learning about herself and this man who claimed to be hers.

At no time, though, did he mention Joy...or Louise.

They became aware of two people who entered the ward and stood at the end of the bed. Les looked up. Pat and Jim were there holding flowers and chocolates.

Les stood up for Pat to take his seat.

"You remember Pat and Jim?" he said to Ruth.

She smiled at them uncertainly.

"They're the friends I've been telling you about."

"We were here last night," Pat said. "Don't you remember?"

"Last night?" Ruth was vague. "I'm sorry…"

Pat exchanged glances with Les.

Jim's eyebrows were raised in question.

Les shook his head slightly.

Les called in to his local fish and chip shop and ordered some grilled fish. The shop was busy as Les waited, flicking through a newspaper left on a bench. Joy's face looked up at him from page five. It started his hands shaking and the pain started up again. It had been too long between meals. *Suspected suicide…he read…Police have taken statements from up to 100 people including…the bayside town of Frankston is continuing to grapple with the horrific death of the teenager…with police appealing to locals, truck drivers and commuters to report any activity on the night at the railway station, on the highway or in the area near Olivers Hill…anything they may have seen, however insignificant…*

"Les, mate. You okay?"

The face of the proprietor shoved through the blur of words that had frozen across Les's mind.

"Eh?"

"You're looking pretty lousy, mate."

Someone whispered behind him, "It was his daughter that died the other night at Olivers Hill, poor bugger."

He turned to see two men talking at the counter. When they saw him turn, they looked up at the menu board, embarrassed, their backs to him.

"Les? You want to come inside and sit down for a bit?"

"No. No," he looked up at the parcel of fish and chips in front of him. "This mine?"

"Yeah."

"How much?"

"Don't worry, mate. On the house. Go home and eat it. Before it gets cold."

His legs and arms felt like tree trunks—heavy and stiff—as he climbed out of the truck. His feet dragged as he willed them towards the back door and he swayed on them as he opened it. The cold, dark house was uninviting in its silent mustiness. He turned on the kitchen light and the room bounced into stark brightness. There were no enticing cooking odours, no welcoming call or rushing, excited footsteps, no hugs or kisses, no television blaring, no strains of music. He had no appetite, although his stomach continued with its constant rumbling and he rubbed at his chest that burned and scraped in painful waves. It was important to eat, though, he remembered, and he opened up the parcel and broke off a piece of fish with his fingers. His mouth was dry, lacking the saliva to push the fish past his throat, but sipping on a glass of milk thrust it down, one piece after the next. He ate a few chips, but the rest ended up in the bin keeping the Devilled Beef company.

His elbows rested on the table, his shoulders sagging over them, his head in his hands. After a few minutes, he started to feel slightly better, and he looked up and around the room, thinking that he would nudge himself off the chair, brush his teeth and collapse in a heap on his bed.

It was then he noticed that he'd carried the newspaper with him from the fish and chip shop. A morbid impulse had him turn the pages over until he found the article again. Oh, how he wished he would wake up and find it was all just a nightmare. He flicked the next few pages over idly, willing himself to get up, yet staying there, searching for any news of Gunter Schwartz. *There!* A small article jumped out at him.

DETECTIVE SAYS GOODBYE TO VIOLINIST

D/Sgt. George Chambers, well known in Western Australia for his campaign to close unresolved cases of violent crime, visited an old friend today in Prince Henry's Hospital. Mr Gunter Schwartz, who collapsed into a coma on 8th May, and whose baby daughter was stolen in Perth thirteen years ago, has failed to regain consciousness. The whereabouts of Mr Schwartz's other daughter remains unknown. The detective expressed his sorrow at Mr Schwartz's seemingly hopeless condition and assured his Victorian counterparts of his eagerness to assist them in their investigations. D/Sgt. Chambers leaves Melbourne tonight to appear as Crown witness in the Stuart murder trial in its third day in Perth.

A long, ragged sigh escaped Les's lips. *So far he hasn't connected the photo of Joy...no Ursula...with Schwartz. Thank Christ the photo's not in colour.*

Then he saw Joy's handbag where he'd left it hanging on a chair. He picked it up and tipped the contents out on the table. Amongst the clutter of teenage indispensables, he noticed the absence of the pill bottle, which he remembered putting in the bag before he dropped it over the cliff. He supposed the police or the coroner had taken them out. Of course, they'd look for traces of the drug in her body, and they'd know where it came from—Ruth's bottle. He hoped they'd assume the girl took them of her own volition and, from what the newspaper was saying, suicide was one way they were thinking.

He wondered if there'd be an inquest—whether he'd be able to keep up the pretence under closer scrutiny. The police officers had been very patient—even kind with him—up until now. Their phone calls and tactful questions had made it easier for him to cope, to find the time to think of the right answers. It seemed like such an uncomplicated case. A depressed teenager, taking her own life. No, there hadn't been anyone hanging around. Nothing suspicious. No boyfriends. He'd seen the police going from house to house and, from what Olive had told him, they'd been to the school as well. They'd asked about him and Ruth and their relationship with Joy. If there were any signs of trouble. If he'd beaten her. If he'd hit Ruth, even. If he was a faithful husband. Doctor Armstrong said he'd be talking to them too, and from what he'd said, he would be unwittingly playing into Les's hands. No, they appeared to be just an ordinary family, a decent family, whose women suffered mental illness. So far luck had been with him—if you could call it luck.

Les woke up at six o'clock the next morning, still fully-clothed, with no recollection of even getting to his bedroom. He was woken by the telephone, its insistent ringing shattering his temporary hibernation.

He padded out to the lounge room and picked up the receiver.
"Yeah, hello?"
There was a long silence as he yawned, waiting.
"Hello?"
The sound of the receiver at the other end being put quietly back on the cradle was unmistakable.

Hands touching him, patting him, guiding him, were the only sensations he was conscious of during the funeral, other than his confusion over the grief he felt for the girl that was supposed to be his daughter lying in the flower-draped coffin. The minister's voice droned over the top of Les's head, falling like a warm mist that you could shred with your fingers. Faces with mouths that opened and closed on fetid breath, uttering words that he couldn't understand. Eyes that leaked into handkerchiefs. The red-brown coffin gleamed in the multi-coloured light cast by stained glass windows above. Flowers that once had life, now cut short to wither like the body they covered.

The earth is cold and water seeps through the sides of the gaping hole cut to accept the coffin. It sinks reluctantly, cautiously, as if sensing its demise along with the sleeping child it holds.

Hearts hugging grief and guilt accompany its journey.

The man hangs his head in shame.

The girl kneels to touch the coffin as if to send her love with it.

Merciful blackness folds her body to the grass.

Tears prick behind his eyes but fail to reach far enough around to smooth the grit that lacerates with each movement to left and right. He blinks dry eyelids over his exhausted, empty eyes. A cheese and gherkin sandwich is pushed between his fingers. The smell reaches his nostrils and he gags. The clink of glass and crockery offend his ears, along with the laughter—yes, laughter—and sympathetic murmurs pressed between breathing bodies that celebrate those thirteen years. The sandwich falls from his fingers as he closes his eyes. He shuts out the now and soars with the past, as silent tears seep from between the lashes that rest on his cheeks.

Joy turned to follow her uncle onto the aircraft after one last look at her father. A hostess noticed her tears and touched her shoulder in sympathy.

Harry turned back to see if Joy was following him. "Over this way, Jim."

She scowled at him.

He shrugged and looked at his boarding pass and counted along the seats until he found their places.

"Here we go," he said. "You take the window seat."

She edged across the seats and flopped down into the one next to the window. They were just in front of the wing, so she had an un-impeded view of the terminal. Her father's figure looked tiny from where she sat. He stood apart from the other people waving in the direction of her plane. She leaned her forehead against the window focusing intently through her tears and the two layers of glass. *Oh, Dad, why are you doing this? Why?*

Harry ran his hand over his near-bald pate and settled into his seat, grateful to be out of the cold Melbourne wind. *Crikey, it's bloody freezing! Glad to get back to the sun.* He did up his seatbelt and turned to Joy to tell her to do the same, but changed his mind. With four unruly children of his own, he instinctively knew that she would be better off left alone. It could wait, he thought.

It was quite some time before Joy composed herself, sat back in her seat and turned to Harry. The aircraft taxied along the runway, gaining speed for takeoff.

"Hang on, mate. She's gonna go up," Harry grinned at her.

With that, the plane shuddered and left the ground. Her surprise as she leaned close to the window and then looked back at him, made him laugh.

"Told ya."

"Wow!"

She felt the push back into her seat as the aircraft climbed, mo-mentarily forgetting her problems. The muffled sounds of the cabin and the shaking of the seats and the paraphernalia in the galley had her looking around her, then out of the window again as the ground slipped away. Slight bumps settled as the aircraft climbed over cotton wool to brilliant blue sky and then levelled out.

Joy felt her ears block and covered them with her hands.

"Yawn," Harry said with a grin. "It'll make your ears pop."

She looked at him doubtfully as he stretched a huge yawn across his face. She found herself yawning involuntarily and heard the rushing sound of the engines as her ears popped.

"Worked, eh?"

"Yes."

"Told ya."

She looked at him candidly. "You look a bit like Dad."

"I should," he laughed. "I'm the good lookin' one though."

His ready humour was infectious and, despite herself, she found her mouth turning up into a grin.

"I don't know about that," she commented honestly.

"Beauty's in the eyes of the beholder, so they say," he said, pulling a face and then he tugged at her beanie.

She was reminded of her hacked hair and pulled the beanie down low over her ears again. The contact was broken and she looked out of the window, her body turned away from him.

Until a meal was served, neither of them spoke. *Stupid bugger*, he chastised himself, then he relaxed back in his seat and closed his eyes, falling asleep in moments.

Joy stole glances at her new uncle, wondering how long she would have to be in his company, what his family was like—if he had any—and where they were going. She soon tired of the cloudy landscape and fossicked inside the pouch on the back of the seat in front of her. The TAA flight magazine held her interest for some time, and then she remembered with regret the books her father had given her. Her act of defiance—leaving them discarded on the floor of the truck—had hurt only herself. *Bugger*.

"Penny for 'em," Harry said, his eyes popping open an hour later with the landing of the aircraft.

"Umm."

He looked outside. "Sydney."

"How do you know?"

"There," he pointed. "Large as life."

"Huh."

"Did you see the bridge?"

"What bridge?"

"Don't they teach you anything in that hick town of yours?"

She looked at him blankly.

"The Harbour Bridge."

"No. I didn't see it," she replied haughtily.

"Well, we'll have a look out for it when we take off again."

She looked at him in surprise. "We're not staying here?"

"Struth, no. I wouldn't live in this dump."

"Where are we going?"

"God's good country."

"And where's that?" she asked sarcastically.

"Bloody outback, mate. Queensland."

Half an hour out of Sydney, Joy settled back into her seat whilst Harry plunged into a steady snoring punctuated by loud whistles. She glanced at him from time to time, stifling giggles at his sound effects. In profile, he looked a lot like her dad, but without the hair. At least she wasn't with a complete stranger. He was blood, wasn't he?

She wondered why her father had never mentioned Uncle Harry. He seemed a nice enough man, but maybe they'd had a fight years ago and only just patched it up. Or maybe they'd lost touch, living so far apart. Still, her dad had no other family. You'd think the brothers would have kept in touch. Their mother and father had died, just like her mum's parents too. Joy was the only girl in school who didn't have any grandparents. That's why she'd adopted Pat and Jim Lewis as her substitute grandparents.

If Uncle Harry was married and had children, then she'd have some real cousins, wouldn't she? *Oh, who gives a bugger anyway,* she thought as her sense of betrayal returned. *Don't want to meet anyone. Just want to go home.*

Her thoughts went to Louise—what she was doing, where she was, if she was missing Joy too. It would have been fun if they were travelling together on this plane, having a holiday.

Harry awoke at the aroma of food. He sat up to take the tray the hostess offered him.

"Struth, I'm hungry. I could eat a horse and chase the jockey."

He looked at Joy.

"What about you, mate?"

Joy accepted her tray and realised that she was hungry too.

"Yes, I am."

She watched him as he took out the cutlery from a cellophane packet.

"Get stuck into it, mate, or I'll eat yours too," he grinned.

The lights below them looked to Joy like a fairyland. She imagined that she was an angel drifting down through the clouds about to bestow gifts on all the children of the city. *Fat chance.* She turned to

Harry who had fallen asleep again, and she gave him a tentative elbow in the ribs.

"Brisbane, I think," she said, indicating with her head towards the window.

He leaned over her. "Sure is."

She looked out with him, their heads almost touching. "It looks so pretty," she breathed.

"Yeah. Not bad this flying caper, is it?"

"I never imagined it would be like this...so...easy. It's hard to imagine you're all the way up here. You could be in a bus."

"Expensive bloody bus ride," he snorted.

"Not much traffic, either," she laughed.

The warm air was a welcome greeting as they descended the steps that were pushed up to the aircraft doorway.

"It smells different," Joy commented.

"Tropical."

A dozen questions were bursting for release from Joy's lips, but she refused to allow herself any—what she regarded as—weakness. She didn't want to show any interest at the risk of appearing remotely happy, or even enjoying herself. No, she would wait and see things happen of their own accord. She didn't want Uncle Harry to report back to her father that she was okay, that he didn't need to worry about her.

She tagged along behind him as he met up with a man of about his age, who she learned was a pilot, even though he wasn't wearing a uniform. She gathered that the man was going to fly them to a place called Longreach. They were going in something called a Cessna. The man paid very little attention to Joy as he chatted with Harry and looked up some details written on sheets of paper on a clipboard.

Before long, the man led the way out of the airport and they walked across the tarmac to a small aircraft.

Joy tugged at Harry's sleeve. "Are we going on this?"

"Yeah, mate. Little beauty, eh?"

"Is it safe?"

Joy's doubts were overcome as the Cessna took off into the night sky and settled into an uneventful flight. It was a lot noisier inside this aircraft and she was relieved that she wouldn't have to talk to the two men in the seats in front of her. They talked amongst themselves, their words unintelligible to her over the sound of the engine. She looked out at the flat landscape, lit softly by a full moon in a cloudless sky. Now and again she noticed flickering lights as they flew over a small town or a group of houses in the middle of nowhere. The hypnotic droning of the engine caught at her weariness and pulled her into a light sleep.

A change in the tone of the engine and her ears blocking brought her back to consciousness. She yawned as she noticed they were descending towards a sizeable group of lights.

"Is this Longreach?" she shouted at Harry, tapping him on the shoulder.

"What?" he shouted back.

"Longreach?"

"Yeah, mate. Home."

The Cessna bounced lightly on the tarmac and came to a halt outside a small terminal building. Joy looked around her curiously as she got out of the aircraft, surprised that there were very few people around. Harry clapped the pilot on the back, shook hands with him, and then turned to Joy.

"Jim, old mate," he grinned at her. "Let's go." He nodded towards the terminal entrance. "Can't keep the wife waiting."

"Wife?"

"Yeah, even an ugly bugger like me's got one."

He led the way inside to where a large woman, with grey hair that was once blonde, stood beaming a huge smile between chubby, red cheeks. Joy saw that the corners of the woman's mouth drew so far back that the gums around her teeth were visible, even at the back of her mouth.

"Gidday, love," Harry planted a kiss on his wife's cheek.

He leaned towards Joy. "This is your Auntie June."

"Hello, love," Auntie June's teeth fairly popped out of her mouth as she bent over rolls of fat that restricted her movement downwards.

"Hello," Joy said in a small voice.

"How was your trip up?"

"Long," Harry said. "And I could do with a good shower."

"I'll bet you'd like one too, love," Auntie June said sympathetically.

"And a decent bite to eat," Harry rubbed at his stomach.

"Didn't they feed you on the plane?"

"Yeah. Just enough for a sparrow."

'Oh, you." Auntie June gave Harry a decent thump on the back.

"Struth, woman," he grunted. "You'll kill me one day." He staggered against a wall, pretending hurt.

Joy looked from one to the other, wondering at their antics. She'd never seen a pair like them. Auntie June saw the expression on her face and a raucous laugh erupted from her wide-open mouth. The noise filled the building as her body jiggled in random directions like a too-soft jelly.

"Come on, or you'll bring the building down," Harry said, putting his elbows out.

Auntie June hooked her arm through the left one, and Harry gestured with his right elbow at Joy. She looked around her in confusion as he kept shaking it.

"Take it, love, or it'll drop off," Auntie June shrieked.

Joy slipped her arm hesitatingly through the proffered elbow, and she was swooped out of the building on a tide of laughter and crazy dancing around and around until she felt dizzy. They stopped in front of a Holden station wagon. Harry jerked the back door open and Joy found herself in a heap on the back seat. "Welcome to Longreach," she heard as the door slammed behind her.

Chapter 48

The station wagon drove smoothly along the wide main street—Eagle Street, Joy's aunt told her—and then turned and travelled a few blocks along until pulling into the driveway of a large weatherboard house. The front yard was littered with engines, bicycle parts, bits of scrap metal, forty-four gallon drums, corrugated iron, and other items that were a mystery to Joy.

She got out of the station wagon, hooking her bag over a shoulder, and picked her way through what she could see of the mess in the light of the street lamp. Harry and June led the way to the front door. As Harry touched the doorknob, it was ripped out of his hand and the door was flung open.

"Surprise!"

A crowd of young faces in various states of dirtiness bobbed up and down in front of them, all shouting at the same time. A dog pushed its way between their legs barking excitedly, its tail wagging furiously. A cat jumped up on the shoulder of one of the children and regarded Joy solemnly.

"I told you little buggers to go to bed, didn't I?" Auntie June bellowed, laughing at the same time.

"Useless," Uncle Harry shook his head.

"Well, come in, love. Might as well meet 'em now as tomorrow." Auntie June pushed Joy towards the children.

"What's his name?" one of them shouted over the din.

"Carol," Uncle Harry shouted back.

"Carol's a funny name for a boy," another said, breaking into a fit of laughter.

"Carol's a girl," Auntie June said sternly.

"What's she wearing boy's clothes for then?"

"Never you mind," Auntie June swiped at the child.

Joy followed them into the kitchen at the back of the house, where she sank down onto a chair somewhat overawed by the sudden appearance of so many people all shouting at once.

"Shut up or I'll belt ya," Uncle Harry yelled.

There was an abrupt silence, which even the dog respected.

"Right," Uncle Harry glared around him from face to face. "This is your cousin, Carol." He pointed at two of the eldest children. "These are Tom and Lenny."

Joy looked at each of them in total confusion. "They look the same"

"Yeah, little buggers are twins. The terrible two, we call 'em. They're both as bad as each other. Tom's the eldest…"

"He's an old fart," yelled Lenny.

"…by two minutes and forty seconds," Uncle Harry continued. "They're thirteen…same as you."

"Cuppa, love?" Auntie June held up a teapot.

"Thanks," Joy said, her mouth suddenly dry.

"And this is Pammy."

"She's a girl," yelled Tom, "but you wouldn't know it. Looks like a boy, like you do."

Joy couldn't help but agree. Pammy was dressed in jeans and T-shirt—her chest was still flat—covered in as much dirt as the boys, and with hair cut boyishly short.

"She's eleven, and you'll be sharing her room…"

"What?" Pammy exploded. "Since when?"

"Since now, you selfish little bugger," her father glared at her.

"Why can't she sleep in Pete's room?" Pammy shouted.

"Because she's sleeping in yours. No arguments."

Uncle Harry started to unbuckle his belt.

"All right, all right," Pammy sat down on a chair, sulking.

"Sorry…" Joy started to say.

"Ignore the little brat," Auntie June said, plonking a mug of tea in front of Joy. The tea slopped over the rim, making a puddle on the table. Her aunt wiped it up with her sleeve.

"Next is old Pete here, who's ten. He's the brainy one. Reads all the time."

"Oh, do you?" Joy said hopefully. "I like reading too."

The boy regarded Joy without speaking. His face was scrubbed clean and his T-shirt was neatly tucked in.

"Doesn't say much," her uncle said. "Too busy thinking."

Suddenly Joy's mug was knocked out of her hand and onto the floor as the cat jumped up onto her shoulder, frightening the wits out of her. The tea splashed in all directions.

"Oh, I'm…"

"Don't worry about it," Auntie June laughed. "Bloody cat's always doing that." She grabbed Pammy by the arm. "Clean it up. There's a good girl."

"Why me?" Pammy whinged.

"'Cause your mother told you to," her father yelled.

"Why don't you ask the boys for a change?" she said, stuck to her seat.

Harry reached for his belt again.

"All right, all right."

"That's Maggie," Auntie June said, reaching over to pat the cat which was rubbing around Joy's neck. "Maggie 'cause she's black and white, like a magpie."

"And this is Rover," Tom said, hugging the kelpie dog. "He's my best mate."

"No, he's mine," yelled Lenny.

"Mine." Tom pushed Lenny away from the dog.

"Mine."

Lenny pushed him back and they ended up in a heap on the floor where Pammy was making a pretence of cleaning up the spilt tea. Harry stood up and grabbed the two boys by an ear each. They stopped struggling.

"That's better," their father grinned.

Maggie purred loudly at Joy's neck. It was such a warm feeling having the cat take to her like that; she tickled it under the chin and around the ears. Suddenly the beanie popped off her head and they all gasped in amazement.

"Jesus!" Tom and Lenny said at the same time.

"Stop swearing," their mother frowned as she looked at Joy's hair.

Pammy started to giggle and her father whacked her lightly across the top of her head. Pete stood with his mouth open.

Though Auntie June tried hard, she couldn't stop herself from laughing. It bubbled up from somewhere deep inside her until it was expelled in a rush, accompanied by a frenzied disturbance of her body in a mixture of wobbles and jerks and undulations of the fat that covered it. The laughter was so infectious that the rest of the family joined in, as well as Rover with an ecstatic barking. Even Pete laughed, in a quiet sort of way, and Maggie jumped off Joy's shoulder to stand on the floor as if to get a better view of the ghastly haircut.

"Oh. Oh." Joy sprung off her chair, mortified. "Oh, I hate you. I hate you all!" And she burst out of the kitchen door and fell down the back stairs.

Nursing a bruised elbow, Joy lay tucked under the bedclothes with only her nose peeping out. She had the pillow over her head as she faced the wall. She knew Pammy was asleep—had been for the past half hour or so—but still hesitated to turn over in case one of the horrible family came in to laugh at her again. She supposed they were all asleep by now, but she didn't trust them. *I'll never forgive Dad for sending me up here. Never.*

The smell of bacon cooking wafted into Joy's nostrils, breaking into her dreams, and stirred her into wakefulness. She looked through the curtain of her eyelashes and was glad to see that she was alone in the bedroom. Now she could inspect her surroundings, which were in the same state of chaos as the rest of the house. Broken toys lay discarded amongst clothes that had fallen to the floor. Drawers were half-open and wardrobe doors spilled out the contents in a confusion of what looked like years of mess. Joy thought longingly of her own room with her beautiful desk, *Blue Eyes*, book-laden shelves, lace curtains that let in the fresh sea air. She blinked back tears that threatened.

The door burst open with a crash.

"Come on, lazy bones. If you're late for breakfast, you go hungry."

Pammy slammed the door shut again and Joy could hear her thumping footsteps going towards the kitchen.

Joy's stomach rumbled. *Traitor.* She got out of bed and pulled her jeans on, then went into the bathroom and splashed her face and washed her hands. The face that looked back at her in the mirror appeared different, but she imagined that was because of the hair that surrounded it—or the lack of. She pulled a face and tossed her head in defiance. She'd stop wearing the beanie and dare them to laugh at her again. *Okay, let them,* she glared at herself. *I won't give them the satisfaction of seeing me cry again.*

The kitchen was a riot of sound and movement. The whole family was seated at the table, shovelling food into their mouths as if it was their last meal. Even the dog and cat were busy at their bowls on the floor.

"Come and tuck in, love," Auntie June beamed, waving her to sit in the chair beside her.

Joy could see mashed bits of egg and bacon at the back of her aunt's mouth when her lips drew back to smile. She shuddered.

"There's plenty there, and more cooking on the stove," her aunt said.

A toaster popped up with a clunk and one of the twins jumped up to get the slices. He added them to a stack already on a plate, and put more in the toaster. Joy noticed that her cousins were taking surreptitious looks at her hair, but she ignored them. They must have been told to shut up about it, she thought with satisfaction. She held her head high and her back straight as she ate her breakfast. It surprised her how hungry she was and her aunt and uncle nodded approvingly at her appetite.

After breakfast, Joy helped Auntie June with the dishes and then went back to the bedroom and made her bed.

"What'd you do that for?" Pammy said.

"What?"

"Make your bed."

"Well, don't you?"

"What for?"

"Aren't you supposed to?"

"Yeah."

"Well?"

"What are you? A goodie goodie, or something?"

"No. Just been brought up properly."

Later that day, Uncle Harry took Joy and the children with him to his garage. It was a block away from the main street and looked to be a busy place with cars, trucks, tractors and other machines that Joy had never seen before, inside the building and out.

"Go and have a look at the town," he told her. "Show her around, Pammy."

"Do I have to?"

"Yeah. You have to."

"Shit," Pammy mumbled under her breath.

"What'd you say?"

"Nothing."

"Didn't sound like it to me."

"Come on," Pammy grabbed Joy's arm.

They wandered down the block and turned into Eagle Street, Joy looking around her with interest. She stopped in front of Solleys Department Store.

"Come on," Pammy whinged after some moments.

"Aren't you interested in dresses?"

"What for?"

"Oh, you're too young," Joy sniffed.

"Bull shit."

"Charming."

Joy continued to study the dresses in the window. Pammy ambled away.

"Suit yourself," she called back over her shoulder.

"I will."

She watched Pammy cross over the street and join up with her brothers. After a good few minutes, Joy proceeded along the street until she came to a newsagency. She wandered inside, ignoring the startled looks of the people who regarded her hair. *Bugger them.* A copy of *True Confessions* caught her eye and she flicked through it. It was one she had at home. She realised she hadn't brought her bag with her and wouldn't be able to buy anything even if she wanted to.

She hesitated at the doorway, hoping that her cousins were out of sight by now. Then she noticed the *Courier Mail,* a Brisbane newspaper. The headline didn't interest her and she flicked the pages over absent-mindedly, at the same time as she looked up and down the street to see if the coast was clear. She failed to notice a small article at the bottom right of the third page. It read:

IN BRIEF - VICTORIA

BODY OF GIRL FOUND IN PORT PHILIP BAY

The body of a teenaged girl was found yesterday washed up on the beach at Frankston, a suburb of Melbourne. Police are investigating.

"Can I help you, miss?"

"No, just looking," Joy said as she dropped the paper back down on the stack. She stepped out into the street and walked in the opposite direction to the one taken by her cousins.

Chapter 49

It was lunchtime before Joy wandered back to Harry's garage, after having spent the time dodging her cousins as well as exploring the Eagle Street shops.

"Thought we'd lost ya," Harry called out from under a truck.

"Just looking around."

"Hungry?"

"So so."

"Where're the others?"

"I don't know."

She squatted down and looked under the truck. Harry grinned at her, his teeth white in a tanned, grimy face.

"Pass me that wrench, will ya?"

"This?" She held it out to him.

"Yeah," he said in surprise. "Didn't think a city slicker would know what a wrench was."

"My dad taught me all about tools and things."

"Did he now?"

He worked on in silence for a time while she watched him.

"What's your mum like?"

"My mum?"

"Yeah. You've got one, haven't you?"

She laughed. "Yes."

"Well?"

Joy thought about it. "She's got dark hair, very pale skin, slim..."

"Yeah, yeah. I get the picture. But what's she like? You know, her personality."

"Oh. She's a terrific dressmaker. Very clever with her hands. And a good cook."

"What's your favourite?"

"Lemon meringue pie," she said without hesitation.

"Sour?"

"No—sweet." A strong image of Ruth filled her mind. "You know, she has a certain way of looking at you when you're talking to her. She stops what she's doing and just listens. Like there's nothing else on earth more important than what you're saying at that moment." A pang of homesickness for her mother stopped her.

"Not many do that."

"No," she agreed, "they don't."

"Is she easygoing?"

"She was before..." Joy bit her lip.

"Before what?"

"Oh, nothing."

"Come on, spit it out."

Suddenly the peace was shattered as four pairs of legs surrounded them. Joy looked up to see her cousins.

"Where'd you get to?" Pammy demanded.

"What about you?" Joy shot back.

Harry slid out from under the truck. "All right. Let's get home for some lunch."

They all piled into the station wagon and arrived back at the house where June had a huge platter of sandwiches waiting for them.

Although the family argued constantly, and her cousins always seemed to be doing the wrong thing, there was obviously a lot of affection shared between them. Grins lurked around cheeky faces as the children responded to the good-natured scoldings of their parents. Despite the many clouts and slaps they received, they seemed to get just as many hugs to compensate, so sulking and grudges hardly appeared in their world.

Joy hated and envied them at the same time. She felt like an intruder as she watched the family's antics, and missed the feeling of belonging in her own small family. She'd never thought about belonging. It was something she took for granted. Her parents would always be there—her friends would, too—and they loved her for who she was. She was comfortable around them. Not like this—in someone else's house where she didn't belong. This was awful.

Joy watched the twins wrestling with their father, while Pammy taunted them at the top of her voice, leaning against her mother, who was in fits of laughter as Tom and Lenny's arms and legs wriggled all over Harry. Rover, not to miss out on the action, kept jumping up at them, leaping higher and higher each time, barking furiously. It looked to Joy as if he was laughing too, with his tongue lolling out of his mouth with its corners drawn back. Pete sat on his chair watching his brothers' antics, clutching a book in his armpit. The cat had jumped up on his shoulder and sat glaring at them all with the utmost disdain on its face. Joy sympathised with it. She didn't even try to put a smile on her face. *Why should I?*

She got up and went to the chaotic bedroom she shared with Pammy. The only tidy part of it was her bed. She sat down on it with her chin in her hands, fighting back tears.

"You want to read my book?"

Joy looked up to see Pete standing in the doorway, holding out his book to her.

"What is it?" she said without interest.

"*Puzzle for the Secret Seven.*"

"I've read it."

"Oh." He looked disappointed.

"Sorry." She was contrite. "I've read just about every Enid Blyton book."

"Me too."

"Really?" She looked at him, surprised.

Pete nodded.

"You like reading that much?"

He nodded again.

"I was reading a new book," she said wistfully. "It's different to Enid Blyton's books though. It's called *The Diary of Anne Frank.* Have you heard of it?"

He shook his head.

"Didn't think so."

She looked around the room. "Does Pammy read?"

Pete's face broke into a smirk. "No way."

"I left my books...that book...in Dad's truck."

"Why?"

"'Cause I'm stupid, that's why." She blinked back tears. Why the book was so important to her, she wasn't really sure, but it was just another disaster on top of everything else. She had identified with the Jewish girl, who had received her first diary on her thirteenth birthday, and likened her own situation with Anne's. *We're both in hiding,* she thought, *only she knows why, and I don't.*

"Dad gave me that book," she said flatly, looking down at the floor.

Pete stared at her and then walked out of the room to return in a few moments with a handful of books. He passed them to her.

"Here."

Her look was grateful. "Thanks," she sniffed, and sat down on her bed with them in her lap. "Why aren't you at school?" she asked, gesturing for him to sit beside her.

"Holidays."

"How come?"

He shrugged.

"You must start earlier than we do in Victoria."

He swung his legs up and down a few times over the edge of the bed, then looked at her. "What grade are you in?"

"I'm in high school. Second form."

"Oh. You'll go to State High."

"What do you mean?"

"At Hospital Hill. That's where the high school kids go."

She stared at him. "I'm not going to any school here. I won't be here long enough."

"That's not what Dad told us. He reckons you'll be going to school with the Terrible Two when the holidays are over."

"What!"

She jumped up suddenly, the books falling off her lap. They both crouched down to pick them up and bumped their heads together.

They heard the clump-clump of footsteps approaching. Pammy thumped on the door-frame.

"Mum says you have to go to the shop."

"What for?" Pete asked her.

"Bread or something," she shrugged.

He stood up, rubbing his forehead.

Pammy watched him for a moment. "What're you doing in my room?"

"Nothing," he said, darting a look at Joy.

"What're all those stupid books doing here?" she demanded.

"I asked him for a lend," Joy said quickly.

"Well, just stay out of my room," Pammy shouted after Pete as he left the bedroom. "Bloody little square," she mumbled to herself.

Joy saw through the window that Harry was in the back yard searching for some parts amongst what looked to her like a pile of rubble. She was outside in a moment.

"Uncle Harry?"

"Yeah?"

"How long am I going to be here?"

He slowly turned to face her, his hands full of nuts and bolts. "You sick of us already?"

"No...I mean...it's just that Pete said you thought I was going to go to school up here." Her mouth felt dry and perspiration dripped between her shoulder blades as she looked at him anxiously. "I'll be back home soon."

He looked down at his hands, turning a nut over and over between his fingers.

"Won't I?" Her voice trembled.

"Don't rightly know, love. That's up to your dad."

"But he said it wouldn't be for long," she insisted. "Well? How long?"

"How long is a piece of string?" he said, pulling a face.

"You mean, you don't even know?"

"Nope."

He looked at her through the hole in the middle of the nut.

"I don't believe this!" she exploded.

Neither do I, he thought grimly.

She blinked away tears of fury and stalked back inside the house.

Gutsy little bugger.

Joy lay staring at the ceiling, swiping angrily at tears that betrayed her turmoil. Her cousins had gone off without her—she didn't care where—and the house was quiet, except for Auntie June thumping around in the laundry. She heard Uncle Harry still sorting through the parts outside, but refused to allow herself to look out of the window in case he saw her and thought she was looking for his company. The phone rang shrilly.

Auntie June called out to Uncle Harry, "Will you get that, Harry, love? It's probably the boys wanting you back in the garage."

Joy heard the back door open on rusty hinges and slam shut behind him as he walked inside. She could hear the murmur of his voice and, after a few minutes, "Carol? Hey Carol? Phone for you."

Her heart began to beat faster and her mouth went dry again. *It has to be Dad.* She hurried to the lounge room and took the phone from Uncle Harry wordlessly. He patted her lightly on the back and walked outside to his station wagon and drove off. She put the receiver to her ear and waited. The breathing in the earpiece was loud but she didn't speak.

"Jo...Carol? Is that you love?"

Carol, is it? Bugger him!

"Carol? Can you hear me?"

"My name is Joy," she hissed into the speaker, "or have you forgotten me already?" Her voice dripped with sarcasm.

"Princess, you know we can't call you that anymore..."

"Why bother to call me anything?"

She slammed the receiver down and walked slowly back to the bedroom.

Auntie June stuck her head out of the laundry as she passed. "Everything okay, Carol?"

Joy ignored her and closed the bedroom door with a bang.

Half an hour later, Joy slipped into the bathroom quietly and washed her face with cold water. She hoped no one would see that she'd been crying. Auntie June was out at the clothesline, and Joy let herself out of the front door without being seen. She walked quickly along Swan Street, and away from Eagle Street, looking over her shoulder a few times to make sure she wasn't being followed. It was a warm day; the sun felt good on her body as her steps slowed to a more relaxed pace. *It'd be cold in Chelsea now.* Her thoughts returned to the phone call and she imagined her father sitting in the lounge room looking stunned at the receiver after she'd hung up on him. *Serve him bloody-well right.* Then she remembered how strange the line had sounded, with noises of traffic in the background, and realised that he'd made the call from a phone box. *What would he do that for?*

Chapter 50

Heading in a north-westerly direction, Joy found herself walking along a highway. Everywhere she looked the land was flat. It extended out to an unbroken horizon that seemed to hold up a painted curtain of brilliant blue. She looked up and then over her head. The blue barrel arched over to the opposite horizon. It was the same sky that sat over Chelsea, she knew, but her home was dropped below the horizon to the south, out of reach. It was so quiet here, apart from the occasional car or truck that passed her, and she longed for the familiar soft whisper of waves on sand.

If she'd been here with her parents on a holiday, visiting Uncle Harry and Auntie June and her cousins for a week or so, then it would have been different. She'd have explored the township eagerly, played with her cousins, had long chats with her aunt and uncle, getting to know them. Then she'd have said goodbye with a tear in her eye, and written to them occasionally, remembering what a great holiday she'd had in the outback.

Instead, she was stuck here for goodness knows how long—alone, confused, fed-up. Did her father really think she was going to like it here? How on earth could she? Under these circumstances? Never! Especially with such a barmy family. Well...most of them. Uncle Harry wasn't so bad. Neither was little Pete. *At least he reads books.*

For the umpteenth time, she wondered about Ursula. *She must think I'm so rude,* Joy thought ashamedly, remembering that she'd actually been asleep when her dad had dropped Ursula off at her home. *I wonder if she's rung?* What would her father tell Ursula if she did? That she just went off on a holiday? That she had forgotten to mention it? That she didn't really want to see her again? Or something equally disastrous? Joy thought her father was acting strangely enough to do just that.

Could you catch mental illness? That's what her mother had, hadn't she? Could her father get it from her? Maybe that's why her father wasn't making sense. *If there's a library in this crappy place, I'll look it up,* she decided. What would you look under? Contagious diseases? Mental illness?

A group of grey wallabies hopped between some low scrub not far from Joy. They stopped and looked at her as she walked steadily along the highway. It seemed that they were having a chinwag about her, like whether or not they thought she belonged in the landscape. *Do I have 'City Slicker' written on my forehead?* She slowed her steps and turned off the highway to approach them.

"Come on, Wally," she clicked her tongue at them. "I won't hurt you."

Unhurriedly, they bounded away from her in long leaps, seemingly confident that she had no hope of ever catching up with them.

"All right. I know when I'm not wanted," she sulked. "Not even my own father wants me."

She trudged on without further pause, not knowing where she was going, but feeling as if she was walking away from her problems. The residential area of the township was behind her as she approached a river, where the highway crossed over it in the form of a bridge. A sign told her that it was the Thomson River. She made her way down the riverbank to sit on a rock platform. Clumps of coolibah trees clung to the cracked, dry, straw-coloured soil, their roots reaching towards the water holes that made up the river. A few dead trees provided ghostly grey perches for chattering birds that squabbled over their pecking order. Joy wished that her problems were as simple as theirs.

The sun gradually slipped off its blue perch and dipped into the horizon, throwing up a golden ruffle so that the human eye would remember where it had been. Then the blue streaked into pink, then gold, then orange, then red, and the colours bled into the water holes. The rest of the landscape—the Mitchell grass, the low bushes, the sparse clumps of trees—all became black cutouts, placed there by some primitive artist.

She had been sitting there, hardly moving, watching nature flaunting its best attributes. She was afraid to leave and yet afraid to stay. *They must be looking for me*, she thought. Were they worried about her? Would they send the Police out for her? Would they be angry? *I don't care if they go crook at me. Bugger them.* She decided she'd spend the night there by the river, although she shivered at the thought of being alone in the outback. Rustlings in the bushes and grass had made her look around many a time during the daylight hours, but now it was suddenly dark the rustlings took on a more ominous quality. She also shivered in her T-shirt—a feeble protection against the abrupt drop in temperature.

Headlights coming towards her stabbed the darkness. A vehicle pulled up on the bridge. A door opened and, in the weak interior light, Joy saw Uncle Harry's lean figure getting out of the station wagon.

"You there Carol?" he called out, swinging a torch back and forth along the riverbanks.

She ducked behind a bush. Something shook the leaves and then brushed against her hand. A squeal escaped her and she darted up to her feet. The torchlight hit her full in the face and she put her arm up to cover it.

"There you are."

He picked his way down the riverbank to join her.

"Thought you might be here," he said quietly. "Good spot, hey?"

"It's all right," she replied, scuffing her feet on the dry earth.

"Hungry?"

"Not really," she lied.

"Been eating the roos, have ya?"

She stifled a giggle.

"Did ya leave any for me? I'm starving," he said.

She looked across the riverbed to the other side. The red sky was slowly fading to black and the first stars were waking up, like the lights of a city being slowly turned on, street by street, suburb by suburb.

"Look, Carol…"

"Don't call me that!"

"All right. What's your real name?"

"Joy," she said in a small voice.

"It'll be our secret then…Joy…but I'm gonna have ta call you Carol when anyone else is around. That's what your dad wanted."

"Fat lot he cares."

"Look…Joy, I reckon he cares a bloody lot about you. He wouldn't have gone to so much bloody trouble if he didn't. He's got his reasons."

"I don't understand them. They don't make sense."

"He'll explain it all to you. When he's good and ready, I guess."

"And when's that going to be? Next year?"

"Jesus, I don't rightly know."

He sensed that she was crying.

"Are we that bad you can't put up with us?" He waited. "For a while?"

He could just make out her profile against the darkening sky. Her head was down and her hands were up to her eyes. He took a step closer and reached out tentatively. She was inside his embrace and crying against his chest before either of them had time to think about it. They stayed that way until the last hint of red had left the sky and the noises of the outback night smothered the sound of her weeping.

Before Joy went to sleep that night, she determined that she would try to get along with her cousins and make the most of her time in Longreach. The next morning, however, her plans were dashed before she hardly had time to blink. She was vaguely aware that something had entered her bed near her feet, and she raised her head off the pillow where her face had been buried in sleep. Yes! There was something there. She felt it tickle her ankle. Turning over quickly, she caught a glimpse of two heads bobbing down below the end of her bed. Now she was fully awake and conscious of the fact that something was wriggling around her legs.

She screamed and jumped out of the bed, flinging the bedclothes back as she did. Two large lizards scurried over the edge of the bed as the Terrible Two broke into shrieks of laughter, jumping up and down with glee. Pammy sat up in bed laughing so much she started coughing until she dry retched.

"You...you...buggers," Joy ground out. "I'll get you for that."

"So, what're you gonna do, hey?" the twins yelled in unison. They grabbed the lizards and darted out of the bedroom with them.

"And you can shut up," she turned on Pammy.

Pammy caught her breath and continued to laugh, holding onto her stomach. "You should have seen the look on your face."

"Shut up, I said. Shut up."

"Make me," Pammy taunted, suddenly laughing no more, her eyes narrowed.

Rage took hold of Joy. Her heart thudded as blood rushed to her head.

Pammy pointed at her hair and started to laugh again.

"Baldy, baldy," she taunted. "Had a fight with the lawn mower?"

With that, Joy grabbed hold of Pammy's hair and yanked as hard as she could. A tuft came out in her hand and she looked at it in surprise.

Pammy shrieked in pain, "You bitch! You bloody bitch!"

The door slammed open.

"What's going on here?" Auntie June looked furious.

The hot dishwater floated steam up into Joy's face as she leant over the sink. Her hands had gone wrinkly from the amount of dishes she'd had to wash. She didn't mind though—despite the fact that it was supposed to be a punishment—because it gave her time to be alone without having to talk to any of them. She wondered when dishes were ever washed in this house; she hadn't seen anyone doing them before. She looked out of the window and smirked at Pammy who was bent over a garden bed wildly crowded with weeds. That'd take her hours and hours, Joy thought. *Serve her bloody-well right.*

Auntie June and Uncle Harry had tried to look serious, after she and those rotten kids had explained what the ruckus was about. She could tell that the punishments were only a token—that it'd probably happen again—and she heard her uncle and aunt laughing in the other room. *Well, they might think it funny, but I don't.*

Uncle Harry had gone to work with the Terrible Two. They had to clean out his garage apparently, and weren't too thrilled about it judging by the scowls on their faces. Their father returned to the house for something else he needed from the rubbish pile in the backyard when the phone rang. Joy heard him talking quietly, as she held a plate suspended over the suds, when he poked his head around the doorway.

"Phone for you, Carol."

She glared at him.

"Well?" His eyebrows shot up to the creases in his forehead.

"Who is it?" she asked sarcastically.

"Your dad, love."

She turned her back on him and put another plate into the water, scrubbing at it furiously. "I'm not interested."

"Oh, come on. He's your dad."

"I don't want to speak with him," she said slowly and distinctly.

He shrugged and returned to the phone.

Joy heard him say, "Crikey, Les, she doesn't want to talk to you. What do you want me to do?"

There was a pause and then, "Yeah. No use forcing the kid."

She pushed the kitchen door shut and began clattering the remaining dishes around furiously as she fought tears.

Lunch was a fairly sombre affair compared to the usual chaos. Joy knew that her cousins hated her.

"I wish you'd never come here," Pammy had spat out at her when her parents were out of earshot.

Joy was sure that was how the others felt too. "So do I," she'd returned with equal venom.

Even though the disastrous beginning to the day had really been Tom and Lenny's fault, Joy felt responsible. It wouldn't have happened if she wasn't there, and none of them would be feeling so unhappy if she hadn't reacted so frantically. If she'd shut up, maybe laughed a little—no, that'd be taking it too far—nobody would have been in trouble.

She was also feeling guilty about her father. Like Uncle Harry said last night, he was probably doing what he was because he really had to. Even though she didn't understand it all, he really did love her—didn't he? Nothing had happened that would change that. Up until the day before her birthday, everything had been fine between them. Always had been. He'd said he still loved her and, by ringing again, he showed that he hadn't forgotten her. *Maybe he really is sick—like Mum. Maybe Mum going off the rails set him off and he doesn't know how to handle everything.* No, she'd try to be more understanding and get along with these cretins who were her cousins. She could pretend, couldn't she? After all, it wouldn't be forever—would it?

Her cousins all disappeared from the house after lunch when Uncle Harry went back to work. Auntie June said she was going over to the neighbours for a while and Joy had declined her offer to accompany her.

"No, thanks. I'll just read a bit." She held up a book that Pete had lent her.

"All right, love. Just make yourself at home."

Joy watched her aunt manoeuvre her way through the front yard, dodging the bits and pieces scattered everywhere. It was surprising that a woman of her bulk could move in such a nimble manner. She reached the gate unscathed and, with a tug at her toosmall T-shirt that accentuated every roll of fat, and a pat at her thick, grey hair, she headed for the neighbour's house.

Joy turned back from the window into the lounge room, knocking the telephone table over. The phone clattered to the floor and she looked up quickly to see if Auntie June had heard it. A metallic voice sounded loud in the now quiet house. "Number please." Joy put the phone back on the table and put the receiver to her ear. Almost without thinking, she asked for the number of her home in Chelsea. Her heart beat at an alarming rate.

"Hello? Hello?" Her father's voice was unmistakable, though he sounded sleepy—like he'd just woken up.

She started to cry, smothering the sound as best she could.

"Who's this?" he said, his voice louder.

She listened mutely, not daring to speak. She knew he would be angry for disobeying him. He'd told her not to use the telephone.

"Hello? I said, hello." He sounded impatient now.

There was a pause and she could hear his breathing.

"Is that you, love?" he whispered.

She put the phone down slowly.

"I miss you, Dad," she cried into her hands.

Joy sat on the sofa and cried until there were no tears left. She felt exhausted and lonely. If only Louise were here. They'd have a good cry together and talk and talk until they sat in a comfortable silence, their arms linked. Her *Sweet Pea*. Just to hear her voice would be enough. Dare she ring? She'd only listen. She wouldn't talk. She'd just listen to her *Sweet Pea* say hello and then hang up. She'd feel better then.

She watched her hand as it clutched the receiver of the phone and pick it up. The voice asked her again what number she wanted. She listened to the...ring, ring...ring, ring...ring, ring...until the operator said that no one was at home. The last ring was cut off as the operator disconnected the call. Then she remembered her dad had told her that Louise had gone away—hadn't he?

An hour later, Pete found Joy sitting in the back yard on an old tyre, staring into space.

"What're you doing?" he asked.

"Nothing much."

"I'm going to the library. You want to come?"

"There's a library here?"

He nodded.

Joy felt at ease with Pete; they walked the few blocks back to Eagle Street without the need of having to say a lot. He stopped in front of a double-storied, old wooden building, with a sign that said *School of Arts.*

"Is this it?" she asked.

At his nod, they went inside the building where they both spent an enjoyable hour exploring the shelves. The librarian obviously knew Pete well by the warm welcome she gave him.

One book that Joy selected was *Black Beauty*.

"Oh, you'll love that one, dear," a woman of about fifty years commented as she paused at a table where Joy was trying to decide which books to borrow. She also had a pile of books to take out.

Joy looked up from her seat. "I've read it before, but I love it so much, I could read it over and over."

Large bright blue eyes peered at her through the glass of modern frames. The eyes smiled, as did the thin, brightly painted lips.

"Me too. Though it's a while since I've read that one." The woman hesitated and then sat down beside Joy. "I haven't seen you before. Are you visiting Longreach?"

"Yes." Joy tried not to pull a face. "Not for long though."

"Where're you staying?"

"With the Bakers...Harry Baker and June Baker."

"Oh, he looks after the ambulances, trucks, and things at the hospital. He's a very good mechanic."

"Is he?"

The woman nodded. "Are they relatives of yours, dear?"

"My uncle and aunt."

"Oh, I see," she said thoughtfully. "That's young Pete Baker you're with?"

"Yes. He loves reading like I do. He brought me here."

The woman smiled again. "Good on him."

Joy thought what a friendly lady she was. She made Joy feel like she was her friend, even though they'd never met before.

"And what books do you like to read?" the woman asked.

Joy showed her the books she'd selected: *Great Expectations, Hard Times, Robinson Crusoe, The Merchant of Venice.*

"You like Dickens too!" the woman said. "And Shakespeare?"

"No." Joy pulled a face. "I hate Shakespeare. I don't understand him."

"Why are you reading him then?"

"We're doing it for school next term. I thought I may as well try and read it first to see if I could make any sense of it."

"Yes, I know. Shakespeare can be difficult," she said in sympathy. "But all these books are quite old. You don't read modern books?"

"Well, I was reading *The Diary of Anne Frank* but I forgot to bring it with me. They don't have a copy here."

"I've got one. I could lend it to you."

"Gee, that'd be great! I was sorry I couldn't go on with it."

"Well, you can come over to my place anytime and I'll give it to you."

"Thanks so much." Joy looked over at Pete who was immersed in a book at another table. "Do you live far from the Bakers?"

"I live and work at the hospital. It's only a few blocks from here. Longreach isn't all that big, you know." She looked at her watch. "My goodness, I must get back. Nice talking to you, dear." She stood up. "What's your name?"

"J...Carol."

"All right, Carol. I'll expect you when I see you."

Joy watched the woman check out two books at the desk and walk out of the library. She noticed what a beautiful figure the woman had, and she liked the way her hair shone so brightly in the sunlight. It was a deep, mahogany-coloured red—tinted, Joy supposed. There was a faint lingering of her perfume. *What a glamorous lady.* Joy was already looking forward to visiting her. Maybe Longreach had some good points.

Walking home, Pete and Joy talked about the books they had chosen and about the woman with whom Joy had struck up the conversation.

"Gee, I forgot to ask her her name," Joy said.

"That's Matron Edwards. She works at the hospital."

"I liked her."

Pete nodded in agreement. "Yes, she's a nice lady."

"Is she married?"

"No. They reckon she hates men."

They heard the last of the mourners leave Olive's place in their cars, and then there was nothing except for the loud ticking of the kitchen clock. They sat in the lounge room, staring at the floor or the red candles glowing in the gas fire. Words seemed a sacrilege to her memory—a blatant disregard for the thoughts that scurried through their minds—and they sat in silence for another half-hour.

Finally, Pat shook herself out of her stupor and put down the cup and saucer that she had held balanced on her knee.

"Les?"

He slowly raised his head and looked at her through red-rimmed eyes.

"Les, the police...they came and talked to us, you know."

He continued to regard her without replying.

Jim frowned, making a shushing signal, but she ignored him.

"I'm sorry to be talking about it now, but I thought you ought to know."

"What?" Les rasped out. He coughed and said again, "What?"

"Because you'd told them I was the last person to see her...alive."

Les nodded.

"Well, there wasn't much I could tell them, really. I mean, she was such a happy kid when I said goodbye to her..." Tears welled in her eyes, but she swallowed hard and continued. "...with finding the brooch and all. Why she would commit...suicide...like they're suggesting...is beyond me. She was a pretty normal kid, I told them. Except when she had those phantom pains, of course. Growing pains, probably." She flushed under Les's gaze. "But they asked about Ruth. Her problems. So many questions."

"I know," Les said quietly.

"I feel awful..."

"Don't," Les reassured her. "Doc Armstrong thinks she might have got Ruth's problems. Puberty...that stuff."

"But I could have done something..."

"What could you have done?" Jim put in.

"Talked to her. Spent more time with her."

"Pat," Les said, "you've got enough on your plate as it is. Neither Ruth or Joy are your problem."

"But they're like my own. All three of you are."

"Thanks. I appreciate that."

"I should have seen…" she cried, tears flooding her cheeks.

"What?" Jim asked, putting his arm around her shoulder.

"That there was something wrong. How could I have been so blind?"

"Don't torture yourself, darl," Jim comforted her.

"There must have been a sign that day. Something she said. Maybe she'd been trying to tell me and I didn't understand."

"Please," Les said, taking her hands in his own, "don't do this to yourself. Whatever it was, she kept it to herself." He paused to look in the direction of Joy's room. "The police…they wanted her diaries. I didn't want to give them to the officers. I knew she'd hate it. But there was nothing in them. Except for the problems with her mother. She wrote a lot about that. Maybe it was getting her down more than we thought."

He looked at the fire, avoiding their eyes. "You know they found a bottle of Ruth's tablets in her bag."

"What?" Pat asked in surprise.

"Joy must have pinched them."

"Why would she do that?"

Les shrugged. "I don't know. But there were a few missing out of the bottle."

"How do you know?"

"They said so," Les said, looking back at them. "They traced the bottle back to the chemist. They were the ones that I bought that morning for Ruth."

Jim hesitated, clearing his throat. "Has the coroner given a cause of death yet?"

"Yeah." Les leaned back against the sofa, raking his hair with his fingers.

"And?"

"Multiple injuries and drowning."

"But…?"

"She had a lot of bruising…as you saw, Jim. There were blows to the head…from the fall probably."

"Do you think she jumped?"

Les put his hand to his chest. The pains were coming back. "I guess so. I mean there's no sign of any…interference with her."

"But how could she have got there?" Pat sighed. "I've asked myself over and over. All that way from the station. Did she walk there? Did someone give her a lift? And if so, who?"

"The police have asked me all that," Les shook his head. "I don't know. Why she'd even go there in the first place, is beyond me, unless she'd planned it."

No one spoke for several moments until a thought occurred to Pat.

"Why buy the present for Louise then?" she asked. "If she knew she wasn't going to see her again, why bother?"

"They were pretty close. Maybe something changed her mind on the way home. Something might have triggered off a mental seizure or something..." Les gasped, clutching his chest.

Pat made sure that Les's pain was under control before they left. He lay back on the sofa, the silence of the house descending upon him like a cloying blanket, where he was condemned to suffer recurring images of Ursula's body tumbling over the cliff face at Olivers Hill.

For the next few days Les stumbled through a fog of automatic obligations—answering the constant questions of the police, mumbling thanks to sympathetic neighbours and friends, visiting Ruth, attempting to ring Joy, organising his workload. His mind was numbed; it was as if someone else was walking around in his body, and he was looking at it performing all the necessary tasks without him. He'd even failed to react when he read another newspaper article about Chambers' probing into Ursula's whereabouts all the way from Perth. There was an inevitability about it that he was powerless to fight.

Each time he rang Joy, she refused to talk with him. He knew, even before he asked for the number, that she wouldn't. He tried to steel himself against the hurt, but it stabbed at him, adding to the weight of guilt and betrayal. He knew he deserved no less.

Ruth's treatment had her in her own fog, escaping reality and living in a world that obviously had gaps in it. Chunks of memory had been exorcised, tucked away where they could no longer harm her. She looked forward to her husband's visits, and those of Pat and Jim, because the time they spent with her made her feel that there was some other life that she could return to.

Each morning, when the hospital staff came to collect her for another treatment, she fought and screamed in vain, desperately afraid of the electrodes that would shatter her very self. On one occasion, as she was being wheeled into the treatment room, her arms shot out and gripped the sides of the doorway in a futile effort to resist. After that, she was restrained with leather straps that had her arms tightly bound at her sides. Her teeth, biting hard into the mouth guard, would stop her screams as the electric current surged between her temples, and her body jerked with involuntarily convulsions. Her mind would scream before the next shock seared her again. *Let me die.*

Louise sat for hours on the front steps of her house, staring at nothing, always waiting for Les. It was as if his presence was the only tenuous living link left of Joy that she could grasp. She saw each time he left the house, each time he returned, heard his back door open and slam shut, heard the truck's motor turn over, saw him collect the mail from his letterbox. His hand would rise in greeting and she would half-rise to talk to him, touch him, but he would turn away, be gone again, and she would sink back onto the step, hardly feeling the pain of her numb buttocks.

Olive allowed Louise to deal with her grief in her own way. She understood Louise's need to cling to Les because, with Ruth in hospital, it was almost as if she, too, were dead. Les had asked Olive not to visit Ruth—at least not yet, he'd said—because the association with Olive and Louise could trigger Ruth's memories of Joy. Although Olive understood, she felt cut off too. After all, Ruth had been her friend—despite the one time Olive and Les had betrayed that friendship—and Olive missed Ruth.

Not for the first time, Olive wondered what would have happened if she'd not had her diaphragm, if she'd fallen pregnant from that one night with Les. She'd have kept it, of course, and she'd have kept quiet about the fact that it wasn't Jack's. If it had been a boy, would it have looked like Les? Would it have been obvious to him? What if Ruth stayed in hospital for the rest of her life? What if Les sought Olive out for comfort...for love? Would she give him that comfort? Of course she would—and she'd have what was rightfully Ruth's. And then she would flush with shame at her treachery and push all thoughts of Les and her unremitting lust for him back to the dark recesses of her mind. How could she think like that when poor Ruth was suffering such horrendous torture in hospital? *Some friend I am,* she'd chide herself as she wondered if she'd go mental, too, if it had been Louise who'd died. Even the thought of it was too hard to get her mind around. No wonder Ruth had blocked it out.

Sometimes Olive would sit on the front steps with Louise. Their shoulders would touch, the warmth of their bodies giving each other comfort, and they would link arms and rock slightly to the rhythm of their grief. There was nothing to say. Nothing that could bring Joy back. Olive would look towards the beach and see the image of the red-haired girl sprinting along the sand with Louise, head back laughing, splashing in the water, building sandcastles, hugging Louise. *Oh, God, where's the justice?*

Louise saw Joy's face amongst the sweet pea, the colours of the flowers radiating in her hair as it billowed around her face. She saw the daisies linked around Joy's neck; the window that would frame Joy's head as it poked out to whistle or call softly over the fence; her hobbling steps over the stones on the road; her excitement over catching buckets of crabs on the jetty. Sometimes, sitting beside her mother, it felt like it was Joy's warmth that seeped into her clothes, and tears would fill her eyes yet again. *How can I ever go to school again without you, Tooth Fairy?*

Les's pain diminished with each day until he had learned how to control it. His exhaustion lessened and he was able to lift his head out of the numbness that had dragged at him like quicksand. After another week, he was told of the coroner's finding that Joy had committed suicide. The relief—to be able to let go and breathe again without the fear of detection, without the ordeal of an inquest—left him shaking and washed out. He sat on the jetty and cried and laughed and cried, thinking that the seagulls were the only witness to his outpourings of emotion. He failed to see Louise sitting at a distance, watching, listening, feeling, remembering.

One morning, Louise heard Les's back door slam shut, heard his footsteps scrunch along the gravel driveway, saw him come around the side of the house and then walk out into the street and hesitate at her front gate. They regarded each other for some moments, not speaking, until he cleared his throat as he opened the gate.

"Louise, I've been thinking."

She waited as he sat down.

"I've been clearing out a few things. I thought...with Joy's stuff..." he faltered, "you might like to take your pick. I mean, you were her best friend. She'd want you to have it."

Louise's eyes filled with ready tears. "Oh, Mr Bacon," she whimpered, her grief too painful to bear, "do you really think she would?"

He nodded. "If it's all right with your mum. We'd better talk to her. See if she thinks you've got the room."

"Room?"

"For the desk," he said quietly.

"What?" She sprang to her feet in surprise. "Her desk?"

"Yeah, love."

"But that's her desk."

"Yeah. But where she is now," he said looking away from Louise, "she can't use it."

"You want me to keep it?" She was incredulous.

"I know she'd hate anyone else to have it other than you. I certainly would."

Les got to his feet and they stood together looking towards the beach. His arms went around her, holding her, as she sobbed into his chest, and he fought back his own tears. They were still there when Olive opened the front door. Her hand reached out tentatively to Les and he included her in his embrace. She, too, found comfort in his maleness, his familiarity. No words were necessary between these three people who grieved for the same girl in their own different ways.

Chapter 52

Ruth's face lit up at the sight of Les strolling into the ward. She knew he was her husband—he'd told her so—and she was the envy of the patients in the other three beds. They commented on his good looks and strong physique, how devoted to her he was, how he visited every night, how he always brought her flowers. Sometimes, memories of a life with him would flash through her mind. She knew he was a very good carpenter because she remembered a beautiful chest of drawers, a polished dining table, an exquisite roll-top desk, and she associated them with him. She could see his hands caressing the wood as he shaped and beautified it. Then images of his hands—on her body—would make her blush as she remembered how they'd made her feel. If she looked at his mouth she could recall how it felt on hers, and she longed to be alone so that he would cover her with kisses again. Maybe then everything would come back to her.

"Ruth," he said, as he sat on the chair beside the bed and held her hand, "you look so much better now. Less tired."

"Yes, since they've cut down those awful treatments."

"None today?"

"No."

"Good. Look, I've been talking with Doc Armstrong. He reckons I can get you out of here in a week or so."

"Really?" Her eyes shone.

"Yeah," he smiled at her.

She liked the way his dimple deepened when he smiled. She would have liked to touch it, but wasn't sure if she should.

"I've missed you so much," he said quietly, looking at her face with longing. *No, I mustn't rush her*, he chided himself. He resisted an impulse to trace her profile, remembering how the feel of the bump on her nose would excite him, and how he would become lost in her brown eyes that always had a giggle bubbling behind them. *I'm falling in love again.*

Her head was tilted to one side, listening, waiting.

"Anyway," he shook himself, "I thought maybe we could start again. You know, a change of scenery."

She continued to regard him in silence, and he smiled again at the familiar way she did this.

"So...how would you feel about selling up and going somewhere completely different?" *Away from Chambers.*

"Les," she laughed. "It makes no difference to me as I hardly remember where we live anyway. If you want to go somewhere else, that's fine by me. But, without familiar places and things, will I ever get my memory back?"

"Oh, sure you will. The doctors reckon the change'll do you good," he lied. "You'll recover quicker."

Louise knelt down beside the grave. The headstone stood out amongst the older marble and granite stones and crosses. Her fingers traced the letters of the name—Joy Bacon—and dropped to the next line that said: 13 years.

"Here you are, Louie," Olive said, handing her the bunch of roses. "I'll wait over there," she indicated with her head towards a bench seat under a tree in the park. "Take your time."

Louise took the flowers and placed them carefully in the receptacle.

Sorry they're not sweet pea, but it's not their time. I'll bring you some in the summer. Promise.

She sat back on her heels and looked at the mound.

You know your dad gave me the desk, don't you? Do you mind? I promise to look after it. I'm looking after Blue Eyes too, but I guess you know that already. I found the birthday card you made for me in one of the secret compartments. It's so pretty! The dried sweet pea and the fern are still stuck on okay. I like the painting you did of my house...and me sticking my head through the window...looks just like me. Sometimes I stick my head through the window and look for you, but you aren't there anymore. I wish I could be with you. It's a whole month already. I miss you. Do you miss me?

Sister Margaret Mary sat with her hands folded in her lap, waiting for Les to go on. They were alone now. He'd told her about Ruth's hospitalization, her short-term memory loss, her fragile state. He'd related the trauma of selling the house as well as his business, and that Joy had been staying with friends in the meantime. As he'd done so, he'd watched Sister Margaret Mary's face for any telltale signs of suspicion, but there was nothing. He let his breath out slowly and carefully, relief flooding him. It was more than he'd dared hope that neither she nor any of the other sisters had seen the news about Joy's supposed death. Or was she pretending? He dared to search her eyes but they looked back at him, sympathizing, without any expression of shock or disbelief.

He sighed. "So the doctor suggested we leave the area...give her a new start...so that her relationship with Joy might improve."

"What does the dear child think about it all?"

"She's...looking forward to the move."

"And you?"

He ran his fingers through his hair. "Yeah, I reckon. What else can I do?"

She leaned over to take his hands in her own.

"We've missed you, Les Bacon, and we'll miss you more."

"Ta, sister. I'll miss you too."

"Is there any hope that we'll see Joy again? And finally meet dear Ruth before you leave?"

"Sorry, sister. We just ran out of time."

"I understand," she said quietly.

Les stood. "So I guess this is it."

"You will write? Let us know how things are?"

"Yeah," he lied.

"I'll write back to you when you give me your new address."

"I'd like that," he said wistfully.

She made the sign of the cross and touched him lightly on the forehead. "May God go with you."

Impulsively, he hugged her, and planted a kiss on her cheek.

"Oh, sorry," he jumped back awkwardly, the imprint of her thin shoulders burning his hands.

"Don't apologise, Les Bacon," she smiled. "It's not very often I get a hug."

His eyes misted over before he had the chance to see hers do the same. He walked out of Aggie's Place with a huge ache in his throat. He swallowed hard and turned back to see her hand raised in farewell.

"But why so far away? Why New Zealand?" Pat asked, wringing her hands.

"That's just it. It's far enough away not to have any reminders of Joy," Les replied. "I hope."

"Well, we'll just have to save up and go and visit you," she said turning to Jim. "Don't you think?"

"It'd be a nice change from Albury. We've done it every year for the last umpteen dozen years. I reckon your sister could do without us at least once in a while," he grinned.

"You'll send us your address as soon as you can, won't you?" Pat asked Les anxiously.

"Yeah."

"You won't forget?"

"No."

"Ah, here she is," Jim said loudly as Ruth rejoined them. "Did you find the magazine you wanted?"

"Yes." She held out the *Women's Weekly*. "It should keep me occupied on the plane."

"Are you excited?" Pat asked her.

"Yes. I've never been on a plane, have I, Les?" she asked, looking at him for confirmation.

"No, love," he smiled down at her. "You haven't. Neither have I, for that matter."

"Oh, I wish I was going with you," Pat sighed.

"You see?" Jim joked. "She's always trying to get away from me."

"Oh you." She jabbed him in the ribs.

They all looked up as a speaker announced Les & Ruth's flight. Tears jumped to Pat's eyes and she threw her arms around Ruth.

"Oh, Ruth, we're going to miss you and Les so much!"

Ruth stood quietly in Pat's embrace. Her hands moved up to Pat's shoulders tentatively and she hugged the older woman back. She knew they were close friends, but she lacked the grief of parting that Pat was feeling.

"Yes, yes," Pat stood back, embarrassed. "Forgive a silly old fool."

"Hey," Les said, picking her up in a hearty embrace. "Nothing to forgive. We're going to miss you like mad."

"Good luck, old son," Jim slapped Les on the shoulder.

They shook hands.

"Look after this boy of yours," Jim said to Ruth. "He's a beaut bloke."

"Yes, I think so too," she said seriously.

Les picked up their cabin bags and made for the departure gate with his arm through Ruth's. They turned back to see Pat crying unashamedly, mopping at her eyes with a bright red handkerchief. Jim sniffed and shuffled around on his feet, trying to look nonchalant.

Such nice people, Ruth thought. *I would have liked to know them better.*

Les smiled at them and turned away. He felt ashamed as he heard Pat call out, "Don't forget to write."

I wish I could.

Chapter 53

Louise looked at her watch and then back at her mother.

"They've taken off now, haven't they?"

"I think so," Olive replied, looking at her own watch.

"I still don't understand it."

"He had his reasons."

Olive continued to iron the pillowslip she'd been working on.

"All I wanted to do was say goodbye. Wave at the plane."

"I know, Louie," Olive said, "but he thought it best for Mrs Bacon."

"I wouldn't have upset her."

"I know you wouldn't have intentionally, but Mr Bacon said the doctors insisted that nothing remind her of Joy."

"I wouldn't have said anything," Louise persisted.

"Of course you wouldn't have, but the sight of you might have triggered some memories. After all, you and Joy were inseparable—like twins."

"I suppose so." Louise struggled with tears that were always ready. She sighed. "I miss her."

Olive left the ironing, sat down beside Louise and kissed her. "I know. It'll take a long time before you can think of her without feeling so sad."

"It didn't with Dad, though."

"Well, that was different. You weren't all that close."

Louise hesitated. "He was an awful man, wasn't he?"

Olive looked out of the window, unpleasant memories clouding her eyes. "Yes, he was."

"I feel guilty, not feeling anything."

"You don't need to."

"I mean, he was my father, but he was so horrible to you. He hit you. He got drunk all the time." She looked at her mother. "I knew about his secretary."

"Did you?"

Louise nodded. "Did that hurt you?"

"Not really. I was beyond caring by that time."

"Why did you marry him in the first place?"

"God, I don't know. Stupid, I guess."

"Why couldn't you have married someone like Mr Bacon?"

Louise walked into her rearranged bedroom where *Blue Eyes* sat atop Joy's roll-top desk. She sat at the desk and leaned over to open one of the secret compartments in which she kept a diary. She turned the pages until she found where she'd last left off. Taking up her fountain pen she began:

10th June 1968

Mum says I shouldn't feel guilty about not caring about Dad. I still do though. It's not a very daughter-type thing to do, is it? And no matter how long it takes, I'll never get over losing Tooth Fairy. She loved her dad so much. I should try to take a feather out of her cap, but I can't when it comes to my father. I can't forget the times he hit Mum and she slept in the spare room. I'll never get married. Men can be absolute beasts. I'm crook on Mr Bacon a bit - sorry Tooth Fairy, if you're listening - because I reckon it wouldn't have caused trouble if I'd said goodbye to Mrs Bacon. I never saw her again. Never! She's Tooth Fairy's mother, after all. I just wanted to give her a hug. I'll tell her that when she writes to us. She will, won't she? I wonder if she's better now. Mum says she doesn't remember Tooth Fairy. How sad. But then I suppose it'd be sadder still if she remembered that she didn't have Tooth Fairy any more. Electric shocks must be awful. I hope I never have to have them. I'd cry, I think. I wonder if the shocks would take away my nightmares? If they did, it might be worth giving it a go, even though I'd be terribly scared. Mum could come in and hold my hand, couldn't she? Otherwise, how do you get rid of nightmares? I wish they'd go away. If I dreamt of Tooth Fairy in a happy way, then I wouldn't mind so much. Who's the man who pushed her over? The one I see in the dreams? NO ONE can tell me she did it herself. SHE WASN'T LIKE THAT. I know her - knew her - and she couldn't have done it. Wouldn't have done it. She'd have told me otherwise. I knew all her secrets. Didn't I, Tooth Fairy? And why would she be wearing someone else's clothes? I don't understand. Mr Bacon didn't seem to be interested and everyone else thought I

was imagining it. Well, I WASN'T!! They think I'm
just a kid. That I don't know anything. Well, I do.

His right eye followed the movement across the end of his bed. Yes,
there it was again. The white blur took shape and he realised it was
the morning nurse. By recognizing the individual staff member, and
the time of day by the amount of natural light in his room, he could
guess whether it was a weekday or weekend. Today was Saturday,
he thought. He liked the nurse who was on today. Her hands were
gentler than those of the weekday nurses when she bathed him. She
talked to him, too, as if he was capable of listening. The others just
talked around him, not to him. They even talked about him, not caring to lower their voices. They treated him like a vegetable, as if he
had no feelings, no ability to hurt.

"Morning Mr Schwartz. How did you sleep?"

She bent over him and pushed his hair back. He felt her nails
scrape lightly over his scalp. It felt so good that he wondered if the
skin stood up in goose bumps.

"My, you could do with a hair cut, don't you think?"

She cocked her head from one side to the other, looking at him
closely.

"I think you parted it."

She flicked his hair over to the right and then to the left.

"Yes. It seems to fall to the right."

Her fingers raked through the hair and she watched as it fell
into a natural parting.

"Can you see me with those beautiful green eyes of yours?"

She smiled into his eyes and he smiled back with his mind. He
wondered if the smile managed to reach his eyes.

"I think you can," she whispered intimately. "They don't think
so," she said, looking towards the doorway, "but I do."

He felt a draft on his body as she drew the covers back.

"How about a nice wash to freshen you up? You'll feel much better then."

With all his might, he tried to tell her how good that would feel.
He felt the words form in his mind; he played with them until he
knew they were right, then he tried to push them towards his lips.
If he'd been pushing a fully laden truck up a hill before this had
happened to him, it would have been easier than trying to utter
those few words. The connection between his brain's commands and
the actual doing was just not there. A tear oozed out of a tear duct
and washed over his eye.

"Oh, Mr Schwartz. Are you crying?" She dabbed at his eye with a face washer. "Or is your eye just leaking a little?"

For another of the countless times he'd thought it, he wondered why this had happened to him, and how much longer it would go on. *When will I ever get better?* Was this a permanent thing—*mein Gott!*—or would he gradually be released from this purgatory? His fear was a thing to push aside or he felt he would go mad—at least the fear for himself—but the fear for Ursula was worse. It gnawed at him constantly. *Where is my liebling? Is she safe?* His inability to find her—even ask about her—frustrated him, horrified him. *Even Sergeant Chambers couldn't find her and has gone back to Perth.*

He remembered the photograph of Ursula in the newspaper, but was convinced that it wasn't her. He hadn't given anyone a photograph of his daughter, and he didn't recognize it—the pose, the background, the school uniform she was in, the style in which her hair was cut. But the most telling fact for him was the missing birthmark. Not that it was an obvious mark, but by the position of the girl's head, tilted up as she smiled into the camera, it would have been visible. At times he asked himself if he'd had enough time to tell from the quick glimpse of the photograph he'd had. But he knew, he just knew, that she wasn't Ursula. So, if she wasn't Ursula, there was only one other person she could be: the missing twin.

Gunter reasoned that one of his daughters had been killed. *Which one?* He grieved for her, grieved for Hannah, grieved for himself. Either way, he had to stay alive. He had to survive this...this appalling situation in which he found himself. He had to wait until he was set free from his prison, to somehow find his remaining daughter.

He set his jaw in his mind's eye, and vowed to himself that he would not give up. *No, never!* He would wait, for however long it took, until something, someone...a miracle?...unlocked his body. He'd been through hell before and survived it. He'd have to do it all again. He'd lost his parents, his sister, Hannah, then his unseen daughter. And he was damned if he was going to abandon whichever one of his daughters was still alive. An image of Hannah sprung to his mind, and he promised her that he would never give up hope. He would find their daughter. She was all he had left.

His thoughts were interrupted by the gentle ministrations of the nurse and her friendly chatter.

"If I find the time," she said in a conspiratorial manner, "I'll come in and read to you. Maybe I'll come in when I have my lunch break. You don't mind if I eat my sandwich in here, do you?"

No, mein lieber Freundin. I don't mind at all.

Joy sat outside on the old tyre in the backyard. It had become her favourite place for cogitating, being away from the chaos of the house. None of her cousins seemed to go out there, except for Pete, who sometimes joined her to sit and kick his heels against the tyre, waiting for her to go for a walk with him. It was still early. The smell of bacon cooking reached her nostrils. It wouldn't be long before she was called in to have breakfast with the rest of them. The house had woken up.

Her thoughts were in turmoil. Tonight they were coming. Her mum and dad would be here in Longreach. *Finally, after a whole month, I'll have my parents back.* Well, at least, she hoped so. *Then I can get out of this dump.* This was her last day at school. Even though she'd argued with Uncle Harry and Auntie June, they wouldn't give in; they'd made her go.

"Wednesday is a school day," they'd said.

"Yes, but what's the point if I'm leaving anyway?" she'd insisted.

"I promised your father you'd go to school, and that's all there is to it," Uncle Harry had shrugged.

Joy knew him well enough by now to know that he wasn't about to give in.

I'll tell those creeps what I think of them, she promised herself, thinking of the pleasure she would get out of ticking off the school bullies for the last time. The thought of going back to her school in Chelsea, seeing Sweet Pea again and sitting on the jetty with her, sitting at her desk and sleeping in her own bed, made her feel far more cheerful. At least this horrible time was nearly over.

The first day Joy had walked into the school grounds of the Longreach State High School, she was on the receiving end of cruel remarks about her hair. Curiosity about the new girl from the 'big smoke down south' attracted genuinely interested and genuinely bullying attention.

"What are you wearing a beanie for?" one girl demanded.

"She's got a cold in the head," someone sniggered.

"Maybe that's their uniform down south," another jeered.

"You can't wear that here."

"Looks spaz."

"Probably is."

"Who do you belong to?"

"Someone said she's with the twins."

"Oh bugger, not another Baker."

Joy tugged her beanie lower over her ears as she tried in vain to ignore the taunting. Tom and Lenny had dumped her as soon as they'd arrived at the school, not wanting to have anything to do with their Victorian cousin, so she faced the tough world of the school yard on her own. She made for the entrance of the double-storied red brick building, hiding her distress behind a cold, stiff mask.

Quick fingers snatched the beanie off her head and there was a sudden silence, followed by sniggering, giggling and then raucous laughter.

"No wonder she's wearing it."

"Jeez. What a mess!"

A voice of authority interrupted them.

"What's going on here?"

"Just welcoming the new girl," a quick thinker said, staring at Joy, daring her to contradict the lie.

The law of the school yard jungle won. Joy said nothing.

The teacher took Joy under her wing and they went inside the building.

You'll keep, Joy thought.

Over the following weeks, Joy—or Carol the Barrel, as she was known—fought a battle of survival that only the pupils of the school were aware of. The teachers failed to suspect that things were not quite right with the intelligent girl from Melbourne, as she kept to herself, did her homework and caused no trouble in the classroom. Outside, in the schoolyard, things were very different.

Because she was obviously the most advanced student for her age at the school, the local children resented her, and her haircut was the perfect way in which they could tease her. Her only means of defence was to hit back verbally:

"Hey Spaz, you're moulting," someone taunted.

"Jeez, it must be catching, only it's your brains moulting," she retorted.

Or to simply ignore them and bury her head in a book.

"Carol the Barrel, what's that you're reading? *Mother Goose?*"

"Would you like me to read it to you? Though I think it might be a bit advanced for a pea brain like you," she snorted.

She would turn away and, with a Dickens book held up over her face, shut out the taunts. They would soon tire of her absorbed silence in her book, and look for fairer game that bit back.

Each morning she entered the school grounds hefting a larger chip on her shoulder than the previous day. Her manner became sullen, defensive, superior. She had no friends and had no intention of making any. *If I'm not staying here, why make the effort?*

But she did make a friend outside of school. She waited a few days after her first visit to the library, and then walked over the road to the hospital that was opposite the school. With some trepidation, Joy lingered around the entrance. *What if she's changed her mind?*

"Yes, love. Can I help you?" asked a nurse hurrying along the corridor with a kidney bowl in her hand.

"Ah, yes. The matron…Matron Edwards. I guess she's busy." Joy turned as if to go. "I'll come back some other time."

"No, it's all right, love. She was in her office last time I saw her. Hang on just a minnie."

Joy hovered uncertainly, then sat down on a chair. She picked up a magazine.

A whiff of perfume met her nostrils.

"Carol! How nice to see you again."

Joy stood to greet the matron. The starched, white uniform suited the woman's shapely figure.

"Hello," Joy said, suddenly shy.

"You've come for *The Diary of Anne Frank?*"

"Well, if that's okay."

"Of course. Come and have a cuppa with me. I'll show you my place."

She led the way as they left the main building and entered a small house, which was her residence.

"Tea or coffee?" the older woman asked. "I never know with you young people. Or would you prefer a soft drink?"

"No, tea's fine, thanks."

Joy followed her into the kitchen.

"What are you reading at the moment?"

"*Hard Times.*"

"And are *you* having a hard time?"

Joy looked at her surprised.

"How did you…?"

"Oh, call it women's intuition, or something exotic like that."

She held out a milk bottle.

"White? Sugar?"

"No. Just sugar, thanks."

Joy's eyes suddenly filled with tears and she blinked them away, embarrassed. *Stop it!* She looked at the floor, away from the matron's gaze.

"Come and see my book collection, such as it is."

They carried their cups into the lounge room. A huge bookcase overflowed onto the floor and piles of books were lined up in neat stacks along the wall.

"Gee," Joy exclaimed, "you've got heaps!"

"And that's not all of them," the matron laughed. "My garage is full of them in I don't know how many cartons."

"Really?"

Joy was already exploring the bookshelves. Her hands stopped at favourite books, or known titles and authors.

"See anything you like?"

"I'll say!"

"Well, whatever interests you, you can borrow," the older woman said over her shoulder as she disappeared into the kitchen. "Oh, the *Anne Frank* is on the coffee table," she called out. "I had it out ready for you."

Joy passed an enjoyable hour with Matron Edwards, talking about books and their favourite characters. She talked about Chelsea and her friend, Louise. She talked about her mother, and what a clever dressmaker she was; about her father and his skill with woodturning; about her desk and its secret compartments.

"You sound like you miss all that," Matron Edwards commented.

Joy nodded, sudden homesickness clutching at her stomach.

"You're here just on a holiday?"

"Sort of," Joy nodded. "Just while Mum gets better. She's a bit...disturbed at times."

"Oh."

"Nothing too drastic. She just overreacts sometimes." She hesitated. "Well, quite often, actually. She's...having shock treatment at the moment."

"Oh, the poor dear."

"Does it hurt?"

"A bit."

Joy bit her lip.

"Don't worry, dear. I'm sure she's in good hands."

Joy finished *The Diary of Anne Frank* within a couple of days. She decided to return it and hopefully borrow something else.

"What did you think of it?" Matron Edwards asked her as they sat down over a cup of tea.

"Very sad at the end," Joy said. "I mean, when you know that she died and she didn't know she was going to die. She had such high hopes of being a writer. I'll bet if she'd lived, she'd be a terrific writer now selling lots of books."

"Quite probably."

"And she was so well educated. Fancy learning all that stuff when you're hidden away like that. She knew far more than I'll ever know, and she was the same age as me when her dad gave the diary to her." Joy took a sip of her tea and continued. "I feel such a dunce compared with someone like her."

"Why, dear?"

"Because there's so much I don't know."

Matron Edwards laughed. "You've got your whole life ahead of you. You'll catch up with Anne Frank before you know it."

"I just can't get her out of my mind. We've got so much in common."

"Really? In what way? Of course not that you're in hiding…"

"No. Of course not," Joy said, a little too loudly.

The older woman regarded her for a moment.

"Are you?"

"No. Why would I be?"

"No reason."

There was an awkward silence until the matron broke it.

"What happened to your hair, dear?"

Joy's hand went up to her head involuntarily.

"Oh that."

"It's none of my business, but there's an excellent cutter here at Petite Madam. She'd be able to get it into some sort of shape for you so that it'd grow out better. I could take you."

"Oh, I can't…"

"My shout. No…" she put up her hand, "it's my idea. I'd like to do it. A girl's got to look after her appearance. Your hair is such a beautiful colour too." She fingered her own mahogany-tinted hair. "I wish mine was that shade. I might try it one day."

"What's your real colour?"

"God, it's so long since I've seen it, I've almost forgotten. A mousy brown. No character."

Joy looked at the other woman's hair closely. "This suits you, though. It makes your eyes look really pretty."

"Thank you, dear. Now how about it? Will you accept my offer?"

"I don't know that I should."

"Should hasn't got anything to do with it. Let's call it a birthday present. When's your birthday?"

"Last week."

Matron Edwards' hairdresser rolled her eyes in despair when she saw the mess Joy's hair was in.

"Strike a light, what happened?"

"The butcher did it," Joy replied sullenly.

"Sorry," the woman recovered, "it's just a bit of a disaster."

"Really?" Joy did a good job of perfect sarcasm.

"Come on now," the matron urged, afraid that Joy would walk out. "Can you fix it?" she asked the hairdresser.

"Well," the younger woman sighed, toying with Joy's hair thoughtfully, "I can certainly have a go at it."

An hour later, Joy left the salon with her hair quite a bit shorter, but she looked a lot happier with herself.

Joy took to calling in at the hospital nearly every day after school. If Matron Edwards was busy, she would either wait for her or return the next day. The time she spent at the matron's house was an escape from the antagonism she had to face constantly with Pammy. She would have preferred to share a bedroom with Pete, but his room was so small that she knew it wasn't practical to even suggest it and, besides, Pete—sympathetic to her as he was—would probably be horrified at the thought of sharing his room with a girl. So Joy tried to be out of the bedroom when Pammy was in it. As a result, Joy spent a lot of her time out in the backyard, reading in the library, or walking down to the Thomson River where she would sit and think about the change in her father's behaviour. The rest of the time—apart from attending school—she spent with the matron who made her feel special.

"Have you always lived in Longreach?" Joy asked her one day.

"Goodness gracious, no. I came from Western Australia...oh, about twelve, thirteen years ago."

"Huh, you're another person I've met lately who comes from there," Joy commented. "Funny, I never knew any West Australians before, and suddenly you're the third."

"Oh? Who else do you know from there?"

"Well, my uncle and aunt...the Bakers...of course. Not my cousins, though. They were born here."

"Yes. I was at the birth of the younger two."

"Oh, really?"

"Yes, after I finished nursing my cousin's daughter. She was very ill for quite some time. They were on a cattle station, you know, but they moved around a bit and I liked it here. The job came up at the hospital and I grabbed it with both hands."

"Were you ever married?"

"No," Matron Edwards said, looking at her hands. "I was close to it once—back in Perth—but he was a rotter, a real stinker."

"Sorry," Joy said, embarrassed.

"Well, that's in the past."

"But, no one since?" Joy persisted. "I mean, you're such a beautiful lady..."

"My gracious," she laughed. "There aren't a lot of men around here who have the same sorts of interests that I do. I'm getting a bit long in the tooth now for all that anyway."

"I don't think so. I think you're just marvellous."

"Well, enough of me, young lady. What about the other person?"

"What person?"

"From Western Australia?"

"Oh, yes. I met someone in Melbourne just last week. She was from Perth. She'd just moved to Victoria with her dad, who's a violinist." Joy's eyes lit up with excitement as she remembered Ursula. "She's very refined, I think. She can play the violin too. Jeez, wouldn't that be terrific? She knows all those classical composers." Joy pulled a face. "I don't know much about them myself, but when I go back to Melbourne, I'm going to meet her again and she'll play the violin for me and teach me all about classical music. Maybe I can go to the Town Hall and see her dad play sometime."

"Is she an older girl?"

"No. Funny thing is, we're the same age. Exactly the same age. Same birthday. And not just that. Guess what?"

"What?"

"We look exactly the same. Just like twins. It's impossible, of course, but it's uncanny. The same hair, the same eyes, the same height. Everything."

"That is uncanny. You're not related, or anything?"

"No. We've never been to Perth, and she'd never been to Melbourne. Her dad's German anyway. We don't have any German blood in our family."

Matron Edwards frowned, "You say you've never been to Perth?"

"No."

"But Harry Baker is your uncle?"

"Yes."

"Whose brother is he—your father or mother's?"

"Oh," Joy looked surprised. "My dad's."

"So your dad is from Perth then?"

"No," Joy said thoughtfully. "He reckons he's never been there."

"Maybe your Uncle Harry wasn't originally from Perth."

"I don't know," Joy grimaced. "I must ask him. Strange isn't it?"

"There's probably a simple explanation."

Joy looked at her watch. "Hell! I'll be late for tea if I don't hurry."

The matron stood. "It's been lovely chatting, as usual."

"Yes." Joy hesitated. "I'll miss you when I go back home. I've enjoyed your company so much."

"Me too, dear."

"Can we keep in touch? You know, write letters?"

"Oh, I'd love that. I'll imagine you sitting at that magnificent desk of yours. Maybe you can even send me a photograph of it."

"I'll get Louise to take it as soon as I get home. She's always taking photos."

Winnie Edwards stood in the doorway of her small house, watching the figure of the red-haired girl, who turned to wave again as she crossed the railway line, and headed for Ibis Street. Something nagged at her. She couldn't quite get to it. *I'll miss that lovely kid,* she thought sadly. *Maybe I'll go and visit her one day in Melbourne. Who knows?* She wondered about the girl's parents—about the mentally ill mother, and the father who'd shunted the child off to the Baker family, *for God's sake,* so that he could cope with his wife. There was a great sadness about the child, and she evaded questions—like that disastrous haircut, for instance—as if she was protecting someone. *Well,* Winnie reminded herself, *it's not my business.*

Chapter 55

The droning of the aircraft had lulled Ruth into a light sleep, her body resting against Les's shoulder as they flew over the arid outback. Although his body was tired, his mind whirled in frantic turmoil.

He wondered why Ruth asked so few questions about what they were doing and where they were going. It reminded him of their flight across the Nullarbor when she had placed her trust in him and gone along with whatever he'd suggested. Like then, this time he went ahead with his plans without offering any explanation unless she asked. His answers gave her the barest information, but she accepted them, smiling at him quietly, and appeared to be content to enjoy the moment. There wasn't a trace of suspicion in her eyes, not an argument, never a hesitation.

Her lack of curiosity puzzled him during their night in Auckland and day in Brisbane before boarding the flight for Longreach. The doctors had told him that it would take some time before she was back to normal again, and he accepted that, but her manner seemed so strange. He knew that memories were gradually returning to her stunned brain, that her feelings for him had been restored, and she appeared to be taking all that in her stride. It was as if the present was all that interested her, that the past was something that would catch up eventually—and she didn't really care if it did today or sometime far off—and the future was something that would just happen. She'd wait and see.

"There you go, Mr and Mrs Paton," the woman had said as she handed Les his tickets at Auckland Airport. "Enjoy your flight."

"Paton?" Ruth had looked momentarily puzzled. "Oh, of course, I must have forgotten."

Have I forgotten anything? Go over it again: name change—yes, on driver's licence, Joy's school reports, Ruth's medical reports. The bottom part of the 'B' scrubbed out okay on most of them. A bit dicey on the tablet bottles. Go over them again later. The 'c' was easy enough to extend to a 't'. No problems getting Ruth to accept Paton. What about Joy?

He sensed a change in the engines as the aircraft sank subtly towards the earth and his stomach tightened with nerves.

What'll her reaction be when she sees Joy? Will it all come back?

Ruth stirred in response to the blocking of her ears.

"Are we there?" she asked, looking up at him.

"Almost," he replied, squeezing her back into his chest. He kissed the top of her head.

She's been so happy these past few days. Jesus, don't let anything stuff it up for her. Don't let her go off again.

"Oh, look," Ruth pointed out of the window, "you can see some houses now. You said your brother will be there to meet us?"

"Him and his wife, June."

"I still don't remember him, you know."

"Oh, you haven't seen him for donkey's years."

Joy, don't do the wrong thing, love. If only you'd let me talk to you.

"Les, what's the surprise? Won't you tell me?"

"No, love."

"It wouldn't be a surprise then, eh?" she said, pretending to pout.

Twenty minutes later, they entered the small terminal building where Harry and June beamed welcoming smiles at them.

"Good on yer, old son. You made it," Harry said, slapping his brother on the back.

"This is my wife, Ruth." Les pushed her forward.

"I'm June, love," said the big woman, giving Ruth a warm hug. "Hello Les," she said, giving him a squeeze against her rolls of fat. "Good to see you again."

"We've got the little lady outside waiting in the wagon," Harry said.

Les frowned at him and rolled his eyes towards Ruth.

"Yeah, well," Harry changed the subject quickly. "This your first time in Longreach, Ruth?"

"Yes. I've never been to Queensland before."

"Oh, it's a good spot," June laughed loudly. "Plenty of sunshine. Plenty of cattle. Plenty of sheep." Her body jiggled in unison with her mirth.

Ruth found herself staring at June's mouth; the more it drew back in laughter, the more of its nether regions could be seen, and it was difficult to tear her eyes away. It was a privileged view of someone's gums and teeth, but Ruth wondered if she could sit looking at it when June was eating. The thought revolted her and she suppressed a shudder. Les caught her eyes in conspiracy and they looked quickly away from each other before they burst out laughing.

"Why don't you two go on out to the wagon? It's a Holden," Harry said. "I've got a few things to pick up—parts and so on. We'll be out there directly."

"We'll get your luggage," June said, pushing them towards the exit.

Les put his arm around Ruth and steered her towards the door.

"Now comes the surprise," he said quietly.

Les spotted Joy's rigid, blank face staring out of the back window. She studied them as they neared the wagon, her body unmoving, tense.

"Is it this Holden?" Ruth asked.

"Yes, love."

"Oh, who's the girl? One of Harry and June's?"

"No."

He opened the back door and Joy got out. Tears spilled down her cheeks as she looked from Les to Ruth.

"Mum?" she said in a small voice.

Ruth looked backwards, as if expecting someone else to claim the girl.

"Oh, Mum!"

And with that, Joy wrapped her arms around Ruth and sobbed into her shoulder.

"I'm so happy to see you," Joy sobbed. "I've missed you so much."

Ruth stood stiffly, unsure how to react. Her arms went instinctively around the girl's body. There was something familiar about her.

"Why's she calling me Mum?" Ruth whispered to Les. "I thought we didn't have any children?"

Joy's head snapped up. She had heard. Her eyes glared at Les as she moved away from her parents, backing up against the wagon.

"What have you told her?" she demanded, hiccuping violently. "What lies have you been telling her?"

"Shush, princess. I'll explain everything soon."

"Explain! Explain!" she shouted. "All you ever say is that you'll explain and you bloody-well don't."

"Don't swear," he frowned.

"Why not?" Her head went up defiantly, her tears drying. "What do you care? You send me to this crappy place and forget about me for a month. Then you turn up here and have the cheek to tell me not to swear."

"Les?" Ruth looked from one to the other.

"It's all right, love," he said, taking her arm. "Look, we'll sort this out. She's just a little upset at the moment."

"A little," Joy snorted.

"Les, is this girl my…daughter?"

"Mum?" Joy's cry was one of anguish. "Don't you know me?"

"I…"

"I'm Joy. Your daughter. Look at me."

Ruth took in the sea-green eyes, the fair, yet sun-tanned skin, the short curly red hair, the slim healthy body.

"What have you done to her?" Joy shouted at Les.

"Nothing, she's just…"

"She doesn't even know me. You call that nothing?"

This was not the happy reunion that Les had envisaged. With a sinking feeling, he knew that he'd botched it up. *If only I knew more about women,* he told himself, in the mistaken belief that this disaster was a female thing rather than a psychological problem. His understanding of a teenaged girl's needs and expectations was as inadequate as his grasp of Ruth's fragile mental state. The enormity of his bungling sat on him, weighing him down like a mantle of pain that seeps into flesh and bones, the blood sluggish, leaden, clogging. He just didn't know what to do.

Ruth's eyes widened as memory fragments rushed through her mind. The pull of a baby's mouth on her nipple; a naked baby lying on a towel on a beach; a red-haired child sorting and threading buttons; a child walking away from her into a school building; a young girl swimming in sparkling blue water; a smiling girl twirling around in a party dress; a body found in the water…

Ruth started to shake. Her whole body was overcome with jerking spasms that threatened to throw her off her feet.

"That smell," she whispered.

"What smell?" Les asked.

She stretched her arm and hand out towards Joy, as if warding off demons. "You're dead. You're dead. You're dead."

Joy stared at her in horror.

"Ruth, love…" Les put his arms around her, trying to stop the shaking.

"Dead. Dead. Dead. Dead. Dead."

"Stop it!" Joy screamed at her. "Tell her to stop it, Dad."

"Joy's dead. Joy's dead," Ruth chanted. "Dead. Dead. You're dead."

"Mum, it's me. Joy," she cried, reaching out to touch Ruth.

Ruth shrank away from her.

"I'm alive, Mum. I'm not dead." She turned to Les. "Why does she think I'm dead?"

Suddenly Ruth broke away from Les and started to run. She headed for the road, oblivious of where she was going, with Les and Joy chasing after her.

Harry and June came out of the terminal building and were surprised to see the three of them hurtling past, away from the car.

"Les?" Harry called after him.

"What the...?" June stared at them, speechless.

They heard a piercing scream as Joy caught up with Ruth and grabbed her by the arm. It appeared, from where they stood, to be Ruth who was the one who had screamed. Les caught up with them a split second later, and shouted something at Ruth. Then the scream surged again on the still air, building in volume until it filled their ears. They saw Les slap his wife. The scream stopped abruptly and she slumped to the ground.

Harry sprinted across to them, with June ploughing over the ground behind him.

Joy stood looking down at Les as he cradled Ruth's head in his hands.

"You hit her," she screamed at him. "You hit my mother."

She knelt down and took Ruth away from him.

"Mum? Mum? Are you all right?"

Ruth opened her eyes to see Joy's face close to hers. The short red hair framed a face that she loved—had loved.

Then a part of her brain snapped shut, closing in the image of a girl she treasured above all else. The image was surrounded by a protective wall that would let nothing in or out. Already the image had lost its contact with the outside world—the world of her consciousness.

Her eyes stared through a frosted window that recognised nothing, felt nothing, heard nothing.

The mind behind the eyes had retreated to a world that included no one else, and drifted into oblivion's custody.

Part Three

"Forgiveness
is the fragrance
the violet sheds
on the heel
that has crushed it."

Anonymous

The woman flicked her hair back as she descended the steps of the Family Court. She squinted at the sun and fished into her handbag for sunglasses. She could see her car parked further along the street but hesitated momentarily; she might walk for a bit—perhaps even have a celebratory drink somewhere. Relief was in her light footsteps; she was liberated at last!

A man walking in the opposite direction turned to watch her as she crossed the road. She was an attractive woman of medium height with a generous figure not given to overweight. Her hair hung thickly over her shoulders—a deep chestnut that shone in the sunlight—contrasting with the bright green of her sleeveless dress. The hemline stopped at her knees, showing off a pair of shapely legs that narrowed to fine ankles. Her jewellery was sparse, but expensive, and her matching high-heeled sandals and handbag were made of soft Italian leather. The man whistled appreciatively and she tossed her head with a grin, her brown eyes laughing at him.

She walked to the main shopping area, browsing casually at the window displays. The smell of coffee reached her nostrils; she decided to have a cup outside and took a seat at a table on the footpath in the sun. She watched the passers-by, wondering about their lives, studying the faces of the women who mostly looked disgruntled. *Get a divorce*, she told them silently. *Nothing like it.*

She looked down at the travel brochures that she'd taken out of her handbag. *Norfolk Island or Bali*. Forty-three was as good an age as any to get a divorce and escape to an island to forget. She'd need a lot of books for that.

Louise had returned to her maiden name, Fletcher, as soon as she'd separated from her husband the year before. It had felt good—a sloughing off of the weight of her unhappy married years. She felt like her own person again, no longer having to tolerate the selfish tantrums of her husband. She often wondered why she had married David Pointer in the first place. Oh, he was glamorous, of course, and handsome in an exotic throw-back-from-Polynesia-way, and he had appeared to be a man on the move with challenging goals. But once he'd reached middle management, he'd stopped dead and floundered into decline.

It didn't take Louise long to figure out that David was gambling as well as drinking heavily. She supposed that one problem fed upon the other. Their joint bank account balance steadily decreased until there was very little left in it to make their house payments. *Thank goodness Mum told me to have my own account,* Louise had thought gratefully.

Arguments became a daily occurrence, increasing in intensity over the nine years they were married, until, frustrated at his impotence to dominate Louise verbally, David resorted to violence. Having been an independent woman before she'd met David, Louise had vowed never to make the same mistake that her mother had—that is, staying and putting up with it. She reasoned that she didn't have to, whereas her mother had had very little choice with no career to speak of.

When Louise finished high school, she'd been offered a job working as a full-time assistant to a leading photographer who had recently moved his premises to the business district of Melbourne. Louise had worked for Mr Watson for two years on a part-time basis, on weekends and school holidays, at his studio in Chelsea. Always one to record every special moment on film herself, she had been determined to learn more about photography, and she'd pestered the man constantly until he'd allowed her into his studio. He never regretted his decision, as she was an apt pupil who took a keen interest in every stage of the photographic process.

His business comprised mostly of portraiture and wedding photography, and Louise became—even while she was still at school—an invaluable assistant when she often smoothed the ruffled feathers of panicking brides-to-be confronted with his particularly acerbic personality. Mr Watson had a certain aversion to wedding photography, being mainly interested in serious portraiture, and regarded brides as frivolous creatures who spent far too much money on themselves. But when in his studio, minutely studying the faces and aspects of his subjects, he was a totally different man. He was finicky about the slightest detail, sending Louise back to the subject time and again to move an article of clothing an inch to the left, arranging a fold, readjusting the hair, or fluffing up a sleeve. She would hold her breath as Mr Watson took one frame after another, hoping that the subject would remain patient, until ultimately he would be satisfied with his work. And always the final result would be a masterpiece.

In the darkroom, Louise never tired of watching the magical appearance of images on paper as they emerged from the washes. In the dim, red-tinted light, she was lost in the world of chemicals and dripping prints pegged onto strings stretched across the room. Faces looked at her in the silence—faces of people she hardly knew, and yet their personalities were captured in that split second Mr Watson had seen them exposed, forever stamped on the film. It was that one split second that fascinated Louise, because those faces could be entirely different on either side of it. The mask they portrayed to the world could be—and probably was—that of another person, but when Mr Watson saw it, he erased the mask and revealed the real character behind it.

On her fifteenth birthday Louise graduated from her Brownie box camera to a more modern device which took coloured photographs. Then, on her seventeenth, she was overjoyed to receive a 35mm single-lens reflex camera from her mother.

"How could you afford it?" Louise had asked.

"Well, I managed," Olive had replied. "A few extra baskets of ironing, some more hours at the corner shop...after all, it looks like you're going to be a famous photographer one day. You may as well start on something decent to work with."

Louise had hugged her tightly. "I can't wait to show Mr Watson."

Her collection of photographs had grown so much that she had a row of neatly stacked large photo albums standing up along the top of her roll-top desk. *Blue Eyes* had run out of room on the desk and was relegated to a softer perch—that of Louise's bed.

Louise's favourite subjects to photograph were people, plants and shells. With her new camera, and a telephoto lens that Mr Watson gave her for her birthday along with his advice, she produced some quite extraordinary work.

"You're becoming quite a passable photographer," he'd said one day when a close-up that she'd taken of a raindrop on a pink sweet pea emerged in the darkroom.

"Such high praise," Louise had laughed, not used to flattery from her normally taciturn boss.

"Well, don't get a swollen head," he'd mumbled, embarrassed.

He turned away from her to study the photograph and then examined another one that was of Olive taken through a slit in tissue paper. The result was an ethereal study of an attractive woman who dissolved into the edges of a cloudy frame. He held it up to the red light, moving it around to see it from every angle. His mouth opened as if to say something, but he closed it again as he saw Louise's head bent over a tray.

"Humph!"

"What?" she asked, looking up.

"Nothing."

When Mr Watson decided to move his premises to the city, Louise was heart-broken. Even though she regarded him as a 'crusty old sod', she loved him. He had taught her so much, and always treated her with the utmost respect—almost to the point of formality—but she knew she'd burrowed under his skin, as he had hers.

"Time to move on, Louise," he'd said, "before it gets too late."

"But what about Mrs Watson?" Louise had asked. "Does she want to move all the way up there?"

"It's only South Yarra, not the end of the world. Besides, it'll be closer to the studio for me, and the shopping is better for my wife."

"I'll miss you," Louise said, swallowing her emotion, not wanting to embarrass either of them. "The job and all."

"Yes, I'll have to get myself an assistant," he said, looking at her sideways.

"Oh." The hurt showed plainly in her voice.

She was surprised to see her mother turn up at the studio that same afternoon.

"What are you doing here?" she asked Olive.

"Mr Watson rang me. He wants to talk about something."

"What?" Louise whispered.

"I don't know."

She watched her mother go into Mr Watson's office. He closed the door firmly after telling Louise to go on with rearranging a backdrop. Twenty minutes later, they re-emerged from the office, Olive with a huge smile on her face. Louise's eyebrow went up in question, looking from one to the other.

Mr Watson cleared his throat. "Your mother and I have been dis-cussing you."

Louise waited.

He continued, "I've asked what her aspirations are for you when you leave school." He looked at Olive for confirmation. "She says she wants you to be a photographer because that's what you want." Olive nodded and then he pursed his lips thoughtfully. "Well?"

"Well what?"

"Yes, girl. Is that what you want?"

"Of course it is. It's the only thing I've ever wanted."

"Well, then. I've asked your mother's permission to offer you a full-time job when I move up to the city."

Louise's mouth dropped open.

"Shut it, girl. You'll catch flies," he said sternly.

"A real job? You mean to work for you in the city?"

"Yes," he said stiffly.

"You mean it?"

"I'm not in the habit of proposing falsehoods."

"Oh, Mr Watson. How can I thank you?"

Louise went to hug him, then thought better of it. Excitement shone from every pore of her body.

"Just work hard, young lady."

"Oh, I will. I will."

The next five years had served as an invaluable apprenticeship with Mr Watson, Louise gaining a reputation of her own as a fine photographer. Her boss encouraged her creativity and, although compliments from him were few and far between, he provided every avenue for her talents with his clients, often sending her for jobs that he was not interested in. As a result, Louise was in demand for wedding photography, and eventually made a name for herself as a nature photographer, having won a string of awards and distinctions at the AIPP Australian Professional Photography Awards. It had been a natural progression to becoming a published writer, producing bestsellers that featured some of her prize-winning portraits, landscapes, macro work, and advice for the hobbyist up to the professional.

The Collins Street studio gradually became known as *the* place for creative portraiture photography, and the clientele came to include politicians, actors, opera singers, and other prominent members of society. Neither of Mr Watson's sons was interested in the business, so Louise had free reign to express her interest in it. Although Mr Watson was not a demonstrative man, he regarded Louise as a daughter and repaid her unquestioning loyalty by offering her a partnership.

By the time Mr Watson was ready to retire, Louise was practically running the flourishing business single-handedly. He stood down without regret, happy that the studio was in her capable hands.

"You've never let me down," he said gruffly, twirling the champagne glass that she'd thrust in his hand.

"No reason to," she'd replied with a lump in her throat. "You've been too good to me."

He looked at her through sentimental eyes—a rare expression that he'd unwittingly allowed to escape. "I couldn't have asked for a more loyal assistant."

"Go on," she said, pushing an elaborately-wrapped parcel into his hands, "open it before we both start bawling."

"Rubbish," he said, clearing his throat.

She smiled at him. "You old softy."

He slowly opened the parcel to find two airline tickets in a box. "What's this?"

"The holiday you've been promising to take that poor suffering wife of yours on for as long as I've known you."

"I couldn't possibly accept..."

"Well, you'll have to," she said sternly. "I've paid for them and they're in your names. They won't refund the money."

For the first time in their working relationship, he bent over and kissed her cheek.

"Thanks boss. That's all I've been waiting for," she grinned.

"Nonsense," he said, blinking suddenly wet lashes.

Louise had been living in Frankston for the best part of a year since she and David had separated. She'd never liked living closer to the city where they'd bought a house; she found the traffic noises, the air pollution, the frantic pace, too much on top of working in the city during the day. She had missed the quiet life on the bay, the soft sound of the waves as they met the shoreline, the clear pure air. It had only taken her a week of house hunting to find just the right place—a cottage on Olivers Hill with sweeping views of the bay.

"Louie, can you afford this?" Olive had asked when Louise took her to see it.

"Probably not," Louise had laughed. "It's just about cleaned me out. But who cares? I've only got myself to spend my squillions on."

"True, but you know you could come back and live with me."

"What—and cramp your style? I'd have to live amongst the ironing baskets. You'd hate me within a week."

Secretly, Louise was unsure if it was wise to be so close to the scene of Joy's death, but somehow she felt it was a link that drew them together, even if only in spirit.

"Aren't you being a little morbid, Louie?" Olive had asked her shrewdly.

"Maybe. Maybe not," Louise had shrugged.

There wasn't a day that passed since Joy went out of her life that she didn't think of her, miss her, grieve for her. Sometimes she found herself walking along the beach and would climb the rocks and sit for hours staring into the water, wondering whether Joy had suffered at the end of her young life. Even at the age of forty-three, Louise still spoke to Joy in her mind. It was a lifelong friendship that parting had not erased. But because of this friendship, Louise had never been able to permit anyone else close enough to her heart to call them friend—acquaintance, yes, but soul mate, no. Deep down she believed that friendships never lasted, so if you didn't let anyone in, you wouldn't get hurt. She supposed the failure of her relationship with David was her fault. He'd been in love with her— very much so—but she only loved him; she wasn't 'in love' with him. He'd known, of course, and that's probably why he started drinking, she thought, and gambling, and womanizing. *A lot like Dad.* Many a time, Louise wondered why her mother had never remarried or even gone out with another man. *Heaven knows she was attractive enough.* Louise had noticed men looking Olive over with lust in their eyes, but her mother had never shown an inkling of interest...ever. *Maybe she's been carrying a torch for someone else—but there's no one I've ever seen—or, more likely, she's been put off by her miserable existence with Dad.*

She pulled into the driveway of her home and sat for a moment looking out at the bay through the frame and lens made by her car window. The turquoise surface was unruffled, shimmering in the sunlight. Sails floated like tethered butterfly wings from the masts of brightly coloured yachts, the hulls parting the water smoothly, leaving thin trails of white foam that appeared to chase after them.

The scene reminded Louise of the days she and Joy had spent sitting on the beach making sandcastles, or swinging their legs over the edge of the jetty. She remembered dancing around Joy with her box camera, capturing her friend's image from every angle: Joy laughing into the lens; pretending to be a model with a mock pout and holding her hair up from her neck; hanging upside down from the ladder off the end of the jetty; spouting water from her mouth as she surfaced the water; her head sticking out of the sand after Louise had buried her; eyes peeping out from under a bucket...

Louise sighed. *If only you were here to talk to. To share my new-found freedom.* She felt like celebrating with someone, but there was no one she could think of who would understand how she felt.

Only her mother would, but Olive was in Sydney visiting her sister, as she did every year at this time.

The phone sounded shrilly from inside the cottage as she fumbled at the door.

"Hello?" Her armload of books fell onto the floor. "Bugger!"

"Louie? Are you okay?"

"Oh, hi Mum. I thought it might be you," she said, bending over to rescue the books. She turned the pages back that had been bent in the fall.

"What happened?"

"Oh, I just dropped a pile of books I was carrying in. It's all right."

"More books?" Olive laughed. "You're hopeless."

"I know. Absolutely. But I didn't buy these. I got them from your place when I called in to check if all was okay. You remember the ones Mr Bacon gave us? The ones in my old room?"

"Don't tell me you actually decided to read them...after all these years."

"I had a touch of the guilts. Thought I'd take them away with me."

"What'd you get?"

"Oh, a Ruth Park...*The Harp in the South*...a Jack London...passed on *Black Beauty*...but I fell across *My Love Must Wait*..."

"Sounds like a Mills and Boon."

"Oh, yeah, Mum. As if..." She put the rest of the books on a coffee table. "No, that one by Ernestine Hill—about Matthew Flinders. Some others...*Anne Frank* too."

"Sounds like you're set." Olive paused. "How'd it go today?"

"Fine. I'm a free woman again."

"Congratulations." There was a moment's hesitation. "Are you really all right? Do you want me to come back?"

"No, Mum. Thanks."

Louise held the phone between her head and shoulder as she poured herself a good measure of Campari and filled the tall glass with soda water.

She took a sip. "I feel as if I've just been let out of a cage."

"No regrets?"

"No. Funny, but I don't even feel sad. I guess I did my grieving over the marriage while David and I were still together."

She put a CD on and stood at the window looking over the bay. Mozart's *Requiem* filled the room, and she saluted.

"Here's to you, Wolfgang. The only worthwhile male on this bloody planet. And you're dead too."

The bitter pink liquid cooled her throat and she sat down at the coffee table to inspect her books.

Chapter 57

Louise sat up in bed surrounded by a disarray of travel brochures. *Come on, make an executive decision. Stop stuffing around.* She yawned as she sorted them into a pile for Norfolk Island and a pile for Bali. *Okay, okay. Norfolk Island it is.* She pushed them onto the floor and turned the bedside light off. The bright red numbers of her clock faintly illuminated the room. It was eleven-thirty. As her eyes adjusted to the darkened surroundings, she could see through her open doorway the outline of *Blue Eyes* sitting on top of the roll-top desk in the lounge room. Louise always left the curtains open in the lounge room as the windows faced out onto the bay. She liked to watch the stars from her bed on cloudless nights. The frame of the lounge room window was like the frame of a lens that looked out on an ever-changing skyscape.

Ever since she was thirteen, she would look for the brightest star in the sky and pretend that it was Joy. It comforted her to talk to her friend before she fell asleep; it had become a habit—like some people prayed before they went to bed, she'd thought. Thirty years later, she was still doing it. Sometimes she felt a little silly, and would ignore the star for a few nights, but an overpowering guilt would soon draw her back to her whispered conversations again.

I think I'm happy with Norfolk Island. What do you think? It'll be peaceful, and that's what I'm after...peace. I'll just sit on that white beach at Emily Bay—looks good in the brochures, eh? The water can't be that blue, can it? I'm going to read until my eyes drop out. What luxury! No work, no clients, for a couple of weeks. I might even leave the gear home. No...can't do that. I'd regret it. Just take the Canon...well, a few extra lenses wouldn't hurt.

She turned on her side and closed her eyes, but tangled images of the magistrate in the Family Court; David shouting at her with his hand raised; sitting at the kitchen table with her mother; wet photographs hanging in her darkroom; swimming in the water with Joy at Chelsea beach; all conspired to deny her sleep.

One eye opened and she saw that it was midnight. *Shut up will you,* she chided her restless brain. She lay on her back and stared at the ceiling. A slight breeze ruffled the leaves of a pink bougainvillea that draped a pergola outside. It was a bougainvillea that flowered six months of the year, providing a colourful backdrop for the many barbecues she'd promised herself to have but never seemed to get around to. There was always next year, once she was more settled, she thought. She'd invite the Watsons and her mother. They'd have a great time catching up on all the news while they consumed huge quantities of tiger prawns and healthy salads and washed it all down with peninsula wines. She pulled a face in the dark. *Who are you kidding?*

Olive was forever expressing concern over the fact that her daughter had no friends her own age—no male prospects either.

"You'll end up an old maid," she'd warn.

"Mum, I believe an old maid is a woman who's remained single beyond the normal marrying age. I hardly fit that picture, though I may as well be one."

"You could still have children…"

"Yeah, right, Mum. At forty-three? I don't think so."

But her mother was right…she really didn't have any friends. It wasn't something that she thought about often as she told herself that she wasn't lonely. It was only sometimes—like New Year's Eve—when she was aware that she had no one to throw her arms around and share kisses with. She'd shrug it off as nonsense and thank her lucky stars that she didn't have to put up with a man who would mess up her bathroom and snore in her ear, as well as betray and beat her.

She met many female clients in her studio—women who'd have liked to form a friendship with the successful photographer and often invited her to luncheons, dinners, parties and sporting clubs. There were the matchmakers who had the *ideal* man for her, those who were difficult to discourage with a firm but polite refusal. And there were the school reunions which she rejected out of hand, not wishing to be involved in cheerful gatherings where the absence of her lost friend would be all the more noticeable. There had been few times when Louise had allowed a tentative association with a female of seemingly like mind; her personal space felt invaded before too long and she would quietly and graciously slip out of the other's life. Louise valued her privacy where her emotional ramparts shielded her from the loss of another relationship.

Over the next few days, Louise paid for her holiday, picked up the tickets, and made sure that everything, which had to be done before she left, was sorted out. She had given a list of instructions to her assistant.

"Will you stop worrying?" Claire complained. "Everything'll be fine."

"I know," Louise said, biting her lip. "Just don't forget to get the proofs to my editor for..."

"Louise, please please please, go and have a holiday. If I run into any trouble, I'll ring you."

"Now you've got the number...?"

"Yes," Claire laughed, "along with the Fire Brigade, the Police, the Ambulance, the State Emergency Services...and this pile of brochures," she said tapping them with a manicured fingernail, "as to where what and how you are staying."

"Okay, okay. I surrender," Louise laughed, relaxing slightly.

"Have you packed?" Claire said with a smirk on her face. "Bet you haven't."

"Well, you've won that one."

"Go on, boss." Claire walked around her desk and gently coaxed Louise towards the door. "Give yourself the rest of the day to get ready. At least put in a toothbrush...and some bathers."

Louise let herself into the silent house and stood for some moments looking out of the window. The bay glittered in the November sunlight; the beach was crowded with young mothers frolicking in the shallows with their pre-school children; older people helped build sandcastles with—Louise surmised—their grandchildren.

Not likely to have any of those, she thought as she regarded the children. *Just like you, Tooth Fairy, eh? Funny how life turns out. I could have sworn we'd have had kids. Sit on the beach with them. Teach them how to make the best sandcastles. Baby-sit for each other. Fancy marrying an impotent man! I wonder if he hadn't been, and we'd had a couple of kids, if we'd still be together.*

She shrugged with a toss of her head, turning away from the scene below, and switched the radio on to the ABC. Margaret Throsby introduced her next selection—the *Gaité Parisienne.* As it filled the room, the music's gaiety was infectious. *Okay, holiday time.* The suitcase was at the top of her walk-in robe. She took it down and opened it out on her bed. *Hell, how long's it been since I last used it?*

She hummed along with the music as she selected various items of clothing, shoes, handbags, hairdryer. *Oh, the books.* They were still on the coffee table where she'd left them some days back. She mixed herself a Campari and soda and then took the drink, along with the stack of books, back into the bedroom and examined them carefully.

Okay, leave out the Dickens...no, put it back. Leave out the Morris West; the Durrell...no, it'll give me a laugh; the Eleanor Dark...maybe; the Anne Frank...a bit depressing?

The front cover fell back as Louise opened the *Diary of Anne Frank*. An inscription caught her eye as she turned over the first few pages:

Dear SP,

You see? I think of you all the time! I hate all
this—missing our party today—not giving you the
brooch. When I give you this book, I'll tell you everything. Cross my heart and spit.

TF

Louise's drink tipped out of her hand, unnoticed. The liquid spread in a pink puddle on the beige carpet, at first squatting on the surface like a jelly, and then slowly sinking into the pile. The wild, giddy abandon of Offenbach's cancan matched the stampede of Louise's heartbeats that roared in her ears as she stared at the childish handwriting.

The phone rang unheeded on the bedside table beside her. It rang eleven times, and then stopped. A few moments later, it rang another ten times and stopped again. The cancan quieted into the barcarolle as Louise tried to get a hold of herself. Her hands shook as she reread the inscription. Her hair prickled her scalp and goose bumps raised the skin on her arms. *I'd know that handwriting anywhere!*

She looked wildly around her and jumped up from the bed. Her bare foot stood on the wet carpet and she looked down at the puddle stupidly. Taking the book into the lounge room, she put it on the roll-top desk and pushed the dividing wall between two pigeonholes. The panel at the rear wall of the desk opened to reveal a tiny note book, its pages filled with childish handwriting. A lock of dark chestnut hair, tied with a fragment of gold ribbon fell out from be- tween two ripped pages. She recognised it as her own hair.

Louise took out another book—a diary—which had belonged to an older Joy. The writing was slightly different from that of the first book, more formed, with the words joining. She flicked over the pages, searching for the abbreviation of their pet names. *There!*

> Went swimming with SP. We won the sandcastle competition!

The elaborate curves of the letters 'SP' were unmistakable. Louise remembered how Joy had been fascinated with calligraphy and other decorative forms of writing. She would curl capital letters around at the ends, and fill the spaces with miniscule flowers, using coloured pencils, until the letters were almost unrecognizable. Louise had teased her about it until she, too, started to decorate her own writing, but she lacked Joy's artistry. There was a photo somewhere that Louise had taken with her Brownie camera. It was a black and white photo of a beautiful plaque Joy had made of Ruth and Les's names one Christmas. It had hung in their kitchen, Louise remembered.

She studied the 'SP' in the diary and the 'SP' in the inscription. They were definitely the same. The inside of both 'P's was filled with minute flowers. Louise marvelled at how Joy had had the patience to fill the 'P' nearly every time she wrote it. That inscription was written by Joy. Louise was convinced of it.

The 'SP', of course, is Sweet Pea, and the 'TF' has to be Tooth Fairy. How many people would write that inside a book? And the mention of the brooch, the party, crossing the heart and spitting…yes, that's Joy all right.

Louise held the *Diary of Anne Frank* and the diary that was Joy's to her chest as she gazed out of the window. Her eyes came to rest on the rocks at the base of Olivers Hill. This was where Joy had died. Thirty years ago. And yet…

How could Joy have written that? If she'd intended to commit suicide, why would she say she'd give the book to SP and tell her everything?

A cold chill went through Louise's body and she shuddered despite the warmth of the sun shining through the window. If she was dead before her birthday, how could she write: *missing our party today*?

Louise picked up the telephone receiver on the desk and punched a button quickly. She waited.

"Claire? Cancel my holiday. I'm not going."

Chapter 58

The phone rang again, as if determined to shake Louise out of her stupor. She had ignored it each time it rang—its insistence hardly impacting upon her state of confusion—her eyes fixed on the rocks below. She turned, frowning, towards the intrusion, and picked it up with a trembling hand.

"Yes?"

"I've been trying to get you for hours. Claire said you left the office ages ago." Olive waited. "Are you all right?"

"Umm."

"What do you mean...umm? Have you been drinking?"

"Not much."

Olive hesitated. "You worry me, you know. You've been working too hard. I'm glad that you're going away, though. It'll do you good. You might even meet a nice..."

"I'm not going."

"But you're leaving tomorrow morning! I rang to wish you bon voyage."

"Mum, can you come home? Earlier than you planned?"

"Well..."

"I know you enjoy your time with Auntie Joan, and I'm sorry to ask you. But..." she chewed her lip, "I really need you, Mum."

"Of course I'll come, Louie." There was a momentary silence. "Are you ill?"

"No."

"Has David been pestering you again?"

"No, Mum. Nothing like that."

"Well, what is it?"

"I'll tell you when you get here. How soon can you come?"

"Well, tomorrow I guess. There are plenty of seats this time of the year."

"Good. Let me know and I'll pick you up at the airport."

"All right, love."

"And, Mum?"

"Yes?"

"Do you still have that scrap book? You know...the one you put all those clippings in...about Joy."

The next day, Louise frustrated her mother by refusing to tell her why she'd asked her to end her holiday so abruptly until they arrived at Olive's house. Once they were seated on the couch together, with the scrapbook on their laps, Louise told a sceptical Olive what she had discovered.

"Look...here it is. See for yourself."

She took the *Diary of Anne Frank* out of her handbag, along with Joy's diary, and pointed out the identical writing.

Olive regarded her daughter with concern. "Louie, don't you think this a huge coincidence? I mean, how could it possibly be? And you've only got to look at these articles...these photos from the papers...to know that she died. There's no denying it." She took Louise's hand in hers, turning it over and tracing the lifeline. "Yours is a long one. Hers must have been short."

"I don't believe that crap, Mum," Louise said, taking her hand away. "And you don't either."

"You've never been able to let it rest, have you?"

Louise shook her head, swallowing a lump. "No, Mum. It's never left me in peace. Deep down I've never believed it."

"What do you mean?"

"Little things," she shrugged, "...unanswered questions. But I was only a kid. No one would listen to me."

"What things?"

"The clothes, for instance...they weren't hers."

Olive went to interrupt but Louise waved her hand.

"Look, we knew everything about each other. Everything. I knew each item of clothing she owned and wore. And those clothes—even though they were the right size—they weren't hers. Joy never had a lime green jumper..."

"How would..."

"I know? I just did. You know how close we were. And those flares...they were very similar, but the embroidery on them, near the hem, it was different. The platforms were new too. Joy's were about a year old and they'd worn down a bit, like mine had. Don't you remember when we pestered the life out of you and Mrs Bacon to get the platforms when we were twelve?"

"Yes," Olive said slowly, memories flooding back, "I do, now you come to mention it."

"And the beads—they were a darker green to go with the jumper. Joy didn't have dark green ones. She had light green beads, and they were shorter."

"Perhaps the clothes had been mixed up at the funeral parlour?"

"Mum, how many girls Joy's size drowned or committed suicide that day in Port Phillip Bay?"

"Okay, okay," Olive conceded.

"And I know, I just know, Joy would not have committed suicide."

"How?"

"Because she was the most together kid I knew."

"Perhaps you were just prejudiced...you know, clouded by friendship."

"Mum, listen to me." She stood and began to pace in front of the couch. "She was as happy as a pig in shit—about our birthday party and the frocks her mum was making for us—and guilty as hell because she hadn't been able to find me a birthday present. I knew that was why she went up to Bentleigh, even though no one told me until later. I saw her go. I guessed that she'd meet Mrs Lewis up there. I was surprised, though, that her mum had let her go alone."

She stopped momentarily and looked out of the lounge room window and over the fence to the Bacon house. Perching herself on the side of an armchair, she sighed. Her mother waited for her to go on.

"And that rubbish about inheriting her mother's mental condition? Utter nonsense! She was nothing like her mother. Didn't even look like her. And their personalities were so different. She was more like Mr Bacon, if anything."

Louise sat down again beside her mother.

"She was a strong, mentally-with-it girl. She'd had to be. Don't you remember what her mum put her through so many times?"

Olive nodded agreement.

"But she got through it, with the help of her dad. And me." Joy's diary was in her hand again. "She told me everything, and it was no different to what's in this. If she'd been contemplating suicide, I would have known about it." She laughed with a slight snort. "She'd probably have asked me to do it with her. She wouldn't have wanted to do it alone."

Opening the diary, Louise flicked through the last pages that had been written on. "See these entries? The last one was on the night before she disappeared. She says: *Can't wait for the party and the big surprise.* Does that sound suicidal to you?"

"No, it doesn't," Olive replied quietly. "You don't think it could have been murder, do you? But the Coroner said it was suicide."

"Yes, well, mistakes have been made before. I think it was made to look like suicide."

"Why? Who on earth...?"

"I don't know, Mum, and I don't know if it was murder either. I've done a lot of thinking about this over the past twenty-four hours and I'd bet you anything that body in the cemetery isn't Joy's. I don't know how I'm going to do it, but I'm going to get to the bottom of it."

Louise drove home later that day and spent a couple of hours reading every article in the scrapbook. *Now what do I do?* She connected to the Internet and typed in: *How do I trace a dead person's family?* She learned that she should start with the death certificate, and looked up the Registry of Births, Deaths & Marriages. *Okay, so I can get it there.*

At nine the next morning, Louise entered the Registry in Collins Street. When she was handed the certificate she found no new information there, other than Ruth Bacon's maiden name, which had been entered as Rogers. Joy's birthplace was Adelaide, South Australia, which Louise already knew. *Okay, that's something to go on with.*

Arriving home again, she turned on her computer and found the site for Births, Deaths & Marriages in South Australia. *Hell!* She read that she would not be able to obtain a birth certificate for Joy as she was not a relative. It was the same for a marriage certificate of the Bacons. She picked up the phone.

"Mum?"

"Yes, Louie."

"Are you sure Mr and Mrs Bacon never gave you a forwarding address in New Zealand?"

"Positive."

The old hurt returned. "Thirty years and they never contacted us. Never. Some friends."

"I know. It's like they wiped us," Olive agreed.

"You can sort of understand...wanting to forget and everything...but you'd think a letter or two wouldn't have been too much to expect."

"I tried, remember?"

"Yes. And I've still got that returned letter I sent them with just New Zealand on the envelope. 'Insufficient address'." Louise sighed, looking out over the bay. "The Lewises didn't hear from them either, did they?"

"No. They were so hurt."

"You don't think they might have died in an accident or something?"

"God, I don't know. Maybe they did."

"I'll see if I can find out, though I've got no idea where to start."

"I wouldn't have the faintest, either."

"I suppose I could go to a family history society. Some brochures I picked up at Births, Deaths & Marriages say to start that way."

Louise found her local family history society and was lucky enough to visit their rooms on a day when they were open.

"Can I help you?" asked an elderly man, looking up from a table cluttered with an array of books and maps.

"I'm trying to find someone," she said. "I thought you might be able to give me some ideas on how to go about it."

Louise explained her mission, while the man regarded her with lively, interested eyes.

"Well, you've got a problem with the birth certificate. Other than going to the Police and getting them to request it for you...and I'm not sure they'll get involved on such slim evidence..."

"I know it's just..."

"I'm not doubting you, dear, but the Police might. They would possibly want something more concrete. And our microfiche only go as far as 1922 for births in South Australia. The same for the marriages—they only go to 1937—so you can't even look them up for registration numbers."

"What do you mean?"

"I'll show you," he said, leading the way to a darkened room where half a dozen people were peering into microfiche readers.

He indicated boxes of microfiche, each labelled with state names or countries, and he explained how to select the era wanted and then how to look up the surname.

"It's time consuming, but sometimes it can be rewarding. You find people you never expected to, and in places you never dreamed they'd be."

"Can I have a go?"

"Sure, if you need any help, just give us a yell."

Not really knowing what she was looking for, Louise chose a microfiche for deaths in South Australia—as their cut-off point was more recent, being 1970—and looked for the name Bacon. Perhaps Les's parents would be there, she reasoned. She turned on the machine's light, and inserted the plastic fiche between two plates of glass. Columns of names, dates and numbers, appeared on a blue background and she adjusted the focus to bring the details into view. The few Bacons gave no clue and, working out the years of death, she doubted that they could have been Les's parents. She tried Rogers, but there were so many of them, that she had no idea if she was looking at Ruth's parents or not. *This is hopeless.*

"Any luck?"

Louise turned to see the kindly man standing near, watching her.

"No," she said dejectedly, "I don't really know what I'm looking for, and I can't look in the time frame I need for either the birth or the marriage."

"Umm, that's unfortunate," he said. "Are you sure it was South Australia?"

"That's what it says on my friend's death certificate."

"Yes, I see, but sometimes—and you'd be surprised how often— incorrect details appear on birth and death certificates. Not so much on marriage certificates, because both parties are actually there. Sometimes the informants get things wrong for a variety of reasons—they could be upset, in the case of a death, or they may not even know all the details and make them up—or they could be lying."

"Oh, I see," Louise said slowly.

"So, why don't you look up the other states of Australia, just in case? Some of them have later cut-off dates. You never know what you might find."

In due course Louise went through the Victorian, New South Wales and Queensland fiches, without success. She looked at her watch. The rooms were closing in fifteen minutes. *Should I bother with Western Australia?* Her hands hesitated over the box of microfiche. *May as well*, she conceded. There appeared another sea of Bacons and Rogers in the deaths and, without more information, she had nothing to link them with Les or Ruth. *What's the point?* She decided to stop wasting her time and put the fiche back.

"Ten minutes, people," the man called out from the front desk.

Most of the researchers at the microfiche readers began to pack up, turning off the lights and returning the fiche to the boxes. A woman pushed past her and returned a fiche to the marriages section. It hadn't been put back neatly and Louise juggled it into the tight box. The one behind it was for marriages in 1952, Aa-Br. *Oh, bugger it.* She took it out quickly and pushed it into her machine. The focus had to be adjusted every time she moved the poor-quality fiche. She was irritated as she searched the columns, straining her eyes to read the screen. Two Bacons appeared—a Frederick and a Ronald. Having realised that some of the fiche were not in strictly alphabetical order, she searched up and down a few rows, just in case, when the name 'Lesley' jumped out at her.

MARRIAGES, 1952

Baker, Lesley T., Perth 1084 M

Baker? No. Can't be. She returned to the box, obeying a hunch, and pulled out a fiche for Qu-Ru.

"Finished in there?" The voice was impatient.

"Yes, yes," Louise called back. "Just a sec."

The screen lit up as she put the fiche in and a blur of white letters whizzed past her eyes as she searched up and down the columns. *There!*

MARRIAGES, 1952

Rogers, Ruth, Perth 788 F

Gotcha! She quickly wrote down the details in her notebook from both microfiche and returned them to the box.

"Look!" she showed the man as he packed up his notes. "I may have found something. What are those numbers, though, and do the 'M' and 'F' stand for male and female?"

"Yes, male and female is right, and the numbers are the registration numbers of the marriage certificate. If you were family, you could apply for the certificate using that number."

"The name's wrong, though," Louise pointed out. "Baker, not Bacon."

"Close enough," the man smiled at her. "Like I said, they could have changed their name."

"Do you think it's them?"

"It's a pretty fair bet, looking at the death certificate here. Her name's right, and the only difference with his is the surname."

"It's Perth, though, not Adelaide."

"In my experience, one of the first things you learn when you become involved with family history, is that most people have a skeleton in their cupboard. The trick is in finding it and working out who it belongs to."

Louise searched his face.

"You know," he said, "I wouldn't be surprised if it's them. From what you've told me, a lot didn't add up, and then not hearing from them again..."

"That was really strange, because we were so close, you know."

He tapped her notebook. "Look, something you could do...go to the State Library in the city and look through the birth notices in the Adelaide newspapers, just in case. Then try the West Australian newspapers when your friend was born. She might turn up there. Try the hospitals—see if there's any record of her. Failing that, you might see if you can get the Police on side to search the records, especially with these names here, and the different surname."

He opened the door for her as she went out. He locked the door behind him and they stood on the steps of the building, having to shout over the noise of the traffic on Nepean Highway.

"While you're at the State Library, have a look at the newspapers at around the time your friend died. I know you said you've got a scrapbook, but look at the other news. Stuff that doesn't have anything to do with her. Something might jump out at you."

"Like what?"

"I don't know, dearie, but you'll know if and when you see it. And you've got the Internet, you said?"

Louise nodded.

"Look, that's about one of the best tools you could have. Get on it and type in genealogy. A hundred thousand sites'll come up. Sift through them. You might even turn those people up. Have a look at New Zealand. If they went there, as you said, you might find some evidence of them there. Try the electoral rolls, newspapers, cemeteries, deaths. I don't think the immigration authorities can help you, though, because you could travel in and out of New Zealand from Australia without a passport back then. Worth a try though."

Back home, she mixed herself a drink and looked down at the rocks at the base of Olivers Hill. *So, maybe your name wasn't Bacon after all.* Somehow, there was an element of hope in Louise's heart—a hope that she might unravel the tangled web that surrounded Joy's life and death, and the lives of her parents. Perhaps then she could let her friend rest in peace.

She turned to a blown-up photograph of Joy and herself that hung on a wall of her lounge room. It was the one that had appeared in the newspapers—the one that Ruth had taken on Joy and Louise's first day of high school. Louise had taken out the background and blended their two faces into a surreal landscape of rocks and stormy sea. "Morbid, obsessive," Olive had said. But Louise liked it for the metaphor it represented of life and death. *Perhaps I am morbid and obsessed.*

From her position on the wall, Joy's eyes seemed to smile into Louise's, as if trying to tell her something. *You've got a secret and it's up to me to find out what it is.*

Chapter 59

Louise went to the city and had herself installed in front of a microfilm machine at the State Library. The motion of the film continually winding past her eyes left her giddy and slightly sick. Joy's face jumped out at her a number of times as she examined the newspapers in May of 1968. Taking the advice she'd received, she skipped reading the articles about Joy. She'd read them all before anyway.

She saw articles on the deaths of Australian soldiers in Vietnam; the anti-war demonstration outside the United States consulate in Melbourne; the policies of the new Prime Minister, John Gorton; talk of the athletes who would represent Australia in the Mexican Olympic Games in October; Rod Laver's hopes for the Wimbledon Tennis Tournament the following month. *Interesting, but nothing to do with Joy Bacon.*

A purse snatcher caught at Flinders Street Station; a lost dog reunited with his owner after walking fifty-seven miles; a house fire in Malvern where a three-year-old child perished; a musician found unconscious on the floor of his flat; an horrific car accident in which an elderly couple lost their lives. *Nothing.*

Louise searched for a month on either side of Joy's supposed death until her eyes hurt and then asked to see the microfilm of an Adelaide newspaper for 1955.

Finding the birth notices in the *Advertiser*, she looked for a Joy Bacon or Joy Baker in May and, then finding no success, she retraced her steps and searched six months before and then six months after. The feeling of motion sickness had returned worse than before. She didn't know how much more she could take, especially as she was having no luck at all.

No point hanging around the Adelaide papers. She's not there. I'll try Perth. But when she asked for Perth microfilm, she was dismayed to find that they had to be ordered twenty-four hours in advance—because they were in hard copy—so that they could be extracted from their storage space. *Well, at least I won't feel sick*, she thought with relief, although she chaffed at the delay.

Back in the library the next day, she referred to her notebook, aware that she was blundering her way through the public records without much idea of what she was doing. All she could go on was what the family history man had told her, so she searched again for any notice of a birth in Joy's name, but nothing appeared even re-motely like it on the fragile pages. She wondered if she would have to contact the hospitals in Perth to see if they had any records and whether they would even allow her to access them.

Without the feeling of motion sickness in front of the microfilm readers, Louise decided to take the time to read through the papers around the time of Joy's birth. Maybe something would turn up. If not, she'd call it a day and go home and get onto the Internet again to begin her New Zealand search.

The only news item that caught her interest was one about the kidnapping of a baby—a twin, in fact—from a Perth hospital. She read the articles with a feeling of great sympathy towards the Ger-man immigrant whose wife had died in childbirth and whose child had disappeared. *How awful.* She shook her head in disbelief at the man's rotten luck. *As if he hadn't suffered enough in Auschwitz.* She read on, hunting the pages for anything about a Lesley Baker or Bacon, a Ruth Rogers or Baker or Bacon, a Joy Baker or Bacon. *Nothing.*

Her eyes were tired and her neck ached from bending over the pages for so long. She was reluctant to give up the bound newspa-pers, feeling that the clues were probably in front of her but she just couldn't see them.

"Is there something else you need?" asked the attendant behind the desk.

"Yes, some New Zealand papers," Louise said.

"Same period?"

"No...June 1968 and onwards."

"That's fine. They'll be ready for you to view tomorrow."

"Not today?" she asked, dismayed.

"Sorry, you need to give the same notice as the others, because they're on hard copy, like the *West Australian*."

Louise's sleep was restless that night, with interwoven dreams of Joy as a five year-old holding a crushed bunch of sweet pea; col-umns of names flickering on blue screens; waves smashing on rocks; tombstones rising from sandy beaches; a faceless person running through silent streets holding a baby...

She sat up in bed abruptly, all traces of sleep dissolved in an in-stant. The outline of *Blue Eyes'* figure against the night sky ap-peared ghostly, almost floating, from its perch atop the desk. Some-thing tickled Louise's mind as she looked at the doll. She couldn't make out the facial features in the darkness, but she realised the doll's face had been the one on the face of the baby in her dream. The story about the kidnapping of the twin baby darted through her head, and she held onto it before it vanished again into recesses she could not reach. *Schwartz!*

Her feet dropped over the side of her bed; she padded out to the lounge room and curled up on the sofa, looking out of the window. The moon picked out the silver tips of small waves that surged on the bay's surface. They were like the shreds of information that surged inside her head, rising to the surface and then sinking back into oblivion. *Think.* The name Schwartz niggled at her. *That was the name of that poor man who lost his wife and child, wasn't it? Yes. What?* She tapped her head as if to dislodge the elusive thought. *What?*

She remembered the headline:

FATHER COLLAPSES WHEN DAUGHTER STOLEN!

It was something to do with that.
Then her brain made the connection:

MUSICIAN COLLAPSES

That man who was found unconscious on the floor of his flat. His name was Schwartz! I'm sure of it.

Louise stopped at her mother's house on the way back to the city the following morning.

"Want some company?" Olive asked her.

"Oh, Mum, I was hoping you'd say that. Sometimes I think I'm going mad with all these things running around inside my head. I wonder if I'm imagining it all, so your input would be great."

Olive studied her daughter's face with concern. "You haven't had much sleep, have you?"

Louise shook her head. "Can't. Too much going on."

"What about that holiday you were going to have?"

"Well, I'm using that time to find Joy."

"What do you mean, find Joy?"

"Just that, Mum. I don't think she was dead at all, and whether she's still alive or not remains to be seen, but I'm going to find out."

"But why would they have...?"

Louise looked at her as she trailed off. "I've got no idea. I can't imagine any reasonable explanation for it. It's weird. Screwy."

"They might still be in New Zealand," Olive offered.

"Who knows?" She hooked her arm through Olive's. "Fancy a trip to New Zealand?"

Louise and Olive perched on the edge of their chairs as they examined the screen in front of them.

"I wish I could remember the date," Louise said. "I know it was around the time Joy was supposed to have died."

She turned the handle again and another page whizzed past their eyes.

"There! Look, Mum," she said excitedly, pointing to the headline. "I was right. The name *is* Schwartz!"

They read the article closely.

MUSICIAN COLLAPSES

Residents of a block of flats in Grange Road, Kew, discovered Mr Gunter Schwartz lying unconscious on the floor of his flat yesterday morning. He was taken by ambulance to Prince Henry's Hospital in St. Kilda Road, where he is undergoing tests. He has not yet regained consciousness. Newly arrived to Melbourne, Mr Schwartz was a prominent violinist with the West Australian Symphony Orchestra. It is believed that he was about to take up a position with the Melbourne Symphony.

"Yes, but what's that got to do with anything?"

"Don't you see? It's the same man who lost his wife and baby in Perth!"

"Yes..."

"A bit much of a co-incidence, don't you think? Those twins were born at the same time Joy was and he turns up here at the same time Joy's body was found in the bay."

"What could he have to do with Joy, though?"

Louise could hardly keep still in her seat. "Look, I think that there's no such person as Joy Bacon or Baker. I think if I looked for the next hundred years—even if I went to Perth to do it—she wouldn't appear in any birth records, in hospitals...anywhere."

"You're so sure?"

"Yes. And you know who I think she is?"

Olive hoped that Louise wasn't going to be hurt all over again, but she couldn't help but be infected by her daughter's excitement.

"Who?"

"The missing twin!"

"I was afraid you were going to say that."

"Why afraid?"

"Because you've got no proof...nothing to go on."

"Yes I have."

"What?"

"The surviving twin..." Louise grabbed her mother and hugged her tightly, "...the newspapers said that baby had red curly hair."

Late that night Louise sat wearily at her computer rubbing her eyes after having searched the Internet for clues as to Les and Ruth's whereabouts. She figured that if she could find them, then she would find Joy—or at least she would find out what had happened to her. She was staggered at the amount of genealogical information there was on the Internet and waded her way through one site after another, typing in Bacon and Baker but, without more specific information, ended up almost drowning in a sea of names.

She found the sites for the New Zealand Electoral Commission and Immigration Service, and sent emails asking if she could access their records to see if she could find evidence of Les and Ruth's existence in New Zealand. Wondering how long it would take them to reply, she then looked up the telephone directory and was horrified at the amount of Bacons and Bakers listed. She searched through the cemetery records that were available, just in case she found that either of them had died there, but without success.

Looking down on the rocks at the base of Olivers Hill, she wondered about the girl found dead there, especially after seeing the article Olive had pointed out on the microfilm earlier that day.

Louise had gone outside the library to take some deep breaths and walk off the giddiness brought on by viewing the film. Olive had decided to stay on in the meantime and search the newspapers for anything else about the Schwartz man. When Louise had returned, her mother greeted her excitedly, her voice higher than her normally husky timbre.

"Louie, I found something. Look!"

Louise bent over the screen to read:

MISSING GIRL

Mr Gunter Schwartz, found unconscious at his home six days ago, has been transferred to the Zion Nursing Home where he will be cared for until, hopefully, he recovers from a deep coma. It has been ascertained that he arrived in Melbourne with a daughter, whose whereabouts are unknown. Any person with information about Miss Schwartz should contact Police.

"I knew it!" Louise exclaimed. "She was here." She tapped her forehead, thinking for a few moments. "You know something? I reckon Mr Bacon knew about them coming here—maybe Gunter Schwartz had been looking for him—and something happened to that poor girl. If Joy was still alive and reading books after we were supposed to have our party, it must have been the other twin who died. Not Joy. But why they would pretend it was Joy who died..."

"It doesn't make sense," Olive agreed.

"No, but it would explain why they left the country." Louise sat back in her chair and rubbed at her forehead. "Oh, I know they said they wanted to start afresh...get away from the memories...but remember how Mr Bacon wouldn't let me visit Mrs Bacon? And we weren't allowed to go to the airport to say goodbye?" Olive nodded. "Well, maybe Mrs Bacon wasn't even in the hospital. Maybe she was somewhere else with Joy. You didn't go to the hospital, did you?"

"No," Olive said thoughtfully. "He asked me not to."

"That's it, then. They had Joy stashed somewhere and she went off to New Zealand with them."

Sleep was difficult to achieve as Louise's mind ran riot over the avenues she had explored to find any clues about the Bacons. It was going to be harder than she had at first believed.

Her thoughts returned to the Schwartz man, and she wondered if he had come out of the coma and, if so, was he still alive, and where? She would have to check at the nursing home to see if their records showed where he had gone when he left there. Then she would have to try to trace him. She remembered that he was a musician. Perhaps she could find him through the Melbourne Symphony. Yes, she'd try that.

It was a muggy night and she moved around her bed trying to find a cool place between the sheets. She got up and walked into the lounge room where the moon cast a silvery light onto Joy's diary and the *Diary of Anne Frank* sitting on the coffee table. Louise picked them up and took them to the sofa with her.

I know you're out there somewhere. Alive. You must be. It'd be too cruel otherwise...finding your message...building up my hopes. Imagine if I find you!

The moon sank slowly out of view as dawn shuffled hesitantly across the bay's surface and the rooftops. A dog barked somewhere and Louise stirred from her position on the sofa where she had fallen into a light slumber. She went back to her bed and fell instantly asleep.

The phone rang adamantly, burrowing through the layers of sleep. The ringing became part of her dream...*her hand reaching out for the phone to find no one there*...until her ears prodded her into consciousness.

"Louie. Did I wake you?"

"It's okay, Mum," Louise said, looking at her clock. "I should have been up ages ago anyway."

"Any luck with your search on the net last night?"

"Not really."

"What about the New Zealand phone directory?"

"Yes," Louise laughed, sitting up in bed. "You should have seen the number of entries. Over two thousand Bakers and nearly two hundred Bacons."

"Hell!"

"Yes, my sentiments exactly."

"I've been thinking...do you think you should go to the Police?"

"What, with an anonymous message scribbled in a book that just so happens to have been in your bookcase for a hundred years, and the wild imaginings of a sleep-starved divorcee?"

"And her mother."

"Sorry...and her mother."

Neither of them said anything for a few moments, both sorting through their thoughts, then Olive broke the silence.

"Do you think the answer could be in Perth?"

"It's an old trail, Mum," Louise said, tapping her forehead. "I honestly don't know. It probably only leads to Melbourne anyway. I think New Zealand's the go. I mean, that's where they went. They must be there somewhere."

"Yes, but where? With that many Bacons and Bakers, it would take a while to find them."

"Carpenters? Builders?"

"Yes, I see what you mean. He'd have to earn a living."

"She was a dressmaker too."

"And a damned good one, at that."

Louise looked out of the window at a magpie sitting on her fence, its head raised in song. The sound of its carolling entered her open window and she smiled with pleasure as its mate joined it. They cleaned each other's beaks and leaped into the air to fly up to the branches of an old eucalyptus tree.

"Now, how about that trip to New Zealand?"

Despite her sixty-three years, Olive managed to keep up with the hectic schedule her daughter set over the following week in New Zealand.

They called upon various branches of family history societies to search microfiche of deaths and marriages, as well as school and hospital registers, wills and post office directories. Both women strained their eyes over the readers, hour after hour, day after day. It was a laborious task that got them nowhere. Each night they returned to their hotel room discouraged and frustrated, conscious of the fact that they had so little to base their research upon. They could find no record of any carpenter or builder whose name was remotely like that of Les's. There was a dressmaker by the name of R. Bacon in Christchurch, but when Louise rang, she found that the woman was a Ruby. One day they drove down to Wellington in the hope that something might turn up on the hard copies of old electoral rolls retained by the National Library but, like every other avenue they searched, they drew a blank.

"You realise, of course," Olive pointed out over lunch one day, "that they could have changed their name again. If they did it once, I suppose there was nothing to stop them doing it again."

"Not being able to get to the immigration records either…I mean, you wouldn't know if they left the country or not. Though, if they did, I'd imagine they'd go anywhere but Australia."

"So what's left to us?"

"The phone?"

"Oh, hell," Olive said. "I knew that was coming."

The following day they spent in their hotel room with the Internet directory printout Louise had brought with her of all the Bacons and Bakers in New Zealand. She had whittled it down to eighty-three.

They finished the day hoarse and tearful, their ears red and sore after being held up to a telephone receiver for the best part of seven hours.

"Not even one," Louise complained. "Not one bloody Aussie out of the lot of them."

"It was worth a try, love. Don't be too discouraged. We'll just have to try something else."

"What though?" Louise stood at the window looking out over the city. "I just can't think what else to do here. We may as well go home tomorrow."

Upon their return to Melbourne, Louise spent a day back in her studio trying to find the real person hidden behind the mask of a politician's wife who posed self-consciously in front of Louise's lenses.

"Imagine you're being fed peeled grapes by Richard Gere or Superman," Louise suggested. "Open your mouth a bit more...that's it...imagine he's naked."

The woman scowled.

"Come on, Leticia, you can do better than that," Louise coaxed, thinking that some women could be really pathetic. Why did they want these so-called glamour shots? Far better to be themselves rather than try to look sexy. *She's got all the dynamic personality of an empty aspirin bottle.*

Two hours later Louise assured the woman that the photos would be fantastic.

"Liar," Claire mouthed.

Louise thankfully shut the door after the woman and then arranged for any outstanding jobs to be postponed, except for a wedding shoot for a regular client. There were proofs to look over, cheques to sign, letters to dictate and invitations to decline—much to Claire's displeasure.

"No, you're not talking me into going to that bunfight again this year," Louise said, tossing her thick hair back.

Claire wagged her finger at her in mock disapproval. "All the top photographers go. You should be seen there. You might even pick up an award or two or three."

"Do I care?"

Claire pulled a face at her, thinking of the already huge collection of awards that Louise had. Argument lost.

Louise then made an appointment to visit the Zion Nursing Home that sprawled across the block between St. Kilda and Punt Roads.

"Look, I don't know if you can help me or not," she told the woman from the residents accounts department. "I'm trying to find out if you would still have the records on a person who was admitted here in 1968."

"Oh, that's a long time ago."

"Yes, I know," Louise smiled encouragingly.

"If they didn't stay here very long, we wouldn't have any records..."

"Not even a forwarding address?"

"No," the woman shrugged, her thin pencilled eyebrows drawing
together. "But if they stayed longer, say a couple of years, then we
would have records."

"A forwarding address?"

"Next of kin details we would have."

"Oh, I see." Louise bit her lip, frowning. "What about if they died
here?"

"Yes, we would have those records."

"Well, can we give it a try?"

"Of course," the woman smiled. "What name is it?"

"A Mr Schwartz."

"Oh, Mr Schwartz? You mean Gunter Schwartz?"

"Yes. Do you remember the name?"

"Of course I do." Her deep-set eyes widened, accentuating the
fine lines at their corners. "Everyone knows Mr Schwartz."

"Really?" Louise's heart skipped a beat, and her hands began to
tremble. She put them in front of her, gripping the edge of the desk.

"Yes, he's our oldest resident."

"You mean...he's here? He's still alive?"

He knew it was raining before he saw it, when the nurse opened the
curtain, by the sound of its tapping on the window of his room. The
icy drops lunged at the glass like transparent darts, then joined in
rivulets to writhe sinuously down to the window ledge. He watched
as the rivulets joined to make wider tributaries, taking the dust
with them, and distorting the images of the naked tree branches
and buildings outside. There were no leaves left on the closer tree
branches. The wind and rain had taken the last ones during the
night. It reminded him of the O'Henry story about the leaf painted
on a wall by a dying artist. Perhaps someone should have painted
more leaves on the branches for him—though he had no intention of
dying. He would cling to life as long as it took.

The daddy-long-legs was no longer above the window where it
had been the night before. His eye moved around, searching the
ceiling. The cobweb hanging from the light fitting had still escaped
the notice of the cleaners. It could only be seen in a certain light—
like now when the morning light encountered its delicate threads.
No, the spider was not there either. *Ah! There it is.* The fine long
legs were splayed out across the corner of the room, where the

wooden built-in wardrobe met the painted wall. One leg appeared to wave to him. *Yes, I see you.* The spider was his silent companion who accepted him for what he was, without pity, without scorn.

The sun glared at him through the window. Even with his eye shut, the white dazzle blinded him, the sun's orb a negative picture imprinted on his eyelid. The heat penetrated his body. He could feel beads of sweat oozing from the pores of his skin, forming runnels that snaked off the edges of his body and soaking the sheet under him.

He turned inward, to where huge rollers from the vast Indian Ocean pounded the sands of the West Australian coast. Ursula beckoned to him from the water, and he walked across the hot sand to the shallows where he paused, savouring the sudden shock of the cool water on his feet. His toes separated to allow the water between them, and he wriggled them in the soft, wet sand. A tiny crab scuttled across his left foot, and disappeared under the sand. Ursula splashed at him, laughing. The sun dazzled his eyes when he looked at its many-hued reflections bouncing off her red hair. The water reached his knees. He walked in further and gasped as it washed over his genitals, then he raised himself on his toes and leapt into the air to dive into the water. The impact of the cold water on his head and shoulders made him shudder momentarily and then he wallowed in the refreshing water that cooled his blood.

He felt it drip on his face. Cool, wet, soft.

"There. That must feel better, Mr Schwartz," a voice broke over his fantasy. "You're burning up."

The nurse with the short dark hair took the face washer away. He could hear water being swished around in something, then dripping, then the face washer came back wetter, and she dabbed it over his forehead, his eyelids, his cheeks. She took it away again, and then it returned refreshed to cool his neck, his shoulders, his chest. He saw the number tattooed on his left forearm as she lifted it. *My companion for life,* he thought with disgust.

"You've got that sun in your eyes again," she observed, as she stood back and it hit him in the eye. "Here, I'll close the blind for a bit."

The leaves had started to fall again. He tried to count them as they fell and followed their flight until they disappeared from his window's view. If he was turned the other way he couldn't see them and, when they turned him back to face the window, he would be surprised to see how many had gone—just in a few hours. He knew how many had gone from whichever branch he singled out for that day. It took him sometimes an hour or more to count them and most of the time he wasn't really sure if he'd counted each and every one. Sometimes he would be in the middle of counting when a nurse would come in and turn him, or take him into the bathing room.

They would wheel him down the long corridor that had polished white linoleum on the floor but that he never saw from his position. He knew the ceiling and upper walls of the corridor very well. Long fluorescent tubes lit the way when it was dark, and red lights were set into the top of each door frame, which would light up if someone pressed a buzzer in their room. His red light never lit up. He couldn't press the buzzer.

The bath stuck out at right angles from a small tiled corner section in the bathing room. They would lower him into the water and he would feel clean again. He'd lost count of how many times his thin, naked body was attended to in that cold, white room. They would hold his head back and wash his hair; sometimes soap would get into his eye and he would blink hoping that they would wash it out. Some of them were rough with his limbs and talked over him, as if he were an animal in the bath. Some were gentler, and some actually talked to him.

He was in a single room where the only sound was that of his own breathing and the sounds that came in from the people passing in the corridor or the traffic outside on Punt Road. At times white uniforms would group around his bed and talk about his condition. Vegetative state, they called it, and coma. *So that's what's wrong with me. I'm in a coma. But shouldn't I be unconscious?*

The face of an old man sometimes hovered over his bed. A receding hairline led back to snowy-white hair that curled around the man's ears. He wore thick glasses in heavy frames, perched on a red indentation on top of a bulbous nose that had copious amounts of hair tufting out of the nostrils. He always smiled. Every time.

"Mr Ruben," a nurse would say, "are you in here bothering Mr Schwartz again?"

And she would lead Mr Ruben to the adjoining room, through the bathroom that they shared—or at least that Mr Ruben enjoyed on his own, as Gunter had never used the toilet or basin in there.

Leave him here so that I can look at him, Gunter would tell her with his mind. Mr Ruben sometimes talked to Gunter about the old days before the war, about his family, about Birkenau where he'd been held captive, about those condemned to vanish in the course of selections on the platform, about his being forced to tattoo the left forearms of his fellow prisoners, about survival. It didn't seem to bother him that Gunter couldn't answer. And then the nurses would find him and take him back to his room.

On more than one occasion Gunter was taken from the building in which he existed.

"Chest infection," he heard them say. "Get the ambulance."

He would be wheeled down the long corridor, past the nurses' station, and bumped into a lift. For a few moments he would be out in the sunshine, if he was lucky to be transferred on a good day, and he would look up at the sky and wish he could float up and stay there, free of his body forever. The warmth of the sun on his face was a luxury. Then he would be jostled inside an ambulance and taken to Prince Henry's, not far away.

Despite his discomfort and desperate battle to breathe, he enjoyed his sojourns to the hospital. There were new faces for him to study, new voices to listen to, new rooms to examine inch by inch. Once his infection was cleared up, he would be transferred back to his room in the nursing home. He would scrutinize the trees outside his window, hour after hour, familiarising himself with the changes that had occurred while he'd been away. He would look for familiar cobwebs to see if they'd been discovered and removed, and track the movements of the spiders who shared his room. But when he had completed his tasks, depression would flatten his enthusiasm and he would escape his surroundings in dreams of his choosing.

One day the nurse with the short dark hair—which was now turning grey—came in with something that would have given him cause to kiss her if he'd been able to. She came in with a portable radio.

"I don't need it, Mr Schwartz. My son gave me a new one for my birthday. And because you were a violinist, I thought you'd like to hear some music." She bent close to his ear and whispered, "I know they reckon you can't hear, but I think you can."

She put the radio on his bedside table and fiddled with the knobs. Pop music bounced into the room in cut-off shreds as she turned the dial; a race caller shouted his excitement over horses thundering along a track; advertisements and jingles sliced past his ears...and then a piano.

"Ah, I think this'd be to your liking," she smiled over him so that he could see her face. "The ABC should be the thing. You'll get the news as well as the music. At least you'll know what's going on in the world."

And that was how Gunter kept track of the time, the months and the years that crept slowly past his window. He stayed suspended in his body, in a prison that he could not break free of. World events entered the room and he had all the time in the world to turn them over in his mind, examine them, digest them, laugh or cry over them. But when classical music played, it soothed his frustrated mind and transported him to other places and other times in his life: the concert halls, the orchestras, the practice sessions with Ursula, the students he taught...the face of his beloved Hannah as she watched him play.

He knew that he'd been there for a very long time. One New Year's Eve ran into the next and he would add another year to his deteriorating body. *Hold on. You must hold on.* He would allow nothing, nothing to finish him off, although he was so tired, so discouraged. He had to wait for something to release him—someone to realise that he was alive inside his body, that he wasn't in a coma. *But how long can I wait?*

In March 1992, Gunter realised he had reached seventy years of age when he woke to the sound of *Happy Birthday* being sung to him. One of the nurses actually kissed his cheek.

"Just in case, Mr Schwartz," she whispered after she'd kissed him. "You can't have a seventieth and not get a kiss, eh?"

"Waste of time," the other nurse said. "He can't hear you."

"How do you know?" the one who'd kissed him retorted. "He might drift in and out. Anyway, if my dad were alive, I'd have liked someone to kiss him on his birthday."

Good girl.

Later, the rabbi prayed at the side of his bed; Gunter wondered why he bothered.

God has turned his face away from me.

Gunter closed his eye wearily.

Hannah, wait for me.

He willed himself to leave the body that kept him prisoner. In dreams he embraced Hannah, he held his daughters, he was reunited with his parents and sister—he smiled again. He tuned his violin carefully and played duets with Ursula, performed with the orchestra, bowed to the applause. He came to resent the return to his cage, resent the ministrations of the medical staff, resent the shattering of his dreams...but most of all, he resented his beating heart. *Stop! Stop! Stop!* The times that he opened his eye were very few now. Curiosity had left him. Hope had left him. He had given up.

"Mr Schwartz? I've brought someone to see you." The voice was one he recognised. It belonged to the day shift nurse, Marta. He liked her. She sometimes read to him. He opened his eye warily, regretful of leaving the other world that she had plucked him from.

A face came into view over his bed. It was a female, late thirties he thought, no lines as yet in the face, friendly brown eyes, thick dark hair that was drawn back behind her head, a generous mouth painted a red that matched the bodice of her dress. Perfume reached his nostrils. *Expensive.* Her left hand went up to push a stray lock of hair back. *No rings.* Red-painted nails. *Another social worker? Occupational therapist? Maybe.*

He was surprised at her mouth. It trembled. Like she was about to cry. He could sense her breathing was shallow, and there was an urgency about her, as if she was excited about something. *No, not a staff member. Why is she looking at me like that?*

"Mr Schwartz, I'm going to leave your visitor with you. Her name's Louise Fletcher."

Louise turned to Marta. "Can he hear me?"

"They say not, dear, but I think he can. Look at his eye following us, and he does react to sound."

Marta stroked Gunter's forehead affectionately. "I'm very fond of this poor man, you know. He's been here for so long, and just hangs on despite the experts who seem to have forgotten about him."

"Mr Schwartz? I'll be back soon," Marta smiled. "Don't you go getting up to any mischief while I'm gone. You don't often get such pretty visitors."

Gunter smiled inside his head.

Louise turned her head to watch Marta leave the room, and Gunter saw that her hair was caught up in a roll with a tortoise-shell comb. She turned back and looked at him for a long time before speaking.

"Mr Schwartz." She licked her lips nervously. "I don't know if you can hear me or not, but I'm going to talk anyway."

He sensed that she was about to say something terribly important. He felt his heart begin to race as his eye fixed on hers, willing her to go on.

"I know that you came from Perth where you lost your wife in childbirth. I also know that your wife gave birth to twins, and that one of them was stolen. I know that you never found her."

Louise looked at him, saw the quivering mouth, the eye fixed on her, the still, helpless body. *Is there a mind in there? Should I go on?*

Inside Gunter's body alarm bells were sounding. His mind screamed at her. *Don't stop!* Here was someone who knew about his past.

"Mr Schwartz," she said, moving around the bed to get to the side where his open eye was closest. "I know about the other twin. I knew her. She was my best friend."

Chapter 62

Louise stood back to watch for any reaction to her words. The face of the man remained like a mask, unmoving, except for small involuntary twitches of the mouth. The eye regarded her steadily. She thought there was expression in it, but how could she tell for sure?

She turned as the sound of footsteps hurried past the doorway and, when she turned back to the man lying in the bed, she found that he was still looking at her.

"Can I hold your hand?" She was hesitant, embarrassed. "If I hold your hand, will you squeeze it if you can hear me?"

She picked up a hand that was surprisingly light in weight. The joints looked huge under soft, transparent, paper-thin skin. Blue veins stood out in knots. She traced them with her forefinger before sliding her fingers into his palm and then closing his hand over her own. The intimacy of the shared warmth of their hands touched her. *This is something a lens can never capture.*

"Mr Schwartz? Can you squeeze my hand?"

His body lay still.

"Please try. Try as hard as you can."

Mein Gott, if I tried any harder I think I would burst! Can't you feel that?

Gunter felt her hand inside his. It felt so soft, so young. He screamed at his brain. *Squeeze. Squeeze.* The order left its place of conception to begin its lightening flight through electric paths to complete the task, but no sooner did it reach the brain stem, than an impenetrable obstacle halted it. There was nowhere for it to go, and it dissolved as fast as it was created. The arm that should have responded with tightening tendons and muscles lay flaccid on the yellow bedspread. The hand that covered Louise's was without the slightest movement. Gunter could only stare back at her pleading eyes, willing her to read his thoughts.

"Oh, well. They did warn me," she said to herself quietly, sighing. "Stupid of me."

She withdrew her hand from his, and moved to the window to look out over Punt Road. The traffic noises floated up to Gunter's room, breaking the silence of their shared frustrations. Louise felt torn—should she sit beside him and tell him everything she knew about Joy, or should she leave the poor man in peace? *He probably can't hear me anyway.* She noticed that his eye kept on following her as she began to pace the room, so she deliberately moved from the window to the door and back again. *Yes, he is looking at me.* She stood next to him and waved her hand slowly up and down, and side to side. His eye followed her hand.

"You are awake in there. I'm sure of it."

Her voice sounded harsh to her and she swallowed. *Don't yell and treat him like an idiot.* She drew up a chair and sat close to him.

"Look, I'm going to tell you everything I know."

His eye blinked.

"Hey! Does that mean yes?"

With enormous effort he blinked again.

Louise took his hand in hers.

"You poor man." There was a huge lump in her throat.

She leant on the bedspread and began to speak slowly and clearly.

"When I was five, Joy Bacon came to live next door to me. We lived in Chelsea—that's a seaside suburb—in a short street that leads right to the beach. I remember being so excited that a girl my age was moving in next door. Even before I met her, I was desperately hoping we'd be best friends and I'd finally have someone to play with. The first time I saw her, I was overcome—in my childish way—by her beauty. Her green eyes...hey, yours are almost the same colour...were such an unusual shade, as was her hair. My God, her hair...it shone in the sunlight—all different shades of red and gold—and I just couldn't imagine that anyone so pretty would want to be friends with me. I guess it was then that my interest in photography first started...not that I knew it then. That's what I am—a photographer, I mean. If I could have captured the colour and texture of her hair and her eyes that day, I would have. I wanted to put it in a box and tie it up with a big green ribbon. I was afraid the colour would change when she became older but, of course, it didn't."

Louise paused, searching the face of the man on the bed. There was no clue as to whether he could hear her but she felt a connection, tenuous though it was. *Is it wishful thinking?* Her heart went out to Gunter. *Do I feel this way because I think he's Joy's real father? Would I feel like this if he wasn't?*

"We were such good friends right from the start, sharing everything together. We read the same books, swapped clothes, went to school together. You know, we spent hours and hours on the beach—swimming, talking, making sandcastles. We were very good at that—making sandcastles. We won such a lot of competitions. And we had no secrets from each other. Absolutely none."

Louise sighed as she delved back into the past. "So many happy memories, and then to be cut off so suddenly…"

She stopped as she bit her lip.

"No, I mustn't get off the track. I should tell it all chronologically, shouldn't I?"

He willed her to go on. He didn't care how she told him, as long as she didn't stop telling him about Joy Bacon in that warm, throaty voice of hers.

"Joy's parents were nice people, especially Mr Bacon." She pulled a face. "Not like my own father…but that's another story. Anyway, Mrs Bacon was nice too, but not quite…you know…normal. What I mean is, she was over-protective about Joy. Obsessive, really. She loved that girl to death. They both did, but Mr Bacon wasn't obsessive like she was. The first day we started school was ghastly. She embarrassed the hell out of Joy by the way she clung to her in the schoolyard. It was like she was losing her for good."

Gunter closed his eye. He knew the pain of losing someone.

"Oh, you poor thing," Louise exclaimed. "I've tired you out, haven't I?"

No! No!

She stood, taking her hand away from his.

"I'll come back another day if I can."

Please don't go!

"Would you like that?"

He ordered his eye to blink.

"If that means yes, then I will come," she decided. A thought came to her. "I could bring photos of her."

Yes!

"You could see whether you thought it was the other twin or not. That would prove it, wouldn't it? I mean, if anyone would know, you would."

Another blink.

"It did say in the newspaper articles that they were identical."

She looked at him closely.

"But just how you could tell me is our biggest hurdle, I think."

They regarded each other for some moments before she straightened and picked up her handbag. It was puzzling to her why she felt so reluctant to leave him.

"Goodbye, Mr Schwartz."

He watched her walk to the door and hesitate, turning back to look at him. He caught the smile that revealed her warmth and sincerity.

"I'll see you again soon."

I hope so.

Outside the room, she leaned against the wall for a moment, fighting the urge to go back and give him a hug. *Don't be ridiculous*, she chided herself. *You don't even know the man.*

At the nurses' station of the palliative ward, Louise waited to speak with someone. She noticed there were about ten people in reclining chairs around the quiet day room. It was a cheerful area with sunlight streaming in through glass-tiled walls. *I wonder if they ever bring Mr Schwartz out here?*

"How did you get on with Mr Schwartz?" A nurse walked up to her.

"Oh, fine. I think."

"Are you related somehow?" the nurse asked hopefully.

"No," Louise looked back at his room. "Does he have many visitors?"

"None at all, besides medical staff."

"How awful."

"Well, it doesn't matter anyway. He's a PVS patient. Probably doesn't have any idea what's going on."

"What's that?"

"Persistent vegetative state—they display wakefulness without awareness."

"You don't think he's conscious some of the time? I mean, he follows you with his eye."

"No. It's a reflex movement."

"What happened to him?"

"A massive stroke."

"Thirty years ago?"

"Yes," the nurse said. "It's amazing how he's hung on this long, but these survivors of the holocaust," she indicated the patients lying motionless in the chairs, "they're tough. They had to be. And the Jewish community looks after its aged population—survival is still paramount to us."

Louise looked at the tired, wasted bodies—some awake and staring ahead of them, others with mouths gaping and their heads back against pillows in slumber. *Why are they hanging on?* She realised how little she knew about what people such as they had suffered, and their instinct to survive.

"Can I visit him again?"

"Sure. Though don't expect any response. He's incapable of any kind of communication. All we can do is try to make him comfortable until he goes...and I don't think that's too far off."

Louise drove back to Frankston deep in thought. *Reflex movement, she said. Yet I'd swear he was watching me.* She decided to look up strokes on the Internet. There was a wealth of information, but not a lot about Gunter's condition. After reading about the symptoms of stroke, Louise suspected that what he had suffered was a brain stem stroke, which had caused his paralysis. She read about comas and persistent vegetative state, from which she learned that many patients have open, moving eyes but that they are incapable of sensation or thought. *But if that's the case, why did he blink at me in the right places? Just co-incidence?*

Her neck and back hurt from sitting in front of the computer screen for so long, and she paused for a while to stretch her muscles and pour herself a drink. As always, she was drawn to the window-framed panorama of the bay. Its waters reached towards the horizon where the sun had begun its descent into night. Molten metallic ripples glazed the water's surface as it fluttered towards the rocks at the base of Olivers Hill. *If his brain wasn't alert, why would he hang around for so long? He should have died years ago. He's defied them.* She sipped the bitter Campari slowly. *Unless he's waiting for something...or someone.*

Back to the computer, she settled down to read more about persistent vegetative state. Through various links, she discovered a site that set her pulse racing. She encountered information about a rare condition called Locked-in Syndrome.

> "...consciousness and cognition are retained but movement and communication are impossible because of severe paralysis of the voluntary motor system. Patients with this syndrome can usually establish limited communication through eye-movement signals...By definition, patients in a persistent vegetative state are unaware of themselves or their environment. They are non-cognitive, nonsentient, and incapable of conscious experience. There is, however, a biological limitation to the certainty of this definition, since we can only infer the presence or absence of consciousness in another person...an error might occur if a pa-

tient in a locked-in state...was wrongly judged to be unaware. Thus, it is theoretically possible that a patient who appears to be in a persistent vegetative state retains awareness but shows no evidence of it. In the practice of neurology, this possibility is sufficiently rare that it does not interfere with a clinical diagnosis carefully established by experts...In rare cases, it may be difficult to distinguish a persistent vegetative state from a severe locked-in state. Under such unusual circumstances, a patient may not be able to express behavioural responses to painful stimuli or the responses may be extremely difficult to detect; the absence of a response cannot be taken as proof of the absence of consciousness."

"Oh shit!"

Louise sat back in her chair, staring in amazement at the screen. She tapped at her forehead.

Could Gunter Schwartz be locked-in?

The phone rang twelve times until it was picked up.

"What time is it?" asked a sleepy Olive.

"Oh. Sorry," Louise said, looking at her watch. "It's one-thirty."

"In the morning?"

"Yes. I didn't realise how late it was. Look, go back to sleep. I'll talk to you tomorrow."

"I'm awake now, Louie. What is it?"

"I've been on the net."

"Do you sleep at all these days?"

"Not much," Louise laughed.

"I'll bet you're not eating either."

"Don't be such a worry-wart."

"Can't help it. You're precious to me, you know."

"Thanks, Mum. Same here."

"Well, go on. Tell me all about it."

Some hours later, Louise was sipping a hot mug of coffee at the kitchen table in her mother's house. Pages of downloaded information about locked-in syndrome were spread out on the table in front of them, along with a thin paper-backed book entitled *The Diving-Bell & the Butterfly*.

"I was at Robinson's Bookshop first thing," Louise said, after swallowing a mouthful of toast, "and was lucky they had a copy on their shelves. Anyway, I sat in the car and read it. It didn't take long, because it's pretty short, but I'm staggered—really staggered—at what an amazing feat it is. Jean-Dominique Bauby, who wrote it, had been locked-in. I mean, that man couldn't utter a word, move an inch, except for blinking his eye. He dictated the whole book to his assistant who kept on reciting the alphabet until he blinked, and whatever letter it was he blinked at she would write it down until they formed words and sentences."

Olive picked up the book, and flicked through the pages.

"You've got to read it, Mum. It's fantastic."

"I'm hooked already," Olive said, absorbed with the first page.

"It's inspirational. I reckon if he could achieve that—writing a book while locked-in—then no one has an excuse to give up on anything. So, I'm going to find Joy, and I don't care what it takes to do it. And if I can get that poor man to communicate—unlock him, so to speak—then I'll do that as well."

Louise picked up a large envelope from the passenger seat of her car. Her hair was hot from the sun shining on it through the car window; it gleamed in healthy chestnut hues as it bounced around her shoulders. The temperature had already reached twenty-five degrees Celsius. It was going to be a hot one. *He won't feel it though,* she thought with sympathy for the helpless man on the fourth floor above her. *I wonder how long it is since he's felt the sun on his face.* She entered the building and took the lift up to the palliative ward.

Gunter was floating somewhere amongst Mozart's *Violin Concerto No. 1*. He had all the rest to go through today. He'd already been through his favourites of Tchaikovsky and Beethoven. His right hand gripped the bow of his violin strongly as he guided it across the strings. The pleasant smell of resin was potent in his nostrils. Hannah sat watching him over the rim of her champagne glass as she absorbed the notes written by a young Mozart. The bubbles leapt up and wet the outline of her nostrils. She giggled and wiped her nose with a lace handkerchief before taking another sip. Ursula stood beside him, holding her own violin. She played in harmony with him, perfectly. Her sister was a pace behind her, in the shadows...

"It's Louise Fletcher to see you again, Mr Schwartz," Marta announced brightly as she led Louise into the room. "Lucky man, eh?"

What? He sank back to Mozart. *Don't interrupt the concerto.*

"Would you like a coffee or tea?" Marta asked Louise.

The music began to fade. *Yes please. Hot and strong with plenty of sugar.*

"No, thanks. I'll be squelching if I have any more," Louise replied.

That throaty voice! Gunter's eye opened and searched frantically for its owner. *Is that her?*

Louise walked around to the side of the bed where his right eye was open. Her lightly-tanned face hovered over him and her mouth opened into a wide grin. It was such an infectious grin that he automatically grinned back, but it failed to reach his lips. Her perfume replaced the smell of resin, and when she began to speak he relinquished his hold on the concerto to listen to her.

"Nice to see you again, Mr Schwartz."

How I've waited for you!

Marta left the room, closing the door behind her.

Louise slipped her hand into his, and gently pressed his hand over hers. It was such a delightful feeling for him to feel her warmth. He couldn't remember the last time anyone had held his hand, other than to take his pulse.

"I've brought those photos I promised to show you." She held up the bulging envelope for him to see.

You wonderful girl.

"Lots of them. And I've been doing a bit of research and if you are conscious in there," she said, lightly touching his forehead, "I'm going to try to get you to communicate with me."

How?

"But I'll come to that later." She took her hand away and emptied the photographs onto the bedspread, then selected one. "Now this one was taken by my mother when Joy and I had our first birthday party together. We were five then."

She held up a black and white photograph of the two girls with arms linked and their cheeks puffed up as they blew out two rows of five candles on a cake.

"Perhaps that's not such a good one as our faces are distorted."

She whipped the photograph away from his line of sight.

No. Let me see!

"Here, this one's better."

A close-up came into view of Louise and Joy. They were laughing as they pointed to the camera.

Ursula!

"We always shared our birthday parties because we were born a day apart. Pity they're in black and white, but you can see how she looked, eh?"

Mein Gott, she is exactly like Ursula!

"Oh, here's a good one."

The black and white photograph was quickly replaced with a colour one. It was an eight year-old Joy putting the finishing touches to an elaborately-decorated sandcastle. She had a look of surprise on her face as she looked at something or someone beyond the frame of the photograph. Her hair was tied back in a ponytail, the sunlight catching all its shades of red and gold. Curly wisps had escaped their confinement to flutter in a breeze that lifted them. Her eyes reflected the green of the shallows behind her.

This is the Ursula of the Perth beaches. This is the Ursula I have held in my arms, comforted when she felt pain, laughed with when she was happy. This is the daughter I have loved. Oh, how I miss her.

He looked from the photograph to Louise, who had been watching him closely for any reaction. She noticed that his upper eyelid had sagged slightly over his eyeball as a tear oozed its way out of the tear-duct. She quickly took a mirror out of her handbag and looked at one of her eyes in it. *Be happy.* She saw that her eye opened wide. *Sad.* The upper lid sagged.

"Mr Schwartz, do you feel sad to see that photo?"

Oh yes, so sad. My daughters…both of them…are gone. Where are they?

"I hope I'm not upsetting you. Should I pack up and leave?" she said deliberately.

No. Stay!

His eye opened slightly, and she copied the movement in her mirror by feigning alarm.

"It's okay, I'll hang around as long as you'll put up with me."

The eye sagged more than before.

Relief. She looked in the mirror and saw that her eye had sagged into the same position.

One by one, Louise picked up each photograph and placed it in front of Gunter's eye. She allowed him several minutes for each one, conscious of the fact that she might be tiring him. As she held up the photographs, she described the scene, the event, who had taken the photo, and the time in Joy's life. After he had studied close to thirty images of Joy, Louise noticed that his eye was closing and that he was looking through a mere slit.

"I'm sorry, I've worn you out."

With a tremendous effort, Gunter opened his eye and tried to say, *Yes I'm tired, lovely lady, but pleasantly so. I wish you would stay. Will you come back? Soon?*

"Can I visit you again? We could try some other ways to communicate then." She brought her face close to his. "I wish you could tell me, Mr Schwartz," she whispered. "I really do."

So do I.

"You know something? I really believe that you're awake in there. I don't believe you are in a persistent vegetative state for one moment. Have you heard of locked-in syndrome?"

She paused to see if there was any change in the position of his eyelid. It opened imperceptibly.

"I think that's what you've got, but I'll tell you about it next time."

Please.

She placed her hand inside his own.

"Goodbye for now."

She walked to the door and turned back with a smile. His eye was open, but only just. As soon as the door closed behind her, he slumped into unconsciousness where Hannah waited for him. When Marta came into the room to turn him, he stayed in his other world. He was still there when they bathed him the next morning.

Chapter 63

The delicious aroma of a roast dinner greeted Louise as she rang the bell at the front door of her mother's house.

"You're determined to fatten me up, aren't you?" she laughed when Olive opened the door to her. She marvelled at her mother's still curvaceous body dressed in fashionable three-quarter pants and a bright top. *Never lets herself go.*

"I'll bet you haven't eaten today," Olive scolded, "or yesterday."

"I ate something or other."

"Look at you. Your clothes are hanging off you."

Louise looked down in surprise. "I guess you're right."

"See?"

"I am feeling hungry, now I come to think of it."

"Good," Olive said preceding Louise into the kitchen. "It's just about ready." She poured them each a glass of shiraz. "Now tell me about your visit to Mr Schwartz before I die from curiosity."

Louise recounted the time she spent with Gunter, talking in detail about what she took to be his reactions to her questions and the photographs of Joy.

"Did you tell him about the locked-in syndrome?"

"I mentioned it, but he was getting really tired. I can go on with it the next time I visit."

"What about the nurses? Did you ask them if he might have it?"

Louise shook her head. "No. I'd rather wait a bit until I'm sure. They might throw me out if they think I'm interfering too much. I mean they don't really know why I'm there anyway. There's one nice nurse there—Marta—who seems to think he's more than a vegetable. She told me she reads to him sometimes."

"Oh, that's nice of her, especially considering the fact she doesn't know if he can hear her or not."

"That's what I thought. I might have a chat with her about it. See if she's heard of locked-in syndrome. From what I've gathered, not many people have."

Olive took another sip of her wine, jammed side combs back into her hair, and got up from the table to dish up. Louise automatically moved beside her to stir the gravy.

"I read the book," Olive said, indicating *The Diving Bell & the Butterfly*, which sat on a chair near the backdoor. "Don't forget to take it home."

"What'd you think of it?"

"Remarkable. I'll never complain about anything again in my life."

"You will, you know. That's human nature."

"But it's a humbling experience to read that man's story. What a brave fellow."

"Yes. It's a privilege to read it—sharing his inner turmoil. And he's made the rest of the world aware of it now."

"So what's next, Louie?"

"I guess keep on visiting Mr Schwartz…see if I can establish contact. I'm going to try the alphabet with him—see if it works like it did for Bauby."

"You realise it could take you months, if you have any success at all?"

They sat at the table with their plates piled high.

"How am I supposed to eat all that?" Louise complained.

"Eat what you can't eat, and don't eat what you can."

Louise laughed. "You know, you always confused the hell out of me whenever you said that."

"I know," Olive laughed with her.

They ate in silence for some moments.

"You're right, you know," Louise said.

"What about?"

"It could take me months…maybe years. And what if he won't talk?"

"Why wouldn't he?"

"It occurred to me that he might be the one who had something to do with Joy's disappearance, or the death of the other twin."

Olive looked at Louise aghast. "I'd never thought of that."

"Then I'll really be stuck. I mean, how do I know that his reactions were what I interpreted? It might have been the complete opposite. He might be panicking inside thinking the game's up."

"If he's the guilty one."

"Yes."

"What do you think?"

"My gut feeling?"

Olive nodded as she held the wine bottle up with a raised eyebrow, but Louise placed her hand over her glass.

"I think that Gunter Schwartz is desperate to communicate. Don't ask me why. I just feel it—a sort of bond. If he were guilty of a crime, why would he wait so long in the condition he's in? It'd be easier to give up and escape the consequences. I think there's a pretty tough man in that body, just waiting for a miracle of some sort. It's like he's got a job to do, and then he could let go. You know—die."

"You've summed that up pretty quickly."

"With only two visits?"

Olive nodded.

"Yes, I know. A bit presumptuous of me, eh?"

"Just a tad."

Louise pushed some beef onto her fork and covered it with gravy. "You're saying I should be more cautious before jumping to any conclusions?"

"More or less."

"You're probably right." She chewed on the meat thoughtfully and washed it down with the last of her wine. "I tend to think that the Bacons—or Bakers, or whoever they are—are more likely to be the culprits in this whole mystery."

"That's the way it seems," Olive agreed.

"I think I will have a drop more, Mum," Louise said holding her glass up. "Just a half."

"Anyway, what I'd been thinking," Olive said, pouring the wine, "was that you should find out a bit more about the kidnapping— read more articles in the West Australian newspapers. You'd perhaps find a missing link."

"Like what?"

"Oh, I don't know…maybe talk to the police there…"

"But would they listen to me?"

"If the case had never been solved, they might."

They finished their meal without speaking for some moments, each occupied with her own thoughts.

Louise broke the silence. "There was a detective mentioned a couple of times in those clippings."

"You could try to contact him."

"I wonder if he's still around."

Louise let herself into her house and switched on a lamp that stood on the desk.

"Hi, Blue Eyes," she said routinely to the doll. "Been up to any mischief today?"

The bottle of Campari was almost empty.

"You naughty girl," she said holding up the bottle. "You've been at it again, eh?" She poured the contents into a long glass and topped it up with soda water from the refrigerator. "May as well join you," Louise said, saluting the doll.

She paused for a moment to look out at the bay, never ceasing to be fascinated by its ever-changing moods. The moon touched its surface with silvery tentacles on a shifting tapestry of lurching corrugations. The rocks stood out against the water, outlined sharply by the moon's radiance.

I'm talking to a doll. She took a sip of her drink. *I think I'm going bonkers.*

Her notebook lay on the coffee table. She opened it and leafed through the pages until she found the articles that she'd photocopied at the State Library and had then stuck into the book. They were from Perth newspapers dated 9th May 1955:

FATHER COLLAPSES WHEN DAUGHTER STOLEN!

After the tragic death of his wife in childbirth, (Mrs Hannah Schwartz, 21 years of age) a further calamity struck the grieving husband, Mr Gunter Schwartz. What should have been a joyous event for the Schwartzes turned into a ghastly nightmare of death and abduction. The birth of a set of female twins would have perhaps been some comfort to the hapless father had not a vile criminal stolen one of the tiny babies. Detective Sergeant George Chambers told the press that, "Mr Schwartz never even had a chance to see the baby. She had disappeared from the hospital nursery while he was paying his respects to his deceased wife." When told the news of the kidnapping, Mr Schwartz collapsed and had to be revived by medical staff at Prince Alfred Hospital.

BABY TAKEN BY FIEND!

Detective Sergeant Chambers, assigned to the case of the Schwartz twin, holds grave fears for the safety of the newborn baby girl. D/Sgt. Chambers reported that, "The stolen twin has disappeared without a trace. We have set up investigations where staff in and around the hospital are being interrogated, and we have foot patrols in the vicinity." Chambers said, "Only the lowest of nefarious persons could have committed a crime such as this. But I hasten to assure the public that the offender will be brought to justice. There is no doubt in my mind about that." Mr Gunter Schwartz was unavailable for comment.

And on 10th May, 1955:

STILL NO SIGN OF KIDNAPPED TWIN

Police presence is very evident on the streets of Perth as the search for the Schwartz baby girl continues into its third day. The hearts of all Perth residents, as indeed the hearts of all Australians, go out to the father of the missing baby. German immigrants from the death camp Auschwitz, Gunter and Hannah Schwartz had settled quietly and happily in Perth since arriving in 1945. Mr Schwartz had resumed his musical career by joining the West Australian Symphony Orchestra as a violinist. Questions being raised are how Mr Schwartz will bring up the surviving baby on his own, and whether the death penalty should be imposed when the kidnapper is caught if the baby does not survive.

Louise studied the photo of Hannah and Gunter underneath the article. *What a handsome couple. No wonder Joy was so pretty. Her mother's hair looks the same. Same high cheek bones, same long neck.* Louise tilted the photo towards the lamplight. They look to be so much in love. She sighed as she tried to immerse herself into the outdoor scene where Gunter smiled at his laughing wife. She envied their intimacy, grudgingly admitting to herself that she wished the same for her life—a man who could make her light up like Hannah did. *He doesn't exist...not for me.*

She bit her lip as she thought of the mere shell that survived in the bed at the nursing home. Gone was the virile man of the photograph whose firm chin demonstrated strength, yet supported lines of hardship and sorrow in the face above it. She thought of the skeletal head with its few tufts of hair in contrast with the precisely-parted, abundant straight hair of his younger days. Gone was the lean face, now replaced by shrunken parchment skin that displayed every vein, bruise and blemish lying just beneath it. Gone was the expression of happiness in the eyes of the young Gunter as he gazed at his wife with love. Now the expression was one of retreat into another world, turned into itself, absorbed inside dreams, hopelessness—except when she showed him the photos of Joy. His eye had come to life. The expression was one of hope.

She returned to her notebook. There she found a small article that she'd stuck into it, dated Saturday 18th June 1955:

NO NEW LEADS ON

KIDNAPPING

D/Sgt. George Chambers, of the Western Australian Police Service, indicated last night that even though the investigation into the disappearance of the Schwartz baby has been wound down, he will never give up the hunt for the missing twin girl. "I will leave no stone unturned, no clue left uninvestigated, even if I have to hunt down the kidnapper—or murderer—in my own time." The father, Mr Schwartz, is caring for the other twin alone. He remains unavailable for comment. D/Sgt. Chambers went on to say that he, "...will never rest until this case is solved. Someone, somewhere, must have the answer to the disappearance of the child. And I mean to catch that person before I die."

Okay, so I ring George Chambers.

Chapter 64

The White Pages on the Internet revealed twenty-one Chambers in Perth with an initial 'G', either in combination with another person or alone. *I wonder how old he was in 1955 and what he'd be now? Where do I start?*

Because of the three hours time difference between Melbourne and Perth, Louise figured that she could get a few phone calls in before it was too late in the evening in Western Australia.

"Hello?"

"Oh, hello. I'm ringing from Melbourne…"

"Yes?"

"I'm looking for a George Chambers. He was a policeman but he'd probably be retired."

"There's no George here."

"Sorry to have troubled you."

She punched in the next number.

"Yeah?"

"Hello. I'm calling George Chambers. Is your G. Chambers a George?"

"No."

The receiver at the other end was banged down loudly and she looked at hers in surprise.

"No need to get shirty."

She tried again.

"Good evening, this is Margaret Chambers."

"Oh, hi. I'm looking for George Chambers. Is your husband a George?"

"No, dear. I'm sorry. You must have the wrong number."

"Thank you."

After having successfully connected to seventeen of the twenty-one G. Chambers without finding the George she was after, she sat back thoughtfully drumming her fingers on her forehead. *What do I do now?*

Back on the computer, Louise found the website for the Western Australia Police Service. She drafted an email to them:

> Would you please be able to put me into contact
> with a retired Detective Sergeant George Cham-

bers who worked on the Schwartz kidnapping case
in 1955?

The following morning, Louise was surprised to see that she'd slept
so late. She yawned and stretched luxuriously in bed as she shook
off the last clinging footprints of sleep that had walked across her
mind during the night. A shower, fresh grapefruit juice, half an
avocado mashed onto a thick piece of wholegrain toast, and a large
mug of black tea, had her awake and ready for whatever challenges
might be thrown at her feet.

She rang her office.

"Claire?"

"Hi boss. Enjoying your holiday?"

"Sort of," Louise said as she touched *Blue Eyes'* tiny fingers with
her own. The paint on the nails remained as bright as when Louise
had first been given the doll. The still, blue eyes stared at her, momentarily distracting her thoughts.

"Where are you?"

"Oh," Louise said. "I'm at home."

"You disappoint me."

"Why?"

"I thought you'd be off on some exotic island in the middle of the
Pacific having a great time with some gorgeous hunk, and relaxing."

Louise laughed. "Wrong on all points. Look, can you manage for
a bit longer without me?"

They discussed various outstanding jobs and worked out a re-
scheduling of them, as well as other minor problems.

"I don't suppose the wedding shoot's been cancelled?" Louise
asked hopefully.

"You wish."

"Okay, just research the exteriors for me and I'll ring in each day
and see how things are."

"Are you going away?" Claire was curious as to what Louise was
up to.

"Might be. I'll let you know."

Over the next hour, Louise sorted through all the photographs of
Joy that she possessed, choosing three when Joy was five, eight and
twelve. She scanned them and worked for some time on the computer overlapping the three images to create a montage that represented the developing face of her friend. When she was satisfied

with it, she printed out a colour copy. Then she connected to the Internet. There was a message from Western Australia:

> We regret to advise that as a matter of policy no personal information about present or past detectives is released to members of the public.

"Bugger!"

The phone shrilled, breaking into her thoughts.

It was Olive. "How'd you get on with the articles? Did you find anything?"

Louise brought her mother up to date on what she had found out, as well as the latest stumbling block. "...so I don't know which way to turn next."

"It's getting hard, isn't it?"

"You could say that."

They were both quiet for some moments, then Olive spoke.

"What about the State Library?"

"I thought of that, but I'd be reading newspapers for years looking for something and having no idea if there was anything at all."

"Why don't you give them a ring? They might have something to suggest."

They hung up, and Louise spoke to a helpful woman at the State Library who, once she understood the difficulty of Louise's search, suggested she visit the library to look up the Perth electoral rolls for the detective's name and address in the years from 1955 onwards. She explained that Louise would be able to trace him from one address to the next, assuming he moved, and also learn if he was married or not as the wife's name would appear with his at the same address.

Louise rang her mother back.

"Feel like a trip into the city this arvo?"

"I was just getting ready," Olive said.

"You must be psychic."

Louise negotiated the heavy peak hour traffic on the way home from the State Library. She and Olive were elated at their success, small though it was. They had been able to trace George Chambers on the electoral rolls through the years until 1972 when he no longer appeared. A staff member at the library had explained that a person's absence from the roll usually indicated the person had died. Disappointed, they looked in further years, but his name never reappeared. They did learn, however, George's wife's name—Dorothy Edna Chambers—and she consistently showed on the roll until the late 1980s when her name also failed to reappear.

In the Genealogy Section of the library, Louise looked up George's death on microfiche and found it confirmed in 1972. The indexes only reached as far as 1980 for deaths in Western Australia, so she couldn't look up Dorothy's death.

"How can you be sure she's dead, though?" Olive asked. "She just might have stopped voting, if she's not fit enough."

They then turned to the Perth telephone directory and found six D. Chambers listed.

"I'll have a go at ringing them when I get home," Louise said. "One of them just might be her. She probably wouldn't know anything about the case but, what the hell, I'll ring her anyway."

The second call that Louise tried that night was a D. Chambers at Riverton Retirement Village.

The voice that answered after eight rings was feeble. "Hello?"

"Hello, is that Mrs Chambers? Mrs Dorothy Chambers?"

"Yes. Who is this?"

"My name's Louise Fletcher. I'm ringing from Melbourne."

"Oh, dear. It's not about Victor, is it?"

"Who?"

"Victor Green. My nephew."

"I'm sorry...?"

"He's been so ill, you know," the old lady said slowly.

"I...I'm sorry to hear that."

"Yes, it's the chemotherapy. He's got no hair left, they told me."

"That's awful."

"And not only that, he feels so nauseous all the time. Day and night."

"You must be very worried." *How did I get into this conversation?*

"Yes. He's the only nephew I have left, you know." Dorothy's voice had picked up strength as she continued. "I only had the one sister. She's passed on now, God rest her soul, and there's just me...and Ivy, of course. What a wonderful daughter she's been. She comes at least twice a week to see me, even though she's got her own family and the business to run. And Jeff's busy with the agency. Do you know him?"

"No, I..."

"Oh, he's such a good husband to Ivy. Always has been. And such a wonderful father to those children. Well, they're not really children any more, are they? Colin's working, of course, and Rebecca's finishing school this year. But you'd know that anyway, wouldn't you?"

"No, I don't..."

"She was only here yesterday with a new pile of books for me, dear child. She loves reading. Just like her grandfather."

"Who?"

"Rebecca. Though I can't say I like everything she brings me, but I wouldn't tell her that. Some of those books have, you know, a lot of sex in them. It's a bit much, isn't it?"

"Yes..."

"I mean, there was none of that in *Gone With The Wind*, was there? Of course, you could read it into it, but it wasn't spelled out for you. A bit of mystery doesn't hurt anyone..."

"Mrs Chambers..."

"...but she means well. I try and read everything she brings me so that we can sit and talk about it. She talks nineteen to the dozen. Loves a good chat. Such a treasure, that child."

Take a breath! Please!

"Mrs Chambers, I'm ringing about your husband."

"George?"

"Yes."

"Oh, he's been gone a long time now. I remember the date so well because..."

"Mrs Chambers, I wonder if you remember the Schwartz kidnapping? It was the case about the twin who was stolen from Prince Alfred Hospital."

"Oh dear, yes. Such a tragic thing."

"Your husband was the detective assigned to the case, wasn't he?"

"Yes." The voice of the old woman hesitated. "He was never the same after that one." She paused for a moment. "Who is this calling again?"

"Louise Fletcher."

"Who?"

"I...I'm a sort of friend of Gunter Schwartz, the father of those twins."

"He's in Melbourne? You did say Melbourne?"

"Yes."

"Did he find the missing baby?"

"Not exactly. I think I have, though."

"Are you the police?"

"No. I'm just trying to help Mr Schwartz. I was hoping to speak with your husband, but he's..."

"Yes, you left it a bit late, dear."

"Yes."

Mrs Chambers heard the disappointment in Louise's voice. "Is there anything I can help you with?"

"I don't really know," Louise floundered. "I just wanted to start from the beginning—learn all the details about the case—so that I can piece together the information I have."

"Would George's old scrap book be of any use?"

"Scrap book?"

"Yes, he used to keep a scrap book for every case he had. He'd paste in clippings, reports, notes—anything at all that would sort out his thoughts. He often solved cases that way, being able to see the information in front of him. He was such a good policeman, you know. Such a good one."

"I'm sure he was, Mrs Chambers."

"I gave them all back to the police force after his heart attack, but not that one. The Schwartz one. It was a part of him. He took it personally that he never found that devil who took the baby. Never a trace, you know. Nothing."

"You still have the scrap book?"

"I've got it right here. When are you coming to look at it?"

"Oh..." Louise fumbled, not having thought that far ahead, "...I...I'm not sure." She looked at the calendar. "Would the day after tomorrow be okay?"

The next morning Louise arrived at the nursing home. She was glad to see that Marta was working that shift.

"Has anyone ever thought it might be locked-in syndrome that he's got?"

Marta looked at her in consternation. "What's that?"

Louise shook her head. "It's unbelievable how hardly anyone's heard of it. Not that I blame you for that," she hurried on to say, "but look at this," she held out a folder of information on locked-in syndrome, "and see what you think. I can leave it with you for a while."

"Thanks," Marta replied slowly, leafing through the pages.

"I know you're close to him. I thought you'd be the best person to show it to."

"Okay, I'll have a read of it."

"And this too," Louise said, handing Marta *The Diving Bell & The Butterfly*. "Have you read it?"

"No."

"You'll never be the same again once you finish it. And if I'm right about this, it might pull Mr Schwartz out of his prison."

"How did you…?"

"It's a long story. I'll tell you about it after you've read the stuff."

The two women regarded each other with liking, realising they were both on the same side.

"How is he?"

"Not good," Marta frowned. "He's slowly slipping away. His eye hardly opens at all now. I don't know if you're too late with all this," she said, holding up the information Louise had given her.

"Well, all I can do is try." Louise took the rolled-up photograph from a cardboard cover and opened it out. "I've got a present for him."

"What a beautiful picture! Who is it?"

"His daughter."

The fog was harder to swim out of. It dragged at his body. A dead weight. It filled his lungs, his stomach, his bladder, his bowel. His arteries and veins were clogged with it. And when he opened his eye, it clouded his vision.

"Mr Schwartz, it's Marta here."

Such a good girl. All these years…

"And your friend, Louise Fletcher, is back to see you again."

Louise Fletcher!

The sound of footsteps on the polished floor reached his bed.

Mein Gott…is she here?

He pushed the heavy fog from his eyelid and forced it open to a bare slit. A movement caught in his vision and he tracked it as Louise neared him. He felt her fingers slide into his palm and then she gently wrapped his fingers around her hand.

It's her!

"I have a present for you, Mr Schwartz." She waited anxiously for some reaction but his eye had closed again. "Something different for you to look at. It's your daughter—my friend, Joy. I've combined three of the best photos I have of her into one big picture."

His eye remained closed under the weight of the fog that quietly rolled across him.

"Can you please try? Please?" She was near to tears. "I'm trying so hard, Mr Schwartz, to find out everything I can to tell you. I want to find her—for both of us. But you mustn't give up. I know it's difficult for you. You must be tired. But you've waited this long. Surely a bit longer?"

Open. Open. Slowly, his eyelid opened again. His vision cleared to the sight of Ursula as he remembered her. She changed before him from a young child through to an adolescent, then back to the child. She appeared to be moving, talking, breathing. *Mein liebling!*

A thin stream of tears slowly trickled from his eye duct, washing the fog to the sides of his vision.

"You see?" Louise whispered to Marta, who was watching closely. "He's reacting to his daughter. It's not coincidence or reflex. I'm sure of it after what I've found out."

"I hope you're right."

Louise spoke up. "Marta is going to stick the picture up in front of you on the wall here, Mr Schwartz, so you can see it as often as you want. Would you like that?"

Yes. Yes.

"I have to go away for a few days. I'm going to Perth."

Perth?

"But I promise to come back and see you as soon as I return. I hope to have some more news for you then." She gently squeezed his hand. "I'll be very disappointed if I find you've given up when I come back. We're so close," she lied, "to discovering the truth. Hang in there. Please?"

I'll try.

The fog reclaimed him so quickly that he failed to feel Louise's fingers slip out of his palm.

She enjoyed the drive out to Riverton, travelling along the Kwinana Freeway, which ran alongside the Swan River for a stretch, then crossing the Canning River before exiting and turning left onto the Leach Highway. The village extended back to the Canning River from the highway. Thirty units lined the property's road, winding around a large pond feature and branched off in little culs-de-sac. Dorothy Chambers' unit was at the entrance to one of them that was bright with tiny front gardens crammed with flowers of every colour in the spectrum.

No sooner had she pressed a button set into the wall with the name Chambers printed underneath it, than a mauve-rinsed, well-rounded lady opened the door. Dorothy Chambers leaned heavily on a walking frame and, though it was apparent that moving around was difficult for her, a ready smile lit her face in welcome. Louise noticed that the old lady's lipstick matched a pink cardigan she wore over a pretty blue and white patterned dress. An antique gold brooch was pinned to the cardigan. Her white shoes had low one-inch heels, and were spotless. *She does look after herself. I'm impressed.*

"Mrs Chambers? I'm Louise Fletcher."

"Yes, dear. I've been waiting for you. Come in. Come in."

The old lady made slow progress through a small hallway and into a living area that looked over the river. The room was bright and tastefully decorated with Renaissance prints and antique furniture. Family photographs appeared on every available space on the walls, and flower-filled vases perched on a coffee table and bookcase.

"What a lovely home you have, Mrs Chambers."

"Yes, I have been lucky," Dorothy puffed heavily, as she sat in a large recliner. "I bought the first one in the village before they were even built."

"Ah, so that's why you have the best view."

Louise's gaze was caught by an over-stuffed children's scrapbook that rested on the coffee table. The name 'Schwartz' was written on the cover in large black letters. Also set out on the coffee table was a silver tray with matching coffee pot, milk jug and sugar bowl, as well as tiny flowered china cups and saucers and a plate of truffles and shortbread biscuits.

Dorothy asked Louise to pour out the coffee and then plunged into a long, yet quite breathless speech about the history of the retirement village, who lived there, what they were up to, and how many were close to death's door. Three cups of coffee later, and half the plate of sweets eaten, Dorothy paused for breath. Louise's head was spinning with the effort of keeping up with the leaping tangents the older woman's conversation took.

The temptation to reach out and touch the scrapbook was torture for Louise. She could feel her eyes glazing over as Dorothy lingered over her parent's courtship and marriage in England, how they migrated to Australia, how her father survived the First World War, despite his many and varied injuries, and her mother's eventual death from consumption.

Blissfully, the telephone rang. Before Dorothy picked it up, she said to Louise, "Why don't you have a look at George's scrapbook in the meantime?"

Louise grabbed up the book as soon as Dorothy began her phone conversation. The pages were covered in large, bold words put down heavily in dark blue ink or thick pencil. Newspaper cuttings, photographs, maps, diagrams, arrows, words crossed out, words rewritten, exclamation marks, and many question marks made up the pattern of George Chambers' investigation.

There were lists of names, areas, suspects, biographies. The hospital staff were listed individually—with at least a page for each person—and a detailed analysis of their backgrounds, personalities, prior convictions (if any, that the hospital might have missed), duties at the hospital, whereabouts at the time of the disappearance of the baby, were all recorded. Ticks and crosses accompanied each item, and some points were underlined in red ink. At the bottom of each page, the words GUT FEELING were written and mostly a 'Yes' or a 'No' followed.

The inner crease of some pages had captured a few strands of straight dark hair that had belonged to George, Louise surmised. She picked them out with her nails and rubbed them between the tips of her fingers. Somehow, they bridged the gap between the years and made her search more personal, as if those parts of him were there to guide her.

Dorothy had launched into a detailed story of her neighbour's latest catastrophe with the person with whom she was speaking. "...and his car blew up. Yes. Well, that's what he said. I didn't hear any explosion but..."

Louise opened her notebook and began to scribble down anything that she thought might be of use, but she realised it was going to take her too long if she went right through the book. She took a single-lens reflex camera out of a black camera bag that she'd brought with her, and clipped a 50mm lens onto it. *Could do with a copy stand and lights, but this'll have to do.* Next, she extended the legs of a folding tripod and screwed the camera onto it. The faint familiar whistle of the flash unit sounded as she turned it on.

The scrapbook was open at a double spread of small photographs of Gunter Schwartz, his wife, the surviving baby, as well as articles with hand-written annotations beside them. Louise positioned the tripod and camera over the pages and photographed them. She turned the page over and photographed a detailed biography of Gunter and Hannah. Here she learned the baby's name—Ursula— and that the name given to the stolen baby was Rachel. *So that's Joy's real name.* The images of Ursula were exactly the same as those which Louise remembered of Joy's baby photos, even though it was such a long time since she'd seen them. But there was no doubt in her mind that Joy was the missing twin.

As Dorothy continued with her telephone conversation, looking in Louise's direction from time to time when the unit flashed, Louise steadily ran through the pages that interested her. She worked quickly and competently, hoping that she would get through the pages before Dorothy finished talking. One film was quickly filled, and she deftly replaced it and resumed capturing the history of the Schwartz kidnapping case.

"…so I really must get back to my visitor…"

Five more minutes!

"…she'll think me terribly rude…"

No! No!

"…but it's so nice to hear from you, dear. And when are you…?"

Yes…chat a bit longer.

Dorothy sidetracked herself again and turned back to the telephone table for a few more minutes. Louise worked at a frantic pace. The flash batteries were running low. She flipped new ones into the flash unit. *Three more pages to go.*

"…and you'll call in next week? All right, dear. I'll look forward to that. Bye bye for now."

The flash exploded on the last page as Dorothy put the receiver down.

"So sorry about that, Louise. I haven't heard from my cousin, Edith, for so long. I didn't like to put her off."

"Oh, that's fine, Mrs Chambers," Louise assured her, exhausted now. "I had plenty to keep me occupied."

"Did you get what you need?"

"I think so. I'm terribly grateful to you."

"I hope it helps your investigations. Where did you say you were from again? The Melbourne Police?"

"No. I'm a friend of Mr Schwartz."

"Oh, yes. That poor man. You know, when that little mite was taken from the hospital..."

Four hours later, Louise let herself into her hotel room and switched on a lamp to examine the prints. Her thoughts whirled around excitedly. *Will there be anything in the scrapbook that'll help? What if there's not? What'll I do then? This trip may have been a wild goose chase.*

Using a magnifying glass she examined and read every item she had photographed. Not really knowing what she was looking for, it was an arduous task, although she was genuinely interested in the case and in learning about Gunter's background. Not for the first time, pity for him swept through her, now more so as she discovered so much tragedy in his life. *How has he survived all this?*

The minutes and hours passed by without her being aware of how late it had become. Her admiration for George Chambers grew as she deciphered his notes and scribblings, his meticulous attention to any minute piece of information, and his understanding and summing up of people's characters as he interviewed them. Those people came alive in her mind. She could almost hear them speak.

As she finished looking at the last print, she sat back and gazed over the treetops in the park opposite her window. The night sky was alive with stars that danced across its velvet blackness. *Are you out there, or are you closer than that? Hell, I'd give anything to know if you're dead or alive. Have I imagined this whole thing?* Then she remembered the inscription:

> You see? I think of you all the time! I hate all this—missing our party today—not giving you the brooch. When I give you this book, I'll tell you everything. Cross my heart and spit.

No—you have to be alive!

Louise stared at the stars through her window as she lay in bed in the darkened room. Her eyes were tired and she had a slight headache. *Nothing.* After going through the prints again, selecting some and discarding others, she had nothing to go on. Except...

She sat up in bed. A name kept on popping up in her mind. Winnie Edwards. The nurse who'd been on duty when the baby disappeared. There were copious notes about her. She'd been the person most under suspicion to begin with until George, in his wisdom, had decided she was not the culprit. The details of her reactions to the questioning; the attitudes of the staff toward her; his discovery of her affair with Anthony Oxford—and the subsequent birth of her illegitimate child at Geraldton Hospital, which George did not mention that he knew of to Winnie; all pointed to her guilt. He knew she had lied in Geraldton about being married, that she had given her baby up for adoption, that she probably ached for it every time she worked with someone else's baby, and yet George recorded his gut feeling that she was not the one who had kidnapped the baby.

Could George have been wrong? Could his gut feeling have betrayed him in this case? There was a forwarding address in Queensland. Winnie was to work for her cousin in an outback town near Longreach. *Perhaps I should try to follow that up,* Louise thought, wondering whether the nursing sister was still alive. And whether she could tell Louise anything, if she was alive, was doubtful. *If she had anything to do with it, would she tell me anyway? Or is Winnie Edwards, the nurse, really Ruth Bacon?*

Chapter 66 Melbourne

Louise took the early morning flight back to Melbourne from Perth. A sense of urgency pushed her to return home to see Gunter. *What if he dies in the meantime?* She called in at Olive's house, on the way back from Tullamarine Airport, where she spread the prints out on the kitchen table into sorted groups. Olive took them up one by one and examined them carefully.

"So, what do you think?" Louise looked at her mother expectantly.

"Umm…I see why you couldn't tell me much on the phone. There's a lot in these." She put the prints down. "Do you want to leave them with me and I'll have a good look at them after you've gone?"

Louise hesitated, searching her mother's face. At sixty-three, Olive still looked like a woman in her early fifties. The profuse dark hair had very few grey strands. Fine lines spread out from the corners of her eyes—a result of a lifetime's sense of humour, despite her disastrous marriage—and her neck had lost some of its elasticity. *Still, for her age, she looks terrific. She must get tired though.*

"Would you?"

"Of course I would. You know that."

Louise drove home and unpacked her few items of luggage before connecting to the Internet. She looked in the White Pages for a W. Edwards in Longreach, Queensland. *None. What if she's a Mary Winifred, or a Gertrude Winifred, or a Doreen Winifred? Or what if she's dead?* Her hand hovered over the telephone buttons, and then she pushed the numbers for M.W. Edwards. Her heart was racing.

"Hello?"

"Yes, I'm looking for a Winnie Edwards. Am I on the right number?"

"Sorry. No one here by that name, love. Are you sure you've got the right Edwards?" The male voice was layered with a strong outback accent.

"No, I'm not. The lady I'm looking for would be a bit past middle age, I think. She was a nursing sister. But she's possibly not even alive…"

"Yeah, you're probably after old Matron Edwards. She used to run the hospital here."

"Oh?"

"Hang on a sec, love. I'll ask the boss."

Louise heard the man put down the receiver and call out to someone. "Hey, Marion, you know if old Matron Edwards is still in the land of the living?" He paused as a muffled voice answered him. "Yeah? Oh, yeah?" The receiver was picked up again. "You there, love?"

"Yes, I'm here," Louise replied.

"Yeah, old Matron Edwards. She's still kicking on."

"Really?" Louise found it hard to contain her excitement.

"She's not the full two bob, though. You know what I mean?"

"Ah..."

"Round the twist."

"Oh."

"You a relative?"

"No. I'm...a friend of a friend. I wanted to look her up."

"Well, she's at the Pioneers Hostel on Sparrow Street. It's a nursing home now for the old folk."

"Right," she said slowly. "You wouldn't know if she could have visitors or not?"

"Don't see why not, love. But she's as nutty as a fruitcake. You wouldn't get much sense out of her."

"That's okay." She hesitated. "You wouldn't happen to know if she's got any family up in Longreach, would you?"

"Not that I know of. I don't think she ever married."

She hung up and leaned back in her chair, fingers tapping her forehead. *So, she's as nutty as a fruitcake, eh? That figures. She was when I last saw her too, but her name wasn't Winnie then.*

She made herself a Campari and soda, then picked up the receiver again.

"Mum?"

"Louie. I was just about to ring you. It must be mental telepathy."

"So, what'd you think about the prints?"

"Interesting stuff."

"I know what you mean."

"But nothing much to go on."

"You're right about that."

"But I have a gut feeling."

"One of George Chambers'?" Louise prompted.

"No, actually. I don't know if I agree with him entirely."

"Go on. I think I know what you're going to say."

"Winnie Edwards?" Olive replied excitedly. "Is that it?"

"Yes. What're you thinking?"

"She's about all we've got. There's something funny about it. I mean, I don't understand why our detective discounted her. She was a perfect candidate after giving birth to that child and giving it up for adoption. It might have been harder for her than she'd imagined. I don't know what I'd have done if I'd had to give you up...probably gone out and stole the first baby I saw!"

"There you are." Louise was triumphant. "We're on the exact same wavelength, Mum."

"So, did you ring Longreach?"

Louise laughed, choking on her drink. "You're miles ahead of me."

"Well?"

"Yes, I rang Longreach, and I spoke to a fellow there who told me that a Matron Edwards is still alive and living in a nursing home there."

"Really?"

"Yes, but she's around the twist."

"Insane?"

"Something like that."

There was a silence between the two.

"Funny, isn't it?" Louise said, breaking the silence. "We knew someone else who was around the twist."

"Ruth..." Olive breathed.

"Got it in one!"

Louise had just got into bed when something else occurred to her. *What if Matron Edwards is Ruth Bacon? What about Les Bacon...and Joy? They'd have to be there too, wouldn't they?*

She reconnected to the Internet. After a few minutes, the White Pages came up with nine Bacons, but none were in Longreach itself. They were as far as Yeppoon and Rockhampton. *Where the hell's Yeppoon anyway?* Rockhampton, she knew, was a large town some six hundred-odd kilometres east of Longreach. Her atlas showed her that Yeppoon was on the coast, thirty-six kilometres from Rockhampton. *Could they have gone there?* She looked at the map thoughtfully. *No...there aren't any L. Bacons or Rs or Js.*

What about Bakers? She typed in the word and waited for the page to come up. Six Bakers. No Ls or Rs but what about the J.T.? Could that be Joy? What would the T. stand for? I don't think she had a second name. Louise looked at the clock. It was 11.49 p.m.

Bugger...too late to ring. Her hands were shaking as she turned off the lamp.

Louise woke late to a bright cloudless sky. The beach was already jam-packed with Sunday swimmers. She had slept well and woke with an appetite, which was a welcome change. As well as her usual grapefruit juice and avocado on toast, she tucked into scrambled eggs.

Come on; don't put it off any longer. She was afraid to ring the J.T. Baker for two reasons—if it wasn't Joy, then she'd be disappointed, and if it was, what would she say? *Hi there, it's your long-lost friend, Louise here, otherwise known as Sweet Pea to you. Where've you been the rest of my life?* Sudden anger and resentment mixed with hope and fear.

Do it. She pushed the numbers.

"Hello?"

The voice was female. Young. Too young.

"Ah, am I speaking with Joy Baker?"

"Who?"

"Oh, I'm sorry. I must have the wrong number. I was after Joy Baker."

"No, I'm Jenny Baker."

"Sorry to have troubled you."

The click at the other end was audible as Louise slowly replaced the receiver. Her heart gradually returned to its normal pace. *A stiff drink'd be good.* Her watch reminded her she had no time to waste, so she gathered her things together instead and drove to her mother's house.

"Are you sure you're up to this?" she asked Olive when they buckled up their seat belts in Louise's car.

Olive nodded. "I really want to meet him. I feel I know so much about him now. And it's the only way we can do it with you going up to Longreach."

A young nurse showed them into Gunter's room. The sun streamed through the window, falling just short of the print of Joy's three faces that hung on the wall. Olive noticed that it was the only decoration in the whole room. A shelf ran a wall's length and she thought of the things that sat on the shelves in the other rooms they had passed: cards, flowers in vases, ornaments, photos in frames, even balloons. *What a sad room this is,* she thought.

"He's been turned a half-hour ago," the nurse said, "so we won't disturb you for another hour. If you need me, just ring the bell."

"Thank you," Louise said as she neared the bed.

"He looks worse," she whispered to Olive, fear gripping her heart.

She moved around to his right side, motioning her mother to follow. Her fingers slipped into his palm and she carefully closed his hand over hers as she'd done the other times.

"Mr Schwartz? It's Louise Fletcher here again. Can you hear me?"

There was no response from his eye.

"I've brought someone else to visit you...my mum. Her name's Olive."

She leaned over and stroked his forehead very softly. His veins stood out darkly under the fragile skin tightly drawn across the bone of his skull. The closed eyes were sunken into dark sockets and they moved slightly, back and forth, back and forth, in some reflex motion of dreams.

"Mr Schwartz? Can you try to wake up? I need to speak with you."

The eye movements became erratic.

"You want me to find your Rachel, don't you?"

He had been hovering around the mouth of the slowly swirling tunnel, trying to decide if now was the time to enter it. He knew that once he did he would never return. The sides of the tunnel were like black cotton wool, soft and inviting, and the urge to let go, to become a part of the tunnel, was stronger each time he had visited it. To enter it imparted no fear—only a feeling of finality.

Rachel? Did someone say Rachel?

"...and I know she was Ursula's sister." Louise waited some moments. "You know that I'm trying to find her," she repeated. "Your Rachel—my Joy."

He felt himself tugged away from the tunnel, back to his room and the throaty voice that was now familiar to him. Light entered as he prised his top eyelid away from the bottom one. A blurred bright red image was in front of him. He blinked to clear his vision and saw the top half of Louise as she sat in front of him. She was wearing a red silk, short-sleeved blouse, with a small oval brooch pinned to the left breast. As she bent closer to him, he read the word *Louise* engraved upon it, and he noticed a spray of multi-coloured flowers curved around the left edge of the brooch.

Louise!

"Hello there," she smiled at him, flicking her hair back over her shoulder. "You're awake."

You came back.

"I've been to Perth and I've brought my mum along with me."

Your mother?

"Go on Mum," she said softly, pushing Olive into his view.

He saw an attractive older version of Louise with thick, dark hair pulled back off her face with tortoiseshell combs. Her hazel eyes regarded him affably.

"Hello, Mr Schwartz," she said in a deep, warm voice. "I've heard so much about you from Louie...Louise. She's very fond of you."

Fond of me? Why?

Louise came back into view, alongside her mother.

"I know so much about you now. I hope you don't mind. I've been reading George Chambers' scrapbook about the case—when your daughter was kidnapped. His widow showed it to me."

The detective? Widow?

Olive held up a few black and white prints in front of him. "Louise photographed most of the pages so that we could try to find something, anything, that would give us a clue."

"And the only thing we've come up with," Louise chipped in, "is the name Winnie Edwards."

The nurse.

"Do you remember anything about her?"

He tried to blink.

The two women regarded him for some moments, and then Louise went on.

"Well, anyway, I've brought this to see if we can get some sort of communication going with you."

She held up an alphabet board in front of her chest. He stared at it.

"I'm going to point to some letters and I want you to blink, if you can, if I point at the right letter. For example, let's start with your name."

She pointed at the G, and waited for what seemed like an hour before there was the slightest flicker.

"Was that a blink?"

Mein Gott, yes. I'm trying. It's so hard!

She pointed to the U.

He willed his eyelid to move, but it began sliding back to a closed position and he couldn't open it again.

So tired. Open! He pushed at it with his fists, his stomach, his heart, but it wouldn't open again. Every effort made him more exhausted, and it was a struggle to stay conscious. A tear leaked out from between his lids.

"Never mind," Louise said, trying to keep the disappointment out of her voice. "We'll try again another time."

He heard the rustling of clothing as Louise got up from her chair.

"I'm having to go away again...to Longreach. That's up in Queensland. I have a lead or two up that way and I have to go there to find out for myself."

If only I could open this eye.

"If it's all right with you, Mr Schwartz," Olive said, "I would like to visit you every day while Louise is away. Perhaps we could try with the alphabet again, when you're less tired. Or I could read to you. Something like that."

"So, what do you think?" Louise asked.

There! I see you again.

"You're back!"

Yes, just a little.

"You'll like Mum." Louise hugged Olive. "She's a likeable person. Really nice."

"Stop it," Olive coloured, despite herself.

"And she's helping us find your Rachel."

How did you...?

Louise held up one of the prints. "I found her name here, in this article from a newspaper. It says you named her Rachel, after your wife's mother. And I know Ursula's name now too."

She took his hand, stroking the back of it softly.

"You look after yourself while I'm away, eh?" She found herself struggling with tears again. *Why do I feel like this every time I say goodbye to him?* "No giving up on me now. You hang in there. Mum'll help you."

Dear girl.

"I'll be gone a couple of days, I think, at the most."

With a supreme effort, he held his eyelid open just long enough to see mother and daughter disappear through the doorway of his room, then the light shut off as he retreated from the conscious world.

The mouth of the tunnel swirled below him. He was pulled towards it and he began to revolve around the edges in the same slow movement. It would be a relief to relinquish his last feeble hold on his shell—the barely-alive framework that still breathed, pulsed, voided. But Louise wanted him to stay. No, he couldn't let go yet. Reluctantly, he pulled himself away from the tunnel and drifted to the world in between where sound and light still intruded. Just a little longer...

Chapter 67   Longreach

The connection time between flights was only long enough for Louise to ring Claire briefly for messages, and then she boarded a Flight West aircraft in Brisbane for Longreach. The two-hour flight dragged as she looked down at the soft-hued browns and greens that are the essence of the outback. Try as she might, she failed to concentrate on reading over the edited proofs she'd brought with her with so much hinging on this visit to Longreach. *What if I've come up on a wild goose chase?* As the aircraft descended towards the earth, it passed over the Australian Stockman's Hall of Fame, the white curved roofs in stark contrast with their brown surrounds. Within minutes, the plane touched down at Longreach Airport.

A taxi took her to the Starlight Motel in Wonga Street, which was close to the township, the railway station, the hospital and the airport. It was also close to the Pioneers Hostel—Louise could see on her map that she could walk to it easily. In fact, it appeared that one could walk around most of the township without having to use a car. She realised she would feel the heat, walking around Longreach on a thirty-six degree day, but consoled herself with the fact that the motel had a pool.

Putting together some of the photographs of the scrapbook pages, and some of the best she had of Joy at various stages of her short life, Louise shoved them into her carry bag, and stepped out into the afternoon heat. She crossed the railway line and walked along Jabiru Street, passing the hospital, and turned left into Tern, crossed Cassowary and entered Sparrow Street.

She hesitated in front of the single-storied red brick building. *Here goes.* A staff member came across her inside the entrance.

"Excuse me," Louise said, "I'm wanting to visit Winnie Edwards."

"Winnie?"

"Yes please."

"How nice! She doesn't get many visitors these days," the nurse smiled warmly. "Are you a relative?"

"No. A friend of a friend."

"But you know what to expect, do you?"

"What do you mean?"

"She's a dementia patient."

At Louise's blank look, she continued, "They forget things like names, conversations, recent events."

"What about past events?"

"Oh, their long-term memory is amazing. They go right back, they do."

"I see..."

"But she's a lovely old thing."

Louise felt shattered. She'd been expecting someone a little irrational, but the memory loss was something she hadn't thought of.

"I think she's out in the garden, sitting in the shade," the nurse said, steering Louise along a corridor that led out to an enclosed area. "Yes, there she is."

They walked outside to where Winnie sat in a wheel chair, twirling a plucked flower between her thumb and forefinger.

"Winnie, dear, you have a visitor."

Bright blue eyes looked up at Louise. The expression in them was without curiosity. It was almost as if she'd been expecting her. An automatic smile, that was decorated with a thick wobbly line of red lipstick, pulled the corners of the mouth up to where lines creased the old face. Her now-thin hair was a faded chestnut at the ends, and the roots showed white on a pink scalp.

It's not her!

Louise pulled a nearby chair over to where Winnie sat. She felt stunned—even affronted—that the old woman was not Ruth Bacon. She'd been so sure and now had to rethink her approach.

"I'll leave you to it then," the nurse said, and disappeared back inside the building.

"Hello, Matron Edwards."

"You can call me Winnie," the old lady whispered, leaning close to Louise conspiratorially. "Did you see them?"

"Who?"

"The others."

"Ah..."

"So they let you through, did they?"

"Ah, yes."

The blue eyes looked at Louise keenly through thick lenses. "I'm worn out too."

"Are you?"

"Been at it all day."

"At what?"

"You know...making beds, checking IVs, prepping patients." Winnie looked around her and drew Louise closer by pulling at her arm. "They took a lot in today."

"Did they?"

She nodded. "The place is full. We're having to send some over to Fremantle."

"I see..." Louise nodded sagely. "So what's the name of this hospital?"

"It's the...you know...the..." Winnie drifted off, and began twirling the flower again.

"Prince Alfred?"

"Yes! Yes!"

Louise looked at her carefully. "Isn't that where that baby disappeared?"

Winnie looked at her sideways, then slid her eyes downward to look at the flower. She mumbled something unintelligible.

"Pardon?" Louise asked, trying to establish eye contact again.

"...blame me." Winnie shook her head. "It wasn't though. Nothing to do with me. Told them that. He believed me."

"Who?"

"That nice detective."

"George Chambers?"

"Yes. That's the one." She rolled the name on her tongue. "George Chambers. He was a real man." She looked at Louise. "Do you know him?"

"No. I'm sorry..."

"Too late. He's married anyway."

"So I believe."

Louise opened her bag. "I've got some photos to show you."

"Good, I like photos. Is it that nice detective?"

"No. It's a little girl."

"Me?"

"No," Louise smiled. "It's a friend of mine."

"What's her name?"

"Joy...or Rachel."

"Don't you know her name?" Winnie asked, suddenly wary.

"Well, yes. It's just that she had two names."

"I've got two—Winnie and Edwards."

"So have I. Mine are Louise and Fletcher."

"Louise? I've heard that before."

"Well, I guess I'm not the only Louise in the world."

Louise held out the small pile of photographs, and Winnie took them from her.

"What a pretty child," she exclaimed, pointing at Joy blowing out the candles on a cake. "Five candles. And that's you there beside her. You haven't changed at all."

"You think so?"

Winnie nodded as she put that photograph down and picked up the one that was used in the newspapers when Joy disappeared.

"Oh, there's Carol!"

Louise looked at her startled.

"Carol?"

"Yes, my little friend Carol. Her hair's longer here, though. My, wasn't it a fright when she came here. But we fixed it up after a few weeks. She liked my colour hair, she said." The old lady patted her own hair. She was in her forties again, and sat up stiffly, pushing her chest out. "Has it grown back?"

"Has what grown back?"

"Her hair, silly," Winnie snorted.

"Ah...yes."

"You played the violin for her."

"Violin?" Louise asked, confused.

"Yes. Your father plays too."

"...not really."

"You don't look a bit like her, though."

"Should I?"

"That's what she said."

"That I look like her?"

"Like twins." Winnie looked at Louise sideways. "Your hair's not red."

"No. This is my natural colour."

Winnie leaned close to Louise's ear. "Mine's a mousy brown," she whispered. "Don't tell them, though."

"No, I won't," Louise whispered back, looking over her shoulder involuntarily.

Footsteps approached them.

"Can I get you ladies a cold drink, or a cup of tea or coffee?"

Winnie held up her hand. "Tea please."

"Okay, same as usual," the woman said. "And what about your guest?"

"A glass of cold water would be lovely, thanks."

"You're not too hot out here, Winnie love?"

"No. No. No," Winnie chanted.

When the drinks arrived, Louise returned to the subject of the mysterious Carol.

"So, when did you last see Carol?"

"Who's Carol?"

"You know—your friend with the red hair," Louise said, putting the photograph of Joy back onto the old lady's lap.

"No. Don't know Carol."

And no matter how Louise tried to steer the conversation around to Carol, Winnie would not, or could not, find her in her memory bank.

Bugger it. The connection's dropped out.

Winnie's eyes were drooping; the flower fell out of her right hand as she lapsed into a doze. Her breathing became heavy as her head lurched towards her chest.

Louise sat looking at her, wondering whether she should stay or go. She felt frustrated and impatient to talk to the old lady after apparently having recognised the photograph of Joy. *But...Carol? And a violin? What was she on about?* Louise frowned. *How would she know Joy? Did they come up here to Longreach? But...why? They were in New Zealand, weren't they? And she said I didn't look like Carol. Why was I supposed to? And like twins?*

She began to pace the garden, perspiration soaking the back of her dress and armpits. Looking at the sleeping woman from time to time, she gritted her teeth in irritation. *If that bloody woman hadn't come with the drinks, I might have got more out of Winnie.* After half an hour, the nurse who had brought Louise to the garden joined her.

"Aren't you boiling out here?"

"Yes," Louise agreed. "But I was waiting for Winnie to wake up."

"Oh, she'll be out to it for a while. She sleeps a lot these days."

"Doesn't she feel the heat?"

"No, she loves it. But I'm taking her inside so she doesn't get burnt." The nurse pushed Winnie along the path that led to the building. "How was the conversation?"

Louise laughed. "Confusing."

"Yes. Some days she makes absolute sense, and others she's away with the fairies. It's working out the difference between what's reality and what's fantasy is the hard thing."

"I know what you mean."

They entered the building and walked down a passageway with four-bed wards leading off it.

"Here we are," the nurse said, turning into one of the rooms. "This is where Winnie lives."

She pushed the wheelchair to a position beside a window and put a call button onto Winnie's lap.

"She'll ring us when she wakes up."

"How long do you think that'd be?"

"Right on dinner time," the nurse grinned. "I reckon her nose tells her. She's pretty good on the tooth still."

"Is she alert after dinner?" Louise asked. "I mean, can I come back and see her again then?"

"Sure."

The water in the motel's pool was invigorating. Louise dived in cleanly, swimming almost the full length underwater before breaking the surface. She sighed with relief, revelling in the coolness of the water after the heat of the day. She had the pool to herself and made the most of it.

She decided to eat in her room while she sorted out her thoughts by jotting down points from the conversation with Winnie in her notebook.

- CAROL? (Joy/Rachel?)

- Her hair was a fright. Has it grown back?

- Me and my father play the <u>VIOLIN</u>?????

- She (Carol?) said I look like her?

- Like TWINS?

- My hair's not red.

- If Carol/Joy here, Les & Ruth must have left NZ

The violin? Of course! Gunter Schwartz plays the violin. Did she know him? Why did she expect me to look like Joy? She knew I wasn't, but Carol had told her I should. Why would Joy/Rachel/Carol be in Longreach and visiting the very person who had some stake in the kidnapping case? Winnie's older than I expected. Could she be Joy's grandmother and Ruth Bacon her daughter?

She walked back to the nursing home and found Winnie in a lounge area with half a dozen other people looking at the television.

"You can talk to her here, or take her for a walk in her wheel chair, if you like," one of the nurses said. "She likes moving about."

"All right," Louise said. "Hello, Winnie. Would you like to go for a walk?"

"Who is she?" Winnie whispered to the nurse.

"Your visitor from this afternoon," the nurse replied. "Louise."

"No," Winnie shook her head. "Don't know any Louise."

"That's okay, Winnie love. She'll take you for a walk anyway."

Louise manoeuvred the wheelchair between the other patients and wheeled it out to the garden where the heat was less intense than it had been earlier.

"You were telling me about Carol," Louise prompted her.

"Such a sad child, except when she was talking about books. She said you read books too."

"She said I did? Yes, I do. I love books."

"I leant her mine. She read dozens of them in the month she was here."

"She was here for a month," Louise repeated slowly. "Did she stay with you?"

"Gracious me, no. She stayed with her uncle and aunt."

"And who were they, Winnie?" Louise's heart was beating so rapidly; it felt like it would burst out of her chest.

"The Bakers. Harry and June. A rough lot, that. She didn't belong with them. She was miserable waiting for her mother to get over the shock treatment."

"You know about that?"

"Yes," the old lady nodded. "She wasn't well, poor thing. Must've been pretty bad. She survived the trip though."

Louise was breathless. "What trip was that?"

"When they left here…"

"They came here?" *From New Zealand?*

"Oh, yes dear. The poor girl couldn't make that long trip on her own, could she?"

"Did they live here too?"

"No. They just collected her. No one even saw them. They came and went just like that," she said, trying to snap her fingers but not succeeding. Her hand returned heavily to her lap, as if it were tired.

"What about the Bakers…Harry and June, you said?"

"Umm…?"

"Do they still live here?"

"Well, of course. Carol only left yesterday. Of course they live here. People don't shift in a day, you know. I'd have known. Young

Pammy's due in for her ears to be unblocked again." She fumbled around for something in her pocket. "I've got a note of it here somewhere. Where's my appointment book?"

"You must have left it on your desk," Louise guessed.

"Yes. Yes. That kiddie always has problems with her ears. I don't know how many times I've washed wax out of them. Probably doesn't clean them. It looks like half the outback's in them."

"Winnie, you said that Carol thought I looked like her...like a twin."

"No. That other girl."

"And who was that?"

"Who was what?" Winnie yawned.

"The other girl."

"What other girl?"

"The one you said looked like me."

"You don't look like anyone I know."

Winnie, come back!

"Who played the violin?" Louise tried, hoping to get there another way.

"Violin?" Winnie looked vague.

"Yes, you said I play the violin and so does my father."

"Who are you?"

"Louise."

The wait for Winnie's reply was interminable. "You live next door, don't you?"

"Yes."

"You were having a party. Such pretty frocks, too. Carol drew them for me. You both had one."

She was buried in hers.

"And the violin?"

"Her father plays it at the Town Hall. She's going to see him play."

"How does Carol know that?"

"The girl told her."

"The girl who looks like Carol?"

"Yes, her twin."

Calm down! Calm down!

"She met a girl who looked like her twin?"

Winnie yawned again and moved restlessly in her wheelchair. She picked at her dress, rolling the fabric between her thumb and forefinger.

"Winnie?"

The old lady looked up at Louise.

"Do you know where Carol is now?"

Winnie leaned forward to touch Louise's skirt.

"Nice colour. I always like bright colours. I'm going to have a new dress made for my birthday. You can come if you like."

"Well, thank you, Winnie. I'd like that. Can Carol come too?"

A smile broke over the old lady's face. "Yes. Can you bring her?"

"I'd love to. Do you know where I can find her?"

"Yes." Winnie nodded seriously. "I've got her address."

"You do?"

"It's on her letters."

"You've got letters from her?" Louise had trouble controlling herself. Her impulse was to jump up and down and scream with delight, but she was afraid she would break Winnie's train of thought.

"Yes. You could bring that girl Louise too. She's Carol's best friend."

Chapter 68

It took all of Louise's willpower to remain calm.

"Can we go and look up that address, Winnie?"

"What time are we leaving?" The old lady peered at her watch, which flipped around the loose skin on her thin arm.

"Leaving?"

"We mustn't be late. They're always cross if you are."

"Late," Louise said slowly, trying to stay with the roller coaster ride inside Winnie's mind. *Where's she gone now?*

"We're late, we're late, for a very important date." Winnie sang in a high, thin voice. She had a mischievous grin on her face.

"No, we mustn't be late," Louise agreed. "Let's go right now." She turned the wheelchair around and pushed it towards Winnie's room. "Are you ready for our date?"

"How's my lipstick?" Winnie leaned back in the chair so that Louise could see her mouth.

"Perfect."

"And my hair?"

Louise patted it down at the back. "Lovely."

"Oh, good. We have to make a grand entrance."

"Yes, of course."

They entered the ward where two of the other patients were already in bed. They watched as Louise pushed Winnie to the side of her bed. There was a bedside table and a single wardrobe beside it.

"Is this where you keep your letters, Winnie?"

"What letters?" Winnie suddenly looked suspicious.

"The ones that Carol sent you," Louise said gently. "Remember?"

Winnie glared at her. "How do you know about them?"

"Ah...she told me she sent you some. She asked me to tell you to show them to me so I can tell her you've still got them and they're safe."

Winnie smiled smugly. "Oh, yes. I've got them."

"You have?"

"They're very safe," the old lady whispered. "No one knows their secret hiding place, except me."

"Well, that's good. I can tell J...ah...Carol that. She'll be so pleased."

"You'll tell her?"

"Would you like me to?"

"Yes," Winnie nodded.

Louise crouched down beside Winnie and whispered, "So if you show them to me now, I can tell her they're safe. Okay?"

Winnie looked at Louise for a long moment. The blue eyes seemed to bore into Louise and she felt embarrassed at having to play the childish game, but she held her gaze afraid to break the subject of the moment. *If Winnie loses the plot again, how'll I get to those letters?*

"They're inside the shoe box," Winnie whispered. "The navy blue high heels."

"All right. I'll get the box out."

Louise opened the wardrobe to see a neat stack of shoeboxes arranged along the base of it. She opened the lid of one of them: white low heels. The box underneath: brown court shoes. The next: burgundy one-inch heels. The next on the right: black two-inch. The one underneath: cream flats. The next: navy blue high heels. She took the box out and laid it on Winnie's lap.

The old hands trembled as they took the shoes out of the box. "Very comfy shoes," she commented. Tissue paper lined the box and Winnie lifted it up to reveal two letters lying flat on the bottom.

Only two?

Louise recognised the handwriting. She resisted the urge to snatch them up and rip them open.

Winnie took them out and hugged them to her. "I'm waiting for the next one."

The postmark was legible on one of the envelopes. It was dated 15 July 1968. *Now I know for sure—she didn't die!*

"She owes you one?" Louise asked.

"Yes. I got this one last week." She held one up for Louise to see.

"Oh, okay. Well, let's make sure you've got the right address."

"I do. I do."

"She told me she might be moving, so can we compare the address on the letter to the one I have?"

Winnie handed the envelope to Louise. As Louise took it, her heart pounded heavily inside her chest; it roared in her ears. Turning it over, she saw written in Joy's handwriting: *C. Paton, Primrose Street, Townsville, Qld.* She fumbled with the folded blue-lined pages inside the envelope. Tears filled her eyes as she began to read:

12th July 1968

Dear Matron Edwards,

I know I promised to write as soon as we got back home but we had such a long trip IN THE COM-PLETE OPPOSITE DIRECTION !!! and only got here (Townsville) a couple of days ago. I am so sick of all this, and I really HATE my parents now. I wish I could tell you why, but I've been sworn to secrecy. Aside from Louise, who I'll probably NEVER see again, you're my only REAL FRIEND. I hated Longreach, but now I feel so lonely with no one to talk to, except my parents, and who would want to talk to them? Not that I can blame Mum all that much. She's really spaz now. But Dad is the PITS. I'll never forgive him for...

Suddenly the pages were ripped out of Louise's hand.

"That's enough. That's enough. It's mine. Not yours."

Louise blinked in surprise, being dragged back from her friend's torment so long ago to the reality of the old demented lady who clutched at the letters.

"I'm sorry. I didn't mean to..."

"Well is it?"

"Is it?" Louise was puzzled.

"The address," Winnie hissed at her. "You were only supposed to read the address. She wouldn't like it."

"No. Of course..."

"Are you going to tell on her?" Winnie demanded, almost shouting.

"No. I wouldn't do that. Not..."

"Don't you tell on her."

"Please, Winnie," Louise said quietly, putting her hand out to touch the old woman's arm.

Winnie shrank back from her.

"Don't you touch me. They sent you, didn't they?" Her voice was shrill and full of hatred.

"Winnie dear, are you losing your temper again?"

"She's going to tell on me," Winnie whined.

Quick footsteps entered the room and Louise turned to see a nurse behind them.

"Is she now?" the nurse said turning to wink at Louise. "And why would she do that?"

"She's finding out secrets."

"Oh, we've all got secrets," the nurse jollied her along, "I've got some too. If you're a good girl, then I'll tell you mine in the morning. How about that?"

"Would you?" Winnie smiled at her. "Big ones?"

"Great big whoppers."

The two women in the other beds had woken—one was crying quietly in her bed, and the other was making attempts to get out of hers.

"Come on Mary Kathleen," the nurse said, guiding her back into her bed, "it's way past your bedtime."

"I'm so sorry for upsetting them..." Louise said softly.

"Don't worry. Winnie gets a bit aggressive when she's tired. She'll be right as rain in the morning. And she won't even remember you've been here."

Louise walked back to the motel wearily. *Primrose Street. Primrose Street*, she kept on reminding herself. *Paton? Paton?* She halted momentarily as she suddenly realised what she'd seen on the envelope. *It said C. Paton. Not Bacon. They changed their name again?* Tears poured unheeded down her face as she walked, thinking of what she had read from the first page of the letter. *If only I'd been able to read the rest.* Her heart went out to her lost and lonely friend who had expected never to see her again. *Why?* Joy had sounded so full of resentment. *If only I'd known she was in Townsville. We could have written, at least.*

By the time Louise reached her motel room, gut-wrenching sobs erupted from her contorted mouth. She cried for the loss of her friend again. This time it hurt even more knowing that Joy had still been alive thirty years ago—perhaps still was—and had not contacted her once. *Had our friendship meant so little?* Or was there something else that held Joy back? Something that being 'sworn to secrecy' bound her for the rest of her life? Louise thought of the countless times she had cried over Joy's death, how she had talked to her in her mind nearly every night before going to sleep, how she had visited the gravesite every birthday and anniversary of Joy's death. What about the grief she had suffered, never able to let go of Joy's memory, almost to the point of obsession? Why did Joy put her through all that? Was it simply 'out of sight out of mind'? *No, I won't believe that.*

Louise deliberately closed the curtains of her room before going to bed. She didn't wish to look out on the stars, or to have a conversation in her bruised mind with Joy. Her thoughts returned to the long phone conversation she'd had with her mother who had been sympathetic about her feelings.

"I think I'd feel pretty hurt over it too," Olive had said quietly.

Louise pulled herself together enough to relate the story of her visits with Winnie and what she'd learned about Joy's movements.

"Are you going to see her uncle up there?"

"Who?"

"The uncle she was staying with," Olive reminded her.

"Oh, I'd forgotten all about it."

"Do you remember the names?"

"Harry and…something or other."

"But you had a listing of them from the Internet, didn't you?"

"You're right. I have. Just a sec…" Louise said as she sorted through her notes. "Yes, here it is. It was the J.T. I was fooled by. Of course the H. & J. didn't mean a thing. June…Harry and June. Yes, that's who they were."

"So they're still there then?"

"Hopefully." Louise thought about it for a moment. "Yes, I'll go and tackle them. See what I can find out."

"What about Winnie Edwards? Are you going back to see her?"

"I'll try again but, Mum, she's exhausting. It's like walking a tightrope."

"Put me down if I ever get like that, will you Louie?"

"Don't talk like that."

"You never know."

They talked around the subject for some minutes and then the conversation switched to Gunter and Olive's visit that day.

"How was he?"

"About the same as yesterday. I took him some sweet pea. Held them under his nose for quite a while until he reacted to the perfume. At least I think he did. I told him the whole story about you giving them to Joy the day they shifted in next door. He opened his eye for a few minutes and it leaked. Whether it was tears, as in crying, or just watery eyes, I don't know. There was a Beethoven symphony on while I was there, so I closed the door of his room and turned it up as loud as I dared. I didn't speak then and just listened to it with him…that's if he was, but I just got the feeling he was."

"That's how I feel, even after the few times I've visited. Like he's listening to everything you do. He just doesn't have the strength any more to show us."

"I told him I'd read him a book, perhaps reading a chapter or two each day. Then I discussed with him…well, it was a one-sided discussion really…about what book I should read. I listed umpteen dozen books until it suddenly hit me—*The Diving-Bell & the Butterfly*. What could be more perfect?"

"But Marta's still got it."

"I saw her there. She was on duty. She's read it already."

"What'd she think?"

"She cried."

"So, I know what she thought."

"Exactly," Olive said. "She thought it a great idea that I read it to him. It might make him see how he can communicate more, from the words of that poor Frenchman, than how you or I could explain it."

"Terrific."

"I spent so long there, I got caught in the peak hour rush on the train and it took me ages to get home. It was worth it though. A young student was clutching your latest book and I tapped him on the shoulder and told him my daughter put it together."

Louise laughed. "Skite."

"And then I fell asleep on the train and almost missed my stop."

"I'm sorry to put you through all this, travelling to the city every day."

"Don't even think of it. It's giving me something useful to do for a change. If I can help that poor man, I'll get as much out of it as he does."

"Mum, I love you."

"I love you too. Now you get a good night's rest. You've got another big day ahead of you."

"Yes Mum."

The nurses' station was unattended when Louise entered the dementia area. She waited for some minutes until an old gentleman snuck up behind her and threaded his arm through hers. He appeared agitated, hopping from one foot to the other.

"You got a cigarette?"

"No, I'm sorry. I don't smoke," she replied.

"Well, can you get me some?"

"I…don't know if…"

"They're up there," he pointed to a locked cupboard on the wall behind the desk. "They keep them there."

"We could ask one of the nurses."

He tut-tutted with impatience. "No. You can get me one now."

"I don't have the keys," she said.

"Don't you have them in your pocket?"

"Leo," a voice came from behind them. "Are you being naughty again trying to get some cigarettes?"

"No. No. No," he said, hopping away from them with a most peculiar gait.

The nurse laughed. "Leo will pester anyone in sight to get him a smoke."

Louise laughed with her. "I'm glad you turned up."

"You here to see Winnie again?"

Louise followed the nurse to Winnie's room.

"Winnie love, it's that lady…" She turned to Louise. "What's your name again?"

"Louise."

"It's Louise to see you, love."

Winnie was seated by the window, bending over something on her lap. She looked up furtively, trying to hide what it was she was holding.

"What you got there Winnie?" the nurse said.

"Nothing." The reply was sullen.

"Can I see the nothing?"

"No."

"Are you sure about that? It might be important."

"No."

"I've got a new lipstick to show you," the nurse teased. She whispered to Louise, "You can always get around her with lipsticks."

"Where?" Winnie looked hopeful.

"Here." The nurse took a lipstick out of her pocket and held it out. "Take it."

Winnie forgot about the contents of her lap as she reached out for the lipstick. Confetti scattered and floated down to the floor around her. It was mostly blue with little lines on it, and what looked like letters for decoration.

"What's all this?" the nurse said as Winnie swivelled the lipstick up out of the casing. "Have you been ripping up someone's letters?"

Louise turned pale as she recognised the paper that Joy had written upon. The pages had been ripped into tiny shreds. It would be impossible to put them together again.

"Have you got hold of Mary Kathleen's mail again?" She muttered to herself, "How she gets to it is beyond me."

Louise sat down on a nearby chair with a thump.

"Are you okay, love?" A cool hand felt her forehead. "Has the heat got to you?"

"Maybe," Louise sighed. "I just feel a little faint."

"Here," the nurse said, pushing a glass of water up to Louise's face, "this'll help. Just take a few deep breaths."

Louise gulped at the water. The dizziness faded and she stood unsteadily. "I think I'll leave the visit for now, if that's all right."

She hesitated before the gate of the large weatherboard house in Ibis Street. The front yard was a confusion of scrap metal, engine parts, cardboard cartons and other paraphernalia. Louise had never seen such a mess in a front yard, much less try to pick her way over it. There was no doorbell, so she knocked on the wall nearest the door. A dog barked somewhere as footsteps approached from inside the house.

"Gidday."

A tall, thin man stood before her with a cigarette dangling between his lips. He reminded her of the stick figures in Russell Drysdale's paintings of the harsh life in the Australian outback. His leathery skin was the same earthy colour of the paintings. A dimple thrust a large cleft into his chin. She recognised it as almost identical to the one she remembered belonging to Les Bacon.

"Yeah?" he said with an amused look in his eyes.

She noticed that one was grey and the other blue. *Unusual.*

"Oh, I...er..."

"Spit it out, love. It can't be that hard."

A deep breath. "I wonder if you can help me. I'm trying to find a friend of mine."

"Who's that, love?" He scratched at his bald head, then kicked back with his right foot. Louise heard a yelp. "Get back in there, you silly bloody mongrel," he growled at something behind him. "Yeah, who're you looking for?"

"Joy Bacon, Baker...or Paton."

His eyebrows shot up to join deep furrows in his forehead.

"Who'd you say?"

"Joy Bacon. Or she may have been using your surname—Baker."

"Never heard of her," he said evenly, leaning against the doorframe.

"But I believe she stayed with you for a month."

"Nope."

"Thirty years ago."

"Nope."

"What about Carol Bacon or Baker or Paton?"

There was the slightest hesitation. "Nope."

"I was told she did."

The eyes narrowed as they regarded the attractive, well-dressed woman in front of him.

"Who told you that?"

"A resident of Longreach."

"Nope."

"I believe Carol Bacon is your niece."

"Nope."

"Look. I know she stayed here. I can check it out with the Police here."

"She's not my niece."

"Who is she then?"

"A mate's daughter."

"So your mate's daughter stayed with you?"

"Yep."

"Do you know where she is now?"

"Nope."

"What about your brother?"

"Haven't got one."

He turned to go inside the house.

"Les Baker isn't your brother?"

He looked at her carefully, then answered slowly. "My brother died years ago. And his name wasn't Les."

"No kidding? Funny about that—did you both go to the same shop for your dimples?"

He turned deliberately and opened the door. The snout of a dog pushed between the doorframe and the edge of the door.

"You hungry, Mutt? There's a nice juicy piece of skirt out there."

Louise glared at him, then turned on her heel and picked her way as gracefully as she could through the rubbish. She closed the gate unhurriedly, and tossed her hair back over her shoulders. *You don't frighten me, you bully.* She heard the door slam behind her.

She walked the two blocks to Eagle Street and found a travel centre there.

"What's the quickest way I can get to Townsville?"

Fifteen minutes later, Louise walked out of the travel centre with a ticket in her handbag.

I wonder where the Police Station is? She looked up and down the street and strode out purposefully to her left.

473

The Police Station on Galah Street looked tempting. *Why don't I go in and dump it all on them?* Louise hesitated, then turned away. *No, who'd believe me anyway?*

Olive picked up the receiver on the second ring.

"What did you find out?" she asked eagerly.

Louise brought her up to date on Winnie tearing up the letters, and her disappointment and frustration at not having had the opportunity to read them.

"Still, at least you know where Joy went."

"I'm flying to Townsville tomorrow afternoon."

"No surprises there."

They talked about Harry's laconic reception to Louise's questions.

"Are you sure he was Les's brother?" Olive asked.

"Definitely...by his voice and the dimple in the chin. Same brand," Louise commented. "You know, I walked over to the Police Station. I was going to go in and give it all to them. Let them sort it out."

"You didn't though."

"No." Louise took a long sip of her drink. "How could I prove any of this? They'd probably think me a menopausal freak who's got nothing better to do than look for people who are well and truly dead. I mean, there's the death certificate and grave to prove it."

"Cynic."

"Yes, I know, Mum." Louise sighed. "Anyway, I decided to wait until I had more to go on. So I won't look so bloody silly."

"Have you thought about what you'll do if you find them tomorrow?" Olive said carefully. "I mean, you don't know what sort of reception you'd get."

"Yes, I've thought of that. I don't really know. Play it by ear, I guess."

"Louie?"

"Yes?"

"Be careful."

The next day her aircraft rose over the township of Longreach and headed for Townsville. The flat landscape spread out endlessly below her with made roads and dirt tracks leading to huge cattle stations and other outback towns. She felt excited, nervous, apprehensive. *Am I really going to see her after all these years? Will she be as happy to see me as I will be her? If they'd changed their name again, will Les Bacon—or whoever he is—be civil? Violent? Dangerous? After all, he must've been hiding something.*

Gradually the countryside took on the greener aspect of the tropics as her aircraft flew over the Ross River during the descent. She had time to see the coastline at Cleveland Bay and the city centre before landing. *Is she down there looking up at my plane?*

Louise checked into her hotel room on the Strand, which had a view of Magnetic Island across the water. There were ten Patons in the telephone directory. None of them were L. or R. There was one C.

"Hello?" It was a male voice.

"I'm looking for a Carol Paton," Louise said breathlessly. "Am I on the right number?"

"No. I'm C. Paton, but I'm no Carol," he laughed. "I'm Chris."

"Sorry to have troubled you," she replied, disappointment deflating her excitement.

She opened the directory again. There were four Bacons, none of which had the required initial. There were five Bakers, one of which was an L.

"Lorna Baker," said a bright female voice that rose on the last syllable.

"Sorry, I've got the wrong number."

"You're welcome," was the sung response.

Might have known it.

Louise walked up and down both sides of Primrose Street without the faintest idea which house it could be. *Why didn't she put the number on the envelope?*

She knocked on the door of a house halfway down the street. A buxom, elderly woman opened the door, wiping her hands on an apron.

"Yes?"

"I'm sorry to bother you, but I'm looking for a friend of mine and I don't know the number in Primrose Street."

"Well, I've lived here for the best part of forty years," the woman replied, peering at Louise through thick lenses, studying her pointedly. "I know just about everyone in the neighbourhood, except for some in the rented houses up near Ryan Street. What's the name, dear?"

"Paton. Carol Paton."

"Oh, I don't think there's anyone by that name." She smoothed out her apron and smiled. "Of course, it might be the renting people. They've only been there for four months, one lot, and the others opposite them have been there for about a year."

"No. My friend moved here about thirty years ago."

"Thirty years, you say?"

Louise nodded hopefully.

The woman looked up and down the street as if to see Louise's friend appear there. "What name did you say again?"

"Carol Paton," Louise reminded her. "And her parents are Les and Ruth."

"No, I would have known. I've been here for forty years. Did I tell you that?"

"Yes, you did."

"Yes...well I would have known them. I know everyone around here."

Louise turned as if to go, then hesitated. "Ah, they might have been known as Bacon or Baker," she said hopefully.

"No," the woman replied decisively. "No Bacons, but there's a Baker three blocks away. Not in Primrose Street though. Nice young couple with a baby girl." Her voice dropped to a whisper. "Born out of wedlock, I heard. Such a shame. You wouldn't think to look..."

"No, that wouldn't be them," Louise interrupted her. "Well, thank you anyway."

The woman watched as Louise walked back towards her hotel, waiting to see if she would go into any of the other houses. Satisfied that Louise had taken her word for it as the expert on the neighbourhood, she went back inside to carry on with her cooking.

Bugger, bugger, bugger. Louise's gait had lost its enthusiasm as she continued along the footpaths looking down at her feet rather than taking an interest in her surroundings. She fought back tears of frustration.

Her stomach rumbled loudly, reminding her of her neglect, and she turned into a restaurant close to her hotel. The mackerel was cooked just the way she liked it, in a spicy butter sauce, accompanied by a green salad, but try as she might, she couldn't finish it. *How the hell am I going to find her now?* The glass of chardonnay tasted like vinegar.

Back in her room, Louise looked up the secondary schools in the area, placing them on her map of Townsville. She narrowed them down to two possible candidates that were the closest to Primrose Street: Townsville State High School, which was the nearest, and Pimlico State High School. She would ring them in the morning. *One of them would have to have records of a Carol Paton attending the school, wouldn't they?*

Olive did her best to cheer her daughter during their phone conversation, but Louise felt depressed with her lack of success.

"You know, I get so close and then another obstacle jumps up in front of me," she complained. "It feels like I'm not meant to find her."

"You're not becoming fatalistic on me, are you?"

"No, I suppose not." Louise sipped at her drink. She noticed that the bottle was half-empty already. *Got to stop this.*

"You're not drinking too much, are you?"

"Mind reader."

"It's not worth it, you know."

She pushed the bottle out of reach. "You're right. I'll pull myself together and get on with it."

"I visited Gunter Schwartz again today."

"Oh, I'm sorry! I'm so full of my own miseries; I didn't even think to ask about him. How is he?"

"The same. Though I think he's listening to the book as I read it to him. I don't read too much—just a few chapters at a time to give him something to think about. He opened his eye a few times and really stared at me. It gave me such an eerie feeling, like a bond has established between us."

"That's how I felt too."

"Yes, I know what you mean now. I talked about what you're doing, where you are, who you've spoken to—the nurse and her ripping up the letters, Les's brother and his dog, and so on. He had his eye open then for quite a few minutes. I'm sure he heard it all."

"Well, either way—whether Mr Schwartz was involved in the disappearance of Joy or not—he'd be interested."

"I don't think he's a bad man."

"Neither do I." Louise laughed. "Are we being silly, sentimental fools?"

"No, not a bit of it," Olive laughed back.

Louise called the Townsville State High School the next morning. A helpful receptionist put her through to the Principal who took down the details of Louise's request.

"I'll get a member of staff to look it up and call you back right away."

She waited for fifteen minutes and picked up the receiver of the phone as soon as it rang.

"I'm sorry, but there's no record of a Carol Paton, Bacon or Baker ever having attended this school," came the reply. "I looked up a Joy with the same surnames, but no luck."

She put down the receiver almost savagely. *I don't believe this!*

Looking at her map, she saw that Pimlico State High School would have been an easy bus ride from Primrose Street, and then a short walk along Fulham Road to the school. *Here we go again.* Her heart began to pound as she dialled the number.

The Principal at the Pimlico school was equally helpful, promising to call back after a morning meeting. Just before twelve, the phone rang.

He was apologetic. "I don't have much to tell you, really."

Bugger. Not again.

"There's a Carol Paton recorded as having started school here in 1968, like you said, but she left suddenly after two weeks."

"Left?" Her mouth suddenly went dry.

"Yes, without any explanation. I wasn't here at the time, but the Principal of the day has made an entry saying that she never turned up again and, upon enquiring at the house, found the family had up and gone."

"They must have been frightened off by something or someone," Olive agreed when Louise rang her.

"But where do I look now?" Louise wailed, close to tears.

"God, they could be anywhere." Olive's voice revealed her exasperation.

"I know. They could have gone in any direction...including overseas."

"New Zealand again?"

"Could be," Louise sighed. "We didn't think to look for Paton."

"We didn't know about Paton."

"He was a very clever man, our Les Bacon. He waltzed in and out of New Zealand without a trace and covered his tracks every time something frightened him. Despite myself, I'm beginning to feel a grudging admiration for him."

"Me too," Olive agreed. "And in those days you didn't need a passport to go to New Zealand from Australia. Though I wonder how long his money would have lasted."

"Do you know how much he had?"

"Well, he sold the house, which they'd paid off," Olive said slowly, "and the truck—though he wouldn't have got much for that. It was pretty old. And the business. He would have got something for the goodwill. How much though, I've got no idea. He sold as much of the furniture as he could—besides the desk, of course—and anything else they had. He must've had a fair swag when they left."

"Okay, so assuming he still had money, could he have afforded to cart them off to New Zealand again?"

"Back to the Internet?"

Louise looked longingly at the brandy bottle. "Yes, I guess so."

"Are you coming home?"

"I think so. I can't think of anything else I can do here, and I have to prepare for the wedding shoot, damn it."

It was a relief to be back in her own home, looking out across the familiar scene of Port Phillip Bay. *To hell with it*, she thought, as she made herself a long Campari and soda, and then settled down in front of the computer screen.

The white pages produced over five hundred Patons, dotted over various areas of the north and south islands of New Zealand. Eleven were L. Patons. Louise decided to call them.

"Gidday," said a rough male voice. *An Aussie?* Her heart pounded.

"Hello, could I speak with Les?"

"Who?"

"Les Paton?"

"No Les here, love." He hiccuped.

"You're L. Paton?"

"Yeah. Larry's the name. Drinking's the game."

"I must have the wrong number."

"Hey," he chortled. "You sound a bit of all right. What're you doing tonight?"

"Tucking up in my own bed."

"Can I join you?"

"Have you got a ticket to Australia?"

"No, love. Is that the price?"

"No, that's where I'm ringing from."

God save me. She rolled her eyes to the ceiling and took a swig of her Campari.

"Hello, can I help you?" The voice was female, young.

"Yes, I'm looking for Les Paton."

"We don't have a Les Paton here. My husband is Laurie Paton. Who's speaking please?"

"Oh, I'm calling from Australia."

"Goodness!"

"Yes, I'm looking for an old friend."

"Well, unless he's Laurie, we can't help you."

"You wouldn't know a Ruth Paton? Or a Joy Paton?"

"No."

"Or a Les Bacon or Baker?"

"What's this? The million dollar quiz?"

"No. I'm just desperate."

The other nine L. Patons produced more or less the same result. Considering that there were fifty R. Patons, fifteen C. Patons and forty-three J. Patons, Louise decided to give up. She rose from her chair and paced the room.

I'm only surmising that they went to New Zealand. Maybe they're still in Australia. But where? She looked at a map of Australia. *Where would I go if I was running from Townsville?* She examined the names of outback towns. *No. In small communities they'd be noticed. He'd probably go for a capital city. But which one?* She went back to the computer and typed Paton in the white pages for Brisbane. The answer came back that there were too many entries to list. She tried the four different initials, but it was the same problem.

She poured herself another drink—stronger this time—and saluted the photograph of Joy on the wall. *I give up. You're going to stay dead.* She put a CD on. It was Mahler's 9th Symphony. Tinged with themes of his own approaching death, the bitterness and despair of the music matched Louise's frame of mind as she buried Joy again.

She awoke on the couch in the living room. Her mouth tasted revolting and her stomach heaved in protest. She made it just in time to the toilet and brought up the remainder of her stomach contents. *Charming.* Her head buzzed and she felt giddy.

The phone rang.

"Hello?" she said faintly.

"Louie? Have you been running?"

"No."

"You sound like you're panting."

"I am. I've just been sick."

"What is it, love? What's made you sick like that?"

"Drunk and disorderly." Louise's voice was bitter. "A hangover."

There was a short silence.

I've disappointed her.

"What happened?"

"Oh, Mum," Louise started to cry. "It's no good. I can't do this anymore. It's just too hard." She reached for a tissue and blew her nose. "It's like looking for a needle in a haystack."

"I was afraid…"

"They've been swallowed up by the white pages. Gobbled into oblivion," Louise cried. "They don't exist anymore. I don't care anymore. They can go to hell for all I care."

"You don't mean that," Olive said quietly.

"Yes I do, Mum," Louise sobbed. "I do."

"What about Gunter Schwartz?"

"What...?"

"Are you going to drop him now?"

Louise looked at the telephone in stunned silence. She felt ashamed.

"No," she said eventually.

"I didn't think so."

They could hear each other's breathing.

"I'm going to visit him after lunch," Olive said firmly. "Are you coming?"

Olive held up the alphabet board. "I'm going to try what Bauby did with his assistant. Let's say I'm your assistant today. You must try. I know you're very tired and it's a lot to ask but, Mr Schwartz, this is our best shot. I know you can do it."

Gunter dredged up the strength to blink. *I understand. I understand.* His eye swivelled to the left to catch sight of Louise. *She looks unhappy. She doesn't say much today.*

Olive pointed to each letter and said it out loud before moving on slowly to the next one. "A...B...C...D..." She paused. "Think about what you would like to say. Just one word would do."

Gunter watched her hand and listened to her clear voice. He had pushed the fog aside and mustered all his strength for her visit. He'd been pleasantly surprised to see Louise with her, but sensed instantly that something was terribly wrong. Neither woman said anything to enlighten him. *What can I say to them?*

Olive started again. "A...B...C...D...E...F...G...H..."

Gunter blinked.

"H?" she asked excitedly. "Did you blink on H?"

Push! Push! His eyelid blinked again.

"Louie, what do you think?"

Louise bent closer. "I think so. Can you confirm that again, Mr Schwartz? Is that an H?"

Mein Gott! Yes. He blinked again.

"Yes!" Both women jumped up and hugged each other.

"Okay, okay. We've got an H. I'll start again," Olive said clearly. "A...B...C...D...E..."

Gunter blinked again.

"E? Is that E?"

Yes. He blinked.

"E. We have HE." Olive was ecstatic.

She worked slowly along the alphabet until she reached the letter L. Gunter blinked.

"L? Can you blink again if that's correct?"

He blinked again.

"My God, Louie, I'll be a monkey's uncle if what's happening isn't real."

"Me too. Go on, Mum," Louise urged her.

"Right—now we have HEL. Let's keep going."

Olive said each letter out loud until she reached L again and Gunter blinked.

"Hell? Is that what you're saying?" Louise asked.

Gunter stared at her, unblinking. *No.*

"I guess that means no," Olive put in. "But we can't be absolutely sure."

"What about," Louise chipped in, "nothing for no, and one blink for yes?"

"Okay, let's try that," Olive agreed. "Mr Schwartz, if you say no, please don't blink. If you are saying yes, please blink."

They watched him anxiously as he stared back at them unblinking for some moments.

"Okay, we'll take that as a no." Olive picked up the board again. "Here we go again. So we're adding onto HELL, is that right?"

Gunter blinked once.

She recited the alphabet until he blinked at the letter O.

"Hello? Is that what you said? Hello?" She was incredulous.

He blinked.

"Oh, my God. You said hello!" Olive started to cry, and Louise joined in. "You said hello to us."

Gunter blinked again as tears leaked out from his eye ducts.

As one, the two women bent over Gunter and kissed him on the cheek. They wiped his tears of happiness as well as their own and then, like children, they hugged and kissed each other, dancing around the room.

"What's all this?" a mock stern voice broke in. It was Marta.

"Marta. You'll never guess," Louise almost shouted.

"What?"

"Mr Schwartz said hello to us. He's communicating!"

Hello! Hello! Hello!

Chapter 71 — Melbourne to Broadbeach

On the way home, Louise had to stop the car twice to get out and vomit, her earlier nausea having returned.

Olive watched her daughter with concern. "I think you'd better stay the night."

They arrived safely at Olive's house, where she had Louise rest on the couch in the lounge room in front of the television.

"Now don't you move, or I'll smack your bottom."

Louise hiccuped and laughed at the same time. "Long time since you did that. I'd like to see you try."

Olive prepared a bland meal that Louise picked at but managed to keep down under the threat of a visit from her mother's local doctor.

"I'm all right," she assured Olive.

"No you're not. You need a damned good holiday."

"I just had one."

"What? Running around New Zealand, Western Australia and then Queensland? At a rate of knots? You call that a holiday?"

"Well..."

"You haven't had a decent rest for years." Olive was stern. "You're run down. The business has taken a lot out of you..."

"I like it."

"Yes, I know you do. But everyone needs a break." Olive took both Louise's hands in her own. "You've been under a lot of strain with this search for Joy. You're riding on your nerves."

"I'll be fine. Besides, there's Gunter Schwartz..."

"Look, just for once will you listen to me? You won't be any good to him if you're sick."

"But what about...?"

"I can keep working with him. I have up to now, haven't I?"

"Yes."

"Well then. End of argument." Olive stood up. "Tomorrow morning we make a booking for you to go away for at least a week. Maybe two."

"Mum, I can't. I've got the wedding to do...remember?"

The view from Louise's hotel room was spectacular with rollers crashing upon miles and miles of white beach, and the Casino and Pacific Fair perched on islands around which canals wound in crazy patterns. The hinterland provided a high solid backdrop to the west, behind which hid the theme parks and Brisbane. Below the hotel was a diverse range of boutique shops, restaurants, bars, movie theatres and department stores. *Pity I'm not on a break*, she thought as she gazed out from her balcony. The beach was crowded with holidaymakers who were taking advantage of the sun and the surf. The towers of Surfers Paradise gleamed white in the bright sunlight.

The day of the wedding was long, hot and exhausting. Trying to coax the best out of a nervous, spoiled and overtired bride was frustrating and Louise reminded herself to never again do favours for her clients against her better judgement. The settings in and around the elegant Main Beach resort were ideal with its picturesque lush palm gardens, sparkling blue lagoon and Broadwater frontage. Louise made the most of the surroundings, convincing the bride and her attendants to get into the water before dressing—only after the bride's father had threatened to disinherit his daughter if she failed to follow Louise's instructions to the letter. A perfectly executed coiffure, perfectly arranged wedding attire, and a couple of outrageously expensive glasses of French champagne downed two hours later, had the bride in a more cooperative mood. She sailed through the ceremony, posing for Louise's lenses like a perfectly trained Barbie doll, gliding elegantly on the arm of her new husband around the pool that reflected gold lights in the still blue water. By the time Louise packed up her lenses and made her getaway, she was giddy with fatigue.

The blue waters of the Pacific Ocean looked inviting, but weariness kept Louise on her balcony the following morning, reclining in a deck chair with a book open on her lap. But she couldn't concentrate. Her eyes kept returning to the beach where a red-haired woman lay stretched out on a bright yellow towel. From Louise's vantage point, the woman could have been any age. *What if it's her?* She tore her eyes away from the scene below her. *Stop it. You've put that behind you.* She read the page that she'd already read three times. It still didn't register. She stole another look and saw the woman turn over, exposing her face to the sun. Louise's eyes strained to focus on the woman's features. *You're paranoid*, she thought in disgust. *Cut it out.*

I'll explore the shops, she told herself, as she put on a pair of sandals and let herself out of her room. The lift was empty and she stared at herself in the mirror as it descended the eight floors. The woman who looked back at her was a stranger with red-rimmed, dark-circled eyes, and a gaunt face with an exhausted, haunted expression. It was a shock to see herself like that.

For some time she browsed in boutiques and specialty shops before strolling onto the beach. *I'll just stick my toes in the water*, she lied to herself, walking in the direction of the red-haired woman. She was still there, lying on the yellow beach towel, but she'd turned on her stomach again and her face was hidden from view. The hair was curly and exactly the same shade of red that Joy had. Louise walked down to the water's edge and paddled in the shallows for some moments, turning back constantly to make sure the woman was still there. At last she saw her turn over again and slowly made her way up the sand to where she could see the woman's face. It was an unlined face of about twenty, and the eyes that looked up at Louise were a deep brown. Feeling ridiculous, Louise walked past the red head and continued on back to the shops.

Having decided to stay on for a few days to recover, the hours rolled into each other in a blur of countless words on pages as she read one book after another. She read stretched out on the beach, on her bed, on her balcony, at tables of restaurants, on park lawns, and gradually the tension eased. Food was tolerable again and she was sleeping better. She avoided alcohol, except for a glass of wine with her meals. The rest of the time she drank copious amounts of chilled water. Her skin took on a healthy colour from exposure to the sun as she reclined on the beach each day, allowing her body to melt into the sand and her mind roam free with the characters of the books she read. She refused to think about Joy, pushing the nagging reminders away before they took hold to depress her again. The only concession to Joy's memory she would allow was concern for Joy's father—Gunter Schwartz.

Each night Louise rang her mother and Olive would bring her up to date on Gunter's progress. The words—though requiring extreme effort on Gunter's part and extreme patience on Olive's—kept coming slowly, bridging the gap in his communication with the rest of the human race. The lure of the swirling black tunnel and Hannah was less compelling, and his periods of consciousness were longer than before. He had thanked Olive for what she was doing and enquired after the sad-looking Louise because her vitality had seemed to disappear when he last saw her. Olive skirted the subject, without actually telling him that Joy's trail had gone cold.

"How can I tell him, Louie?" Olive said. "It's what he's hanging out for."

"I don't know, Mum. It's a bit like cheating him, isn't it?"

"Yes and no. Sometimes I think we should have let him die in peace…"

"But would it have been peace?" Louise felt depressed again.

"I wonder if it would have mattered after all those years. Though he's told me that's what kept him alive—hope that he would see one of them again."

"I feel really bad about that," Louise said quietly.

"Stop it, Louie. You did your best."

"Yes, well, it wasn't good enough, was it?" She sighed. "What about the nursing home staff? Are they doing tests and things?"

"Marta put a bomb under them and they've actually taken notice. There's a stream of doctors, physiotherapists, social workers and so on, in and out of his room all day. I have trouble getting a moment alone with him. He's the wonder boy now."

"That's terrific, Mum."

"But you know something? He won't talk to anyone else, except for Marta. He just lies there with his eye open staring at them. He won't blink a message though."

"Why?"

"He told me that he's very disappointed in the medical profession. For thirty years they treated him like a vegetable—except for Marta—and he's not about to make them famous by telling them anything."

"Stubborn old coot."

"That's what kept him alive."

"You're right," Louise conceded. "What an incredible man."

"I asked him about the police."

"What'd he say?"

"No. Without George Chambers he doesn't want them involved. He wants you to find her."

"Oh, hell." Tension gripped Louise's stomach.

"Now, look," Olive said sternly. "Don't you go getting yourself all uptight again. You did all you could. It's cost you a pretty penny as well."

"I knew all that money I'd earned would come in handy one day." Louise was without regret.

"I think what we're going to have to do is just kid him that you're still following up leads." Her voice dropped so that Louise had to strain to hear her. "He can't last much longer."

"I could go to the police," Louise said hopefully. "He wouldn't have to know."

"Perhaps you're right."

"As soon as I get back to Melbourne I'll go and talk to them. They'd have to listen now."

The day before Louise was due to return to Melbourne, she strolled along the streets surrounding the hotel, exploring the many shops. She looked up as the monorail glided high over the highway towards Jupiters Casino. *I haven't done that yet.* She entered the Oasis Shopping Centre and climbed the stairs to the top floor to board the monorail when it next swept into the airy space where giant paper butterflies hung suspended from the ceiling. The view was spectacular as she was taken out over the highway. Traffic hurried under her on its way to Surfers Paradise, or in the opposite direction towards Coolangatta. Small boats meandered along the canals, trailing their wake behind them like temporary signatures on the water. Bulging at the seams with eager tourists, resplendent tall hotels stood like concertinaed bellows overlooking the Pacific Ocean. Their long shadows cast surreal images of their measure on the sand.

She wandered through the dim, smoky world of the gambler in a cacophonous lair of clinking chips and muted voices. Engrossed faces studied balls spinning dizzily around wheels, or cards flicked artfully onto green baize tables, or flickering screens that tumbled images in rows of luck or loss. *This isn't for me*, she grimaced as she struggled for breath in the choking atmosphere. It was a relief to return to the platform, where the tropical air was fresh, to wait for the monorail.

The shops at the Oasis failed to excite her interest and she wandered back to her hotel, picking up her messages on the way. A woman preceded her into the lift with a newspaper under her arm. She punched a button and looked at Louise with an eyebrow raised.

"What floor?"

"Oh...eight, thanks."

The doors glided to a close silently as the woman opened her newspaper. Louise's gaze fell onto the open page of *The Gold Coast Bulletin* where the headline announced:

GOLD COAST BUSINESS EXCELLENCE AWARDS SECOND TO NONE

Thirty years in the business, and it shows. Voted the Best Businesswoman of the year, Carol Paton, proprietor of the popular *Second to None* book-shop, rose over a class field of entrants to win the...

Louise felt her stomach lurch as her eyes took in the photo that accompanied the article.

"You said eight, didn't you?" The voice reached her from a long way off. "The eighth floor?"

Louise looked stupidly at the woman in the lift.

"You wanted to get off here?" The woman snapped the newspaper shut, irritated as Louise looked from her to the paper. Her finger was on the *Door Open* button.

"Here?" The sound of her pulse was loud in her ears. It pushed at her eyes and choked the air from her lungs.

"Are you ill?" The woman's voice was a little softer.

"Can I have your paper?"

The second hand bookshop was one block from her hotel. In the window display was a little book on a stand facing her. On the front cover was a picture of an antique camera. She recognised it as an 1880s Lancaster Gem Camera. The polished mahogany and brass camera, with its brass mounted lenses for taking postage stamp pictures, was one she had inherited from Mr Watson. He had given it to her when he had left the business. As she studied the cover through the glass window, a hand appeared beside it to place another book on a stand.

Louise looked up to the face that hovered above the hand. It was surrounded by shoulder-length, red curly hair. The woman looked to be the same age as Louise. The half-smile on the woman's lips slowly dropped back into harsh lines that were deep on either side of her mouth. The colour drained out of the face, so that it looked like chalky parchment. The eyes that met Louise's through the glass were sea green. They widened in shock.

My search is ended.

Louise and the woman stared openly at each other for several moments that seemed an eternity. A wave of giddiness swept over Louise so that she had to brace herself against the shop window. The movement broke the spell and the woman drew her head back quickly from the window display and disappeared into the dim interior of the shop.

Louise took a deep breath and opened the door just as a closed sign was about to be hung on it. She pushed at the door and stepped inside. There were no other customers. The woman retreated behind the counter, her back to Louise, holding herself stiffly as she fiddled with some books on a shelf.

"Excuse me?" Louise neared the counter.

"Yes?" the woman said, not turning around.

"Are you...? I mean..."

"You're after a book? One in the window?" The voice was curt, businesslike.

"No. I mean, yes. The camera book."

The woman hurried to the window, keeping her face turned from Louise. She lifted the book and its stand out of the display area with shaking hands and, as she turned back to the counter, dropped them.

"Here..." Louise stooped to help her.

"It's all right," the woman said harshly.

She retrieved the book and the stand from the floor and walked briskly back to the counter, keeping her head down all the time. Louise studied the hair that showed some white at the temples. It was drawn back off her face by a clasp at the crown and the rest fell in soft curls to the woman's shoulders. Her skin was a light tan over naturally pale skin. She was slim, to the point of skinny, her shoulders sticking out sharply from her sleeveless pale orange dress. Her nails were cut short, unpolished, and the fingers were long, artistic. They were busy putting the book into a small plastic bag that had the name *Second to None* printed on it. The hand turned over, palm upwards, waiting for the price of the book.

"That'll be eight dollars fifty, thanks." Her voice was crisp, light, the words rushed; she bit her bottom lip.

Louise fumbled in her bag for her wallet. She opened it and took out a ten-dollar bill. She held it close to her chest, not extending her arm towards the woman who looked up in surprise.

The long neck led up to high cheekbones that reminded Louise of the photos of Hannah she'd seen. The sea green eyes were as Louise remembered them, except for the expression. It had grown up.

"Joy..."

"Pardon?" The eyes turned a steely grey-green. The mouth thinned, appearing bloodless.

"Joy, it's me. Louise."

"You've mistaken me for someone else."

"What?"

"I don't know any Louise."

Anger thrust a red-hot wave through Louise's stomach. It spread up through her chest and into her neck. It exploded into her head.

"Bullshit you don't!"

"I beg your pardon?" The eyes were now slits.

"How dare you stand there and lie to me bare-faced and tell me you don't know who the hell I am. After all these bloody years of thinking you were dead, grieving over you, never accepting the fact that you'd disappeared and left me alone, and then searching all over Australia for you, and then I find you here! Don't tell me you don't know who I am. I sure as hell know who you are," she yelled, jabbing a finger at her. "You're Joy Bacon, or Baker, or Paton, or Carol whatever. And you're not getting away from me this time until I get a bloody good explanation."

They regarded each other, Louise breathless from her shouted tirade, the other woman holding her breath. A car's horn blared from outside, making them both jump. Joy darted to the door of the shop and locked it. She rotated the closed sign towards the street, then turned around leaning her back on the door.

Slowly, an anguished wailing escaped from her mouth, rising in pitch until it filled the shop. The stiffness of her stance dissolved into submission, her shoulders slumping towards her arms that hugged her body. She slid down the door until she reached the floor and her elbows rested on her knees, her hands covering her face. Great tearing sobs racked her body with thirty years of misery at losing her childhood and her friend, thirty years of looking over her shoulder, thirty years of never being able to share her thoughts with anyone she could trust enough, thirty years of anger. Her body characterised defeat, utter sadness and relief.

Louise took several steps forward, tears streaming down her face. She knelt down beside her childhood friend and their arms went out to each other as they embraced, crying thirty years of tears on each other's shoulders.

The two women sat in the back room of the shop, surrounded by books that told of love, hate, friendship, deception, revenge, murder and grief. They told of families split asunder, they told of loyalty and obsession, and they told of fate and chance. But none of them held the story of Joy's life and origins. That was something that only the two of them could piece together. Louise went first.

She told Joy how she had read *The Diary of Anne Frank* by chance and read the inscription written by Tooth Fairy all those years ago. She told of her growing realisation that her friend hadn't died and of her quest for the truth by searching public records and the leads that had taken her to New Zealand and Western Australia, as well as outback and tropical Queensland. She told of the despair and frustration when she had lost the trail.

She took Joy's hands in her own, looking her in the eyes searchingly. "Do you know about your real father?" she asked carefully.

"A little."

"Do you know that he's still alive?"

"What?" Joy was stunned. "He said...Dad said...that he'd died in 1968."

"No, he didn't. He's in Melbourne. My mum is with him."

Fresh tears stung Joy's eyes. "Does he know about me?"

"Yes. I've told him everything. I showed him photos."

"He's alive? Really alive?"

"Only just," Louise said softly. "He's been waiting for you."

Joy's sharp intake of breath was the only sound in the quiet shop. Traffic noises seeped through the walls but the women were deaf to them, as if the shop had been transported to where nothing existed but the two of them.

"Why didn't he...?"

"He couldn't." Louise swallowed a lump in her throat. "He's been locked-in for thirty years."

"In gaol?"

"No. Inside his body."

"What?"

"He had a massive brain stem stroke and became totally paralysed. It was thought he was a vegetable all those years, but he was in a rare state called 'locked-in syndrome'. He was locked inside his body—able to see, hear, think—but no one knew it."

"Jesus. How awful."

"Yes."

"For thirty years?"

Louise nodded. "And you know what kept that man alive? You."

Joy sat with her head bowed for some time, turning over in her mind what she had learned.

"So she really was my twin?"

"Yes."

"Dad actually told me the truth about that? I wasn't sure whether to believe him or not."

"Yes."

"Jesus."

They sat in silence for a few minutes until Louise asked, "Why didn't you want to admit who you were?" Uncertain hurt tinged her voice.

The harsh, bitter lines around Joy's mouth deepened. She shook her head as if to clear it, then took a deep breath.

"Until I was certain that I couldn't fool you, I had to pretend. It was too dangerous."

"For whom?"

"Mum and Dad."

"Where are they?"

"Here."

Louise looked around her as if they would spring out of the walls.

"No," Joy grimaced. "We live here in Broadbeach. Not far from the shop." She picked at her fingernails nervously. "I've been dreading this day for most of my life."

"Why?"

"I just didn't know what I'd do. Run again? I'm almost relieved it's happened at last. I knew you straight away, as soon as I saw you out there on the footpath. I always knew I'd recognise you. You haven't changed a bit, you know." She smiled. "Still as pretty as the last time I saw you."

Louise opened her mouth to respond, but Joy interrupted her. "No, don't say it. It wouldn't be true. I see this face in the mirror every day. I'd swap it for yours like a shot. If you've been hurt and bitter and betrayed during the past thirty years, it doesn't show." She went on. "I don't think you know what happened that day, do you?"

"No."

"Well, I'll tell you. But you won't like it."

Joy told the story at first from her point of view—the bewilderment, the fear, the sense of loss for Louise, home, the familiar—and then she picked up the account from when Ruth had seen her at Longreach airport.

"She was like a walking zombie. Worse than when you knew her. You remember when she'd go off the deep end when there was a kidnapping or a shark attack?" At Louise's nod she continued. "Well, this was different. It was like someone had turned the lights out. Nobody home. Dad had really stuffed it up. He had no idea about women. He still doesn't."

"What do you mean?"

"Well, he thought her problems were 'women's problems'—not psychological. He didn't know enough about it. He wasn't educated, after all. He didn't realise that you can't tell a mentally-unhinged person their daughter is dead, and then produce her again. Hey presto…here's your daughter. She's not dead after all. She's been resurrected." Joy snorted her derision. "I'm such a bloody miracle. Look at me. I'm alive again." Tears welled in her eyes.

Louise made as if to stop her.

"No, it's okay," Joy sniffed. "It's a relief to have someone to talk to about it after all this time."

She busied herself preparing hot drinks and then sat down again, waiting for the kettle to boil.

"Mum had gone right off her tree and Dad didn't know what to do with her. He had me—a rebellious teenager—screaming at him, and a brother and sister-in-law who wanted some explanations. It's a wonder he didn't go into La-La Land as well. It might have been easier. One thing I'll say for Dad," she said sarcastically, "is he doesn't give up. Good old Dad. Loyal to the family to the bitter end. We were all he had, after all."

She bounced off her seat at the sound of the kettle whistling. With mugs in hand, she returned to Louise.

"So right there, in the middle of the bloody outback, we all sat on the ground and Dad spilled the whole story." She paused for a moment, digging out the old memories. "Did you know that Mum…Ruth…had a stillbirth?"

"No."

"No, I don't suppose you would. Mum doesn't know either."

"How…?"

"Oh, Dad was very good at that. He covered up Mum's delusional depression...yes; I've looked it up...after she stole the baby—me. She went through about two weeks of post-natal depression. Couldn't come to grips with it. Then, goodness gracious me," her tone was dripping with sarcasm again, "this red-haired baby turns up. Suddenly Mum is her old self again. Happy, smiling. So Dad decides to go along with it. Poor old Gunter Schwartz has lost his wife in childbirth and he still has one to bring up on his own. Why not take the burden of the other twin off his hands? Such a good man, my dad. My pretend dad."

She stopped as someone tried the front door. "Piss off. I'm busy," she said, more to herself than the potential customer who couldn't see her. Louise was surprised at her coarseness and the venom in her voice.

"Not nice, eh?" Joy hadn't missed Louise's reaction.

"No, it's..." Louise finished off lamely.

"It's okay. I know who I am."

Joy settled back in her seat and continued.

"So Dad carts Mum and me over the Nullarbor in a truck. Imagine that. A pretty good feat in 1955. I'll give him that. It was a ghastly trip, apparently, but they loved it. Their real honeymoon," she sniggered. "So they set up house in Bentleigh for a few years and then moved to Chelsea. He covered their tracks so well that there was nothing to connect them with the kidnapping. He almost convinced himself that I was their baby. But after she lost her baby she was never the full two bob. As long as he protected her from anything that would ruffle her feathers, she was okay. You saw that yourself. My going to school was the first thing that upset the apple cart. You remember our first day?"

"Yes, I do."

"How could you forget it? I couldn't. For the first time I wished your mum was mine. My mum embarrassed the shit out of me. If I could have traded mums that would have been the day." She paused for a minute to blow her nose and wipe her eyes. "This is like drawing teeth," she admitted.

"Are you sure you're up to this?" Louise asked.

Joy laughed. "It's cathartic. Can you stand it though?"

"Of course I can. This is what I've been trying to find out."

"Okay. You asked for it." The bravado in her voice was shadowed by the tormented expression in her eyes. "Did you know that Dad drugged Mum every time she went off the deep end?"

"Mum told me."

"Yeah, well, he had to do it more often as the years went by. The wife he knew and loved was slipping away from him." She hesitated. "Then comes our thirteenth birthday. You know, I really wanted to get you something special for your birthday. Something you would always treasure." Tears began to slide down her face again. "So I talked Mum into letting me go to Bentleigh to find something. I met Pat Lewis there. Do you remember her?"

"Very well."

"Well, I met her and we had a lovely day looking everywhere for a present for you." A faraway look was in Joy's eyes as she returned to that day so long ago. "Then we went into a jeweller's shop and a brooch jumped out at me. It was perfect. It had sweet pea on it. I remember it so well." She shook her head sadly. "I wish you could have seen it."

"But I did," Louise exclaimed. "I have it still."

"You do?"

"Yes. You had my name engraved on it."

"Jesus, he actually told the truth about that too. Dad told me he gave it to you."

"Yes, he did."

"And the desk?"

"That and the brooch—and *Blue Eyes*—are my most treasured possessions," Louise said softly.

"You've got *Blue Eyes*?"

Louise nodded, not certain if Joy would be pleased or not.

"Oh, I'm so happy about that. I thought she'd ended up in some no-name's place and probably on the tip by now."

"No," Louise laughed, relieved. "She sits on the desk and is one of the last things I look at every night. I even talk to her."

Joy's eyebrows shot up. "Really?"

"Yes. And you know what?"

"What?"

"I've talked to you in my head nearly every night since you disappeared." Louise felt a little silly admitting this fact to the woman in front of her who she realised she hardly knew.

"What'd you say?"

"Things."

"Like what?"

"Where are you? Can you see me?" Sudden tears sprang to Louise's eyes as she relived the hurt and sense of loss. She hung her head to hide them.

Joy put down her mug and crouched beside Louise's chair, putting her arms around her. "I'm sorry."

They stayed that way, bridging the years of absence, tentatively feeling their way around the friendship they had shared.

"Do you want to go on?" Louise asked finally.

"All right." Joy stood up and sat back on her chair. She looked up at the ceiling as she gathered her thoughts. "So Pat Lewis saw me off on the platform of Bentleigh station while I pretended I was waiting for my train. I remember pulling the brooch out of my bag and looking at it again. I was so excited thinking about what your reaction would be when you opened the present. I just knew you'd like it..."

"I did. I do."

"And then I met up with Ursula, as we'd secretly arranged. I met her the day before at Chelsea when she was on the platform. She stood there looking at me across the road, and I couldn't believe what I saw. It was like looking in a mirror. It was weird. We spent the most incredible time on the beach comparing ourselves. I felt so close to her. Not like with you...I mean, we were soul mates, and you can't get much closer than that...but with her, it was like meeting myself. We didn't know then that we were twins." Joy looked down at the floor. "I doubt she ever knew." She paused for a moment, then got up to pace the room. "In Bentleigh Dad was supposed to pick me up at a certain time but he arrived early and caught Ursula and me together. He was really funny...peculiar, not ha-ha. I guess this was the moment he'd always dreaded, though not expected. As soon as he saw Ursula, he knew who she was, though he didn't tell us that. He picked us up and drugged us. Can you believe that? He actually drugged us. It's a wonder he didn't kill us. They were Mum's pills."

"But why?"

"To give him time to think. He was riding by the seat of his pants. He had no idea what to do."

"He told you all this?"

"He had to. He had me screaming at him and his brother and Auntie June looking daggers at him."

"So what did he do?"

"He killed her!"

"What?"

"Just like that. He chucked her over some cliff."

"Hell!"

"He says it wasn't an easy decision...bravo for him...but he had to do it 'to protect the family'. That's what he said. That if he'd allowed Ursula to live, the whole thing would have come out. Her dad—our dad—would have realised who I was, and then that Les and Ruth Bacon were the ones who'd stolen me. Ruth would have ended up in the funny farm—probably having a lobotomy—and Les would have gone to gaol. And I would have ended up with a real father who I didn't know and a twin sister. We couldn't let that happen, could we? So he tossed her overboard. Then he made out that it was me who had died. I mean, we were identical, weren't we? End of story."

"What was your reaction to all of this?"

"Well, I freaked out, didn't I? I mean, suddenly the father you've had for thirteen years turns out not to be your father, and your mother isn't your mother, and your pretend father turns out to be a bloody murderer. I used to love him so much. I thought he was the most handsome dad this side of the black stump and, no offence, but he was so much nicer than yours..."

"Amen to that."

"...and suddenly he turns into this monster. I really hated him for that. I just hated him."

"What about Harry and June?"

"How did you know their names?"

"I met him."

"Not a bad stick."

"He was horrible."

"Well, rightfully, he was furious that Dad had involved them in a murder. Auntie June went right off her tree. Then when they calmed down, Uncle Harry said it was nothing to do with them and Dad could just bugger off. Dad said he'd be glad to, but with Mum like she was he didn't want to draw attention to her and ultimately to Uncle Harry. So Uncle Harry bundled us all in his station wagon and took us to his garage. He had a Falcon that he said would clear the bumps in the road. Without so much as a fond farewell, he filled the tank up with petrol, gave us a water bottle, pointed in the direction of Muttaburra, and walked away from us. That was it."

"Muttaburra?"

"That's on some God-awful dirt road to a little place called Prairie. It took us a couple of days to get there. Dad kept on stopping and checking on Mum who did absolutely nothing. She didn't speak, didn't eat, drink, or anything. Dad was beside himself. He kept on trying to pour water down her throat but she didn't swallow. Some of it must have trickled down, because she survived the trip, though Christ knows how. It must have been another day or so before we reached Charters Towers, where the road improved, and then on to Townsville."

"How were things between you and your dad on the trip?"

"Next to zero. No…below zero."

"Oh, I see."

"I just kept on thinking of what he'd done. And then there was you. He said if I contacted you, your mum would tell the police and then we'd all be thrown in gaol. You know, the old emotional blackmail trick. Well, at thirteen, what answer do you have to that? He said I was to forget you—like you'd died. Like you thought I had." She looked down at her fingers, picking some dead skin away from one of the nails. "You know, I rang you a couple of times."

"But…"

"No—I hung up without saying anything. I heard your voice though." She swallowed hard. "I cried so much each time that I stopped doing it. I was scared I'd get caught too."

"If only…"

"I know."

"What about your real father?"

"Oh, Dad said that he'd seen a notice in the paper about him collapsing and probably dying. There was nothing else about him afterwards, and by that time we were all out of the State." Joy looked at Louise. "Lucky, wasn't it?"

Louise felt uncomfortable under such causticity. "I guess so."

Joy held up her mug. "Another one?"

"Thanks." Louise handed her the mug. "Why did you only stay in Townsville for a few weeks?"

"You found that out too?" Joy was incredulous. "You have been busy."

"I saw one of your letters to Winnie Edwards."

"What?" Joy spun around from the sink. "Matron Edwards? Is she still alive?"

"Oh yes. Very much so."

"In Longreach?"

"In the dementia ward of the nursing home."

"Oh. I liked her."

"She liked you very much." Louise recounted the story of her visits with Winnie and the eventual tearing-up of Joy's two letters. "I only had the chance to see the address on the back of the envelope."

"Primrose Street…"

"That's right. No number, though, which had me guessing for a while. I got it from the school when I found out you didn't return and your father had whisked you all off again. There was absolutely nothing to point me in any direction after that. I was really depressed then. I'd given up."

"No wonder." Joy sat down again. "I'd promised to write to Matron Edwards. I didn't tell Dad because I knew he'd forbid me to. When I wrote the first letter I didn't put the number of the street on, telling the Matron not to write to me just yet. It was when I put the number on the second letter, she replied to me. Dad just happened to be in the front yard when the postie came. Rotten luck, eh? He went through me like a dose of salts. Threatened to thrash me with a cane—something he'd never done—if I ever contacted anyone again. So that night he packed everything in the Falcon and we took off for..."

Just then the phone rang. Both women looked up and listened to it.

"Aren't you going to answer it?" Louise asked Joy.

She went out to the counter and picked up the receiver.

"Second to None, good morning." She listened for a moment, then looked at her watch. "You're right, it is afternoon...no, we're closed today...tomorrow? Yes, I think so...some unexpected delivery problems...okay, see you then."

Joy resumed her seat and pressed on with her story. "So we came here. To Broadbeach."

"Why here?"

"Dad figured that with such a shifting population—you know, all the holiday makers—and it being such a fast-growing area, first of all, we wouldn't be noticed, and secondly, there'd be plenty of work for him. Right on both counts."

"So you've been here for thirty years?"

"Yes."

"What about your mum. I mean, Ruth?"

"Oh, she's okay. As long as nothing upsets her. She still thinks of me as her little girl and if I'm around her she thinks everything's okay. We make sure she takes her medication, and she could fool just about anyone she's normal."

"What about the shock treatment?"

"She doesn't remember anything. She's blocked the whole miserable episode out of her memory, like the stillbirth." Joy looked thoughtful. "Wish I could do that. It's a handy mechanism."

"And what about your...Les?"

"He's going on for seventy. Still does a couple of odd jobs around the neighbourhood. He's such a bloody good wood turner that the jobs keep on rolling in. He's happy doing that."

"And you?"

"Me?" She shrugged. "I'd get pissed off with Dad now and again and think of leaving—maybe starting afresh somewhere else. I actually made the move once but it was a disaster," she said, pulling a face. "Went to Sydney. Got a flat and a job in a bookshop, but I felt so bloody guilty leaving Mum because she went on a downward spiral of depression. Dad had to dope her up to the hilt to stop her having to go into the funny farm. I was in touch with him, of course, and realised I was attached to them more firmly than I'd believed. I felt I owed them something...don't ask me what...maybe my upbringing, my food and shelter, my unique education in how to avoid capture. You know how it is." She spread her hands. "So I came back, full of resentment, got another job, thought about going again, but it never happened." She picked savagely at the quick of a finger nail. "I tried to make some friends—you know—those creatures called men." Her teeth bit a piece of loose skin from her finger. She sighed. "Never married. Can't do."

"Why not?"

"Mum'd have a fit if I left her. And no bloke in his right mind would marry into our small family. He'd have to spend the wedding night in my little room and the rest of his life as well. In the meantime I've got this glorious place..." she indicated the shop with a sweep of her arms, "No. I really love it. Do you still like books?"

"Of course. And that's indirectly how I found you."

"Imagine that, eh? My little message getting through to you after all those years. What a huge coincidence. I didn't give that book another thought, you know, other than that I wanted to finish it. It never occurred to me that..."

The rattling of the front door interrupted her.

"Can't they read the closed sign?"

"He's pretty insistent," Louise said, poking her head around the corner.

Joy stood up and went into the shop. "All right, all right. I'm coming."

Suddenly everything went quiet. Louise looked around the corner of the back room again. Joy had stopped halfway to the door. Louise heard a faint "shit" and then Joy turned her head back towards Louise.

"Brace yourself," she said, "the shit's about to hit the fan."

"What?"

"It's Dad."

Chapter 73   Broadbeach to Melbourne

Joy opened the door to a thickset man whose head almost touched the top of the doorframe. He was dressed in builder's overalls and was carrying some tools and short pieces of wood.

"Are you all right, love? Why're you closed?" He stooped down to kiss her.

"Oh, Dad. I forgot about the shelves," Joy replied, a little nervously. "No, I'm okay. I've got a visitor and I didn't want to be disturbed."

"A visitor?" Les straightened to look around the shop.

Louise walked into the public space from the back room. As she walked towards him, she marvelled at how little he'd changed. His hair had receded slightly, showing more of a tanned creased forehead, and the sandy colour was liberally peppered with silver strands. His face was heavily lined around the mouth and his dimple shot out a V formation above its deep cleft in his chin. His neck was loose, resembling the skin of a plucked chicken. His grey eyes smiled in conjunction with the mouth that revealed large worn teeth. It was an open, enquiring smile. If he'd been anyone else, she probably would have liked him.

Les looked at the attractive woman walking towards him. She exuded poise, sophistication, sensuality and class. A whiff of expensive perfume preceded her and he sniffed it appreciatively. A woman like this flustered him, making him feel overlarge and oafish. And this woman looked dangerous.

"Sorry, love," he turned to Joy. "I'm interrupting..."

"Dad, I'd like you to meet her."

Louise stood in front of Les, still appraising him with her eyes. She kept her arms stiffly at her sides, ignoring his outstretched hand. She smiled, but the parted lips and upturned corners of her mouth failed to spread the friendliness into her eyes. They were dark brown. Threatening.

There's something about her, he thought, drawn into her gaze.

The silence in the shop was palpable, awkward.

Louise broke the silence. "Hello, Mr Bacon. Or, should I say Paton...or Baker?"

The hairs stood up on his scalp as her warm, throaty voice dripped into his ears. "Olive?"

"Almost right...Louise. And the name's still Fletcher."

"Jesus Christ!"

"Exactly."

Les looked at Joy wordlessly.

"The game's up, Dad," she said in a hard voice.

"Did you honestly think," Louise said quietly, "that you'd get away with it forever?"

"I..."

"Though God knows you were clever enough. You had me running in circles."

"What're you going to do?" he asked, his body sagging in defeat. He knew she had him, just by her presence there.

She noticed that his face suddenly looked older and his eyes held an expression of utter hopelessness. She indicated the back room. "Why don't we go in and have a cosy chat about it?"

Les dropped his tools and the wood where he stood and followed them. For a split second Louise wondered if she should be afraid of him, but she felt no threat. Joy put the kettle on and prepared three mugs for tea and coffee. Les sat opposite Louise. They stared at each other, listening to the ordinary sounds of Joy's tinkering at the sink. They waited until the hot drinks were made.

"Mr Bacon, Joy and I think we've pretty-much got the whole story now. A pretty sordid story it is, too." Louise sighed heavily. "I should hate you for what you've done to me...to Joy. You've put us through thirty years of misery. Do you realise that?"

He dropped his gaze from hers, ashamed.

"I suppose you do," she continued. "Though I guess you've been in your own kind of hell for the best part of forty-three years. Am I right?"

Les shrugged. He wasn't looking for sympathy.

"But how could you, how *could* you deprive Joy of a normal childhood, much less take away the life of her twin sister?" Her voice rose. "And never mind the fact that you tore her," she indicated Joy, "and me apart. We were so close—you knew that—and you knew what I suffered thinking she was dead. Hell, you went through that whole disgusting charade with me, with Mum, with Mrs Bacon...everyone!" She tossed her hair back impatiently as tears ran unheeded down her face. "You robbed us of the chance to have a normal life. You know that? How could Joy possibly settle down, meet some *normal* man and have some kids? How could I? I've never let anyone get close enough to me, let alone my poor excuse of a husband."

Les shook his head from side to side, looking at the floor between his feet.

Anger blazed in her eyes as her dialogue took flight. "And it's not just two lives you've ruined—what about Ursula? I knew her sister better than she ever could. They were *twins*, for God's sake, *twins*. That poor kid never had a chance. She didn't grow up even to have a shitty life of grief and loss like we did," she said pointing at Joy and herself. "At least she should have had that chance, have some kids, give her poor father—who'd suffered unimaginable horrors in Auschwitz, as well as losing his wife—some grandchildren to dandle on his knee. And those two sisters could have shared so so much but you took that away from them." Her voice dropped to a throaty whisper. "How *could* you?"

Joy held onto her mug of untouched coffee, her eyes bleak in the company of reawakened pain.

Louise sighed again. "And your wife—what you put that poor woman through. With the right medication at the very beginning, back in Perth, she might have been okay. You could have had a normal life, the two of you, without hurting anyone else." She regarded him thoughtfully. "It must have taken a lot of strength to do what you did—when Mrs Bacon stole the baby. I've often wondered why you didn't give Joy straight back to Mr Schwartz. You could have pleaded insanity for your wife."

Les's head came up. "And her end up in a loony bin? No way."

"I see."

Joy cleared her throat and spoke up. "Dad's always loved Mum, to the point of obsession I guess. There's never been anyone else for him. I think that's been behind all of it, hasn't it, Dad?"

An expression of utter hopelessness filled his eyes. He nodded slowly.

"And he still loves her."

"Yeah." Les dug his fingers through his hair. The two women could hear him raking his scalp savagely.

"Stop it, Dad. You'll end up looking like Uncle Harry."

"No, you're bigger. Not bald," Louise commented.

Les looked surprised.

"She's met him, Dad," Joy said. "She's been to Longreach. She's been to Perth. She's even been to New Zealand on a wild goose chase."

"Why?"

"Because I found out Joy didn't die in 1968."

"How'd you do that?"

And so Louise recounted the story of *The Diary of Anne Frank* and the inscription that led her upon her investigations. Joy filled in her part of how she had written the inscription supposing that she would personally be giving the book to Louise.

"I remember buying that book and giving it to you," he said to Joy.

"Funny how things bounce back, eh Dad?"

"Without that book, I would have stayed in ignorance of this whole thing," Louise added.

They each thought about that, sipping on their drinks in silence.

"Tell him about the other thing, Louise," Joy prompted.

"What thing?"

"You know. The person who your mum's with."

"Oh, yes." She looked hard at Les. "Do you realise that Gunter Schwartz is still alive?"

"What?" A vein throbbed in Les's neck as he stared at Louise in shock.

"Yes, he's in Melbourne." She crossed her legs and sat back in her chair. "He wants to see his daughter."

"But you're my..." he said to Joy, tears filling his eyes.

"Daughter?" Joy smirked. "I don't think so. Surrogate daughter—you know, the stand-in for the stillborn. On loan from Auschwitz."

Les gasped as if hit in the gut. A spasm of pain staggered across his face. It was a pain he hadn't felt for a long time.

"Oh, Dad, I'm sorry," Joy started to cry. She crouched down beside him, putting her arms around him. "I didn't mean it." She looked up at Louise. "He's been a wonderful father most of the time. Oh, I know he's done some dreadful things. But haven't we all? And his reasons were basically good, though how you can justify murder I don't know. I've never wanted for anything and, except for the time when he...when he...you know...did that to Ursula, I've always been protected by him. He was just looking after Mum the best way he knew how. God knows she needed him."

She turned to Les who had tears pouring down his face. "Dad, I really hated you then—when it happened. But not anymore. I thought I did until now. You know, I've been bitter and twisted all my life, hating something you did, rather than what you are." She hesitated. "I didn't know that until just this minute. I've been so busy feeling sorry for myself, seeing the worst in you and not appreciating the best." She stroked his face. "And there is more of the best."

"Princess," he murmured quietly, "I don't think anyone else will think that, least of all the cops. I just don't know what'll happen to your mum."

Louise felt embarrassed as Les and Joy held each other, both crying for what was to come, for the pain of their separation that they knew they couldn't avoid. They had both accepted the inevitable—that Les would be brought to justice and he would be separated from his beloved Ruth. The family unit that he had gone to such lengths to hold together would now be shattered. Louise knew instinctively that there was no fight left in Les. He had come to the end of the road.

Les looked at Louise. "When are they coming?"

"Who?"

"The cops."

Her eyes searched his for a long moment, her anger now depleted. "They're not."

Joy sat back on her heels in astonishment. "What did you say?"

Louise looked from one to the other. "Mr Schwartz doesn't want them brought into it after all this time—he's too tired for all that—and, now, I don't think I do either. When I first realised what you'd done, I was full of hate and revenge. I thought if I ever found you I'd have the police onto you so fast you wouldn't have time to think. I even thought you might be violent." She sighed, tears coming to her own eyes. Her voice shook as she continued. "But I think we've all suffered enough, for such a long time. I don't think I would've wanted to be in your shoes, Mr Bacon. I don't even know what I'd have done in your shoes. I don't condone it, of course, but who am I to judge? I guess you've been your own judge and jury, and by God you've stuck by that poor wife of yours and Joy here."

She stopped to swipe at her tears. Joy silently handed her a tissue.

"He is a good man, Louise," Joy said evenly.

Louise looked at her for a long time, then shook her head. "No, I won't call the police. It won't bring Ursula back or change anything."

Les slumped in his chair, his eyes closed. Pain ground at his stomach.

Joy mouthed the words 'thank you' as she put her arms around him.

The aircraft climbed steadily, leaving the Gold Coast and the Patons behind it. Louise turned from the window as the seat belt sign went off. So much had happened in the past few weeks, and yet it wasn't finished. There was still Gunter Schwartz. She settled back in her seat, listening to the throb of the engines, and her throat ached thinking of those she had left behind.

"You all right?" said the voice beside her.

Louise turned her head and smiled. "Yes, just a little weary after everything. What about you?"

"I'm excited," Joy replied. "Scared."

"Of course you are." Louise touched Joy's arm.

"I just don't know what I'll say to him. What if I disappoint him?"

"After all the years he's waited? I don't think so."

"I can't wait to see the photos of them."

"You know, I travelled with the photos everywhere I went until I flew to the Gold Coast." Louise laughed. "I was up here to work, so I had nothing to remind me of you. Then what happens? You pop up right in front of my eyes."

"I'm so glad you came," Joy sighed. "It's a huge weight been chipped off my shoulders. No more living in fear." She leaned closer to Louise. "How can I thank you for letting Dad go?"

"You already have."

"You're a very forgiving person."

"I think you're pretty forgiving yourself."

"Why?"

"Well," Louise said, "when I first walked into your shop you sounded so bitter, so full of hate, so cynical. Then your dad turns up and you give him a hard time and then do a complete turn around and forgive him. That's a big ask. I don't know if I could have done it."

"I think you would have." Joy smiled ruefully. "He's a decent man. A very misguided, uneducated man. He loves my mother to bits. And she loves him. Whatever they had when they were young, it stuck to him like glue. They were always faithful to each other. But if he wasn't around, she'd never survive. Oh, I know she's got a fixation about me, but he's the one she turns to. He's the one who stands like a pillar of strength to support her, never mind what it costs him."

"If only I'd met a man who loved me like that," Louise said wistfully.

"Mum's lucky, but I don't know if she knows that anymore."

"I would have liked to see her again."

"I know, but you understand..."

"Yes—a reminder of the past, something that could trigger her off."

"She's been on such an even keel for so long now, Dad didn't want to risk it. Just my leaving for a while was bad enough, but he'll placate her. He can do that."

The Qantas airbus landed at Tullamarine Airport on a perfect summer day. Joy found Melbourne to be a new place, not having spent much time in the city itself when she was a child. As they drove past the older Essendon Airport, memories flooded back of her fury over her haircut, meeting Harry for the first time, parting from Les, her mental chaos. Her hands unclenched as they passed the windsocks that pointed towards the terminal.

Louise drove expertly along the Nepean Highway, pointing out various landmarks to Joy. Once they crossed Mordialloc Creek, the short streets leading onto the beach flashed past with a glimpse of blue water over white sand. Joy began to feel at home again.

At Chelsea they turned into Sandalwood Avenue. Neither spoke as Louise swung the car into the driveway of her mother's house. The white picket fence was still standing and, where it separated the two houses, it was covered with sweet pea. Joy bit her lip as she looked at her old house. The window of her old room had vertical blinds now, and the house was painted green instead of white. But at a stretch of her imagination, she could see her head sticking out as she whistled to Louise to go for a swim. The sweet pea waved their multi-coloured flowers in the gentle sea breeze, as if in greeting. *You're home. You're home.*

They stood on the front steps, Joy taking in the fresh salty air, looking towards the beach and the jetty. Memories rushed in, one on top of the other, and she grieved for the intervening years that should have been hers and Louise's together. They turned as the door opened and Olive held out her arms. Joy went into them, joined by Louise, and they stayed there, three women crying in the warmth and comfort of each other's bodies, each knowing what the other felt.

The interior of Olive's house had hardly changed. Joy felt as if she were walking back in time as she took in each room, each item, and the smell of it. Lace curtains swayed at open windows and vases full of sweet pea sat at every available space; their perfume filled the rooms and Joy smiled, biting her lip, at Olive's thoughtfulness.

"For you," Olive said simply.

"I know." Fresh tears welled in her eyes. "I don't think I've cried so much in all my life as I have in the past few days."

"Do you good," Olive smiled. "It'll wash the cobwebs away."

They all sat down to dinner and talked until the early hours of the morning, catching up as women do, renewing and healing their friendship.

Finally, Louise stood. "I think we'd better be going."

"Yes, you've got a big day ahead of you tomorrow," Olive said to Joy.

Joy took a deep breath as she stood up. She let it out slowly. "Yes, I have."

Louise pointed to the rocks below Olivers Hill through her lounge room window. "That's where it happened." The clear moonlight accentuated the rocks as the waves broke on them. They looked cruel with knife-sharp edges.

Joy shuddered. "It makes it so real now. I'd tried not to imagine it. Tried to push it out of my mind..."

"I'm sorry..."

"No. This is only one of the things I have to face."

Joy looked away from the view as she accepted a glass of water. It was then she noticed the huge photograph of herself and Louise blended into rocks and waves. She studied it for a long time before speaking.

"This is what you felt?"

"Yes."

"It's beautiful. But I'm glad it's a lie."

"So am I," Louise smiled. "I never thought you'd ever be standing here with me." She suddenly put her hands over Joy's eyes. "Don't look."

"Promise." Joy giggled.

"Spit on it?"

"Here?"

"No, perhaps not," Louise laughed. "I'll take your word for it."

She took her hands away and, when she was sure Joy still had her eyes closed, she took *Blue Eyes* from the desk and put the doll in Joy's hands. "You can open them now."

Joy started to laugh and cry at the same time.

"What're you doing? Laughing or crying?" Louise was crying too.

"Both."

Joy hugged *Blue Eyes*. She touched the doll's hair, minute white teeth, tiny fingers, feet, and turned it over and back again to hear it cry: "Mummy".

"You've looked after her so well."

"I had to. She belonged to my best friend."

"And the desk." Joy ran her fingers over the polished wood, marvelling at its beauty, taking in every remembered nook and cranny. Her hand hesitated over the middle shelf.

"Go on," Louise urged her. "You remember how."

Joy gripped the dividing wall between two of the pigeonholes and pushed it inwards. They heard a faint click before a panel opened behind the rear wall of the desk. Her eyes shone.

"See what's in there," Louise said.

Joy slid her hand between the two larger drawers on the bottom shelf and felt around inside the compartment. She pulled out a notebook.

"You know what that is, don't you?"

Joy turned it over in her hand. "My diary."

Then she burst into tears again.

They spent what was left of the night sitting on the couch, exploring photograph albums that stacked up on the floor as they went through each one. Then followed the photographs that Louise had taken of George Chambers' scrapbook, as well as her own notebook with everything she had learned about Joy's history. Looking out over the bay, they talked in muted voices, learning about each other, making up for lost time. Finally, they fell asleep leaning against each other, with the moonlight casting a soft glow on their faces. Their heads were together, like in the photograph above them, but now they were older, both were alive, and nothing was going to part them again.

Chapter 74

Louise stirred on the couch, surprised to find herself there still. *Hell, did we stay here all night?* She groaned softly, her stiff muscles protesting as she turned to see Joy asleep beside her. The face in repose had softened its bitter lines, become more youthful. Above her friend was the photograph of them as thirteen year-olds, and Louise compared the face of the sleeping Joy to her younger self. *Ah, there's such innocence in those young eyes, but now there's sadness behind those closed lids.* In her head Louise began to move fragments of each face into a montage of images that would represent the movement of time and identities.

Joy opened her eyes to see Louise studying her closely.

"Do I pass?"

Louise laughed. "With flying colours."

"What were you looking at?"

"Just you—how you have and haven't changed. How much you look like your mother with your high cheek bones."

"I wish I'd known her," Joy said wistfully. "And Ursula."

"I know. Well, at the very least you'll meet your real father."

Joy's eyes widened with concern. "What'll I call him?"

"Gee, I don't know. Dad? Father?"

"Mr Schwartz?"

"Oh, come on," Louise scolded her. "You can hardly call him that."

"But we're strangers." She hesitated. "What if he doesn't like me?"

"Joy, how could he not like you?" Louise hugged her. "He loves you. You're his daughter."

"But Ursula was the one he knew. He probably wishes I was her."

"Yes, but he never ever saw you. He told Mum that if there was one last person he could see, it would be you."

"Really?"

"Yes." Louise held up a photograph of Hannah, putting it close to Joy's head. "It would be like seeing an older Hannah. It's eerie."

The drive to the nursing home seemed to take forever after Louise and Joy picked Olive up from her Chelsea home. There was very little conversation in the car, each busy with her own thoughts.

Louise steered the car into a parking space, turned off the engine and leaned against the back of her seat. She looked over at Joy.

"Ready?"

Joy bit her lip. "I don't know how to handle this."

Olive leaned across from the back seat, putting her hand on Joy's shoulder. "Just go with your heart. It'll work out fine."

They entered the building and took the lift up to the palliative ward. Marta was busy at the nurses' station. She looked up and, when she saw Joy, her mouth dropped open.

"You're..."

Louise smiled. "Yes, this is Joy."

"You found her!"

"By accident—it's a long story. I'll tell you later."

The introductions done, Marta led the way to Gunter's room. Tears filled her eyes as she kept looking at Joy.

"I'm sorry, it's just that..."

"I know," Joy said gently. "You've been so good to him for so long. Louise told me."

Olive stopped Marta before they entered the room. "How is he today?"

"Very tired. He's been so busy defying the specialists, refusing to talk to them, that he's used up a lot of energy." She leaned against the doorframe, dropping her voice to a whisper. "I had a quick word with him a while ago. He's just about given up hope. He told me he'll wait until he sees you once more," she said to Louise, "and then he'll let go. He seemed depressed." She turned to Joy. "He's waited so long for you."

"Perhaps I should have told him yesterday," Olive said, "but I wanted it to be a surprise."

"It won't be too much of a shock for him?" Joy asked.

Marta sighed. "Look, even if it is, he's ready to go. But he'll be happy."

"You mean...?" Joy whispered.

"Yes," Marta nodded. "This could be a pretty traumatic experience for you. Do you think you're up to it?"

Tears spilled from Joy's eyes unheeded. "I'll have to be, won't I? I mean, compared to what he's been through, any trauma on my part will be next to nothing."

"We'll be here for you," Louise said, linking her arm through Joy's.

Olive took Joy's other arm.

Joy looked from one to the other. "Thanks," she whispered. She took a deep breath, blinking her tears away. "Okay, I'm ready."

Marta pushed the door open. The room was bright with sunshine that highlighted the colours of the many flowers in vases around the room. Their perfume filled the air. Where the sun touched the wall, it fell upon the large photograph of the three Joys. Joy turned to Louise with a question in her eyes. Louise nodded.

"Mr Schwartz?" Marta said brightly. "It's Marta here. Can you hear me?"

He was turned on his left side, with pillows at his back holding him in position. The other three women were on Gunter's blind side. Joy bit her lip savagely as she took in the sunken eyes in dark deep sockets, the skeletal head, the thin parted lips, the loose wrinkled skin of the neck. *I wish I'd known you before.* His hands appeared huge, as though transparent parchment had been wrapped around a collection of lifeless bones that poked at the surface. Purple bruises and dark brown age spots freckled the parchment that continued over wrist bones that led up to stick-thin arms, one marred by a numbered tattoo.

Louise broke away from her mother and Joy, and walked around to face Gunter.

"Louise is back to see you, Mr Schwartz," Marta said. "Are you going to say hello to her?"

The fog swirled around him. Today it was very thick. Thicker than yesterday. Thicker than all the other days—and cold. It muffled the sounds around him. It softened the pain of disappointment. It lay over him. It enveloped him. It was beginning to merge with him as it dragged him towards the swirling tunnel. Hannah was there. He'd glimpsed her. And Ursula. And his parents. And his sister.

Louise sat down beside the bed and slipped her fingers into his palm. She watched his face, with its closed eyes, carefully.

But wait. A sensation of warmth radiated somewhere. Somewhere that belonged to him. Somewhere a long way from here.

"Mr Schwartz," she said, "It's Louise here."

The warmth connected with a hand that used to belong to him. It spread to his blood vessels, stirring their sluggish drift to nowhere. And the warmth hovered around his eardrum as her voice dripped into his head.

"I've brought you a present. Something very special. Something you want more than anything else."

It's Louise.

From somewhere inside him—or was it from the other world?—came the strength to lift, lift, lift his eyelid. The fog surged in front of his vision, and then peeled away to reveal her face close to his.

"Hello there," she said. "Welcome back."

Why is she crying?

"I made a promise to you. Do you remember?"

He blinked.

"I always keep my promises."

Louise turned as she saw a movement had caught his eye. Someone was walking around behind her and coming towards him.

Joy trembled violently as she neared Gunter. Tears poured down her face as she looked at him.

Louise got up from her seat and Joy sat down where she had been.

Hannah!

"Father?" she said.

Father?

"It's me...your Rachel."

He stared at the face that was Hannah, and yet not Hannah. The red curly hair was the same, though white threads sprouted amongst it. The long neck, with pale skin more tanned than he remembered, led gracefully up to a high-cheek-boned face. Harsh lines on either side of the mouth now marred the soft contours of that face. The eyes were the same sea-green that was borrowed from the shallows surrounding the great continent that had become his home—but their expression reminded him of what he had seen in the eyes of the people of Auschwitz.

Rachel? This is my liebling? My lost liebling?

"I've so wanted to meet you," Joy sobbed. "Ever since I found out the truth, I've wanted to know my real father."

Don't cry, my liebling.

She held his hand in hers—the final link between them. The shared warmth of their fingers bonded them—a mere skin's thickness apart—as the blood coursed through the veins of both father and daughter.

"There's so much I want to say. So much I would love to hear you say." The tightness in her throat choked her.

He blinked rapidly, swivelling his eye towards Olive, who had come into his line of vision.

"Hello, Mr Schwartz," she said, leaning over the bed. "You want to talk?"

He blinked once.

"All right." She touched Joy on the arm. "Do you remember how to do it?"

"I think so," Joy sniffed. Marta handed her a tissue and she blew her nose before continuing. "Father...Louise and Mrs Fletcher have told me about the alphabet. Can you do it with me without the board?"

Gunter blinked.

"That means yes," Olive said quietly.

Joy started to recite the alphabet. Gunter stared at her, concentrating hard. When she came to the letter "M" he blinked.

Ten minutes later, they had a sentence: *My daughter, how I have missed you.*

"If only I'd known," Joy replied, guilt flooding through her.

Gunter began to blink again. It was a long laborious process. *You are like your mother.*

"Yes, I've seen her at last. Louise showed me a photo."

I love her so much.

"You must have missed her terribly all these years."

No, she is with me.

"And my sister?"

She also.

"Are you angry with my...Les and Ruth Bacon?"

No.

"After what they did to you?"

Did they love you?

"Yes."

Were they good to you?

"Yes."

I forgive them.

Joy cried, overwhelmed by his generosity. She thought how grateful Les would be to know that.

"Thank you."

He was tired. The time between each blink as he constructed the next sentence lengthened. *I wish I could embrace you.*

"Can I hold you instead?"

Yes.

She looked to Marta who nodded. Very gently, she slid her arm under his pillow, coming into contact with hard shoulder blades. *There's nothing of him.* She slowly lowered her body onto the edge of the bed beside him. She felt a rail go up behind her to stop her falling off. Her other arm went around his shoulder and they lay facing each other, their faces inches apart. His weak, stale breath hardly reached her.

"Am I hurting you?"

I love you.

"Oh, Father," she cried, "I love you too."

I am happy at last.

Tears escaped Gunter's eyes as he filled his mind with the vision of his daughter. It would have to last him until she joined him in eternity. To have her with him at last was a joy that saturated his being. He hugged it to him as the smell of her entered his nostrils and the feel of her light touch on his shoulder reminded him that he still had a body. He knew he would be relinquishing it before long.

Joy noticed that the time between each of his breaths appeared gradually to be spaced longer apart. His body heaved with those breaths that robbed the last of his borrowed strength. She heard a whisper close to her ear, "It won't be long now," and knew it was Marta. She clenched her jaw hard to banish the sobs that she was concerned could distress him.

His eye fixed desperately upon his daughter, conveying the love he had kept for her for forty-three years.

"Must you go now?" she asked him.

Yes.

"Are you afraid?"

No.

"Are you alone?"

Your mother and sister are here.

There was a long, long pause between breaths.

They love you.

His body shuddered as his lungs rattled in another heaving, ponderous gasp. Small jerking movements crept across his face. His eye began to close.

"Father? Can you hear me?"

He prodded his eye open. *Yes.*

"Will you be with me until I die?"

Always my daughter.

A great silent sigh surged through his tired body. It was a sigh of contentment, of release. At last his journey was at an end.

Music swelled until it filled the room. A solo violin soared, each note perfection. It lifted him through the fog and to the mouth of the swirling tunnel. He looked back to see his body lying cold and stiff on the white sheets. The warm soft body of his lost daughter lay curled beside it. She was crying, as were the other three women whom he had grown to love. *Don't cry, my liebling. I will be with my Hannah at last.*

Hannah reached out for him at the end of the tunnel and this time he did not hesitate. He let go and drifted into the soft darkness.

Chapter 75　　　Melbourne to Broadbeach

The celebrant's last words died on the breeze. They stood there—Joy, Louise, Olive and Marta—looking down at the gleaming coffin that lay on top of another that had already been there for thirty years. The elongated sheath of flowers stretched protectively over the lid; their bright splashes of colour made a kaleidoscope of the tears that fell towards them. A handful of sweet pea fluttered from hands to coffin landing with a leafy plop, like the soft breath of a baby.

The lie that stood in concrete above the open ground mocked the silent tears. *Joy Bacon 13 years.*

As one, the four women turned away from the grave.

"I wish I could change that," Joy whispered, still shocked at seeing her own epitaph on the headstone.

"I don't see how," Louise replied.

They arrived in Sandalwood Avenue—three women dressed in black, whose figures stood out dramatically against the white sand. They breathed in the warm, salty air as they gazed wordlessly out across the bay. Their tears dried as their arms linked in love and friendship.

Joy cleared her throat. "I don't know how to thank the two of you."

"There's no need," Louise smiled.

"We were just glad we could be there with him in his last weeks of life," Olive sighed. "He was a very courageous man, your father."

"And because of you two," Joy continued, "he died in peace."

They walked along the water's edge, each holding their shoes in their hands, digging their feet into the wet sand. Sea gulls scattered out of their way to flit across the water and land on the waves, bobbing like white plastic toys with moving eyes.

"Do you know what you're going to do yet?" Olive asked Joy.

"What else can I do but go back to Mum and Dad?" Joy said, watching the gulls. "They're waiting for me."

"Any regrets?" Louise followed her gaze.

"No, except for one thing."

"What's that?"

"I wish I could see Nana…if she's still alive. At least I could tell her none of it was her fault."

Olive thought about that for a moment. "She'd be pretty old, Joy. She was old enough to be my mother."

"Yes, well, I couldn't see her anyway, even if she was alive, could I?"

Louise looked at Joy. "Not really."

"The police'd be onto Dad and Mum like a shot."

"Joy..." Olive said suddenly, "...have you thought about Marta and the hospital?"

"What?"

"They know who you are."

"Oh, Jesus." Joy's face suddenly drained of colour. "Do you think...?"

"I don't know." Olive shook her head.

"I'd better get back to the Gold Coast soon then," Joy decided. "At least give Dad time to figure out what they'll do. Can I ring him from your place now?"

"Of course you can."

They began to walk towards the house when Louise stopped them.

"What about the stuff in the boot, Joy?" she said. "Aren't you going to look at it?"

"I'd forgotten," Joy replied. "Yes. Look, I'll ring Dad first—he'll want to know what's happened down here—and then we can go through it."

They washed the sand off their feet at the back door and Joy went inside to ring Les. Louise and Olive stayed outside, allowing Joy her privacy.

After several minutes, Joy walked slowly out to where mother and daughter strolled amongst the veggie patch. They looked at her questioningly.

"No answer," she said, frowning.

"They must've gone shopping or something," Louise offered.

"They usually leave the answering machine on."

"People forget." Olive put her arm around Joy. "Don't worry."

"His mobile didn't answer either."

They looked at each other for several moments.

"I've got a bad feeling here," Joy pointed at her stomach. "Something's wrong. Maybe Mum's in hospital because I'm away. Or Dad's had an accident. What'd happen to Mum then?" Her face was ashen.

"Look," Olive said, "try again later. They're bound to be home and wonder what you're worrying about. There must be a simple explanation."

"Well…"

"Come on," Louise took her arm. "Let's get your father's things out of the boot in the meantime."

They carried the four cardboard cartons, two suitcases and two violin cases into the house. Joy trembled as she undid the clasps on a suitcase. It contained a collection of Gunter's clothes. Even though they had been in the suitcase for thirty years, they looked crisp and clean and were folded precisely. A faint whiff of cologne or talcum powder mixed with the mustiness. The other suitcase held Ursula's clothes—Joy recognised each garment as having the same taste in colour and style as she had had when thirteen.

"How could I throw these out?" she said tearfully.

"You don't have to," Olive said. "Give yourself time to decide what you'll do with them. You've got the rest of your life to do that."

Joy held a blouse up to her face. "It's almost the same as the green one I had with the long sleeves. Do you remember?"

Louise nodded. "The one with the Peter Pan collar?"

"Yes, that's the one." She hugged the blouse. "These are part of her."

Next she went through the cardboard cartons. They contained shoes, handbags, books of music, papers, a few trinkets of jewellery, and photographs.

"Look." Joy held up a frame. "It's my mother and father."

It was a head to waist shot of a young Gunter standing behind Hannah with his arms around her. She was dressed in white with tiny flowers pinned in her hair, and she held a bouquet of flowers at her waist. She was displaying a ring on the third finger of her left hand.

"It must have been their wedding day," Louise smiled.

"Don't they look happy?" Olive had tears in her eyes.

There was a studio photograph of Ursula as a baby, propped up against a satin backdrop.

"That's me," Joy cried. "Exactly the same."

Another frame held a photograph of Gunter with Ursula sitting on his knee. They were laughing as they looked at something behind the camera. On the back of the frame was written: *Gunter 40 years Ursula 7 years.*

A shoebox full of photographs was an unexpected treasure. The three women spent a long time examining them and speculating about who the other people were who shared those captured moments with Gunter and Ursula. A short lifetime for Ursula that ended abruptly in 1968, as well as for her father.

Joy picked up one of the violin cases. It appeared the older of the two. She unlocked the clasp and opened the lid, which held two long bows. They gasped at the sight of a magnificent violin encased in blue velvet. The instrument's varnish gleamed a polished red-brown. Her fingers carefully lifted it out, curling around the fingerboard. A string vibrated softly at the contact. The unfamiliar smell of resin was pleasant in her nostrils. The chin rest beckoned her to it, and she gingerly fitted her chin onto it. Tears filled her eyes as she looked at Louise and Olive.

"It suits you," Louise said softly.

Joy took in every detail of the violin, marvelling at the skill of the craftsman who created it. "It's so beautiful," she breathed, thinking of the magnificent creations that Les turned out from pieces of quality wood. "And it's so personal. An extension of what he was." She returned it to its resting place. "I'm never going to sell it...even if it is one of those expensive Italian ones. You know what? I'm going to learn to play it."

"Good for you." Olive voiced her approval.

"Even if I never play it well, it'll stay in the family...small though it is."

"He'd be happy about that, I think," Louise agreed.

The other case was less worn, and when Joy opened it, they noticed that the lining was red.

"This must have been Ursula's," Joy said softly. "Look, there's a hanky."

A white lace handkerchief was tucked into the resin compartment. Joy took the instrument from the case and held it up to the light of the window. The wood was a lighter colour than that of Gunter's violin—a streaked blonde wood that glowed in the light. She handed it to Louise.

"I want you to have this," she said.

"What?"

"Perhaps you can learn to play it," Joy smiled.

"I couldn't take this..."

"Yes, you could." Joy was firm. "If it hadn't been for you, we wouldn't be sitting here now. Look, even if you never play it, just keep it. For her."

"I don't know what to say," Louise choked.

"Say nothing."

They sat back on the couch, looking at the collection of memorabilia.

"That's all that's left of three lives," Joy said sadly. "I'm on my own now."

"You've got Les and Ruth," Olive reminded her.

"Yes, I have, haven't I?"

"And you've got us," Louise said hopefully.

"Oh, of course I have." Joy hugged them both. "That makes me the luckiest woman alive."

Over the next few hours, Joy attempted to ring Les and Ruth again, but still there was no answer.

"I'm really worried now," she told Louise and Olive. "It's not like Dad at all. I can always contact him. I'm flying back first thing in the morning."

"Would you like me to come too?" Louise offered.

Joy looked at her for a long moment. "No," she said slowly, "I think it best that I do this alone. He'll be feeling pretty miserable about the whole thing, wondering about my meeting my real father, about you two, about the risk of discovery—lots of things. Mum won't know anything, of course. She'll just be a bit frantic because I'm not there."

"What about later?" Louise asked. "Are you going to stay with them or make a new life for yourself?"

"They need me," Joy said simply.

"Yes."

"But you and I...we've found each other again. We can holiday together, visit each other, talk on the phone, send emails."

"Of course we can. But, Joy, promise me something?"

"Anything."

"If your dad gets the wind up and you all go into hiding again, please don't hide from me. Your secret is safe with Mum and me."

"Definitely," Olive agreed.

"Just don't bury yourself again. Don't leave me in the dark."

"No, I wouldn't do that to you."

"No matter how risky it is?"

"Never. I'd find a way to make contact."

"Promise?"

"Promise," Joy smiled. "You want me to spit on it, Sweet Pea?"

"Don't you go spitting on my carpet," Olive said sternly.

The taxi pulled up in front of Joy's home in Broadbeach. The house was situated at the end of a street touching the sand that rimmed the Pacific Ocean. Rollers curled inwards on their sweep towards the beach, rising up like the heads of cobras before striking the water underneath that fed their energy. Bronzed bodies defied the rollers' strength by riding them triumphantly on magical boards that seemed stuck to the watery surfaces. The breeze was soft on Joy's face as she picked up her suitcase and walked along the pathway to the front door.

Dad's home, at least, she thought, as she noticed Les's Ford ute parked at the end of the driveway. *Why're all the windows closed? They must've just got home or something.* She heard the hum of the air conditioner on her parents' bedroom wall. *Funny—it's not that hot today.* She judged the temperature to be in the high twenties. The humidity was oppressive, but that never bothered either of her parents. *Mum's sick. Got a temperature. That's it—she's been in hospital.*

"Dad? Mum?" she called out as she fitted her key into the front door and pushed it open. "Where are you? What're you up to?"

He must be in the garage.

She put her suitcase down outside her own bedroom and walked towards her parents' bedroom. She tapped softly on the door.

"Yoo-hoo. Can I come in?"

She waited, then knocked again.

"I'm coming, ready or not."

The handle protested loudly as she turned it. *Dad really should fix this. It's been this way for ages.*

A blast of very cold air hit her in the face as she entered the room.

"God, it's freezing in here, Mum. You'll catch your death..."

She stopped when she saw her parents lying asleep in their bed. Les had his arms around Ruth, whose head rested on his shoulder.

"Oh, sorry," she whispered.

What're they asleep for at this time of the day?

A feeling of utter dread pulled her stomach muscles tight.

She crept up to the side of the bed and looked down at Les and Ruth. Their faces were a dull grey.

They were not breathing.

"Oh, no! Please no," she mouthed. "Please don't do this. Oh, Dad...Mum. Not this way."

She touched their faces. They were cold. Les's mouth was slightly open as his cheek rested on the top of Ruth's head who looked as if she had just fallen asleep.

Oh, Dad. She looked down at him with understanding. *Couldn't you have run away again instead?*

As the realisation of what Les had done slowly crept over her, soaking into her body and mind like a sponge slowly filling with water, she slumped over her parents. She felt their stiff cold bodies under the sheet. The steady hum of the air conditioner and the pounding of the waves outside the window muffled her sobs of grief.

It was quite some time later when she raised her head and reached over for a tissue from a box on the bedside table. Her hand brushed against something that fell to the floor. It was an envelope.

With shaking hands, she picked it up and read, "To our daughter, Joy" written in Les's handwriting. She turned the envelope over and eased out a thick wad of pages.

Dear Princess,

I know finding our bodies will be a terrible shock to you. I'm sorry I had to put you through this. I hoped by having the air conditioner on full blast that at least the smell of the dead will be postponed for some days.

Princess, I've reached the end of the road. I knew it would happen one day. You can't get away with what I did forever. I did some pretty terrible things but as you know I did them mostly for your mother. That's no excuse of course but you know I'd have done just about anything to make her happy. In a way that's selfish, because whatever made her happy made me happy. You said I was obsessive about her and you're probably right. You see she and I were the only people in the world that cared about us. Our parents didn't give a shit about us as you know. Then you came along—right or wrong—and we had you to love. And Jesus how we loved you and still do.

I want you to show this letter to the cops. It's a shame that this won't be private—just between you and me—but they need to know that what I did had nothing to do with you. You just shut up because I told you to. What could a kid your age do anyway? And then you kept your mouth shut to protect your mother.

Tell them I admit that I went along with the kidnapping of you. Your mother took you from the hospital because she really thought you were hers. She was a bit bonkers—no, quite a bit bonkers—when she did that. She'd had that dead baby and she lost her mind for a couple of weeks until she saw you in the hospital with that toy she'd made in the bassinet. Naturally she'd think you were hers seeing that toy with you. When I saw her with you all her personality had come back. She was my Ruth again. And what could that poor sod do with two babies I thought? Well, that's how I justified it. So we cleared out of WA and got to Vic where we brought you up. Ruth had no idea you weren't really hers. She never remembered that her baby had died.

But when your twin turned up I just didn't know what to do. If you'd asked me if I was capable of killing someone before, I would have laughed in your face. I'm not a violent person. Never was. But I knew that if you and she got together with her father then he'd put two and two together and come up with the right answer. There'd only be one result of that— gaol for me and the funny farm for your mother. I wouldn't have cared so much for myself, but what would your mother have done with her funny head? And what about you my Princess? At thirteen would you have settled into your "real" family? I honestly don't know.

Well, now that Louise has discovered us and gone to so much trouble to find out the truth, it leaves me with no choice. Not that I blame her, mind you, and you shouldn't either. She's just a smart lady who worked it out for herself. Once the cops find out about it all they'll be up here looking to throw me to the sharks. Well, I'm beating them to it. At least this way your mother and I will go together, just like it should be. She won't suffer, if that's any consolation, and neither will I, though I deserve to. That pill bottle on the bedside table won't have many left in it. It was a full bottle. I've been saving them up for ages now just *in case this happened. Your mum will just go to sleep and I'll follow her.*

Princess, don't be too sad. Who knows? Maybe you'll be really pissed off with me. You've got every right to. Jesus how you socked it to me on the way to Townsville. Even though I was feeling real shithouse then about having to tell you everything, I really admired your guts. You gave me everything I deserved and more. But over the years since then I think you forgave me a bit and we were a pretty good family weren't we? You gave your mother and me everything any bloke and his missus could ever want in a kid. You're smart and pretty and very loyal. I'm grateful to you for that because if you hadn't been we'd all have been in the clink by now.

Thanks for being our daughter, even though you had no choice in it, because we love you. Jesus how we love you. And I wish I could give you a great big hug now and say goodbye properly but that wouldn't work would it?

Wherever your mum and me are now, we'll be looking out for you. You know I don't hold any great shakes on this religion stuff, but if I'm wrong about it then we're either up there or I'll more likely be down the other way. But if there's anything left of what's inside me and your mum—you know that soul stuff— then we'll hang around you, if that's okay, and make sure you're all right. But if it ends right here then I'll say goodbye and send you a kiss, as I know your mum would, and say I hope I didn't make your life too hard, that I'm sorry you didn't get to have a normal life and was stuck with us. Now you'll be free to do something with yourself. I really hope you meet some nice bloke who'll take care of you and love you even half as much as we do. You're getting a bit long in the tooth, but try and have a baby. Some women your age still can have them so give it a go. Having a baby is the best thing that can happen to a woman and her husband. It gives you a family and that's what's important. But for

Christ's sake marry a man who's got his own family then you'll have a bigger one. Have plenty of kids then you'll have lots of grandchildren to make your old age a happy one. You hear me?

I love you Princess.

Dad.

Epilogue

Joy stood back to admire her handiwork. The two marble miniature violins settled slowly into the wet concrete.

"What do you think?" She looked up at Louise and Olive.

"I think they're beautiful," Louise smiled.

"Perfect," Olive agreed.

The inscription on the new headstone stood out clearly in the afternoon light as it slanted across the marble.

Here lie Gunter Schwartz (1922-1998)
and his beloved daughter Ursula (1955-1968)
Reunited at last to journey to the stars where
Gunter's adored wife and Ursula's mother,
Hannah (1934-1955), awaits them
Remembered with love by their daughter & sister, Rachel

The walk across the cemetery grounds to the garden setting for cremated remains was a short one. They found the rock easily. It was at the edge of a lake where a fountain shot a cascade of water into the air. A mother duck bustled around her ducklings as they fossicked at the water's edge. The name Baker stood out clearly on its plaque set into the rock.

Joy knelt down to place fresh flowers in the receptacle set into the granite block that held the memorial plaque.

We remember with love
Lesley Thomas Baker (1930-1998)
and his adored wife
Ruth (née Rogers) Baker (1935-1998)
Devoted parents of Joy
Much loved friends of Louise & Olive
As in life they are joined together in death
May their love be peaceful at last

At the left side of the plaque was an engraving of a tiny roll-top desk. At the right was a tiny *Blue Eyes* dressed in a frilly dress.

"I think they're happy now," Joy said softly as healing tears made their way down her cheeks, "especially that their ashes are mingled."

Joy and Louise sat on the edge of the jetty, looking across the bay. Seagulls squawked as they dived for fish and squabbled in mid air to keep their catch. The water was calm, translucent. Sand crabs scurried across the bottom of the bay, intent upon their own survival. The two women bent over the jetty. Their rippling reflections looked up at them—reflections of times past mirrored in older faces—until a school of tiny fish hurried across the images, shattering them.

The two friends turned to each other and hugged. Then they stood up and walked back to where Olive waited for them at the door of her house. Their arms went around each other and they went inside the house and closed the front door behind them.

531

www.ingramcontent.com/pod-product-compliance
Lightning Source LLC
Chambersburg PA
CBHW020513110726

47899CB00004B/1101